Great Thrillers

Great Thrillers

Ice Station Zebra
Alistair MacLean

The Eagle has Landed
Jack Higgins

The Tightrope Men
Desmond Bagley

COLLINS
St James's Place, London

Ice Station Zebra
first published in Great Britain in 1963 by Collins
Publishers
© Normandy Investment Ltd., 1963

The Eagle Has Landed
first published in Great Britain in 1975 by Collins
Publishers
© Jack Higgins 1975

The Tightrope Men
first published in Great Britain in 1973 by Collins
Publishers
© L. J. Jersey Ltd 1973

ISBN 0 00 243298 6

Typeset by CCC, printed and bound in Great
Britain by
William Clowes (Beccles) Limited, Beccles and
London.

Contents

Ice Station Zebra

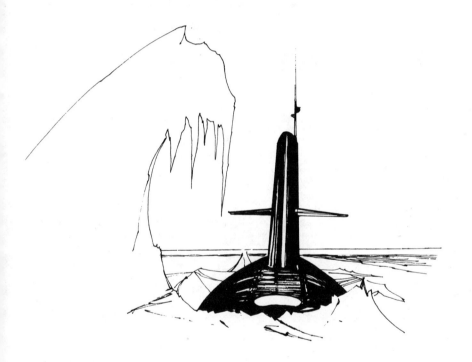

Alistair MacLean

1

Commander James D. Swanson of the United States Navy was short, plump and crowding forty. He had jet-black hair topping a pink cherubic face, and with the deep permanent creases of laughter lines radiating from his eyes and curving round his mouth he was a dead ringer for the cheerful, happy-go-lucky extrovert who is the life and soul of the party where the guests park their brains along with their hats and coats. That, anyway, was how he struck me at first glance but on the reasonable assumption that I might very likely find some other qualities in the man picked to command the latest and most powerful nuclear submarine afloat I took a second and closer look at him and this time I saw what I should have seen the first time if the dank grey fog and winter dusk settling down over the Firth of Clyde hadn't made seeing so difficult. His eyes. Whatever his eyes were they weren't those of the gladhanding wisecracking *bon vivant*. They were the coolest, clearest grey eyes I'd ever seen, eyes that he used as a dentist might his probe, a surgeon his lancet or a scientist his electronic microscope. Measuring eyes. They measured first me and then the paper he held in his hand but gave no clue at all as to the conclusions arrived at on the basis of measurements made.

'I'm sorry, Dr. Carpenter.' The south-of-the-Mason-Dixon-line voice was quiet and courteous, but without any genuine regret that I could detect, as he folded the telegram back into its envelope and handed it to me. 'I can accept neither this telegram as sufficient authorisation nor yourself as a passenger. Nothing personal, you know that: but I have my orders.'

'Not sufficient authorisation?' I pulled the telegram from its cover and pointed to the signature. 'Who do you think this is – the resident window-cleaner at the Admiralty?'

It wasn't funny, and as I looked at him in the failing light I thought maybe I'd overestimated the depth of the laughter lines in the face. He said precisely: 'Admiral Hewson is commander of the Nato Eastern Division. On Nato exercises I come under his command. At all other times I am responsible only to Washington. This is one of those other times. I'm sorry. And I must point out, Dr. Carpenter, that you could have arranged for anyone in London to send this telegram. It's not even on a naval message form.'

He didn't miss much, that was a fact, but he was being suspicious about nothing. I said: 'You could call him up by radio-telephone, Commander.'

'So I could,' he agreed. 'And it would make no difference. Only accredited American nationals are allowed aboard this vessel – and the authority must come from Washington.'

'From the Director of Underseas Warfare or Commander Atlantic Submarines?' He nodded, slowly, speculatively, and I went on: 'Please radio them and ask them to contact Admiral Hewson. Time is very short, Commander.' I might have added that it was beginning to snow and that I was getting colder by the minute, but I refrained.

He thought for a moment, nodded, turned and walked a few feet to a portable dockside telephone that was connected by a looping wire to the long dark shape lying at our feet. He spoke briefly, keeping his voice low, and hung up. He barely had time to rejoin me when three duffel-coated figures came hurrying up an adjacent gangway, turned in our direction and stopped when they reached us. The tallest of the three tall men, a lean rangy character with wheat-coloured hair and the definite look of a man who ought to have had a horse between his legs, stood slightly in advance of the other two. Commander Swanson gestured towards him.

'Lieutenant Hansen, my executive officer. He'll look after you till I get back.' The commander certainly knew how to choose his words. 'I don't need looking after,' I said mildly. 'I'm all grown up now and I hardly ever feel lonely.'

'I shall be as quick as I can, Dr. Carpenter,' Swanson said. He hurried off down the gangway and I gazed thoughtfully after him. I put out of my mind any idea I might have had about the Commander U.S. Atlantic Submarines picking his captains from the benches in Central Park. I had tried to effect an entrance aboard Swanson's ship and if such an entrance was unauthorised he didn't want me taking off till he'd found out why. Hansen and his two men, I guessed, would be the three biggest sailors on the ship.

The ship. I stared down at the great black shape lying almost at my feet. This was my first sight of a nuclear-engined submarine and the *Dolphin* was like no submarine that I had ever seen. She was about the same length as a World War II long-range ocean-going submarine but there all resemblance ceased. Her diameter was at least twice that of any conventional submarine. Instead of having the vaguely boat-shaped lines of her predecessors, the *Dolphin* was almost perfectly cylindrical in design: instead of the usual V-shaped bows, her fore end was completely hemispherical. There was no deck, as such: the rounded sheer of sides and bows rose smoothly to the top of the hull then fell as smoothly away again, leaving only a very narrow fore-and-aft working space so dangerously treacherous in its slippery convexity that it was permanently railed off in harbour. About a hundred feet back from the bows the slender yet massive conning-tower reared over twenty feet above the deck, for all the world like the great dorsal fin of some monstrous shark:

half-way up the sides of the conning-tower and thrust out stubbily at right angles were the swept-back auxiliary diving planes of the submarine. I tried to see what lay farther aft but the fog and the thickening snow swirling down from the north of Loch Long defeated me. Anyway, I was losing interest. I'd only a thin raincoat over my clothes and I could feel my skin start to gooseflesh under the chill fingers of that winter wind.

'Nobody said anything about us having to freeze to death,' I said to Hansen. 'That naval canteen there. Would your principles prevent you from accepting a cup of coffee from Dr. Carpenter, that well-known espionage agent?'

He grinned and said: 'In the matter of coffee, friend, I have no principles. Especially tonight. Someone should have warned us about those Scottish winters.' He not only looked like a cowboy, he talked like one: I was an expert on cowboys as I was sometimes too tired to rise to switch off the TV set. 'Rawlings, go tell the captain that we are sheltering from the elements.'

While Rawlings went to the dockside phone Hansen led the way to the nearby neon-lit canteen. He let me precede him through the door then made for the counter while the other sailor, a red-complexioned character about the size and shape of a polar bear, nudged me gently into an angled bench seat in one corner of the room. They weren't taking too many chances with me. Hansen came and sat on the other side of me, and when Rawlings returned he sat squarely in front of me across the table.

'As neat a job of corralling as I've seen for a long time,' I said approvingly. 'You've got nasty suspicious minds, haven't you?'

'You wrong us,' Hansen said sadly. 'We're just three friendly sociable guys carrying out our orders. It's Commander Swanson who has the nasty suspicious mind, isn't that so, Rawlings?'

'Yes, indeed, Lieutenant,' Rawlings said gravely. 'Very security-minded, the captain is.'

I tried again. 'Isn't this very inconvenient for you?' I asked. 'I mean, I should have thought that every man would have been urgently required aboard if you're due to sail in less than two hours' time.'

'You just keep on talking, Doc,' Hansen said encouragingly. There was nothing encouraging about his cold blue Arctic eyes. 'I'm a right good listener.'

'Looking forward to your trip up to the ice-pack?' I inquired pleasantly.

They operated on the same wavelength, all right. They didn't even look at one another. In perfect unison they all hitched themselves a couple of inches closer to me, and there was nothing imperceptible about the way they did it either. Hansen waited, smiling in a pleasantly relaxed fashion until the waitress had deposited four steaming mugs of coffee on the table, then said in the same encouraging tone: 'Come again, friend. Nothing we like to hear better than top classified information being bandied about in canteens. How the hell do *you* know where we're going?'

I reached up my hand beneath my coat lapel and it stayed there, my right wrist locked in Hansen's right hand.

'We're not suspicious or anything,' he said apologetically. 'It's just that we submariners are very nervous on account of the dangerous life we lead. Also, we've a very fine library of films aboard the *Dolphin* and every time a character in one of those films reaches up under his coat it's always for the same reason and that's not just because he's checking to see if his wallet's still there.'

I took his wrist with my free hand, pulled his arm away and pushed it down on the table. I'm not saying it was easy, the U.S. Navy clearly fed its submariners on a high protein diet, but I managed it without bursting a blood-vessel. I pulled a folded newspaper out from under my coat and laid it down. 'You wanted to know how the hell I knew where you were going,' I said. 'I can read, that's why. That's a Glasgow evening paper I picked up in Renfrew Airport half an hour ago.'

Hansen rubbed his wrist thoughtfully, then grinned. 'What did you get your doctorate in, Doc? Weight-lifting? About that paper – how could you have got it in Renfrew half an hour ago?'

'I flew down here. Helicopter.'

'A whirlybird, eh? I heard one arriving a few minutes ago. But that was one of ours.'

'It had U.S. Navy written all over it in four-foot letters,' I conceded, 'and the pilot spent all his time chewing gum and praying out loud for a quick return to California.'

'Did you tell the skipper this?' Hansen demanded.

'He didn't give me the chance to tell him anything.'

'He's got a lot on his mind and far too much to see to,' Hansen said. He unfolded the paper and looked at the front page. He didn't have far to look to find what he wanted: the two-inch banner headlines were spread over seven columns.

'Well, would you look at this.' Lieutenant Hansen made no attempt to conceal his irritation and chagrin. 'Here we are, pussy-footing around in this God-forsaken dump, sticking-plaster all over our mouths, sworn to eternal secrecy about mission and destination and then what? I pick up this blasted Limey newspaper and here are all the top-secret details plastered right across the front page.'

'You are kidding, Lieutenant,' said the man with the red face and the general aspect of a polar bear. His voice seemed to come from his boots.

'I am not kidding, Zabrinski,' Hansen said coldly, 'as you would appreciate if you had ever learned to read. "Nuclear submarine to the rescue," it says. "Dramatic dash to the North Pole." God help us, the North Pole. And a picture of the *Dolphin*. And of the skipper. Good lord, there's even a picture of me.'

Rawlings reached out a hairy paw and twisted the paper to have a better look at the blurred and smudged representation of the man before him. 'So there is. Not very flattering, is it, Lieutenant? But a speaking likeness, mind you, a speaking likeness. The photographer has caught the essentials perfectly.'

'You are utterly ignorant of the first principles of photography,' Hansen said witheringly. 'Listen to this lot. "The following joint statement was issued simultaneously a few minutes before noon (G.M.T.) today in both London and Washington: 'In view of the critical condition of the survivors of Drift Ice Station Zebra and the failure either to rescue or contact them by conventional means, the United States Navy has willingly agreed that the United States nuclear submarine *Dolphin* be dispatched with all speed to try to effect contact with the survivors.'

'"The *Dolphin* returned to its base in the Holy Loch, Scotland, at dawn this morning after carrying out extensive exercises with the Nato naval forces in the Eastern Atlantic. It is hoped that the *Dolphin* (Commander James D. Swanson, U.S.N., commanding) will sail at approximately 7 p.m. (G.M.T.) this evening.

'"The laconic understatement of this communique heralds the beginning of a desperate and dangerous rescue attempt which must be without parallel in the history of the sea or the Arctic. It is now sixty hours——"'

'"Desperate,"' you said, Lieutenant?' Rawlings frowned heavily. '"Dangerous," you said? The captain will be asking for volunteers?'

'No need. I told the captain that I'd already checked with all eighty-eight enlisted men and that they'd volunteered to a man.'

'You never checked with me.'

'I must have missed you out. Now kindly clam up, your executive officer is talking. "It is now sixty hours since the world was electrified to learn of the disaster which has struck Drift Ice Station Zebra, the only British meteorological station in the Arctic, when an English-speaking ham radio operator in Bodo, Norway, picked up the faint S.O.S. from the top of the world.

'"A further message, picked up less than twenty-four hours ago by the British trawler *Morning Star* in the Barents Sea makes it clear that the position of the survivors of the fuel oil fire that destroyed most of Drift Ice Station Zebra in the early hours of Tuesday morning is desperate in the extreme. With their oil fuel reserves completely destroyed and their food stores all but wiped out, it is feared that those still living cannot long be expected to survive in the twenty-below temperatures – fifty degrees of frost – at present being experienced in that area.

'"It is not known whether all the prefabricated huts, in which the expedition members lived, have been destroyed.

'"Drift Ice Station Zebra, which was established only in the late summer of this year, is at present in an estimated position of 85° 40′ N. 21° 30′ E., which is only about three hundred miles from the North Pole. Its position cannot be known with certainty because of the clockwise drift of the polar ice-pack.

'"For the past thirty hours long-range supersonic bombers of the American, British and Russian air forces have been scouring the polar ice-pack searching for Station Zebra. Because of the uncertainty about the Drift Station's actual position, the complete absence of daylight in the Arctic at this time of year and the extremely bad weather conditions, they were unable to locate the station and forced to return."'

'They didn't have to locate it,' Rawlings objected. 'Not visually. With the instruments those bombers have nowadays they could home in on a humming-bird a hundred miles away. The radio operator at the Drift Station had only to keep on sending and they could have used that as a beacon.'

'Maybe the radio operator is dead,' Hansen said heavily. 'Maybe his radio has packed up on him. Maybe the fuel that was destroyed was essential for running the radio. All depends what source of power he used.'

'Diesel-electric generator,' I said. 'He had a standby battery of Nife cells. Maybe he's conserving the batteries, using them only for emergencies. There's also a hand-cranked generator, but its range is pretty limited.'

'How do you know that?' Hansen asked quietly. 'About the type of power used?'

'I must have read it somewhere.'

'You must have read it somewhere.' He looked at me without expression, then turned back to his paper. '"A report from Moscow,"' he read on, '"states that the atomic-engined *Dvina*, the world's most powerful ice-breaker, sailed from Murmansk some twenty hours ago, and is proceeding at high speed towards the Arctic pack. Experts are not hopeful about the outcome for, at this late period of the year, the ice-pack has already thickened and compacted into a solid mass which will almost certainly defy the efforts of any vessel, even those of the *Dvina*, to smash its way through.

'"The use of the submarine *Dolphin* appears to offer the only slender hope of life for the apparently doomed survivors of Station Zebra. The odds against success must be regarded as heavy in the extreme. Not only will the *Dolphin* have to travel several hundred miles continuously submerged under the polar ice-cap, but the possibilities of its being able to break through the ice-cap at any given place or to locate the survivors are very remote. But undoubtedly if any ship in the world can do it it is the *Dolphin*, the pride of the United States Navy's nuclear submarine fleet."'

Hansen broke off and read on silently for a minute. Then he said: 'That's about all. A story giving all the known details of the *Dolphin*. That, and a lot of ridiculous rubbish about the enlisted men in the *Dolphin*'s crew being the élite of the cream of the U.S. Navy.'

Rawlings looked wounded. Zabrinski, the polar bear with the red face, grinned, fished out a pack of cigarettes and passed them around. Then he became serious again and said: 'What are those crazy guys doing up there at the top of the world anyway?'

'Meteorological, lunkhead,' Rawlings informed him. 'Didn't you hear the lieutenant say so? A big word, mind you,' he conceded generously, 'but he made a pretty fair stab at it. Weather station to you, Zabrinski.'

'I still say they're crazy guys,' Zabrinski rumbled. 'Why do they do it, Lieutenant?'

'I suggest you ask Dr. Carpenter about it,' Hansen said dryly. He stared through the plate-glass windows at the snow whirling greyly through the gathering darkness, his eyes bleak and remote, as if he were already visualising the doomed men drifting to their death in the frozen immensity of the polar ice-cap. 'I think he knows a great deal more about it than I do.'

'I know a little,' I admitted. 'There's nothing mysterious or sinister about what I know. Meteorologists now regard the Arctic and the Antarctic as the two great weather factories of the world, the areas primarily responsible for the weather that affects the rest of the hemispheres. We already know a fair amount about Antarctic conditions, but practically nothing about the Arctic. So we pick a suitable ice-floe, fill it with huts crammed with technicians and all sorts of instruments and let them drift around the top of the world for six months or so. Your own people have already set up two or three of those stations. The Russians have set up at least ten, to the best of my knowledge, most of them in the East Siberian Sea.'

'How do they establish those camps, Doc?' Rawlings asked.

'Different ways. Your people prefer to establish them in winter-time, when the pack freezes up enough for plane landings to be made. Someone flies out from, usually, Point Barrow in Alaska and searches around the polar pack till they find a suitable ice-floe – even when the ice is compacted and frozen together into one solid mass an expert can tell which pieces are going to remain as good-sized floes when the thaw comes and the break-in begins. Then they fly out all huts, equipment, stores and men by ski-plane and gradually build the place up.

'The Russians prefer to use a ship in summer-time. They generally use the *Lenin*, a nuclear-engined ice-breaker. It just batters its way into the summer pack, dumps everything and everybody on the ice and takes off before the big freeze-up starts. We use the same technique for Drift Ice Station Zebra – our one and only ice station. The Russians lent us the *Lenin* – all countries are only too willing to co-operate on meteoreological research as everyone benefits by it – and took us pretty deep into the ice-pack north of Franz Josef Land. Zebra has already moved a good bit from its original position – the polar ice-cap, just sitting on top of the Arctic Ocean, can't quite manage to keep up with the west-east spin of the earth so that it has a slow westward movement in relation to the earth's crust. At the present moment it's about four hundred miles due north of Spitzbergen.'

'They're still crazy,' Zabrinski said. He was silent for a moment then looked speculatively at me. 'You in the Limey navy, Doc?'

'You must forgive Zabrinski's manners, Dr. Carpenter,' Rawlings said coldly. 'But he's been denied the advantages that the rest of us take for granted. I understand he was born in the Bronx.'

'No offence,' Zabrinski said equably. 'Royal Navy, I meant. Are you, Doc?'

'Attached to it, you might say.'

'Loosely, no doubt.' Rawlings nodded. 'Why so keen on an Arctic holiday, Doc? Mighty cool up there, I can tell you.'

'Because the men on Drift Station Zebra are going to be badly in need of medical aid. If there are any survivors, that is.'

'We got our own medico on board and he's no slouch with a stethoscope, or so I've heard from several who have survived his treatment. A well-spoken-of quack.'

'Doctor, you ill-mannered lout,' Zabrinski said severely.

'That's what I meant,' Rawlings apologised. 'It's not often that I get the chance to talk to an educated man like myself, and it just kinda slipped out. The point is, the *Dolphin's* already all buttoned up on the medical side.'

'I'm sure it is.' I smiled. 'But any survivors we might find are going to be suffering from advanced exposure, frostbite and probably gangrene. The treatment of those is rather a speciality of mine.'

'Is it now?' Rawlings surveyed the depths of his coffee cup. 'I wonder how a man gets to be a specialist in those things?'

Hansen stirred and withdrew his gaze from the darkly-white world beyond the canteen windows.

'Dr. Carpenter is not on trial for his life,' he said mildly. 'The counsel for the prosecution will kindly pack it in.'

They packed it in. This air of easy familiarity between officer and men, the easy camaraderie, the mutually tolerant disparagement with the deceptively misleading overtones of knock-about comedy, was something very rare in my experience but not unique. I'd seen it before, in first-line R.A.F. bomber crews, a relationship found only among a close-knit, close-living group of superbly trained experts each of whom is keenly aware of their complete interdependence. The casually informal and familiar attitude was a token not of the lack of discipline but of the complete reverse: it was the token of a very high degree of self-discipline, of the regard one man held for another not only as a highly-skilled technician in his own field but also as a human being. It was clear, too, that a list of unwritten rules governed their conduct. Off-hand and frequently completely lacking in outward respect though Rawlings and Zabrinski were in their attitude towards Lieutenant Hansen, there was an invisible line of propriety over which it was inconceivable that they would ever step: for Hansen's part, he scrupulously avoided any use of his authority when making disparaging remarks at the expense of the two enlisted men. It was also clear, as now, who was boss.

Rawlings and Zabrinski stopped questioning me and had just embarked upon an enthusiastic discussion of the demerits of the Holy Loch in particular and Scotland in general as a submarine base when a jeep swept past the canteen windows, the snow whirling whitely, thickly, through the swathe of the headlights. Rawlings jumped to his feet in mid-sentence, then subsided slowly and thoughtfully into his chair.

'The plot,' he announced, 'thickens.'

'You saw who it was?' Hansen asked.

'I did indeed. Andy Bandy, no less.'

'I didn't hear that, Rawlings,' Hansen said coldly.

'Vice-Admiral John Garvie, United States Navy, sir.'

'Andy Bandy, eh?' Hansen said pensively. He grinned at me. 'Admiral Garvie, Officer Commanding U.S. Naval Forces in Nato. Now this is very interesting, I submit. I wonder what he's doing here.'

'World War III has just broken out,' Rawlings announced. 'It's just about time for the Admiral's first martini of the day and no lesser crisis———'

'He didn't by any chance fly down with you in that chopper from Renfrew this afternoon?' Hansen interrupted shrewdly.

'No.'

'Know him, by any chance?'

'Never even heard of him until now.'

'Curiouser and curiouser,' Hansen murmured.

A few minutes passed in desultory talk – the minds of Hansen and his two men were obviously very much on the reason for the arrival of Admiral Garvie – and then a snow-filled gust of chilled air swept into the canteen as the door opened and a blue-coated sailor came in and crossed to our table.

'The captain's compliments, Lieutenant. Would you bring Dr. Carpenter to his cabin, please?'

Hansen nodded, rose to his feet and led the way outside. The snow was beginning to lie now, the darkness was coming down fast and the wind from the north was bitingly chill. Hansen made for the nearest gangway, halted at its head as he saw seamen and dockyard workers, insubstantial and spectral figures in the swirling flood-lit snow, carefully easing a slung torpedo down the for'ard hatch, turned and headed towards the after gangway. We clambered down and at the foot Hansen said: 'Watch your step, Doc. It's a mite slippery hereabouts.'

It was all that, but with the thought of the ice-cold waters of the Holy Loch waiting for me if I put a foot wrong I made no mistake. We passed through the hooped canvas shelter covering the after hatch and dropped down a steep metal ladder into a warm, scrupulously clean and gleaming engine-room packed with a baffling complexity of grey-painted machinery and instrument panels, its every corner brightly illuminated with shadowless fluorescent lighting.

'Not going to blindfold me, Lieutenant?' I asked.

'No need.' He grinned. 'If you're on the up and up, it's not necessary. If you're not on the up and up it's still not necessary, for you can't talk about what you've seen – not to anyone that matters, that is – if you're going to spend the next few years staring out from behind a set of prison bars.'

I saw his point. I followed him for'ard, our feet soundless on the black rubber decking past the tops of a couple of huge machines readily identifiable as turbo-generator sets for producing electricity. More heavy banks of instruments, a door, then a thirty-foot-long very narrow passageway. As we passed along its length I was conscious of a heavy vibrating hum from beneath my feet. The *Dolphin's* nuclear reactor had to be somewhere. This would be it, here. Directly beneath us. There were circular hatches on the passageway deck and those could only be covers for the heavily-leaded glass windows, inspection ports which would provide the nearest and only approach to the nuclear furnace far below.

The end of the passage, another heavily-clipped door, and then we were into what was obviously the control centre of the *Dolphin*. To the left was a partitioned-off radio room, to the right a battery of machines and dialled panels of incomprehensible purpose, straight ahead a big chart table. Beyond that again, in the centre, were massive mast housings and, still farther on, the periscope stand with its twin periscopes. The whole control room was twice the size of any I'd ever seen in a conventional submarine but, even so, every square inch of bulkhead space seemed to be taken up by one type or another of highly-complicated looking machines or instrument banks: even the deckhead was almost invisible, lost to sight above thickly twisted festoons of wires, cables and pipes of a score of different kinds.

The for'ard port side of the control room was for all the world like a replica of the flight-deck of a modern multi-engined jet airliner. There were two separate yoke aircraft-type control columns, facing on to banks of hooded calibrated dials. Behind the yokes were two padded leather chairs, each chair, I could see, fitted with safety-belts to hold the helmsman in place. I wondered vaguely what type of violent manœuvres the *Dolphin* might be capable of when such safety-belts were obviously considered essential to strap the helmsman down.

Opposite the control platform, on the other side of the passageway leading forward from the control room, was a second partitioned-off room. There was no indication what this might be and I wasn't given time to wonder. Hansen hurried down the passage, stopped at the first door on his left, and knocked. The door opened and Commander Swanson appeared.

'Ah, there you are. Sorry you've been kept waiting, Dr. Carpenter. We're sailing at six-thirty, John.' – This to Hansen. 'You can have everything buttoned up by then?'

'Depends how quickly the loading of the torpedoes goes, Captain.'

'We're taking only six aboard.'

Hansen lifted an eyebrow, made no comment. He said: 'Loading them into the tubes?'

'In the racks. They have to be worked on.'

'No spares?'

'No spares.'

Hansen nodded and left. Swanson led me into his cabin and closed the door behind him.

Commander Swanson's cabin was bigger than a telephone booth, I'll say that for it, but not all that much bigger to shout about. A built-in bunk, a folding washbasin, a small writing-bureau and chair, a folding camp-stool, a locker, some calibrated repeater instrument dials above the bunk and that was it. If you'd tried to perform the twist in there you'd have fractured yourself in a dozen places without ever moving your feet from the centre of the floor.

'Dr. Carpenter,' Swanson said, 'I'd like you to meet Admiral Garvie, Commander U.S. Nato Naval Forces.'

Admiral Garvie put down the glass he was holding in his hand, rose from the only chair and stretched out his hand. As he stood with his feet together, the far from negligible clearance between his knees made it easy to understand the latter part of his 'Andy Bandy' nickname: like Hansen, he'd have been at home on the range. He was a tall florid-faced man with white hair, white eyebrows and a twinkle in the blue eyes below: he had that certain indefinable something about him common to all senior naval officers the world over, irrespective of race or nationality.

'Glad to meet you, Dr. Carpenter. Sorry for the – um – lukewarm reception you received, but Commander Swanson was perfectly within his rights in acting as he did. His men have looked after you?'

'They permitted me to buy them a cup of coffee in the canteen.'

He smiled. 'Opportunists all, those nuclear men. I feel that the good name of American hospitality is in danger. Whisky, Dr. Carpenter?'

'I thought American naval ships were dry, sir.'

'So they are, my boy, so they are. Except for a little medicinal alcohol, of course. My personal supply.' He produced a hip-flask about the size of a canteen, reached for a convenient tooth-glass. 'Before venturing into the remoter fastnesses of the Highlands of Scotland the prudent man takes the necessary precautions. I have to make an apology to you, Dr. Carpenter. I saw your Admiral Hewson in London last night and had intended to be here this morning to persuade Commander Swanson here to take you aboard. But I was delayed.'

'Persuade, sir?'

'Persuade.' He sighed. 'Our nuclear submarine captains, Dr. Carpenter, are a touchy and difficult bunch. From the proprietary attitude they adopt towards their submarines you'd think that each one of them was a majority shareholder in the Electric Boat Company of Groton, where most of those boats are built.' He raised his glass. 'Success to the commander and yourself. I hope you manage to find those poor devils. But I don't give you one chance in a thousand.'

'I think we'll find them, sir. Or Commander Swanson will.'

'What makes you so sure?' He added slowly: 'Hunch?'

'You could call it that.'

He laid down his glass and his eyes were no longer twinkling. 'Admiral Hewson was most evasive about you, I must say. Who are you, Carpenter? *What* are you?'

'Surely he told you, Admiral? Just a doctor attached to the navy to carry out——'

'A naval doctor?'

'Well, not exactly. I——'

'A civilian, is it?'

I nodded, and the admiral and Swanson exchanged looks which they were at no pains at all to conceal from me. If they were happy at the prospect of having aboard America's latest and most secret submarine a man who was not only a foreigner but a civilian to boot, they were hiding it well. Admiral Garvie said: 'Well, go on.'

'That's all. I carry out environmental health studies for the services. How men react to extremes of environmental conditions, such as in the Arctic or the tropics, how they react to conditions of weightlessness in simulated space flight or to extremes of pressure when having to escape from submarines. Mainly——'

'Submarines.' Admiral Garvie pounced on the word. 'You have been to sea in submarines, Dr. Carpenter. Really sailed in them, I mean?'

'I had to. We found that simulated tank escapes were no substitute for the real thing.'

The admiral and Swanson looked unhappier than ever. A foreigner – bad. A foreign civilian – worse. But a foreign civilian with at least a working knowledge of submarines – terrible. I didn't have to be beaten over the head to see their point of view. I would have felt just as unhappy in their shoes.

'What's your interest in Drift Ice Station Zebra, Dr. Carpenter?' Admiral Garvie asked bluntly.

'The Admiralty asked me to go there, sir.'

'So I gather, so I gather,' Garvie said wearily. 'Admiral Hewson made that quite plain to me already. Why *you*, Carpenter?'

'I have some knowledge of the Arctic, sir. I'm supposed to be an expert on the medical treatment of men subjected to prolonged exposure, frostbite and gangrene. I might be able to save lives or limbs that your own doctor aboard might not.'

'I could have half a dozen such experts here in a few hours,' Garvie said evenly. 'Regular serving officers of the United States Navy, at that. That's not enough, Carpenter.'

This was becoming difficult. I tried again. I said: 'I know Drift Station Zebra. I helped select the site. I helped establish the camp. The commandant, a Major Halliwell, has been my closest friend for many

years.' The last was only half the truth but I felt that this was neither the
time nor the place for over-elaboration.

'Well, well,' Garvie said thoughtfully. 'And you still claim you're just
an ordinary doctor?'

'My duties are flexible, sir.'

'I'll say they are. Well then, Carpenter, if you're just a common-or-
garden sawbones, how do you explain this?' He picked a signal form
from the table and handed it to me. 'This has just arrived in reply to
Commander Swanson's radioed query to Washington about you.'

I looked at the signal. It read: 'Dr. Neil Carpenter's bona-fides beyond
question. He may be taken into your fullest, repeat fullest, confidence.
He is to be extended every facility and all aid short of actually
endangering the safety of your submarine and the lives of your crew.' It
was signed by the Director of Naval Operations.

'Very civil of the Director of Naval Operations, I must say.' I handed
back the signal. 'With a character reference like this, what are you
worrying about? That ought to satisfy anyone.'

'It doesn't satisfy me,' Garvie said heavily. 'The ultimate responsibility
for the safety of the *Dolphin* is mine. This signal more or less gives you *carte
blanche* to behave as you like, to ask Commander Swanson to act in ways
that might be contrary to his better judgment. I can't have that.'

'Does it matter what you can or can't have? You have your orders.
Why don't you obey them?'

He didn't hit me. He didn't even bat an eyelid. He wasn't activated by
pique about the fact that he wasn't privy to the reason for the seeming
mystery of my presence there, he was genuinely concerned about the
safety of the submarine. He said: 'If I think it more important that the
Dolphin should remain on an active war footing rather than go haring off
on a wild-goose chase to the Arctic, or if I think you constitute a danger
to the submarine, I can countermand the D.N.O.'s orders. I'm the C.-in-
C. on the spot. And I'm not satisfied.'

This was damnably awkward. He meant every word he said and he
didn't look the type who would give a hoot for the consequences if he
believed himself to be in the right. I looked at both men, looked at them
slowly and speculatively, the unmistakable gaze, I hoped, of a man who
was weighing others in the balance: what I was really doing was thinking
up a suitable story that would satisfy both. After I had given enough time
to my weighing-up – and my thinking – I dropped my voice a few
decibels and said: 'Is that door soundproof?'

'More or less,' Swanson said. He'd lowered his own voice to match
mine.

'I won't insult either of you by swearing you to secrecy or any such

rubbish,' I said quietly. 'I want to put on record the fact that what I am
about to tell you I am telling you under duress, under Admiral Garvie's
threat to refuse me transport if I don't comply with his wishes.'

'There will be no repercussions,' Garvie said.

'How do you know? Not that it matters now. Well, gentlemen, the
facts are these. Drift Ice Station Zebra is officially classed as an Air
Ministry meteorological station. Well, it belongs to the Air Ministry all
right, but there's not more than a couple of qualified meteorologists
among its entire personnel.'

Admiral Garvie refilled the toothglass and passed it to me without a
word, without a flicker of change in his expression. The old boy certainly
knew how to play it cool.

'What you will find there,' I went on, 'are some of the most highly
skilled men in the world in the fields of radar, radio, infra-red and
electronic computers, operating the most advanced instruments ever
used in those fields. We know now, never mind how, the count-down
succession of signals the Russians use in the last minute before launching
a missile. There's a huge dish aerial in Zebra that can pick up and
amplify any such signals within seconds of it beginning. Then long-
range radar and infra-red home in on that bearing and within three
minutes of the rocket's lift-off they have its height, speed and course pin-
pointed to an infinitesimal degree of error. The computers do this, of
course. One minute later the information is in the hands of all the anti-
missile stations between Alaska and Greenland. One minute more and
solid fuel infra-red homing anti-missile rockets are on their way: then the
enemy missiles will be intercepted and harmlessly destroyed while still
high over the Arctic regions. If you look at a map you will see that in its
present position Drift Ice Station Zebra is sitting practically on Russia's
missile doorstep. It's hundreds of miles in advance of the present DEW
line – the distant early warning system. Anyway, it renders the DEW
line obsolete.'

'I'm only the office boy around those parts,' Garvie said quietly. 'I've
never heard of any of this before.'

I wasn't surprised. I'd never heard of any of it myself either, not until
I'd just thought it up a moment ago. Commander Swanson's reactions, if
and when we ever got to Drift Station Zebra, were going to be interesting.
But I'd cross that bridge when I came to it. At present, my only concern
was to get there.

'Outside the Drift Station itself,' I said, 'I doubt if a dozen people in the
world know what goes on there. But now you know. And you can
appreciate how vitally important it is to the free world that this base be
maintained in being. If anything has happened to it we want to find out

just as quickly as possible *what* has happened so that we can get it operating again.'

'I still maintain that you're not an ordinary doctor.' Garvie smiled. 'Commander Swanson, how soon can you get under way?'

'Finish loading the torpedoes, move alongside the *Hunley*, load some final food stores, pick up extra Arctic clothing and that's it, sir.'

'Just like that? You said you wanted to make a slow-time dive out in the loch to check the planes and adjust the underwater trim – those missing torpedoes up front are going to make a difference you know.'

'That's before I heard Dr. Carpenter. Now I want to get up there just as fast as he does, sir. I'll see if immediate trim checks are necessary: if not, we can carry them out at sea.'

'It's your boat,' Garvie acknowledged. 'Where are you going to accommodate Dr. Carpenter, by the way?'

'There's space for a cot in the Exec's and Engineer's cabin.' He smiled at me. 'I've already had your suitcase put in there.'

'Did you have much trouble with the lock?' I inquired.

He had the grace to colour slightly. 'It's the first time I've ever seen a combination lock on a suitcase,' he admitted. 'It was that, more than anything else – and the fact that we couldn't open it – that made the admiral and myself so suspicious. I've still got one or two things to discuss with the admiral, so I'll take you to your quarters now. Dinner will be at eight tonight.'

'I'd rather skip dinner, thanks.'

'No one ever gets seasick on the *Dolphin*, I can assure you.' Swanson smiled.

'I'd appreciate the chance to sleep instead. I've had no sleep for almost three days and I've been travelling non-stop for the past fifty hours. I'm just tired, that's all.'

'That's a fair amount of travelling.' Swanson smiled. He seemed almost always to be smiling, and I supposed vaguely that there would be some people foolish enough to take that smile always at its face value. 'Where were you fifty hours ago, Doctor?'

'In the Antarctic.'

Admiral Garvie gave me a very old-fashioned look indeed, but he let it go at that.

2

When I awoke I was still heavy with sleep, the heaviness of a man who has slept for a long time. My watch said nine-thirty, and I knew it must be the next morning, not the same evening: I had been asleep for fifteen hours.

The cabin was quite dark. I rose, fumbled for the light switch, found it and looked around. Neither Hansen nor the engineer officer was there: they must have come in after I had gone to sleep and left before I woke. I looked around some more, and then I listened. I was suddenly conscious of the almost complete quiet, the stillness, the entire lack of any perceptible motion. I might have been in the bedroom of my own house. What had gone wrong? What hold-up had occurred? Why in God's name weren't we under way? I'd have sworn the previous night that Commander Swanson had been just as conscious of the urgency as I had been.

I had a quick wash in the folding Pullman-type basin, passed up the need for a shave, pulled on shirt, trousers and shoes and went outside. A few feet away a door opened to starboard off the passage. I went along and walked in. The officers' wardroom, without a doubt, with one of them still at breakfast, slowly munching his way through a huge plateful of steak, eggs and French fries, glancing at a magazine in a leisurely fashion and giving every impression of a man enjoying life to the luxurious full. He was about my own age, big, inclined to fat – a common condition, I was to find, among the entire crew who ate so well and exercised so little – with close-cropped black hair already greying at the temples and a cheerful intelligent face. He caught sight of me, rose and stretched out a hand.

'Dr. Carpenter, it must be. Welcome to the wardroom. I'm Benson. Take a seat, take a seat.'

I said something, appropriate but quick, then asked: 'What's wrong? What's been the hold-up? Why aren't we under way?'

'That's the trouble with the world today,' Benson said mournfully. 'Rush, rush, rush. And where does all the hurry get them? I'll tell you——'

'Excuse me. I must see the captain.' I turned to leave but he laid a hand on my arm.

'Relax, Dr. Carpenter. We *are* at sea. Take a seat.'

'At sea? On the level? I don't feel a thing.'

'You never do when you're three hundred feet down. Maybe four hundred. I don't,' he said expansively, 'concern myself with those trifles.

I leave them to the mechanics.'

'Mechanics?'

'The captain, engineer officer, people like those.' He waved a hand in a generously vague gesture to indicate the largeness of the concept he understood by the term 'mechanics'. 'Hungry?'

'We've cleared the Clyde?'

'Unless the Clyde extends to well beyond the north of Scotland, the answer to that is, yes, we have.'

'Come again?'

He grinned. 'At the last check we were well into the Norwegian Sea, about the latitude of Bergen.'

'This is still only Tuesday morning?' I don't know if I looked stupid: I certainly felt it.

'It's still only Tuesday morning.' He laughed. 'And if you can work out from what kind of speed we have been making in the last fifteen hours we'd all be obliged if you'd keep it to yourself.' He leaned back in his seat and lifted his voice. 'Henry!'

A steward, white-jacketed, appeared from what I took to be the pantry. He was a tall thin character with a dark complexion and the long lugubrious face of a dyspeptic spaniel. He looked at Benson and said in a meaningful voice: '*Another* plate of French fries, Doc?'

'You know very well that I never have more than one helping of that carbohydrated rubbish,' Benson said with dignity. 'Not, at least, for breakfast. Henry, this is Dr. Carpenter.'

'Howdy,' Henry said agreeably.

'Breakfast, Henry,' Benson said. 'And, remember, Dr. Carpenter is a Britisher. We don't want him leaving with a low opinion of the chow served up in the United States Navy.'

'If anyone aboard this ship has a low opinion of the food,' Henry said darkly, 'they hide it pretty well. Breakfast. The works. Right away.'

'Not the works, for heaven's sake,' I said. 'There are some things we decadent Britishers can't face up to first thing in the morning. One of them is French fries.'

He nodded approvingly and left. I said: 'Dr. Benson, I gather.'

'Resident medical officer aboard the *Dolphin*, no less,' he admitted. 'The one who's had his professional competence called into question by having a competing practitioner called in.'

'I'm along for the ride. I assure you I'm not competing with anyone.'

'I know you're not,' he said quickly. Too quickly. Quickly enough so that I could see Swanson's hand in this, could see him telling his officers to lay off quizzing Carpenter too much. I wondered again what Swanson was going to say when and if we ever arrived at the Drift Station and he found out just how fluent a liar I was. Benson went on, smiling: 'There's no call for even one medico aboard this boat, far less two.'

'You're not overworked?' From the leisurely way he was going about his breakfast it seemed unlikely.

'Overworked! I've sickbay call once a day and no one ever turns up – except the morning after we arrive in port with a long cruise behind us and then there are liable to be a few sore heads around. My main job, and what is supposed to be my speciality, is checking on radiation and atmosphere pollution of one kind or another – in the olden submarine days the atmosphere used to get pretty foul after only a few hours submerged but we have to stay down for months, if necessary.' He grinned. 'Neither job is very exacting. We issue each member of the crew with a dosimeter and periodically check a film badge for radiation dosage – which is invariably less than you'd get sitting on the beach on a moderately warm day.

'The atmospheric problem is even easier. Carbon dioxide and carbon monoxide are the only things we have to worry about. We have a scrubbing machine that absorbs the breathed-out carbon dioxide from the atmosphere and pumps it out into the sea. Carbon monoxide – which we could more or less eliminate if we forbade cigarette smoking, only we don't want a mutiny on our hands when we're three hundred feet down – is burned to monoxide by a special heater and then scrubbed as usual. And even that hardly worries me – I've a very competent engineman who keeps those machines in tip-top condition.' He sighed. 'I've a surgery here that will delight your heart, Dr. Carpenter. Operating table, dentist's chair, the lot, and the biggest crisis I've had yet is a cigarette burn between the fingers sustained by a cook who fell asleep during one of the lectures.'

'Lectures?'

'I've got to do something if I'm not to go round the bend. I spend a couple of hours a day keeping up with all the latest medical literature but what good is that if you don't get a chance to practise it? So I lecture. I read up about places we're going to visit and everyone listens to those talks. I give lectures on general health and hygiene and some of them listen to those. I give lectures on the perils of over-eating and under-exercise and no one listens to those. I don't listen to them myself. It was during one of those that the cook got burned. That's why our friend Henry, the steward, adopts his superior and critical attitude towards the eating habits of those who should obviously be watching their eating habits. He eats as much as any two men aboard but owing to some metabolic defect he remains as thin as a rake. Claims it's all due to dieting.'

'It all sounds a bit less rigorous than the life of the average G.P.'

'It is, it is.' He brightened. 'But I've got one job – a hobby to me – that the average G.P. can't have. The ice-machine. I've made myself an expert on that.'

'What does Henry think about it?'

'What? Henry?' He laughed. 'Not that kind of ice-machine. I'll show you later.'

Henry brought food and I'd have liked the *maîtres d'hôtel* of some allegedly five-star hotels in London to be there to see what a breakfast should be like. When I'd finished and told Benson that I didn't see that his lectures on the dangers of overweight were going to get him very far, he said: 'Commander Swanson said you might like to see over the ship. I'm at your complete disposal.'

'Very kind of you both. But first I'd like to shave, dress and have a word with the captain.'

'Shave if you like. No one insists on it. As for dress, shirt and pants are the rig of the day here. And the captain told me to tell you that he'd let you know immediately anything came through that could possibly be of any interest to you.'

So I shaved and then had Benson take me on a conducted tour of this city under the sea: the *Dolphin*, I had to admit, made any British submarine I'd ever seen look like a relic from the Ice Age.

To begin with, the sheer size of the vessel was staggering. So big had the hull to be to accommodate the huge nuclear reactor that it had internal accommodation equivalent to that of a 3,000-ton surface ship, with three decks instead of the usual one and lower hold found in the conventional submarine. The size, combined with the clever use of pastel paints for all the accommodation spaces, working spaces and passageways, gave an overwhelming impression of lightness, airiness and, above all, spaciousness.

He took me first, inevitably, to his sickbay. It was at once the smallest and most comprehensively equipped surgery I'd ever seen, whether a man wanted a major operation or just a tooth filled, he could have himself accommodated there. Neither clinical nor utilitarian, however, was the motif Benson had adopted for the decoration of the one bulkhead in his surgery completely free from surgical or medical equipment of any kind – a series of film stills in colour featuring every cartoon character I'd ever seen, from Pop-eye to Pinocchio, with, as a two-foot square centrepiece, an immaculately cravatted Yogi Bear industriously sawing off from the top of a wooden signpost the first word of a legend which read 'Don't feed the bears'. From deck to deckhead, the bulkhead was covered with them.

'Makes a change from the usual pin-ups,' I observed.

'I get inundated with those, too,' Benson said regretfully. 'Film librarian, you know. Can't use them, supposed to be bad for discipline. However. Lightens the morgue-like atmosphere, what? Cheers up the sick and suffering, I like to think – and distracts their attention while I turn up page 217 in the old textbook to find out what's the matter with them.'

From the surgery we passed through the wardroom and officers' quarters and dropped down a deck to the crew's living quarters. Benson took me through the gleaming tiled washrooms, the immaculate bunk-room, then into the crew's mess hall.

'The heart of the ship,' he announced. 'Not the nuclear reactor, as the uninformed maintain, but here. Just look at it. Hi-fi, juke box, record player, coffee machine, ice-cream machine, movie theatre, library and the home of all the card-sharps on the ship. What chance has a nuclear reactor against this lot? The old-time submariners would turn in their graves if they could see this: compared to the prehistoric conditions they lived in we must seem completely spoiled and ruined. Maybe we are, then again maybe we're not: the old boys never had to stay submerged for months at a time. This is also where I send them to sleep with my lectures on the evils of over-eating.' He raised his voice for the benefit of seven or eight men who were sitting about the tables, drinking coffee, smoking and reading. "You can observe for yourself, Dr. Carpenter, the effects of my lectures on dieting and keeping fit. Did you ever see a bunch of more out-of-condition fat-bellied slobs in your life?"

The men grinned cheerfully. They were obviously well used to this sort of thing: Benson was exaggerating and they knew it. Each of them looked as if he knew what to do with a knife and fork when he got them in his hands, but that was about as far as it went. All had a curious similarity, big men and small men, the same characteristic as I'd seen in Zabrinski and Rawlings – an air of calmly relaxed competence, a cheerful imperturbability, that marked them out as being the men apart that they undoubtedly were.

Benson conscientiously introduced me to everyone, telling me exactly what their function aboard ship was and in turn informing them that I was a Royal Navy doctor along for an acclimatisation trip. Swanson would have told him to say this, it was near enough the truth and would stop speculation on the reason for my presence there.

Benson turned into a small compartment leading off the mess hall. "The air purification room. This is Engineman Harrison. How's our box of tricks, Harrison?"

'Just fine, Doc, just fine. CO reading steady on thirty parts a million.'

He entered some figures in a log book, Benson signed it with a flourish, exchanged a few more remarks and left.

'Half my day's toil done with one stroke of the pen,' he observed. 'I take it you're not interested in inspecting sacks of wheat, sides of beef, bags of potatoes and about a hundred different varieties of canned goods.'

'Not particularly. Why?'

'The entire for'ard half of the deck beneath our feet – a storage hold, really – is given up mainly to that. Seems an awful lot, I know, but then a hundred men can get through an awful lot of food in three months, which is the minimum time we must be prepared to stay at sea if the need arises. We'll pass up the inspection of the stores, the sight of all that food just makes me feel I'm fighting a losing battle all the time, and have a look where the food's cooked.'

He led the way for'ard into the galley, a small square room all tiles and glittering stainless steel. A tall, burly, white-coated cook turned at our entrance and grinned at Benson. 'Come to sample today's lunch, Doc?'

'I have not,' Benson said coldly. 'Dr. Carpenter, the chief cook and my arch-enemy, Sam MacGuire. What form does the excess of calories take that you are proposing to thrust down the throats of the crew today?'

'No thrusting required,' said MacGuire happily. 'Cream soup, sirloin of beef, no less, roast potatoes and as much apple pie as a man can cope with. All good nourishing food."

Benson shuddered. He made to leave the galley, stopped and pointed at a heavy bronze ten-inch tube that stood about four feet above the deck of the galley. It had a heavy hinged lid and screwed clamps to keep the lid in position. 'This might interest you, Dr. Carpenter. Guess what?'

'A pressure cooker?'

'Looks like it, doesn't it? This is our garbage disposal unit. In the old days when a submarine had to surface every few hours garbage disposal was no problem, you just tipped the stuff over the side. But when you spend weeks on end cruising at three hundred feet you can't just walk up to the upper deck and tip the waste over the side: garbage disposal becomes quite a problem. This tube goes right down to the bottom of the *Dolphin.* There's a heavy watertight door at the lower end corresponding to this one, with interlocking controls which make it impossible for both doors to be open at the same time – it would be curtains for the *Dolphin* if they were. Sam here, or one of his henchmen, sticks the garbage into nylon mesh or polythene bags, weighs them with bricks——'

'Bricks, you said?'

'Bricks. Sam, how many bricks aboard this ship?'

'Just over a thousand at the latest count, Doc.'

'Regular builder's yard, aren't we?' Benson grinned. 'Those bricks are to ensure that the garbage bags sink to the bottom of the sea and not float to the surface – even in peacetime we don't want to give our position away to anyone. In go three or four bags, the top door is clamped shut and the bags pumped out under pressure. Then the outer door is closed again. Simple.'

'Yes.' For some reason or other this odd contraption had a curious fascination for me. Days later I was to remember my inexplicable interest in it and wonder whether, after all, I wasn't becoming psychic with advancing years.

'It's not worth all that attention,' Benson said good-humouredly. 'Just an up-to-date version of the old rubbish chute. Come on, a long way to go yet.'

He led the way from the galley to a heavy steel door set in a transverse bulkhead. Eight massive clips to release, then replace after we had passed through the doorway.

'The for'ard torpedo storage room.' Benson's voice was lowered, for at least half of the sixteen or so bunks that lined the bulkheads or were jammed up close to the torpedoes and racks were occupied and every man occupying them was sound asleep. 'Only six torpedoes as you can see. Normally there's stowage for twelve plus another six constantly kept loaded in the torpedo tubes. But those six are all we have just now. We had a malfunction in two of our torpedoes of the newest and more or less untested radio-controlled type – during the Nato exercises just ended – and Admiral Garvie ordered the lot removed for inspection when we got back to the Holy Loch. The *Hunley*, that's our depot ship, carries experts for working on those things. However, they were no sooner taken off yesterday morning than this Drift Station operation came our way and Commander Swanson insisted on having at least six of them put back on straight away.' Benson grinned. 'If there's one thing a submarine skipper hates it's putting to sea without his torpedoes. He feels he might just as well stay at home.'

'Those torpedoes are still not operational?'

'I don't know whether they are nor not. Our sleeping warriors here will do their best to find out when they come to.'

'Why aren't they working on them now?'

'Because before our return to the Clyde they were working on them for nearly sixty hours non-stop trying to find out the cause of the malfunction – and if it existed in the other torpedoes. I told the skipper that if he wanted to blow up the *Dolphin* as good a way as any was to let those torpedo-men keep on working – they were starting to stagger around like zombies and a zombie is the last person you want to have working on the highly-complicated innards of a torpedo. So he pulled them off.'

He walked the length of the gleaming torpedoes and halted before another steel door in a cross bulkhead. He opened this, and beyond, four feet away, was another such heavy door set in another such bulkhead. The sills were about eighteen inches above deck level.

'You don't take many chances in building these boats, do you?' I asked. 'It's like breaking into the Bank of England.'

'Being a nuclear sub doesn't mean that we're not as vulnerable to underwater hazards as the older ships,' Benson said. 'We are. Ships have been lost before because the collision bulkheads gave way. The hull of the *Dolphin* can withstand terrific pressures, but a relatively minor tap from a sharp-edged object can rip us wide like an electric can-opener. The biggest danger is surface collision which nearly always happens at the bows. So, to make doubly sure in the event of a bows collision, we have those double collision bulkheads – the first submarine ever to have them. Makes fore and aft movements here a bit difficult but you've no idea how much more soundly we all sleep at night.'

He closed the after door behind him and opened the for'ard one: we found ourselves in the for'ard torpedo room, a narrow cramped compartment barely long enough to permit torpedoes to be loaded or withdrawn from their tubes. Those tubes, with their heavy-hinged rear doors, were arranged close together in two vertical banks of three. Overhead were the loading rails with heavy chain tackles attached. And that was all. No bunks in here and I didn't wonder: I wouldn't have liked to be the one to sleep for'ard of those collision bulkheads.

We began to work our way aft and had reached the mess hall when a sailor came up and said that the captain wanted to see me. I followed him up the wide central stairway into the control room, Dr. Benson a few paces behind to show that he wasn't being too inquisitive. Commander Swanson was waiting for me by the door of the radio room.

'Morning, Doctor. Slept well?'

'Fifteen hours. What do you think? And breakfasted even better. What's up, Commander.' Something was up, that was for sure: for once, Commander Swanson wasn't smiling.

'Message coming through about Drift Station Zebra. Has to be decoded first but that should take minutes only.' Decoding or not, it seemed to me that Swanson already had a fair idea of the content of that message.

'When did we surface?' I asked. A submarine loses radio contact as soon as it submerges.

'Not since we left the Clyde. We are close on three hundred feet down right now.'

'This is a *radio* message that's coming through?'

'What else? Times have changed. We still have to surface to transmit but we can receive down to our maximum depth. Somewhere in Connecticut is the world's largest radio transmitter using an extremely low frequency which can contact us as this depth far more easily than any other radio can contact a surface ship. While we're waiting, come and meet the drivers.'

He introduced me to some of his control centre crew – as with Benson it seemed to be a matter of complete indifference to him whether it was officer or enlisted man – finally stopped by an officer sitting just aft of the periscope stand, a youngster who looked as if he should still be in high school. 'Will Raeburn,' Swanson said. 'Normally we pay no attention to him but after we move under the ice he becomes the most important man on the ship. Our navigation officer. Are we lost, Will?'

'We're just there, Captain.' He pointed to a tiny pin-point of light on the Norwegian Sea chart spread out below the glass on the plotting-table. 'Gyro and sins are checking to a hair.'

'Sins?' I said.

'You may well look surprised, Dr. Carpenter,' Swanson said. 'Lieutenant Raeburn here is far too young to have any sins. He is referring to S.I.N.S. – Ship's Inertial Navigational System – a device once used for guiding intercontinental missiles and now adapted for submarine use, specifically nuclear submarines. No point in my elaborating, Will's ready to talk your head off about it if he manages to corner you.' He glanced at the chart position. 'Are we getting along quickly enough to suit you, Doctor?'

'I still don't believe it,' I said.

'We cleared the Holy Loch a bit earlier than I expected, before seven,' Swanson admitted. 'I had intended to carry out some slow-time dives to adjust trim – but it wasn't necessary. Even the lack of twelve torpedoes up in the nose didn't make her as stern-heavy as I'd expected. She's so damned big that a few tons more or less here or there doesn't seem to make any difference to her. So we just came haring on up——'

He broke off to accept a signal sheet from a sailor, and read through it slowly, taking his time about it. Then he jerked his head, walked to a quiet corner of the control centre and faced me as I came up to him. He still wasn't smiling.

'I'm sorry,' he said. 'Major Halliwell, the commandant of the Drift Station – you said last night he was a very close friend of yours?'

I felt my mouth begin to go dry. I nodded, took the message from him. It read: 'A further radio message, very broken and difficult to decipher, was received 0945 Greenwich Mean Time from Drift Ice Station Zebra by the British trawler *Morning Star*, the vessel that picked up the previous broadcast. Message stated that Major Halliwell, Officer Commanding, and three others un-named critically injured or dead, no indication who or how many of the four are dead. Others, number again unknown, suffering severely from burns and exposure. Some message about food and fuel, atmospheric conditions and weakness in transmission made it quite indecipherable. Understood from very garbled signal that survivors in one hut, unable to move because of weather. Word "icestorm" clearly picked up. Apparent details of wind speed and temperature but unable to make out.

'*Morning Star* several times attempted contact Drift Station Zebra immediately afterwards. No acknowledgment.

'*Morning Star*, at request of British Admiralty, has abandoned fishing grounds and is moving closer in to Barrier to act as listening post. Message ends.'

I folded the paper and handed it back to Swanson. He said again: 'Sorry about this, Carpenter.'

'Critically injured or dead,' I said. 'In a burnt-out station on the ice-cap in winter, what's the difference?' My voice fell upon my ears as the voice of another man, a voice flat and lifeless, a voice empty of all emotion. 'Johnny Halliwell and three of his men. Johnny Halliwell. Not the kind of man you would meet often, Commander. A remarkable man. Left school at fifteen when his parents died to devote himself to the support of a brother eight years younger than himself. He slaved, he scraped, he sacrificed, he devoted many of the best years of his life to doing everything for his younger brother, including putting him through a six-year University course. Not till then did he think of himself, not till then did he get married. He leaves a lovely wife and three marvellous kids. Two nieces and a nephew not yet six months old.'

'Two nieces——' He broke off and stared at me. 'Good God, your brother? *Your* brother?' He didn't, for the moment, seem to find anything peculiar in the difference of surname.

I nodded silently. Young Lieutenant Raeburn approached us, an odd expression of anxiety on his face, but Swanson abruptly waved him away without seeming even to glance in his direction. He shook his head slowly and was still shaking it when I said abruptly: 'He's tough. He may be one of the survivors. He may live. We must get Drift Station Zebra's position. We *must* get it.'

'Maybe they haven't got it themselves,' Swanson said. You could see he was grateful for something to talk about. 'It *is* a drifting station, remember. The weather being what it is, it may have been days since they got their last fixes – and for all we know their sextants, chronometers and radio direction finders have been lost in the fire.'

'They must know what their latest fix was, even although it was a week ago. They must have a fairly accurate idea of the speed and direction of their drift. They'll be able to provide approximate data. The *Morning Star* must be told to keep transmitting non-stop with a continuous request for their position. If you surface now, can you contact the *Morning Star*?'

'I doubt it. The trawler must be the best part of a thousand miles north of us. His receiver wouldn't be big enough to pull us in – which is another way of saying that our transmitter is too small.'

'The B.B.C. have plenty of transmitters that are big enough. So have the Admiralty. Please ask one or other to contact the *Morning Star* and ask it to make a continuous send for Zebra's position.'

'They could do that themselves direct.'

'Sure they could. But they couldn't hear the reply. The *Morning Star* can – if there's any reply. And she's getting closer to them all the time.'

'We'll surface now.' Swanson nodded. He turned away from the chart table we'd been standing beside and headed for the diving stand. As he passed the plotting table he said to the navigator: 'What was it you wanted, Will?'

Lieutenant Raeburn turned his back on me and lowered his voice, but my hearing has always been a little abnormal. He whispered: 'Did you see his face, Captain? I thought he was going to haul off and clobber you one.'

'I thought the same thing myself,' Swanson murmured. 'For a moment. But I think I just happened to be in his line of vision, that's all.'

I went forward to my cabin and lay down in the cot.

3

'There it is, then,' said Swanson. 'That's the Barrier.'

The *Dolphin*, heading due north, her great cylindrical bulk at one moment completely submerged, the next showing clear as she rolled heavily through the steep quartering seas, was making less than three knots through the water, the great nuclear-powered engines providing just enough thrust to the big twin eight-foot propellers to provide steerage way and no more: thirty feet below where we stood on the bridge the finest sonar equipment in the world was ceaselessly probing the waters all around us but even so Swanson was taking no chances on the effects of collision with a drifting ice-block. The noonday Arctic sky was so overcast that the light was no better than that of late dusk. The bridge thermometer showed the sea temperature as 28°F., the air temperature as – 16°F. The gale-force wind from the north-east was snatching the tops off the rolling steel-grey waves and subjecting the steep-walled sides of the great conning-tower – sail, the crew called it – to the ceaseless battering of a bullet-driven spray that turned to solid ice even as it struck. The cold was intense.

Shivering uncontrollably, wrapped in heavy duffel-coat and oilskins and huddled against the illusory shelter of the canvas wind-dodger, I followed the line of Swanson's pointing arm: even above the high, thin, shrill whine of the wind and the drum-fire of the flying spray against the sail, I could hear the violent chattering of his teeth. Less than two miles away a long, thin, greyish-white line, at that distance apparently smooth and regular, seemed to stretch the entire width of the northern horizon. I'd seen it before and it wasn't much to look at but it was a sight a man never got used to, not because of itself but because of what it represented, the beginning of the polar ice-cap that covered the top of the world, at this time of year a solid compacted mass of ice that stretched clear from where we lay right across to Alaska on the other side of the world. And we had to go under that mass. We had to go under it to find men hundreds of miles away, men who might be already dying, men who might be already dead. Who probably were dead. Men, dying or dead, whom we had to seek out by guess and by God in that great wasteland of ice stretching out endlessly before us, for we did not know where they were.

The relayed radio message we had received just forty-nine hours previously had been the last. Since then, there had been only silence. The trawler *Morning Star* had been sending almost continuously in the intervening two days, trying to raise Drift Station Zebra, but out of that bleak desert of ice to the north had come nothing but silence. No word, no signal, no faintest whisper of sound had come out of that desolation.

Eighteen hours previously the Russian atomic-engined *Dvina* had reached the Barrier and had started on an all-out and desperate attempt to smash its way into the heart of the ice-cap. In this early stage of winter the ice was neither so thick nor so compacted as it would be at the time of its maximum density, in March, and the very heavily armoured and powerfully engined *Dvina* was reputed to be able to break through ice up to a thickness of eighteen feet: given fair conditions, the *Dvina* was widely believed to be capable of battering its way to the North Pole. But the conditions of the rafted ice had proved abnormal to a degree and the attempt a hopeless one. The *Dvina* had managed to crash its way over forty miles into the ice-cap before being permanently stopped by a thick wall of rafter ice over twenty feet in height and probably more than a hundred deep. The *Dvina*, according to reports, had sustained heavy damage to its bows and was still in the process of extricating itself, with the greatest difficulty, from the pack. A very gallant effort that had achieved nothing except an improvement in East-West relations to an extent undreamed of for many years.

Nor had the Russian effort stopped there. Both they and the Americans had made several flights over the area with front-line long-range bombers. Through the deep overcast and driving ice- and snow-filled winds those planes had criss-crossed the suspected area a hundred times, searching with their fantastically accurate radar. But not one single radar sighting had been reported. Various reasons had been put forward to explain the failure, especially the failure of the Strategic Air Command's B52 bomber whose radar was known to be easily capable of picking out a hut against contrasting background from ten thousand feet and in pitch darkness. It had been suggested that the huts were no longer there: that the radar's eye was unable to distinguish between an ice-sheathed hut and the thousands of ice-hummocks which dot the polar cap in winter; and that they had been searching in the wrong area in the first place. The most probable explanation was that the radar waves had been blurred and deflected by the dense clouds of ice-spicules blowing over the area. Whatever the reason, Drift Ice Station Zebra remained as silent as if no life had ever been there, as lost as if it had never existed.

'There's no percentage in staying up here and getting frozen to death.' Commander Swanson's voice was a half-shout, it had to be to make him heard. 'If we're going under that ice, we might as well go now.' He turned his back to the wind and stared out to the west where a big broad-beamed trawler was rolling heavily and sluggishly in the seas less than a quarter of a mile away. The *Morning Star*, which had closed right up to the edge of the ice-pack over the last two days, listening, waiting, and all in vain, was about to return to Hull: her fuel reserves were running low.

'Make a signal,' Swanson said to the seaman by his side. '"We are about to dive and proceed under the ice. We do not expect to emerge for minimum four days, are prepared to remain maximum fourteen."' He turned to me and said: 'If we can't find them in that time . . .' and left the sentence unfinished.

I nodded, and he went on: '"Many thanks for your splendid co-operation. Good luck and a safe trip home."' As the signalman's lamp starting chattering out its message, he said wonderingly: 'Do those fishermen trawl up in the Arctic the entire winter?'

'They do.'

'The whole winter. Fifteen minutes and I'm about dead. Just a bunch of decadent Limeys, that's what they are.' A lamp aboard the *Morning*

Star flickered for some seconds and Swanson said: 'What reply?'

'"Mind your heads under that ice. Good luck and goodbye."'

'Everybody below,' Swanson said. As the signalman began to strip the canvas dodger I dropped down a ladder into a small compartment beneath, wriggled through a hatch and down a second ladder to the pressure hull of the submarine, another hatch, a third ladder and then I was on the control deck of the *Dolphin*. Swanson and the signalman followed, then last of all Hansen, who had to close the two heavy watertight doors above.

Commander Swanson's diving technique would have proved a vast disappointment to those brought up on a diet of movie submarines. No frenzied activity, no tense steely-eyed men hovering over controls, no Tannoy calls of 'Dive, dive, dive,' no blaring of klaxons. Swanson reached down a steel-spring microphone, said quietly: 'This is the captain. We are about to move under the ice. Diving now,' hung up and said: 'Three hundred feet.'

The chief electronics technician leisurely checked the rows of lights indicating all hatches, surface openings and valves closed to the sea. The disc lights were out: the slot lights burned brightly. Just as leisurely he rechecked them, glanced at Swanson and said: 'Straight line shut, sir.' Swanson nodded. Air hissed loudly out of the ballast tanks, and that was it. We were on our way. It was about as wildly exciting as watching a man push a wheelbarrow. And there was something oddly reassuring about it all.

Ten minutes later Swanson came up to me. In the past two days I'd come to know Commander Swanson fairly well, like him a lot and respect him tremendously. The crew had complete and implicit faith in him. I was beginning to have the same thing. He was a kindly genial man with a vast knowledge of every aspect of submarining, a remarkable eye for detail, an even more remarkably acute mind and an imperturbability that remained absolute under all conditions. Hansen, his executive officer and clearly no respecter of persons, had said flatly that Swanson was the best submarine officer in the Navy. I hoped he was right: that was the kind of man I wanted around in conditions like these.

'We're about to move under the ice now, Dr. Carpenter,' he said. 'How do you feel about it?'

'I'd feel better if I could see where we were going.'

'We can see,' he said. 'We've the best eyes in the world aboard the *Dolphin*. We've got eyes that look down, around, ahead and straight up. Our downward eye is the fathometer or echosounder that tells us just how deep the water below our keel is – and as we have about five thousand feet of water below our keel at this particular spot we're hardly

likely to bump into underwater projections and its use right now is
purely a formality. But no responsible navigation officer would ever
think of switching it off. We have two sonar eyes for looking around and
ahead, one sweeping the ship, another searching out a fifteen-degree
path on either side of the bow. Sees everything, hears everything. You
drop a spanner on a warship twenty miles away and we know all about
it. Fact. Again it seems purely a formality. The sonar is searching for
underwater ice stalactites forced down by the pressure of rafted ice
above, but in five trips under the ice and two to the Pole I've never seen
underwater stalactites or ridges deeper than two hundred feet, and we're
at three hundred feet now. But we still keep them on.'

'You might bump into a whale?' I suggested.

'We might bump into another submarine.' He wasn't smiling. 'And
that would be the end of both of us. What with the Russian and our own
nuclear submarines busy criss-crossing to and fro across the top of the
world the underside of the polar ice-cap is getting more like Times
Square every day.'

'But surely the chances——'

'What are the chances of mid-air collision to the only two aircraft
occupying ten thousand square miles of sky? On paper, they don't exist.
There have been three such collisions this year already. So we keep the
sonar pinging. But the really important eye, when you're under the ice,
is the one that looks up. Come and have a squint at it.'

He led the way to the after starboard end of the control room where
Dr. Benson and another man were busy studying a glassed-in eye-level
machine which outwardly consisted of a seven-inch-wide moving ribbon
of paper and an inked stylus that was tracing a narrow straight black line
along it. Benson was engrossed in adjusting some of the calibrated
controls.

'The surface fathometer,' Swanson said. 'Better known as the ice-
machine. It's not really Dr. Benson's machine at all, we have two trained
operators aboard, but as we see no way of separating him from it without
actually court-martialling him, we take the easy way out and let him be.'
Benson grinned, but his eye didn't leave the line traced out by the stylus.
'Same principle as the echo-sounding machine, it just bounces an echo
back from the ice – when there is any. That thin black line you see means
open water above. When we move under the ice the stylus has an added
vertical motion which not only indicates the presence of ice but also gives
us its thickness.'

'Ingenious,' I said.

'It's more than that. Under the ice it can be life or death for the *Dolphin*.
It certainly means life or death for Drift Station Zebra. If we ever get its

position we can't get at it until we break through the ice and this is the only machine that can tell us where the ice is thinnest.'

'No open water at this time of year? No leads?'

'Polynyas, we call them. None. Mind you, the ice-pack is never static, not even in winter, and surface pressure changes can very occasionally tear the ice apart and expose open water. With air temperatures such as you get in winter you can guess how long the open water stays in a liquid condition. There's a skin of ice on it in five minutes, an inch in an hour and a foot inside two days. If we get to one of those frozen-over polynyas inside, say, three days, we've a fair chance of breaking through.'

'With the conning-tower?'

'That's it. The sail. All new nuclear subs have specially strengthened sails designed for one purpose only – breaking through Arctic ice. Even so we have to go pretty gently as the shock, of course, is transmitted to the pressure hull.'

I thought about this a bit then said: 'What happens to the pressure hull if you come up too fast – as I understand may happen with a sudden change in salinity and sea temperature – and you find out at the last minute that you've drifted away from the indicated area of thin ice and have ten solid feet of the stuff above you?'

'That's it,' he said. 'Like you say, it's the last minute. Don't even think about such things, far less talk about them: I can't afford to have nightmares on this job.' I looked at him closely, but he wasn't smiling any more. He lowered his voice. 'I don't honestly think that there is one member of the crew of the *Dolphin* who doesn't get a little bit scared when we move in under the ice. I know I do. I think this is the finest ship in the world, Dr. Carpenter, but there are still a hundred things that can go wrong with it and if anything happens to the reactor or the steam turbines or the electrical generators – then we're already in our coffin and the lid screwed down. The ice-pack above is the coffin lid. In the open sea most of those things don't matter a damn – we just surface or go to snorkel depth and proceed on our diesels. But for diesels you need air – and there's no air under the ice-pack. So if anything happens we either find a polynya to surface in, one chance in ten thousand at this time of year, before our standby battery packs up or – well, that's it.'

'This is all very encouraging,' I said.

'Isn't it?' He smiled, none too soon for me. 'It'll never happen. What's the worthy Benson making all the racket about?'

'Here it is,' Benson called. 'The first drift-block. And another. And another! Come and have a look, Doctor.'

I had a look. The stylus, making a faint soft hissing sound, was no longer tracing out a continuously horizontal line but was moving rapidly up and down across the paper, tracing out the outline of the block of ice passing astern of us. Another thin straight line, more agitated vertical movements of the stylus, and again another block of ice had gone. Even as I watched the number of thin horizontal lines became fewer and fewer and shorter and shorter until eventually they disappeared altogether.

'That's it, then,' Swanson nodded. 'we'll take her deep now, real deep, and open up all the stops.'

When Commander Swanson had said he was going to hurry, he'd meant every word of it. In the early hours of the following morning I was awakened from a deep sleep by a heavy hand on my shoulder. I opened my eyes, blinked against the glare of the overhead light, then saw Lieutenant Hansen.

'Sorry about the beauty sleep, Doc,' he said cheerfully. 'But this is it.'

'This is what?' I said irritably.

'85° 35' north, 21° 20' east – the last estimated position of Drift Station Zebra. At least, the last estimated position with estimated correction for polar drift.'

'Already?' I glanced at my watch, not believing it. 'We're there already?'

'We have not,' Hansen said modestly, 'been idling. The skipper suggests you come along and watch us at work.'

'I'll be right with you.' When and if the *Dolphin* managed to break through the ice and began to try her one in a million chance of contacting Drift Station Zebra, I wanted to be there.

We left Hansen's cabin and had almost reached the control room when I lurched, staggered and would have fallen but for a quick grab at a handrail that ran along one side of the passageway. I hung on grimly as the *Dolphin* banked violently sideways and round like a fighter plane in a tight turn. No submarine in my experience had ever been able to begin to behave even remotely in that fashion. I understood now the reasons for the safety belts on the diving control seats.

'What the hell's up?' I said to Hansen. 'Avoiding some underwater obstruction ahead?'

'Must be a possible polynya. Some place where the ice is thin, anyway. As soon as we spot a possible like that we come around like a chicken chasing its own tail just so we don't miss it. It makes us very popular with the crew, especially when they're drinking coffee or soup.'

We passed into the control room. Commander Swanson, flanked by the navigator and another man, was bent over the plotting table, examining something intently. Farther aft a man at the surface fathometer was reading out ice thickness figures in a quiet unemotional voice. Commander Swanson looked up from the chart.

'Morning, Doctor. John, I think we may have something here.'

Hansen crossed to the plot and peered at it. There didn't seem to be much to peer at – a tiny pin-point of light shining through the glass top of the plot and a squared sheet of chart paper marked by a most unseamanlike series of wavering black lines traced out by a man with a pencil following the track of the tiny moving light. There were three red crosses superimposed on the paper, two very close together, and just as Hansen was examining the paper the crewman manning the ice-machine – Dr. Benson's enthusiasm for his toy did not, it appeared, extend to the middle of the night – called out 'Mark!' Immediately the black pencil was exchanged for a red and a fourth cross made.

'"Think" and "may" are just about right, Captain,' Hansen said. 'It looks awfully narrow to me.'

'It looks the same way to me, too,' Swanson admitted. 'But it's the first break in the heavy ice that we've had in an hour, almost. And the farther north we go, the poorer our chances. Let's give it a go. Speed?'

'One knot,' Raeburn said.

'All back one-third,' Swanson said. No sharp imperatives, not ever, in the way Swanson gave his orders, more a quiet and conversational suggestion, but there was no mistaking the speed with which one of the crewmen, strapped into the diving-stand bucket seat, leaned forward to telegraph the order to the engine-room. 'Left full rudder.'

Swanson bent over to check the plot, closely watching the tiny pin-point of light and tracing pencil move back towards the approximate centre of the elongated quadrangle formed by the four red crosses. 'All stop,' he went on. 'Rudder amidships.' A pause then: 'All ahead one-third. So. All stop.'

'Speed zero,' Raeburn said.

'120 feet,' Swanson said to the diving officer, 'but gently, gently.'

A strong steady hum echoed in the control centre. I asked Hansen: 'Blowing ballast?'

He shook his head. 'Just pumping the stuff out. Gives a far more precise control of rising speed and makes it easier to keep the sub on an even keel. Bringing a stopped sub up on a dead even keel is no trick for beginners. Conventional subs never try this sort of thing.'

The pumps stopped. There came the sound of water flooding back into the tanks as the diving officer slowed up the rate of ascent. The sound faded.

'Secure flooding,' the diving officer said. 'Steady on 120 feet.'

'Up periscope,' Swanson said to the crewman by his side. An overhead lever was engaged and we could hear the hiss of high-pressure oil as the hydraulic piston began to lift the starboard periscope off its seating. The gleaming cylinder rose slowly against the pressure of the water until finally the foot of the periscope cleared its well. Swanson opened the hinged handgrips and peered through the eyepiece.

'What does he expect to see in the middle of the night at this depth?' I asked Hansen.

'Never can tell. It's rarely completely dark, as you know. Maybe a moon, maybe only stars – but even starlight will show as a faint glow through the ice – if the ice is thin enough.'

'What's the thickness of the ice above, in this rectangle?'

'The sixty-four thousand dollar question,' Hansen admitted, 'and the answer is that we don't know. To keep that ice-machine to a reasonable size the graph scale has to be very small. Anything between four and forty inches. Four inches we go through like the icing on a wedding cake: forty inches and we get a very sore head indeed.' He nodded across the Swanson. 'Doesn't look so good. That grip he's twisting is to tilt the periscope lens upwards and that button is for focusing. Mean's he's having trouble in finding anything.'

Swanson straightened. 'Black as the earl of hell's waistcoat,' he said conversationally. 'Switch on hull and sail floodlights.'

He stooped and looked again. For a few seconds only. 'Peasoup. Thick and yellow and strong. Can't see a thing. Let's have the camera, shall we?'

I looked at Hansen, who nodded to a white screen that had just been unshuttered on the opposite bulkhead. 'All mod cons, Doc. Closed circuit TV. Camera is deck mounted under toughened glass and can be remotely controlled to look up or round.'

'You could do with a new camera, couldn't you?' The TV screen was grey, fuzzy, featureless.

'Best that money can buy,' Hansen said. 'It's the water. Under certain conditions of temperature and salinity it becomes almost completely opaque when floodlit. Like driving into a heavy fog with your headlights full on.'

'Floodlights off,' Swanson said. The screen became quite blank. 'Floodlights on.' The same drifting misty grey as before. Swanson sighed and turned to Hansen. 'Well, John?'

'If I were paid for imagining things,' Hansen said carefully, 'I could imagine I see the top of the sail in that left corner. Pretty murky out there, Captain. Heigh-ho for the old blind man's bluff, is that it?'

'Russian roulette, I prefer to call it.' Swanson had the clear unworried face of a man contemplating a Sunday afternoon in a deck-chair. 'Are we holding position?'

'I don't know.' Raeburn looked up from the plot. 'It's difficult to be sure.'

'Sanders?' This to the man at the ice-machine.

'Thin ice, sir. Still thin ice.'

'Keep calling. Down periscope.' He folded the handles up and turned to the diving officer. 'Take her up like we were carrying a crate of eggs atop the sail and didn't want to crack even one of them.'

The pumps started again. I looked around the control room. Swanson excepted, everyone was quiet and still and keyed-up. Raeburn's face was beaded with sweat and Sanders's voice was too calm and impersonal by half as he kept repeating: 'Thin ice, thin ice,' in a low monotone. You could reach out and touch the tension in the air. I said quietly to Hansen: 'Nobody seems very happy. There's still a hundred feet to go.'

'There's forty feet,' Hansen said shortly. 'Readings are taken from keel level and there's sixty feet between the keel and the top of the sail. Forty feet minus the thickness of the ice – and maybe a razor-sharp or needle-pointed stalactite sticking down ready to skewer the *Dolphin* through the middle. You know what that means?'

'That it's time I started getting worried too?'

Hansen smiled, but he wasn't feeling like smiling. Neither was I, not any more.

'Ninety feet,' the diving officer said.

'Thin ice, thin ice,' Sanders intoned.

'Switch off the deck flood, leave the sail flood on,' Swanson said. 'And keep that camera moving. Sonar?'

'All clear,' the sonar operator reported. 'All clear all round.' A pause, then: 'No, hold it, hold it! Contact dead astern!'

'How close?' Swanson asked quickly.

'Too close to say. Very close.'

'She's jumping!' the diving officer called out sharply. '80, 75.' The *Dolphin* had hit a layer of colder water or extra salinity.

'Heavy ice, heavy ice!' Sanders called out urgently.

'Flood emergency!' Swanson ordered – and this time it was an order.

I felt the sudden build-up of air pressure as the diving officer vented the negative tank and tons of sea-water poured into the emergency diving tank, but it was too late. With a shuddering, jarring smash that sent us staggering the *Dolphin* crashed violently into the ice above, glass tinkled, lights went out and the submarine started falling like a stone.

'Blow negative to the mark!' the diving officer called. High pressure air came boiling into the negative tank – at our rate of falling we would have been flattened by the sea-pressure before the pumps could even have begun to cope with the huge extra ballast load we had taken aboard in seconds. Two hundred feet, two hundred and fifty and we were still falling. Nobody spoke, everybody just stood or sat in a frozen position staring at the diving stand. It required no gift for telepathy to know the thought in every mind. It was obvious that the *Dolphin* had been struck aft by some underwater pressure ridge at the same instant as the sail had hit the heavy ice above: if the *Dolphin* had been holed aft this descent wasn't going to stop until the pressure of a million tons of water had crushed and flattened the hull and in a flicker of time snuffed out the life of every man inside it.

'Three hundred feet,' the diving officer called out. 'Three fifty – and she's slowing! She's slowing.'

The *Dolphin* was still falling, sluggishly passing the four-hundred-foot mark, when Rawlings appeared in the control room, tool-kit in one hand, a crate of assorted lamps in the other.

'It's unnatural,' he said. He appeared to be addressing the shattered lamp above the plot which he had immediately begun to repair. 'Contrary to the laws of nature, I've always maintained. Mankind was never meant to probe beneath the depths of the ocean. Mark my words, those new-fangled inventions will come to a bad end.'

'So will you, if you don't keep quiet,' Commander Swanson said acidly. But there was no reprimand in his face, he appreciated as well as any of us the therapeutic breath of fresh air that Rawlings had brought into that tension-laden atmosphere. 'Holding?' he went on to the diving officer.

The diving officer raised a finger and grinned. Swanson nodded, swung the coil-spring microphone in front of him. 'Captain here,' he said calmly. 'Sorry about that bump. Report damage at once.'

A green light flashed in the panel of a box beside him. Swanson touched a switch and a loudspeaker in the deckhead crackled.

'Manœuvring room here.' The manœuvring room was in the after end of the upper level engine-room, towards the stern. 'Hit was directly above us here. We could do with a box of candles and some of the dials and gauges are out of kilter. But we still got a roof over our heads.'

'Thank you, Lieutenant. You can cope?'

'Sure we can.'

Swanson pressed another switch. 'Stern room?'

'We still attached to the ship?' a cautious voice inquired.

'You're still attached to the ship,' Swanson assured him. 'Anything to report?'

'Only that there's going to be an awful lot of dirty laundry by the time we get back to Scotland. The washing-machine's had a kind of fit.'

Swanson smiled and switched off. His face was untroubled, he must

have had a special sweat-absorbing mechanism on his face, I felt I could
have done with a bath towel. He said to Hansen: 'That was bad luck. A
combination of a current where a current had no right to be, a
temperature inversion where a temperature inversion had no right to be,
and a pressure ridge where we least expected it. Not to mention the
damned opacity of the water. What's required is a few circuits until we
know this polynya like the backs of our hands, a small offset to allow for
drift and a little precautionary flooding as we approach the ninety-foot
mark.'

'Yes, sir. That's what's required. Point is, what are we going to do?'

'Just that. Take her up and try again.'

I had my pride so I refrained from mopping my brow. They took her
up and tried again. At 200 feet and for fifteen minutes Swanson juggled
propellers and rudder till he had the outline of the frozen polynya above
as accurately limned on the plot as he could ever expect to have it. Then
he positioned the *Dolphin* just outside one of the boundary lines and gave
an order for a slow ascent.

'One twenty feet,' the diving officer said. 'One hundred ten.'

'Heavy ice,' Sanders intoned. 'Still heavy ice.'

Sluggishly the *Dolphin* continued to rise. Next time in the control room,
I promised myself, I wouldn't forget that bath towel. Swanson said: 'If
we've overestimated the speed of the drift, there's going to be another
bump I'm afraid.' He turned to Rawlings who was still busy repairing
lights. 'If I were you, I'd suspend operations for the present. You may
have to start all over again in a moment and we don't carry all that
number of spares aboard.'

'One hundred feet,' the diving officer said. He didn't sound as unhappy
as his face looked.

'The water's clearing,' Hansen said suddenly. 'Look.'

The water had cleared, not dramatically so, but enough. We could see
the top corner of the sail clearly outlined on the TV screen. And then,
suddenly, we could see something else again, heavy ugly ridged ice not
a dozen feet above the sail.

Water flooded into the tanks. The diving officer did not have to be told
what to do, we'd gone up like an express lift the first time we'd hit a
different water layer and once like that was enough in the life of a
submarine.

'Ninety feet,' he reported. 'Still rising.' More water flooded in, then the
sound died away. 'She's holding. Just under ninety feet.'

'Keep her there.' Swanson stared at the TV screen. 'We're drifting
clear and into the polynya – I hope.'

'Me too,' Hansen said. 'There can't be more than a couple of feet between the top of the sail and that damned ugly stuff.'

'There isn't much room,' Swanson acknowledged. 'Sanders?'

'Just a moment, sir. The graph looks kinda funny – no, we're clear.' He couldn't keep the excitement out of his voice. 'Thin ice!'

I looked at the screen. He was right. I could see the vertical edge of a wall of ice move slowly across the screen, exposing clear water above.

'Gently, now, gently,' Swanson said. 'And keep that camera on the ice wall at the side, then straight up, turn about.'

The pumps began to throb again. The ice wall, less than ten yards away, began to drift slowly down past us.

'Eighty-five feet,' the diving officer reported. 'Eighty.'

'No hurry,' Swanson said. 'We're sheltered from that drift by now.'

'Seventy-five feet.' The pumps stopped, and water began to flood into the tanks. 'Seventy.' The *Dolphin* was almost stopped now, drifting upwards as gently as thistledown. The camera switched upwards, and we could see the top corner of the sail clearly outlined with a smooth ceiling of ice floating down to meet it. More water gurgled into the tanks, the top of the sail met the ice with a barely perceptible bump and the *Dolphin* came to rest.

'Beautifully done,' Swanson said warmly to the diving officer. 'Let's try giving that ice a nudge. Are we slewing?'

'Bearing constant.'

Swanson nodded. The pumps hummed, pouring out water, lightening ship, steadily increasing positive buoyancy. The ice stayed where it was. More time passed, more water pumped out, and still nothing happened. I said softly to Hansen: 'Why doesn't he blow the main ballast? You'd get a few hundred tons of positive buoyancy in next to no time and even if that ice is forty inches thick it couldn't survive all that pressure at a concentrated point.'

'Neither could the *Dolphin*,' Hansen said grimly. 'With a suddenly induced big positive buoyancy like that, once she broke through she'd go up like a cork from a champagne bottle. The pressure hull might take it, I don't know, but sure as little apples the rudder would be squashed flat as a piece of tin. Do you want to spend what little's left of your life travelling in steadily decreasing circles under the polar ice-cap?'

I didn't want to spend what little was left of my life in travelling in steadily decreasing circles under the ice-cap so I kept quiet. I watched Swanson as he walked across to the diving stand and studied the banked dials in silence for some seconds. I was beginning to become a little apprehensive about what Swanson would do next: I was beginning to realise, and not slowly either, that he was a lad who didn't give up easily.

'That's enough of that lot,' he said to the diving officer. 'If we go through now with all this pressure behind us we'll be airborne. This ice is even thicker than we thought. We've tried the long steady shove and it hasn't worked. A sharp tap is obviously what is needed. Flood her down, but gently, to eighty feet or so, a good sharp whiff of air into the ballast tanks and we'll give our well-known imitation of a bull at a gate.'

Whoever had installed the 240-ton air-conditioning unit in the *Dolphin* should have been prosecuted, it just wasn't working any more. The air was very hot and stuffy – what little there was of it, that was. I looked around cautiously and saw that everyone else appeared to be suffering from this same shortage of air, all except Swanson, who seemed to carry his own built-in oxygen cylinder around with him. I hoped Swanson was keeping in mind the fact that the *Dolphin* had cost 120 million dollars to build. Hansen's narrowed eyes held a definite core of worry and even the usually imperturbable Rawlings was rubbing a bristly blue chin with a hand the size and shape of a shovel. In the deep silence after Swanson had finished speaking the scraping noise sounded unusually loud, then was lost in the noise of water flooding into the tanks.

We stared at the screen. Water continued to pour into the tanks until we could see a gap appear between the top of the sail and the ice. The pumps started up, slowly, to control the speed of descent. On the screen, the cone of light thrown on to the underside of the ice by the flood-lamp grew fainter and larger as we dropped, then remained stationary, neither moving nor growing in size. We had stopped.

'Now,' said Swanson. 'Before that current gets us again.'

There came the hissing roar of compressed air under high pressure entering the ballast tanks. The *Dolphin* started to move sluggishly upwards while we watched the cone of light on the ice slowly narrow and brighten.

'More air,' Swanson said.

We were rising faster now, closing the gap to the ice all too quickly for my liking. Fifteen feet, twelve feet, ten feet.

'More air,' Swanson said.

I braced myself, one hand on the plot, the other on an overhead grab bar. On the screen, the ice was rushing down to meet us. Suddenly the picture quivered and danced, the *Dolphin* shuddered, jarred and echoed hollowly along its length, more lights went out, the picture came back on the screen, the sail was still lodged below the ice, then the *Dolphin* trembled and lurched and the deck pressed against our feet like an ascending elevator. The sail on the TV vanished, nothing but opaque white taking its place. The diving officer, his voice high with strain that had not yet found relief, called out: 'Forty feet, forty feet.' We had broken through.

'There you are now,' Swanson said mildly. 'All it needed was a little perseverance.' I looked at the short plump figure, the round good-humoured face, and wondered for the hundredth time why the nerveless iron men of this world so very seldom look the part.

I let my pride have a holiday. I took my handkerchief from my pocket, wiped my face and said to Swanson: 'Does this sort of thing go on all the time?'

'Fortunately, perhaps, no.' He smiled. He turned to the diving officer. 'We've got our foothold on this rock. Let's make sure we have a good belay.'

For a few seconds more compressed air was bled into the tanks, then the diving officer said: 'No chance of her dropping down now, Captain.'

'Up periscope.'

Again the long gleaming silver tube hissed up from its well. Swanson didn't even bother folding down the hinged handles. He peered briefly into the eyepiece, then straightened.

'Down periscope.'

'Pretty cold up top?' Hansen asked.

Swanson nodded. 'Water on the lens must have frozen solid as soon as it hit that air. Can't see a thing.' He turned to the diving officer. 'Steady at forty?'

'Guaranteed. And all the buoyancy we'll ever want.'

'Fair enough.' Swanson looked at the quartermaster who was shrugging his way into a heavy sheepskin coat. 'A little fresh air, Ellis, don't you think?'

'Right away, sir.' Ellis buttoned his coat and added: 'Might take some time.'

'I don't think so,' Swanson said. 'You may find the bridge and hatchways jammed with broken ice but I doubt it. My guess is that that ice is so thick that it will have fractured into very large sections and fallen outside clear of the bridge.'

I felt my ears pop with the sudden pressure change as the hatch swung up and open and snapped back against its standing latch. Another more distant sound as the second hatch-cover locked open and then we heard Ellis on the voice-tube.

'All clear up top.'

'Raise the antennæ,' Swanson said. 'John, have them start transmitting and keep transmitting until their fingers fall off. Here we are and here we stay – until we raise Drift Ice Station Zebra.'

'If there's anyone left alive there,' I said.

'There's that, of course,' Swanson said. He couldn't look at me. 'There's always that.'

4

This, I thought, death's dreadful conception of a dreadful world, must have been what had chilled the hearts and souls of our far-off Nordic ancestors when life's last tide slowly ebbed and they had tortured their failing minds with fearful imaginings of a bleak and bitter hell of eternal cold. But it had been all right for the old boys, all they had to do was to imagine it, we had to experience the reality of it and I had no doubt at all in my mind as to which was the easier. The latter-day Eastern conception of hell was more comfortable altogether, at least a man could keep reasonably warm there.

One thing sure, nobody could keep reasonably warm where Rawlings and I were, standing a half-hour watch on the bridge of the *Dolphin* and slowly freezing solid. It had been my own fault entirely that our teeth were chattering like frenzied castanets. Half an hour after the radio room had started transmitting on Drift Ice Station Zebra's wavelength and all without the slightest whisper by way of reply or acknowledgment, I had suggested to Commander Swanson that Zebra might possibly be able to hear us without having sufficient power to send a reply but that they might just conceivably let us have an acknowledgment some other way. I'd pointed out that Drift Stations habitually carried rockets – the only way to guide home any lost members of the party if radio communication broke down – and radio-sondes and rockoons. The sondes were radio-carrying balloons which could rise to a height of twenty miles to gather weather information: the rockoons, radio rockets fired from balloons, could rise even higher. On a moonlit night such as this, those balloons, if released, would be visible at least twenty miles away: if flares were attached to them, at twice that distance. Swanson had seen my point, called for volunteers for the first watch and in the circumstances I hadn't had much option. Rawlings had offered to accompany me.

It was a landscape – if such a bleak, barren and featureless desolation could be called a landscape – from another and ancient world, weird and strange and oddly frightening. There were no clouds in the sky, but there were no stars either: this I could not understand. Low on the southern horizon a milky misty moon shed its mysterious light over the dark lifelessness of the polar ice-cap. Dark, not white. One would have expected moonlit ice to shine and sparkle and glitter with the light of a million crystal chandeliers – but it was dark. The moon was so low in the sky that the dominating colour on the ice-cap came from the blackness of the long shadows cast by the fantastically ridged and hummocked ice:

and where the moon did strike directly the ice had been so scoured and abraded by the assaults of a thousand ice-storms that it had lost almost all its ability to reflect light of any kind.

This ridged and hummocked ice-cap had a strange quality of elusiveness, of impermanence, of evanescence: one moment there, definitively hard and harsh and repellent in its coldly contrasting blacks and whites, the next, ghost-like, blurring, coalescing and finally vanishing like a shimmering mirage fading and dying in some ice-bound desert. But this was no trick of the eye or imagination, it was the result of a ground-level ice-storm that rose and swirled and subsided at the dictates of an icy wind that was never less than strong and sometimes gusted up to gale force, a wind that drove before it a swirling rushing fog of billions of needle-pointed ice-spicules. For the most part, standing as we were on the bridge twenty feet above the level of the ice – the rest of the *Dolphin* might never have existed as far as the eye could tell – we were above this billowing ground-swell of ice particles; but occasionally the wind gusted strongly, the spicules lifted, drummed demonaically against the already ice-sheathed starboard side of the sail, drove against the few exposed inches of our skin with all the painfully stinging impact of a sand-blaster held at arm's length; but unlike a sand-blaster, the pain-filled shock of those spear-tipped spicules was only momentary, each wasp-like sting carried with it its own ice-cold anæsthetic and all surface sensation was quickly lost. Then the wind would drop, the furious rattling on the sail would fade and in the momentary contrast of near-silence we could hear the stealthy rustling as of a million rats advancing as the ice-spicules brushed their blind way across the iron-hard surface of the polar cap. The bridge thermometer stood at −21°F. – 53° of frost. If I were a promoter interested in developing a summer holiday resort, I thought, I wouldn't pay very much attention to this place.

Rawlings and I stamped our feet, flailed our arms across our chests, shivered non-stop, took what little shelter we could from the canvas windbreak, rubbed our goggles constantly to keep them clear, and never once, except when the ice-spicules drove into our faces, stopped examining every quarter of the horizon. Somewhere out there on those frozen wastes was a lost and dying group of men whose lives might depend upon so little a thing as the momentary misting up of one of our goggles. We stared out over those shifting ice-sands until our eyes ached. But that was all we had for it, just aching eyes. We saw nothing, nothing at all. The ice-cap remained empty of all signs of life. Dead.

When our relief came Rawlings and I got below with all the speed our frozen and stiffened limbs would allow. I found Commander Swanson sitting on a canvas stool outside the radio room. I stripped off outer clothes, face coverings and goggles, took a steaming mug of coffee that had appeared from nowhere and tried not to hop around too much as the blood came pounding back into arms and legs.

'How did you cut yourself like that?' Swanson asked, concern in his voice. 'You've a half-inch streak of blood right across your forehead.'

'Flying ice, it just looks bad.' I felt tired and pretty low. 'We're wasting our time transmitting. If the men on Drift Station Zebra were without any shelter it's no wonder all signals ceased long ago. Without food and shelter no one could last more than a few hours in that lot. Neither Rawlings nor I is a wilting hothouse flower but after half an hour up there we've both just about had it.'

'I don't know,' Swanson said thoughtfully. 'Look at Amundsen. Look at Scott, at Peary. They *walked* all the way to the Poles.'

'A different breed of men, Captain. Either that or the sun shone for them. All I know is that half an hour is too long to be up there. Fifteen minutes is enough for anyone.'

'Fifteen minutes it shall be.' He looked at me, face carefully empty of all expression. 'You haven't much hope?'

'If they're without shelter, I've none.'

'You told me they had an emergency power pack of Nife cells for powering their transmitter,' he murmured. 'You also said those batteries will retain their charge indefinitely, years if necessary, irrespective of the weather conditions under which they are stored. They must have been using that battery a few days ago when they sent out their first S.O.S. It wouldn't be finished already.'

His point was so obvious that I didn't answer. The battery wasn't finished: the men were.

'I agree with you,' he went on quietly. 'We're wasting our time. Maybe we should just pack up and go home. If we can't raise them, we'll never find them.'

'Maybe not. But you're forgetting your directive from Washington, Commander.'

'How do you mean?'

'Remember? I'm to be extended every facility and all aid short of actually endangering the safety of the submarine and the lives of the crew. At the present moment we're doing neither. If we fail to raise them I'm prepared for a twenty-mile sweep on foot round this spot in the hope of locating them. If that fails we could move to another polynya and repeat the search. The search area isn't all that big, there's a fair chance, but a chance, that we might locate the station eventually. I'm prepared to stay up here all winter till we do find them.'

'You don't call that endangering the lives of my men? Making extended searches of the ice-cap, on foot, in mid-winter?'

'Nobody said anything about endangering the lives of your men.'

'You mean – you mean you'd go it alone.' Swanson stared down at the deck and shook his head. 'I don't know what to think. I don't know whether to say you're crazy or whether to say I'm beginning to understand why they – whoever "they" may be – picked you for the job, Dr Carpenter.' He sighed, then regarded me thoughtfully. 'One moment you say there's no hope, the next that you're prepared to spend the winter here, searching. If you don't mind my saying so, Doctor, it just doesn't make sense.'

'Stiff-necked pride,' I said. 'I don't like throwing my hand in on a job before I've even started it. I don't know what the attitude of the United States Navy is on that sort of thing.'

He gave me another speculative glance, I could see he believed me the way a fly believes the spider on the web who has just offered him safe accommodation for the night. He smiled. He said: 'The United States Navy doesn't take offence all that easily, Dr Carpenter. I suggest you catch a couple of hours' sleep while you can. You'll need it all if you're going to start walking towards the North Pole.'

'How about yourself? You haven't been to bed at all tonight.'

'I think I'll wait a bit.' He nodded towards the door of the radio room. 'Just in case anything comes through.'

'What are they sending? Just the call sign?'

'Plus request for position and a rocket, if they have either. I'll let you know immediately anything comes through. Good night, Dr Carpenter. Or rather, good morning.'

I rose heavily and made my way to Hansen's cabin.

The atmosphere round the 8 a.m. breakfast table in the wardroom was less than festive. Apart from the officer on deck and the engineer lieutenant on watch, all the *Dolphin*'s officers were there, some just risen from their bunks, some just heading for them, none of them talking in anything more than monosyllables. Even the ebullient Dr. Benson was remote and withdrawn. It seemed pointless to ask whether any contact had been established with Drift Station Zebra, it was painfully obvious that it hadn't. And that after almost five hours' continuous sending. The sense of despondency and defeat, the unspoken knowledge that time had run out for the survivors of Drift Station Zebra hung heavy over the wardroom.

No one hurried over his meal – there was nothing to hurry for – but by and by they rose one by one and drifted off, Dr. Benson to his sick-bay call, the young torpedo officer, Lieutenant Mills, to supervise the efforts of his men who had been working twelve hours a day for the past two days to iron out the faults in the suspect torpedoes, a third to relieve Hansen, who had the watch, and three others to their bunks. That left only Swanson, Raeburn and myself. Swanson, I knew, hadn't been to bed at all the previous night, but for all that he had the rested clear-eyed look of a man with eight solid hours behind him.

The steward, Henry, had just brought in a fresh pot of coffee when we heard the sound of running footsteps in the passageway outside and the quartermaster burst into the wardroom. He didn't quite manage to take the door off its hinges, but that was only because the Electric Boat Company put good solid hinges on the doors of their submarines.

'We got it made!' he shouted, and then perhaps recollecting that enlisted men were expected to conduct themselves with rather more decorum in the wardroom, went on: 'We've raised them, Captain, we've raised them!'

'What!' Swanson could move twice as fast as his comfortable figure suggested and he was already half-out of his chair.

'We are in radio contact with Drift Ice Station Zebra, sir,' Ellis said formally.

Commander Swanson got to the radio room first, but only because he had a head start on Raeburn and myself. Two operators were on watch, both leaning forward towards their transmitters, one with his head bent low, the other with his cocked to one side, as if those attitudes of concentrated listening helped them to isolate and amplify the slightest sounds coming through the earphones clamped to their heads. One of them was scribbling away mechanically on a signal pad. DSY, he was writing down, DSY repeated over and over again. DSY. The answering call-sign of Drift Station Zebra. He stopped writing as he caught sight of Swanson out of the corner of one eye.

'We've got 'em, Captain, no question. Signal very weak and intermittent but——'

'Never mind the signal!' It was Raeburn who made this interruption without any by-your-leave from Swanson. He tried, and failed, to keep the rising note of excitement out of his voice and he looked more than ever like a youngster playing hooky from high school. 'The bearing? Have you got their bearing? That's all that matters.'

The other operator swivelled in his seat and I recognised my erstwhile guard, Zabrinski. He fixed Raeburn with a sad and reproachful eye.

'Course we got their bearing, Lieutenant. First thing we did. O-forty-five, give or take a whisker. North-east, that is.'

'Thank you, Zabrinski,' Swanson said dryly. 'O-forty-five is north-east. The navigating officer and I wouldn't have known. Position?'

Zabrinski shrugged and turned to his watchmate, a man with a red face, leather neck and a shining polished dome where his hair ought to have been. 'What's the word, Curly?'

'Nothing. Just nothing.' Curly looked at Swanson. 'Twenty times I've asked for his position. No good. All he does is send out his call-sign. I don't think he's hearing us at all, he doesn't even know we're listening, he just keeps sending his call-sign over and over again. Maybe he hasn't switched his aerial in to "receive".'

'It isn't possible,' Swanson said.

'It is with this guy,' Zabrinski said. 'At first Curly and I thought that it was the signal that was weak, then we thought it was the operator who was weak or sick, but we were wrong, he's just a ham-handed amateur.'

'You can tell?' Swanson asked.

'You can always tell. You can——' He broke off, stiffened and touched his watchmate's arm.

Curly nodded. 'I got it,' he said matter-of-factly. 'Position unknown, the man says.'

Nobody said anything, not just then. It didn't seem important that he couldn't give us his position, all that mattered was that we were in direct contact. Raeburn turned and ran forward across the control room. I could hear him speak rapidly on the bridge telephone. Swanson turned to me.

'Those balloons you spoke of earlier. The ones on Zebra. Are they free or captive?'

'Both.'

'How do the captive ones work?'

'A free-running winch, nylon cord marked off in hundreds and thousands of feet.'

'We'll ask them to send a captive balloon up to 5,000 feet,' Swanson decided. 'With flares. If they're within thirty or forty miles we ought to see it, and if we get its elevation and make an allowance for the effect of wind on it, we should get a fair estimate of distance ... What is it, Brown?' This to the man Zabrinski called 'Curly'.

'They're sending again,' Curly said. 'Very broken, fades a lot. "God's sake, hurry." Just like that, twice over. "God's sake, hurry."'

'Send this,' Swanson said. He dictated a brief message about the balloons. 'And send it real slow.'

Curly nodded and began to transmit. Raeburn came running back into the radio room.

'The moon's not down yet,' he said quickly to Swanson. 'Still a degree or two above the horizon. I'm taking a sextant up top and taking a moon-sight. Ask them to do the same. That'll give us the latitude difference and if we know they're o-forty-five of us we can pin them down to a mile.'

'It's worth trying,' Swanson said. He dictated another message to Brown. Brown transmitted the second message immediately after the first. We waited for the answer. For all of ten minutes we waited. I looked at the men in the radio room, they all had the same remote withdrawn look of men who are there only physically, men whose minds are many miles away. They were all at the same place and I was too, wherever Drift Ice Station Zebra was.

Brown started writing again, not for long. His voice this time was still matter-of-fact, but with overtones of emptiness. He said: '"All balloons burnt. No moon."'

'No moon.' Raeburn couldn't hide the bitterness, the sharpness of his disappointment. 'Damn! Must be pretty heavy overcast up there. Or a bad storm.'

'No,' I said. 'You don't get local weather variations like that on the ice-cap. The conditions will be the same over 50,000 square miles. The moon is down. For them, the moon is down. Their latest estimated position must have been pure guesswork, and bad guesswork at that. They must be at least a hundred miles farther north and east than we had thought.'

'Ask them if they have any rockets,' Swanson said to Brown.

'You can try,' I said. 'It'll be a waste of time. If they are as far off as I think, their rockets would never get above our horizon. Even if they did, we wouldn't see them.'

'It's always a chance, isn't it?' Swanson asked.

'Beginning to lose contact, sir,' Brown reported. 'Something there about food but it faded right out.'

'Tell them if they have any rockets to fire them at once,' Swanson said. 'Quickly, now, before you lose contact.'

Four times in all Brown sent the message before he managed to pick up a reply. Then he said: 'Message reads: 'Two minutes.' Either this guy is pretty far through or his transmitter batteries are. That's all. "Two minutes," he said.'

Swanson nodded wordlessly and left the room. I followed. We picked up coats and binoculars and clambered up to the bridge. After the warmth and comfort of the control room, the cold seemed glacial, the flying ice-spicules more lancet-like than ever. Swanson uncapped the gyro-repeater compass, gave us the line of o-forty-five, told the two men who had been keeping watch what to look for and where.

A minute passed, two minutes, five. My eyes began to ache from staring into the ice-filled dark, the exposed part of my face had gone completely numb and I knew that when I removed those binoculars I was going to take a fair bit of skin with them.

A phone bell rang. Swanson lowered his glasses, leaving two peeled and bloody rings around his eyes – he seemed unware of it, the pain wouldn't come until later – and picked up the receiver. He listened briefly, hung up.

'Radio room,' he said. 'Let's get below. All of us. The rockets were fired three minutes ago.'

We went below. Swanson caught sight of his face reflected in a glass gauge and shook his head. 'They must have shelter,' he said quietly. 'They must. Some hut left. Or they would have been gone long ago.' He went into the radio room. 'Still in contact?'

'Yeah.' Zabrinski spoke. 'Off and on. It's a funny thing. When a dicey contact like this starts to fade it usually gets lost and stays lost. But this guy keeps coming back. Funny.'

'Maybe he hasn't even got batteries left,' I said. 'Maybe all they have is a hand-cranked generator. Maybe there's no one left with the strength to crank it for more than a few moments at a time.'

'Maybe,' Zabrinski agreed. 'Tell the captain that last message, Curly.'

'"Can't late many tours,"' Brown said. 'That's how the message came through. "Can't late many tours." I think it should have read "Can't last many hours." Don't see what else it can have been.'

Swanson looked at me briefly, glanced away again. I hadn't told anyone else that the commandant of the base was my brother and I knew he hadn't told anyone either. He said to Brown: 'Give them a time-check. Ask them to send their call-signs five minutes every hour on the hour. Tell them we'll contact them again within six hours at the most, maybe only four. Zabrinski, how accurate was that bearing?'

'Dead accurate, Captain. I've had plenty of re-checks. O-forty-five exactly.'

Swanson moved out into the control centre. 'Drift Station Zebra can't see the moon. If we take Dr. Carpenter's word for it that weather conditions are pretty much the same all over, that's because the moon is below their horizon. With the elevation we have of the moon, and knowing their bearing, what's Zebra's minimum distance from us?'

'A hundred miles, as Dr. Carpenter said,' Raeburn confirmed after a short calculation. 'At least that.'

'So. We leave here and take a course o-forty. Not enough to take us very far from their general direction but it will give us enough offset to take a good cross-bearing eventually. We will go exactly a hundred miles and try for another polynya. Call the executive officer, secure for diving.' He smiled at me. 'With two cross-bearings and an accurately measured base-line, we can pin them down to a hundred yards.'

'How do you intend to measure a hundred miles under the ice?

Accurately, I mean?'

'Our inertial navigation computer does it for me. It's very accurate, you wouldn't believe just how accurate. I can dive the *Dolphin* off the eastern coast of the United States and surface again in the Eastern Mediterranean within five hundred yards of where I expect to be. Over a hundred miles I don't expect to be twenty yards out.'

Radio aerials were lowered, hatches screwed down and within five minutes the *Dolphin* had dropped down from her hole in the ice and was on her way. The two helmsmen at the diving stand sat idly smoking, doing nothing: the steering controls were in automatic interlock with the inertial navigation system which steered the ship with a degree of accuracy and sensitivity impossible to human hands. For the first time I could feel a heavy jarring vibration rumbling throughout the length of the ship: 'can't last many hours' the message had said: the *Dolphin* was under full power.

I didn't leave the control room that morning. I spent most of the time peering over the shoulder of Dr. Benson who had passed his usual five minutes in the sick-bay waiting for the patients who never turned up and then had hurried to his seat by the ice-machine. The readings on that machine meant living or dying to the Zebra survivors. We had to find another polynya to surface in to get a cross-bearing on Zebra's position: no polynya, no cross-bearing: no cross-bearing, no hope. I wondered for the hundredth time how many of the survivors of the fire were still alive. From the quiet desperation of the few garbled messages that Brown and Zabrinski had managed to pick up I couldn't see that there would be many.

The pattern traced out by the hissing stylus on the chart was hardly an encouraging sight. Most of the time it showed the ice overhead to be of a thickness of ten feet or more. Several times the stylus dipped to show thicknesses of thirty to forty feet, and once it dipped down almost clear of the paper, showing a tremendous inverted ridge of at least 150 feet in depth. I tried to imagine what kind of fantastic pressures created by piled-up log-jams of rafted ice on the surface must have been necessary to force ice down to such a depth: but I just didn't have the imagination to cope with that sort of thing.

Only twice in the first eighty miles did the stylus trace out the thin black line that meant thin ice overhead. The first of those polynyas might have accommodated a small rowing boat, but it would certainly never have looked at the *Dolphin*: the other had hardly been any bigger.

Shortly before noon the hull vibration died away as Swanson gave the order for a cutback to a slow cruising speed. He said to Benson: 'How does it look?'

'Terrible. Heavy ice all the way.'

'Well, we can't expect a polynya to fall into our laps straight away,' Swanson said reasonably. 'We're almost there. We'll make a grid search. Five miles east, five miles west, a quarter-mile farther to the north each time.'

The search began. An hour passed, two, then three. Raeburn and his assistant hardly ever raised their heads from the plotting table where they were meticulously tracing every movement the *Dolphin* was making in its criss-cross search under the sea. Four o'clock in the afternoon. The normal background buzz of conversation, the occasional small talk from various groups in the control centre, died away completely. Benson's occasional 'Heavy ice, still heavy ice,' growing steadily quieter and more dispirited, served only to emphasise and deepen the heavy brooding silence that had fallen. Only a case-hardened undertaker could have felt perfectly at home in that atmosphere. At the moment, undertakers were the last people I wanted to think about.

Five o'clock in the afternoon. People weren't looking at each other any more, far less talking. Heavy ice, still heavy ice. Defeat, despair, hung heavy in the air. Heavy ice, still heavy ice. Even Swanson had stopped smiling, I wondered if he had in his mind's eye what I now constantly had in mine, the picture of a haggard, emaciated, bearded man with his face all but destroyed with frostbite, a frozen, starving, dying man draining away the last few ounces of his exhausted strength as he cranked the handle of his generator and tapped out his call-sign with lifeless fingers, his head bowed as he strained to listen above the howl of the ice-storm for the promise of aid that never came. Or maybe there was no one tapping out a call-sign any more. They were no ordinary men who had been sent to man Drift Ice Station Zebra but there comes a time when even the toughest, the bravest, the most enduring will abandon all hope and lie down to die. Perhaps he had already lain down to die. Heavy ice, still heavy ice.

At half past five Commander Swanson walked across to the ice-machine and peered over Benson's shoulder. He said: 'What's the average thickness of that stuff above?'

'Twelve to fifteen feet,' Benson said. His voice was low and tired. 'Nearer fifteen, I would say.'

Swanson picked up a phone. 'Lieutenant Mills? Captain here. What is the state of readiness of those torpedoes you're working on? . . . Four? . . . Ready to go? . . . Good. Stand by to load. I'm giving this search another thirty minutes, then it's up to you. Yes, that is correct. We shall attempt to blow a hole through the ice.' He replaced the phone.

Hansen said thoughtfully: 'Fifteen feet of ice is a helluva lot of ice.

And that ice will have a tamping effect and will direct ninety per cent of the explosive force down the way. You think we *can* blow a hole through fifteen feet of ice, Captain?'

'I've no idea,' Swanson admitted. 'How can anyone know until we try it?'

'Nobody ever tried to do this before?' I asked.

'No. Not in the U.S. Navy, anyway. The Russians may have tried it, I wouldn't know. They don't,' he added dryly, 'keep us very well informed on those matters.'

'Aren't the underwater shock waves liable to damage the *Dolphin?*' I asked. I didn't care for the idea at all, and that was a fact.

'If they do, the Electric Boat Company can expect a pretty strong letter of complaint. We shall explode the warhead electronically about one thousand yards after it leaves the ship – it has to travel eight hundred yards anyway before a safety device unlocks and permits the warhead to be armed. We shall be bows-on to the detonation and with a hull designed to withstand the pressures this one is, the shock effects should be negligible.'

'Very heavy ice,' Benson intoned. 'Thirty feet, forty feet, fifty feet. Very, very heavy ice.'

'Just too bad if your torpedo ended up under a pile like the stuff above us just now,' I said. 'I doubt if it would even chip off the bottom layer.'

'We'll take care that doesn't happen. We'll just find a suitably large layer of ice of normal thickness, kind of back off a thousand yards and then let go.'

'Thin ice!' Benson's voice wasn't a shout, it was a bellow. 'Thin ice. No, by God, clear water! Clear water! Lovely clear, clear water!'

My immediate reaction was that either the ice-machine or Benson's brain had blown a fuse. But the officer at the diving panel had no such doubts for I had to grab and hang on hard as the *Dolphin* heeled over violently to port and came curving round, engines slowing, in a tight circle to bring her back to the spot where Benson had called out. Swanson watched the plot, spoke quietly and the big bronze propellers reversed and bit into the water to bring the *Dolphin* to a stop.

'How's it looking now, Doc?' Swanson called out.

'Clear, clear water,' Benson said reverently. 'I got a good picture of it. It's pretty narrow, but wide enough to hold us. It's long, with a sharp left-hand dog-leg, for it followed us round through the first forty-five degrees of our curve.'

'One fifty feet,' Swanson said.

The pumps hummed. The *Dolphin* drifted gently upwards like an airship rising from the ground. Briefly, water flooded back into the tanks.

The *Dolphin* hung motionless.

'Up periscope,' Swanson said.

The periscope hissed up slowly into the raised position. Swanson glanced briefly through the eyepiece, then beckoned me. 'Take a look,' he beamed 'As lovely a sight as you'll ever see.'

I took a look. If you'd made a picture of what could be seen above and framed it you couldn't have sold the result even if you added Picasso's name to it: but I could see what he meant. Solid black masses on either side with a scarcely lighter strip of dark jungle green running between them on a line with the fore-and-aft direction of the ship. An open lead in the polar pack.

Three minutes later we were lying on the surface of the Arctic Ocean, just under two hundred and fifty miles from the Pole.

The rafted, twisted ice-pack reared up into contorted ridges almost fifty feet in height, towering twenty feet above the top of the sail, so close you could almost reach out and touch the nearest ridge. Three or four of those broken and fantastically hummocked ice-hills we could see stretching off to the west and then the light of the floodlamp failed and we could see no more. Beyond that there was only blackness.

To the east we could see nothing at all. To have stared out to the east with opened eyes would have been to be blinded for life in a very few seconds: even goggles became clouded and scarred after the briefest exposure. Close in to the *Dolphin*'s side you could, with bent head and hooded eyes, catch, for a fleeting part of a second, a glimpse of black water, already freezing over: but it was more imagined than seen.

The wind, shrieking and wailing across the bridge and through raised antennæ, showed at consistently over 60 m.p.h. on the bridge anemometer. The ice-storm was no longer the gusting, swirling fog of that morning but a driving wall of stiletto-tipped spears, near-lethal in its ferocity, high speed ice-spicule lances that would have skewered their way through the thickest cardboard or shattered in a second a glass held in your hand. Over and above the ululating threnody of the wind we could hear an almost constant grinding, crashing and deep-throated booming as millions of tons of racked and tortured ice, under the influence of the gale and some mighty pressure centre, heaven knew how many hundreds of miles away, reared and twisted and tore and cracked, one moment forming another rafted ridge as a layer of ice, perhaps ten feet thick, screeched and roared and clambered on to the shoulders of another and then another, the next rending apart in indescribably violent cacophony to open up a new lead, black wind-torn water that started to skim over with ice almost as soon as it was formed.

'Are we both mad? Let's get below.' Swanson cupped his hands to my ear and had to shout, but even so I could hardly hear him above that hellish bedlam of sound.

We clambered down into the comparatively sudden stillness of the control room. Swanson untied his parka hood and pulled off scarf and goggles that had completely masked his face. He looked at me and shook his head wonderingly.

'And some people talk about the white silence of the Arctic. My God, a boilermaker's shop is like a library reading-room compared to that lot.' He shook his head again. 'We stuck our noses out a few times above the ice-pack last year, but we never saw anything like this. Or heard it. Winter-time, too. Cold, sure, damned cold, and windy, but never so bad that we couldn't take a brief stroll on the ice, and I used to wonder about those stories of explorers being stuck in their tents for days on end, unable to move. But I know now why Captain Scott died.'

'It is pretty nasty,' I admitted. 'How safe are we here, Commander?'

'That's anybody's guess,' Swanson shrugged. 'The wind's got us jammed hard against the west wall of this polynya and there's maybe fifty yards of open water to starboard. For the moment we're safe. But you can hear and see that pack is on the move, and not slowly either. The lead we're in was torn open less than an hour ago. How long? Depends on the configuration of the ice, but those polynyas can close up damned quickly at times, and while the hull of the *Dolphin* can take a fair old pressure, it can't take a million tons of ice leaning against it. Maybe we can stay here for hours, maybe only for minutes. Whichever it is, as soon as that east wall comes within ten feet of the starboard side we're dropping down out of it. You know what happens when a ship gets caught in the ice.'

'I know. They get squeezed flat, are carried round the top of the world for a few years then one day are released and drop to the bottom, two miles straight down. The United States Government wouldn't like it, Commander.'

'The prospects of further promotion for Commander Swanson would be poor,' Swanson admitted. 'I think——'

'Hey!' The shout came from the radio room. 'Hey, c'm here.'

'I rather think Zabrinski must be wanting me,' Swanson murmured. He moved off with his usual deceptive speed and I followed him into the radio room. Zabrinski was sitting half-turned in his chair, an ear-to-ear beam on his face, the earphones extended in his left hand. Swanson took them, listened briefly, then nodded.

'DSY,' he said softly. 'DSY, Dr. Carpenter. We have them. Got the bearing? Good.' He turned to the doorway, saw the quartermaster. 'Ellis, ask the navigating officer to come along as soon as possible.'

'We'll pick 'em all up yet, Captain,' Zabrinski said jovially. The smile on the big man's face, I could see now, didn't extend as far as his eyes. 'They must be a pretty tough bunch of boys out there.'

'Very tough, Zabrinski,' Swanson said absently. His eyes were remote and I knew he was listening to the metallic cannonading of the ice-spicules, a billion tiny pneumatic chisels drumming away continuously against the outer hull of the submarine, a sound loud enough to make low speech impossible. 'Very tough. Are you in two-way contact?'

Zabrinski shook his head and turned away. He'd stopped smiling. Raeburn came in, was handed a sheet of paper and left for his plotting table. We went with him. After a minute or two he looked up, and said: 'If anyone fancies a Sunday afternoon's walk, this is it.'

'So close?' Swanson asked.

'So very close. Five miles due east give or take half a mile. Pretty fair old bloodhounds, aren't we?'

'We're just lucky,' Swanson said shortly. He walked back to the radio room. 'Talking to them yet?'

'We've lost them altogether.'

'Completely?'

'We only had 'em a minute, Captain. Just that. Then they faded. Got weaker and weaker. I think Doc Carpenter here is right, they're using a hand-cranked generator.' He paused, then said idly: 'I've a six-year-old-daughter who could crank one of those machines for five minutes without turning a hair.'

Swanson looked at me, then turned away without a word. I followed him to the unoccupied diving stand. From the bridge access hatch we could hear the howl of the storm, the grinding ice with its boom and scream that spanned the entire register of hearing. Swanson said: 'Zabrinski put it very well. . . . I wonder how long this damnable storm is going to last?'

'Too long. I have a medical kit in my cabin, a fifty-ounce flask of medicinal alcohol and cold-weather clothes. Could you supply me with a thirty-pound pack of emergency rations, high protein high-calorie concentrates? Benson will know what I mean.'

'Do you mean what I think you mean?' Swanson said slowly. 'Or am I just going round the bend?'

'What's this about going round the bend?' Hansen had just come through the doorway leading to the for'ard passageway, and the grin on his face was clear enough indication that though he'd caught Swanson's last words he'd caught neither the intonation nor the expression on Swanson's face. 'Very serious state of affairs, going round the bend. I'll have to assume command and put you in irons, Captain. Something about it in regulations, I dare say.'

'Dr. Carpenter is proposing to sling a bag of provisions on his back and proceed to Drift Station Zebra on foot.'

'You've picked them up again?' Just for the moment Hansen had forgotten me. 'You really got them? And a cross-bearing?'

'Just this minute. We've hit it almost on the nose. Five miles, young Raeburn says.'

'My God! Five miles. Only five miles!' Then the elation vanished from voice and face as if an internal switch had been touched. 'In weather like this it might as well be five hundred. Even old Amundsen couldn't have moved ten yards through this stuff.'

'Dr. Carpenter evidently thinks he can improve on Amundsen's standards,' Swanson said dryly. 'He's talking about walking there.'

Hansen looked at me for a long and considering moment, then turned back to Swanson. 'I think maybe it's Doc Carpenter we should be clapping in the old irons.'

'I think maybe it is,' Swanson said.

'Look,' I said. 'There are men out there on Drift Station Zebra. Maybe not many, not now, but there are some. One, anyway. Men a long way past being sick. Dying men. To a dying man it takes only the very smallest thing to spell out the difference between life and death. I'm a doctor, I know. The smallest thing. An ounce of alcohol, a few ounces of food, a hot drink, some medicine. Then they'll live. Without those little things they will surely die. They're entitled to what smallest aid they can get, and I'm entitled to take whatever risks I care to see they get it. I'm not asking anyone else to go, all I'm asking is that you implement the terms of your orders from Washington to give me all possible assistance without endangering the *Dolphin* or its crew. Threatening to stop me is not my idea of giving assistance. And I'm not asking you to endanger· your submarine or the lives of your men.'

Swanson gazed at the floor. I wondered what he was thinking of: the best way to stop me, his orders from Washington, or the fact that he was the only man who knew that the commandant on Zebra was my brother. He said nothing.

'You must stop him, Captain,' Hansen said urgently. 'Any other man you saw putting a pistol to his head or a razor to his throat, you'd stop that man. This is the same. He's out of his mind, he's wanting to commit suicide.' He tapped the bulkhead beside him. 'Good God, Doc, why do you think we have the sonar operators in here on duty even when we're stopped. So that they can tell us when the ice wall on the far side of the polynya starts to close in on us, that's why. And *that's* because it's impossible for any man to last thirty seconds on the bridge or see an inch against the ice-storm up there. Just take a quick twenty-second trip up there, up on the bridge, and you'll change your mind fast enough, I guarantee.'

'We've just come down from the bridge,' Swanson said matter-of-factly.

'And he still wants to go? It's like I say, he's crazy.'

'We could drop down now,' Swanson said. 'We have the position. Perhaps we can find a polynya within a mile, half a mile of Zebra. That would be a different proposition altogether.'

'Perhaps you could find a needle in a haystack,' I said. 'It took you six hours to find this one, and even at that we were lucky. And don't talk about torpedoes, the ice in this area is rafted anything up to a hundred feet in depth. Pretty much all over. You'd be as well trying to blast your way through with a ·22. Might be twelve hours, might be days before we could break through again. I can get there in two-three hours.'

'If you don't freeze to death in the first hundred yards,' Hansen said. 'If you don't fall down a ridge and break your leg. If you don't get blinded in a few minutes. If you don't fall into a newly-opened polynya that you can't see, where you'll either drown or, if you manage to get out, freeze solid in thirty seconds. And even if you do survive all those things, I'd be grateful if you'd explain to me exactly how you propose to find your way blind to a place five miles away. You can't carry a damn' great gyro weighing about half a ton on your back, and a magnetic compass is useless in those latitudes. The magnetic north pole is a good bit *south* of where we are now and a long way to the west. Even if you *did* get some sort of bearing from it, in the darkness and the ice-storm you could still miss the camp – or what's left of it – by only a hundred yards and never know it. And even if by one chance in a million you do manage to find your way there, how on earth do you ever expect to find your way back again. Leave a paper-trail? A five-mile ball of twine. Crazy is hardly the word for it.'

'I may break a leg, drown or freeze,' I conceded. 'I'll take my chance on that. Finding my way there and back is no great trick. You have a radio bearing on Zebra and know exactly where it lies. You can take a radio bearing on any transmitter. All I have to do is to tote a receiver-transmitter radio along with me, keep in touch with you and you can keep me on the same bearing as Zebra. It's easy.'

'It would be,' Hansen said, 'except for one little thing. We don't have any such radio.'

'I have a twenty-mile walkie-talkie in my case,' I said.

'Coincidence, coincidence,' Hansen murmured. 'Just happened to bring it along, no doubt. I'll bet you have all sorts of funny things in that case of yours, haven't you, Doc?'

'What Dr. Carpenter has in his case is really no business of ours,' Swanson said in mild reproof. He hadn't thought so earlier. 'What does concern us is his intention to do away with himself. You really can't expect us to consent to this ridiculous proposal, Dr. Carpenter.'

'No one's asking you to consent to anything,' I said. 'Your consent is not required. All I'm asking you to do is to stand to one side. And to arrange for that food provision pack for me. If you won't, I'll have to manage without.'

I left and went to my cabin. Hansen's cabin, rather. But even although it wasn't my cabin that didn't stop me from turning the key in the lock as soon as I had passed through the door.

Working on the likely supposition that if Hansen did come along soon he wasn't going to be very pleased to find the door of his own cabin locked against him, I wasted no time. I spun the combination lock on the case and opened the lid. At least three-quarters of the available space was taken up by Arctic survival clothing, the very best that money could buy. It hadn't been my money that had bought it.

I stripped off the outer clothes I was wearing, pulled on long open-mesh underwear, woollen shirt and cord breeches, then a triple-knit wool parka lined with pure silk. The parka wasn't quite standard, it had a curiously shaped suède-lined pocket below and slightly to the front of the left armpit, and a differently shaped suède-lined pocket on the right-hand side. I dug swiftly to the bottom of my case and brought up three separate items. The first of these, a nine-millimetre Mannlicher-Schoenauer automatic, fitted into the left-hand pocket as securely and snugly as if the pocket had been specially designed for it, which indeed it had: the other items, spare magazine clips, fitted as neatly into the right-hand pocket.

The rest of the dressing didn't take long. Two pairs of heavy-knit woollen socks, felt undershoes and then the furs – caribou for the outer parka and trousers, wolverine for the hood, sealskin for the boots and reindeer for the gloves, which were pulled on over other layers of silk gloves and woollen mittens. Maybe a polar bear would have had a slight edge over me when it came to being equipped to survive an Arctic blizzard, but there wouldn't have been much in it.

I hung snow-mask and goggles round my neck, stuck a rubberised waterproofed torch into the inside pocket of the fur parka, unearthed my walkie-talkie and closed the case. I set the combination again. There was no need to set the combination any more, not now that I had the Mannlicher-Schoenauer under my arm, but it would give Swanson

something to do while I was away. I shoved my medicine case and a steel
flask of alcohol in a rucksack and unlocked the door.

Swanson was exactly where I'd left him in the control room. So was
Hansen. So were two others who had not been there when I had left,
Rawlings and Zabrinski. Hansen, Rawlings, and Zabrinski, the three
biggest men in the ship. The last time I'd seen them together was when
Swanson had whistled them up from the *Dolphin* in the Holy Loch to see
to it that I didn't do anything he didn't want me to do. Maybe
Commander Swanson had a one-track mind. Hansen, Rawlings, and
Zabrinski. They looked bigger than ever.

I said to Swanson: 'Do I get those iron rations or not?'

'One last formal statement,' Swanson said. His first thoughts, as I came
waddling into the control centre, must have been that a grizzly bear was
loose inside his submarine, but he hadn't batted an eyelid. 'For the
record. Your intentions are suicidal, your chances are non-existent. I
cannot give my consent.'

'All right, your statement is on record, witnesses and all. The iron
rations.'

'I cannot give my consent because of a fresh and dangerous
development. One of our electronic technicians was carrying out a
routine calibration test on the ice-machine just now and an overload coil
didn't function. Electric motor burnt out. No spares, it will have to be
rewired. You realise what that means. If we're forced to drop down I
can't find my way to the top again. Then it's curtains for everybody –
everybody left above the ice, that is.'

I didn't blame him for trying, but I was vaguely disappointed in him:
he'd had time to think up a better one than that. I said: 'The iron rations,
Commander. Do I get them?'

'You mean to go through with this? After what I've said?'

'Oh, for God's sake. I'll do without the food.'

'My executive officer, Torpedoman Rawlings and Radioman Zabrinski,' Swanson said formally, 'don't like this.'

'I can't help what they like or don't like.'

'They feel they can't let you go through with it,' he persisted.

They were more than big. They were huge. I could get past them the
way a lamb gets past a starving lion. I had a gun all right but with that
one-piece parka I was wearing I'd practically have to undress myself to
get at it and Hansen, in that Holy Loch canteen, had shown just how
quickly he could react when he saw anyone making a suspicious move.
And even if I did get my gun out, what then? Men like Hansen, like
Rawlings and Zabrinski, didn't scare. I couldn't bluff them with a gun.
And I couldn't use the gun. Not against men who were just doing their

duty.

'They *won't* let you go through with it,' Swanson went on, 'unless, that is, you will permit them to accompany you, which they have volunteered to do.'

'Volunteered,' Rawlings sniffed. 'You, you, and you.'

'I don't want them,' I said.

'Gracious, ain't he?' Rawlings asked of no one in particular. 'You might at least have said thanks, Doc.'

'You are putting the lives of your men in danger, Commander Swanson. You know what your orders said.'

'Yes. I also know that in Arctic travels, as in mountaineering and exploring, a party has always double the chances of the individual. I also know that if it became known that we had permitted a civilian doctor to set off on his own for Drift Station Zebra while we were all too scared to stir from our nice warm sub, the name of the United States Navy would become pretty muddy.'

'What do your men think of your making them risk their lives to save the good name of the submarine service?'

'You heard the captain,' Rawlings said. 'We're volunteers. Look at Zabrinski there, anyone can see that he is a man cast in a heroic mould.'

'Have you thought of what happens,' I said, 'if the ice closes in when we're away and the captain has to take the ship down?'

'Don't even talk of it,' Zabrinski urged. 'I'm not all that heroic.'

I gave up. I'd no option but to give up. Besides, like Zabrinski, I wasn't all that heroic and I suddenly realised that I would be very glad indeed to have those three men along with me.

5

Lieutenant Hansen was the first man to give up. Or perhaps 'give up' is wrong, the meaning of the words was quite unknown and the thought totally alien to Hansen; it would be more accurate to say that he was the first of us to show any glimmerings of common sense. He caught my arm, brought his head close to mine, pulled down his snow mask and shouted: 'No farther, Doc. We must stop.'

'The next ridge,' I yelled back. I didn't know whether he'd heard me or not. As soon as he'd spoken he'd pulled his mask back up into position again to protect the momentarily exposed skin against the horizontally driving ice-storm, but he seemed to understand for he eased his grip on the rope round my waist and let me move ahead again. For the past two and a half hours Hansen, Rawlings and I had each taken his turn at being the lead man on the end of the rope, while the other three held on to it some ten yards behind, the idea being not that the lead man should guide the others but that the others should save the life of the lead man, should the need arise. And the need already had arisen, just once. Hansen, slipping and scrambling on all-fours across a fractured and upward sloping raft of ice, had reached gropingly forward with his arms into the blindness of the night and the storm and found nothing there. He had fallen eight vertical feet before the rope had brought him up with a vicious jerk that had been almost as painful for Rawlings and myself, who had taken the brunt of the shock, as it had been for Hansen. For nearly two minutes he'd dangled above the wind-torn black water of a freshly opened lead before we'd managed to drag him back to safety. It had been a close thing, far too close a thing, for in far sub-zero temperatures with a gale-force wind blowing, even a few seconds' submersion in water makes the certainty of death absolute, the process of dissolution as swift as it is irreversible. In those conditions the clothes of a man pulled from the water become a frozen and impenetrable suit of armour inside seconds, an armour that can neither be removed nor chipped away. Petrified inside this ice-shroud, a man just simply and quickly freezes to death – in the unlikely event, that is, of his heart having withstood the thermal shock of the body surface being exposed to an almost instantaneous hundred degree drop in temperature.

So now I stepped forward very cautiously, very warily indeed, feeling the ice ahead of me with a probe we'd devised after Hansen's near accident – a chopped-off five-foot length of rope which we'd dipped into the water of the lead then exposed to the air until it had become as rigid as a bar of steel. At times I walked, at times I stumbled, at times, when a brief lull in the gale-force wind, as sudden as it was unexpected, would catch me off balance I'd just fall forward and continue on hands and knees, for it was quite as easy that way. It was during one of those periods when I was shuffling blindly forward on all-fours that I realised that the wind had, for the time being, lost nearly all of its violence and that I was no longer being bombarded by that horizontally driving hail of flying ice-spicules. Moments later my probe made contact with some solid obstacle in my path: the vertical wall of a rafted ice ridge. I crawled thankfully into its shelter, raised my goggles and pulled out and switched on my torch as the others came blindly up to where I lay.

Blindly. With arms outstretched they pawed at the air before them like sightless men, which for the past two and a half hours was exactly what they had been. For all the service our goggles had given us we might as well have stuck our heads in gunny sacks before leaving the *Dolphin*. I looked at Hansen, the first of the three to come up. Goggles, snow-mask, hood, clothing – the entire front part of his body from top to toe was deeply and solidly encrusted in a thick and glittering layer of compacted ice, except for some narrow cracks caused by joint movements of legs and arms. As he drew close to me I could hear him splintering and crackling a good five feet away. Long ice-feathers streamed back from his head, shoulders and elbows; as an extra-terrestrial monster from one of the chillier planets, such as Pluto, he'd have been a sensation in any horror movie. I suppose I looked much the same.

We huddled close together in the shelter of the wall. Only four feet above our heads the ice-storm swept by in a glittering grey-white river. Rawlings, sitting on my left, pushed up his goggles, looked down at his ice-sheathed furs and started to beat himself with his fist across the chest to break up the covering. I reached out a hand and caught his arm.

'Leave it alone.' I said.

'Leave it alone?' Rawlings's voice was muffled by his snow-mask, but not so muffled that I couldn't hear the chattering of his teeth. 'This damn' suit of armour weighs a ton. I'm out of training for this kind of weight-lifting, Doc.'

'Leave it alone. If it weren't for that ice, you'd have frozen to death by this time: it's insulating you from that wind and the ice-storm. Let's see the rest of your face. And your hands.'

I checked him and the two others for frost-bite, while Hansen checked me. We were still lucky. Blue and mottled and shaking with the cold, but no frost-bite. The furs of the other three might not have been quite as fancy as mine, but they were very adequate indeed. Nuclear subs always got the best of everything, and Arctic clothing was no exception. But although they weren't freezing to death I could see from their faces and hear from their breathing that they were pretty far gone in exhaustion. Thrusting into the power of that ice-storm was like wading upstream against the current of a river of molasses: that was energy-sapping enough, but the fact that we had to spend most of our time clambering over, slipping on, sliding and falling across fractured ice or making detours round impassable ridges while being weighed down with forty-pound packs on our back and heaven only knew how many additional pounds of ice coating our furs in front had turned our trudge across that contorted treacherous ice into a dark and frozen nightmare.

'The point of no return, I think,' Hansen said. His breathing, like Rawlings's, was very quick, very shallow, almost gasping.

'We can't take much more of this, Doc.'

'You ought to listen to Dr. Benson's lectures a bit more,' I said reprovingly. 'All this ice-cream and apple pie and lolling around in your bunks is no training for this sort of thing.'

'Yeah?' he peered at me. 'How do *you* feel?'

'A mite tired,' I admitted. 'Nothing much to speak of.' Nothing much to speak of, my legs felt as if they were falling off, that was all, but the goad of pride was always a useful one to have to hand. I slipped off my rucksack and brought out the medicinal alcohol. 'I suggest fifteen minutes' break. Any more and we'll just start stiffening up completely. Meantime, a little drop of what we fancy will help keep the old blood corpuscles trudging around.'

'I thought medical opinion was against alcohol in low temperatures,' Hansen said doubtfully. 'Something about opening the pores.'

'Name me any form of human activity,' I said, 'and I'll find you a group of doctors against it. Spoilsports. Besides, this isn't alcohol, it's very fine Scotch whisky.'

'You should have said so in the first place. Pass it over. Not too much for Rawlings and Zabrinski, they're not used to the stuff. Any word, Zabrinski?'

Zabrinski, with the walkie-talkie's aerial up and one earphone tucked in below the hood of his parka, was talking into the microphone through cupped hands. As the radio expert, Zabrinski had been the obvious man to handle the walkie-talkie and I'd given it to him before leaving the submarine. This was also the reason why Zabrinski wasn't at any time given the position of lead man in our trudge across the pack ice. A heavy fall or immersion in water would have finished the radio he was carrying slung on his back: and if the radio were finished then so would we be, for without the radio not only had we no hope of finding Drift Station Zebra, we wouldn't have a chance in a thousand of ever finding our way back to the *Dolphin* again. Zabrinski was built on the size and scale of a medium-sized gorilla and was about as durable; but we couldn't have treated him more tenderly had he been made of Dresden china.

'It's difficult,' Zabrinski said. 'Radio's O.K., but this ice-storm causes such damn' distortion and squeaking – no, wait a minute, though, wait a minute.'

He bent his head over the microphone, shielding it from the sound of the storm, and spoke again through cupped hands. 'Zabrinski here . . . Zabrinski. Yeah, we're all kinda tuckered out, but Doc here seems to think we'll make it. . . . Hang on, I'll ask him.'

He turned to me. 'How far do you reckon we've come, they want to know.'

'Four miles.' I shrugged. 'Three and a half, four and a half. You guess it.'

Zabrinski spoke again, looked interrogatively at Hansen and myself, saw our headshakes and signed off. He said: 'Navigating officer says we're four-five degrees north of where we should be and that we'll have to cut south if we don't want to miss Zebra by a few hundred yards.'

It could have been worse. Over an hour had passed since we'd received the last bearing position from the *Dolphin* and, between radio calls, our only means of navigating had been by judging the strength and direction of the wind in our faces. When a man's face is completely covered and largely numb it's not a very sensitive instrument for gauging wind direction – and for all we knew the wind might be either backing or veering. It could have been a lot worse and I said so to Hansen.

'It could be worse,' he agreed heavily. 'We could be travelling in circles or we could be dead. Barring that, I don't see how it could be worse.' He gulped down the whisky, coughed, handed the flask top back to me. 'Things look brighter now. You honestly think we can make it?'

'A little luck, that's all. You think maybe our packs are too heavy? That we should abandon some of it here?' The last thing I wanted to do was to abandon any of the supplies we had along with us: eighty pounds of food, a stove, thirty pounds of compressed fuel tablets, 100 ounces of alcohol, a tent, and a very comprehensive medical kit; but if it was to be abandoned I wanted the suggestion to be left to them, and I was sure they wouldn't make it.

'We're abandoning nothing,' Hansen said. Either the rest or the whisky had done him good, his voice was stronger, his teeth hardly chattering at all.

'Let the thought die stillborn,' Zabrinski said. When first I'd seen him in Scotland he had reminded me of a polar bear and now out here on the ice-cap, huge and crouched in his ice-whitened furs, the resemblance was redoubled. He had the physique of a bear, too, and seemed completely tireless; he was in far better shape than any of us. 'This weight on my bowed shoulders is like a bad leg: an old friend that gives me pain, but I wouldn't be without it.'

'You?' I asked Rawlings.

'I am conserving my energy,' Rawlings announced. 'I expect to have to carry Zabrinski later on.'

We pulled the starred, abraded and now thoroughly useless snow-goggles over our eyes again, hoisted ourselves stiffly to our feet and moved off to the south to find the end of and round the high ridge that here blocked our path. It was by far the longest and most continuous ridge we'd encountered yet, but we didn't mind, we required to make a good offing to get us back on course and not only were we doing just that but we were doing it in comparative shelter and saving our strength by so doing. After perhaps four hundred yards the ice wall ended so abruptly, leading to so sudden and unexpected an exposure to the whistling fury of the ice-storm that I was bowled completely off my feet. An express train couldn't have done it any better. I hung on to the rope with one hand, clawed and scrambled my way back on to my feet with the help of the other, shouted a warning to the others, and then we were fairly into the wind again, holding it directly in our faces and leaning far forward to keep our balance.

We covered the next mile in less than half an hour. The going was easier now, much easier than it had been, although we still had to make small detours round rafted, compacted and broken ice: on the debit side, we were all of us, Zabrinski excepted, pretty far gone in exhaustion, stumbling and falling far more often than was warranted by the terrain and the strength of the ice-gale: for myself, my leaden dragging legs felt as if they were on fire, each step now sent a shooting pain stabbing from ankle clear to the top of the thigh. For all that, I think I could have kept going longer than any of them, even Zabrinski, for I had the motivation, the driving force that would have kept me going hours after my legs would have told me that it was impossible to carry on a step farther. Major John Halliwell. My elder, my only brother. Alive or dead. Was he alive or was he dead, this one man in the world to whom I owed everything I had or had become? Was he dying, at that very moment when I was thinking of him, was he dying? His wife, Mary, and his three children who spoilt and ruined their bachelor uncle as I spoilt and ruined them: whatever way it lay they would have to know, and only I could tell them. Alive or dead? My legs weren't mine, the stabbing fire that tortured them belonged to some other man, not to me. I had to know, I had to know, and if I had to find out by covering whatever miles lay between me and Drift Ice Station Zebra on my hands and knees, then I would do just that. I would find out. And over and above the tearing anxiety as to what had happened to my brother there was yet another powerful motivation, a motivation that the world would regard as of infinitely more importance than the life or death of the commandant of the station. As infinitely more important than the living or dying of the score of men who manned that desolate polar outpost. Or so the world would say.

The demented drumming of the spicules on my mask and ice-sheathed furs suddenly eased, the gale wind fell away and I found myself standing in the grateful shelter of an ice-ridge even higher than the last one we'd used for shelter. I waited for the others to come up, asked Zabrinski to make a position check with the *Dolphin* and doled out some more of the medicinal alcohol. More of it than on the last occasion. We were in more need of it. Both Hansen and Rawlings were in a very distressed condition, their breath whistling in and out of their lungs in the rapid, rasping, shallow panting of a long-distance runner in the last tortured moments of his final exhaustion. I became gradually aware that the speed of my own breathing matched theirs almost exactly, it required a concentrated effort of will-power to hold my breath even for the few seconds necessary to gulp down my drink. I wondered vaguely if perhaps Hansen hadn't had the right of it, maybe the alcohol wasn't good for us. But it certainly tasted as if it were.

Zabrinski was already talking through cupped hands into the microphone. After a minute or so he pulled the earphones out from under his parka and buttoned up the walkie-talkie set. He said: 'We're either good or lucky or both. The *Dolphin* says we're exactly on the course we ought to be on.' He drained the glass I handed him and sighed in satisfaction. 'Well, that's the good part of the news. Here comes the bad part. The sides of the polynya the *Dolphin* is lying in are beginning to close together. They're closing pretty fast. The captain estimates he'll have to get out of it in two hours. Two at the most.' He paused, then finished slowly: 'And the ice-machine is still on the blink.'

'The ice-machine,' I said stupidly. Well, anyway, I felt stupid, I don't know how I sounded. 'Is the ice——?'

'It sure is, brother,' Zabrinski said. He sounded tired. 'But you didn't believe the skipper, did you, Dr. Carpenter? You were too clever for that.'

'Well, that's a help,' Hansen said heavily. 'That makes everything just perfectly splendid. The *Dolphin* drops down, the ice closes up, and there we are, the *Dolphin* below, us on top and the whole of the polar ice-cap between us. They'll almost certainly never manage to find us again, even if they do fix the ice-machine. Shall we just lie down and die now or shall we first stagger around in circles for a couple of hours and then lie down and die?'

'It's tragic,' Rawlings said gloomily. 'Not the personal aspect of it, I mean the loss to the United States Navy. I think I may fairly say, Lieutenant, that we are – or were – three promising young men. Well, you and me, anyway. I think Zabrinski there had reached the limit of his potentialities. He reached them a long time ago.'

Rawlings got all this out between chattering teeth and still painful gasps of air. Rawlings, I reflected, was very much the sort of person I would like to have by my side when things began to get awkward, and it looked as if things were going to become very awkward indeed. He and Zabrinski had, as I'd found out, established themselves as the homespun if slightly heavy-handed humorists on the *Dolphin*; for reasons known only to themselves both men habitually concealed intelligences of a high order and advanced education under a cloak of genial buffoonery.

'Two hours yet,' I said. 'With this wind at our back we can be back in the sub in well under an hour. We'd be practically blown back there.'

'And the men on Drift Station Zebra?' Zabrinski asked.

'We'd have done our best. Just one of those things.'

'We are profoundly shocked, Dr. Carpenter,' Rawlings said. The tone of genial buffoonery was less noticeable than usual.

'Deeply dismayed,' Zabrinski added, 'by the very idea.' The words were light, but the lack of warmth in the voice had nothing to do with the bitter wind.

'The only dismaying thing around here is the level of intelligence of certain simple-minded sailors,' Hansen said with some asperity. He went on, and I wondered at the conviction in his voice: 'Sure, Dr. Carpenter thinks we should go back. But that doesn't include him. Dr. Carpenter wouldn't turn back now for all the gold in Fort Knox.' He pushed himself wearily to his feet. 'Can't be much more than half a mile to go now. Let's get it over with.'

In the backwash of light from my torch I saw Rawlings and Zabrinski glance at each other, saw them shrug their shoulders at the same moment. Then they, too, were on their feet and we were on our way again.

Three minutes later Zabrinski broke his ankle.

It happened in an absurdly simple fashion, but for all its simplicity it was a wonder that nothing of the same sort had happened to any of us in the previous three hours. After starting off again, instead of losing our bearing by working to the south or north until we had rounded the end of the ice ridge blocking our path, we elected to go over it. The ridge was all of ten feet high but by boosting and pulling each other we reached the top without much difficulty. I felt my way forward cautiously, using the ice-probe – the torch was useless in that ice-storm and my goggles completely opaque. After twenty feet crawling across the gently downward sloping surface I reached the far side of the ridge and stretched down with the probe.

'Five feet,' I called to the others as they came up. 'It's only five feet.' I swung over the edge, dropped down and waited for the others to follow. Hansen came first, then Rawlings, both sliding down easily beside me. What happened to Zabrinski was impossible to see, he either misjudged his distance from the edge or a sudden easing of the wind made him lose his footing. Whatever the cause, I heard him call out, the words whipped away and lost by the wind, as he jumped down beside us. He seemed to land squarely and lightly enough on his feet, then cried out sharply and fell heavily to the ground.

I turned my back to the ice-storm, raised the useless snow-goggles and pulled out my torch. Zabrinski was half-sitting, half-lying on the ice, propped up on his right elbow and cursing steadily and fluently and, as far as I could tell because of the muffling effect of his snow-mask, without once repeating himself. His right heel was jammed in a four-inch crack on the ice, one of the thousands of such fractures and fissures that criss-crossed the pressure areas of the pack: his right leg was bent over at an angle to the outside, an angle normally impossible for any leg to assume. I didn't need to have a medical diploma hung around my neck to tell that the ankle was gone: either that or the lowermost part of the tibia, for the ankle was so heavily encased in a stout boot with lace binding that most of the strain must have fallen on the shin-bone. I hoped it wasn't a compound fracture, but it was an unreasonable hope: at that acute angle the snapped bone could hardly have failed to pierce the skin. Compound or not, it made no immediate difference, I'd no intention of examining it: a few minutes' exposure of the lower part of his leg in those temperatures was as good a way as any of ensuring that Zabrinski went through the rest of his life with one foot missing.

We lifted his massive bulk, eased the useless foot out of the crack in the ice and lowered him gently to a sitting position. I unslung the medical kit from my back, knelt beside him and asked: 'Does it hurt badly?'

'No, it's numb, I hardly feel a thing.' He swore disgustedly. 'What a crazy thing to do. A little crack like that. How stupid can a man get?'

'You wouldn't believe me if I told you,' Rawlings said acidly. He shook his head. 'I prophesied this, I prophesied this. I said it would end up with me carrying this gorilla here.'

I laid splints to the injured leg and taped them as tightly as possible over the boot and the furs, trying not to think of the depth of trouble we were in now. Two major blows in one. Not only had we lost the indispensable services of the strongest man in our party, we now had an extra 220 lbs. – at least – of weight, of deadweight, to carry along with us. Not to mention his 40-lb. pack. Zabrinski might almost have read my thoughts.

'You'll have to leave me here, Lieutenant,' he said to Hansen. His teeth were rattling, with shock and cold. 'We must be almost there now. You can pick me up on the way back.'

'Don't talk rubbish,' Hansen said shortly. 'You know damn' well we'd never find you again.'

'Exactly,' Rawlings said. His teeth were like Zabrinski's, stuttering away irregularly like an asthmatic machine-gun. He knelt on the ice to support the injured man's bulk. 'No medals for morons. It says so in the ship's articles.'

'But you'll never get to Zebra,' Zabrinski protested. 'If you have to carry me——'

'You heard what I said,' Hansen interrupted. 'We're not leaving you.'

'The lieutenant is perfectly correct,' Rawlings agreed. 'You aren't the hero type, Zabrinski. You haven't the face for it, for one thing. Now clam up while I get some of this gear off your back.'

I finished tightening the splints and pulled mittens and fur gloves back on my silk-clad but already frozen hands. We shared out Zabrinski's load among the three of us, pulled goggles and snow-masks back into position, hoisted Zabrinski to his one sound leg, turned into the wind and went on our way again. It would be truer to say that we staggered on our way again.

But now, at last and when we most needed it, luck was with us. The ice-cap stretched away beneath our feet level and smooth as the surface of a frozen river. No ridges, no hummocks, no crevasses, not even the tiny cracks one of which had crippled Zabrinski. Just billiard flat unbroken ice and not even slippery, for its surface had been scoured and abraded by the flying ice-storm.

Each of us took turns at being lead man, the other two supporting a Zabrinski who hopped along in uncomplaining silence on one foot. After maybe three hundred yards of this smooth ice, Hansen, who was in the lead at the moment, stopped so suddenly and unexpectedly that we bumped into him.

'We're there!' he yelled above the wind. 'We've made it. We're there! Can't you smell it?'

'Smell what?'

'Burnt fuel oil. Burnt rubber. Don't you get it?'

I pulled down my snow-mask, cupped my hands to my face and sniffed cautiously. One sniff was enough. I hitched up my mask again, pulled Zabrinski's arm more tightly across my shoulder and followed on after Hansen.

The smooth ice ended in another few feet. The ice sloped up sharply to a level plateau and it took the three of us all of what pitifully little strength remained to drag Zabrinski up after us. The acrid smell of burning seemed to grow more powerful with every step we took. I moved forward, away from the others, my back to the storm, goggles down and sweeping the ice with semicircular movements of my torch. The smell was strong enough now to make my nostrils wrinkle under the mask. It seemed to be coming from directly ahead. I turned round into the wind, protectively cupped hand over my eyes, and as I did my torch struck something hard and solid and metallic. I lifted my torch and vaguely through the driving ice I could just make out the ghostly hooped steel skeleton, ice-coated on the windward side, fire-charred on the leeward side, of what had once been a nissen-shaped hut.

We had found Drift Ice Station Zebra.

I waited for the others to come up, guided them past the gaunt and burnt-out structure, then told them to turn backs to wind and lift their goggles. For maybe ten seconds we surveyed the ruin in the light of my torch. No one said anything. Then we turned round into the wind again.

Drift Station Zebra had consisted of eight separate huts, four in each of two parallel rows, thirty feet between the two rows, twenty feet between each two huts in the rows – this to minimise the hazard of fire spreading from hut to hut. But the hazard hadn't been minimised enough. No one could be blamed for that. No one, except in the wildest flights of nightmarish imagination, could have envisaged what must indeed have happened – exploding tanks and thousands of gallons of blazing oil being driven through the night by a gale-force wind. And, by a double inescapable irony, fire, without which human life on the polar ice-cap cannot survive, is there the most dreaded enemy of all: for although the entire ice-cap consists of water, frozen water, there is nothing that can melt that water and so put out the fire. Except fire itself. I wondered vaguely what had happened to the giant chemical fire-extinguishers housed in every hut.

Eight huts, four in each row. The first two on either side were completely gutted. No trace remained of the walls, which had been of two layers of weather-proofed bonded ply that had enclosed the insulation of shredded glass-fibre and kapok: on all of them even the aluminium-sheeted roofs had disappeared. In one of the huts we could see charged and blackened generator machinery, ice-coated on the windward side, bent and twisted and melted almost out of recognition: one could only wonder at the furnace ferocity of the heat responsible.

The fifth hut – the third on the right-hand side – was a gutted replica of the other four, the framing even more savagely twisted by the heat. We were just turning away from this, supporting Zabrinski and too sick at heart even to speak to each other, when Rawlings called out something unintelligible. I leaned closer to him and pulled back my parka hood.

'A light!' he shouted. 'A light. Look, Doc – across there!'

And a light there was, a long narrow strangely white vertical strip of light from the hut opposite the charred wreck by which we stood. Leaning sideways into the storm we dragged Zabrinski across the intervening gap. For the first time my torch showed something that was more than a bare framework of steel. This was a hut. A blackened, scorched and twisted hut with a roughly nailed-on sheet of plywood where its solitary window had been, but nevertheless a hut. The light was coming from a door standing just ajar at the sheltered end. I laid my hand on the door, the one unscorched thing I'd seen so far in Drift Station Zebra. The hinges creaked like a rusty gate in a cemetery at midnight and the door gave beneath my hand. We passed inside.

Suspended from a hook in the centre of the ceiling a hissing Coleman lamp threw its garish light, amplified by the glittering aluminium ceiling, over every corner and detail of that eighteen by ten hut. A thick but transparent layer of ice sheathed the aluminium roof except for a three-foot circle directly above the lamp, and the ice spread from the ceiling down the plywood walls all the way to the floor. The wooden floor, too, was covered with ice, except where the bodies of the men lay. There may have been ice under them as well. I couldn't tell.

My first thought, conviction rather, and one that struck at me with a heart-sapping sense of defeat, with a chill that even the polar storm outside had been unable to achieve, was that we had arrived too late. I had seen many dead men in my life, I knew what dead men looked like, and now I was looking at just that many more. Shapeless, huddled, lifeless forms lying under a shapeless mass of blankets, mackinaws, duffels and furs, I wouldn't have bet a cent on my chances of finding one heart-beat among the lot of them. Lying packed closely together in a rough semicircle at the end of the room remote from the door, they were utterly still, as unmoving as men would be if they had been lying that way for a frozen eternity. Apart from the hissing of the pressure-lamp there was no sound inside the hut other than the metallic drumfire of the ice-spicules against the ice-sheathed eastern wall of the hut.

Zabrinski was eased down into a sitting position against a wall. Rawlings unslung the heavy load he was carrying on his back, unwrapped the stove, pulled off his mittens and started fumbling around for the fuel tablets. Hansen pulled the door to behind him, slipped the buckles of his rucksack and wearily let his load of tinned food drop to the floor of the shack.

For some reason, the voice of the storm outside and the hissing of the Coleman inside served only to heighten the deathly stillness in the hut, and the unexpected metallic clatter of the falling cans made me jump. It made one of the dead men jump, too. The man nearest to me by the left-hand wall suddenly moved, rolled over and sat up, bloodshot faded eyes staring out unbelievingly from a frost-bitten, haggard and cruelly burnt face, the burns patchily covered by a long dark stubble of beard. For long seconds he looked at us unblinkingly, then, some obscure feeling of pride making him ignore the offer of my outstretched arm, he pushed himself shakily and with obvious pain to his feet. Then the cracked and peeling lips broke into a grin.

'You've been a bleedin' long time getting here.' The voice was hoarse and weak and cockney as the Bow Bells themselves. 'My name's Kinnaird. Radio operator.'

'Whisky?' I asked.

He grinned again, tried to lick his cracked lips, and nodded. The stiff tot of whisky went down his throat like a man in a barrel going over the Niagara Falls, one moment there, the next gone for ever. He bent over, coughing harshly until the tears came to his eyes, but when he straightened life was coming back into those same lack-lustre eyes and colour touching the pale emaciated cheeks.

'If you go through life saying "Hallo" in this fashion, mate,' he observed, 'then you'll never lack for friends.' He bent and shook the shoulder of the man beside whom he had been lying. 'C'mon, Jolly, old boy, where's your bleedin' manners. We got company.'

It took quite a few shakes to get Jolly, old boy, awake, but when he did come to he was completely conscious and on his feet with remarkable speed in the one case and with remarkable nimbleness in the other. He was a short, chubby character with china-blue eyes, and although he was as much in need of a shave as Kinnaird, there was still colour in his face and the round good-humoured face was far from emaciated: but frost-bite had made a bad mess of both mouth and nose. The china-blue eyes, flecked with red and momentarily wide in surprise, crinkled into a grin of welcome. Jolly, old boy, I guess, would always adjust fast to circumstances.

'Visitors, eh?' His deep voice held a rich Irish brogue. 'And damned glad we are to see you, too. Do the honours, Jeff.'

'We haven't introduced ourselves,' I said. 'I'm Dr. Carpenter and this——'

'Regular meeting of the B.M.A., old boy,' Jolly said. I was to find out later that he used the phrase 'old boy' in every second or third sentence, a mannerism which went strangely with his Irish accent.

'Dr. Jolly?'

'The same. Resident medical officer, old boy.'

'I see. This is Lieutenant Hansen of the United States Navy submarine *Dolphin*——'

'Submarine?' Jolly and Kinnard stared at each other, then at us. 'You said "submarine," old top?'

'Explanations can wait. Torpedoman Rawlings. Radioman Zabrinski.' I glanced down at the huddled men on the floor, some of them already stirring at the sound of voices, one or two propping themselves up on their elbows. 'How are they?'

'Two or three pretty bad burn cases,' Jolly said. 'Two or three pretty far gone with cold and exhaustion, but not so far gone that food and warmth wouldn't have them right as rain in a few days. I made them all huddle together like this for mutual warmth.'

I counted them. Including Jolly and Kinnaird, there were twelve all told. I said: 'Where are the others?'

'The others?' Kinnaird looked at me in momentary surprise, then his face went bleak and cold. He pointed a thumb over his shoulder. 'In the next hut, mate.'

'Why?'

'Why?' He rubbed a weary forearm across bloodshot eyes. 'Because we don't fancy sleeping with a roomful of corpses, that's why.'

'Because you don't——' I broke off and stared down at the men at my feet. Seven of them were awake now, three of them propped on elbows, four still lying down, all seven registering various degrees of dazed bewilderment: the three who were still asleep – or unconscious – had their faces covered by blankets. I said slowly: 'There were nineteen of you.'

'Nineteen of us,' Kinnaird echoed emptily. 'The others – well, they never had a chance.'

I said nothing. I looked carefully at the faces of the conscious men, hoping to find among them the one face I wanted to see, hoping perhaps that I had not immediately recognised it because frost-bite or hunger or burns had made it temporarily unrecognisable. I looked very carefully indeed and I knew that I had never seen any of those faces before.

I moved over to the first of the three still sleeping figures and lifted the blanket covering the face. The face of a stranger. I let the blanket drop. Jolly said in puzzlement: 'What's wrong? What do you want?'

I didn't answer him. I picked my way round recumbent men, all staring uncomprehendingly at me, and lifted the blanket from the face of the second sleeping man. Again I let the blanket drop and I could feel my mouth go dry, the slow heavy pounding of my heart. I crossed to the third man, then stood there hesitating, knowing I must find out, dreading what I must find. Then I stooped quickly and lifted the blanket. A man with a heavily bandaged face. A man with a broken nose and a thick blond beard. A man I had never seen in my life before. Gently I spread the blanket back over his face and straightened up. Rawlings, I saw, already had the solid-fuel stove going.

'That should bring the temperature up to close to freezing,' I said to Dr. Jolly. 'We've plenty of fuel. We've also brought food, alcohol, a complete medical kit. If you and Kinnaird want to start in on those things now I'll give you a hand in a minute. Lieutenant, that was a polynya, that smooth stretch we crossed just before we got here? A frozen lead?'

'Couldn't be anything else.' Hansen was looking at me peculiarly, a wondering expression on his face. 'These people are obviously in no fit state to travel a couple of hundred yards, far less four or five miles. Besides, the skipper said he was going to be squeezed down pretty soon. So we whistle up the *Dolphin* and have them surface at the back door?'

'Can he find that polynya – without the ice-machine, I mean?'

'Nothing simpler. I'll take Zabrinski's radio, move a measured two hundred yards to the north, send a bearing signal, move two hundred yards to the south and do the same. They'll have our range to a yard. Take a couple of hundred yards off that and the *Dolphin* will find itself smack in the middle of the polynya.'

'But still under it. I wonder how thick that ice is. You had an open lead to the west of the camp some time ago, Dr. Jolly. How long ago?'

'A month. Maybe five weeks. I can't be sure.'

'How thick?' I asked Hansen.

'Five feet, maybe six. Couldn't possibly break through it. But the captain's always had a hankering to have a go with his torpedoes.' He turned to Zabrinski. 'Still fit to operate that radio of yours?'

I left them to it. I'd hardly been aware of what I'd been saying, anyway. I felt sick and old and empty and sad, and deathly tired. I had my answer now. I'd come 12,000 miles to find it, I'd have gone a million to avoid it. But the inescapable fact was there and now nothing could ever change it. Mary, my sister-in-law and her three wonderful children – she would never see her husband again, they would never see their father again. My brother was dead and no one was ever going to see him again. Except me. I was going to see him now.

I went out, closing the door behind me, moved round the corner of the hut and lowered my head against the storm. Ten seconds later I reached the door of the last hut in the line. I used the torch to locate the handle, twisted it, pushed and passed inside.

Once it had been a laboratory: now it was a charnel house, a house of the dead. The laboratory equipment had all been pushed roughly to one side and the cleared floor space covered with the bodies of dead men. I knew they were dead men, but only because Kinnaird had told me so: hideously charred and blackened and grotesquely misshapen as they were, those carbonised and contorted lumps of matter could have been any form of life or indeed no form of life at all. The stench of incinerated flesh and burnt diesel fuel was dreadful. I wondered which of the men in the other hut had had the courage, the iron resolution, to bring those grisly burdens, the shockingly disfigured remains of their former comrades into this hut. They must have had strong stomachs.

Death must have been swift, swift for all of them. Theirs had not been the death of men trapped by fire, it had been the death of men who had themselves been on fire. Caught, drenched, saturated by a gale-borne sea of burning oil, they must have spent the last few seconds of life as incandescently blazing human torches before dying in insane screaming agony. They must have died as terribly as men can ever die.

Something about one of the bodies close to me caught my attention. I stooped and focused the torch beam on what had once been a right hand, now no more than a blackened claw with the bone showing through. So powerful had been that heat that it had warped, but not melted, the curiously shaped gold ring on the third finger. I recognised that ring, I had been with my sister-in-law when she had bought it.

I was conscious of no grief, no pain, no revulsion. Perhaps, I thought dully, those would come later when the initial shock had worn off. But I didn't think so. This wasn't the man I remembered so well, the brother to whom I owed everything, a debt that could never now be repaid. This charred mass of matter before me was a stranger, so utterly different from the man who lived on in my memory, so changed beyond all possibility of recognition that my numbed mind in my exhausted body just could not begin to bridge the gap.

As I stood there, staring down, something ever so slightly off-beat about the way the body lay caught my professional attention. I stooped low, very low, and remained bent over for what seemed a long time. I straightened, slowly, and as I did I heard the door behind me open. I whirled round and saw that it was Lieutenant Hansen. He pulled down his snow-mask, lifted up his goggles, looked at me and then at the man at my feet. I could see shock draining expression and colour from his face. Then he looked up at me.

'So you lost out, Doc?' I could hardly hear the husky whisper above the voice of the storm. 'God, I'm sorry.'

'What do you mean?'

'Your brother?' He nodded at the man at my feet.

'Commander Swanson told you?'

'Yeah. Just before we left. That's why we came.' His gaze moved in horrified fascination over the floor of the hut, and his face was grey, like old parchment. 'A minute, Doc, just a minute.' He turned and hurried through the doorway.

When he came back he looked better, but not much. He said: 'Commander Swanson said that that was why he had to let you go.'

'Who else knows?'

'Skipper and myself. No one else.'

'Keep it that way, will you? As a favour to me.'

'If you say so, Doc.' There was curiosity in his face now, and puzzlement, but horror was still the dominant expression. 'My God, have you ever seen anything like it?'

'Let's get back to the others,' I said. 'We're doing nobody any good by staying here.'

He nodded without speaking. Together we made our way back to the other hut. Apart from Dr. Jolly and Kinnaird, three other men were on their feet now: Captain Folsom, an extraordinarily tall thin man with savagely burnt face and hands who was second in command of the base; Hewson, a dark-eyed taciturn character, a tractor driver and engineer who had been responsible for the diesel generators, and a cheerful Yorkshireman, Naseby, the camp cook. Jolly, who had opened my medical kit and was applying fresh bandages to the arms of one of the men still lying down, introduced them, then turned back to his job. He didn't seem to need my help, not for the moment, anyway. I heard Hansen say to Zabrinski: 'In contact with the *Dolphin?*'

'Well, no.' Zabrinski stopped sending his call-sign and shifted slightly to ease his broken ankle. 'I don't quite know how to put this, Lieutenant, but the fact is that this little ol' set here seems to have blown a fuse.'

'Well, now,' Hansen said heavily. 'That *is* clever of you, Zabrinski. You mean you can't raise them?'

'I can hear them, they can't hear me.' He shrugged, apologetically. 'Me and my clumsy feet, I guess. It wasn't just only my ankle that went when I took that tumble out there.'

'Well, can't you repair the damn' thing?'

'I don't think so, Lieutenant.'

'Damn it, you're supposed to be a radioman.'

'That's so,' Zabrinski acknowledged reasonably. 'But I'm not a magician. And with a couple of numbed and frozen hands, no tools, an old-type set without a printed circuit and the code signs in Japanese – well, even Marconi would have called it a day.'

'*Can* it be repaired?' Hansen insisted.

'It's a transistor set. No valves to smash. I expect it could be repaired. But it might take hours, Lieutenant – I'd even have to fake up a set of tools first.'

'Well, fake them. Anything you like. Only get that thing working.'

Zabrinski said nothing. He held out the headphones to Hansen. Hansen looked at Zabrinski, then at the phones, took them without a word and listened briefly. Then he shrugged, handed back the phones and said: 'Well, I guess there *is* no hurry to repair that radio.'

'Yeah,' Zabrinski said. 'Awkward, you might say, Lieutenant.'

'What's awkward,' I asked.

'Looks as if *we're* going to be next on the list for a rescue party,' Hansen said heavily. 'They're sending a more or less continuous signal: "Ice closing rapidly, return at once."'

'I was against this madness from the very beginning,' Rawlings intoned from the floor. He stared down at the already melting lumps of frozen tinned soup and stirred it moodily with a fork. 'A gallant attempt, men, but foredoomed to failure.'

'Keep your filthy fingers out of that soup and kindly clam up,' Hansen said coldly. He turned suddenly to Kinnaird. 'How about *your* radio set. Of course, that's it. We have fit men here to crank your generator and——'

'I'm sorry.' Kinnaird smiled the way a ghost might smile. 'It's not a hand-powered generator, that was destroyed, it's a battery set. The batteries are finished. Completely finished.'

'A battery set, you said?' Zabrinski looked at him in mild surprise. 'Then what caused all the power fluctuations when you were transmitting?'

'We kept changing over the nickel cadmium cells to try to make the most of what little power was left in them: we'd only fifteen left altogether, most of them were lost in the fire. That caused the power fluctuations. But even Nife cells don't last for ever. They're finished, mate. The combined power left in those cells wouldn't light a pencil torch.'

Zabrinski didn't say anything. No one said anything. The ice-spicules drummed incessantly against the east wall, the Coleman hissed, the solid-fuel stove purred softly: but the sole effect of those three sounds was to make the silence inside seem that little bit more absolute. No one looked at his neighbours, everyone stared down at the floor with a fixed and steadfast gaze of an entomologist hunting for traces of woodworm. Any newspaper printing a picture taken at that instant wouldn't have found it any too easy to convince its readers that the men on Drift Ice Station Zebra had been rescued just ten minutes previously, and rescued from certain death at that. The readers would have pointed out that one might have expected a little more jubilation in the atmosphere, a touch, perhaps, of lighthearted relief, and they wouldn't have been far wrong at that, there wasn't very much gaiety around.

After the silence had gone on just that little too long I said to Hansen: 'Well, that's it, then. We don't have to hire any electronic computer to work this one out. Someone's got to get back to the *Dolphin* and get back there now. I'm nominating myself.'

'No!' Hansen said violently, then more quietly: 'Sorry, friend, but the skipper's orders didn't include giving permission to anyone to commit suicide. You're staying here.'

'So I stay here,' I nodded. This wasn't the time to tell him I didn't need his permission for anything, far less was it the time to start flourishing the Mannlicher-Schoenauer. 'So we all stay here. And then we all die here. Quietly, without any fighting, without any fuss, we just lie down and die here. I suppose you reckon that comes under the heading of inspiring leadership. Amundsen would have loved that.' It wasn't fair, but then I wasn't feeling fair-minded at the moment.

'Nobody's going any place,' Hansen said. 'I'm not my brother's keeper, Doc, but for all that I'll be damned if I let you kill yourself. You're not fit, none of us is fit to make the return trip to the *Dolphin* – not after what we've just been through. That's one thing. The next thing is that without a transmitter from which the *Dolphin* can pick up our directional bearings, we could never hope to find the *Dolphin* again. The third thing is that the closing ice will probably have forced the *Dolphin* to drop down before anyone could get half-way there. And the last thing is that if we failed to find the *Dolphin* either because we missed her or because she was gone, we could never make our way back to Zebra again: we wouldn't have the strength and we would have nothing to guide us back anyway.'

'The odds offered aren't all that attractive,' I admitted. 'What odds are you offering on the ice-machine being repaired?'

Hansen shook his head, said nothing. Rawlings started stirring his soup again, carefully not looking up, he didn't want to meet the anxious eyes, the desperate eyes, in that circle of haggard and frost-bitten faces any more than I did. But he looked up as Captain Folsom pushed himself away from the support of a wall and took a couple of unsteady steps towards us. It didn't require any stethoscope to see that Folsom was in a pretty bad way.

'I am afraid that we don't understand,' he said. His voice was slurred and indistinct, the puffed and twisted lips had been immobilised by the savage charring of his face: I wondered bleakly how many months of pain would elapse, how many visits to the surgeon's table, before Folsom could show that face to the world again. In the very remote event, that was, of our ever getting him to hospital. 'Would you please explain? What is the difficulty?'

'Simply this,' I said. 'The *Dolphin* has an ice fathometer, a device for measuring the thickness of the overhead ice. Normally, even if Commander Swanson – the captain of the *Dolphin* – didn't hear from us, we could expect him on our doorstep in a matter of hours. He has the position of this Drift Station pinned down pretty closely. All he would have to do is to drop down, come under us here, start a grid search with his ice fathometer and it would be only minutes before he would locate the relatively thin ice out in that lead there. But things aren't normal. The ice-machine has broken down and if it stays that way he'll never find that lead. That's why I want to go back there. Now. Before Swanson's forced to dive by the closing ice.'

'Don't see it, old boy,' Jolly said. 'How's that going to help? Can *you* fix this ice what-you-may-call-it.'

'I don't have to. Commander Swanson knows his distance from this camp give or take a hundred yards. All I have to do is to tell him to cover the distance less quarter of a mile and loose off a torpedo. That ought——'

'Torpedo?' Jolly asked. 'Torpedo? To break through the ice from beneath?'

'That's it. It's never been tried before. I suppose there's no reason why it shouldn't work if the ice is thin enough and it won't be all that thick in the lead out there. I don't really know.'

'They'll be sending planes, you know, Doc,' Zabrinski said quietly. 'We started transmitting the news as soon as we broke through and everybody will know by now that Zebra has been found – at least, they'll know exactly where it is. They'll have the big bombers up here in a few hours.'

'Doing what?' I asked. 'Sculling around uselessly in the darkness up above? Even if they do have the exact position, they still won't be able to see what's left of this station because of the darkness and the ice-storm. Perhaps they can with radar. It's unlikely, but even if they do, what then? Drop supplies? Maybe. But they won't dare drop supplies directly on us for fear of killing us. They'd have to drop them some distance off – and even a quarter-mile would be too far away for any chance we'd ever have of finding stuff in those conditions. As for landing – even if weather conditions were perfect, no plane big enough to have the range to fly here could ever hope to land on the ice-cap. You know that.'

'What's your middle name, Doc?' Rawlings asked dolefully. 'Jeremiah?'

'The greatest good of the greatest number,' I said. 'The old yardstick, but there's never been a better one. If we just hole up here without making any attempt to help ourselves and the ice-machine remains useless, then we're all dead. All sixteen of us. If I make it there safely, then we're all alive. Even if I don't, the ice-machine may be fixed and there would only be one lost then.' I started pulling on my mittens. 'One is less than sixteen.'

'We might as well make it two.' Hansen sighed and began to pull on his own gloves. I was hardly surprised. When he'd last spoken he'd talked at first of 'you' having no chance and finished by saying that 'we' had none and it hadn't required any phychiatrist to follow his quick shift in mental orientation: whatever men like Hansen were hand-picked for, it wasn't for any predilection for shifting the load to others' shoulders when the going became sticky.

I didn't waste time arguing with him.

Rawlings got to his feet.

'One skilled volunteer for the soup-stirring,' he requested. 'Those two wouldn't get as far as the door there without my holding their hands. I shall probably get a medal for this. What's the highest decoration awarded in peace-time, Lieutenant?'

'There are no medals given for soup-stirring, Rawlings,' Hansen said, 'which is what you are going to keep on doing. You're staying right here.'

'Uh-uh.' Rawlings shook his head. 'Prepare yourself to deal with your first mutiny, Lieutenant. I'm coming with you. I can't lose. If we get to the *Dolphin* you'll be too damned glad and happy to have made it to dream of reporting me, apart from being a fair-minded man who will have to admit that our safe arrival back at the ship will be entirely due to Torpedoman Rawlings.' He grinned. 'And if we don't make it – well, you can't very well report it, can you, Lieutenant?'

Hansen walked across to him. He said quietly: 'You know that there's more than an even chance that we won't reach the *Dolphin.* That would leave twelve pretty sick men here, not to mention Zabrinski with a broken ankle, and with no one to look after them. They must have one fit man to look after them. You couldn't be that selfish now, could you, Rawlings? Look after them, will you? As a favour to me?'

Rawlings looked at him for long seconds, then squatted down and started stirring the soup again.

'As a favour to me, you mean,' he said bitterly. 'O.K., I'll stay. As a favour to me. Also to prevent Zabrinski tripping over his legs again and breaking another ankle.' He stirred the soup viciously. 'Well, what are you waiting for? The skipper may be making up his mind to dive any minute.'

He had a point. We brushed off protests and attempts to stop us made by Captain Folsom and Dr. Jolly and were ready to leave in thirty seconds. Hansen was through the door first. I turned and looked at the sick and emaciated and injured survivors of Drift Station Zebra. Folsom, Jolly, Kinnaird, Hewson, Naseby and seven others. Twelve men altogether. They couldn't all be in cahoots together, so it had to be a single man, maybe two, acting in concert. I wondered who those men might be, those men I would have to kill, that person or persons who had murdered my brother and six other men on Drift Ice Station Zebra.

I pulled the door to behind me and followed Hansen out into the dreadful night.

6

We had been tired, more than tired, even before we had set out. We had been leaden-legged, bone-weary, no more than a short hand-span from total exhaustion. But for all that we flitted through the howling darkness of that night like two great white ghosts across the dimly seen whiteness of a nightmare lunar landscape. We were no longer bowed under the weight of heavy packs. Our backs were to that gale-force wind so that for every laborious plodding step we had made on our way to Zebra we now covered five, with so little a fraction of our earlier toil that at first it seemed all but effortless. We had no trouble in seeing where we were going, no fear of falling into an open lead or of crippling ourselves against some unexpected obstacle, for with our useless goggles removed and powerful torch beams dancing erratically ahead of us as we jog-trotted along, visibility was seldom less than five yards, more often near to ten. Those were the physical aids that helped us on our way but even more sharply powerful as a spur to our aching legs was that keen and ever-growing fear that dominated our minds to the exclusion of all else, the fear that Commander Swanson had already been compelled to drop down and that we would be left to die in that shrieking wasteland: with our lacking both shelter and food, the old man with the scythe would not be keeping us waiting too long.

We ran, but we did not run too fast, for to have done that would have been to have the old man tapping us on the shoulder in very short order indeed. In far sub-zero temperatures, there is one thing that the Eskimo avoids as he would the plague – over-exertion; in those latitudes more deadly, even, than the plague itself. Too much physical effort while wearing heavy furs inevitably results in sweat, and when the effort ceases, as eventually cease it must, the sweat freezes on the skin: the only way to destroy that film of ice is by further exertion, producing even more sweat, the beginnings of a vicious and steadily narrowing circle that can have only one end. So though we ran it was only at a gentle jog-trot, hardly more than a fast walk: we took every possible precaution against overheating.

After half an hour, perhaps a little more, I called for a brief halt in the shelter of a steep ice-wall. Twice in the past two minutes Hansen had stumbled and fallen where there hadn't appeared to be any reason to stumble and fall: and I had noticed that my own legs were more unsteady than the terrain warranted.

'How are you making out?' I asked.

'Pretty bushed, Doc.' He sounded it, too, his breathing quick and rasping and shallow. 'But don't write me off yet. How far do you reckon we've come?'

'Three miles, near enough.' I patted the ice-wall behind us. 'When we've had a couple of minutes I think we should try climbing this. Looks like a pretty tallish hummock to me.'

'To try to get into the clear above the ice-storm?' I nodded my head and he shook his. 'Won't do you any good, Doc. This ice-storm must be at least twenty feet thick, and even if you do get above it the *Dolphin* will still be below it. She's only got the top of her sail clear above the ice.'

'I've been thinking,' I said. 'We've been so lost in our own woes and sorrows that we have forgotten about Commander Swanson. I think we have been guilty of underestimating him pretty badly.'

'It's likely enough. Right now I'm having a full-time job worrying about Lieutenant Hansen. What's on your mind?'

'Just this. The chances are better than fifty-fifty that Swanson believes we are on the way back to the *Dolphin*. After all, he's been ordering us to return for quite some time; and if he thinks we didn't get the order because something has happened to us or the radio, he'll still figure that we will be returning.'

'Not necessarily. Radio or not, we might still be pushing on for Drift Station Zebra.'

'No. Definitely not. He'll be expecting us to be smart enough to figure it the way he would; and smart enough to see that that is the way he *would* figure it. He would know that if our radio broke down before we got to Zebra that it would be suicidal for us to try to find it without radio bearing – but that it *wouldn't* be suicidal for us to try to make it back to the *Dolphin*, for he would be hoping that we would have sufficient savvy to guess that he would put a lamp in the window to guide the lost sheep home.'

'My God, Doc, I believe you've got it! Of course he would, of course he would. Lordy, lordy, what am I using for brains?' He straightened and turned to face the ice-wall.

Pushing and pulling, we made it together to the top. The summit of the rafted ice hummock was less than twenty feet above the level of the ice-pack and not quite high enough. We were still below the surface of that gale-driven river of ice-spicules. Occasionally, for a brief moment of time, the wind force would ease fractionally and let us have a brief glimpse of the clear sky above but only occasionally and for a fraction of a second. And if there was anything to be seen in that time, we couldn't see it.

'There'll be other hummocks,' I shouted in Hansen's ear. 'Higher hummocks.' He nodded without answering. I couldn't see the expression on his face but I didn't have to see it. The same thought was in both our minds: we could see nothing because there was nothing to see. Commander Swanson hadn't put a lamp in the window, for the window was gone, the *Dolphin* forced to dive to avoid being crushed by the ice.

Five times in the next twenty minutes we climbed hummocks, and five times we climbed down, each time more dejected, more defeated. By now I was pretty far gone, moving in a pain-filled nightmare: Hansen was in even worse case, lurching and staggering around like a drunken man. As a doctor, I knew well of the hidden and unsuspected resources that an exhausted man can call on in times of desperate emergency; but I knew, too, that those resources are not limitless and that we were pretty close to the end. And when that end came we would just lie down in the lee of an ice-wall and wait for the old man to come along: he wouldn't keep us waiting long.

Our sixth hummock all but defeated us. It wasn't that it was hard to climb, it was well ridged with foot and hand holds in plenty, but the sheer physical effort of climbing came very close to defeating us. And then I dimly began to realise that part of the effort was due to the fact that this was by far the highest hummock we had found yet. Some colossal pressures had concentrated on this one spot, rafting and log-jamming the ice-pack until it had risen a clear thirty feet above the general level: the giant underwater ridge beneath must have stretched down close on two hundred feet towards the black floor of the Arctic.

Eight feet below the summit our heads were in the clear: on the summit itself, holding on to each other for mutual support against the gale, we could look down on the ice-storm whirling by just beneath our feet: a fantastic sight, a great grey-white sea of undulating turbulence, a giant rushing river that stretched from horizon to horizon. Like so much else in the high Arctic the scene had an eerie and terrifying strangeness about it, a mindless desolation that belonged not to earth but to some alien and long-dead planet.

We scanned the horizon to the west until our eyes ached. Nothing. Nothing at all. Just that endless desolation. From due north to due south, through 180°, we searched the surface of that great river; and still we saw nothing. Three minutes passed. Still nothing. I began to feel the ice running in my blood.

On the remote off-chance that we might already have by-passed the

Dolphin to the north or south, I turned and peered towards the east. It wasn't easy, for that far sub-zero gale of wind brought tears to my eyes in an instant of time; but at least it wasn't impossible, we no longer had to contend with the needle-pointed lances of the ice-spicules. I made another slow 180° sweep of the eastern horizon, and again, and again. Then I caught Hansen's arm.

'Look there,' I said. 'To the north-east. Maybe quarter of a mile away, maybe half a mile. Can you see anything?'

For several seconds Hansen squinted along the direction of my outstretched hand, then shook his head. 'I see nothing. What do you think you see?'

'I don't know. I'm not sure. I can imagine I see a very faint touch of luminescence on the surface of the ice-storm there, maybe just a fraction of a shade whiter than the rest.'

For a full half-minute Hansen stared out through cupped hands. Finally he said: 'It's no good. I don't see it. But then my eyes have been acting up on me for the past half-hour. But I can't even *imagine* I see anything.'

I turned away to give my streaming eyes a rest from that icy wind and then looked again. 'Damn it,' I said, 'I can't be sure that there is anything there; but I can't be sure that there isn't, either.'

'What do you fancy it would be?' Hansen's voice was dispirited, with overtones of hopelessness. 'A light?'

'A searchlight shining vertically upwards. A searchlight that's not able to penetrate that ice-storm.'

'You're kidding yourself, Doc,' Hansen said wearily. 'The wish father to the thought. Besides, that would mean that we had already passed the *Dolphin*. It's not possible.'

'It's not impossible. Ever since we started climbing those damned ice-hummocks I've lost track of time and space. It *could* be.'

'Do you still see it?' The voice was empty, uninterested, he didn't believe me and he was just making words.

'Maybe my eyes are acting up, too,' I admitted. 'But, damn it, I'm still not sure that I'm not right.'

'Come on, Doc, let's go.'

'Go where?'

'I don't know.' His teeth chattered so uncontrollably in that intense cold that I could scarcely follow his words. 'I guess it doesn't matter very much where——'

With breath-taking abruptness, almost in the centre of my imagined patch of luminescence and not more than four hundred yards away, a swiftly climbing rocket burst through the rushing river of ice-spicules and climbed high into the clear sky trailing behind it a fiery tale of glowing red sparks. Five hundred feet it climbed, perhaps six hundred, then burst into a brilliantly incandescent shower of crimson stars, stars that fell lazily back to earth again, streaming away to the west on the wings of the gale and dying as they went, till the sky was colder and emptier than ever before.

'You still say it doesn't matter very much where we go?' I asked Hansen. 'Or maybe you didn't see that little lot?'

'What I just saw,' he said reverently, 'was the prettiest ol' sight that Ma Hansen's little boy ever did see – or ever will see.' He thumped me on the back, so hard that I had to grab him to keep my balance. 'We got it made, Doc!' he shouted. 'We got it made. Suddenly I have the strength of ten. Home sweet home, here we come.'

Ten minutes later we were home.

'God, this is wonderful,' Hansen sighed. He stared in happy bemusement from the captain to me to the glass in his hand to the water dripping from the melting ice on his furs on to the corticene decking of the captain's tiny cabin. 'The warmth, the light, the comfort and home sweet home. I never thought I'd see any of it again. When the rocket went up, Skipper, I was just looking around to pick a place to lay me down and die. And don't think I'm joking, for I'm not.'

'And Dr. Carpenter?' Swanson smiled.

'Defective mental equipment somewhere,' Hansen said. 'He doesn't seem to know how to set about giving up. I think he's just mule-headed. You get them like that.'

Hansen's slightly off-beat, slightly irrational talk had nothing to do with the overwhelming relief and relaxation that comes after moments of great stress and tension. Hansen was too tough for that. I knew that and I knew that Swanson knew it also. We'd been back for almost twenty minutes now, we'd told our story, the pressure was off, a happy ending for all seemed in sight and normalcy was again almost the order of the day. But when the strain is off and conditions are back to normal a man has time to start thinking about things again. I knew only too well what was in Hansen's mind's eye, that charred and huddled shapelessness that had once been my brother. He didn't want me to talk about him, and for that I didn't blame him; he didn't want me even to think about him, although he must have known that that was impossible. The kindest men nearly always are like that, hard and tough and cynical on the outside, men who have been too kind and shown it.

'However it was – ' Swanson smiled – 'you can consider yourselves two of the luckiest men alive. That rocket you saw was the third last we had;

it's been a regular fourth of July for the past hour or so. And you reckon Rawlings, Zabrinski and the survivors on Zebra are safe for the present?'

'Nothing to worry about for the next couple of days.' Hansen nodded. 'They'll be O.K. Cold, mind you, and a good half of them desperately in need of hospital treatment, but they'll survive.'

'Fine. Well, this is how it is. This lead here stopped closing in about half an hour ago, but it doesn't matter now, we can drop down any time and still hold our position. What does matter is that we have located the fault in the ice-machine. It's a damnably tricky and complicated job and I expect it will take several hours yet to fix. But I think we'll wait until it is fixed before we try anything. I'm not too keen on this idea of making a dead reckoning approach to this lead near Zebra then loosing off a shot in the dark. Since there's no desperate hurry, I'd rather wait till we got the ice fathometer operating again, make an accurate survey of this lead then fire a torpedo up through the middle. If the ice is only four or five feet thick there, we shouldn't have much trouble blowing a hole through.'

'That would be best,' Hansen agreed. He finished off his medicinal alcohol – an excellent bourbon – rose stiffly to his feet and stretched. 'Well, back to the old treadmill again. How many torpedoes in working order?'

'Four, at the last count.'

'I may as well go help young Mills load them up now. If that's O.K. by you, Skipper.'

'It is not O.K. by me,' Swanson said mildly, 'and if you'll take a quick gander at that mirror there you'll understand why. You're not fit to load a slug into an airgun far less a torpedo into its tube. You haven't just been on a Sunday afternoon stroll, you know. A few hours' sleep, John, then we'll see.'

Hansen didn't argue. I couldn't imagine anyone arguing with Commander Swanson. He made for the door. 'Coming, Doc?'

'In a moment. Sleep well.'

'Yeah. Thanks.' He touched me lightly on the shoulder and smiled through bloodshot and exhausted eyes. 'Thanks for everything. Good night, all.'

When he was gone Swanson said: 'It was pretty wicked out there to-night?'

'I wouldn't recommend it for an old ladies' home Sunday afternoon outing.'

'Lieutenant Hansen seems to imagine he's under some kind of debt to you,' he went on inconsequentially.

'Imagination, as you say. They don't come any better than Hansen. You're damned lucky to have him as an exec.'

'I know that.' He hesitated, then said quietly: 'I promise you I won't mention this again – but, well, I'm most damnably sorry, Doctor.'

I looked at him and nodded slowly. I knew he meant it, I knew he had to say it, but there's not much you can say in turn to anything like that. I said: 'Six others died with him, Commander.'

He hesitated again. 'Do we – do we take the dead back to Britain with us?'

'Could I have another drop of that excellent bourbon, Commander? Been a very heavy run on your medicinal alcohol in the past few hours, I'm afraid.' I waited till he had filled my glass then went on: 'We don't take them back with us. They're not dead men, they're just unrecognisable and unidentifiable lumps of charred matter. Let them stay here.'

His relief was unmistakable and he was aware of it for he went on hurriedly, for something to say: 'All this equipment for locating and tracking the Russian missiles. Destroyed?'

'I didn't check.' He'd find out for himself soon enough that there had been no such equipment. How he'd react to that discovery in light of the cock-and-bull story I'd spun to himself and Admiral Garvie in the Holy Loch I couldn't even begin to guess. At the moment I didn't even care. It didn't seem important , nothing seemed important, not any more. All at once I felt tired, not sleepy, just deathly tired, so I pushed myself stiffly to my feet, said good night and left.

Hansen was in his bunk when I got back to his cabin, his furs lying where he had dropped them. I checked that he was no longer awake, slipped off my own furs, hung them up and replaced the Mannlicher-Schoenauer in my case. I lay down in my cot to sleep, but sleep wouldn't come. Exhausted though I was, I had never felt less like sleep in my life.

I was too restless and unsettled for sleep, too many problems coming all at once were causing a first-class log-jam in my mind. I got up, pulled on shirt and denim pants, and made my way to the control room. I spent the better part of what remained of the night there, pacing up and down, watching two technicians repairing vastly complicated innards of the ice-machine, reading the messages of congratulation which were still coming in, talking desultorily to the officer on deck and drinking endless cups of coffee. It passed the night for me and although I hadn't closed an eye I felt fresh and almost relaxed by the time morning came.

At the wardroom breakfast table that morning everyone seemed quietly cheerful. They knew they had done a good job, the whole world was telling them they had done a magnificent job, and you could see that they all regarded that job as being as good as over. No one appeared to doubt Swanson's ability to blow a hole through the ice. If it hadn't been for the presence of the ghost at the feast, myself, they would have been positively jovial.

'We'll pass up the extra cups of coffee this morning, gentlemen,' Swanson said. 'Drift Station Zebra is still waiting for us and even although I'm assured everyone there will survive, they must be feeling damned cold and miserable for all that. The ice-machine has been in operation for almost an hour now, at least we hope it has. We'll drop down right away and test it and after we've loaded the torpedoes – two should do it, I fancy – we'll blow our way up into this lead at Zebra.'

Twenty minutes later the *Dolphin* was back where she belonged, 150 feet below the surface of the sea – or the ice-cap. After ten minutes' manœuvring, with a close check being kept on the plotting table to maintain our position relative to Drift Station Zebra, it was clear that the ice-machine was behaving perfectly normally again, tracing out the inverted ridges and valleys in the ice with its usual magical accuracy. Commander Swanson nodded his satisfaction.

'That's it, then.' He nodded to Hansen and Mills, the torpedo officer. 'You can go ahead now. Maybe you'd like to accompany them, Dr. Carpenter. Or is loading torpedoes old hat to you?'

'Never seen it,' I said truthfully. 'Thanks, I'd like to go along.' Swanson was as considerate towards men as he was towards his beloved *Dolphin* which was why every man in the ship swore by him. He knew, or suspected that, apart from the shock I felt at my brother's death, I was worried stiff about other things: he would have heard, although he hadn't mentioned it to me and hadn't even asked me how I had slept, that I'd spent the night prowling aimlessly and restlessly about the control room: he knew I would be grateful for any distraction, for anything that would relieve my mind, however temporarily, of whatever it was that was troubling it. I wondered just how much that extraordinarily keen brain knew or guessed. But that was an unprofitable line of thought so I put it out of my mind and went along with Hansen and Mills. Mills was another like Raeburn, the navigation officer; he looked to me more like a college undergraduate than the highly competent officer he was, but I supposed it was just another sign that I was growing old.

Hansen crossed to a panel by the diving console and studied a group of lights. The night's sleep had done Hansen a great deal of good and, apart from the abraded skin on his forehead and round the cheekbones where the ice-spicules of last night had done their work, he was again his normal cheerfully-cynical relaxed self, fresh and rested and fit. He waved his hand at the panel.

'The torpedo safety lights, Dr. Carpenter. Each green light represents a closed torpedo tube door. Six doors that open to the sea – bow caps, we call them – six rear doors for loading the torpedoes. Only twelve lights but we study them very, very carefully – just to make sure that all the lights are green. For if any of them were red – any of the top six, that is, which represent the sea doors – well, that wouldn't be so good, would it?' He looked at Mills. 'All green?'

'All green,' Mills echoed.

We moved for'ard along the wardroom passage, and dropped down the wide companionway into the crew's mess. From there we moved into the for'ard torpedo storage room. Last time I'd been there, on the morning after our departure from the Clyde, nine or ten men had been sleeping in their bunks; now all the bunks were empty. Five men were waiting for us: four ratings and a Petty Officer Bowen whom Hansen, no stickler for protocol, addressed as Charlie.

'You will see now,' Hansen observed to me, 'why officers are more highly paid than enlisted men, and deservedly so. While Charlie and his gallant men skulk here behind two sets of collision bulkheads, we must go and test the safety of the tubes. Regulations. Still, a cool head, and an iron nerve: we do it gladly for our men.'

Bowen grinned and unclipped the first collision bulkhead door. We stepped over the eighteen-inch sill, leaving the five men behind, and waited until the door had been clipped up again before opening the for'ard collision bulkhead door and stepping over the second sill into the cramped torpedo room. This time the door was swung wide open and hooked back on a heavy standing catch.

'All laid down in the book of rules,' Hansen said. 'The only time the two doors can be opened at the same time is when we're actually loading the torpedoes.' He checked the position of metal handles at the rear of the tubes, reached up, swung down a steel-spring microphone and flicked a switch. 'Ready to test tubes. All manual levers shut. All lights showing green?'

'All lights still green.' The answering voice from the overhead squawk box was hollow, metallic, queerly impersonal.

'You already checked,' I said mildly.

'So we check again. Same old book of rules.' He grinned. 'Besides, my grandpa died at ninety-seven and I aim to beat his record. Take no chances and you run no risk. What are they to be, George?'

'Three and four.' I could see the brass plaques on the circular rear doors of the tubes, 2, 4 and 6 on the port side, 1, 3 and 5 on the starboard. Lieutenant Mills was proposing to use the central tubes on each side.

Mills unhooked a rubber torch from the bulkhead and approached number 3 first. Hansen said: 'Still no chances. First of all George opens the test cock in the rear door which will show if there is any water at all in the tubes. Shouldn't be, but sometimes a little gets past the bow caps. If the test cock shows nothing, then he opens the door and shines his torch up to examine the bow cap and see that there is no obstruction in the tube. How's it, George?'

'O.K., number three.' Three times Mills lifted the test cock handle and no trace of water appeared. 'Opening the door now.'

He hauled on the big lever at the rear, pulled it clear and swung back the heavy circular door. He shone his torch up the gleaming inside length of the tube, then straightened. 'Clean as a whistle and dry as a bone.'

'That's not the way he was taught to report it,' Hansen said sorrowfully. 'I don't know what the young officers are coming to these days. Right, George, number four.'

Mills grinned, secured the rear door on number 3 and crossed to number 4. He lifted the test cock handle and said: 'Oh-oh.'

'What is it?' Hansen asked.

'Water,' Mills said tersely.

'Is there much? Let's see.'

'Just a trickle.'

'Is that bad?' I asked.

'It happens,' Hansen said briefly. He joggled the handle up and down and another spoonful of water appeared. 'You can get a slightly imperfect bow-cap and if you go deep enough to build up sufficient outside pressure you can get a trickle of water coming in. Probably what has happened in this case. If the bow-cap was open, friend, at this depth the water would come out of that spout like a bullet. But no chances, no chances.' He reached for the microphone again. 'Number four bow-cap still green? We have a little water here.'

'Still green.'

Hansen looked down at Mills. 'How's it coming?'

'Not so much now.'

'Control centre,' Hansen said into the microphone. 'Check the trim chit, just to make sure.'

There was a pause, then the box crackled again.

'Captain here. All tubes showing "Empty." Signed by Lieutenant Hansen and the foreman engineer.'

'Thank you, sir.' Hansen switched off and grinned. 'Lieutenant Hansen's word is good enough for me any day. How's it now?'

'Stopped.'

'Open her up.'

Mills tugged the heavy lever. It moved an inch or two, then stuck. 'Uncommon stiff,' he commented.

'You torpedomen never heard of anything called lubricating oil?' Hansen demanded. 'Weight, George, weight.'

Mills applied more weight. The lever moved another couple of inches. Mills scowled, shifted his feet to get maximum purchase and heaved just as Hansen shouted: 'No! Stop! For God's sake, stop!'

He was too late. He was a lifetime too late. The lever snapped clear, the heavy circular rear door smashed open as violently as if it had been struck by some gigantic battering ram and a roaring torrent of water burst into the for'ard torpedo room. The sheer size, the enormous power and frightening speed of that almost horizontally travelling column of water was staggering. It was like a giant hosepipe, like one of the outlet pipes of the Boulder Dam. It caught up Lieutenant Mills, already badly injured by the flailing sweep of that heavy door and swept him back across the torpedo room to smash heavily against the after bulkhead; for a moment he half stood there, pinned by the power of that huge jet, then slid down limply to the deck.

'Blow all main ballast!' Hansen shouted into the microphone. He was hanging on to a rear torpedo door to keep from being carried away and even above the thunderous roar of the waters his voice carried clearly. 'Emergency. Blow all main ballast. Number four tube open to the sea. Blow all main ballast!' He released his grip, staggered across the deck, trying to keep his balance in the madly swirling already foot-deep waters. 'Get out of here, for God's sake.'

He should have saved his energy and breath. I was already on my way out of there. I had Mills under the arms and was trying to drag him over the high sill of the for'ard collision bulkhead and I was making just no headway at all. The proper trim of a submarine is a delicate thing at the best of times and even after these few seconds the nose of the *Dolphin*, heavy with the tons of water that had already poured in, was beginning to cant sharply downwards: trying to drag Mills and at the same time keep my balance on that sloping deck with knee-high water boiling around me was more than I could do; but suddenly Hansen had Mills by the feet and I stumbled off-balance, tripped over the high sill and fell backwards into the confined space between the two collision bulkheads, dragging Mills after me.

Hansen was still on the other side of the bulkhead. I could hear him cursing steadily, monotonously and as if he meant it as he struggled to unhook the heavy door from its standing catch. Because of the steep downward pitch of the *Dolphin*'s deck he had to lean all his weight against the massive steel door to free the catch, and with his insecure footing among the swirling waters on that sloping slippery deck he was obviously having the devil's own time trying to release it. I let Mills lie, jumped

over the sill, flung my shoulder against the door and with the suddenly
added pressure the latch clicked free. The heavy door at once swung
half-shut, carrying us along with it and knocking us both off our feet into
the battering-ram path of that torrent still gushing from number 4 tube.
Coughing and spluttering we scrambled upright again, crossed the sill
and, hanging on to a clip handle apiece, tried to drag the door shut.

Twice we tried and twice we failed. The water boiled in through the
tube and its level was now almost lipping the top of the sill. With every
second that passed the downward angle of the *Dolphin* increased and with
every extra degree of steepness the task of pulling that door uphill
against the steadily increasing gravity became more and more difficult.

The water began to spill over the sill on to our feet.

Hansen grinned at me. At least, I thought for a moment he was
grinning, but the white teeth were clamped tightly together and there
was no amusement at all in his eyes. He shouted above the roar of the
water: 'It's now or never.'

A well-taken point. It was indeed now or never. At a signal from
Hansen we flung our combined weights on to those clip-handles each
with one hand to a clip while the other braced against the bulkhead to
give maximum purchase. We got the door to within four inches. It swung
open. We tried again. Still four inches and I knew that all our strength
had gone into that one.

'Can you hold it for a moment?' I shouted.

He nodded. I shifted both hands to the lower corner clip, dropped to
the deck, braced my feet against the sill and straightened both legs in one
convulsive jerk. The door crashed shut, Hansen jammed his clip home,
I did the same with mine and we were safe. For the moment we were safe.

I left Hansen to secure the remaining clips and started knocking the
clips of the after collision bulkhead door. I'd only got as far as the first one
when the others started falling off by themselves. Petty Officer Bowen
and his men, on the other side of that door, needed no telling that we
wanted out of there just as fast as possible. The door was pulled open and
my ear-drums popped with the abrupt fall in air pressure. I could hear
the steady echoing roar of air blasting into the ballast tanks under high
pressure. I hoisted Mills by the shoulders, strong competent hands lifted
him out and over the sill and a couple of seconds later Hansen and I were
beside him.

'In God's name!' Petty Officer Bowen said to Hansen. 'What's gone
wrong?'

'Number four tube open to the sea.'

'Jesus!'

'Clip up that door,' Hansen ordered. 'But good.' He left at a dead run, clawing his way up the sharply sloping deck of the torpedo storage room. I took a look at Lieutenant Mills – one short look was all I needed – and followed after Hansen. Only I didn't run. Running wasn't going to help anybody now.

The roar of compressed air filled the ship, the ballast tanks were rapidly emptying, but still the *Dolphin* continued on its deadly dive, arrowing down for the dark depths of the Arctic: not even the massive compressed-air banks of the submarine could hope to cope so soon with the effects of the scores of tons of seawater that had already floored into the for'ard torpedo room: I wondered bleakly if they would ever be able to cope at all. As I walked along the wardroom passage, using the hand-rail to haul myself up that crazily canted deck, I could feel the entire submarine shudder beneath my feet. No doubt about what that was, Swanson had the great turbines turning over at maximum revolutions, the big bronze propellers threshing madly in reverse, trying to bite deep into the water to slow up the diving submarine.

You can smell fear. You can smell it and you can see it and I could do both as I hauled my way into the control centre of the *Dolphin* that morning. Not one man as much as flickered an eye in my direction as I passed by the sonar room. They had no eyes for me. They had no eyes for anybody: tense, strained, immobile, with hunted faces, they had eyes for one thing only – the plummeting needle on the depth gauge.

The needle was passing the six-hundred-feet mark. Six hundred feet. No conventional submarine I'd ever been on could have operated at this depth. Could have survived at this depth. Six hundred and fifty. I thought of the fantastic outside pressure that represented and I felt far from happy. Someone else was feeling far from happy also, the young seaman manning the inboard diving seat. His fists were clenched till the knuckles showed, a muscle was jumping in his cheek, a nerve twitching in his neck and he had the look on his face of a man who sees the bony finger of death beckoning.

Seven hundred feet. Seven hundred and fifty. Eight hundred. I'd never heard of a submarine that had reached that depth and lived. Neither, apparently, had Commander Swanson.

'We have just set up a new mark, men,' he said. His voice was calm and relaxed and although he was far too intelligent a man not to be afraid, no trace of it showed in tone or manner. 'Lowest recorded dive ever, as far as I am aware. Speed of descent?'

'No change.'

'It will change soon. The torpedo room must be about full now – apart from the pocket of air compressed under high pressure.' He gazed at the dial and tapped his teeth thoughtfully with a thumb-nail – this, for

Swanson, was probably the equivalent of going into hysterics. 'Blow the diesel tanks: blow the fresh-water tanks.' Imperturbable though he sounded, Swanson was close to desperation for this was the counsel of despair: thousands of miles from home and supplies, yet jettisoning all the diesel and drinking water, the lack of either of which could make all the difference between life and death. But, at that moment, it didn't matter: all that mattered was lightening ship.

'Main ballast tanks empty,' the diving officer reported. His voice was hoarse and strained.

Swanson nodded, said nothing. The volume of the sound of the compressed air had dropped at least seventy-five per cent and the suddenly comparative silence was sinister, terrifying, as if it meant that the *Dolphin* was giving up the fight. Now we had only the slender reserves of the fresh water and diesel to save us: at the rate at which the *Dolphin* was still diving I didn't see how it could.

Hansen was standing beside me. I noticed blood dripping from his left hand to the deck and when I looked more closely I could see that two of his fingers were broken. It must have happened in the torpedo room. At the moment, it didn't seem important. It certainly didn't seem important to Hansen. He was entirely oblivious of it.

The pressure gauge fell farther and still farther. I knew now that nothing could save the *Dolphin*. A bell rang. Swanson swung down a microphone and pressed a button.

'Engine-room here,' a metallic voice came through. 'We must slow down. Main bearings beginning to smoke, she'll seize up any moment."

'Maintain revolutions.' Swanson swung back the microphone. The youngster at the diving console, the one with the jumping cheek muscles and the nervous twitch, started to mumble, 'Oh, dear God, oh, dear God,' over and over again, softly at first, then the voice climbing up the scale to hysteria. Swanson moved two paces, touched him on the shoulder. 'Do you mind, laddie? I can hardly hear myself think.' The mumbling stopped and the boy sat quite still, his face carved from grey granite, the nerve in his neck going like a trip-hammer.

'How much more of this will she take?' I asked casually. At least, I meant it to sound casual but it came out like the croak of an asthmatic bullfrog.

'I'm afraid we're moving into the realms of the unknown,' Swanson admitted calmly. 'One thousand feet plus. If that dial is right, we passed the theoretical implosion point – where the hull should have collapsed – fifty feet ago. At the present moment she's being subjected to well over a million tons of pressure.' Swanson's repose, his glacial calm, was staggering, they must have scoured the whole of America to find a man like that. If ever there was the right man in the right place at the right time it was Commander Swanson in the control room of a runaway submarine diving to depths of hundreds of feet below what any submarine had ever experienced before.

'She's slowing,' Hansen whispered.

'She's slowing.' Swanson nodded.

She wasn't slowing half fast enough for me. It was impossible that the pressure hull could hold out any longer. I wondered vaguely what the end would be like, then put the thought from my mind, I would never know anything about it, anyway. At that depth the pressure must have been about twenty tons to the square foot; we'd be squashed as flat as flounders before our senses could even begin to record what was happening to us.

The engine-room call-up bell rang again. The voice this time was imploring, desperate. 'We must ease up, Captain. Switch gear is turning red hot. We can see it glowing.'

'Wait till it's white hot, then you can complain about it,' Swanson said curtly. If the engines were going to break down they were going to break down; but until they did he'd tear the life out of them in an attempt to save the *Dolphin*. Another bell rang.

'Control room?' The voice was harsh, high-pitched. 'Crew's mess deck here. Water is beginning to come in.' For the first time, every eye in the control room turned away from the depth gauge and fixed itself on that loudspeaker. The hull was giving at last under the fantastic pressure, the crushing weight. One little hole, one tiny threadlike crack as a starting point and the pressure hull would rip and tear and flatten like a toy under a steam-hammer. A quick glance at the strained, shocked faces showed this same thought in every mind.

'Where?' Swanson demanded.

'Starboard bulkhead.'

'How much?'

'A pint or two, just trickling down the bulkhead. And it's getting worse. It's getting worse all the time. For God's sake, Captain, what are we going to do?'

'What are you going to do?' Swanson echoed. 'Mop the damn' stuff up, of course. You don't want to live in a dirty ship, do you?' He hung up.

'She's stopped. She's stopped.' Four words and a prayer. I'd been wrong about every eye being on the loudspeaker, one pair of eyes had never left the depth gauge, the pair belonging to the youngster at the console.

'She's stopped,' the diving officer confirmed. His voice had a shake in it.

No one spoke. The blood continued to drip unheeded from Hansen's crushed fingers. I thought that I detected, for the first time, a faint sheen of sweat on Swanson's brow, but I couldn't be sure. The deck still shuddered beneath our feet as the giant engines strove to lift the *Dolphin* out of these deadly depths, the compressed air still hissed into the diesel and fresh-water tanks. I could no longer see the depth gauge, the diving officer had drawn himself so close to it that he obscured most of it from me.

Ninety seconds passed, ninety seconds that didn't seem any longer than a leap year, ninety interminable seconds while we waited for the sea to burst in to our hull and take us for its own, then the diving officer said: 'Ten feet. *Up.*'

'Are you sure?' Swanson asked.

'A year's pay.'

'We're not out of the wood yet,' Swanson said mildly. 'The hull can still go – it should have gone a damn' long time ago. Another hundred feet – that means a couple of tons less pressure to the square foot – and I think we'll have a chance. At least a fifty-fifty chance. And after that the chances will improve with every foot we ascend; and as we ascend the highly compressed air in the torpedo room will expand, driving out water and so lightening ship.'

'Still rising,' the diving officer said. 'Still rising. Speed of ascent unchanged.'

Swanson walked across to the diving stand and studied the slow movement of the depth gauge dial. 'How much fresh water left?'

'Thirty per cent.'

'Secure blowing fresh-water ballast. Engines all back two-thirds.'

The roar of compressed air fell away and the deck vibration eased almost to nothing as the engine revolutions fell from emergency power to two-thirds full speed.

'Speed of ascent unchanged,' the diving officer reported. 'One hundred feet up.'

'Secure blowing diesel.' The roar of compressed air stopped completely. 'All back one-third.'

'Still rising. Still rising.'

Swanson took a silk handkerchief from his pocket and wiped his face and neck. 'I was a little worried there,' he said to no one in particular, 'and I don't much care who knows it.' He reached for a microphone and I could hear his voice booming faintly throughout the ship.

'Captain here. All right, you can all start breathing again. Everything is under control, we're on our way up. As a point of interest we're still over three hundred feet deeper than the lowest previous submarine dive ever recorded.'

I felt as if I had just been through the rollers of a giant mangle. We all looked as if we'd just been through the rollers of a giant mangle. A voice said: 'I've never smoked in my life, but I'm starting now. Someone give me a cigarette.' Hansen said: 'When we get back to the States do you know what I'm going to do?'

'Yes,' Swanson said. 'You're going to scrape together your last cent, go up to Groton and throw the biggest, the most expensive party ever for the men who built this boat. You're too late, Lieutenant, I thought of it first.' He checked abruptly and said sharply: 'What's happened to your hand?'

Hansen lifted his left hand and stared at it in surprise. 'I never even knew I'd been scratched. Must have happened with that damn' door in the torpedo room. There's a medical supply box there, Doc. Would you fix this.'

'You did a damn' fine job there, John,' Swanson said warmly. 'Getting that door closed, I mean. Couldn't have been easy.'

'It wasn't. All pats on the back to our friend here,' Hansen said. 'He got it closed, not me. And if we hadn't got it closed——'

'Or if I'd let you load the torpedoes when you came back last night,' Swanson said grimly. 'When we were sitting on the surface and the hatches wide open. We'd have been eight thousand feet down now and very, very dead.'

Hansen suddenly snatched his hand away. 'My God!' he said remorsefully. 'I'd forgotten. Never mind this damned hand of mine. George Mills, the torpedo officer. He caught a pretty bad smack. You'd better see him first. Or Doc Benson.'

I took his hand back. 'No hurry for either of us. Your fingers first. Mills isn't feeling a thing.'

'Good lord!' Astonishment showed in Hansen's face, maybe shock at my callousness. 'When he recovers consciousness——'

'He'll never recover consciousness again,' I said. 'Lieutenant Mills is dead.'

'What!' Swanson's fingers bit deeply, painfully into my arm. '"Dead," did you say?'

'That column of water from number four tube came in like an express train,' I said tiredly. 'Flung him right back against the after bulkhead and smashed in the occiput – the back of his head – like an eggshell. Death must have been instantaneous.'

'Young George Mills,' Swanson whispered. His face had gone very pale. 'Poor young beggar. His first trip on the *Dolphin*. And now – just like that. Killed.'

'Murdered,' I said.

'What!' If Commander Swanson didn't watch out with his fingers he'd have my upper arm all black and blue. 'What was that you said?'

'"Murdered," I said. "Murdered," I meant.'

Swanson stared at me for a long moment, his face empty of expression, but the eyes strained and tired and suddenly somehow old. He wheeled, walked across to the diving officer, spoke a few words to him and returned. 'Come on,' he said abruptly. 'You can fix up the lieutenant's hand in my cabin.'

7

'You realise the seriousness of what you are saying?' Swanson asked. 'You are making a grave accusation——'

'Come off it,' I said rudely. 'This is not a court of law and I'm not accusing anyone. All I say is that murder has been done. Whoever left that bow-cap door open is directly responsible for the death of Lieutenant Mills.'

'What do you mean "left the door open"? Who says anyone left the door open? It could have been due to natural causes. And even if – I can't see it – that door had been left open, you can't accuse a man of murder because of carelessness or forgetfulness or because——'

'Commander Swanson,' I said, 'I'll go on record as saying that you are probably the best naval officer I have ever met. But being best at that doesn't mean that you're best at everything. There are noticeable gaps in your education, Commander, especially in the appreciation of the finer points of skulduggery. You require an especially low and devious type of mind for that and I'm afraid that you just haven't got it. Doors left open by natural causes, you say. What natural causes?'

'We've hit the ice a few hefty smacks,' Swanson said slowly. 'That could have jarred it open. Or when we poked through the ice last night a piece of ice, a stalactite, say, could have——'

'Your tubes are recessed, aren't they? Mighty oddly-shaped stalactite that would go down then bend in at a right angle to reach the door – and even then it would only shut it more tightly.'

'The doors are tested every time we're in harbour,' Commander Swanson persisted quietly. 'They're also opened when we open tubes to carry out surface trimming tests in dock. Any dockyard has pieces of waste, rope and other rubbish floating around that could easily have jammed a door open.'

'The safety lights showed the doors shut.'

'They could have been opened just a crack, not enough to disengage the safety contact.'

'Open a crack! Why do you think Mills is dead? If you've ever seen the jet of water that hits the turbine blades in a hydro-electric plant, then you'll know how that water came in. A crack? My God! How are those doors operated?'

'Two ways. Remote control, hydraulic, just press a button: then there are manually-operated levers in the torpedo room itself.'

I turned to Hansen. He was sitting on the bunk beside me, his face pale as I splinted his broken fingers. I said: 'Those hand-operated levers. Were they in the shut position?'

'You heard me say so in there. Of course they were. First thing we always check.'

'Somebody doesn't like you,' I said to Swanson. 'Or somebody doesn't like the *Dolphin*. Or somebody knew that the *Dolphin* was going searching for the Zebra survivors and they didn't like that either. So they sabotaged the ship. You will remember you were rather surprised you didn't have to correct the *Dolphin*'s trim? It had been your intention to carry out a slow-time dive to check the underwater trim because you thought that would have been affected by the fact that you had no torpedoes in the for'ard tubes. But surprise, surprise. She didn't need any correction.'

'I'm listening,' Swanson said quietly. He was with me now. He was with me all the way. He cocked an eyebrow as we heard water flooding back into the tanks. The repeater gauge showed 200 feet, Swanson must have ordered his diving officer to level off at that depth. The *Dolphin* was still canted nose downwards at an angle of about 25°.

'She didn't need any correcting because some of her tubes were already full of water. For all I know maybe number three tube, the one we tested and found O.K. is the only one that is *not* full of water. Our clever little pal left the doors open, disconnected the hand-operated levers so that they appeared to be in the shut position when they were actually open and crossed over a few wires in a junction box so that the open position showed green while the closed showed red. A man who knew what he was about could have done it in a few minutes. Two men who knew what they were about could have done it in no time at all. I'll lay anything you like that, when you're eventually in a position to check, you'll find the levers disconnected, the wires crossed and the inlets of the test-cocks blocked with sealing-wax, quick-drying paint or even chewing-gum so that when the test-cocks were opened nothing would show and you would assume the tubes to be empty.'

'There was a trickle from the test-cock in number four tube,' Hansen objected.

'Low-grade chewing-gum.'

'The murderous swine,' Swanson said calmly. His restraint was far more effective than the most thunderous denunciations could ever have been. 'He could have murdered us all. But for the grace of God and the Groton boatyard shipwrights he would have murdered us all.'

'He didn't mean to,' I said. 'He didn't mean to kill anyone. You had intended to carry out a slow-time dive to check trim in the Holy Loch before you left that evening. You told me so yourself. Did you announce it to the crew, post it up in daily orders or something like that?'

'Both.'

'So. Our pal knew. He also knew that you carried out those checks when the boat is still awash or just under the surface. When you checked the tubes to see if they were O.K., water would come in, too much water to permit the rear doors to be shut again, but not under such high pressure that you wouldn't have time and to spare to close the for'ard collision bulkhead door and make a leisurely retreat in good order. What would have happened? Not much. At the worst you would have settled down slowly to the bottom and stayed there. Not deep enough to worry the *Dolphin*. In a submarine of even ten years ago it might have been fatal for all, because of the limited air supply. Not today when your air purifying machines can let you stay down for months at a time. You just float up your emergency indicator buoy and telephone, tell your story, sit around and drink coffee till a naval diver comes down and replaces the bow-cap, pump out the torpedo room and surface again. Our unknown pal – or pals – didn't mean to kill anyone. But they did mean to delay you. And they would have delayed you. We know now that you could have got to the surface under your own steam, but even so your top brass would have insisted that you go into dock for a day or two to check that everything was O.K.'

'Why should anyone want to delay us?' Swanson asked. I thought he had an unnecessarily speculative look in his eyes, but it was hard to be sure, Commander Swanson's face showed exactly what Commander Swanson wanted it to show and no more.

'My God, do you think I know the answer to that one?' I said irritably.

'No. No, I don't think so.' He could have been more emphatic about it. 'Tell me, Dr. Carpenter, do you suspect some member of the *Dolphin*'s crew to be responsible?'

'Do you really need an answer to that one?'

'I suppose not,' he sighed. 'Going to the bottom of the Arctic Ocean is not a very attractive way of committing suicide, and if any member of the crew had jinxed things he'd damn' soon have unjinxed them as soon as he realised that we weren't going to carry out trim checks in shallow water. Which leaves only the civilian dockyard workers in Scotland – and every one of them has been checked and rechecked and given a top-grade security clearance.'

'Which means nothing. There are plushy Moscow hotels and British and American prisons full of people who had top-grade security clearances. . . . What are you going to do now, Commander? About the *Dolphin*, I mean.'

'I've been thinking about it. In the normal course of events the thing to do would be to close the bow-cap of number four and pump out the torpedo room, then go in and close the rear door of number four. But the bow-cap door won't close. Within a second of John's telling us that number four was open to the sea the diving officer hit the hydraulic button – the one that closes it by remote control. You saw for yourself that nothing happened. It must be jammed.'

'You bet your life it's jammed,' I said grimly. 'A sledge-hammer might do some good but pressing buttons won't.'

'I could go back to that lead we've just left, surface again and send a diver under the ice to investigate and see what he can do, but I'm not going to ask any man to risk his life doing that. I could retreat to the open sea, surface and fix it there, but not only would it be a damned slow and uncomfortable trip with the *Dolphin* canted at this angle, it might take us days before we got back here again. And some of the Drift Station Zebra men are pretty far through. It might be too late.'

'Well, then,' I said. 'You have the man to hand, Commander. I told you when I first met you that environmental health studies were my speciality, especially in the field of pressure extremes when escaping from submarines. I'v done an awful lot of simulated sub escapes, Commander. I do know a fair amount about pressures, how to cope with them and how I react to them myself.'

'How do you react to them, Dr. Carpenter?'

'A high tolerance. They don't worry me much.'

'What do you have in mind?'

'You know damn' well what I have in mind,' I said impatiently. 'Drill a hole in the door of the after collision bulkhead, screw in a high-pressure hose, open the door, shove someone in the narrow space between the two collision bulkheads and turn up the hose until the pressure between the collision bulkheads equals that in the torpedo room. You have the clips eased off the for'ard collision door. When the pressures are equalised it opens at a touch, you walk inside, close number four rear door and walk away again. That's what you had in mind, wasn't it?'

'More or less,' he admitted. 'Except that *you* are no part of it. Every man on this ship has made simulated escapes. They all know the effects of pressure. And most of them are a great deal younger than you.'

'Suit yourself,' I said. 'But age has little to do with the ability to stand stresses. You didn't pick a teenager as the first American to orbit the earth, did you? As for simulated escapes, making a free ascent up a hundred-foot tank is a different matter altogether from going inside an iron box, waiting for the slow build-up of pressure, working under that pressure, then waiting for the slow process of decompression. I've seen young men, big, tough, very, very fit young men break up completely under those circumstances and almost go crazy trying to get out. The combination of physiological and psychological factors involved is pretty fierce.'

'I think,' Swanson said slowly, 'that I'd sooner have you – what do the English say, batting on a sticky wicket – than almost any man I know. But there's a point you've overlooked. What would the Admiral Commanding Atlantic Submarines say to me if he knew I'd let a civilian go instead of one of my own men?'

'If you *don't* let me go, I know what he'll say. He'll say: "'We must reduce Commander Swanson to lieutenant, j.g., because he had on board the *Dolphin* an acknowledged expert in this speciality and refused, out of stiff-necked pride, to use him, thereby endangering the lives of his crew and the safety of his ship."'

Swanson smiled a pretty bleak smile, but with the desperately narrow escape we had just had, the predicament we were still in and the fact that his torpedo officer was lying dead not so many feet away, I hardly expected him to break into gales of laughter. He looked at Hansen: 'What do you say, John?'

'I've seen more incompetent characters than Dr. Carpenter,' Hansen said. 'Also, he gets about as nervous and panic-stricken as a bag of Portland cement.'

'He has qualifications you do not look to find in the average medical man,' Swanson agreed. 'I shall be glad to accept your offer. One of my men will go with you. That way the dictates of common sense and honour are both satisfied.'

It wasn't all that pleasant, not by quite a way, but it wasn't all that terribly bad either. It went off exactly as it could have been predicted it would go off. Swanson cautiously eased the *Dolphin* up until her stern was just a few feet beneath the ice: this reduced the pressure in the torpedo room to a minimum, but even at that the bows were still about a hundred feet down.

A hole was drilled in the after collision bulkhead door and an armoured high-pressure hose screwed into position. Dressed in porous rubber suits and equipped with an aqua-lung apiece, a young torpedoman by the name of Murphy and I went inside and stood in the gap between the two collision bulkheads. High-powered air hissed into the confined space. Slowly the pressure rose: twenty, thirty, forty, fifty pounds to the square inch. I could feel the pressure on lungs and ears, the pain behind the eyes, the slight wooziness that comes from the poisonous effect of breathing pure oxygen under such pressure. But I was used to it, I knew it wasn't going to kill me: I wondered if young Murphy knew that. This was the stage where the combined physical and mental effects became too much for most people, but if Murphy was scared or panicky or suffering from bodily distress he hid it well. Swanson would have picked his best man and to be the best man in a company like that Murphy had to be something very special.

We eased off the clips on the for'ard collision bulkhead door, knocked them off cautiously as the pressures equalised. The water in the torpedo room was about two feet above the level of the sill and as the door came ajar the water boiled whitely through into the collision space while compressed air hissed out from behind us to equalise the lowering pressure of the air in the torpedo room. For about ten seconds we had to hang on grimly to hold the door and maintain our balance while water and air fought and jostled in a seething mælstrom to find their own natural levels. The door opened wide. The water level now extended from about thirty inches up on the collision bulkhead to the for'ard deckhead of the torpedo room. We crossed the sill, switched on our waterproof torches and ducked under.

The temperature of that water was about 28° F. – four below freezing. Those porous rubber suits were specially designed to cope with icy waters but even so I gasped with the shock of it – as well as one can gasp when breathing pure oxygen under heavy pressure. But we didn't linger, for the longer we remained there the longer we would have to spend decompressing afterwards. We half-walked, half-swam towards the fore end of the compartment, located the rear door on number 4 tube and closed it, but not before I had a quick look at the inside of the pressure cock. The door itself seemed undamaged: the body of the unfortunate Lieutenant Mills had absorbed its swinging impact and prevented it from being switched off its hinges. It didn't seem distorted in any way, and fitted snugly into place. We forced its retaining lever back into place and left.

Back in the collision compartment we gave the prearranged taps on the door. Almost at once we heard the subdued hum of a motor as the high-speed extraction pumps into the torpedo room got to work, forcing the water out through the hull. Slowly the water level dropped and as it dropped the air pressure as slowly decreased. Degree by degree the *Dolphin* began to come back on an even keel. When the water was finally below the level of the for'ard sill we gave another signal and the remaining over-pressure air was slowly bled out through the hose. A few minutes later, as I was stripping off the rubber suit, Swanson asked: 'Any trouble?'

'None. You picked a good man in Murphy.'

'The best. Many thanks, Doctor.' He lowered his voice. 'You wouldn't by any chance——'

'You know damned well I would,' I said. 'I did. Not sealing-wax, not chewing-gum, not paint. Glue, Commander Swanson. That's how they blocked the test-cock inlet. The old-fashioned animal hide stuff that comes out of a tube. Ideal for the job.'

'I see,' he said, and walked away.

The *Dolphin* shuddered along its entire length as the torpedo hissed out of its tube – number 3 tube, the only one in the submarine Swanson could safely rely upon.

'Count it down,' Swanson said to Hansen. 'Tell me when we should hit, tell me when we should hear it hit.'

Hansen looked at the stop-watch in his bandaged hand and nodded. The seconds passed slowly. I could see Hansen's lips move silently. Then he said: 'We should be hitting – now,' and two or three seconds later: 'We should be hearing – now.'

Whoever had been responsible for the settings and time calculations on that torpedo had known what he was about. Just on Hansen's second 'now' we felt as much as heard the clanging vibration along the *Dolphin*'s hull as the shock-waves from the exploding war-head reached us. The deck shook briefly beneath our feet but the impact was nowhere nearly as powerful as I had expected. I was relieved. I didn't have to be a clairvoyant to know that everyone was relieved. No submarine had ever before been in the vicinity of a torpedo detonating under the ice-pack: no one had known to what extent the tamping effect of overhead ice might have increased the pressure and destructive effect of the lateral shock waves.

'Nicely,' Swanson murmured. 'Very nicely done indeed. Both ahead one-third. I hope that bang had considerably more effect on the ice than it had on our ship.' He said to Benson at the ice-machine: 'Let us know as soon as we reach that lead, will you?'

He moved to the plotting table. Raeburn looked up and said: 'Five hundred yards gone, five hundred to go.'

'All stop,' Swanson said. The slight vibration of the engines died away. 'We'll just mosey along very carefully indeed. That explosion may have sent blocks of ice weighing a few tons apiece pretty far down into the sea. I don't want to be doing any speed at all if we meet any of them on the way up.'

'Three hundred yards to go,' Raeburn said.

'All clear. All clear all round,' the sonar room reported.

'Still thick ice,' Benson intoned. 'Ah! That's it. We're under the lead. Thin ice. Well, five or six feet.'

'Two hundred yards,' Raeburn said. 'It checks.'

We drifted slowly onwards. At Swanson's orders the propellors kicked over once or twice then stopped again.

'Fifty yards,' Raeburn said. 'Near enough.'

'Ice reading?'

'No change? Five feet, about.'

'Speed?'

'One knot.'

'Position?'

'One thousand yards exactly. Passing directly under target area.'

'And nothing on the ice-machine. Nothing at all?'

'Not a thing.' Benson shrugged and looked at Swanson. The captain walked across and watched the inked stylus draw its swiftly etched vertical lines on the paper.

'Peculiar, to say the least of it,' Swanson murmured. 'Seven hundred pounds of very high-grade amatol in that lot. Must be uncommonly tough ice in those parts. Again to say the least of it. We'll go up to ninety feet and make a few passes under the area. Floodlights on, TV on.'

So we went up to ninety feet and made a few passes and nothing came of it. The water was completely opaque, the floods and camera useless. The ice-machine stubbornly registered four to six feet – it was impossible to be more accurate – all the time.

'Well, that seems to be it,' Hansen said. 'We back off and have another go?'

'Well, I don't know,' Swanson said pensively. 'What say we just try to shoulder our way up?'

'Shoulder our way up?' Hansen wasn't with him: neither was I. 'What kind of shoulder is going to heave five feet of ice to one side?'

'I'm not sure. The thing is, we've been working from unproved assumptions and that's always a dangerous basis. We've been assuming that if the torpedo didn't blow the ice to smithereens it would at least blow a hole in it. Maybe it doesn't happen that way at all. Maybe there's just a big upward pressure of water distributed over a fair area that heaves the ice up and breaks it into pretty big chunks that just settle back into the water again in their original position in the pattern of a dried-up mud hole with tiny cracks all round the isolated sections. But with cracks all round. Narrow cracks, but there. Cracks so narrow that the ice-machine couldn't begin to register them even at the slow speed we were doing.' He turned to Raeburn. 'What's our position?'

'Still in the centre of the target area, sir.'

'Take her up till we touch the ice,' Swanson said.

He didn't have to add any cautions about gentleness. The diving officer took her up like floating thistledown until we felt a gentle bump.

'Hold her there,' Swanson said. He peered at the TV screen but the water was so opaque that all definition vanished half-way up the sail. He nodded to the diving officer. 'Kick her up – hard.'

Compressed air roared into the ballast tanks. Seconds passed without anything happening then all at once the *Dolphin* shuddered as something very heavy and very solid seemed to strike the hull. A moment's pause, another solid shock then we could see the edge of a giant segment of ice sliding down the face of the TV screen.

'Well, now, I believe I might have had a point there,' Swanson remarked. 'We seem to have hit a crack between two chunks of ice almost exactly in the middle. Depth?'

'Forty-five.'

'Fifteen feet showing. And I don't think we can expect to lift the hundreds of tons of ice lying over the rest of the hull. Plenty of positive buoyancy?'

'All we'll ever want.'

'Then we'll call it a day at that. Right, Quartermaster, away you go up top and tell us what the weather is like.'

I didn't wait to hear what the weather was like. I was interested enough in it, but I was even more interested in ensuring that Hansen didn't come along to his cabin in time to find me putting on the Mannlicher-Schoenauer along with my furs. But this time I stuck it not in its special holster but in the outside pocket of my caribou trousers. I thought it might come in handier there.

It was exactly noon when I clambered over the edge of the bridge and used a dangling rope to slide down a great rafted chunk of ice that slanted up almost to the top of the sail. The sky had about as much light in it as a late twilight in winter when the sky is heavy with grey cloud. The air was as bitter as ever, but the weather had improved for all that. The wind was down now, backed round to the north-east, seldom gusting at more than twenty m.p.h., the ice-spicules rising no more than two or three feet above the ice-cap. Nothing to tear your eyes out. To be able to see where you were going on that damned ice-cap made a very pleasant change.

There were eleven of us altogether – Commander Swanson himself, Dr. Benson, eight enlisted men and myself. Four of the men were carrying stretchers with them.

Even seven hundred pounds of the highest grade conventional explosive on the market hadn't managed to do very much damage to the ice in that lead. Over an area of seventy yards square or thereabouts the ice had fractured into large fragments curiously uniform in size and roughly hexagonal in shape but fallen back so neatly into position that you couldn't have put a hand down most of the cracks between the adjacent fragments of ice: many of the cracks, indeed, were already beginning to bind together. A poor enough performance for a torpedo war-head – until you remembered that though most of its disruptive power must have been directed downwards it had still managed to lift and fracture a chunk of the ice-cap weighing maybe 5,000 tons. Looked at in that way, it didn't seem such a puny effort after all. Maybe we'd been pretty lucky to achieve what we had.

We walked across to the eastern edge of the lead, scrambled up on to the ice-pack proper and turned round to get our bearings, to line up on the unwavering white finger of the searchlight that reached straight up into the gloom of the sky. No chance of getting lost this time. While the wind stayed quiet and the spicules stayed down you could see that lamp in the window ten miles away.

We didn't even need to take any bearings. A few steps away and up from the edge of the lead and we could see it at once. Drift Station Zebra. Three huts, one of them badly charred, five blackened skeletons of what had once been huts. Desolation.

'So that's it,' Swanson said in my ear. 'Or what's left of it. I've come a long way to see this.'

'You nearly went a damned sight longer and never saw it,' I said. 'To the floor of the Arctic, I mean. Pretty, isn't it?'

Swanson shook his head slowly, moved on. There were only a hundred yards to go. I led the way to the nearest intact hut, opened the door and passed inside.

The hut was about thirty degrees warmer than the last time I had been there, but still bitterly cold. Only Zabrinski and Rawlings were awake. The hut smelt of burnt fuel, disinfectant, iodine, morphine and a peculiar aroma arising from a particularly repulsive looking hash that Rawlings was industriously churning around in a dixie over the low stove.

'Ah, there you are,' Rawlings said conversationally. He might have been hailing a neighbour who'd phoned a minute previously to see if he could come across to borrow the lawn-mower rather than greeting men he'd been fairly certain he'd never see again. 'The time is perfect – just about to ring the dinner bell, Captain. Care for some Maryland chicken – I think.'

'Not just at the moment, thank you,' Swanson said politely. 'Sorry about the ankle, Zabrinski. How is it?'

'Just fine, Captain, just fine. In a plaster cast.' He thrust out a foot, stiffly. 'The Doc here – Dr. Jolly – fixed me up real nice. Had much trouble last night?' This was for me.

'Dr. Carpenter had a great deal of trouble last night,' Swanson said. 'And we've had a considerable amount since. But later. Bring that stretcher in here. You first, Zabrinski. As for you, Rawlings, you can stop making like Escoffier. The *Dolphin*'s less than a couple of hundred yards from here. We'll have you all aboard in half an hour.'

I heard a shuffling noise behind me. Dr. Jolly was on his feet, helping Captain Folsom to his. Folsom looked even weaker than he had done yesterday: his face, bandaged though it was, certainly looked worse.

'Captain Folsom,' I introduced him. 'Dr. Jolly. This is Commander Swanson, captain of the *Dolphin*. Dr. Benson.'

'*Doctor* Benson, you said, old boy?' Jolly lifted an eyebrow. 'My word, the pill-rolling competition's getting a little fierce in these parts. And Commander. By jove, but we're glad to see you fellows.' The combination of the rich Irish brogue and the English slang of the twenties fell more oddly than ever on my ear; he reminded me of educated Singhalese I'd met with their precise, lilting, standard southern English interlarded with the catch-phrases of forty years ago. Topping, old bean, simply too ripping for words.

'I can understand that.' Swanson smiled. He looked around the huddled unmoving men on the floor, men who might have been living or dead but for the immediate and smoky condensation from their shallow breathing, and his smile faded. He said to Captain Folsom: 'I cannot tell you how sorry I am. This has been a dreadful thing.'

Folsom stirred and said something but we couldn't make out what it was. Although his shockingly burnt face had been bandaged since I'd seen him last it didn't seem to have done him any good: he was talking inside his mouth all right but the ravaged cheek and mouth had become so paralysed that his speech didn't emerge as any recognisable language. The good side of his face, the left, was twisted and furrowed and the eye above almost completely shut. This had nothing to do with any sympathetic neuro-muscular reaction caused by the wickedly charred

right cheek. The man was in agony. I said to Jolly: 'No morphine left?'
I'd left him, I'd thought, with more than enough of it.

'Nothing left,' he said tiredly. 'I used the lot. The lot.'

'Dr. Jolly worked all through the night,' Zabrinski said quietly. 'Eight
hours. Rawlings and himself and Kinnaird. They never stopped once.'

Benson had his medical kit open. Jolly saw it and smiled, a smile of
relief, a smile of exhaustion. He was in far worse case than he'd been the
previous evening. He hadn't had all that much in him when he'd started.
But he'd worked. He'd worked a solid eight hours. He'd even fixed up
Zabrinski's ankle. A good doctor. Conscientious, Hippocratic, anyway.
He was entitled to relax. Now that there were other doctors here, he'd
relax. But not before.

He began to ease Folsom into a sitting position and I helped him. He
slid down himself, his back to the wall. 'Sorry, and all that, you know,' he
said. His bearded frost-bitten face twisted into the semblance of a grin.
'A poor host.'

'You can leave everything to us now, Dr. Jolly,' Swanson said quietly.
'You've got all the help that's going. One thing. All those men fit to be
moved?'

'I don't know.' Jolly rubbed an arm across bloodshot, smudged eyes.
'I don't know. One or two of them slipped pretty far back last night. It's
the cold. Those two. Pneumonia, I think. Something an injured man
could fight off in a few days back home can be fatal here. It's the cold,' he
repeated. 'Uses up ninety per cent of his energy not in fighting illness and
infection but just generating enough heat to stay alive.'

'Take it easy,' Swanson said. 'Maybe we'd better change our minds
about that half-hour to get you all aboard. Who's first for the ambulance,
Dr. Benson?' Not Dr. Carpenter. Dr. Benson. Well, Benson was his own
ship's doctor. But pointed, all the same. A regrettable coolness, as sudden
in its onset as it was marked in degree, had appeared in his attitude
towards me, and I didn't have to be beaten over the head with a heavy
club to guess at the reason for the abrupt change.

'Zabrinski, Dr. Jolly, Captain Folsom and this man here,' Benson said
promptly.

'Kinnaird, radio operator,' Kinnaird identified himself. 'We never
thought you'd make it, mate.' This to me. He dragged himself somehow
to his feet and stood there swaying. 'I can walk.'

'Don't argue,' Swanson said curtly. 'Rawlings, stop stirring that filthy
mush and get to your feet. Go with them. How long would it take you to
run a cable from the boat, fix up a couple of big electric heaters in here,
some lights?'

'Alone?'

'All the help you want, man.'

'Fifteen minutes. I could rig a phone, sir.'

'That would be useful. When the stretcher bearers come back bring blankets, sheets, hot water. Wrap the water containers in the blankets. Anything else, Dr. Benson?'

'Not now, sir.'

'That's it then. Away you go.'

Rawlings lifted the spoon from the pot, tasted it, smacked his lips in appreciation and shook his head sadly. 'It's a crying shame,' he said mournfully. 'It really is.' He went out in the wake of the stretcher bearers.

Of the eight men left lying on the floor, four were conscious. Hewson the tractor-driver, Naseby the cook, and two others who introduced themselves as Harrington. Twins. They'd even been burnt and frost-bitten in the same places. The other four were either sleeping or in coma. Benson and I started looking them over, Benson much more carefully than myself, very busy with thermometer and stethoscope. Looking for signs of pheumonia. I didn't think he'd have to look very far. Commander Swanson looked speculatively around the cabin, occasionally throwing a very odd look in my direction, occasionally flailing his arms across his chest to keep the circulation going. He had to. He didn't have the fancy furs I had and in spite of the solid-fuel stove the place was like an ice-box.

The first man I looked at was lying on his side in the far right-hand corner of the room. He had half-open eyes, just showing the lower arcs of his pupils, sunken temples, marble-white forehead and the only part of his face that wasn't bandaged was as cold as the marble in a winter graveyard. I said: 'Who is this?'

'Grant. John Grant.' Hewson, the dark quiet tractor-driver, answered me. 'Radio operator. Kinnaird's side-kick. How's it with him?'

'He's dead. He's been dead quite some time.'

'Dead?' Swanson said sharply. 'You sure?' I gave him my aloof professional look and said nothing. He went on to Benson: 'Anybody too ill to be moved?'

'Those two here, I think,' Benson said. He wasn't noticing the series of peculiar looks Swanson was letting me have, so he handed me his stethoscope. After a minute I straightened and nodded.

'Third-degree burns,' Benson said to Swanson. 'What we can see of them, that is. Both high temperatures, both very fast, very weak and erratic pulses, both with lung fluids.'

'They'd have a better chance inside the *Dolphin*,' Swanson said.

'You'll kill them getting there,' I said. 'Even if you could wrap them up warmly enough to take them back to the ship, hauling them up to the top of the sail and then lowering them vertically through those hatchways would finish them off.'

'We can't stay out in that lead indefinitely,' Swanson said. 'I'll take the responsibility for moving them.'

'Sorry, Captain.' Benson shook his head gravely. 'I agree with Dr. Carpenter.'

Swanson shrugged and said nothing. Moments later the stretcher bearers were back, followed soon after by Rawlings and three other enlisted men carrying cables, heaters, lamps and a telephone. It took only a few minutes to button the heaters and lamps on to the cable. Rawlings cranked the call-up generator of his field-phone and spoke briefly into the mouthpiece. Bright lights came on and the heaters started to crackle and after a few seconds glow.

Hewson, Naseby and the Harrington twins left by stretcher. When they'd gone I unhooked the Coleman lamp. 'You won't be needing this now,' I said. 'I won't be long.'

'Where are you going?' Swanson's voice was quiet.

'I won't be long,' I repeated. 'Just looking around.'

He hesitated, then stood to one side. I went out, moved round a corner of the hut and stopped. I heard the whirr of the call-up bell, a voice on the telephone. It was only a murmur to me, I couldn't make out what was being said. But I'd expected this.

The Coleman storm lantern flickered and faded in the wind, but didn't go out. Stray ice-spicules struck against the glass, but it didn't crack or break, it must have been one of those specially toughened glasses immune to a couple of hundred degrees' temperature range between the inside and the outside.

I made my way diagonally across to the only hut left on the south side. No trace of burning, charring or even smoke-blackening on the outside walls. The fuel store must have been the one next to it, on the same side and to the west, straight downwind: that almost certainly must have been its position to account for the destruction of all the other huts, and the grotesquely buckled shape of its remaining girders made this strong probability a certainty. Here had been the heart of the fire.

Hard against the side of the undamaged hut was a lean-to shed, solidly built. Six feet high, six wide, eight long. The door opened easily. Wooden floor, gleaming aluminium for the sides and ceiling, big black heaters bolted to the inside and outside walls. Wires led from those and it was no job for an Einstein to guess that they led – or had led – to the now destroyed generator house. This lean-to shed would have been warm night and day. The squat low-slung tractor that took up nearly all the floor space inside would have started at any time at the touch of a switch.

It wouldn't start at the turn of a switch now, it would take three or four blow-torches and the same number of strong men even to turn the engine over once. I closed the door and went into the main hut.

It was packed with metal tables, benches, machinery and every modern device for the automatic recording and interpretation of every conceivable observed detail of the Arctic weather. I didn't know what the functions of most of the instruments were and I didn't care. This was the meteorological office and that was enough for me. I examined the hut carefully but quickly and there didn't seem to be anything odd or out of place that I could see. In one corner, perched on an empty wooden packing-case, was a portable radio transmitter with listening phones – transceivers, they called them nowadays. Near it, in a box of heavy oiled wood, were fifteen Nife cells connected up in series. Hanging from a hook on the wall was a two-volt test lamp. I touched its bare leads to the outside terminals of the battery formed by the cells. Had those cells left in them even a fraction of their original power that test lamp should have burnt out in a white flash. It didn't even begin to glow. I tore a piece of flex from a nearby lamp and touched its ends to the terminals. Not even the minutest spark. Kinnaird hadn't been lying when he had said that his battery had been completely dead. But, then, I hadn't for a moment thought he'd been lying.

I made my way to the last hut – the hut that held the charred remnants of the seven men who had died in the fire. The stench of charred flesh and burnt diesel seemed stronger, more nauseating than ever. I stood in the doorway and the last thing I wanted to do was to approach even an inch closer. I peeled off fur and woollen mittens, set the lamp on a table, pulled out my torch and knelt by the first dead man.

Ten minutes passed and all I wanted was out of there. There are some things that doctors, even hardened pathologists, will go a long way to avoid. Bodies that have been too long in the sea is one: bodies that have been in the immediate vicinity of underwater explosion is another; and men who have literally been burned alive is another. I was beginning to feel more than slightly sick; but I wasn't going to leave there until I was finished.

The door creaked open. I turned and watched Commander Swanson come in. He'd been a long time, I'd expected him before then. Lieutenant Hansen, his damaged left hand wrapped in some thick woollen material, came in after him. That was what the phone call had been about, the Commander calling up reinforcements. Swanson switched off his torch, pushed up his snow-goggles and pulled down his mask. His eyes narrowed at the scene before him, his nostrils wrinkled in involuntary disgust, and the colour drained swiftly from his ruddy cheeks. Both Hansen and I had told him what to expect, but he hadn't been prepared for this: not often can the imagination encompass the reality. For a moment I thought he was going to be sick, but then I saw a slight tinge of colour touch the cheekbones and I knew he wasn't.

'Dr. Carpenter,' he said in a voice in which the unsteady huskiness seemed only to emphasise the stilted formality, 'I wish you to return at once to the ship where you will remain confined to your quarters. I would prefer you went voluntarily, accompanied by Lieutenant Hansen here. I wish no trouble. I trust you don't either. If you do, we can accommodate you. Rawlings and Murphy are waiting outside that door.'

'Those are fighting words, Commander,' I said, 'and very unfriendly. Rawlings and Murphy are going to get uncommon cold out there.' I put my right hand in my caribou pants pocket – the one with the gun in it – and surveyed him unhurriedly. 'Have you had a brainstorm?'

Swanson looked at Hansen and nodded in the direction of the door. Hansen half-turned, then stopped as I said: 'Very high-handed, aren't we? I'm not worth an explanation, is that it?'

Hansen looked uncomfortable. He didn't like any part of this. I suspected Swanson didn't either, but he was going to do what he had to do and let his feelings look elsewhere.

'Unless you're a great deal less intelligent than I believe – and I credit you with a high intelligence – you know exactly what the explanation is. When you came aboard the *Dolphin* in the Holy Loch both Admiral Garvie and myself were highly suspicious of you. You spun us a story about being an expert in Arctic conditions and of having helped set up this station here. When we wouldn't accept that as sufficient authority or reason to take you along with us you told a highly convincing tale about this being an advanced missile-warning outpost and even although it was peculiar that Admiral Garvie had never heard of it, we accepted it. The huge dish aerial you spoke of, the radar masts, the electronic computers – what's happened to them, Dr. Carpenter? A bit insubstantial, weren't they? Like all figments of the imagination.'

I looked at him, considering, and let him go on.

'There never were any of those things, were there? You're up to the neck in something very murky indeed, my friend. What it is I don't know nor, for the moment, do I care. All I care for is the safety of the ship, the welfare of the crew and bringing the Zebra survivors safely back home and I'm taking no chances at all.'

'The wishes of the British Admiralty, the orders from your own Director of Underseas Warfare – those mean nothing to you?'

'I'm beginning to have very strong reservations about the way those orders were obtained,' Swanson said grimly. 'You're altogether too mysterious for my liking, Dr. Carpenter – as well as being a fluent liar.'

'Those are harsh, harsh words, Commander.'

'The truth not infrequently sounds that way. Will you please come?'

'Sorry. I'm not through here yet.'

'I see. John, will you——'

'I can give you an explanation. I see I have to. Won't you listen?'

'A third fairy-story?' A headshake. 'No.'

'And I'm not ready to leave. Impasse.'

Swanson looked at Hansen, who turned to go. I said: 'Well, if you're too stiff-necked to listen to me, call up the bloodhounds. Isn't it just luck, now, that we have three fully-qualified doctors here?'

'What do you mean?'

'I mean this.' Guns have different characteristics in appearance. Some look relatively harmless, some ugly, some businesslike, some wicked-looking. The Mannlicher-Schoenauer in my hand looked just plain downright wicked. Very wicked indeed. The white light from the Coleman glittered off the blued metal, menacing and sinister. It was a great gun to terrify people with.

'You wouldn't use it,' Swanson said flatly.

'I'm through talking. I'm through asking for a hearing. Bring on the bailiffs, friend.'

'You're bluffing, mister,' Hansen said savagely. 'You don't dare.'

'There's too much at stake for me not to dare. Find out now. Don't be a coward. Don't hide behind your enlisted men's backs. Don't order them to get themselves shot.' I snapped off the safety-catch. 'Come and take it from me yourself.'

'Stay right where you are, John,' Swanson said sharply. 'He means it. I suppose you have a whole armoury in that combination-lock suitcase of yours,' he added bitterly.

'That's it. Automatic carbines, six-inch naval guns, the lot. But for a small-size situation a small-size gun. Do I get my hearing?'

'You get your hearing.'

'Send Rawlings and Murphy away. I don't want anyone else to know anything about this. Anyway, they're probably freezing to death.'

Swanson nodded. Hansen went to the door, opened it, spoke briefly and returned. I laid the gun on a table, picked up my torch and moved some paces away. I said: 'Come and have a look at this.'

They came. Both of them passed by the table with the gun lying there and didn't even look at it. I stopped before one of the grotesquely misshapen charred lumps lying on the floor. Swanson came close and stared down. His face had lost whatever little colour it had regained. He made a queer noise in his throat.

'That ring, that gold ring——' he began, then stopped short.

'I wasn't lying about that.'

'No. No, you weren't. I – I don't know what to say. I'm most damnably——'

'It doesn't matter,' I said roughly. 'Look here. At the back. I'm afraid I had to remove some of the carbon.'

'The neck,' Swanson whispered. 'It's broken.'

'Is that what you think?'

'Something heavy, I don't know, a beam from one of the huts, must have fallen——'

'You've just seen one of those huts. They have no beams. There's an inch and half of the vertebræ missing. If anything sufficiently heavy to smash off an inch and a half of the backbone had struck him, the broken piece would be embedded in his neck. It's not. It was blown out. He was shot from the front, through the base of the throat. The bullet went out the back of the neck. A soft-nosed bullet – you can tell by the size of the exit hole – from a powerful gun, something like a .38 Colt or Luger or Mauser.'

'Good God above!' For the first time, Swanson was badly shaken. He stared at the thing on the floor, then at me. 'Murdered. You mean he was murdered.'

'Who would have done this?' Hansen said hoarsely. 'Who, man, who? And in God's name, why?'

'I don't know who did it.'

Swanson looked at me, his eyes strange. 'You just found this out?'

'I found out last night.'

'You found out last night.' The words were slow, far-spaced, a distinct hiatus between each two. 'And all the time since, aboard the ship, you never said – you never showed – my God, Carpenter, you're inhuman.'

'Sure,' I said. 'See that gun there. It makes a loud bang and when I use it to kill the man who did this I won't even blink. I'm inhuman, all right.'

'I was speaking out of turn. Sorry.' Swanson was making a visible effort to bring himself under normal control. He looked at the Mannlicher-Schoenauer, then at me, then back at the gun. 'Private revenge is out, Carpenter. No one is going to take the law into his own hands.'

'Don't make me laugh out loud. A morgue isn't a fit place for it. Besides, I'm not through showing you things yet. There's more. Something that I've just found out now. Not last night.' I pointed to another huddled black shape on the ground. 'Care to have a look at this man here?'

'I'd rather not,' Swanson said steadily. 'Suppose you tell us?'

'You can see from where you are. The head. I've cleaned it up. Small hole in the front, in the middle of the face and slightly to the right: larger exit hole at the back of the top of the head. Same gun. Same man behind the gun.'

Neither man said anything. They were too sick, too shocked to say anything.

'Queer path the bullet took,' I went on. 'Ranged sharply upwards. As if the man who fired the shot had been lying or sitting down while his victim stood above him.'

'Yes.' Swanson didn't seem to have heard me. 'Murder. Two murders. This is a job for the authorities, for the police.'

'Sure,' I said. 'For the police. Let's just ring the sergeant at the local station and ask him if he would mind stepping this way for a few minutes.'

'It's not a job for us,' Swanson persisted. 'As captain of an American naval vessel with a duty to discharge I am primarily interested in bringing my ship and the Zebra survivors back to Scotland again.'

'Without endangering the ship?' I asked. 'With a murderer aboard the possibility of endangering the ship does not arise?'

'We don't know he is – or will be – aboard.'

'You don't even begin to believe that yourself. You know he will be. You know as well as I do why this fire broke out and you known damn' well that it was no accident. If there was any accidental element about it, it was just the size and extent of the fire. The killer may have miscalculated that. But both time and weather conditions were against him: I don't think he had very much option. The only possible way in which he could obliterate all traces of his crime was to have a fire of sufficient proportions to obliterate those traces. He would have got off with it too, if I hadn't been here, if I hadn't been convinced before we left port that something was very far wrong indeed. But he would take very good care that he wouldn't obliterate himself in the process. Like it or not, Commander, you're going to have a killer aboard your ship.'

'But all of those men have been burned, some very severely——'

'What the hell did you expect? That the unknown X would go about without a mark on him, without as much as a cigarette burn, proclaiming to the world that he had been the one who had been throwing matches about and had then thoughtfully stood to one side? Local colour. He *had* to get himself burnt.'

'It doesn't follow,' Hansen said. 'He wasn't going to know that anyone was going to get suspicious and start investigating.'

'You'll be well advised to join your captain in keeping out of the detecting racket,' I said shortly. 'The men behind this are top-flight experts with far-reaching contacts – part of a criminal octopus with tentacles so long that it can even reach out and sabotage your ship in the Holy Loch. Why they did that, I don't know. What matters is that top-flight operators like those *never* take chances. They always operate on the assumption that they *may* be found out. They take every possible precaution against every possible eventuality. Besides, when the fire was at its height – we don't know the story of that, yet – the killer would have had to pitch in and rescue those trapped. It would have seemed damned odd if he hadn't. And so he got burnt.'

'My God.' Swanson's teeth were beginning to chatter with the cold but he didn't seem to notice it. 'What a hellish set-up.'

'Isn't it? I dare say there's nothing in your navy regulations to cover this lot.'

'But what – what are you going to do?'

'We call the cops. That's me.'

'What do you mean?'

'What I say. I have more authority, more official backing, more scope, more power and more freedom of action than any cop you ever saw. You must believe me. What I say is true.'

'I'm beginning to believe it *is* true,' Swanson said in slow thoughtfulness. 'I've been wondering more and more about you in the past twenty-four hours. I've kept telling myself I was wrong, even ten minutes before I kept telling myself. You're a policeman? Or detective?'

'Naval officer. Intelligence. I have credentials in my suitcase which I am empowered to show in an emergency.' It didn't seem the time to tell him just how wide a selection of credentials I did have. 'This is the emergency.'

'But – but you are a doctor.'

'Sure I am. A navy doctor – on the side. My speciality is investigating sabotage in the U.K. armed forces. The cover-up of research doctor is the ideal one. My duties are deliberately vague and I have the power to poke and pry into all sorts of corners and situations and talk to all sorts of people on the grounds of being an investigating psychologist that would be impossible for the average serving officer.'

There was a long silence, then Swanson said bitterly: 'You might have told us before this.'

'I might have broadcast it all over your Tannoy system. Why the hell should I? I don't want to trip over blundering amateurs every step I take. Ask any cop. The biggest menace of his life is the self-appointed Sherlock. Besides, I couldn't trust you, and before you start getting all hot and bothered about that I might add that I don't mean you'd deliberately give me away or anything like that but that you may inadvertently give me away. Now I've no option but to tell you what I can and chance the consequences. Why couldn't you just have accepted that directive from your Director of Naval Operations and acted accordingly?'

'Directive?' Hansen looked at Swanson. 'What directive?'

'Order from Washington to give Dr. Carpenter here *carte blanche* for practically everything. Be reasonable, Carpenter. I don't like operating in the dark and I'm naturally suspicious. You came aboard in highly questionable circumstances. You knew too damn' much about submarines. You were as evasive as hell. You had this sabotage theory all cut and dried. Damn it, man, of course I had reservations. Wouldn't you have had, in my place?'

'I suppose so. I don't know. Me, I obey orders.'

'Uh-huh. And your orders in this case?'

'Meaning what exactly is all this about.' I sighed. 'It would have to come to this. You must be told now – and you'll understand why your Director of Naval Operations was so anxious that you give me every help possible.'

'We can believe this one?' Swanson asked.

'You can believe this one. The story I spun back in the Holy Loch wasn't all malarkey – I just dressed it up a bit to make sure you'd take me along. They did indeed have a very special item of equipment here – an electronic marvel that was used for monitoring the count-down of Soviet missiles and pin-pointing their locations. This machine was kept in one of the huts now destroyed – the second from the west in the south row. Night and day a giant captive radio-sonde balloon reached thirty thousand feet up into the sky – but it had no radio attached. It was just a huge aerial. Incidentally, I should think that this is the reason why the oil fuel appears to have been flung over so large an area – an explosion caused by the bursting of the hydrogen cylinders used to inflate the balloons. They were stored in the fuel hut.'

'Did everybody in Zebra know about this monitoring machine?'

'No. Most of them thought it a device for investigating cosmic rays. Only four people knew what it really was – my brother and the three others who all slept in the hut that housed this machine. Now the hut is destroyed. The free world's most advanced listening-post. You wonder why your D.N.O. was so anxious?'

'Four men?' Swanson looked at me, a faint speculation still in his eye. 'Which four men, Dr. Carpenter?'

'Do you have to ask? Four of the seven men you see lying here, Commander.'

He stared down at the floor then looked quickly away. He said: 'You mentioned that you were convinced even before we left port that something was far wrong. Why?'

'My brother had a top-secret code. We had messages sent by himself – he was an expert radio operator. One said that there had been two separate attempts to wreck the monitor. He didn't go into details. Another said that he had been attacked and left unconscious when making a midnight check and found someone bleeding off the gas from the hydrogen cylinders – without the radio-sonde aerial the monitor would have been useless. He was lucky, he was only out for a few minutes, as long again and he would have frozen to death. In the circumstances did you expect me to believe that the fire was unconnected with the attempts to sabotage the monitor?'

'But how would anyone *know* what it was?' Hansen objected. 'Apart from your brother and the other three men, that is?' Like Swanson, he glanced at the floor and, like Swanson looked as hurriedly away. 'For my money this is the work of a psycho. A madman. A coldly calculating criminal would – well, he wouldn't go in for wholesale murder like this. But a psycho would.'

'Three hours ago,' I said, 'before you loaded the torpedo into number three tube you checked the manually controlled levers and the warning lights for the tube bow-caps. In the one case you found that the levers had been disconnected in the open position: in the other you found that the wires had been crossed in a junction-box. Do you think that was the work of a psycho? Another psycho?'

He said nothing. Swanson said: 'What can I do to help, Dr. Carpenter?'

'What are you willing to do, Commander?'

'I will not hand over command of the *Dolphin*.' He smiled, but he wasn't feeling like smiling. 'Short of that, I – and the crew of the *Dolphin* – are at your complete disposal. You name it, Doctor, that's all.'

'This time you believe my story?'

'This time I believe your story.'

I was pleased about that, I almost believed it myself.

8

The hut where we'd found all the Zebra survivors huddled together was almost deserted when we got back to it – only Dr. Benson and the two very sick men remained. The hut seemed bigger now, somehow, bigger and colder, and very shabby and untidy like the remnants of a church rummage sale where the housewives have trained for a couple of months before moving up to battle stations. Pieces of clothing, bedding, frayed and shredded blankets, gloves, plates, cutlery and dozens of odds and ends of personal possessions lay scattered all over the floor. The sick men had been too sick – and too glad to be on their way – to worry overmuch about taking too many of their various knick-knacks out of there. All they had wanted out of there was themselves. I didn't blame them.

The two unconscious men had their scarred and frost-bitten faces towards us. They were either sleeping or in a coma. But I took no chances. I beckoned Benson and he came and stood with us in the shelter of the west wall.

I told Benson what I'd told the commander and Hansen. He had to know. As the man who would be in the most constant and closest contact with the sick men, he had to know. I suppose he must have been pretty astonished and shaken, but he didn't show it. Doctors' faces behave as doctors tell them to, when they come across a patient in a pretty critical state of health they don't beat their breasts and break into loud lamentations, as this tends to discourage the patient. This now made three men from the *Dolphin*'s crew who knew what the score was—well, half the score, anyway. Three was enough. I only hoped it wasn't too much.

Thereafter Swanson did the talking: Benson would take it better from him than he would from me. Swanson said: 'Where were you thinking of putting the sick men we've sent back aboard?'

'In the most comfortable places I can find. Officers' quarters, crew's quarters, scattered all over so that no one is upset too much. Spread the load, so to speak.' He paused. 'I didn't know of the latest – um – development at the time. Things are rather different now.'

'They are. Half of them in the wardroom, the other half in the crew's mess – no, the crew's quarters. No reason why they shouldn't be fixed up comfortably. If they wonder at this, you can say it's for ease of medical treatment and that they can all be under constant medical watch, like heart patients in a ward. Get Dr. Jolly behind you in this, he seems a co-operative type. And I've no doubt he'll support you in your next move – that all patients are to be stripped, bathed and provided with clean pyjamas. If they're too ill to move, bed-bath. Dr. Carpenter here tells me that prevention of infection is of paramount importance in cases of severe burn injuries.'

'And their clothes?'

'You catch on more quickly than I did.' Swanson grunted. 'All their clothes to be taken away and labelled. All contents to be removed and labelled. The clothes, for anyone's information, are to be disinfected and laundered.'

'It might help if I am permitted to know just what we are looking for,' Benson suggested.

Swanson looked at me.

'God knows,' I said. 'Anything and everything. One thing certain – you won't find a gun. Be especially careful in labelling gloves – when we get back to Britain we'll have the experts test them for nitrates from the gun used.'

'If anyone has brought aboard anything bigger than a postage stamp I'll find it,' Benson promised.

'Are you sure?' I asked. 'Even if you brought it aboard yourself?'

'Eh? Me? What the devil are you suggesting?'

'I'm suggesting that something may have been shoved inside your medical kit, even your pockets, when you weren't looking.'

'Good lord.' He dug feverishly into his pockets. 'The idea never even occurred to me.'

'You haven't the right type of nasty suspicious mind,' Swanson said dryly. 'Off you go. You too, John.'

They left, and Swanson and I went inside. Once I'd checked that the two men really were unconscious, we went to work. It must have been many years since Swanson had policed a deck or parade-ground, far less doubled as scavenger, but he took to it in the manner born. He was assiduous, painstaking, and missed nothing. Neither did I. We cleared a corner of the hut and brought across there every single article that was either lying on the floor or attached to the still ice-covered walls. Nothing was missed. It was either shaken, turned over, opened or emptied according to what it was. Fifteen minutes and we were all through. If there was anything bigger than a matchstick to be found in that room then we would have found it. But we found nothing. Then we scattered everything back over the floor again until the hut looked more or less as it had been before our search. If either of the two unconscious men came to I didn't want him knowing that we had been looking for anything.

'We're no great shakes in the detecting business,' Swanson said. He looked slightly discouraged.

'We can't find what isn't there to be found. And it doesn't help that we don't know what we're looking for. Let's try for the gun now. May be anywhere, he may even have thrown it away on the ice-cap, though I think that unlikely. A killer never likes to lose his means of killing – and he couldn't have been sure that he wouldn't require it again. There aren't so very many places to search. He wouldn't have left it here, for this is the main bunkhouse and in constant use. That leaves only the met. office and the lab. where the dead men are lying.'

'He could have hidden it among the ruins of one of the burnt-out huts,'

Swanson objected.

'Not a chance. Our friend has been here for some months now, and he must know exactly the effect those ice-storms have. The spicules silt up against any object that lies in their path. The metal frameworks at the bases of the destroyed buildings are still in position, and the floors of the huts – or where the wooden floors used to be – are covered with solid ice to a depth of from four to six inches. He would have been as well to bury his gun in quick-setting concrete.'

We started on the meteorological hut. We looked in every shelf, every box, every cupboard and had just started ripping the backs off the metal cabinets that housed the meteorological equipment when Swanson said abruptly: 'I have an idea. Back in a couple of minutes.'

He was better than his word. He was back in a minute flat, carrying in his hands four objects that glittered wetly in the lamplight and smelled strongly of petrol. A gun – a Luger automatic – the haft and broken-off blade of a knife and two rubber-wrapped packages which turned out to be spare magazines for the Luger. He said: 'I guess this was what you were looking for.'

'Where did you find them?'

'The tractor. In the petrol tank.'

'What made you think of looking there?'

'Just luck. I got to thinking about your remark that the guy who had used this gun might want to use it again. But if he was to hide it anywhere where it was exposed to the weather it might have become jammed up with ice. Even if it didn't, he might have figured that the metal would contract so that the shells wouldn't fit or that the firing mechanism and lubricating oil would freeze solid. Only two things don't freeze solid in these sub-zero temperatures – alcohol and petrol. You can't hide a gun in a bottle of gin.'

'It wouldn't have worked,' I said. 'Metal would still contract – the petrol is as cold as the surrounding air.'

'Maybe he didn't know that. Or if he did, maybe he just thought it was a good place to hide it, quick and handy.' He looked consideringly at me as I broke the butt and looked at the empty magazine, then said sharply: 'You're smearing that gun a little, aren't you?'

'Fingerprints? Not after being in petrol. He was probably wearing gloves anyway.'

'So why did you want it?'

'Serial number. May be able to trace it. It's even possible that the killer had a police permit for it. It's happened before, believe it or not. And you must remember that the killer believed there would be no suspicion of foul play, far less that a search would be carried out for the gun.

'Anyway, this knife explains the gun. Firing guns is a noisy business and I'm surprised – I was surprised – that the killer risked it. He might have wakened the whole camp. But he had to take the risk because he'd gone and snapped off the business end of this little sticker here. This is a very slender blade, the kind of blade it's very easy to snap unless you know exactly what you're doing, especially when the extreme cold makes the metal brittle. He probably struck a rib or broke the blade trying to haul it out – a knife slides in easily enough but it can jam against cartilage or bone when you try to remove it.'

'You mean – you mean the killer murdered a *third* man?' Swanson asked carefully. 'With this knife?'

'The third man but the first victim,' I nodded. 'The missing half of the blade will be stuck inside someone's chest. But I'm not going to look for it – it would be pointless and take far too long.'

'I'm not sure that I don't agree with Hansen,' Swanson said slowly. 'I know it's impossible to explain away the sabotage on the boat – but, by God, this looks like the work of a maniac. All this – all this senseless killing.'

'All this killing,' I agreed. 'But not senseless – not from the point of view of the killer. No, don't ask me, I don't know what his point of view was – or is. I know – you know – why he started the fire: what we don't know is why he killed those men in the first place.'

Swanson shook his head, then said: 'Let's get back to the other hut. I'll phone for someone to keep a watch over those sick men. I don't know about you, but I'm frozen stiff. And you had no sleep last night.'

'I'll watch them meantime,' I said. 'For an hour or so. And I've some thinking to do, some very hard thinking.'

'You haven't much to go on, have you?'

'That's what makes it so hard.'

I'd said to Swanson that I didn't have much to go on, a less than accurate statement, for I didn't have anything to go on at all. So I didn't waste any time thinking. Instead I took a lantern and went once again to the lab. where the dead men lay. I was cold and tired and alone, and the darkness was falling and I didn't very much fancy going there, Nobody would have fancied going there, a place of dreadful death which any sane person would have avoided like the plague. And that was why I was going there, not because I wasn't sane, but because it was a place that no man would ever voluntarily visit – unless he had an extremely powerful motivation, such as the intention of picking up some essential thing he had hidden there in the near certainty that no one else would ever go near the place. It sounded complicated, even to me. I was very tired. I made a fuzzy mental note to ask around, when I got back to the *Dolphin*, to find out who had suggested shifting the dead men in there.

The walls of the lab. were lined with shelves and cupboards containing jars and bottles and retorts and test-tubes and such-like chemical junk, but I didn't give them more than a glance. I went to the corner of the hut where the dead men lay most closely together, shone my torch along the side of the room and found what I was looking for in a matter of seconds – a floorboard standing slightly proud of its neighbours. Two of the blackened contorted lumps that had once been men lay across that board. I moved them just far enough, not liking the job at all, then lifted one end of the loose floorboard.

It looked as if someone had had it in mind to start up a supermarket. In the six-inch space between the floor and the base of the hut were stacked dozens of neatly arranged cans – soup, beef, fruit, vegetables, a fine varied diet with all the proteins and vitamins a man could want. Someone had no intention of going hungry. There was even a small pressure-stove and a couple of gallons of kerosene to thaw out the cans. And to one side, lying flat, two rows of gleaming Nife cells – there must have been about forty in all.

I replaced the board, left the lab. and went across to the meteorological hut again. I spent over an hour there, unbuttoning the backs of metal cabinets and peering into their innards, but I found nothing. Not what I had hoped to find, that was. But I did come across one very peculiar item, a small green metal box six inches by four by two, with a circular control that was both switch and tuner, and two glassed-in dials with neither figures nor marking on them. At the side of the box was a brass-rimmed hole.

I turned the switch and one of the dials glowed green, a magic-eye tuning device with the fans spread well apart. The other dial stayed dead. I twiddled the tuner control but nothing happened. Both the magic eye and the second dial required something to activate them – something like a pre-set radio signal. The hole in the side would accommodate the plug of any standard telephone receiver. Not many people would have known what this was, but I'd seen one before – a transistorised homing device for locating the direction of a radio signal, such as emitted by the 'Sarah' device on American space capsules which enables searchers to locate it once it has landed in the sea.

What legitimate purpose could be served by such a device in Drift Ice Station Zebra? When I'd told Swanson and Hansen of the existence of a console for monitoring rocket-firing signals from Siberia, that much of my story, anyway, had been true. But that had called for a giant aerial stretching far up into the sky: this comparative toy couldn't have ranged a twentieth of the distance to Siberia.

I had another look at the portable radio transmitter and the now exhausted Nife batteries that served them. The dialling counter was still tuned in to the waveband on which the *Dolphin* had picked up the distress signals. There was nothing for me there. I looked more closely at the nickel-cadmium cells and saw that they were joined to one another and to the radio set by wire-cored rubber leads with very powerfully spring-loaded saw-tooth clips on the terminals: those last ensured perfect electrical contact as well as being very convenient to use. I undid two of the clips, brought a torch-beam to bear and peered closely at the terminals. The indentations made by the sharpened steel saw-teeth were faint but unmistakable.

I made my way back to the laboratory hut, lifted the loose floorboard again and shone the torch on the Nife cells lying there. At least half of the cells had the same characteristic markings. Cells that looked fresh and unused, yet they had those same markings and if anything was certain it was that those cells had been brand-new and unmarked when Drift Ice Station Zebra had been first set up. A few of the cells were tucked so far away under adjacent floorboards that I had to stretch my hand far in to reach them. I pulled out two and in the space behind I seemed to see something dark and dull and metallic.

It was too dark to distinguish clearly what the object was but after I'd levered up another two floorboards I could see without any trouble at all. It was a cylinder about thirty inches long and six in diameter with brass stopcock and mounted pressure gauge registering 'Full': close behind it was a package about eighteen inches square and four thick, stencilled with the words 'RADIO-SONDE BALLOONS'. Hydrogen, batteries, balloons, corned beef and mulligatawny soup. A catholic enough assortment of stores by any standards; but there wouldn't have been anything haphazard about the choice of that assortment.

When I made it back to the bunkhouse, the two patients were still breathing. That was about all I could say for myself, too, I was shaking with the cold and even clamping my teeth together couldn't keep them from chattering. I thawed out under the big electric heaters until I was only half-frozen, picked up my torch and moved out again into the wind and the cold and the dark. I was a sucker for punishment, that was for sure.

In the next twenty minutes I made a dozen complete circuits of the camp, moving a few yards farther out with each circuit. I must have walked over a mile altogether and that was all I had for it, just the walk and a slight touch of frost-bite high up on the cheekbones, the only part of my face, other than the eyes, exposed to that bitter cold. I knew I had frost-bite for the skin had suddenly ceased to feel cold any more and was quite dead to the touch. Enough was enough and I had a hunch that I was wasting my time anyway. I headed back to the camp.

I passed between the meteorological hut and the lab. and was just level with the eastern end of the bunkhouse when I sensed as much as saw something odd out of the corner of my eye. I steadied the torch-beam on the east wall and peered closely at the sheath of ice that had been deposited there over the days by the ice-storm. Most of the encrustation was of a homogeneous greyish-white, very smooth and polished, but it wasn't all grey-white: it was speckled here and there with dozens of black flecks of odd shapes and sizes, none of them more than an inch square. I tried to touch them but they were deeply imbedded in and showing through the gleaming ice. I went to examine the east wall of the meteorological hut, but it was quite innocent of any such black flecking. So was the east wall of the lab.

A short search inside the meteorological hut turned up a hammer and screw-driver. I chipped away a section of the black-flecked ice, brought it into the bunkhouse and laid it on the floor in front of one of the big electrical heaters. Ten minutes later I had a small pool of water and, lying in it, the sodden remains of what had once been fragments of burnt paper. This was very curious indeed. It meant that there were scores of pieces of burnt paper imbedded in the east wall of the bunkhouse. Just there: nowhere else. The explanation, of course, could be completely innocuous: or not, as the case may be.

I had another look at the two unconscious men. They were warm enough and comfortable enough but that was about all you could say for them. I couldn't see them as fit enough to be moved inside the next twenty-four hours. I lifted the phone and asked for someone to relieve me and when two seamen arrived, I made my way back to the *Dolphin*.

There was an unusual atmosphere aboard ship that afternoon, quiet and dull and almost funereal. It was hardly to be wondered at. As far as the crew of the *Dolphin* had been concerned, the men manning Drift Ice Station Zebra had been just so many ciphers, not even names, just unknowns. But now the burnt, frost-bitten, emaciated survivors had come aboard ship, sick and suffering men each with a life and individuality of his own, and the sight of those wasted men still mourning the deaths of their eight comrades had suddenly brought home to every man on the submarine the full horror of what had happened on Zebra. And, of course, less than seven hours had elapsed since their own torpedo officer, Lieutenant Mills, had been killed. Now, even although the mission had been successful, there seemed little enough reason for celebration. Down in the crew's mess the hi-fi and the juke-box were stilled. The ship was like a tomb.

I found Hansen in his cabin. He was sitting on the edge of his pullman bunk, still wearing his fur trousers, his face bleak and hard and cold. He watched me in silence as I stripped off my parka, undid the empty holster tied round my chest, hung it up and stuck inside it the automatic I'd pulled from my caribou pants. Then he said suddenly: 'I wouldn't take them all off, Doc. Not if you want to come with us, that is.' He looked at his own furs and his mouth was bitter. 'Hardly the rig of the day for a funeral, is it?'

'You mean——'

'Skipper's in his cabin. Boning up on the burial service. George Mills and that assistant radio operator—Grant, wasn't it—who died out there today. A double funeral. Out on the ice. There's some men there already, chipping a place with crowbars and sledges at the base of a hummock.'

'I saw no one.'

'Port side. To the west.'

'I thought Swanson would have taken young Mills back to the States. Or Scotland.'

'Too far. And there's the psychological angle. You could hardly dent the morale of this bunch we have aboard here far less shoot it to pieces, but carrying a dead man as a shipmate is an unhappy thing. He's had permission from Washington ...' He broke off uncertainly, looked quickly up at me and then away again. I didn't have any need of telepathy to know what was in his mind.

'The seven men on Zebra?' I shook my head. 'No, no funeral service for them. How could you? I'll pay my respects some other way.'

His eyes flickered up at the Mannlicher-Schoenauer hanging in its holster, then away again. He said in a quiet savage voice: 'Goddam his black murderous soul. That devil's aboard here, Carpenter. Here. On our ship.' He smacked a bunched fist hard against the palm of his other hand. 'Have you no idea what's behind this, Doc? No idea who's responsible?'

'If I had, I wouldn't be standing here. Any idea how Benson is getting along with the sick and injured?'

'He's all through. I've just left him.'

I nodded, reached up for the automatic and stuck it in the pocket of my caribou pants. Hansen said quietly: 'Even aboard here?'

'Especially aboard here.' I left him and went along to the surgery. Benson was sitting at his table, his back to his art gallery of technicolour cartoons, making entries in a book. He looked up as I closed the door behind me.

'Find anything?' I asked.

'Nothing that I would regard as interesting. Hansen did most of the sorting. You may find something.' He pointed to neatly folded piles of clothing on the deck, several small attache-cases and a few polythene bags, each labelled. 'Look for yourself. How about the two men left out on Zebra?'

'Holding their own. I think they'll be O.K., but it's too early to say yet.' I squatted on the floor, went carefully through all the pockets in the clothes and found, as I had expected, nothing. Hansen wasn't the man to miss anything. I felt every square inch of the lining areas and came up with the same results. I went through the small cases and the polythene bags, small items of clothing and personal gear, shaving kits, letters, photographs, two or three cameras. I broke open the cameras and they were all empty. I said to Benson: 'Dr. Jolly brought his medical case aboard with him?'

'Wouldn't even trust one of your own colleagues, would you?'

'No.'

'Neither would I.' He smiled with his mouth only. 'Your evil influence. I went through every item in it. Not a thing. I even measured the thickness of the bottom of the case. Nothing there.'

'Good enough for me. How are the patients?'

'Nine of them,' Benson said. 'The psychological effect of knowing that they're safe has done them more good than any medication ever could.' He consulted cards on his desk. 'Captain Folsom is the worst. No danger, of course, but his facial burns are pretty savage. We've arranged to have a plastic surgeon standing by in Glasgow when we return. The Harrington twins, both met. officers, are rather less badly burnt, but very weak, from both cold and hunger. Food, warmth and rest will have them on their feet in a couple of days again. Hassard, another met. officer, and Jeremy, a lab. technician, moderate burns, moderate frost-bite, fittest of the lot otherwise—it's queer how different people react so differently to hunger and cold. The other four – Kinnaird, the senior radio operator, Dr. Jolly, Naseby, the cook, and Hewson, the tractor-driver and man who was in charge of the generator – are much of a muchness: they're suffering most severely of all from frost-bite, expecially Kinnaird, all with moderate burns, weak, of course, but recovering fast. Only Folsom and the Harrington twins have consented to become bed-patients. The rest we've provided with rigouts of one sort or another. They're all lying down, of course, but they won't be lying down long. All of them are young, tough, and basically very fit – they don't pick children or old men to man places like Drift Station Zebra.'

A knock came to the door and Swanson's head appeared. He said,

'Hallo, back again,' to me then turned to Benson. 'A small problem of medical discipline here, Doctor.' He stood aside to let us see Naseby, the Zebra cook, standing close behind him, dressed in a U.S. Navy's petty officer's uniform. 'It seems that your patients have heard about the funeral service. They want to go along – those who are able, that is – to pay their last respects to their colleagues. I understand and sympathise, of course, but their state of health——'

'I would advise against it, sir,' Benson said. 'Strongly.'

'You can advise what you like, mate,' a voice came from behind Naseby. It was Kinnaird, the cockney radio operator, also clad in blue. 'No offence. Don't want to be rude or ungrateful. But I'm going. Jimmy Grant was my mate.'

'I know how you feel,' Benson said. 'I also know how *I* feel about it – your condition, I mean. You're in no fit state to do anything except lie down. You're making things very difficult for me.'

'I'm the captain of this ship,' Swanson put in mildly. 'I can forbid it, you know. I can say "No", and make it stick.'

'And you are making things difficult for us, sir,' Kinnaird said. 'I don't reckon it would advance the cause of Anglo-American unity very much if we started hauling off at our rescuers an hour or two after they'd saved us from certain death.' He smiled faintly. 'Besides, look at what it might do to our wounds and burns.'

Swanson cocked an eyebrow at me. 'Well, they're your countrymen.'

'Dr. Benson is perfectly correct,' I said. 'But it's not worth a civil war. If they could survive five or six days on that damned ice-cap, I don't suppose a few minutes more is going to finish them off.'

'Well, if it does,' Swanson said heavily, 'we'll blame you.'

If I ever had any doubt about it I didn't have then, not after ten minutes out in the open. The Arctic ice-cap was no place for a funeral; but I couldn't have imagined a more promising set-up for a funeral director who wanted to drum up some trade. After the warmth of the *Dolphin* the cold seemed intense and within five minutes we were all shivering violently. The darkness was as nearly absolute as it ever becomes on the ice-cap, the wind was lifting again and thin flurries of snow came gusting through the night. The solitary floodlamp served only to emphasise the ghostly unreality of it all, the huddled circle of mourners with bent heads, the two shapeless canvas-wrapped forms lying huddled at the base of an ice-hummock, Commander Swanson bent over his book, the wind and the snow snatching the half-heard mumble from his lips as he hurried through the burial service. I caught barely one word in ten of committal and then it was all over, no meaningless rifle salutes, no empty blowing of bugles, just the service and the silence and the dark shapes of stumbling men hurriedly placing fragments of broken ice over the canvas-sheeted forms. And within twenty-four hours the eternally drifting spicules and blowing snow would have sealed them for ever in their icy tomb, and there they might remain for ever, drifting in endless circles about the North Pole; or some day, perhaps a thousand years from then, an icelead might open up and drop them down to the uncaring floor of the Arctic, their bodies as perfectly preserved as if they had died only that day. It was a macabre thought.

Heads bent against the snow and ice, we hurried back to the shelter of the *Dolphin*. From the ice-cap to the top of the sail it was a climb of over twenty feet up the almost vertically inclined huge slabs of ice that the submarine had pushed upwards and sideways as she had forced her way through. Hand-lines had been rigged from the top of the sail but even then it was a fairly tricky climb. It was a set-up where with the icy slope, the frozen slippery ropes, the darkness and the blinding effect of the snow and ice, an accident could all too easily happen. And happen it did.

I was about six feet up, giving a hand to Jeremy, the lab. technician from Zebra whose burnt hands made it almost impossible for him to climb alone, when I heard a muffled cry above me. I glanced up and had a darkly-blurred impression of someone teetering on top of the sail, fighting for his balance, then jerked Jeremy violently towards me to save him from being swept away as that same someone lost his footing, toppled over backwards and hurtled down past us on to the ice below. I winced at the sound of the impact, two sounds, rather, a heavy muffled thud followed immediately by a sharper, crisper crack. First the body, then the head. I half imagined that I heard another sound afterwards, but couldn't be sure. I handed Jeremy over to the care of someone else and slithered down an ice-coated rope, not looking forward very much to what I must see. The fall had been the equivalent of a twenty-foot drop on to a concrete floor.

Hansen had got there before me and was shining his torch down not on to one prostrate figure as I had expected, but two. Benson and Jolly, both of them out cold.

I said to Hansen: 'Did you see what happened?'

'No. Happened too quickly. All I know is that it was Benson who did the falling and Jolly who did the cushioning. Jolly was beside me only a few seconds before the fall.'

'If that's the case then Jolly probably saved your doctor's life. We'll need to strap them in stretchers and haul them up and inside. We can't leave them out here.'

'Stretchers? Well, yes, if you say so. But they might come round any minute.'

'One of them might. But one of them is not going to come round for a long time. You heard that crack when a head hit the ice, it was like someone being clouted over the head with a fence-post. And I don't know which it is yet.'

Hansen left. I stooped over Benson and eased back the hood of the duffel-coat he was wearing. A fence-post was just about right. The side of his head, an inch above the right ear, was a blood-smeared mess, a three-inch long gash in the purpling flesh with the blood already coagulating in the bitter cold. Two inches farther forward and he'd have been a dead man, the thin bone behind the temple would have shattered under such an impact. For Benson's sake, I hoped the rest of his skull was pretty thick. No question but that this had been the sharp crack I'd heard.

Benson's breathing was very shallow, the movement of his chest barely discernible. Jolly's, on the other hand, was fairly deep and regular. I pulled back his anorak hood, probed carefully over his head and encountered a slight puffiness far back, near the top on the left-hand side. The inference seemed obvious. I hadn't been imagining things when I thought I had heard a second sound after the sharp crack caused by Benson's head striking against the ice. Jolly must have been in the way of the falling Benson, not directly enough beneath him to break his fall in any way but directly enough to be knocked backwards on to the ice and clout the back of his head as he fell.

It took ten minutes to have them strapped in stretchers, taken inside and placed in a couple of temporary cots in the sick-bay. With Swanson waiting anxiously I attended to Benson first, though there was little enough I could do, and had just started on Jolly when his eyes flickered and he slowly came back to consciousness, groaning a bit and trying to hold the back of his head. He made to sit up in his cot but I restrained him.

'Oh, lord, my head.' Several times he squeezed his eyes tightly shut, opened them wide, focused with difficulty on the bulkhead riotous with the colour of Benson's cartoon characters, then looked away as if he didn't believe it. 'Oh, my word, that must have been a dilly. Who did it, old boy?'

'Did what?' Swanson asked.

'Walloped me on the old bean. Who? Eh?'

'You mean to say you don't remember?'

'Remember?' Jolly said irritably. 'How the devil should I . . .' He broke off as his eye caught sight of Benson in the adjacent cot, a huddled figure under the blankets with only the back of his head and a big gauze pack covering his wound showing. 'Of course, of course. Yes, that's it. He fell on top of me, didn't he?'

'He certainly did,' I said. 'Did you try to catch him?'

'Catch him? No, I didn't try to catch him. I didn't try to get out of the way either. It was all over in half a second. I just don't remember a thing about it.' He groaned a bit more then looked across at Benson. 'Came a pretty nasty cropper, eh? Must have done.'

'Looks like it. He's very severely concussed. There's X-ray equipment here and I'll have a look at his head shortly. Damned hard luck on you too, Jolly.'

'I'll get over it,' he grunted. He pushed off my hand and sat up. 'Can I help you?'

'You may not,' Swanson said quietly. 'Early supper then twelve hours solid for you and the eight others, Doctor, and those are *my* doctor's orders. You'll find supper waiting in the wardroom now.'

'Aye, aye, sir.' Jolly gave a ghost of a smile and pushed himself groggily to his feet. 'That bit about the twelve hours sounds good to me.'

After a minute or two, when he was steady enough on his feet, he left. Swanson said: 'What now?'

'You might inquire around to see who was nearest or near to Benson when he slipped climbing over the edge of the bridge. But discreetly. It might do no harm if at the same time you hinted around that maybe Benson had just taken a turn.'

'What are *you* hinting at?' Swanson asked slowly.

'Did he fall or was he pushed? That's what I'm hinting at.'

'Did he fall or . . .' He broke off then went on warily: 'Why should anyone want to push Dr. Benson?'

'Why should anyone want to kill seven—eight, now—men on Drift Ice Station Zebra?'

'You have a point,' Swanson acknowledged quietly. He left.

Making X-ray pictures wasn't very much in my line but apparently it hadn't been very much in Dr. Benson's line either for he'd written down, for his own benefit and guidance, a detailed list of instructions for the taking and development of X-ray pictures. I wondered how he would have felt if he had known that the first beneficiary of his meticulous thoroughness was to be himself. The two finished negatives I came up with wouldn't have caused any furore in the Royal Photographic Society, but they were enough for my wants.

By and by Commander Swanson returned, closing the door behind him. I said: 'Ten gets one that you got nothing.'

'You won't die a poor man,' he nodded. 'Nothing is what it is. So Chief Torpedoman Patterson tells me, and you know what he's like.'

I knew what he was like. Patterson was the man responsible for all discipline and organisation among the enlisted men and Swanson had said to me that he regarded Patterson, and not himself, as the most indispensable man on the ship.

'Patterson was the man who reached the bridge immediately before Benson,' Swanson said. 'He said he heard Benson cry out, swung round and saw him already beginning to topple backwards. He didn't recognise who it was at the time, it was too dark and snowy for that. He said he had the impression that Benson had already had one hand and one knee on the bridge coaming when he fell backwards.'

'A funny position in which to start falling backwards,' I said. 'Most of his body weight must already have been inboard. And even if he did topple outwards he would surely still have had plenty of time to grab the coaming with both hands.'

'Maybe he did take a turn,' Swanson suggested. 'And don't forget that the coaming is glass-slippery with its smooth coating of ice.'

'As soon as Benson disappeared Patterson ran to the side to see what had happened to him?'

'He did,' Swanson said wearily. 'And he said there wasn't a person within ten feet of the top of the bridge when Benson fell.'

'And who *was* ten feet below?'

'He couldn't tell. Don't forget how black it was out there on the ice-cap and that the moment Patterson had dropped into the brightly lit bridge he'd lost whatever night-sight he'd built up. Besides, he didn't wait for more than a glance. He was off for a stretcher even before you or Hansen got to Benson. Patterson is not the sort of man who has to be told what to do.'

'So it's a dead end there?'

'A dead end.'

I nodded, crossed to a cupboard and brought back the two X-rays, still wet, held in their metal clips. I held them up to the light for Swanson's inspection.

'Benson?' he asked, and when I nodded peered at them more closely and finally said: 'That line there—a fracture?'

'A fracture. And not a hair line one either, as you can see. He really caught a wallop.'

'How bad is it? How long before he comes out of this coma—he *is* in a coma?'

'He's all that. How long? If I were a lad fresh out of medical school I'd let you have a pretty confident estimate. If I were a top-flight brain surgeon I'd say anything from half an hour to a year or two, because people who really know what they are talking about are only too aware that we know next to nothing about the brain. Being neither, I'd guess at two or three days—and my guess could be hopelessly wrong. There may be cerebral bleeding. I don't know. I don't think so. Blood-pressure, respiration and temperature show no evidence of organic damage. And now you know as much about it as I do.'

'Your colleagues wouldn't like that.' Swanson smiled faintly. 'This cheerful confession of ignorance does nothing to enhance the mystique of your profession. How about your other patients—the two men still out in Zebra?'

'I'll see them after supper. Maybe they'll be fit enough to be brought there to-morrow. Meanwhile, I'd like to ask a favour of you. Could you lend me the services of your Torpedoman Rawlings? And would you have any objections to his being taken into our confidence?'

'Rawlings? I don't know why you want him, but why Rawlings? The officers and petty officers aboard this ship are the pick of the United States Navy. Why not one of them? Besides, I'm not sure that I like the idea of passing on to an enlisted man secrets denied to my officers.'

'They're strictly non-naval secrets. The question of hierarchy doesn't enter into it. Rawlings is the man I want. He's got a quick mind, quick reflexes, and a dead-pan give-away-nothing expression that is invaluable in a game like this. Besides, in the event—the unlikely event, I hope—of the killer suspecting that we're on to him, he wouldn't look for any danger from one of your enlisted men because he'd be certain that we wouldn't let them in on it.'

'What do you want him for?'

'To keep a night guard on Benson here.'

'On Benson?' A fractional narrowing of the eyes, that could have been as imagined as real, was the only change in Swanson's impassive face. 'So you don't think it was an accident, do you?'

'I don't honestly know. But I'm like yourself when you carry out a hundred and one different checks, most of which you know to be unnecessary, before you take your ship to sea – I'm taking no chances. If it wasn't an accident – then some one might have an interest in doing a really permanent job next time.'

'But how can Benson represent a danger to anyone?' Swanson argued.

'I'll wager anything you like, Carpenter, that Benson doesn't – or didn't – know a thing about them that could point a finger at anyone. If he did, he'd have told me straight away. He was like that.'

'Maybe he saw or heard something the significance of which he didn't then realise. Maybe the killer is frightened that if Benson has time enough to think about it the significance will dawn on him. Or maybe it's all a figment of my overheated imagination: maybe he just fell. But I'd still like to have Rawlings.'

'You shall have him.' Swanson rose to his feet and smiled. 'I don't want you quoting that Washington directive at me again.'

Two minutes later Rawlings arrived. He was dressed in a light brown shirt and overall pants, obviously his own conception of what constituted the well-dressed submariner's uniform, and for the first time in our acquaintance he didn't smile a greeting. He didn't even glance at Benson on his cot. His face was still and composed, without any expression.

'You sent for me, sir?' 'Sir,' not 'Doc.'

'Take a seat, Rawlings.' He sat, and as he did I noticed the heavy bulge in the twelve-inch thigh pocket on the side of his overall pants. I nodded and said: 'What have you got there? Doesn't do much for the cut of your natty suiting, does it?'

He didn't smile. He said: 'I always carry one or two tools around with me. That's what the pocket is for.'

'Let's see this particular tool,' I said.

He hesitated briefly, shrugged and, not without some difficulty, pulled a heavy gleaming drop-forged steel pipe-wrench from the pocket. I hefted it in my hand.

'I'm surprised at you, Rawlings,' I said. 'What do you think the average human skull is made of – concrete? One little tap with this thing and you're up on a murder or manslaughter charge.' I picked up a roll of bandage. 'Ten yards of this wrapped round the business end will automatically reduce the charge to one of assault and battery.'

'I don't know what you're talking about,' he said mechanically.

'I'm talking about the fact that when Commander Swanson, Lieutenant Hansen and I were inside the laboratory this afternoon and you and Murphy were outside, you must have kind of leaned your ear against the door and heard more than was good for you. You know there's something far wrong and though you don't know what your motto is "be prepared". Hence the cosh. Correct?'

'Correct.'

'Does Murphy know?'

'No.'

'I'm a naval intelligence officer. Washington know all about me. Want the captain to vouch for me?'

'Well, no.' The first faint signs of a grin. 'I heard you pull a gun on the skipper, but you're still walking about loose. You must be in the clear.'

'You heard me threaten the captain and Lieutenant Hansen with a gun. But then you were sent away. You heard nothing after that?'

'Nothing.'

'Three men have been murdered on Zebra. Two shot, one knifed.

Their bodies were burned to conceal traces of the crime. Four others died in the fire. The killer is aboard this ship.'

Rawlings said nothing. His eyes were wide, his face pale and shocked. I told him everything I'd told Swanson and Hansen and emphasised that he was to keep it all to himself. Then I finished: 'Dr. Benson here has been seriously hurt. A deliberate attempt, for God knows what reason, may have been made on his life. We don't know. But if it was a deliberate attempt, then it's failed – so far.'

Rawlings had brought himself under control. He said, his voice as empty of expression as his face: 'Our little pal might come calling again?'

'He may. No member of the crew except the captain, the executive officer or I will come here. Anyone else – well, you can start asking him questions when he recovers consciousness.'

'You recommended ten yards of this bandage, Doc?'

'It should be enough. And only a gentle tap, for God's sake. Above and behind the ear. You might sit behind that curtain there where no one can see you.'

'I'm feeling lonesome to-night,' Rawlings murmured. He broke open the bandage, started winding it around the head of the wrench and glanced at the cartoon-decorated bulkhead beside him. 'Even old Yogi Bear ain't no fit companion for me to-night. I hope I have some other company calling.'

I left him there. I felt vaguely sorry for anyone who should come calling, killer or not. I felt, too, that I had taken every possible precaution. But when I left Rawlings there guarding Benson I did make one little mistake. Just one. I left him guarding the wrong man.

The second accident of the day happened so quickly, so easily, so inevitably that it might almost have been just that – an accident.

At supper that evening I suggested that, with Commander Swanson's permission, I'd have a surgery at nine next morning; because of enforced neglect most of the burn wounds were suppurating fairly badly, requiring constant cleaning and changing of coverings: I also thought it about time that an X-ray inspection be made of Zabrinski's broken ankle. Medical supplies in the sickbay were running short. Where did Benson keep his main supplies? Swanson told me and detailed Henry, the steward, to show me where it was.

About ten that night, after I'd returned from seeing the two men out on Zebra, Henry led me through the now deserted control room and down the ladder which led to the inertial navigation room and the electronics space, which abutted on it. He undid the strong-back clamp

on the square heavy steel hatch in a corner of the electronics room and
with an assist from me—the hatch must have weighed about 150 pounds
– swung it up and back until the hatch clicked home on its standing latch.

Three rungs on the inside of the hatch-cover led on to the vertical steel
ladder that reached down to the deck below. Henry went down first,
snapping on the light as he went, and I followed.

The medical storage room, though tiny, was equipped on the same
superbly lavish scale as was everything else on the *Dolphin.* Benson, as
thoroughly meticulous in this as he had been in his outlining of X-ray
procedure, had everything neatly and logically labelled so that it took
me less than three minutes to find everything I wanted. I went up the
ladder first, stopped near the top, stretched down and took the bag of
supplies from Henry, swung it up on the deck above, then reached up
quickly with my free hand to grab the middle of the three rungs welded
on the lower side of the hatch cover to haul myself up on to the deck of
the electronics space. But I didn't haul myself up. What happened was
that I hauled the hatch cover down. The retaining latch had become
disengaged, and the 150-pound dead weight of that massive cover was
swinging down on top of me before I could even begin to realise what
was happening.

I fell half-sideways, half-backwards, pulling the hatch cover with me.
My head struck against the hatch coaming. Desperately I ducked my
head forward – if it had been crushed between the coaming and the
falling cover the two sides of my skull would just about have met in the
middle—and tried to snatch my left arm back inside. I was more or less
successful with my head—I had it clear of the coaming and was ducking
so quickly that the impact of the cover was no more than enough to give
me a slight headache afterwards; but my left arm was a different matter
altogether. I almost got it clear—but only almost. If my left hand and
wrist had been strapped to a steel block and a gorilla had had a go at it
with a sledge-hammer, the effect couldn't have been more agonising. For
a moment or two I hung there, trapped, dangling by my left wrist, then
the weight of my body tore the mangled wrist and hand through the gap
and I crashed down to the deck beneath. Then the gorilla seemed to have
another go with the sledge-hammer and consciousness went.

'I won't beat about the bush, old lad,' Jolly said. 'No point in it with a
fellow pill-roller. Your wrist is a mess – I had to dig half your watch out
of it. The middle and little fingers are broken, the middle in two places.
But the permanent damage, I'm afraid, is to the back of your hand – the
little and ring finger tendons have been sliced.'

'What does that mean?' Swanson asked.

'It means that in his left hand he'll have to get by with two fingers and a thumb for the rest of his life,' Jolly said bluntly.

Swanson swore softly and turned to Henry. 'How in God's name could you have been so damnably careless? An experienced submariner like you? You know perfectly well that you are required to make a visual check every time a hatch cover engages in a standing latch. Why didn't you?'

'I didn't need to, sir.' Henry was looking more dyspeptic and forlorn than ever. 'I heard it click and I gave a tug. It was fixed, all right. I can swear to it, sir.'

'How could it have been fixed? Look at Dr. Carpenter's hand. Just a hair-line engagement and the slightest extra pressure – my God, why can't you people obey regulations?'

Henry stared at the deck in silence. Jolly, who was understandably looking about as washed-out as I felt, packed away the tools of his trade, advised me to take a couple of days off, gave me a handful of pills to take, said a weary good night and climbed up the ladder leading from the electronics space, where he had been fixing my hand. Swanson said to Henry: 'You can go now, Baker.' It was the first time I'd ever heard anyone address Henry by his surname, a sufficient enough token of what Swanson regarded as the enormity of his crime. 'I'll decide what to do about this in the morning.'

'I don't know about the morning," I said after Henry was gone. 'Maybe the next morning. Or the one after that. Then you can apologise to him. You and me both. That cover was locked on its standing latch. *I* checked it visually, Commander Swanson.'

Swanson gave me his cool impassive look. After a moment he said quietly : 'Are you suggesting what I think you are suggesting?'

'Someone took a risk,' I said. 'Not all that much of a risk, though – most people are asleep now and the control room was deserted at the moment that mattered. Someone in the wardroom to-night heard me ask your permission to go down to the medical store and heard you giving your okay. Shortly after that nearly everyone turned in. One man didn't – he kept awake and hung around patiently until I came back from the Drift Station. He followed us down below – he was lucky, Lieutenant Sims, your officer on deck, was taking star-sights up on the bridge and the control room was empty – and he unhooked the latch but left the hatch cover in a standing position. There was a slight element of gambling as to whether I would come up first, but not all that much, it would have been a matter of elementary courtesy, he would have thought, for Henry to see me up first. Anyway, he won his gamble, slight though it was. After that our unknown friend wasn't quite so lucky – I think he expected the damage to be a bit more permanent.'

'I'll get inquiries under way immediately,' Swanson said. 'Whoever was responsible, someone must have seen him. Someone must have heard him leaving his cot——'

'Don't waste your time, Commander. We're up against a highly intelligent character who doesn't overlook the obvious. Not only that but word of your inquiries is bound to get around and you'd scare him under cover where I'd never get at him.'

'Then I'll just keep the whole damned lot under lock and key until we get back to Scotland,' Swanson said grimly. '*That* way there'll be no more trouble.'

'That way we'll *never* find out who the murderer of my brother and the six – seven now – others are. Whoever it is has to be given sufficient rope to trip himself up.'

'Good lord, man, we can't just sit back and let things be done to us.' A hint of testiness in the commander's voice and I couldn't blame him. 'What do we – what do *you* propose to do now?'

'Start at the beginning. To-morrow morning we'll hold a court of inquiry among the survivors. Let's find out all we can about that fire. Just an innocent above-board fact-finding inquiry – for the Ministry of Supply, let us say. I've an idea we might turn up something very interesting indeed.'

'You think so?' Swanson shook his head. 'I don't believe it. I don't believe it for a moment. Look what's happened to you. It's obvious, man, that someone knows or suspects that you're on to them. They'll take damned good care to give nothing away.'

'You think that's why I was clouted to-night?'

'What other reason could there be?'

'Was that why Benson was hurt?'

'We don't know that he was. Deliberately, I mean. May have been pure coincidence.'

'Maybe it was,' I agreed. 'And again maybe it wasn't. My guess, for what it's worth, is that the accident or accidents have nothing at all to do with any suspicions the killer may have that we're on to him. Anyway, let's see what to-morrow brings.'

It was midnight when I got back to my cabin. The engineer officer was on watch and Hansen was asleep so I didn't put on any light lest I disturb him. I didn't undress, just removed my shoes, lay down on the cot and pulled a cover over me.

I didn't sleep. I couldn't sleep. My left arm from the elbow downwards still felt as if it were caught in a bear trap. Twice I pulled from my pocket the pain-killers and sleeping-tablets that Jolly had given me and twice I put them away.

Instead I just lay there and thought and the first and most obvious conclusion I came up with was that there was someone aboard the *Dolphin* who didn't care any too much for the members of the medical profession. Then I got to wondering why the profession was so unpopular and after half an hour of beating my weary brain-cells around I got silently to my feet and made my way on stockinged soles to the sick-bay.

I passed inside and closed the door softly behind me. A red night-light burnt dully in one corner of the bay, just enough to let me see the huddled form of Benson lying on a cot. I switched on the overhead light, blinked in the sudden fierce wash of light and looked at the curtain at the other end of the bay. Nothing stirred behind it. I said: 'Just kind of take your itching fingers away from that pipe-wrench, Rawlings. It's me, Carpenter.'

The curtain was pulled to one side and Rawlings appeared, the pipe-wrench, with its bandage-wrapped head, dangling from one hand. He had a disappointed look on his face.

'I was expecting someone else,' he said reproachfully. 'I was kinda hoping – my God, Doc, what's happened to your arm?'

'Well may you ask, Rawlings. Our little pal had a go at me to-night. I think he wanted me out of the way. Whether he wanted me out of the way permanently or not I don't know, but he near as a toucher succeeded.' I told him what had happened, then asked him: 'Is there any man aboard you can trust absolutely?' I knew the answer before I had asked the question. 'Zabrinski,' he said unhesitatingly.

'Do you think you could pussy-foot along to wherever it is that he's sleeping and bring him here without waking up anyone?'

He didn't answer my questions. He said: 'He can't walk, Doc, you know that.'

'Carry him. You're big enough.'

He grinned and left. He was back with Zabrinski inside three minutes. Three-quarters of an hour later, after telling Rawlings he could call off his watch, I was back in my cabin.

Hansen was still asleep. He didn't wake even when I switched on a side light. Slowly, clumsily, painfully, I dressed myself in my furs, unlocked my case and drew out the Luger, the two rubber-covered magazines and the broken knife which Commander Swanson had found in the tractor's petrol tank. I put those in my pocket and left. As I passed through the control room I told the officer on deck that I was going out to check on the two patients still left out in the camp. As I had pulled a fur mitten over my injured hand he didn't raise any eyebrows, doctors were a law to themselves and I was just the good healer *en route* to give aid and comfort to the sick.

I did have a good look at the two sick men, both of whom seemed to me to be picking up steadily, then said 'goodnight' to the two *Dolphin* crewmen who were watching over them. But I didn't go straight back to the ship. First I went to the tractor shed and replaced the gun, magazines and broken knife in the tractor tank. Then I went back to the ship.

9

'I'm sorry to have to bother you with all these questions,' I said pleasantly. 'But that's the way it is with all government departments. A thousand questions in quadruplicate and each of them more pointlessly irritating than the rest. But I have this job to do and the report to be radioed off as soon as possible and I would appreciate all the information and co-operation you can give me. First off, has anyone any idea at all how this damnable fire started?'

I hoped I sounded like a Ministry of Supply official which was what I'd told them I was – making a Ministry of Supply report. I'd further told them, just to nip any eyebrow-raising in the bud, that it was the Ministry of Supply's policy to send a doctor to report on any accident where loss of life was involved. Maybe this was the case. I didn't know and I didn't care.

'Well, I was the first to discover the fire, I think,' Naseby, the Zebra cook, said hesitantly. His Yorkshire accent was very pronounced. He was still no picture of health and strength but for all that he was a hundred per cent improved on the man I had seen yesterday. Like the other eight survivors of Drift Ice Station Zebra who were present in the wardroom that morning, a long night's warm sleep and good food had brought about a remarkable change for the better. More accurately, like seven others. Captain Folsom's face had been so hideously burnt that it was difficult to say what progress he was making although he had certainly had a good enough breakfast, almost entirely liquid, less than half an hour previously. 'It must have been about two o'clock in the morning,' Naseby went on. 'Well, near enough two. The place was already on fire. Burning like a torch, it was. I——'

'What place?' I interrupted. 'Where were you sleeping?'

'In the cookhouse. That was also our dining-hall. Farthest west hut in the north row.'

'You slept there alone?'

'No. Hewson, here, and Flanders and Bryce slept there also. Flanders and Bryce, they're – they were – lab. technicians. Hewson and I slept at the very back of the hut, then there were two big cupboards, one each side, that held all our food stores, then Flanders and Bryce slept in the dining-hall itself, by a corner of the galley.'

'They were nearest the door?'

'That's right. I got up, coughing and choking with smoke, very groggy, and I could see flames already starting to eat through the east wall of the hut. I shook Hewson then ran for the fire extinguisher – it was kept by the door. It wouldn't work. Jammed solid with the cold, I suppose. I don't know. I ran back in again. I was blind by this time, you never saw smoke like it in your life. I shook Flanders and Bryce and shouted at them to get out then I bumped into Hewson and told him to run and wake Captain Folsom here.'

I looked at Hewson. 'You woke Captain Folsom?'

'I went to wake him. But not straight away. The whole camp was blazing like the biggest Fifth of November bonfire you ever saw and flames twenty feet high were sweeping down the lane between the two rows of huts. The air was full of flying oil, a lot of it burning. I had to make a long swing to the north to get clear of the oil and the flames.'

'The wind was from the east?'

'Not quite. Not that night. South-east, I would say. East-south-east would be more like it, rather. Anyway, I gave a very wide berth to the generator house – that was the one next the dining-hall in the north row – and reached the main bunkhouse. That one you found us in.'

'Then you woke Captain Folsom?'

'He was already gone. Shortly after I'd left the dining-hall the fuel drums in the fuel storage hut – that was the one directly south of the main bunkhouse – started exploding. Like bloody great bombs going off they were, the noise they made. They would have wakened the dead. Anyway, they woke Captain Folsom. He and Jeremy here' – he nodded at a man sitting across the table from him – 'had taken the fire extinguisher from the bunkhouse and tried to get close to Major Halliwell's hut.'

'That was the one directly west of the fuel store?'

'That's right. It was an inferno. Captain Folsom's extinguisher worked well enough but he couldn't get close enough to do any good. There was so much flying oil in the air that even the extinguisher foam seemed to burn.'

'Hold on a minute,' I said. 'To get back to my original question. How did the fire start?'

'We've discussed that a hundred times among ourselves,' Dr. Jolly said wearily. 'The truth is, old boy, we haven't a clue. We know *where* it started all right: match the huts destroyed against the wind direction that night and it could only have been in the fuel store. But how? It's anybody's guess. I don't see that it matters a great deal now.'

'I disagree. It matters very much. If we could find out how it started we might prevent another such tragedy later on. That's why I'm here. Hewson, you were in charge of the fuel store and generator hut. Have you no opinion on this?'

'None. It *must* have been electrical, but how I can't guess. It's possible that there was a leakage from one of the fuel drums and that oil vapour was present in the air. There were two black heaters in the fuel store, designed to keep the temperature up to zero Fahrenheit, so that the oil would always flow freely. Arcing across the make and break of the thermostats might have ignited the gas. But it's only a wild guess, of course.'

'No possibility of any smouldering rags or cigarette ends being the cause?'

Hewson's face turned a dusky red.

'Look, mister, I know my job. Burning rags, cigarette ends – I know how to keep a bloody fuel store——'

'Keep your shirt on,' I interrupted. 'No offence. I'm only doing *my* job.' I turned back to Naseby. 'After you'd sent Hewson here to rouse up Captain Folsom, what then?'

'I ran across to the radio room – that's the hut due south of the cookhouse and west of Major Halliwell's——'

'But those two lab. technicians – Flanders and Bryce, wasn't it—surely you checked they were awake and out of it before you left the dining-hall?'

'God help me, I didn't.' Naseby stared down at the deck, his shoulders hunched, his face bleak. 'They're dead. It's my fault they're dead. But you don't know what it was like inside that dining-hall. Flames were breaking through the east wall, the place was full of choking smoke and oil, I couldn't see, I could hardly breathe. I shook them both and shouted at them to get out. I shook them hard and I certainly shouted loud enough.'

'I can bear him out on that,' Hewson said quietly. 'I was right beside him at the time.'

'I didn't wait,' Naseby went on. 'I wasn't thinking of saving my own skin. I thought Flanders and Bryce were all right and that they would be out the door on my heels. I wanted to warn the others. It wasn't – it wasn't until minutes later that I realised that there was no sign of them. And then – well, then it was too late.'

'You ran across to the radio room. That's where you slept, Kinnaird, wasn't it?'

'That's where I slept, yes.' His mouth twisted. 'Me and my mate Grant, the boy that died yesterday. And Dr. Jolly slept in the partitioned-off east end of the hut. That's where he had his surgery and the little cubby-hole where he carried out his tests on ice samples.'

'So your end would have started to go on fire first?' I said to Jolly.

'Must have done,' he agreed. 'Quite frankly, old chap, my recollection of the whole thing is just like a dream – a nightmare, rather. I was almost asphyxiated in my sleep, I think. First thing I remember was young Grant bending over me, shaking me and shouting. Can't recall what he was shouting but it must have been that the hut was on fire. I don't know what I said or did, probably nothing, for the next thing I clearly remember was being hit on both sides of the face, and not too gently either. But, by jove, it worked! I got to my feet and he dragged me out of my office into the radio room. I owe my life to young Grant. I'd just enough sense left to grab the emergency medical kit that I always kept packed.'

'What woke Grant?'

'Naseby, here, woke him,' Kinnaird said. 'He woke us both, shouting and hammering on the door. If it hadn't been for him Dr. Jolly and I would both have been goners, the air inside that place was like poison gas and I'm sure if Naseby hadn't shouted on us we would never have woken up. I told Grant to waken the doctor while I tried to get the outside door open.'

'It was locked?'

'The damned thing was jammed. That was nothing unusual at night. During the day when the heaters were going full blast to keep the huts at a decent working temperature the ice around the doors tended to melt: at night, when we got into our sleeping-bags, we turned our heaters down and the melted ice froze hard round the door openings, sealing it solid. That happened most nights in most of the huts – usually had to break our way out in the morning. But I can tell you that I didn't take too long to burst it open that night.'

'And then?'

'I ran out,' Kinnaird said. 'I couldn't see a thing for black smoke and flying oil. I ran maybe twenty yards to the south to get some idea of what was happening. The whole camp seemed to be on fire. When you're woken up like that at two in the morning, half-blinded, half-asleep and groggy with fumes your mind isn't at its best, but thank God I'd enough left of my mind to realise that an S.O.S. radio message was the one thing that was going to save our lives. So I went back inside the radio hut.'

'We all owe our lives to Kinnaird.' Speaking for the first time was

Jeremy, a burly red-haired Canadian who had been chief technician on the base. 'And if I'd been a bit quicker with my hands we'd have all been dead.'

'Oh, for Christ's sake, mate, shut up,' Kinnaird growled.

'I won't shut up,' Jeremy said soberly. 'Besides, Dr. Carpenter wants a full report. I was first out of the main bunkhouse after Captain Folsom here. As Hewson said, we tried the extinguisher on Major Halliwell's hut. It was hopeless from the beginning but we had to do it – after all, we knew there were four men trapped in there. But, like I say, it was a waste of time. Captain Folsom shouted that he was going to get another extinguisher and told me to see how things were in the radio room.

'The place was ablaze from end to end. As I came round as close as I could to the door at the west end I saw Naseby here bending over Dr. Jolly, who'd keeled over as soon as he had come out into the fresh air. He shouted to me to give him a hand to drag Dr. Jolly clear and I was just about to when Kinnaird, here, came running up. I saw he was heading straight for the door of the radio room.' He smiled without humour. 'I thought he had gone off his rocker. I jumped in front of him, to stop him. He shouted at me to get out of the way. I told him not to be crazy and he yelled at me – you had to yell to make yourself heard above the roar of the flames – that he had to get the portable radio out, that all the oil was gone and the generator and the cookhouse with all the food were burning up. He knocked me down and the next I saw was him disappearing through that door. Smoke and flames were pouring through the doorway. I don't know how he ever got out alive.'

'Was that how you got your face and hands so badly burnt?' Commander Swanson asked quietly. He was standing in a far corner of the wardroom, having taken no part in the discussion up till now, but missing nothing all the same. That was why I had asked him to be present: just because he was a man who missed nothing.

'I reckon so, sir.'

'I fancy that should earn you a trip to Buckingham Palace,' Swanson murmured.

'The hell with Buckingham Palace,' Kinnaird said violently. 'How about my mate, eh? How about young Jimmy Grant? Can he make the trip to Buckingham Palace? Not now he can't, the poor bastard. Do you know what he was doing? He was still *inside* the radio room when I went back in, sitting at the main transmitter, sending out an S.O.S. on our regular frequency. His clothes were on fire. I dragged him off his seat and shouted to him to grab some Nife cells and get out. I caught up the portable transmitter and a nearby box of Nife cells and ran through the door. I thought Grant was on my heels but I couldn't hear anything, what with the roar of flames and the bursting of fuel drums the racket was deafening. Unless you'd been there you just can't begin to imagine what it was like. I ran far enough clear to put the radio and cells in a safe place. Then I went back. I asked Naseby, who was still trying to bring Dr. Jolly round, if Jimmy Grant had come out. He said he hadn't. I started to run for the door again – and, well, that's all I remember.'

'I clobbered him," Jeremy said with gloomy satisfaction. 'From behind. I had to.'

'I could have killed you when I came round,' Kinnaird said morosely. 'But I guess you saved my life at that.'

'I certainly did, brother.' Jeremy grimaced. 'That was my big contribution that night. Hitting people. After Naseby, here, had brought Dr. Jolly round he suddenly started shouting: "Where's Flanders and Bryce, where's Flanders and Bryce?" Those were the two who had been sleeping with Hewson and himself in the cookhouse. A few others had come down from the main bunkhouse by that time and the best part of a minute had elapsed before we realised that Flanders and Bryce weren't among them. Naseby, here, started back for the cookhouse at a dead run. He was making for the doorway, only there was no doorway left, just a solid curtain of fire where the doorway used to be. I swung at him as he passed and he fell and hit his head on the ice.' He looked at Naseby. 'Sorry again, Johnny, but you were quite crazy at the moment.'

Naseby rubbed his jaw and grinned wearily. 'I can still feel it. And God knows you were right.'

'Then Captain Folsom arrived, along with Dick Foster, who also slept in the main bunkhouse,' Jeremy went on. 'Captain Folsom said he'd tried every other extinguisher on the base and that all of them were frozen solid. He'd heard about Grant being trapped inside the radio room and he and Foster were carrying a blanket apiece, soaked with water. I tried to stop them but Captain Folsom ordered me to stand aside.' Jeremy smiled faintly. 'When Captain Folsom orders people to stand aside – well, they do just that.

'He and Foster threw the wet blankets over their heads and ran inside. Captain Folsom was out in a few seconds, carrying Grant. I've never seen anything like it, they were burning like human torches. I don't know what happened to Foster, but he never came out. By that time the roofs of both Major Halliwell's hut and the cookhouse had fallen in. Nobody could get anywhere near either of those buildings. Besides, it was far too late by then, Major Halliwell and the three others inside the major's hut and Flanders and Bryce inside the cookhouse must already have been dead. Dr. Jolly, here, doesn't think they would have suffered very much – asphyxiation would have got them, like enough, before the flames did.'

'Well,' I said slowly, 'That's as clear a picture of what must have been a very confusing and terrifying experience as we're ever likely to get. It wasn't possible to get anywhere near Major Halliwell's hut?'

'You couldn't have gone within fifteen feet of it and hoped to live,' Naseby said simply.

'And what happened afterwards?'

'I took charge, old boy,' Jolly said. 'Wasn't much to take charge of, though, and what little there was to be done could be done only by myself – fixing up the injured, I mean. I made 'em all wait out there on the ice-cap until the flames had died down a bit and there didn't seem to be any more likelihood of further fuel drums bursting then we all made our way to the bunkhouse where I did the best I could for the injured men. Kinnaird here, despite pretty bad burns, proved himself a first-class assistant doctor. We bedded down the worst of them. Young Grant was in a shocking condition – 'fraid there never really was very much hope for him. And – well, that was about all there was to it.'

'You had no food for the next few days and nights?'

'Nothing at all, old boy. No heat either, except for the standby Coleman lamps that were in the three remaining huts. We managed to melt a little water from the ice, that was all. By my orders everyone remained lying down and wrapped up in what was available in order to conserve energy and warmth.'

'Bit rough on you,' I said to Kinnaird. 'Having to lose any hard-earned warmth you had every couple of hours in order to make those S.O.S. broadcasts.'

'Not only me,' Kinnaird said. 'I'm no keener on frost-bite than anyone else. Dr. Jolly insisted that everyone who could should take turn about at sending out the S.O.S.s. Wasn't hard. There was a pre-set mechanical call-up and all anyone had to do was to send this and listen in on the earphones. If any message came through I was across to the met. office in a flash. It was actually Hewson, here, who contacted the ham operator in Bodo and Jeremy who got through to that trawler in the Barents Sea. I carried on from there, of course. Apart from them there were Dr. Jolly and Naseby, here, to give a hand, so it wasn't so bad. Hassard, too, took a turn after the first day – he'd been more or less blinded on the night of the fire.'

'You remained in charge throughout, Dr. Jolly?' I asked.

'Bless my soul, no. Captain Folsom, here, was in a pretty shocked condition for the first twenty-four hours, but when he'd recovered from that he took over. I'm only a pill-roller, old boy. As a leader of men and a dashing man of action—well, no, quite frankly, old top, I don't see myself in that light at all.'

'You did damned well, all the same.' I looked round the company. 'That most of you won't be scarred for life is due entirely to the quick and highly efficient treatment Dr. Jolly gave you under almost impossible circumstances. Well, that's all. Must be a pretty painful experience for all of you, having to relive that night again. I can't see that we can ever hope to find out how the fire started, just one of those chance in a million accidents, what the insurance companies call an act of God. I'm certain, Hewson, that no shadow of negligence attaches to you and that your theory on the outbreak of fire is probably correct. Anyway, although we've paid a hellishly high cost, we've learnt a lesson – never again to site a main fuel store within a hundred yards of the camp.'

The meeting broke up. Jolly bustled off to the sick-bay, not quite managing to conceal his relish at being the only medical officer aboard who wasn't *hors de combat*. He had a busy couple of hours ahead of him – changing bandages on burns, checking Benson, X-raying Zabrinski's broken ankle and resetting the plaster.

I went to my cabin, unlocked my case, took out a small wallet, relocked my case and went to Swanson's cabin. I noticed that he wasn't smiling quite so often now as when I'd first met him in Scotland. He looked up as I came in in answer to his call and said without preamble: 'If those two men still out in the camp are in any way fit to be moved I want them both aboard at once. The sooner we're back in Scotland and have some law in on this the happier I'll be. I warned you that this investigation of yours would turn up nothing. Lord knows how short a time it will be before someone else gets clobbered. God's sake, Carpenter, we have a murderer running loose.'

'Three things,' I said. 'Nobody's going to get clobbered any more, that's almost for certain. Secondly, the law, as you call it, wouldn't be allowed to touch it. And in the third place, the meeting this morning was of some use. It eliminated three potential suspects.'

'I must have missed something that you didn't.'

'Not that. I knew something that you didn't. I knew that under the floor of the laboratory were about forty Nife cells in excellent condition – but cells that had been used.'

'The hell you did,' he said softly. 'Sort of forgot to tell me, didn't you?'

'In this line of business I never tell anyone anything unless I think he can help me by having that knowledge.'

'You must win an awful lot of friends and influence an awful lot of people,' Swanson said dryly.

'It gets embarrassing. Now, who could have used cells? Only those who left the bunkhouse from time to time to send out the S.O.S.s. That cuts out Captain Folsom and the Harrington twins—there's no question of any of the three of them having left the bunkhouse at any time. They weren't fit to. So that leaves Hewson, Naseby, Dr. Jolly, Jeremy, Hassard and Kinnaird. Take your choice. One of them is a murderer.'

'Why did they want those extra cells?' Swanson asked. 'And if they had those extra cells why did they risk their lives by relying on those dying cells that they did use. Does it make sense to you?'

'There's sense in everything,' I said. If you want evasion, Carpenter has it. I brought out my wallet, spread cards before him. He picked them up, studied them and returned them to my wallet.

'So now we have it,' he said calmly. 'Took quite a while to get round to it, didn't you? The truth, I mean. Officer of M.I.6 Counter-Espionage. Government agent, eh? Well, I won't make any song and dance about it, Carpenter, I've known since yesterday what you must be: you couldn't be anything else.' He looked at me in calm speculation. 'You fellows never disclose your identity unless you have to.' He left the logical question unspoken.

'Three reasons why I'm telling you. You're entitled to some measure of my confidence. I want you on my side. And because of what I'm about to tell you, you'd have known anyway. Have you ever heard of the Perkin-Elmer Roti satellite missile tracker camera?'

'Quite a mouthful,' he murmured. 'No.'

'Heard of Samos? Samos III?'

'Satellite and Missile Observation System?' He nodded. 'I have. And what conceivable connection could that have with a ruthless killer running amok on Drift Station Zebra?'

So I told him what connection it could have. A connection that was not conceivable, not only possible, not only probable, but absolutely certain. Swanson listened very carefully, very attentively, not interrupting even once and at the end of it he leaned back in his chair and nodded. 'You have the right of it, no doubt about that. The question is, who? I just can't wait to see this fiend under close arrest and armed guard.'

'You'd clap him in irons straight away?'

'Good God!' He stared at me. 'Wouldn't you?'

'I don't know. Yes, I do. I'd leave him be. I think our friend is just a link in a very long chain and if we give him enough rope he'll not only hang himself, he'll lead us to the other members of the chain. Besides, I'm not all that sure that there is only one murderer: killers have been known to have accomplices before now, Commander.'

'Two of them? You think there may be two killers aboard my ship?' He pursed his lips and squeezed his chin with a thoughtful hand, Swanson's nearest permissible approach to a state of violent agitation. Then he shook his head definitely. 'There may only be one. If that is so, and I knew who he was, I'd arrest him at once. Don't forget, Carpenter, we've hundreds of miles to go under the ice before we're out into the open sea. We can't watch all six of them all the time and there are a hundred and one things that a man with even only a little knowledge of submarines could do that would put us all in mortal danger. Things that wouldn't matter were we clear of the ice: things that would be fatal under it.'

'Aren't you rather overlooking the fact that if the killer did us in he'd also be doing himself in?'

'I don't necessarily share your belief in his sanity. All killers are a little crazy. No matter how excellent their reasons for killing, the very fact that they do kill makes them a rogue human being, an abnormal. You can't judge them by normal standards.'

He was only half-right, but unfortunately that half might apply in this case. Most murderers kill in a state of extreme emotional once-in-a-lifetime stress and never kill again. But our friend in this case had every appearance of being a stranger to emotional stress of any kind – and, besides, he'd killed a great deal more than once.

'Well,' I said doubtfully. 'Perhaps. Yes, I think I do agree with you.' I refrained from specifying our common ground for agreement. 'Who's your candidate for the high jump, Commander?'

'I'm damned if I know. I listened to every word that was said this morning. I watched the face of each man who spoke – and the faces of the ones who weren't speaking. I've been thinking non-stop about it since and I'm still damned if I have a clue. How about Kinnaird?'

'He's the obvious suspect, isn't he? But only because he's a skilled radio operator. I could train a man in a couple of days to send and receive in morse. Slow, clumsy, he wouldn't know a thing about the instrument he was using, but he could still do it. Any of them may easily have been competent enough to operate a radio. The fact that Kinnaird is a skilled operator may even be a point in his favour.'

'Nife cells were removed from the radio cabin and taken to the laboratory,' Swanson pointed out. 'Kinnaird had the easiest access to them. Apart from Dr. Jolly who had his office and sleeping quarters in the same hut.'

'So that would point a finger at Kinnaird or Jolly?'

'Well, wouldn't it?'

'Certainly. Especially if you will agree that the presence of those tinned foods under the lab. floor also points a finger at Hewson and Naseby, both of whom slept in the cookhouse where the food was stored, and that the presence of the radio-sonde balloon and the hydrogen in the lab. also points a finger at Jeremy and Hassard, one a met. officer and the other a technician who would have had the easiest access to those items.'

'That's right, confuse things,' Swanson said irritably. 'As if they weren't confused enough already.'

'I'm not confusing things. All I'm saying is that if you admit a certain possibility for a certain reason then you must admit similar possibilities for similar reasons. Besides, there are points in Kinnaird's favour. He risked his life to go back into the radio room to bring out the portable transmitter. He risked almost certain suicide when he tried to go in the second time to bring out his assistant, Grant, and probably would have died if Jeremy hadn't clobbered him. Look what happened to that man Foster who went in there immediately afterwards with a wet blanket over his head—*he* never came out.

'Again, would Kinnaird have mentioned the Nife cells if he had any guilt complex about them? But he did. That, incidentally, might have been why Grant, the assistant radio operator, collapsed in there and later died—Kinnaird had told him to bring out the other Nife cells and he was overcome because he stayed there too long looking for things that had already been removed from the hut. And there's one final point: we have Naseby's word for it that the door of the radio room was jammed, presumably by ice. Had Kinnaird been playing with matches a few moments previously, that door wouldn't have had time to freeze up.'

'If you let Kinnaird out,' Swanson said slowly, 'you more or less have to let Dr. Jolly out too.' He smiled. 'I don't see a member of your profession running round filling people full of holes, Dr. Carpenter. Repairing holes is their line of business, not making them. Hippocrates wouldn't have liked it.'

'I'm not letting Kinnaird out,' I said. 'But I'm not going off half-cocked and pinning a murder rap on him either. As for the ethics of my profession – would you like a list of the good healers who have decorated the dock in the Old Bailey? True, we have nothing on Jolly. His part in the proceedings that night seems to have consisted in staggering out from the radio room, falling flat on his face and staying there till pretty near the end of the fire. That, of course, has no bearing upon whatever part he might have taken in the proceedings prior to the fire. Though against that possibility there's the fact of the jammed door, the fact that Kinnaird or Grant would have been almost bound to notice if he had been up to something – Jolly's bunk was at the back of the radio room and he would have had to pass Kinnaird and Grant to get out, not forgetting that he would also have to stop to pick up the Nife cells. And there is one more point in his favour – an apparent point, that is. I still don't think that Benson's fall was an accident and if it was no accident it is difficult to see how Jolly could have arranged it while he was at the foot of the sail and Benson at the top and it's even more difficult to see why he should have stood at the foot of the sail and let Benson fall on top of him.'

'You're putting up a very good defence case for both Jolly and Kinnaird,' Swanson murmured.

'No. I'm only saying what a defence lawyer would say.'

'Hewson,' Swanson said slowly. 'Or Naseby, the cook. Or Hewson *and* Naseby. Don't you think it damned funny that those two, who were sleeping at the back or east side of the cookhouse, which was the first part of the hut to catch fire, should have managed to escape while the other two – Flanders and Bryce, wasn't it – who slept in the middle should have suffocated in there? Naseby said he shouted at them and shook them violently. Maybe he could have shouted and shaken all night without result. Maybe they were already unconscious – or dead. Maybe they had seen Naseby or Hewson or both removing food supplies and had been silenced. Or maybe they had been silenced *before* anything had been removed. And don't forget the gun. It was hidden in the petrol tank of the tractor, a pretty damn' funny place for a man to hide anything. But nothing funny about the idea occurring to Hewson, was there? He was the tractor-driver. And he seems to have taken his time about getting around to warn Captain Folsom. He said he had to make a wide circuit to avoid the flames but apparently Naseby didn't find it so bad when he went to the radio room. Another thing, a pretty telling point, I think, he said that when he was on the way to the bunkhouse the oil drums in the fuel store started exploding. If they only started exploding then how come all the huts – the five that were eventually destroyed, that is – were already uncontrollably on fire. They were uncontrollably on fire because they were saturated by flying oil so the first explosions must have come a long time before then. And, apart from warning Folsom – who had already been warned – Hewson doesn't seem to have done very much after the fire started.'

'You'd make a pretty good prosecuting counsel yourself, Commander. But wouldn't you think there is just too *much* superficially against Hewson? That a clever man wouldn't have allowed so much superficial evidence to accumulate against him? You would have thought that, at least, he would have indulged in a little fire-fighting heroics to call attention to himself?'

'No. You're overlooking the fact that he would never have had reason to expect that there would be any investigation into the causes of the fire. That the situation would never arise where he – or anyone else, for that matter – would have to justify their actions and behaviour if accusations were to be levelled against them.'

'I've said it before and I say it again. People like that *never* take a chance. They always act on the assumption that they *may* be found out.'

'How could they be found out?' Swanson protested. 'How could they possibly expect to have suspicion aroused?'

'You don't think it possible that they suspect that we are on to them?'

'No, I don't.'

'That wasn't what you were saying last night after that hatch fell on me,' I pointed out. 'You said it was obvious that someone was on to me.'

'Thank the lord that all I have to do is the nice uncomplicated job of running a nuclear submarine,' Swanson said heavily. 'The truth is, I don't know what to think any more. How about this cook fellow – Naseby?'

'You think he was in cahoots with Hewson?'

'If we accept the premise that the men in the cookhouse who were not in on this business had to be silenced, and Naseby wasn't, then he must have been, mustn't he? But, dammit, how then about his attempts to rescue Flanders and Bryce?'

'May just have been a calculated risk. He saw how Jeremy flattened Kinnaird when he tried to go back into the radio-room a second time and perhaps calculated that Jeremy would oblige again if he tried a similar but fake rescue act.'

'Maybe Kinnaird's second attempt was also fake,' Swanson said. 'After all, Jeremy had already tried to stop him once.'

'Maybe it was,' I agreed. 'But Naseby. If he's your man, why should he have said that the radio room door was jammed with ice, and that he had to burst it open. That gives Kinnaird and Jolly an out – and a murderer wouldn't do anything to put any other potential suspect in the clear.'

'It's hopeless,' Swanson said calmly. 'I say let's put the whole damn' crowd of them under lock and key.'

'That would be clever,' I said. 'Yes, let's do just that. That way we'll never find out who the murderer is. Anyway, before you start giving up, remember it's even more complicated than that. Remember you're passing up the two most obvious suspects of all – Jeremy and Hassard, two tough, intelligent birds who, if they were the killers, were clever enough to see that *nothing* pointed the finger against them. Unless, of course, there might have been something about Flanders and Bryce that Jeremy didn't want anyone to see, so he stopped Naseby from going back into the cookhouse. Or not.'

Swanson almost glared at me. Watching his submarine plummeting out of control beyond the 1000-feet mark was something that rated maybe the lift of an eyebrow; but this was something else again. He said: 'Very well, then, we'll let the killer run loose and wreck the *Dolphin* at his leisure. I must have very considerable confidence in you, Dr. Carpenter. I feel sure my confidence will not be misplaced. Tell me one last thing.

I assume you are a highly skilled investigator. But I was puzzled by one omission in your questioning. A vital question, I should have thought.'

'Who suggested moving the corpses into the lab. knowing that by doing so he would be making his hiding-place for the cached material a hundred per cent foolproof?'

'I apologise.' He smiled faintly. 'You had your reasons, of course.'

'Of course. You're not sure whether or not the killer is on to the fact that we are on to him. I'm sure. I know he's not. But had I asked that question, he'd have known immediately that there could be only one reason for my asking it. Then he would have known I was on to him. Anyway, it's my guess that Captain Folsom gave the order, but the original suggestion, carefully camouflaged so that Folsom may no longer be able to pin it down, would have come from another quarter.'

Had it been a few months earlier with the summer Arctic sun riding in the sky, it would have been a brilliant day. As it was, there was no sun, not in that latitude and so late in the year, but for all that the weather was about as perfect as it was possible for it to be. Thirty-six hours – the time that had elapsed since Hansen and I had made that savage trip back to the *Dolphin* – had brought about a change that seemed pretty close to miraculous. The knifing east wind had died, completely. That flying sea of ice-spicules was no more. The temperature had risen at least twenty degrees and the visibility was as perfect as visibility on the winter ice-pack ever is.

Swanson, sharing Benson's viewpoint on the crew's over-sedentary mode of existence and taking advantage of the fine weather, had advised everyone not engaged in actual watch-keeping to take advantage of the opportunity offered to stretch their legs in the fresh air. It said much for Swanson's powers of persuasion that by eleven that morning the *Dolphin* was practically deserted; and of course the crew, to whom Drift Ice Station Zebra was only so many words, were understandably curious to see the place, even the shell of the place, that had brought them to the top of the world.

I took my place at the end of the small queue being treated by Dr. Jolly. It was close on noon before he got round to me. He was making light of his own burns and frost-bite and was in tremendous form, bustling happily about the sick-bay as if it had been his own private domain for years.

'Well,' I said, 'the pill-rolling competition wasn't so fierce after all, was it? I'm damned glad there was a third doctor around. How are things on the medical front?'

'Coming along not too badly, old boy,' he said cheerfully. 'Benson's picking up very nicely, pulse, respiration, blood-pressure close to normal, level of unconsciousness very slight now, I should say. Captain Folsom's still in considerable pain, but no actual danger, of course. The rest have improved a hundred per cent, little thanks to the medical fraternity: excellent food, warm beds and the knowledge that they're safe have done them more good than anything we could ever do. Anyway, it's done me a lot of good, by jove!'

'And then,' I agreed, 'all your friends except Folsom and the Harrington twins have followed most of the crew on to the ice and I'll wager that if you had suggested to them forty-eight hours ago that they'd willingly go out there again in so short a time, they'd have called for a strait-jacket.'

'The physical and mental recuperative power of homo sapiens,' Jolly said jovially. 'Beyond belief at times, old lad, beyond belief. Now, let's have a look at that broken wing of yours.'

So he had a look, and because I was a colleague and therefore inured to human suffering he didn't spend any too much time in molly-coddling me, but by hanging on to the arm of my chair and the shreds of my professional pride I kept the roof from falling in on me. When he was finished he said: 'Well, that's the lot, except for Brownell and Bolton, the two lads out on the ice.'

'I'll come with you,' I said. 'Commander Swanson is waiting pretty anxiously to hear what we have to say. He wants to get away from here as soon as possible.'

'Me, too,' Jolly said fervently. 'But what's the commander so anxious about?'

'Ice. You never know the hour or minute it starts to close in. Want to spend the next year or two up here?'

Jolly grinned, thought over it for a bit, then stopped grinning. He said apprehensively: 'How long are we going to be under this damned ice? Before we reach the open sea, I mean?'

'Twenty-four hours, Swanson says. Don't look so worried, Jolly. Believe me, it's far safer under this stuff than among it.'

With a very unconvinced look on his face Jolly picked up his medical kit and led the way from the sick-bay. Swanson was waiting for us in the control room. We climbed up the hatches, dropped down over the side and walked over to the Drift Station.

Most of the crew had already made their way out there. We passed numbers of them on the way back and most of them looked grim or sick or both and didn't even glance up as we passed. I didn't have to guess why they looked as they did; they'd been opening doors that they should have left closed.

With the sharp rise in outside temperature and the effect of the big electric heaters having been burning there for twenty-four hours the bunkhouse hut was now, if anything, overheated, with the last traces of ice long vanished from walls and ceiling. One of the men, Brownell, had recovered consciousness and was sitting up, supported, and drinking soup provided by one of the two men who had been keeping watch over him.

'Well,' I said to Swanson, 'here's one ready to go.'

'No doubt about that,' Jolly said briskly. He bent over the other, Bolton, for some seconds, then straightened and shook his head. 'A very sick man, Commander, very sick. I wouldn't care to take the responsibility of moving him.'

'I might be forced to take the responsibility myself,' Swanson said bluntly. 'Let's have another opinion on this.' His tone and words, I thought, could have been more diplomatic and conciliatory; but if there were a couple of murderers aboard the *Dolphin* there was a thirty-three and a third per cent chance that Jolly was one of them and Swanson wasn't forgetting it for a moment.

I gave Jolly an apologetic half-shrug, bent over Bolton and examined him as best I could with only one hand available for the task. I straightened and said: 'Jolly's right. He is pretty sick. But I think he might just stand the transfer to the ship.'

'"Might just" is not quite the normally accepted basis for deciding the treatment of a patient,' Jolly objected.

'I know it's not. But the circumstances are hardly normal either.'

'I'll take the responsibility,' Swanson said. 'Dr. Jolly, I'd be most grateful if you would supervise the transport of those two men back to the ship. I'll let you have as many men as you want straight away.' Jolly protested some more, then gave in with good grace. He supervised the transfer, and very competent he was about it too. I remained out there a little longer, watching Rawlings and some others dismantling heaters and lights and rolling up cables and, after the last of them was gone and I was alone, I made my way round to the tractor shed.

The broken haft of the knife was still in the tank of the tractor. But not the gun and not the two magazines. Those were gone. And whoever had taken them it hadn't been Dr. Jolly, he hadn't been out of my sight for two consecutive seconds between the time he'd left the *Dolphin* and the time of his return to it.

At three o'clock that afternoon we dropped down below the ice and headed south for the open sea.

10

The afternoon and evening passed quickly and pleasantly enough. Closing our hatches and dropping down from our hardly won foothold in that lead had had a symbolic significance at least as important as the actual fact of leaving itself. The thick ceiling of ice closing over the hull of the *Dolphin* was a curtain being drawn across the eye of the mind. We had severed all physical connection with Drift Ice Station Zebra, a home of the dead that might continue to circle slowly about the Pole for mindless centuries to come; and with the severance had come an abrupt diminution of the horror and the shock which had hung pall-like over ship and its crew for the past twenty-four hours. A dark door had swung to behind us and we had turned our backs on it. Mission accomplished, duty done, we were heading for home again and the sudden upsurge of relief and happiness among the crew to be on their way again, their high anticipation of port and leave, was an almost tangible thing. The mood of the ship was close to that of lighthearted gaiety. But there was no gaiety in my mind, and no peace: I was leaving too much behind. Nor could there be any peace in the minds of Swanson and Hansen, of Rawlings and Zabrinski: they knew we were carrying a killer aboard, a killer who had killed many times. Dr. Benson knew also, but for the moment Dr. Benson did not count: he still had not regained consciousness and I held the very unprofessional hope that he wouldn't for some time to come. In the twilit world of emergence from coma a man can start babbling and say all too much.

Some of the Zebra survivors had asked if they could see around the ship and Swanson agreed. In light of what I had told him in his cabin that morning, he must have agreed very reluctantly indeed, but no trace of this reluctance showed in his calmly smiling face. To have refused their request would have been rather a churlish gesture, for all the secrets of the *Dolphin* were completely hidden from the eye of the layman. But it wasn't good manners that made Swanson give his consent: refusing a reasonable request could have been responsible for making someone very suspicious indeed.

Hansen took them around the ship and I accompanied them, less for the exercise or interest involved than for the opportunity it gave me to keep a very close eye indeed on their reactions to their tour. We made a complete circuit of the ship, missing out only the reactor room, which no one could visit, anyway, and the inertial navigation-room which had been barred to me also. As we moved around I watched them all, and especially two of them, as closely as it is possible to watch anyone without making him aware of your observation, and I learned precisely what I had expected to learn – nothing. I'd been crazy even to hope I'd learn anything; our pal with the gun was wearing a mask that had been forged into shape and riveted into position. But I'd had to do it, anyway: playing in this senior league I couldn't pass up the one chance in a million.

Supper over, I helped Jolly as best I could with his evening surgery. Whatever else Jolly was, he was a damn' good doctor. Quickly and efficiently he checked and where necessary rebandaged the walking cases, examined and treated Benson and Folsom, then asked me to come right aft with him to the nucleonics laboratory in the stern room which had been cleared of deck gear to accommodate the four other bed patients, the Harrington twins, Brownell and Bolton. The sick-bay itself had only two cots for invalids and Benson and Folsom had those.

Bolton, despite Jolly's dire predictions, hadn't suffered a relapse because of his transfer from the hut to the ship – which had been due largely to Jolly's extremely skilful and careful handling of the patient and the stretcher into which he had been lashed. Bolton, in fact, was conscious now and complaining of severe pain in his badly burned right forearm. Jolly removed the burn covering and Bolton's arm was a mess all right, no skin left worth speaking of, showing an angry violent red between areas of suppuration. Different doctors have different ideas as to the treatment of burns: Jolly favoured a salve-coated aluminium foil which he smoothed across the entire burn area then lightly bandaged in place. He then gave him a pain-killing injection and some sleeping tablets, and briskly informed the enlisted man who was keeping watch that he was to be informed immediately of any change or deterioration in Bolton's condition. A brief inspection of the three others, a changed bandage here and there and he was through for the night.

So was I. For two nights now I had had practically no sleep – what little had been left for me the previous night had been ruined by the pain in my left hand. I was exhausted. When I got to my cabin, Hansen was already asleep and the engineer officer gone.

I didn't need any of Jolly's sleeping pills that night.

I awoke at two o'clock. I was sleep-drugged, still exhausted and felt as if I had been in bed about five minutes. But I awoke in an instant and in that instant I was fully awake.

Only a dead man wouldn't have stirred. The racket issuing from the squawk box just above Hansen's bunk was appalling: a high-pitched, shrieking, atonic whistle, two tones and altering pitch every half-second, it drilled stiletto-like against my cringing ear-drums. A banshee in its death agonies could never have hoped to compete with that lot.

Hansen already had his feet on the deck and was pulling on clothes and shoes in desperate haste. I had never thought to see that slow-speaking laconic Texan in such a tearing hurry, but I was seeing it now.

'What in hell's name is the matter?' I demanded. I had to shout to make myself heard above the shrieking of the alarm whistle.

'Fire!' His face was shocked and grim. 'The ship's on fire. And under this goddamned ice!'

Still buttoning his shirt, he hurdled my cot, crashed the door back on its hinges and was gone.

The atonic screeching of the whistle stopped abruptly and the silence fell like a blow. Then I was conscious of something more than silence – I was conscious of a complete lack of vibration throughout the ship. The great engines had stopped. And then I was conscious of something else again: feathery fingers of ice brushing up and down my spine. Why had the engines stopped? What could make a nuclear engine stop so quickly and what happened once it did? My God, I thought, maybe the fire is coming from the reactor room itself. I'd looked into the heart of the uranium atomic pile through a heavily leaded glass inspection port and seen the indescribable unearthly radiance of it, a nightmarish coalescence of green and violet and blue, the new 'dreadful light' of mankind. What happened when this dreadful light ran amok? I didn't know, but I suspected I didn't want to be around when it happened.

I dressed slowly, not hurrying. My damaged hand didn't help me much but that wasn't why I took my time. Maybe the ship was on fire, maybe the nuclear power plant had gone out of kilter. But if Swanson's superbly trained crew couldn't cope with every emergency that could conceivably arise then matters weren't going to be improved any by Carpenter running around in circles shouting: 'Where's the fire?'

Three minutes after Hansen had gone I walked along to the control room and peered in: if I was going to be in the way then this was as far as I was going to go. Dark acrid smoke billowed past me and a voice – Swanson's – said sharply: 'Inside and close that door.'

I pulled the door to and looked around the control room. At least, I tried to. It wasn't easy. My eyes were already streaming as if someone had thrown a bag of pepper into them and what little sight was left them didn't help me much. The room was filled with black evil-smelling smoke, denser by far and more throat-catching than the worst London fog. Visibility was no more than a few feet, but what little I could see showed me men still at their stations. Some were gasping, some were half-choking, some were cursing softly, all had badly watering eyes, but there was no trace of panic.

'You'd have been better on the other side of that door,' Swanson said dryly. 'Sorry to have barked at you, Doctor, but we want to limit the spread of the smoke as much as possible.'

'Where's the fire?'

'In the engine-room.' Swanson could have been sitting on his front porch at home discussing the weather. 'Where in the engine-room we don't know. It's pretty bad. At least, the smoke is. The extent of the fire we don't know, because we can't locate it. Engineer officer says it's impossible to see your hand in front of your face.'

'The engines,' I said. 'They've stopped. Has anything gone wrong?'

He rubbed his eyes with a handkerchief, spoke to a man who was pulling on a heavy rubber suit and a smoke-mask, then turned back to me.

'We're not going to be vaporised, if that's what you mean.' I could have sworn he was smiling. 'The atomic pile can only fail safe no matter what happens. If anything goes wrong the uranium rods slam down in very quick time indeed – a fraction under one-thousandth of a second – stopping the whole reaction. In this case, though, we shut it off ourselves. The men in the manœuvring-room could no longer see either the reactor dials or the governor for the control rods. No option but to shut it down. The engine-room crew have been forced to abandon the engine and manœuvring-rooms and take shelter in the stern room.'

Well, that was something at least. We weren't going to be blown to pieces, ignobly vaporised on the altar of nuclear advancement: good old-fashioned suffocation, that was to be our lot.

'So what do we do?' I asked.

'What we should do is surface immediately. With fourteen feet of ice overhead that's not easy. Excuse me, will you?'

He spoke to the now completely masked and suited man who was carrying a small dialled box in his hands. They walked together past the navigator's chart desk and ice-machine to the heavy door opening on the passage that led to the engine-room over the top of the reactor compartment. They unclipped the door, pushed it open. A dense blinding cloud of dark smoke rolled into the room as the masked man stepped quickly into the passageway and swung the door to behind him. Swanson clamped the door shut, walked, temporarily blinded, back to the control position and fumbled down a roof microphone.

'Captain speaking.' His voice echoed emptily through the control centre. 'The fire is located in the engine-room. We do not know yet whether it is electrical, chemical or fuel oil: the source of the fire has not been pin-pointed. Acting on the principle of being prepared for the worst, we are now testing for a radiation leak.' So that was what the masked man had been carrying, a Geiger counter. 'If that proves negative, we shall try for a steam leak; and if that is negative we shall carry out an intensive search to locate the fire. It will not be easy as I'm told visibility is almost zero. We have already shut down all electrical circuits in the engine-room, lighting included, to prevent an explosion in the event of atomised fuel being present in the atmosphere. We have closed the oxygen intake valves and isolated the engine-room from the air-cleaning system in the hope that the fire will consume all available oxygen and burn itself out.

'All smoking is prohibited until further notice. Heaters, fans and all electrical circuits other than communication lines to be switched off – and that includes the juke-box and the ice-cream machine. All lamps to be switched off except those absolutely essential All movement is to be restricted to a minimum. I shall keep you informed of any progress we may make.'

I became aware of someone standing by my side. It was Dr. Jolly, his normally jovial face puckered and woebegone, the tears flowing down his face. Plaintively he said to me: 'This *is* a bit thick, old boy, what? I'm not sure that I'm so happy now about being rescued. And all those prohibitions – no smoking, no power to be used, no moving around – do those mean what I take them to mean?'

'I'm afraid they do indeed.' It was Swanson who answered Jolly's question for him. 'This, I'm afraid, is every nuclear submarine captain's nightmare come true – fire under the ice. At one stroke we're not only reduced to the level of a conventional submarine – we're two stages worse. In the first place, a conventional submarine wouldn't be under the ice, anyway. In the second place, it has huge banks of storage batteries, and even if it were beneath the ice it would have sufficient reserve power to steam far enough south to get clear of the ice. Our reserve storage battery is so small that it wouldn't take us a fraction of the way.'

'Yes, yes,' Jolly nodded. 'But this no smoking, no moving——'

'That same very small battery I'm afraid, is the only source left to us for power for the air-purifying machines, for lighting, ventilation, heating – I'm afraid the *Dolphin* is going to get very cold in a short time – so we have to curtail its expenditure of energy on those things. So no smoking, minimum movement – the less carbon dioxide breathed into the atmosphere the better. But the real reason for conserving electric energy is that we need it to power the heater, pumps and motors that have to be used to start up the reactor again. If that battery exhausts itself before we get the reactor going – well, I don't have to draw a diagram.'

'You're not very encouraging, are you, Commander?' Jolly

complained.

'No, not very. I don't see any reason to be,' Swanson said dryly.

'I'll bet you'd trade in your pension for a nice open lead above us just now,' I said.

'I'd trade in the pension of every flag officer in the United States Navy,' he said matter-of-factly. 'If we could find a polynya I'd surface, open the engine-room hatch to let most of the contaminated air escape, start up our diesel – it takes its air direct from the engine-room – and have the rest of the smoke sucked out in nothing flat. As it is, that diesel is about as much use to me as a grand piano.'

'And the compasses?' I asked.

'That's another interesting thought,' Swanson agreed. 'If the power output from our reserve battery falls below a certain level, our three Sperry gyro-compasses systems and the N6A – that's the inertial guidance machine – just pack up. After that we're lost, completely. Our magnetic compass is quite useless in these latitudes – it just walks in circles.'

'So we would go around and around in circles, too,' Jolly said thoughtfully. 'For ever and ever under the jolly old ice-cap, what? By jove, Commander, I'm really beginning to wish we'd stayed up at Zebra.'

'We're not dead yet, Doctor. . . . Yes, John?' This to Hansen, who had just come up.

'Sanders, sir. On the ice-machine. Can he have a smoke mask. His eyes are watering pretty badly.'

'Give him anything you like in the ship,' Swanson said, 'just so long as he can keep his eyes clear to read that graph. And double the watch on the ice-machine. If there's a lead up there only the size of a hair, I'm going for it. Immediate report if the ice thickness falls below, say, eight or nine feet.'

'Torpedoes?' Hansen asked. 'There hasn't been ice thin enough for that in three hours. And at the speed we're drifting there won't be for three months. I'll go keep the watch myself. I'm not much good for anything else, this hand of mine being the way it is.'

'Thank you. First you might tell Engineman Harrison to turn off the CO_2 scrubber and monoxide burners. Must save every amp of power we have. Besides, it will do this pampered bunch of ours the world of good to sample a little of what the old-time submariners had to experience when they were forced to stay below maybe twenty hours at a time.'

'That's going to be pretty rough on our really sick men,' I said. 'Benson and Folsom in the sick-bay, the Harrington twins, Brownell and Bolton in the nucleonics lab. right aft. They've got enough to contend with without foul air as well.'

'I know,' Swanson admitted. 'I'm damnably sorry about it. Later on, when – and if – the air gets really bad, we'll start up the air-purifying systems again but blank off every place except the lab. and sick-bay.' He broke off and turned round as a fresh wave of dark smoke rolled in from the suddenly opened after door. The man with the smoke mask was back from the engine-room and even with my eyes streaming in that smoke-filled acrid atmosphere I could see he was in a pretty bad way. Swanson and two others rushed to meet him, two of them catching him as he staggered into the control room, the third quickly swinging the heavy door shut against the darkly-evil clouds of smoke.

Swanson pulled off the man's smoke mask. It was Murphy, the man who had accompanied me when we'd closed the torpedo tube door. People like Murphy and Rawlings, I thought, always got picked for jobs like this.

His face was white and he was gasping for air, his eyes upturned in his head. He was hardly more than half-conscious, but even that foul atmosphere in the control centre must have seemed to him like the purest mountain air compared to what he had just been breathing for within thirty seconds his head had begun to clear and he was able to grin up painfully from where he'd been lowered into a chair.

'Sorry, Captain,' he gasped. 'This smoke-mask was never meant to cope with the stuff that's in the engine-room. Pretty hellish in there, I tell you.' He grinned again. 'Good news, Captain. No radiation leak.'

'Where's the Geiger counter?' Swanson asked quietly.

'It's had it, I'm afraid, sir. I couldn't see where I was going in there, honest, sir, you can't see three inches in front of your face. I tripped and damn' near fell down into the machinery space. The counter did fall down. But I'd a clear check before then. Nothing at all.' He reached up to his shoulder and unclipped his film badge. 'This'll show, sir.'

'Have that developed immediately. That was very well done, Murphy,' he said warmly. 'Now nip for'ard to the mess room. You'll find some really clear air there.'

The film badge was developed and brought back in minutes. Swanson took it, glanced at it briefly, smiled and let out his breath in a long slow whistle of relief. 'Murphy was right. No radiation leak. Thank God for that, anyway. If there had been – well, that was that, I'm afraid.'

The for'ard door of the control room opened, a man passed through, and the door was as quickly closed. I guessed who it was before I could see him properly.

'Permission from Chief Torpedoman Patterson to approach you, sir,' Rawlings said with brisk formality. 'We've just seen Murphy, pretty groggy he is, and both the Chief and I think that youngsters like that shouldn't be——'

'Am I to understand that you are volunteering to go next, Rawlings?' Swanson asked. The screws of responsibility and tension were turned hard down on him, but I could see that it cost him some effort to keep his face straight.

'Well, not exactly volunteering, sir. But – well, who else is there?'

'The torpedo department aboard this ship,' Swanson observed acidly, 'always did have a phenomenally high opinion of itself.'

'Let him try an underwater oxygen set,' I said. 'Those smoke-masks seem to have their limitations.'

'A steam leak, Captain?' Rawlings asked. 'That what you want me to check on?'

'Well, you seemed to have been nominated, voted for and elected by yourself,' Swanson said. 'Yes, a steam leak.'

'That the suit Murphy was wearing?' Rawlings pointed to the clothes on the deck.

'Yes. Why?'

'You'd have thought there would be some signs of moisture or condensation if there had been a steam leak, sir.'

'Maybe. Maybe soot and smoke particles are holding the condensing steam in suspension. Maybe it was hot enough in there to dry off any moisture that did reach his suit. Maybe a lot of things. Don't stay too long in there.'

'Just as long as it takes me to get things fixed up,' Rawlings said confidently. He turned to Hansen and grinned. 'You baulked me once back out there on the ice-cap, Lieutenant, but sure as little apples I'm going to get that little old medal this time. Bring undying credit on the whole ship, I will.'

'If Torpedoman Rawlings will ease up with his ravings for a moment,' Hansen said, 'I have a suggestion to make, Captain. I know he won't be able to take off his mask inside there but if he would give a call-up signal on the engine telephone or ring through on the engine answering telegraph every four or five minutes we'd know he was O.K. If he doesn't, someone can go in after him.'

Swanson nodded. Rawlings pulled on suit and oxygen apparatus and left. That made it the third time the door leading to the engine compartment had been opened in a few minutes and each time fresh clouds of that black and biting smoke had come rolling in. Conditions were now very bad inside the control room, but someone had issued a supply of goggles all round and a few were wearing smoke-masks.

A phone rang. Hansen answered, spoke briefly and hung up.

'That was Jack Cartwright, Skipper.' Lieutenant Cartwright was the main propulsion officer, who'd been on watch in the manœuvring-room and had been forced to retreat to the stern room. 'Seems he was overcome by the fumes and was carried back into the stern room. Says he's O.K. now and could we send smoke-masks or breathing apparatus for himself and one of his men—they can't get at the ones in the engine-room. I told him yes.'

'I'd certainly feel a lot happier if Jack Cartwright was in there investigating in person,' Swanson admitted. 'Send a man, will you?'

'I thought I'd take them myself. Someone else can double on the ice-machine.'

Swanson glanced at Hansen's injured hand, hesitated then nodded. 'Right. But straight through the engine-room and straight back.'

Hansen was on his way inside a minute. Five minutes later he was back again. He stripped off his breathing equipment. His face was pale and covered in sweat.

'There's fire in the engine-room, all right,' he said grimly. 'Hotter than the hinges of hell. No trace of sparks or flames but that doesn't mean a thing, the smoke in there is so thick that you couldn't see a blast furnace a couple of feet away.'

'See Rawlings?' Swanson asked.

'No. Has he not rung through?'

'Twice, but——' He broke off as the engine-room telegraph rang. 'So. He's still O.K. How about the stern room, John?'

'Damn' sight worse than it is here. The sick men aft there are in a pretty bad way, especially Bolton. Seems the smoke got in before they could get the door shut.'

'Tell Harrison to start up his air scrubbers. But for the lab. only. Blank off the rest of the ship.'

Fifteen minutes passed, fifteen minutes during which the engine-room telegraph rang three times, fifteen minutes during which the air became thicker and fouler and steadily less breathable, fifteen minutes during which a completely equipped fire-fighting team was assembled in the control centre, then another billowing cloud of black smoke announced the opening of the after door.

It was Rawlings. He was very weak and had to be helped out of his breathing equipment and his suit. His face was white and streaming sweat, his hair and clothes so saturated with sweat that he might easily have come straight from an immersion in the sea. But he was grinning triumphantly.

'No steam leak, Captain, that's for certain.' It took him three breaths to get that out. 'But fire down below in the machinery space. Sparks flying all over the shop. Some flame, not much. I located it, sir. Starboard high-pressure turbine. The lagging's on fire.'

'You'll get that medal, Rawlings,' Swanson said, 'even if I have to make the damn' thing myself.' He turned to the waiting firemen. 'You heard. Starboard turbine. Four at a time, fifteen minutes maximum. Lieutenant Raeburn, the first party. Knives, claw-hammers, pliers, crowbars, CO_2. Saturate the lagging first then rip it off. Watch out for flash flames when you're pulling it off. I don't have to warn you about the steam pipes. Now on your way.'

They left. I said to Swanson: 'Doesn't sound so much. How long will it take. Ten minutes, quarter of an hour?'

He looked at me sombrely. 'A minimum of three or four hours – if we're lucky. It's hell's own maze down in the machinery space there. Valves, tubes, condensers and miles of that damned steam piping that would burn your hands off if you touched it. Working conditions even normally are so cramped as to be almost impossible. Then there's that huge turbine housing with this thick insulation lagging wrapped all round it – and the engineers who fitted it meant it to stay there for keeps. Before they start they have to douse the fire with the CO_2 extinguishers and even that won't help much. Every time they rip off a piece of charred insulation the oil-soaked stuff below will burst into flames again as soon as it comes into contact with the oxygen in the atmosphere.'

'Oil-soaked?'

'That's where the whole trouble must lie,' Swanson explained. 'Wherever you have moving machinery you must have oil for lubrication. There's no shortage of machinery down in the machine space – and no shortage of oil either. And just as certain materials are strongly hygroscopic so that damned insulation has a remarkable affinity for oil. Where there's any around, whether in its normal fluid condition or in fine suspension in the atmosphere that lagging attracts it as a magnet does iron filings. And it's as absorbent as blotting-paper.'

'But what could have caused the fire?'

'Spontaneous combustion. There have been cases before. We've run over 50,000 miles in this ship now and in that time I suppose the lagging has become thoroughly saturated. We've been going at top speed ever since we left Zebra and the excess heat generated has set the damn' thing off. . . . . John, no word from Cartwright yet?'

'Nothing.'

'He must have been in there for the best part of twenty minutes now.'

'Maybe. But he was just beginning to put his suit on – himself and Ringman – when I left. That's not to say they went into the engine-room straight away. I'll call the stern room.' He did, spoke then hung up, his face grave. 'Stern room says that they have been gone twenty-five minutes. Shall I investigate, sir?'

'You stay right here. I'm not——'

He broke off as the after door opened with a crash and two men came staggering out – rather, one staggering, the other supporting him. The door was heaved shut and the men's masks removed. One man I recognised as an enlisted man who had accompanied Raeburn: the other was Cartwright, the main propulsion officer.

'Lieutenant Raeburn sent me out with the lieutenant here,' the enlisted man said. 'He's not so good, I think, Captain.'

It was a pretty fair diagnosis. He wasn't so good and that was a fact. He was barely conscious but none the less fighting grimly to hang on to what few shreds of consciousness were left him.

'Ringman,' he jerked out. 'Five minutes – five minutes ago. We were going back——'

'Ringman,' Swanson prompted with a gentle insistence. 'What about Ringman?'

'He fell. Down into the machinery space. I – I went after him, tried to lift him up the ladder. He screamed. God, he screamed. I – he——'

He slumped in his chair, was caught before he fell to the floor. I said: 'Ringman. Either a major fracture or internal injuries.'

'Damn!' Swanson swore softly. 'Damn and blast. A fracture. Down there. John, have Cartwright carried through to the crew's mess. A fracture!'

'Please have a mask and suit ready for me,' Jolly said briskly. 'I'll fetch Dr. Benson's emergency kit from the sick-bay.'

'You?' Swanson shook his head. 'Damned decent, Jolly. I appreciate it but I can't let you——'

'Just for once, old boy, the hell with your navy regulations," Jolly said politely. 'The main thing to remember, Commander, is that I'm aboard this ship too. Let us remember that we all – um – sink or swim together. No joke intended.'

'But you don't know how to operate those sets——'

'I can learn, can't I?' Jolly said with some asperity. He turned and left.

Swanson looked at me. He was wearing goggles, but they couldn't hide the concern in his face. He said, curiously hesitant: 'Do you think——'

'Of course Jolly's right. You've no option. If Benson were fit you know very well you'd have him down there in jig-time. Besides, Jolly is a damned fine doctor.'

'You haven't been down there, Carpenter. It's a metal jungle. There isn't room to splint a broken finger far less——'

'I don't think Dr. Jolly will try to fix or splint anything. He'll just give Ringman a jab that will lay him out so that he can be brought up here without screaming in agony in all the way.'

Swanson nodded, pursed his lips and walked away to examine the ice fathometer. I said to Hansen: 'It's pretty bad, isn't it?'

'You can say that again, friend. It's worse than bad. Normally, there should be enough air in the submarine to last us maybe sixteen hours. But well over half the air in the ship, from here right aft, is already practically unbreathable. What we have left can't possibly last us more than a few hours. Skipper's boxed in on three sides. If he doesn't start up the air purifiers the men working down in the machinery space are going to have the devil of a job doing anything. Working in near-zero visibility with breathing apparatus on you're practically as good as blind—the floods will make hardly any difference. If he does start up the purifiers in the engine-room, the fresh oxygen will cause the fire to spread. And, when he starts them up, of course, that means less and less power to get the reactor working again.'

'That's very comforting,' I said. 'How long will it take you to restart the reactor?'

'At least an hour. That's after the fire has been put out and everything checked for safety. At least an hour.'

'And Swanson reckoned three or four hours to put the fire out. Say five, all told. It's a long time. Why doesn't he use some of his reserve power cruising around to find a lead?'

'An even bigger gamble than staying put and trying to put out the fire. I'm with the skipper. Let's fight the devil we know rather than dice with the one we don't.'

Medical case in hand, Jolly came coughing and spluttering his way back into the control centre and started pulling on suit and breathing apparatus. Hansen gave him instruction on how to operate it and Jolly seemed to get the idea pretty quickly. Brown, the enlisted man who'd helped Cartwright into the control centre, was detailed to accompany him. Jolly had no idea of the location of the ladder leading down from the upper engine-room to the machinery space.

'Be as quick as you can,' Swanson said. 'Remember, Jolly, you're not trained for this sort of thing. I'll expect you back inside ten minutes.'

They were back in exactly four minutes. They didn't have an unconscious Ringman with them either. The only unconscious figure was that of Dr. Jolly, whom Brown half-carried, half-dragged over the sill into the control room.

'Can't say for sure what happened,' Brown gasped. He was trembling from the effort he had just made, Jolly must have out-weighed him by at least thirty pounds. 'We'd just got into the engine-room and shut the door. I was leading and suddenly Dr. Jolly fell against me – I reckon he must have tripped over something. He knocked me down. When I got to my feet he was lying there behind me. I put the torch on him. Out cold, he was. His mask had been torn loose. I put it on as best I could and pulled him out.'

'My word,' Hansen said reflectively. 'The medical profession on the *Dolphin is* having a rough time.' He gloomily surveyed the prone figure of Dr. Jolly as it was carried away towards the after door and relatively fresh air. 'All three saw-bones out of commission now. That's very handy, isn't it, Skipper?'

Swanson didn't answer. I said to him: 'The injection for Ringman. Would you know what to give, how to give it and where?'

'No.'

'Would any of your crew?'

'I'm in no position to argue, Dr. Carpenter.'

I opened Jolly's medical kit, hunted among the bottles on the lid rack until I found what I wanted, dipped a hypodermic and injected it in my left forearm, just where the bandage ended. 'Pain-killer,' I said. 'I'm just a softy. But I want to be able to use the forefinger and thumb of that hand.' I glanced across at Rawlings, as recovered as anyone could get in that foul atmosphere, and said: 'How are you feeling now?'

'Just resting lightly.' He rose from his chair and picked up his breathing equipment. 'Have no fears, Doc. With Torpedoman First-Class Rawlings by your side——'

'We have plenty of fresh men still available aft, Dr. Carpenter,' Swanson said.

'No. Rawlings. It's for his own sake. Maybe he'll get two medals now for this night's work.'

Rawlings grinned and pulled the mask over his head. Two minutes later we were inside the engine-room.

It was stiflingly hot in there, and visibility, even with powerful torches shining, didn't exceed eighteen inches, but for the rest it wasn't too bad. The breathing apparatus functioned well enough and I was conscious of no discomfort. At first, that was.

Rawlings took my arm and guided me to the head of the ladder that reached down to the deck of the machinery space. I heard the penetrating hiss of a fire-extinguisher and peered around to locate its source.

A pity they had no submarines in the Middle Ages, I thought, the sight of that little lot down there would have given Dante an extra fillip when he'd started in on his *Inferno.* Over on the starboard side two very powerful floodlamps had been slung above the huge turbine: the visibility they gave varied from three to six feet, according to the changing amount of smoke given off by the charred and smouldering insulation. At the moment, one patch of the insulation was deeply covered in a layer of white foam – carbon dioxide released under pressure immediately freezes anything with which it comes in contact. As the man with the extinguisher stepped back, three others moved forward in the swirling gloom and started hacking and tearing away at the insulation. As soon as a sizable strip was dragged loose the exposed lagging below immediately burst into flame reaching the height of a man's head, throwing into sharp relief weird masked figures leaping backwards to avoid being scorched by the flames. And then the man with the CO_2 would approach again, press his trigger, the blaze would shrink down, flicker and die, and a coat of creamy-white foam would bloom where the fire had been. Then the entire process would be repeated all over again. The whole scene with the repetitively stylised movements of the participants highlit against a smoky oil-veined background of flickering crimson was somehow weirdly suggestive of the priests of a long-dead and alien culture offering up some burnt sacrifice on their bloodstained pagan altar.

It also made me see Swanson's point: at the painfully but necessarily slow rate at which those men were making progress, four hours would be excellent par for the course. I tried not to think what the air inside the *Dolphin* would be like in four hours' time.

The man with the extinguisher – it was Raeburn – caught sight of us, came across and led me through a tangled maze of steam pipes and condensers to where Ringman was lying. He was on his back, very still, but conscious: I could see the movement of the whites of his eyes behind his goggles. I bent down till my mask was touching his.

'Your leg?' I shouted.

He nodded. 'Left?'

He nodded again, reached out gingerly and touched a spot half-way down the shin-bone. I opened the medical case, pulled out scissors, pinched the clothes on his upper arm between finger and thumb and cut a piece of the material away. The hypodermic came next and within two minutes he was asleep. With Rawlings's help I laid splints against his leg and bandaged them roughly in place. Two of the fire-fighters stopped work long enough to help us drag him up the ladder and then Rawlings and I took him through the passage above the reactor room. I became aware that my breathing was now distressed, my legs shaking and my whole body bathed in sweat.

Once in the control centre I took off my mask and immediately began to cough and sneeze uncontrollably, tears streaming down my cheeks. Even in the few minutes we had been gone the air in the control room had deteriorated to a frightening extent.

Swanson said: 'Thank you, Doctor. What's it like in there?'

'Quite bad. Not intolerable, but not nice. Ten minutes is long enough for your fire-fighters at one time.'

'Fire-fighters I have in plenty. Ten minutes it shall be.'

A couple of burly enlisted men carried Ringman through to the sick-bay. Rawlings had been ordered for'ard for rest and recuperation in the comparatively fresh air of the mess-room, but elected to stop off at the sick-bay with me. He'd glanced at my bandaged left hand and said: 'Three hands are better than one, even although two of them do happen to belong to Rawlings.'

Benson was restless and occasionally murmuring, but still below the level of consciousness. Captain Folsom was asleep, deeply so, which I found surprising until Rawlings told me that there were no alarm boxes in the sick-bay and that the door was completely soundproofed.

We laid Ringman down on the examination table and Rawlings slit up his left trouser leg with a pair of heavy surgical scissors. It wasn't as bad as I had feared it would be, a clean fracture of the tibia, not compound: with Rawlings doing most of the work we soon had his leg fixed up. I didn't try to put his leg in traction. When Jolly, with his two good hands, had completely recovered he'd be able to make a better job of it than I could.

We'd just finished when a telephone rang. Rawlings lifted it quickly before Folsom could wake, spoke briefly and hung up.

'Control room,' he said. I knew from the wooden expression on his face that whatever news he had for me, it wasn't good. 'It was for you. Bolton, the sick man in the nucleonics lab., the one you brought back from Zebra yesterday afternoon. He's gone. About two minutes ago.' He shook his head despairingly. 'My God, another death.'

'No,' I said. 'Another murder.'

11

The *Dolphin* was an ice-cold tomb. At half past six that morning, four and a half hours after the outbreak of the fire, there was still only one dead man inside the ship, Bolton. But as I looked with bloodshot and inflamed eyes at the men sitting or lying about the control room – no one was standing any more – I knew that within an hour, two at the most, Bolton would be having company. By ten o'clock, at the latest, under those conditions, the *Dolphin* would be no more than a steel coffin with no life left inside her.

As a ship, the *Dolphin* was already dead. All the sounds we associated with a living vessel, the murmurous pulsation of great engines, the high-pitched whine of generators, the deep hum of the air-conditioning unit, the unmistakable transmission from the sonar, the clickety-clack from the radio room, the soft hiss of air, the brassy jingle from the juke-box, the whirring of fans, the rattle of pots from the galley, the movement of men, the talking of men – all those were gone. All those vital sounds, the heartbeats of a living vessel, were gone; but in their place was not silence but something worse than silence, something that bespoke not living but dying, the frighteningly rapid, hoarse, gasping breathing of lung-tortured men fighting for air and for life.

Fighting for air. The was the irony of it. Fighting for air while there were still many days' supply of oxygen in the giant tanks. There were some breathing sets aboard, similar to the British Built-in Breathing System which takes a direct oxy-nitrogen mixture from tanks, but only a few, and all members of the crew had had a turn at those, but only for two minutes at a time. For the rest, for the more than ninety per cent without those systems, there was only the panting straining agony that leads eventually to death. Some portable closed-circuit sets were still left, but those were reserved exclusively for the fire-fighters.

Oxygen was occasionally bled from the tanks directly into the living spaces and it just didn't do any good at all; the only effect it seemed to have was to make breathing even more cruelly difficult by heightening the atmospheric pressure. All the oxygen in the world was going to be of little avail as long as the level of carbon dioxide given off by our anguished breathing mounted steadily with the passing of each minute. Normally, the air in the *Dolphin* was cleaned and circulated throughout the ship every two minutes, but the giant 200-ton air-conditioner responsible for this was a glutton for the electric power that drove it; and the electricians' estimate was that the reserve of power in the stand-by battery, which alone could reactivate the nuclear power plant, was already dangerously low. So the concentration of carbon dioxide increased steadily towards lethal levels and there was nothing we could do about it.

Increasing, too, in what passed now for air, were the Freon fumes from the refrigerating machinery and the hydrogen fumes from the batteries. Worse still, the smoke was now so thick that visibility, even in the for'ard parts of the ship, was down to a few feet, but that smoke had to remain also, there was no power to operate the electrostatic precipitators and even when those had been tried they had proved totally inadequate to cope with the concentration of billions of carbon particles held in suspension in the air. Each time the door to the engine-room was opened

– and that was progressively oftener as the strength of the fire-fighters ebbed – fresh clouds of that evil acrid smoke rolled through the submarine. The fire in the engine-room had stopped burning over two hours previously; but now what remained of the redly-smouldering insulation round the starboard high-pressure turbine gave off far more smoke and fumes than flames could ever have done.

But the greatest enemy of all lay in the mounting count of carbon monoxide, that deadly, insidious, colourless, tasteless, odourless gas with its murderous affinity for the red blood cells – five hundred times that of oxygen. On board the *Dolphin* the normal permissible tolerance of carbon monoxide in the air was thirty parts in a million. Now the reading was somewhere between four and five hundred parts in a million. When it reached a thousand parts, none of us would have more than minutes to live.

And then there was the cold. As Commander Swanson had grimly prophesied, the *Dolphin*, with the steam pipes cooled down and all heaters switched off, had chilled down to the sub-freezing temperature of the sea outside, and was ice-cold. In terms of absolute cold, it was nothing – a mere two degrees below zero on the centigrade scale. But in terms of cold as it reacted on the human body it was very cold indeed. Most of the crew were without warm clothing of any kind – in normal operating conditions the temperature inside the *Dolphin* was maintained at a steady 22°C. regardless of the temperature outside – they were both forbidden to move around and lacked the energy to move around to counteract the effects of the cold, and what little energy was left in their rapidly weakening bodies was so wholly occupied in forcing their labouring chest muscles to gulp in more and ever more of that foul and steadily worsening air that they had none at all left to generate sufficient animal heat to ward off that dank and bitter cold. You could actually *hear* men shivering, could listen to their violently shaking limbs knocking and rat-tat-tatting helplessly against bulk-heads and deck, could hear the chattering of their teeth, the sound of some of them, far gone in weakness, whimpering softly with the cold: but always the dominant sound was that harsh strangled moaning, a rasping and frightening sound, as men sought to suck air down into starving lungs.

With the exception of Hansen and myself – both of whom were virtually one-handed – and the sick patients, every man in the *Dolphin* had taken his turn that night in descending into the machinery space and fighting that red demon that threatened to slay us all. The number in each fire-fighting group had been increased from four to eight and the time spent down there shortened to three or four minutes, so that efforts could be concentrated and more energy expended in a given length of time; but because of increasingly Stygian darkness in the machinery space, the ever-thickening coils of oily black smoke, and the wickedly cramped and confined space in which the men had to work, progress had been frustratingly, maddeningly slow; and entered into it now, of course, was the factor of that dreadful weakness that now assailed us all, so that men with the strength only of little children were tugging and tearing at the smouldering insulation in desperate near-futility and seemingly making no progress at all.

I'd been down again in the machinery space, just once, at 5.30 a.m. to attend to Jolly who had himself slipped, fallen and laid himself out while helping an injured crewman up the ladder, and I knew I would never forget what I had seen there, dark and spectral figures in a dark and spectral and swirling world, lurching and staggering around like zombies in some half-forgotten nightmare, swaying and stumbling and falling to the deck or down into the bilges now deep-covered in great snowdrifts of carbon dioxide foam and huge smoking blackened chunks of torn-off lagging. Men on the rack, men in the last stages of exhaustion. One little spark of fire, one little spark of an element as old as time itself and all the brilliant technological progress of the twentieth century was set at nothing, the frontiers of a man's striving translated in a moment from the nuclear age to the dark unknown of pre-history.

Every dark hour brings forth its man and there was no doubt in the minds of the crew of the *Dolphin* that that dark night had produced its own here. Dr. Jolly. He had made a swift recovery from the effects of his first disastrous entry into the engine-room that night, appearing back in the control centre only seconds after I had finished setting Ringman's broken leg. He had taken the news of Bolton's death pretty badly, but never either by word or direct look did he indicate to either Swanson or myself that the fault lay with us for insisting against his better judgment on bringing on board the ship a man whose life had been hanging in the balance even under the best of conditions. I think Swanson was pretty grateful for that and might even have got around to apologising to Jolly had not a fire-fighter come through from the engine-room and told us that one of his team had slipped and either twisted or broken an ankle – the second of many minor accidents and injuries that were to happen down in the machinery space that night. Jolly had reached for the nearest closed-circuit breathing apparatus before we could try to stop him and was gone in a minute.

We eventually lost count of the number of trips he made down there that night. Fifteen at least, perhaps many more – by the time six o'clock had come my mind was beginning to get pretty fuzzy round the edges. He'd certainly no lack of customers for his medical skill. Paradoxically enough, the two main types of injury that night were diametrically opposite in nature: burning and freezing, burning from the red-hot lagging – and, earlier, the steam pipes – and freezing from a carelessly directed jet of carbon dioxide against exposed areas of face or hands. Jolly never failed to answer a call, not even after the time he'd given his own head a pretty nasty crack. He would complain bitterly to the captain, old boy, for rescuing him from the relative safety and comfort of Drift Ice Station Zebra, crack some dry joke, pull on his mask and leave. A dozen speeches to Congress or Parliament couldn't have done what Jolly did that night in cementing Anglo-American friendship.

About 6.45 a.m. Chief Torpedoman Patterson came into the control centre. I suppose he walked through the doorway, but that was only assumption, from where I sat on the deck between Swanson and Hansen you couldn't see half-way to the door; but when he came up to Swanson he was crawling on his hands and knees, head swaying from side to side, whooping painfully, his respiration rate at least fifty to the minute. He was wearing no mask of any kind and was shivering constantly.

'We must do something, Captain,' he said hoarsely. He spoke as much when inhaling as when exhaling, when your breathing is sufficiently distressed one is as easy as the other. 'We've got seven men passed out now between the for'ard torpedo room and the crew's mess. They're pretty sick men, Captain.'

'Thank you, Chief.' Swanson, also without a mask, was in as bad a way as Patterson, his chest heaving, his breath hoarsely rasping, tears and sweat rolling down the greyness of his face. 'We will be as quick as possible.'

'More oxygen,' I said. 'Bleed more oxygen into the ship.'

'Oxygen? More oxygen?' He shook his head. 'The pressure is too high as it is.'

'Pressure won't kill them.' I was dimly aware through my cold and misery and burning chest and eyes that my voice sounded just as strange as did those of Swanson and Patterson. 'Carbon monoxide will kill them. Carbon monoxide is what is killing them now. It's the relative proportion of CO_2 to oxygen that matters. It's too high, it's far too high. That's what's going to finish us all off.'

'More oxygen,' Swanson ordered. Even the unnecessary acknowledgment of my words would have cost too much. 'More oxygen.'

Valves were turned and oxygen hissed into the control room and, I knew, into the crew spaces. I could feel my ears pop as the pressure swiftly built up, but that was all I could feel. I certainly couldn't feel any improvement in my breathing, a feeling that was borne out when Patterson, noticeably weaker this time, crawled back and croaked out the bad news that he now had a dozen unconscious men on his hands. I went for'ard with Patterson and a closed-circuit oxygen apparatus – one of the few unexhausted sets left – and clamped it for a minute or so on to the face of each unconscious man in turn, but I knew it was but a •temporary palliative, the oxygen revived them but within a few minutes of the mask being removed most of them slipped back into unconsciousness again. I made my way back to the control room, a dark dungeon of huddled men nearly all lying down, most of them barely conscious. I was barely conscious myself. I wondered vaguely if they felt as I did, if the fire from the lungs had now spread to the remainder of the body, if they could see the first slight changes in colour in their hands and faces, the deadly blush of purple, the first unmistakable signs of a man beginning to die from carbon monoxide poisoning. Jolly, I noticed, still hadn't returned from the engine-room: he was keeping himself permanently on hand, it seemed, to help those men who were in ever increasingly greater danger of hurting themselves and their comrades, as their weakness increased, as their level of care and attention and concentration slid down towards zero.

Swanson was where I'd left him, propped on the deck against the plotting table. He smiled faintly as I sank down beside himself and Hansen.

'How are they, Doctor?' he whispered. A whisper, but a rock-steady whisper. The man's monolithic calm had never cracked and I realised dimly that here was a man who could never crack; you do find people like that, once in a million or once in a lifetime. Swanson was such a man.

'Far gone,' I said. As a medical report it maybe lacked a thought in detail but it contained the gist of what I wanted to say and it saved me energy. 'You will have your first deaths from carbon monoxide poisoning within the hour.'

'So soon?' The surprise was in his red, swollen streaming eyes as well as in his voice. 'Not so soon, Doctor. It's hardly – well, it's hardly started to take effect.'

'So soon,' I said. 'Carbon monoxide poisoning is very rapidly progressive. Five dead within the hour. Within two hours, fifty. At least fifty.'

'You take the choice out of my hands,' he murmured. 'For which I am grateful. John, where is our main propulsion officer. His hour has come.'

'I'll get him.' Hansen hauled himself wearily to his feet, an old man making his last struggle to rise from his deathbed, and at that moment the engine-room door opened and blackened exhausted men staggered into the control room. Waiting men filed out to take their place. Swanson said to one of the men who had just entered: 'Is that you, Will?'

'Yes, sir.' Lieutenant Raeburn, the navigating officer, pulled off his mask and began to cough, rackingly, painfully. Swanson waited until he had quietened a little.

'How are things down there, Will?'

'We've stopped making smoke, Skipper.' Raeburn wiped his streaming face, swayed dizzily and lowered himself groggily to the floor. 'I think we've drowned out the lagging completely.'

'How long to get the rest of it off?'

'God knows. Normally, ten minutes. The way we are – an hour. Maybe longer.'

'Thank you. Ah!' He smiled faintly as Hansen and Cartwright appeared out of the smoke-filled gloom. 'Our main propulsion officer. Mr. Cartwright, I would be glad if you would put the kettle on to boil. What's the record for activating the plant, getting steam up and spinning the turbo-generators?'

'I couldn't say, Skipper.' Red-eyed, coughing, smoke-blackened and obviously in considerable pain, Cartwright nevertheless straightened his shoulders and smiled slowly. 'But you may consider it broken.'

He left. Swanson heaved himself to his feet with obvious weakness – except for two brief inspection trips to the engine-room he had not once worn any breathing apparatus during those interminable and pain-filled hours. He called for power on the broadcast circuit, unhooked a microphone and spoke in a calm clear strong voice: it was an amazing exhibition in self-control, the triumph of a mind over agonised lungs still starving for air.

'This is your captain speaking,' he said. 'The fire in the engine-room is out. We are already reactivating our power plant. Open all watertight doors throughout the ship. They are to remain open until further orders. You may regard the worst of our troubles as lying behind us. Thank you for all you have done.' He hooked up the microphone, and turned to Hansen. 'The worst *is* behind, John – if we have enough power left to reactivate the plant.'

'Surely the worst is still to come,' I said. 'It'll take you how long, three-quarters of an hour, maybe an hour to get your turbine generators going and your air-purifying equipment working again. How long do you think it will take your air cleaners to make any noticeable effect on this poisonous air?'

'Half an hour. At least that. Perhaps more.'

'There you are, then.' My mind was so woolly and doped now that I had difficulty in finding words to frame my thoughts, and I wasn't even sure that my thoughts were worth thinking. 'An hour and a half at least – and you said the worst was over. The worst hasn't even begun.' I shook my head, trying to remember what it was that I had been going to say next, then remembered. 'In an hour and a half one out of every four of your men will be gone.'

Swanson smiled. He actually, incredibly, smiled. He said: 'As Sherlock used to say to Moriarty, I think not, Doctor. Nobody's going to die of monoxide poisoning. In fifteen minutes' time we'll have fresh breathable air thoughout the ship.'

Hansen glanced at me just as I glanced at him. The strain had been too much, the old man had gone off his rocker. Swanson caught our interchange of looks and laughed, the laugh changing abruptly to a bout of convulsive coughing as he inhaled too much of that poisoned smoke-laden atmosphere. He coughed for a long time then gradually quietened down.

'Serves me right,' he gasped. 'Your faces ... Why do you think I ordered the watertight doors opened, Doctor?'

'No idea.'

'John?'

Hansen shook his head. Swanson looked at him quizzically and said: 'Speak to the engine-room. Tell them to light up the diesel.'

'Yes, sir,' Hansen said woodenly. He made no move.

'Lieutenant Hansen is wondering whether he should fetch a strait-jacket,' Swanson said. 'Lieutenant Hansen knows that a diesel engine is never *never* lit up when a submarine is submerged – unless with a snorkel which is useless under ice – for a diesel not only uses air straight from the engine-room atmosphere, it gulps it down in great draughts and would soon clear away all the air in the ship. Which is what I want. We bleed compressed air under fairly high pressure into the forepart of the ship. Nice clean fresh air. We light up the diesel in the after part – it will run rough at first because of the low concentration of oxygen in this poisonous muck – but it will run. It will suck up much of this filthy air, exhausting its gases over the side, and as it does it will lower the atmospheric pressure aft and the fresh air will make its way through from for'ard. To have done this before now would have been suicidal, the fresh air would only have fed the flames until the fire was out of control. But we can do it now. We can run it for a few minutes only, of course, but a few minutes will be ample. You are with me, Lieutenant Hansen?'

Hansen was with him all right, but he didn't answer. He had already left.

Three minutes passed, then we heard, through the now open passageway above the reactor room, the erratic sound of a diesel starting, fading, coughing, then catching again – we learned later that the engineers had had to bleed off several ether bottles in the vicinity of the air intake to get the engine to catch. For a minute or two it ran roughly and erratically and seemed to be making no impression at all on that poisonous air: then, imperceptibly, almost, at first, then with an increasing degree of definition, we could see the smoke in the control room, illuminated by the single lamp still left burning there, begin to drift and eddy towards the reactor passage. Smoke began to stir and eddy in the corners of the control room as the diesel sucked the fumes aft, and more smoke-laden air, a shade lighter in colour, began to move in from the wardroom passageway, pulled in by the decreasing pressure in the control room, pushed in by the gradual build-up of fresh air in the forepart of the submarine as compressed air was bled into the living spaces.

A few more minutes made the miracle. The diesel thudded away in the engine-room, running more sweetly and strongly as air with a higher concentration of oxygen reached its intake, and the smoke in the control room drained steadily away to be replaced by a thin greyish mist from the forepart of the ship that was hardly deserving of the name of smoke at all. And that mist carried with it air, an air with fresh life-giving oxygen, an air with a proportion of carbon dioxide and carbon monoxide that was now almost negligible. Or so it seemed to us.

The effect upon the crew was just within the limits of credibility. It was as if a wizard had passed through the length of the ship and touched them with the wand of life. Unconscious men, men for whom death had been less than half an hour away, began to stir, some to open their eyes: sick, exhausted, nauseated and pain-racked men who had been lying or sitting on the decks in attitudes of huddled despair sat up straight or stood, their faces breaking into expressions of almost comical wonderment and disbelief as they drew great draughts down into their aching lungs and found that it was not poisonous gases they were inhaling but fresh breathable air: men who had made up their minds for death began to wonder how they could ever have thought that way. As air went, I suppose, it was pretty sub-standard stuff and the Factory Acts would have had something to say about it; but, for us, no pine-clad mountain air ever tasted half so sweet.

Swanson kept a careful eye on the gauges recording the air pressure in the submarine. Gradually it sank down to the fifteen pounds at which the atmosphere was normally kept, then below it; he ordered the compressed air to be released under higher pressure and then when the atmospheric pressure was back to normal ordered the diesel stopped and the compressed air shut off.

'Commander Swanson,' I said. 'If you ever want to make admiral you can apply to me for a reference any time.'

'Thank you.' He smiled. 'We have been very lucky.' Sure we had been
lucky, the way men who sailed with Swanson would always be lucky.
We could hear now the sounds of pumps and motors as Cartwright
started in on the slow process of bringing the nuclear power plant to life
again. Everyone knew that it was touch and go whether there would be
enough life left in the batteries for that, but, curiously, no one seemed to
doubt that Cartwright would succeed; we had been through too much to
entertain even the thought of failure now.

Nor did we fail. At exactly eight o'clock that morning Cartwright
phoned to say that he had steam on the turbine blades and that the
Dolphin was a going proposition again. I was glad to hear it.

For three hours we cruised along at slow speed while the air-conditioning
plant worked under maximum pressure to bring the air inside the *Dolphin*
back to normal. After that Swanson slowly stepped up our speed until we
had reached about fifty per cent of normal cruising speed, which was as
fast as the propulsion officer deemed it safe to go. For a variety of
technical reasons it was impractical for the *Dolphin* to operate without all
turbines in commission, so we were reduced to the speed of the slowest
and, without lagging on it, Cartwright didn't want to push the starboard
high-pressure turbine above a fraction of its power. This way, it would
take us much longer to clear the ice-pack and reach the open sea but the
captain, in a broadcast, said that if the limit of the ice-pack was where it
had been when we'd first moved under it – and there was no reason to
think it should have shifted more than a few miles – we should be moving
out into the open sea about four o'clock the following morning.

By four o'clock of that afternoon, members of the crew, working in
relays, had managed to clear away from the machinery space all the
débris and foam that had accumulated during the long night. After that,
Swanson reduced all watches to the barest skeletons required to run the
ship so that as many men as possible might sleep as long as possible. Now
that the exultation of victory was over, now that the almost intolerable
relief of knowing that they were not after all to find their gasping end in
a cold iron tomb under the ice-cap had begun to fade, the inevitable
reaction, when it did come, was correspondingly severe. A long and
sleepless night behind them; hours of cruelly back-breaking toil in the
metal jungle of the machinery space; that lifetime of tearing tension
when they had not known whether they were going to live or die but had
believed they were going to die; the poisonous fumes that had laid them
all on the rack: all of those combined had taken cruel toll of their reserves
of physical and mental energy and the crew of the *Dolphin* were now
sleep-ridden and exhausted as they had never been. When they lay down

to sleep they slept at once, like dead men.

I didn't sleep. Not then, not at four o'clock. I couldn't sleep. I had too much to think about, like how it had been primarily my fault, through mistake, miscalculation or sheer pig-headedness, that the *Dolphin* and her crew had been brought to such desperate straits: like what Commander Swanson was going to say when he found out how much I'd kept from him, how little I'd told him. Still, if I had kept him in the dark so long, I couldn't see that there would be much harm in it if I kept him in the dark just that little time longer. It would be time enough in the morning to tell him all I knew. His reactions would be interesting, to say the least. He might be striking some medals for Rawlings, but I had the feeling that he wouldn't be striking any for me. Not after I'd told him what I'd have to.

Rawlings. That was the man I wanted now. I went to see him, told him what I had in mind and asked him if he would mind sacrificing a few hours' sleep during the night. As always, Rawlings was co-operation itself.

Later that evening I had a look at one or two of the patients. Jolly, exhausted by his Herculean efforts of the previous night, was fathoms deep in slumber, so Swanson had asked if I would deputise for him. So I did, but I didn't try very hard. With only one exception they were sound asleep and none of them was in so urgent need of medical attention that there would have been any justification for waking him up. The sole exception was Dr. Benson, who had recovered consciousness late that afternoon. He was obviously on the mend but complained that his head felt like a pumpkin with someone at work on it with a riveting gun so I fed him some pills and that was the extent of the treatment. I asked him if he had any idea as to what had been the cause of his fall from the top of the sail, but he was either too woozy to remember or just didn't know. Not that it mattered now. I already knew the answer.

I slept for nine hours after that, which was pretty selfish of me considering that I had asked Rawlings to keep awake half the night; but then I hadn't had much option about that, for Rawlings was in the position to perform for me an essential task that I couldn't perform for myself.

Some time during the night we passed out from under the ice-cap into the open Arctic Ocean again.

I awoke shortly after seven, washed, shaved and dressed as carefully as I could with one hand out of commission, for I believe a judge owes it to his public to be decently turned out when he goes to conduct a trial, then breakfasted well in the wardroom. Shortly before nine o'clock I walked into the control room. Hansen had the watch. I went up to him and said quietly so that I couldn't be overheard: 'Where is Commander Swanson?'

'In his cabin.'

'I'd like to speak to him and yourself. Privately.'

Hansen looked at me speculatively, nodded, handed over the watch to the navigator and led the way to Swanson's cabin. We knocked, went in and closed the door behind us. I didn't waste any time in preamble. 'I know who the killer is,' I said. 'I've no proof but I'm going to get it now. I would like you to be on hand. If you can spare the time.'

They'd used up all their emotional responses and reactions during the previous thirty hours so they didn't throw up their hands or do startled double-takes or make any of the other standard signs of incredulousness. Instead Swanson just looked thoughtfully at Hansen, rose from his table, folded the chart he'd been studying and said dryly: 'I think we might spare the time, Dr. Carpenter. I have never met a murderer.' His tone was impersonal, even light, but the clear grey eyes had gone very cold indeed. 'It will be quite an experience to meet a man with eight deaths on his conscience.'

'You can count yourself lucky that it is only eight,' I said. 'He almost brought it up to the hundred mark yesterday morning.'

This time I did get them. Swanson stared at me, then said softly: 'What do you mean?'

'Our pal with the gun also carried a box of matches around with him,' I said. 'He was busy with them in the engine-room in the early hours of yesterday morning.'

'Someone *deliberately* tried to set the ship on fire?' Hansen looked at me in open disbelief. 'I don't buy that, Doc.'

'I buy it,' Swanson said. 'I buy anything Dr. Carpenter says. We're dealing with a madman, Doctor. Only a madman would risk losing his life along with the lives of a hundred others.'

'He miscalculated,' I said mildly. 'Come along.'

They were waiting for us in the wardroom as I'd arranged, eleven of them in all – Rawlings, Zabrinski, Captain Folsom, Dr. Jolly, the two Harrington twins, who were now just barely well enough to be out of bed, Naseby, Hewson, Hassard, Kinnaird and Jeremy. Most of them were seated round the wardroom table except for Rawlings, who opened the door for us, and Zabrinski, his foot still in the cast, who was sitting in a chair in one corner of the room, studying an issue of the *Dolphin Daze*, the submarine's own mimeographed newspaper. Some of them made to get to their feet as we came in but Swanson waved them down. They sat, silently, all except Dr. Jolly who boomed out a cheerful: 'Good morning, Captain. Well, well, this is an intriguing summons. Most intriguing. What is it you want to see us about, Captain?'

I cleared my throat. 'You must forgive a small deception. It is I who want to see you, not the captain.'

'You?' Jolly pursed his lips and looked at me speculatively. 'I don't get it, old boy. Why you?'

'I have been guilty of another small deception. I am not, as I gave you to understand, attached to the Ministry of Supply. I am an agent of the British Government. An officer of M.I.6, counter-espionage.'

Well, I got my reaction, all right. They just sat there, mouths wide open like newly-landed fish, staring at me. It was Jolly, always a fast adjuster, who recovered first.

'Counter-espionage, by jove! Counter-espionage! Spies and cloaks and daggers and beautiful blondes tucked away in the wardrobes – or wardroom, should I say. But why – but why are you *here*? What do you – well, what *can* you want to see us about, Dr. Carpenter?'

'A small matter of murder,' I said.

'Murder!' Captain Folsom spoke for the first time since coming aboard ship, the voice issuing from that savagely burnt face no more than a strangled croak. 'Murder?'

'Two of the men lying up there now in the Drift Station lab. were dead *before* the fire. They had been shot through the head. A third had been knifed. I would call that murder, wouldn't you?'

Jolly groped for the table and lowered himself shakily into his seat. The rest of them looked as if they were very glad that they were already sitting down.

'It seems so superfluous to add,' I said, adding it all the same, 'that the murderer is in this room now.'

You wouldn't have thought it, not too look at them. You could see at a glance that none of those high-minded citizens could possibly be a killer. They were as innocent as life's young morning, the whole lot of them, pure and white as the driven snow.

12

It would be an understatement to say that I had the attention of the company. Maybe had I been a two-headed visitor from outer space, or had been about to announce the result of a multi-million pound sweepstake in which they held the only tickets, or was holding straws for them to pick to decide who should go before the firing squad – maybe then they might have given me an even more exclusive degree of concentration. But I doubt it. It wouldn't have been possible.

'If you'll bear with me,' I began, 'first of all I'd like to give you a little lecture in camera optics – and don't ask me what the hell that has to do with murder. It's got everything to do with it, as you'll find out soon enough.

'Film emulsion and lens quality being equal, the clarity of detail in any photograph depends upon the focal length of the lens – that is, the distance between the lens and the film. As recently as fifteen years ago the maximum focal length of any camera outside an observatory was about fifty inches. Those were used in reconnaissance planes in the later stages of the Second World War. A small suitcase lying on the ground would show up on a photograph taken from a height of ten miles, which was pretty good for those days.

'But the American Army and Air Force wanted bigger and better aerial cameras, and the only way this could be done was by increasing the focal length of the lens. There was obviously a superficial limit to this length because the Americans wanted this camera to fit into a plane – or an orbiting satellite – and if you wanted a camera with a focal length of, say, 250 inches, it was obviously going to be quite impossible to install a twenty-foot camera pointing vertically downwards in a plane or small satellite. But scientists came up with a new type of camera using the folded lens principle, where the light, instead of coming down a long straight barrel, is bounced round a series of angled mirrored corners, which permits the focal length to be increased greatly without having to enlarge the camera itself. By 1950 they'd developed a hundred-inch focal length lens. It was quite an improvement on the World War II cameras which could barely pick up a suitcase at ten miles – this one could pick up a cigarette packet at ten miles. Then, ten years later, came what they called the Perkin-Elmer Roti satellite missile tracker, with a focal length of five hundred inches – equivalent to a barrel type camera forty feet long: this one could pick up a cube of sugar at ten miles.'

I looked inquiringly around the audience for signs of inattention. There were no signs of inattention. No lecturer ever had a keener audience than I had there.

'Three years later,' I went on, 'another American firm had developed this missile tracker into a fantastic camera that could be mounted in even a small-size satellite. Three years' non-stop work to create this camera – but they reckoned it worth it. We don't know the focal length, it's never been revealed: we do know that, given the right atmospheric conditions, a white saucer on a dark surface will show up clearly from 300 miles up in space. This on a relatively tiny negative capable of almost infinite enlargement – for the scientists have also come up with a completely new film emulsion, still super-secret and a hundred times as sensitive as the finest films available on the commerical market today.

'This was to be fitted to the two-ton satellite the Americans called Samos III – Samos for Satellite and Missile Observation System. It never was. This, the only camera of its kind in the world, vanished, hi-jacked in broad daylight and, as we later learned, dismantled, flown from New York to Havana by a Polish jet-liner which had cleared for Miami and so avoided customs inspection.

'Four months ago this camera was launched in a Soviet satellite on a polar orbit, crossing the American middle west seven times a day. Those satellites can stay up indefinitely, but in just three days, with perfect weather conditions, the Soviets had all the pictures they ever wanted – pictures of every American missile launching base west of the Mississippi. Every time this camera took a picture of a small section of the United States another smaller camera in the satellite, pointing vertically upwards, took a fix on the stars. Then it was only a matter of checking map co-ordinates and they could have a Soviet inter-continental ballistic missile ranged in on every launching-pad in America. But first they had to have the pictures.

'Radio transmission is no good, there's far too much quality and detail lost in the process – and you must remember this was a relatively tiny negative in the first place. So they had to have the actual films. There are two ways of doing this – bring the satellite back to earth or have it eject a capsule with the films. The Americans, with their Discoverer tests, have perfected the art of using planes to snatch falling capsules from the sky. The Russians haven't, although we do know they have a technique for ejecting capsules should a satellite run amok. So they had to bring the satellite down. They planned to bring it down some two hundred miles east of the Caspian. But something went wrong. Precisely what we don't know, but our experts say that it could only have been due to the fact that the retro-rockets on one side of the capsule failed to fire when given the radio signal to do so. You are beginning to understand, gentlemen?'

'We are beginning to understand indeed.' It was Jeremy who spoke, his voice very soft. 'The satellite took up a different orbit.'

'That's what happened. The rockets firing on one side didn't slow her up any that mattered, they just knocked her far off course. A new and wobbly orbit that passed through Alaska, south over the Pacific, across Grahamland in Antarctica and directly south of South America, up over Africa and Western Europe, then round the North Pole in a shallow curve, maybe two hundred miles distant from it at the nearest point.

'Now, the only way the Russians could get the films was by ejecting the capsule, for with retro-rockets firing on one side only they knew that even if they did manage to slow up the satellite sufficiently for it to leave orbit, they had no idea where it would go. But the damnably awkward part of it from the Russians' viewpoint was that nowhere in its orbit of the earth did the satellite pass over the Soviet Union or any sphere of Communist influence whatsoever. Worse, ninety per cent of its travel was over open sea and if they brought it down there they would never see their films again as the capsule is so heavily coated with aluminium and Pyroceram to withstand the heat of re-entry into the atmosphere that it was much heavier than water. And as I said, they had never developed the American know-how of snatching falling capsules out of the air – and you will appreciate that they couldn't very well ask the Americans to do the job for them.

'So they decided to bring it down in the only safe place open to them – either the polar ice-cap in the north or the Antarctic in the south. You will remember, Captain, that I told you that I had just returned from the Antarctic. The Russians have a couple of geophysical stations there and, up until a few days ago, we thought that there was a fifty-fifty chance that the capsule might be brought down there. But we were wrong. Their nearest station in the Antarctic was 300 miles from the path of orbit – and no field parties were stirring from home.'

'So they decided to bring it down in the vicinity of Drift Ice Station Zebra?' Jolly asked quietly. It was a sign of his perturbation that he didn't even call me 'old boy'.

'Drift Ice Station Zebra wasn't even in existence at the time the satellite went haywire, although all preparations were complete. We had arranged for Canada to lend us a St. Lawrence ice-breaker to set up the station but the Russians in a burst of friendly goodwill and international co-operation offered us the atomic-powered *Lenin*, the finest ice-breaker in the world. They wanted to make good and sure that Zebra was set up and set up in good time. It was. The east-west drift of the ice-cap was unusually slow this year and almost eight weeks elapsed after the setting up of the station until it was directly beneath the flight trajectory of the satellite.

'You *knew* what the Russians had in mind?' Hansen asked.

'We knew. But the Russians had no idea whatsoever that we were on to them. They had no idea that one of the pieces of equipment which was landed at Zebra was a satellite monitor which would tell Major Halliwell when the satellite received the radio signal to eject the capsule.' I looked slowly round the Zebra survivors. 'I'll wager none of you knew that. But Major Halliwell did – and the three other men who slept in his hut where this machine was located.

'What we did not know was the identity of the member of Zebra's company that had been suborned by the Russians. We were certain someone *must* have been but had no idea who it was. Every one of you had first-class security clearances. But someone was suborned – and that someone, when he arrived back in Britain, would have been a wealthy man for the rest of his days. In addition to leaving what was in effect an enemy agent planted in Zebra, the Soviets also left a portable monitor – an electronic device for tuning in on a particular radio signal which would be activated inside the capsule at the moment of its ejection from the satellite. A capsule can be so accurately ejected 300 miles up that it will land within a mile of its target, but the ice-cap is pretty rough territory and dark most of the time, so this monitor would enable our friend to locate the capsule which would keep on emitting its signal for at least, I suppose, twenty-four hours after landing. Our friend took the monitor and went out looking for the capsule. He found it, released it from its drogue and brought it back to the station. You are still with me, gentlemen? Especially one particular gentleman?'

'I think we are all with you, Dr. Carpenter,' Commander Swanson said softly. 'Every last one of us.'

'Fine. Well, unfortunately, Major Halliwell and his three companions also knew that the satellite had ejected its capsule – don't forget that they were monitoring this satellite twenty-four hours a day. They knew that someone was going to go looking for it pretty soon, but who that someone would be they had no idea. Anyway, Major Halliwell posted one of his men to keep watch. It was a wild night, bitterly cold, with a gale blowing an ice-storm before it, but he kept a pretty good watch all the same. He either bumped into our friend returning with the capsule or, more probably, saw a light in a cabin, investigated, found our friend stripping the film from the capsule and, instead of going quietly away and reporting to Major Halliwell, he went in and challenged this man. If that was the way of it, it was a bad mistake, the last he ever made. He got a knife between the ribs.' I gazed at all the Zebra survivors in turn. 'I wonder which one of you did it? Whoever it was, he wasn't very expert. He broke off the blade inside the chest. I found it there.' I was looking at Swanson and he didn't bat an eyelid. He knew I hadn't found the blade there: he had found the haft in the petrol tank. But there was time enough to tell them that.

'When the man he had posted didn't turn up, Major Halliwell got worried. It must have been something like that. I don't know and it doesn't matter. Our friend with the broken knife was on the alert now, he knew someone was on to him – it must have come as a pretty severe shock, he'd thought himself completely unsuspected – and when the second man the Major sent turned up he was ready for him. He had to kill him – for the first man was lying dead in his cabin. Apart from his broken knife he'd also a gun. He used it.

'Both those men had come from Halliwell's cabin, the killer knew that Halliwell must have sent them and that he and the other man still in the major's cabin would be around in double quick time if the second watcher didn't report back immediately. He decided not to wait for that – he'd burnt his boats anyway. He took his gun, went into Major Halliwell's cabin and shot him and the other man as they lay on their beds. I know that because the bullets in their heads entered low from the front and emerged high at the back – the angle the bullets would naturally take if the killer was standing at the foot of their beds and fired at them as they were lying down. I suppose this is as good a time as any to say that my name is not really Carpenter. It's Halliwell. Major Halliwell was my elder brother.'

'Good God!' Dr. Jolly whispered. 'Good God above!'

'One thing the killer knew it was essential to do right away – to conceal the traces of his crime. There was only one way – burn the bodies out of all recognition. So he dragged a couple of drums of oil out of the fuel store, poured them against the walls of Major Halliwell's hut – he'd already pulled in there the first two men he'd killed – and set fire to it. For good measure he also set fire to the fuel store. A thorough type, my friends, a man who never did anything by halves.'

The men seated around the wordroom table were dazed and shocked, uncomprehending and incredulous. But they were only incredulous because the enormity of the whole thing was beyond them. But not beyond them all.

'I'm a man with a curious turn of mind,' I went on. 'I wondered why sick, burnt, exhausted men had wasted their time and their little strength in shifting the dead men into the lab. Because someone had suggested that it might be a good thing to do, the decent thing to do. The real reason, of course, was to discourage anyone from going there. I looked under the floor-boards and what did I find? Forty Nife cells in first-class condition, stores of food, a radio-sonde balloon and a hydrogen cylinder for inflating the balloon. I had expected to find the Nife cells – Kinnaird, here, has told us that there were a good many reserves, but Nife cells won't be destroyed in a fire. Buckled and bent a bit, but not destroyed. I hadn't expected to find the other items of equipment, but they made everything clear.

'The killer had had bad luck on two counts – being found out and with the weather. The weather really put the crimp on all his plans. The idea was that when conditions were favourable he'd send the films up into the sky attached to a radio-sonde balloon which could be swept up by a

Russian plane: snatching a falling capsule out of the sky is very tricky indeed; snaring a stationary balloon is dead easy. The relatively unused Nife cells our friend used for keeping in radio touch with his pals to let them know when the weather had cleared and when he was going to send the balloon up. There is no privacy on the air-waves, so he used a special code; when he no longer had any need for it he destroyed the code by the only safe method of destruction in the Arctic – fire. I found scores of pieces of charred paper imbedded in the walls of one of the huts where the wind had carried them from the met. office after our friend had thrown the ashes away.

'The killer also made sure that only those few worn-out Nife cells were used to send the S. O. S.s and to contact the *Dolphin*. By losing contact with us so frequently, and by sending such a blurred transmission, he tried to delay our arrival here so as to give the weather a chance to clear up and let him fly off his balloon. Incidentally you may have heard radio reports – it was in all the British newspapers – that Russian as well as American and British planes scoured this area immediately after the fire. The British and Americans were looking for Zebra: the Russians were looking for a radio-sonde balloon. So was the ice-breaker *Dvina* when it tried to smash its way through here a few days ago. But there have been no more Russian planes: our friend radioed *his* friends to say that there was no hope of the weather clearing, that the *Dolphin* had arrived and that they would have to take the films back with them on the submarine.'

'One moment, Dr. Carpenter,' Swanson interrupted in a careful sort of voice. 'Are you saying that those films are aboard this ship now?'

'I'll be very much surprised if they aren't, Commander. The other attempt to delay us, of course, was by making a direct attack on the *Dolphin* itself. When it became known that the *Dolphin* was to make an attempt to reach Zebra, orders went through to Scotland to cripple the ship. Red Clydeside is no more red than any other maritime centre in Britain, but you'll find Communists in practically every shipyard in the country – and, more often than not, their mates don't know what they are. There was no intention, of course, of causing any fatal accident – and, as far as whoever was responsible for leaving the tube doors open was concerned, there was no reason why there should be. International espionage in peacetime shuns violence – which is why our friend here is going to be very unpopular with his masters. Like Britain or America, they'll adopt any legitimate or illegitimate tactic to gain their espionage end – but they stop short of murder, just as we do. Murder was no part of the Soviet plan.'

'Who is it, Dr. Carpenter?' Jeremy said very quietly. 'For God's sake, who is it? There's nine of us here and – do you *know* who it is?'

'I know. And only six, not nine, can be under suspicion. The ones who kept radio watches after the disaster. Captain Folsom and the two Harringtons here were completely immobilised. We have the word of all of you for that. So that, Jeremy, just leaves yourself, Kinnaird, Dr. Jolly, Hassard, Naseby and Hewson. Murder for gain, and high treason. There's only one answer for that. The trial will be over the day it begins: three weeks later it will all be over. You're a very clever man, my friend. You're more than that, you're brilliant. But I'm afraid it's the end of the road for you, Dr. Jolly.'

They didn't get it. For long seconds they didn't get it. They were too shocked, too stunned. They'd heard my words all right, but the meaning hadn't registered immediately. But it was beginning to register now for like marionettes under the guidance of a master puppeteer they all slowly turned their heads and stared at Jolly. Jolly himself rose slowly to his feet and took two paces towards me, his eyes wide, his face shocked, his mouth working.

'Me?' His voice was low and hoarse and unbelieving. '*Me?* Are you – are you mad, Dr. Carpenter? In the name of God, man——'

I hit him. I don't know why I hit him, a crimson haze seemed to blur my vision, and Jolly was staggering back to crash on the deck, holding both hands to smashed lips and nose, before I could realise what I had done. I think if I had had a knife or a gun in my hand then, I would have killed him. I would have killed him the way I would have killed a fer-de-lance, a black widow spider or any other such dark and evil and deadly thing, without thought or compunction or mercy. Gradually the haze cleared from my eyes. No one had stirred. No one had stirred an inch. Jolly pushed himself painfully to his knees and then his feet and collapsed heavily in his seat by the table. He was holding a blood-soaked handkerchief to his face. There was utter silence in the room.

'My brother, Jolly,' I said. 'My brother and all the dead men on Zebra. Do you know what I hope?' I said. 'I hope that something goes wrong with the hangman's rope and that you take a long, long time to die.'

He took the handkerchief from his mouth.

'You're a crazy man,' he whispered between smashed and already puffing lips. 'You don't know what you are saying.'

'The jury at the Old Bailey will be the best judge of that. I've been on to you now, Jolly, for almost exactly sixty hours.'

'What did you say?' Swanson demanded. 'You've known for sixty hours!'

'I knew I'd have to face your wrath some time or other, Commander,' I said. Unaccountably, I was beginning to feel very tired, weary and heart-sick of the whole business. 'But if you had known who he was you'd

have locked him up straightaway. You said so in so many words. I
wanted to see where the trail led to in Britain, who his associates and
contacts would be. I had splendid visions of smashing a whole spy ring.
But I'm afraid the trail is cold. It ends right here. Please hear me out.

'Tell me, did no one think it strange that when Jolly came staggering
out of his hut when it caught fire that he should have collapsed and
remained that way? Jolly claimed that he had been asphyxiated. Well,
he wasn't asphyxiated inside the hut because he managed to come out
under his own steam. Then he collapsed. Curious. Fresh air invariably
revives people. But not Jolly. He's a special breed. He wanted to make it
clear to everyone that he had nothing to do with the fire. Just to drive
home the point, he has repeatedly emphasised that he is not a man of
action. If he isn't, then I've never met one.'

'You can hardly call that proof of guilt,' Swanson interrupted.

'I'm not adducing evidence,' I said wearily. 'I'm merely introducing
pointers. Pointer number two. You, Naseby, felt pretty bad about your
failure to wake up your two friends, Flanders and Bryce. You could have
shaken them for an hour and not woken them up. Jolly, here, used either
ether or chloroform to lay them out. This was after he had killed Major
Halliwell and the three others; but before he started getting busy with
matches. He realised that if he burnt the place down there might be a
long, long wait before rescue came and he was going to make damned
certain that he wasn't going to go hungry. If the rest of you had died from
starvation – well, that was just your bad luck. But Flanders and Bryce lay
between him and the food. Didn't it strike you as very strange, Naseby,
that your shouting and shaking had no effect? The only reason could be
that they had been drugged – and only one man had access to drugs.
Also, you said that both Hewson and yourself felt pretty groggy. No
wonder. It was a pretty small hut and the chloroform or ether fumes had
reached and affected Hewson and yourself – normally you'd have smelt
it on waking up, but the stink of burning diesel obliterates every other
smell. Again, I know this is not proof of any kind.

'Third pointer. I asked Captain Folsom this morning who had given
the orders for the dead men to be put in the lab. He said he had. But, he
remembered, it was Jolly's suggestion to him. Something learnedly
medical about helping the morale of the survivors by putting the charred
corpses out of sight.

'Fourth pointer. Jolly said that *how* the fire started was unimportant.
A crude attempt to side-track me. Jolly knew as well as I did that it was
all-important. I suppose, by the way, Jolly, that you deliberately jammed
all the fire-extinguishers you could before you started the fire. About that
fire, Commander. Remember you were a bit suspicious of Hewson, here,

because he said the fuel drums hadn't started exploding until he was on his way to the main bunkhouse. He was telling the truth. There were no fewer than four drums in the fuel stores that didn't explode – the ones Jolly, here, used to pour against the huts to start the fire. How am I doing Dr. Jolly?'

'It's all a nightmare,' he said very quietly. 'It's a nightmare. Before God, I know nothing of any of this.'

'Pointer number five. For some reason that is unclear to me Jolly wanted to delay the *Dolphin* on its return trip. He could best do this, he reckoned, if Bolton and Brownell, the two very sick men still left out on the station could be judged to be too sick to be transferred to the *Dolphin*. The snag was, there were two other doctors around who might say that they *were* fit to be transferred. So he tried, with a fair measure of success, to eliminate us.

'First Benson. Didn't it strike you as strange, Commander, that the request for the survivors to be allowed to attend the funeral of Grant and Lieutenant Mills should have come from Naseby in the first place, then Kinnaird? Jolly, as the senior man of the party with Captain Folsom, here, temporarily unfit, was the obvious man to make the approach – but he didn't want to go calling too much attention to himself. Doubtless by dropping hints, he engineered it so that someone else should do it for him. Now Jolly had noticed how glass-smooth and slippery the ice-banked sides of the sail were and he made a point of seeing that Benson went up the rope immediately ahead of him. You must remember it was almost pitch dark – just light enough for Jolly to make out the vague outline of Benson's head from the wash of light from the bridge as it cleared the top of the rail. A swift outward tug on the rope and Benson overbalanced. It seemed that he had fallen on top of Jolly. But only seemed. The loud sharp crack I heard a fraction of a second after Benson's body struck was not caused by his head hitting the ice – it was caused by Jolly, here, trying to kick his head off. Did you hurt your toes much, Jolly?'

'You're mad,' he said mechanically. 'this is utter nonsense. Even if it wasn't nonsense, you couldn't prove a word of it.'

'We'll see. Jolly claimed that Benson fell on top of him. He even flung himself on the ice and cracked his head to give some verisimilitude to his story – our pal never misses any of the angles. I felt the slight bump on his head. But he wasn't laid out. He was faking. He recovered just that little bit too quickly and easily when he got back to the sick-bay. And it was then that he made his first mistake, the mistake that put me on to him – and should have put me on guard for an attack against myself. You were there, Commander.'

'I've missed everything else,' Swanson said bitterly. 'Do you want me to spoil a hundred per cent record?'

'When Jolly came to he saw Benson lying there. All he could see of him was a blanket and a big gauze pack covering the back of his head. As far as Jolly was concerned, it could have been anybody – it had been pitch dark when the accident occurred. But what did he say? I remember his exact words. He said: 'Of course, of course. Yes that's it. He fell on top of me, didn't he?' *He never thought to ask who it was* – the natural, the inevitable question in the circumstances. But Jolly didn't have to ask. He knew.'

'He knew.' Swanson stared at Jolly with cold bleak eyes and there was no doubt in his mind now about Jolly. 'You have it to rights, Dr. Carpenter. He knew.'

'And then he had a go at me. Can't prove a thing, of course. But he was there when I asked you where the medical store was, and he no doubt nipped down smartly behind Henry and myself and loosened the latch on the hatch-cover. But he didn't achieve quite the same high degree of success this time. Even so, when we went out to the station next morning he still tried to stop Brownell and Bolton from being transferred back to the ship by saying Bolton was too ill. But you overruled him.'

'I was right about Bolton,' Jolly said. He seemed strangely quiet now. 'Bolton died.'

'He died,' I agreed. 'He died because you murdered him and for Bolton alone I can make certain you hang. For a reason I still don't know, Jolly was still determined to stop this ship. Delay it, anyway. I think he wanted only an hour or two's delay. So he proposed to start a small fire, nothing much, just enough to cause a small scare and have the reactor shut down temporarily. As the site of his fire he chose the machinery space – the one place in the ship where he could casually let something drop and where it would lie hidden, for hours if need be, among the maze of pipes down there. In the sick-bay he concocted some type of delayed action chemical fuse which would give off plenty of smoke but very little flame – there are a dozen combinations of acids and chemicals that can bring this about and our friend will be a highly-trained expert well versed in all of them. Now all Jolly wanted was an excuse to pass through the engine-room when it would be nice and quiet and virtually deserted. In the middle of the night. He fixed this too. He can fix anything. He is a very, very clever man indeed is our pal here; he's also an utterly ruthless fiend.

'Late on the evening of the night before the fire the good healer here made a round of his patients. I went with him. One of the men he treated was Bolton in the nucleonics lab. – and, of course, to get to the nucleonics lab. you have to pass through the engine-room. There was an enlisted man watching over the patients and Jolly left special word that he was to be called at any hour if Bolton became any worse. He was called. I checked with the engine-room staff after the fire. The engineer officer was on watch and two others were in the manœuvring-room but an engineman carrying out a routine lubrication job saw him passing through the engine-room about 1.30 a.m. in answer to a call from the man watching over the patients. He took the opportunity to drop his little chemical fuse as he was passing by the machinery space. What he didn't know was that his little toy lodged on or near the oil-saturated lagging on the housing of the starboard turbo-generator and that when it went off it would generate sufficient heat to set the lagging on fire.'

Swanson looked at Jolly, bleakly and for a long time, then turned to me and shook his head. 'I can't wear that, Dr. Carpenter. This phone call because a patient just happens to turn sick. Jolly is not the man to leave *anything* to chance.

'He isn't,' I agreed. 'He didn't. Up in the refrigerator in the sick-bay I have an exhibit for the Old Bailey. A sheet of aluminimum foil liberally covered with Jolly's fingerprints. Smeared on this foil is the remains of a salve. That foil was what Jolly had bandaged on to Bolton's burnt forearm that night, just after he had given him pain-killing shots – Bolton was suffering very badly. But before Jolly put the salve on the foil he spread on something else first – a layer of sodium chloride – common or garden household salt. Jolly knew that the drugs he had given Bolton would keep him under for three or four hours; he also knew that by the time Bolton had regained consciousness body heat would have thinned the salve and brought the salt into contact with the raw flesh on the forearm. Bolton, he knew, when he came out from the effects of the drugs, would come out screaming in agony. Can you imagine what it must have been like: the whole forearm a mass of raw flesh – and covered with salt? When he died soon after, he died from shock. Our good healer here – a lovable little lad, isn't he?

'Well, that's Jolly. Incidentally, you can discount most of the gallant doctor's heroism during the fire – although he was understandably as anxious as any of us that we survive. The first time he went into the engine-room it was too damned hot and uncomfortable for his liking so he just lay down on the floor and let someone carry him for'ard to where the fresh air was. Later——'

'He'd his mask off,' Hansen objected.

'He took it off. *You* can hold your breath for ten or fifteen seconds – don't you think Jolly can too? Later on, when he was performing his heroics in the engine-room it was because conditions there were better, conditions outside were worse – and because by going into the engine-room he was entitled to a closed-circuit breathing set. Jolly got more clean air last night than any of us. He doesn't mind if he causes someone to die screaming his head off in agony – but he himself isn't going to suffer the slightest degree of hardship. Not if he can help it. Isn't that so, Jolly?'

He didn't answer.

'Where are the films, Jolly?'

'I don't know what you are talking about,' he said in a quiet toneless voice. 'Before God, my hands are clean.'

'How about your fingerprints on that foil with the salt on it?'

'Any doctor can make a mistake.'

'My God! Mistake! Where are they, Jolly – the films?'

'For God's sake leave me alone,' he said tiredly.

'Have it your own way.' I looked at Swanson. 'Got some nice secure place where you can lock this character up?'

'I certainly have,' Swanson said grimly. 'I'll conduct him there in person.'

'No one's conducting anyone anywhere,' Kinnaird said. He was looking at me and I didn't care very much for the way he was looking at me. I didn't care very much either for what he held in his hand, a very nasty looking Luger. It was cradled in his fist as if it had grown there and it was pointing straight between my eyes.

13

'Clever, clever counter-espionage, Carpenter,' Dr. Jolly murmured. 'How swiftly the fortunes of war change, old boy. But you shouldn't be surprised really. You haven't found out anything that actually matters, but surely you should have found out enough to realise that you are operating out of your class. Please don't try anything foolish. Kinnaird is one of the finest pistol shots I have ever known – and you will observe how strategically he's placed so that everyone in the room is covered.'

He delicately patted his still-bleeding mouth with a handkerchief, rose, went behind me and ran his hands quickly down my clothes.

'My word,' he said. 'Not even carrying a gun. You really are unprepared, Carpenter. Turn round, will you, so that your back is to Kinnaird's gun?'

I turned round. He smiled pleasantly then hit me twice across the face with all his strength, first with the back of his right hand and then with the back of the left. I staggered, but didn't fall down. I could taste the salt of blood.

'Can't even call it regrettable loss of temper,' Jolly said with satisfaction. 'Did it deliberately and with malice aforethought. Enjoyed it, too.'

'So Kinnaird was the killer,' I said slowly, thickly. 'He was the man with the gun?'

'Wouldn't want to take all the credit, mate,' Kinnaird said modestly. 'Let's say we sorted them out fifty-fifty.'

'*You* were the one who went out with the monitor to find the capsule.' I nodded. 'That's why you got your face so badly frost-bitten.'

'Got lost,' Kinnaird admitted. 'Thought I'd never find the damned station again.'

'Jolly and Kinnaird,' Jeremy said wonderingly. 'Jolly and Kinnaird. Your own mates. You two filthy murderous——'

'Be quiet,' Jolly ordered. 'Kinnaird, don't bother answering questions. Unlike Carpenter here, I take no pleasure in outlining my *modus operandi* and explaining at length how clever I've been. As you observed, Carpenter, I'm a man of action. Commander Swanson, get on that phone there, call up your control room, order your ship to surface and steam north.'

'You're becoming too ambitious, Jolly,' Swanson said calmly. 'You can't hi-jack a submarine.'

'Kinnaird,' Jolly said. 'Point your gun at Hansen's stomach. When I reach the count of five, pull the trigger. One, two, three——'

Swanson half-raised a hand in acknowledgment of defeat, crossed to the wall-phone, gave the necessary orders, hung up and came back to stand beside me. He looked at me without either respect or admiration. I looked round all the other people in the room. Jolly, Hansen and Rawlings standing, Zabrinski sitting on a chair by himself with the now disregarded copy of the *Dolphin Daze* on his knees, all the others sitting round the table, Kinnaird well clear of them, the gun very steady in his hand. So very steady. No one seemed to be contemplating any heroics. For the most part everyone was too shocked, too dazed, to think of anything.

'Hi-jacking a nuclear submarine is an intriguing prospect – and no doubt would be a highly profitable one, Commander Swanson,' Jolly said. 'But I know my limitations. No, old top, we shall simply be leaving you. Not very many miles from here is a naval vessel with a helicopter on its after deck. In a little while, Commander, you will send a wireless message on a certain frequency giving our position: the helicopter will pick us up. And even if your crippled engine would stand the strain I wouldn't advise you to come chasing after that ship with ideas about torpedoing it or anything of that dramatic ilk. Apart from the fact that you wouldn't like to be responsible for triggering off a nuclear war, you couldn't catch it, anyway. You won't even be able to see the ship, Commander – and if you did it wouldn't matter, anyway. It has no nationality markings.'

'Where are the films?' I asked.

'They're already aboard that naval vessel.'

'They're *what?*' Swanson demanded. 'How in hell's name can they be?'

'Sorry and all that, old boy. I repeat that unlike Carpenter, here, I don't go around shooting off my mouth. A professional, my dear captain, *never* gives information about his methods.'

'So you get off with it,' I said bitterly. My mouth felt thick and swollen.

'Don't see what's to stop us. Crimes don't always come home to roost, you know.'

'Eight men murdered,' I said wonderingly. 'Eight men. You can stand there and cheerfully admit that you are responsible for the deaths of eight men.'

'Cheerfully?' he said consideringly. 'No, not cheerfully. I'm a professional, and a professional never kills unnecessarily. but this time it was necessary. That's all.'

'That's the second time you've used the word "professional",' I said slowly. 'I was wrong on one theory. You weren't just suborned after the Zebra team had been picked. You've been at this game a long time – you're too good not to have been.'

'Fifteen years, old lad,' Jolly said calmly. 'Kinnaird and I – we were the best team in Britain. Our usefulness in that country, unfortunately, is over. I should imagine that our – um – exceptional talents can be employed elsewhere.'

'You admit to all those murders?' I asked.

He looked at me in sudden cold speculation. 'A damned funny question, Carpenter. Of course. I've told you. Why?'

'And do you, Kinnaird?'

He looked at me in bleak suspicion. 'Why ask?'

'You answer my question and I'll answer yours.' At the corner of my range of vision I could see Jolly looking at me with narrowed eyes. He was very sensitive to atmosphere, he knew there was something off-key.

'You know damn' well what I did, mate,' Kinnaird said coldly.

'So there we have it. In the presence of no less than twelve witnesses, you both confess to murder. You shouldn't have done that, you know. I'll answer your question, Kinnaird. I wanted to have an oral confession from you because, apart from the sheet of aluminium foil and something I'll mention in a minute, we have no actual proof at all against either of you. But now we have your confessions. Your great talents are not going to be used in any other sphere, I'm afraid. You'll never see that helicopter or that naval vessel. You'll both die jerking on the end of a rope.'

'What rubbish is this?' Jolly asked contemptuously. But there was worry under the contempt. 'What last-minute despairing bluff are you trying to pull, Carpenter?'

I ignored his question. I said: 'I've been on to Kinnaird, here, for some sixty hours also, Jolly. But I had to play it this way. Without letting you gain what appeared to be the upper hand you would never have admitted to the crimes. But now you have.'

'Don't fall for it, old lad,' Jolly said to Kinnaird. 'It's just some desperate bluff. He never had any idea that you were in on this.'

'When I knew you were one of the killers,' I said to Jolly, 'I was almost certain Kinnaird had to be another. You shared the same cabin and unless Kinnaird had been sapped or drugged he had to be in on it. He was neither. He was in on it. That door wasn't jammed when Naseby ran round to the radio room to warn you – the two of you were leaning all your weight against it to give the impression that it had been closed for hours and that ice had formed.

'By the same token, young Grant, the assistant radio operator, was in cahoots with you – or he wasn't. If he wasn't, he would have to be silenced. He wasn't. So you silenced him. After I'd caught on to the two of you I had a good look at Grant. I went out and dug him up from where we'd buried him. Rawlings and I. I found a great big bruise at the base of his neck. He surprised you in something, or he woke when you knifed or shot one of Major Halliwell's men, and you laid him out. You didn't bother killing him, you were about to set the hut on fire and incinerate him, so killing would have been pointless. But you didn't reckon on Captain Folsom, here, going in and bringing him out – alive.

'That was most damnably awkward for you, wasn't it, Jolly? He was unconscious but when and if he recovered consciousness he could blow the whole works on you. But you couldn't get at him to finish him off, could you? The bunkhouse was full of people, most of them suffering so severely that sleep was impossible for them. When we arrived on the scene you got desperate. Grant was showing signs of regaining consciousness. You took a chance, but not all that much of a chance. Remember how surprised I was to find that you had used up all my morphine? Well, I *was* surprised then. But not now. I know now where it went. You gave him an injection of morphine – and you made damn' sure the hypodermic had a lethal dose. Am I correct?'

'You're cleverer than I thought you were,' he said calmly. 'Maybe I have misjudged you a little. But it still makes no difference, old boy.'

'I wonder. If I'd known about Kinnaird so long why do you think I allowed a situation to develop where you could apparently turn the tables?'

'Apparently is not the word you want. And the answer to your question is easy. You didn't know Kinnaird *had* a gun.'

'No?' I looked at Kinnaird. 'Are you sure that thing works?'

'Don't come that old stuff with me, mate,' Kinnaird said in contempt.

'I just wondered,' I said mildly. 'I thought perhaps the petrol in the tractor's tank might have removed all the lubricating oil.'

Jolly came close to me, his face tight and cold. 'You *knew* about this? What goes on, Carpenter?'

'It was actually Commander Swanson, here, who found the gun in the tank,' I said. 'You had to leave it there because you knew you'd all be getting a good clean-up and medical examination when we got you on board and it would have been bound to be discovered. But a murderer – a professional, Jolly – will never part with his gun unless he is compelled to. I knew if you got the slightest chance you would go back for it. So I put it back in the tank.'

'The hell you did!' Swanson was as nearly angry as I'd ever seen him. 'Forgot to tell me, didn't you?'

'I must have done. That was after I'd cottoned on to you, Jolly. I wasn't *absolutely* sure you had a partner, but I knew if you had it must be Kinnaird. So I put the gun back there in the middle of the night and I made good and certain that you, Jolly, didn't get the chance to go anywhere near the tractor shed at any time. But the gun vanished that following morning when everyone was out sampling the fresh air. So then I knew you had an accomplice. But the real reason for planting that gun, of course, is that without it you'd never have talked. But now you have talked and it's all finished. Put up that gun, Kinnaird.'

'I'm afraid your bluff's run out, mate.' The gun was pointing directly at my face.

'Your last chance, Kinnaird. Please pay attention to what I am saying. Put up that gun or you will be requiring the services of a doctor within twenty seconds.'

He said something, short and unprintable. I said: 'It's on your own head. Rawlings, you know what to do.'

Every head turned towards Rawlings who was standing leaning negligently against a bulkhead, his hands crossed lightly in front of him. Kinnaird looked too, the Luger following the direction of his eyes. A gun barked, the sharp flat crack of a Mannlicher-Schoenauer, Kinnaird screamed and his gun spun from his smashed hand. Zabrinski, holding my automatic in one hand and his copy of the *Dolphin Daze* – now with a neat charred hole through the middle – in the other, regarded his handiwork admiringly then turned to me. 'Was that how you wanted it done, Doc?'

'That was exactly how I wanted it done, Zabrinski. Thank you very much. A first-class job.'

'A first-class job.' Rawlings sniffed. He retrieved the fallen Luger and pointed it in Jolly's general direction. 'At four feet even Zabrinski couldn't miss.' He dug into a pocket, pulled out a roll of bandage and tossed it to Jolly. 'We kinda thought we might be having to use this so we came prepared. Dr. Carpenter said your pal here would be requiring the service of a doctor. He is. You're a doctor. Get busy.'

'Do it yourself,' Jolly snarled. No 'old boy,' no 'old top.' The *bonhomie* was gone and gone for ever.

Rawlings looked at Swanson and said woodenly: 'Permission to hit Dr. Jolly over the head with this little old gun, sir?'

'Permission granted,' Swanson said grimly. But no further persuasion was necessary. Jolly cursed and started ripping the cover off the bandage.

For almost a minute there was silence in the room while we watched Jolly carry out a rough, ready and far from gentle repair job on Kinnaird's hand. Then Swanson said slowly: 'I still don't understand how in the devil Jolly got rid of the film.'

'It was easy. Ten minutes thinking and you'd get it. They waited until we had cleared the ice-cap then they took the films, shoved them in a waterproof bag, attached a yellow dye marker to the bag then pumped it out through the garbage disposal unit in the galley. Remember, they'd been on a tour of the ship and seen it – although the suggestion was probably radioed them by a naval expert. I had Rawlings posted on watch in the early hours of this morning and he saw Kinnaird go into the galley about half past four. Maybe he just wanted a ham sandwich, I don't know. But Rawlings says he had the bag and marker with him when he sneaked in and empty hands when he came out. The bag would float to the surface and the marker stain thousands of square yards of water. The naval ship up top would have worked out our shortest route from Zebra to Scotland and would be within a few miles of our point of exit from the ice-pack. It could probably have located it without the helicopter: but the chopper made it dead certain.

'Incidentally, I was being rather less than accurate when I said I didn't know the reason for Jolly's attempts to delay us. I knew all along. He'd been told that the ship couldn't reach our exit point until such and such a time and that it was vital to delay us until then. Jolly, here, even had the effrontery to check with me what time we would be emerging from the ice-pack.'

Jolly looked up from Kinnaird's hand and his face was twisted in a mask of malevolence.

'You win, Carpenter. So you win. All along the line. But you lost out in the only thing that really mattered. They got the films – the films showing the location, as you said, of nearly every missile base in America. And that was all that mattered. Ten million pounds couldn't buy that information. But we got it.' He bared his teeth in a savage smile. 'We may have lost out, Carpenter, but we're professionals. We did our job.'

'They got the films, all right,' I acknowledged. 'And I'd give a year's salary to see the faces of the men who develop them. Listen carefully, Jolly. Your main reason in trying to cripple Benson and myself was not so much that you could have the say-so on Bolton's health and so delay us: your main reason, your overriding reason, was that you wanted to be the only doctor on the ship so that it could only be you who would carry out the X-ray on Zabrinski's ankle here and remove the plaster cast. Literally everything hinged on that: basically, nothing else mattered. That was why you took such a desperate chance in crippling me when you heard me say I intended to X-ray Zabrinski's ankle the following morning. That was the one move you made that lacked the hall-mark of class – of a professional – but then I think you were close to panic. You were lucky.

'Anyway, you removed the plaster cast two mornings ago and also the films which you had hidden there in oilskin paper when you'd fixed the plaster on to Zabrinski's leg the first night we arrived in Zebra. A perfect hiding-place. You could always, of course, have wrapped them in bandages covering survivors' burns, but that would be too dicey. The cast was brilliant.

'Unfortunately for you and your friends I had removed the original plaster during the previous night, extracted the films from the oiled paper and replaced them with others. That, incidentally, is the second piece of evidence I have on you. There are two perfect sets of prints on the leaders of the satellite films – yours and Kinnaird's. Along with the salt-covered aluminium foil and the confession freely made in front of witnesses that guarantees you both the eight o'clock walk to the gallows. The gallows and failure, Jolly. You weren't even a professional. Your friends will never see those films.'

Mouthing soundless words through smashed lips, his face masked in madness and completely oblivious to the two guns, Jolly flung himself at me. He had taken two steps and two only when Rawlings's gun caught him, not lightly, on the side of the head. He crashed to the floor as if the Brooklyn bridge had fallen on top of him. Rawlings surveyed him dispassionately.

'Never did a day's work that gave me profounder satisfaction,' he said conversationally. 'Except, perhaps, those pictures I took with Dr. Benson's camera to give Dr. Carpenter, here, some negatives to shove inside that oiled paper.'

'Pictures of what?' Swanson asked curiously.

Rawlings grinned happily. 'All those pin-ups in Doc Benson's sickbay. Yogi Bear, Donald Duck, Pluto, Popeye, Snow-White and the seven dwarfs – you name it, I got it. The lot. Each a guaranteed work of art – and in glorious Technicolor.' He smiled a beatific smile. 'Like Doc Carpenter, here, I'd give a year's pay to see their faces when they get around to developing those negatives.'

The Eagle
has Landed

Jack Higgins

AUTHOR'S NOTE

At precisely one o'clock on the morning of Saturday 6 November 1943, Heinrich Himmler, Reichsführer of the SS and Chief of State Police, received a simple message. *The Eagle has landed.* It meant that a small force of German paratroops were at the moment safely in England and poised to snatch the British Prime Minister, Winston Churchill, from the Norfolk country house near the sea, where he was spending a quiet weekend. This book is an attempt to recreate the events surrounding that astonishing exploit. At least fifty per cent of it is documented historical fact. The reader must decide for himself how much of the rest is a matter of speculation, or fiction. . . .

1

Someone was digging a grave in one corner of the cemetery as I went in through the lychgate. I remember that quite clearly because it seemed to set the scene for nearly everything that followed.

Five or six rooks lifted out of the beech trees at the west end of the church like bundles of black rags, calling angrily to each other as I threaded my way between the tombstones and approached the grave, turning up the collar of my trenchcoat against the driving rain.

Whoever was down there was talking to himself in a low voice. It was impossible to catch what he was saying. I moved to one side of the pile of fresh earth, dodging another spadeful, and peered in. 'Nasty morning for it.'

He looked up, resting on his spade, an old, old man in a cloth cap and shabby, mud-stained suit, a grain sack draped across his shoulders. His cheeks were sunken and hollow, covered with a grey stubble, and his eyes full of moisture and quite vacant.

I tried again. 'The rain,' I said.

Some kind of understanding dawned. He glanced up at the sombre sky and scratched his chin. 'Worse before it gets better, I'd say.'

'It must make it difficult for you,' I said. There was at least six inches of water swilling about in the bottom.

He poked at the far side of the grave with his spade and it split wide open, like something rotten bursting, earth showering down. 'Could be worse. They put so many in this little boneyard over the years, people aren't planted in earth any more. They're buried in human remains.'

He laughed, exposing toothless gums, then bent down, scrabbled in the earth at his feet and held up a finger-bone. 'See what I mean?'

The appeal, even for the professional writer, of life in all its infinite variety, definitely has its limits on occasion and I decided it was time to move on. 'I have got it right? This is a Catholic church?'

'All Romans here,' he said. 'Always have been.'

'Then maybe you can help me. I'm looking for a grave or perhaps even a monument inside the church. Gascoigne – Charles Gascoigne. A sea captain.'

'Never heard of him,' he said. 'And I've been sexton here forty-one years. When was he buried?'

'Around sixteen eighty-five.'

His expression didn't alter. He said calmly, 'Ah, well then, before my time, you see. Father Vereker – now he might know something.'

'Will he be inside?'

'There or the presbytery. Other side of the trees behind the wall.'

At that moment, for some reason or other, the rookery in the beech trees above our heads erupted into life, dozens of rooks wheeling in the rain, filling the air with their clamour. The old man glanced up and hurled the finger-bone into the branches. And then he said a very strange thing.

'Noisy bastards!' he called. 'Get back to Leningrad.'

I'd been about to turn away, but paused, intrigued. 'Leningrad?' I said. 'What makes you say that?'

'That's where they come from. Starlings, too. They've been ringed in Leningrad and they turn up here in October. Too cold for them over there in the winter.'

'Is that so?' I said.

He had become quite animated now, took half a cigarette from behind his ear and stuck it in his mouth. 'Cold enough to freeze the balls off a brass monkey over there in the winter. A lot of Germans died at Leningrad during the war. Not shot or anything. Just froze to death.'

By now I was quite fascinated. I said, 'Who told you all that?'

'About the birds?' he said, and suddenly he changed completely, his face suffused by a kind of sly cunning. 'Why, Werner told me. He knew all about birds.'

'And who was Werner?'

'Werner?' He blinked several times, the vacant look appearing on his face again, though whether genuine or simulated it was impossible to tell. 'He was a good lad, Werner. A good lad. They shouldn't have done that to him.'

He leaned over his spade and started to dig again, dismissing me completely. I stayed there for a moment longer, but it was obvious that he had nothing more to say, so, reluctantly, because it had certainly sounded as if it might be a good story, I turned and worked my way through the tombstones to the main entrance.

I paused inside the porch. There was a notice-board on the wall in some sort of dark wood, the lettering in faded gold paint. *Church of St Mary and All the Saints, Studley Constable* across the top and, underneath, the times for Mass and Confession. At the bottom it said *Father Philip Vereker, S.J.*

The door was oak and very old, held together by iron bands, studded with bolts. The handle was a bronze lion's head with a large ring in its mouth and the ring had to be turned to one side before the door opened, which it did finally with a slight, eerie creaking.

I had expected darkness and gloom inside, but instead, found what was in effect a medieval cathedral in miniature, flooded with light and astonishingly spacious. The nave arcades were superb, great Norman pillars soaring up to an incredible wooden roof, richly carved with an assortment of figures, human and animal, which were really in quite remarkable condition. A row of round, clerestory windows on either side at roof level were responsible for a great deal of the light which had so surprised me.

There was a beautiful stone font and on the wall beside it, a painted board listed all the priests who had served over the years, starting with a Rafe de Courcey in 1132 and ending with Vereker again, who had taken over in 1943.

Beyond was a small, dark chapel, candles flickering in front of an image of the Virgin Mary that seemed to float there in the half-light. I walked past it and down the centre aisle between the pews. It was very quiet, only the ruby light of the sanctuary lamp, a fifteenth-century Christ high on his cross down by the altar, rain drumming against the high windows.

There was a scrape of a foot on stone behind me and a dry, firm voice said, 'Can I help you?'

I turned and found a priest standing in the entrance of the Lady Chapel, a tall, gaunt man in a faded black cassock. He had iron-grey hair cropped close to the skull and the eyes were set deep in their sockets as if he had been recently ill, an impression heightened by the tightness of the skin across the cheekbones. It was a strange face. Soldier or scholar, this man could have been either, but that didn't surprise me, remembering from the notice board that he was a Jesuit. But it was also a face that lived with pain as a constant companion if I was any judge and, as he came forward, I saw that he leaned heavily on a blackthorn stick and dragged his left foot.

'Father Vereker?'

'That's right.'

'I was talking to the old man out there, the sexton.'

'Ah, yes, Laker Armsby.'

'If that's his name. He thought you might be able to help me.' I held out my hand. 'My name's Higgins, by the way. Jack Higgins. I'm a writer.'

He hesitated slightly before shaking hands, but only because he had to switch the blackthorn from his right hand to his left. Even so, there was a definite reserve, or so it seemed to me. 'And how can I help you, Mr. Higgins?'

'I'm doing a series of articles for an American magazine,' I said. 'Historical stuff. I was over at St. Margaret's at Cley, yesterday.'

'A beautiful church.' He sat down in the nearest pew. 'Forgive me, I tire rather easily these days.'

'There's a table tomb in the churchyard there,' I went on. 'Perhaps you know it?' "To James Greeve ..."'

He cut in on me instantly. '... who was assistant to Sir Cloudesley Shovel in burning ye ships in Ye Port of Tripoly in "Barbary, January fourteenth, sixteen seventy-six."' He showed that he could smile. 'But that's a famous inscription in these parts.'

'According to my researches, when Greeve was Captain of the *Orange Tree* he had a mate called Charles Gascoigne who later became a captain in the navy. He died of an old wound in sixteen eighty-three and it seems Greeve had him brought up to Cley to be buried.'

'I see,' he said politely, but without any particular interest. In fact, there was almost a hint of impatience in his voice.

'There's no trace of him in Cley churchyard,' I said, 'or in the parish records and I've tried the churches at Wiveton, Glandford and Blakeney with the same result.'

'And you think he might be here?'

'I was going through my notes again and remembered that he'd been raised a Catholic as a boy and it occurred to me that he might have been buried in the faith. I'm staying at the Blakeney Hotel and I was talking to one of the barmen there who told me there was a Catholic church here at Studley Constable. It's certainly an out-of-the-way little place. Took me a good hour to find it.'

'All to no purpose, I'm afraid.' He pushed himself up. 'I've been here at St. Mary's for twenty-eight years now and I can assure you I've never come across any mention of this Charles Gascoigne.'

It had been very much my last chance and I suppose I allowed my disappointment to show, but in any case, I persisted. 'Can you be absolutely sure? What about church records for the period? There might be an entry in the burial register.'

'The local history of this area happens to be a personal interest of mine,' he said with a certain acidity. 'There is not a document connected with this church with which I am not completely familiar and I can assure you that nowhere is there any mention of a Charles Gascoigne. And now, if you'll excuse me. My lunch will be ready.'

As he moved forward, the blackthorn slipped and he stumbled and almost fell. I grabbed his elbow and managed to stand on his left foot. He didn't even wince.

I said, 'I'm sorry, that was damned clumsy of me.'

He smiled for the second time. 'Nothing to hurt, as it happens.' He rapped at the foot with the blackthorn. 'A confounded nuisance, but, as they say, I've learned to live with it.'

It was the kind of remark which required no comment and he obviously wasn't seeking one. We went down the aisle together, slowly because of his foot, and I said, 'A remarkably beautiful church.'

'Yes, we're rather proud of it.' He opened the door for me. 'I'm sorry I couldn't be of more help.'

'That's all right,' I said. 'Do you mind if I have a look around the churchyard while I'm here?'

'A hard man to convince, I see.' But there was no malice in the way he said it. 'Why not? We have some very interesting stones. I'd particularly recommend you to the section at the west end. Early eighteenth-century and obviously done by the same local mason who did similar work at Cley.'

This time he was the one who held out his hand. As I took it, he said, 'You know, I thought your name was familiar. Didn't you write a book on the Ulster troubles last year?'

'That's right,' I said. 'A nasty business.'

'War always is, Mr. Higgins.' His face was bleak. 'Man at his most cruel. Good-day to you.'

He closed the door and I moved into the porch. A strange encounter. I lit a cigarette and stepped into the rain. The sexton had moved on and for the moment I had the churchyard to myself, except for the rooks, of course. *The rooks from Leningrad.* I wondered about that again, then pushed the thought resolutely from my mind. There was work to be done. Not that I had any great hope, after talking to Father Vereker, of finding Charles Gascoigne's tomb, but the truth was there just wasn't anywhere else to look.

I worked my way through methodically, starting at the west end, noticing in my progress the headstones he'd mentioned. They were certainly curious. Sculptured and etched with vivid and rather crude ornaments of bones, skulls, winged hourglasses and archangels. Interesting, but entirely the wrong period for Gascoigne.

It took me an hour and twenty minutes to cover the entire area and at the end of that time I knew I was beaten. For one thing, unlike most country churchyards these days, this one was kept in very decent order. Grass cut, bushes trimmed back, very little that was overgrown or partially hidden from view or that sort of thing.

So, no Charles Gascoigne. I was standing by the newly-dug grave when I finally admitted defeat. The old sexton had covered it with a tarpaulin against the rain and one end had fallen in. I crouched down to pull it back into position and as I started to rise, noticed a strange thing.

A yard or two away, close in to the wall of the church at the base of the tower, there was a flat tombstone set in a mound of green grass. It was early eighteenth-century, an example of the local mason's work I've already mentioned. It had a superb skull and crossbones at its head and was dedicated to a wool merchant named Jeremiah Fuller, his wife and two children. Crouched down as I was, I became aware that there was another slab beneath it.

The Celt in me rises to the top easily and I was filled with a sudden irrational excitement as if conscious that I stood on the threshold of something. I knelt over the tombstone and tried to get my fingers to it, which proved to be rather difficult. But then, quite suddenly, it started to move.

'Come on, Gascoigne,' I said softly. 'Let's be having you.'

The slab slid to one side, tilting on the slope of the mound and all was revealed. I suppose it was one of the most astonishing moments of my life. It was a simple stone, with a German cross at the head – what most people would describe as an iron cross. The inscription beneath it was in German. It read *Hier ruhen Oberstleutnant Kurt Steiner und 13 Deutsche Fallschirmjäger gefallen am 6 November 1943.*

My German is indifferent at the best of times, mainly from lack of use, but it was good enough for this. *Here lies Lieutenant-Colonel Kurt Steiner and 13 German paratroopers, killed in action on the 6th November, 1943.*

I crouched there in the rain, checking my translation carefully but no, I was right, and that didn't make any kind of sense. To start with, I happened to know, as I'd once written an article on the subject, that when the German Military Cemetery was opened at Cannock Chase in Staffordshire in 1967, the remains of the four thousand, nine hundred and twenty-five German servicemen who died in Britain during the First and Second World Wars were transferred there.

Killed in action, the inscription said. No, it was quite absurd. An elaborate hoax on somebody's part. It had to be.

Any further thoughts on the subject were prevented by a sudden outraged cry. 'What in the hell do you think you're doing?'

Father Vereker was hobbling towards me through the tombstones, holding a large black umbrella over his head.

I called cheerfully, 'I think you'll find this interesting, Father. I've made a rather astonishing find.'

As he drew closer, I realised that something was wrong. Something was very wrong indeed, for his face was white with passion and he was shaking with rage. 'How dare you move that stone? Sacrilege – that's the only word for it.'

'All right,' I said. 'I'm sorry about that, but look what I've found underneath.'

'I don't give a damn what you've found underneath. Put it back at once.'

I was beginning to get annoyed myself now. 'Don't be silly. Don't you realise what it says here? If you don't read German then allow me to tell you. "Here lies Lieutenant-Colonel Kurt Steiner and thirteen German paratroopers killed in action sixth November nineteen forty-three." Now don't you find that absolutely bloody fascinating?'

'Not particularly.'

'You mean you've seen it before.'

'No, of course not.' There was something hunted about him now, an edge of desperation to his voice when he added, 'Now will you kindly replace the original stone?'

I didn't believe him, not for a moment. I said, 'Who was he, this Steiner? What was it all about?'

'I've already told you, I haven't the slightest idea,' he said, looking more hunted still.

And then I remembered something. 'You were here in nineteen forty-three, weren't you? That's when you took over the parish. It says so on the board inside the church.'

He exploded, came apart at the seams. 'For the last time, will you replace that stone as you found it?'

'No,' I said. 'I'm afraid I can't do that.'

Strangely enough, he seemed to regain some kind of control of himself at that point. 'Very well,' he said calmly. 'Then you will oblige me by leaving at once.'

There seemed little point in arguing, considering the state of mind he was in, so I said briefly, 'All right, Father, if that's the way you want it.'

I had reached the path when he called, 'And don't come back. If you do I shall call the local police without the slightest hesitation.'

I went out through the lychgate, got into the Peugeot and drove away. His threats didn't worry me. I was too excited for that, too intrigued. Everything about Studley Constable was intriguing. It was one of those places that seem to turn up in North Norfolk and nowhere else. The kind of village that you find by accident one day and can never find again, so that you begin to question whether it ever existed in the first place.

Not that there was very much of it. The church, the old presbytery in its walled garden, fifteen or sixteen cottages of one kind or another scattered along the stream, the old mill with its massive water wheel, the village inn on the opposite side of the green, the Studley Arms.

I pulled into the side of the road beside the stream, lit a cigarette and gave the whole thing a little quiet thought. Father Vereker was lying. He'd seen that stone before, he knew of its significance, of that I was convinced. It was rather ironic when one thought about it. I'd come to

Studley Constable by chance in search of Charles Gascoigne. Instead I'd discovered something vastly more intriguing, a genuine mystery. But what was I going to do about it, that was the thing?

The solution presented itself to me almost instantly in the person of Laker Armsby, the sexton, who appeared from a narrow alley between two cottages. He was still splashed with mud, still had that old grain sack over his shoulders. He crossed the road and entered the Studley Arms and I got out of the Peugeot instantly and went after him.

According to the plate over the entrance, the licensee was one George Henry Wilde. I opened the door and found myself in a stone-flagged corridor with panelled walls. A door to the left stood ajar and there was a murmur of voices, a burst of laughter.

Inside, there was no bar, just a large, comfortable room with an open fire on a stone hearth, several high-backed benches, a couple of wooden tables. There were six or seven customers and none of them young. I'd have said that sixty was about the average age – a pattern that's distressingly common in such rural areas these days.

They were countrymen to the backbone, faces weathered by exposure, tweed caps, gumboots. Three played dominoes watched by two more, an old man sat by the fire playing a mouth-organ softly to himself. They all looked up to consider me with the kind of grave interest close-knit groups always have in strangers.

'Good afternoon,' I said.

Two or three nodded in a cheerful enough way, though one massively-built character with a black beard flecked with grey didn't look too friendly. Laker Armsby was sitting at a table on his own, rolling a cigarette between his fingers laboriously, a glass of ale in front of him. He put the cigarette in his mouth and I moved to his side and offered him a light. 'Hello, there.'

He glanced up blankly and then his face cleared. 'Oh, it's you again. Did you find Father Vereker then?'

I nodded. 'Will you have another drink?'

'I wouldn't say no.' He emptied his glass in a couple of swallows. 'A pint of brown ale would go down very nicely. Georgy!'

I turned and found a short, stocky man in shirt-sleeves standing behind me, presumably the landlord, George Wilde. He seemed about the same age range as the others and was a reasonable enough looking man except for one unusual feature. At some time in his life he'd been shot in the face at close quarters. I'd seen enough gunshot wounds in my time to be certain of that, In his case the bullet had scoured a furrow in his left cheek, obviously taking bone with it as well. His luck was good.

He smiled pleasantly. 'And you, sir?'

I told him I'd have a large vodka and tonic which brought amused looks from the farmers or whatever they were, but that didn't particularly worry me as it happens to be the only alcohol I can drink with any kind of pleasure. Laker Armsby's hand-rolled cigarette hadn't lasted too long so I gave him one of mine which he accepted with alacrity. The drinks came and I pushed his ale across to him.

'How long did you say you'd been sexton up at St. Mary's?'

'Forty-one years.'

He drained his pint glass. I said, 'Here, have another and tell me about Steiner.'

The mouth-organ stopped playing abruptly, all conversation died. Old Laker Armsby stared at me across the top of his glass, that look of sly cunning on his face again. 'Steiner?' he said. 'Why, Steiner was . . .'

George Wilde cut in, reached for the empty glass and ran a cloth over the table. 'Right, sir, time please.'

I looked at my watch. It was two-thirty. I said, 'You've got it wrong. Another half-hour till closing time.'

He picked up my glass of vodka and handed it to me. 'This is a free house, sir, and in a quiet little village like this we generally do as we please without anybody getting too upset about it. If I say I'm closing at two-thirty then two-thirty it is.' He smiled amiably. 'I'd drink up if I were you, sir.'

There was tension in the air that you could cut with a knife. They were all sitting looking at me, hard, flat faces, eyes like stones and the giant with the black beard moved across to the end of the table and leaned on it, glaring at me.

'You heard him,' he said in a low, dangerous voice. 'Now drink up like a good boy and go home, wherever that is.'

I didn't argue because the atmosphere was getting worse by the minute. I drank my vodka and tonic, taking a certain amount of time over it, though whether to prove something to them or myself I'm not certain, then I left.

Strange, but I wasn't angry, just fascinated by the whole incredible affair and by now, of course, I was too far in to draw back. I had to have some answers and it occurred to me that there was a rather obvious way of getting them.

I got into the Peugeot, turned over the bridge and drove up out of the village, passing the church and the presbytery, taking the road to Blakeney. A few hundred yards past the church, I turned the Peugeot into a cart track, left it there and walked back, taking a small Pentax camera with me from the glove compartment of the car.

I wasn't afraid. After all, on one famous occasion I'd been escorted from the Europa Hotel in Belfast to the airport by men with guns in their pockets who'd suggested I got the next plane out for the good of my health and didn't return. But I had and on several occasions; had even got a book out of it.

When I went back to into the churchyard I found the stone to Steiner and his men exactly as I'd left it. I checked the inscription once again and just to make sure I wasn't making a fool of myself, took several photos of it from different angles, then hurried to the church and went inside.

There was a curtain across the base of the tower and I went behind it. Choirboys' scarlet cottas and white surplices hung neatly on a rail, there was an old iron-bound trunk, several bell ropes trailed down through the gloom above and a board on the wall informed the world that on 22 July 1936, a peal of five thousand and fifty-eight changes of Bob Minor was rung at the church. I was interested to note that Laker Armsby was listed as one of the six bell-ringers involved.

Even more interesting was a line of holes cutting across the board which had at some time been filled in with plaster and stained. They continued into the masonry, for all the world like a machine-gun burst, but that was really too outrageous.

What I was after was the burial register and there was no sign of any kind of books or documents there. I went out through the curtain and almost instantly noticed the small door in the wall behind the font. It opened easily enough when I tried the handle and I stepped inside and found myself in what was very obviously the sacristy, a small, oak-panelled room. There was a rack containing a couple of cassocks, several surplices and copes, an oak cupboard and a large, old-fashioned desk.

I tried the cupboard first and struck oil at once. Every kind of ledger possible was in there, stacked neatly on one of the shelves. There were three burial registers and 1943 was in the second one. I leafed through the pages quickly, conscious at once of a feeling of enormous disappointment.

There were two deaths entered during November 1943 and they were both women. I hurriedly worked my way back to the beginning of the year, which didn't take very long, then closed the register and replaced it in the cupboard. So one very obvious avenue was closed to me. If Steiner, whoever he was, had been buried here, then he should have gone into the register. That was an incontrovertible point of English law. So what in the hell did it all mean?

I opened the sacristy door and stepped out, closing it behind me. There were two of them there from the pub. George Wilde and the man with the black beard whom I was disturbed to notice carried a double-barrelled shotgun.

Wilde said gently, 'I did advise you to move on, sir, you must admit that. Now why weren't you sensible?'

The man with the black beard said, 'What in the hell are we waiting for? Let's get this over with.'

He moved with astonishing speed for a man of such size and grabbed hold of the lapels of my trenchcoat. In the same moment the sacristy door opened behind me and Vereker stepped out. God knows where he'd come from, but I was distinctly pleased to see him.

'What on earth's going on here?' he demanded.

Blackbeard said, 'You just leave this to us, Father, we'll handle it.'

'You'll handle nothing, Arthur Seymour,' Vereker said. 'Now step back.'

Seymour stared at him flatly, still hanging on to me. I could have cut him down to size in several different ways, but there didn't seem a great deal of point.

Vereker said again, 'Seymour!' and there was really iron in his voice this time.

Seymour slowly released his grip and Vereker said, 'Don't come back again, Mr. Higgins. It should be obvious to you by now that it wouldn't be in your best interests.'

'A good point.'

I didn't exactly expect a hue and cry, not after Vereker's intervention, but it hardly seemed politic to hang around, so I hurried back to the car at a jog trot. Further consideration of the whole mysterious affair could come later.

I turned into the cart track and found Laker Armsby sitting on the bonnet of the Peugeot rolling a cigarette. He stood up as I approached. 'Ah, there you are,' he said. 'You got away then?'

There was that same look of low cunning on his face again. I took out my cigarettes and offered him one. 'Do you want to know something?' I said. 'I don't think you're anything like as simple as you look.'

He grinned slyly and puffed out smoke in a cloud into the rain. 'How much?'

I knew what he meant instantly, but for the moment, played him along. 'What do you mean, how much?'

'Is it worth to you. To know about Steiner.'

He leaned back against the car looking at me, waiting, so I took out my wallet, extracted a five-pound note and held it up between my fingers. His eyes gleamed and he reached. I pulled back my hand.

'Oh, no. Let's have some answers first.'

'All right, mister. What do you want to know?'

'This Kurt Steiner – who was he?'

He grinned, the eyes furtive again, that sly, cunning smile on his lips. 'That's easy,' he said. 'He was the German lad who came here with his men to shoot Mr. Churchill.'

I was so astonished that I simply stood there staring at him. He snatched the fiver from my hand, turned and cleared off at a shambling trot.

Some things in life are so enormous in their impact that they are almost impossible to take in, like a strange voice on the other end of a telephone telling you that someone you greatly loved has just died. Words become meaningless, the mind cuts itself off from reality for a little while, a necessary breathing space until one is ready to cope.

Which is roughly the state I found myself in after Laker Armsby's astonishing assertion. It wasn't just that it was so incredible. If there's one lesson I've learned in life it's that if you say a thing is impossible, it will probably happen next week. The truth is that the implications, if what Armsby had said was true, were so enormous that, for the moment, my mind was incapable of handling the idea.

It was there. I was aware of its existence, but didn't consciously think about it. I went back to the Blakeney Hotel, packed my bags, paid my bill and started home, the first stop in a journey which, although I didn't realise it then, was to consume a year of my life. A year of hundreds of files, dozens of interviews, travelling halfway round the world. San Francisco, Singapore, the Argentine, Hamburg, Berlin, Warsaw and even – most ironic of all – the Falls Road in Belfast. Anywhere there seemed to be a clue, however slight, that would lead me to the truth and particularly, because he is somehow central to the whole affair, some knowledge, some understanding of the enigma that was Kurt Steiner.

2

In a sense a man called Otto Skorzeny started it all on Sunday 12 September 1943 by bringing off one of the most brilliantly audacious commando coups of the Second World War – thus proving once again to Adolf Hitler's entire satisfaction that he, as usual, had been right and the High Command of the Armed Forces wrong.

Hitler himself had suddenly wanted to know why the German Army did not have commando units like the English ones which had operated so successfully since the beginning of the war. To satisfy him, the High

Command decided to form such a unit. Skorzeny, a young SS lieutenant, was kicking his heels in Berlin at the time after being invalided out of his regiment. He was promoted captain and made Chief of German Special Forces, none of which meant very much, which was exactly what the High Command intended.

Unfortunately for them, Skorzeny proved to be a brilliant soldier, uniquely gifted for the task in hand. And events were soon to give him a chance to prove it.

On 3 September 1943 Italy surrendered, Mussolini was deposed and Marshal Badoglio had him arrested and spirited away. Hitler insisted that his former ally be found and set free. It seemed an impossible task and even the great Erwin Rommel himself commented that he could see no good in the idea and hoped that it wouldn't be put on to his plate.

It wasn't, for Hitler gave it to Skorzeny personally who threw himself into the task with energy and determination and soon discovered that Mussolini was being held in the Sports Hotel on top of the ten-thousand-foot Gran Sasso in the Abruzzi, guarded by two hundred and fifty men.

Skorzeny landed by glider with fifty paratroopers, stormed the hotel and freed Mussolini. He was flown out in a tiny Stork spotter plane to Rome, then transhipped by Dornier to the Wolf's Lair, Hitler's headquarters for the Eastern Front, which was situated at Rastenburg in a gloomy, damp and heavily-wooded part of East Prussia.

The feat earned Skorzeny a hatful of medals, including the Knight's Cross, and started him on a career that was to embrace countless similar daring exploits and make him a legend in his own time. The High Command, as suspicious of such irregular methods as senior officers the world over, remained unimpressed.

Not so the Führer. He was in his seventh heaven, transported with delight, danced as he had not danced since the fall of Paris and this mood was still with him on the evening of the Wednesday following Mussolini's arrival at Rastenburg, when he held a meeting in the conference hut to discuss events in Italy and the Duce's future role.

The map room was surprisingly pleasant, with pine walls and ceiling. There was a circular table at one end surrounded by eleven rush chairs, flowers in a vase in the centre. At the other end of the room was the long map table. The small group of men who stood beside it discussing the situation on the Italian front included Mussolini himself, Josef Goebbels, Reich Minister of Propaganda and Minister for Total War, Heinrich Himmler, Reichführer of the SS, Chief of the State Police and of the State Secret Police, amongst other things, and Admiral Wilhelm Canaris, Chief of Military Intelligence, the Abwehr.

When Hitler entered the room they all stiffened to attention. He was in a jovial mood, eyes glittering, a slight fixed smile on his mouth, full of charm as only he could be on occasion. He descended on Mussolini and shook his hand warmly, holding it in both of his. 'You look better tonight, Duce. Decidedly better.'

To everyone else present the Italian dictator looked terrible. Tired and listless, little of his old fire left in him.

He managed a weak smile and the Führer clapped his hands. 'Well, gentlemen, and what should our next move be in Italy? What does the future hold? What is your opinion, Herr Reichsführer?'

Himmler removed his silver pince-nez and polished their lenses meticulously as he replied. 'Total victory, my Führer. What else? The presence of the Duce here with us now is ample proof of the brilliance with which you saved the situation after that traitor Badoglio signed an armistice.'

Hitler nodded, his face serious, and turned to Goebbels. 'And you, Josef?'

Goebbels' dark, mad eyes blazed with enthusiasm. 'I agree, my Führer. The liberation of the Duce has caused a great sensation at home and abroad. Friend and foe alike are full of admiration. We are able to celebrate a first-class moral victory, thanks to your inspired guidance.'

'And no thanks to my generals.' Hitler turned to Canaris, who was standing looking down at the map, a slight, ironic smile on his face. 'And you, Herr Admiral? You also think this a first-class moral victory?'

There are times when it pays to speak the truth, others when it does not. With Hitler it was always difficult to judge the occasion.

'My Führer, the Italian Battle Fleet now lies at anchor under the guns of the fortress of Malta. We have had to abandon Corsica and Sardinia and news is coming through that our old allies are already making arrangements to fight on the other side.'

Hitler had turned deathly pale, his eyes glittered, there was the faint damp of perspiration on his brow, but Canaris continued, 'As for the new Italian Socialist Republic as proclaimed by the Duce.' Here, he shrugged. 'Not a single neutral country so far, not even Spain, has agreed to set up diplomatic relations. I regret to say, my Führer, that in my opinion, they won't.'

'Your opinion?' Hitler exploded with fury. 'Your opinion? You're as bad as my generals and when I listen to them what happens? Failure everywhere.' He moved to Mussolini, who seemed rather alarmed, and placed an arm around his shoulders. 'Is the Duce here because of the High Command? No, he's here because I insisted that they set up a commando unit, because my intuition told me it was the right thing to do.'

Goebbels looked anxious, Himmler as calm and enigmatic as usual, but Canaris stood his ground. 'I implied no criticism of you personally, my Führer.'

Hitler had moved to the window and stood looking out, hands tightly clenched behind him. 'I have an instinct for these things and I knew how successful this kind of operation could be. A handful of brave men, daring all.' He swung round to face them. 'Without me there would have been no Gran Sasso because without me there would have been no Skorzeny.' He said that as if delivering Biblical writ. 'I don't wish to be too hard on you, Herr Admiral, but after all, what have you and your people at the Abwehr accomplished lately? It seems to me that all you can do is produce traitors like Dohnanyi.'

Hans von Dohnanyi, who had worked for the Abwehr, had been arrested for treason against the state in April.

Canaris was paler than ever now, on dangerous ground indeed. He said, 'My Führer, there was no intention on my part . . .'

Hitler ignored him and turned to Himmler. 'And you, Herr Reichsführer – what do you think?'

'I accept your concept totally, my Führer,' Himmler told him. 'Totally; but then, I'm also slightly prejudiced. Skorzeny, after all, is an SS officer. On the other hand, I would have thought the Gran Sasso affair to be exactly the kind of business the Brandenburgers were supposed to take care of.'

He was referring to the Brandenburg Division, a unique unit formed early in the war to perform special missions. Its activities were supposedly in the hands of Department Two of the Abwehr, which specialised in sabotage. In spite of Canaris's efforts, this elite force had, for the most part, been frittered away in hit-and-run operations behind the Russian lines which had achieved little.

'Exactly,' Hitler said. 'What have your precious Brandenburgers done? Nothing worth a moment's discussion.' He was working himself into a fury again now, and as always at such times, seemed able to draw on his prodigious memory to a remarkable degree.

'When it was originally formed, this Brandenburg unit, it was called the Company for Special Missions, and I remember hearing that von Hippel, its first commander, told them they'd be able to fetch the Devil from Hell by the time he'd finished with them. I find that ironic, Herr Admiral, because as far as I can remember, they didn't bring me the Duce. I had to arrange for that myself.'

His voice had risen to a crescendo, the eyes sparked fire, the face was wet with perspiration. 'Nothing!' he shrieked. 'You have brought me nothing and yet with men like that, with such facilities, you should have been capable of bringing me Churchill out of England.'

There was a moment of complete silence as Hitler glanced from face to face. 'Is that not so?'

Mussolini looked hunted, Goebbels nodded eagerly. It was Himmler who added fuel to the flames by saying quietly, 'Why not, my Führer? After all, anything is possible, no matter how miraculous, as you have shown by bringing the Duce out of Gran Sasso.'

'Quite right.' Hitler was calm again now. 'A wonderful opportunity to show us what the Abwehr is capable of, Herr Admiral.'

Canaris was stunned. 'My Führer, do I understand you to mean . . . ?'

'After all, an English commando unit attacked Rommel's headquarters in Africa,' Hitler said, 'and similar groups have raided the French coast on many occasions. Am I to believe that German boys are capable of less?' He patted Canaris on the shoulder and said affably, 'See to it, Herr Admiral. Get things moving. I'm sure you'll come up with something.' He turned to Himmler. 'You agree, Herr Reichsführer?'

'Certainly,' Himmler said without hesitation. 'A feasibility study at the very least – surely the Abwehr can manage that?'

He smiled slightly at Canaris who stood there, thunderstruck. He moistened dry lips and said in a hoarse voice. 'As you command, my Führer.'

Hitler put an arm around his shoulder. 'Good. I knew I could rely on you as always.' He stretched out his arm as if to pull them all forward and leaned over the map. 'And now, gentlemen – the Italian situation.'

Canaris and Himmler were returning to Berlin by Dornier that night. They left Rastenburg at the same time in separate cars for the nine-mile drive to the airfield. Canaris was fifteen minutes late and when he finally mounted the steps into the Dornier he was not in the best of moods. Himmler was already strapped into his seat and, after a moment's hesitation, Canaris joined him.

'Trouble?' Himmler asked as the plane bumped forward across the runway and turned into the wind.

'Burst tyre.' Canaris leaned back. 'Thanks very much, by the way. You were a great help back there.'

'Always happy to be of service,' Himmler told him.

They were airborne now, the engine note deepening as they climbed. 'My God, but he was really on form tonight,' Canaris said. 'Get Churchill. Have you ever heard anything so crazy?'

'Since Skorzeny got Mussolini out of Gran Sasso, the world will never be quite the same again. The Führer now believes miracles can actually take place and this will make life increasingly difficult for you and me,

Herr Admiral.'

'Mussolini was one thing,' Canaris said. 'Without in any way detracting from Skorzeny's magnificent achievement, Winston Churchill would be something else again.'

'Oh, I don't know,' Himmler said. 'I've seen the enemy newsreels as you have. London one day – Manchester or Leeds the next. He walks the streets with that stupid cigar in his mouth talking to the people. I would say that of all the major world leaders, he is probably the least protected.'

'If you believe that, you'll believe anything,' Canaris said drily. 'Whatever else they are, the English aren't fools. MI five and six employ lots of very well-spoken young men who've been to Oxford or Cambridge and who'd put a bullet through your belly as soon as look at you. Anyway, take the old man himself. Probably carries a pistol in his coat pocket and I bet he's still a crack shot.'

An orderly brought them some coffee. Himmler said, 'So you don't intend to proceed in this affair?'

'You know what will happen as well as I do,' Canaris said. 'Today's Wednesday. He'll have forgotten the whole crazy idea by Friday.'

Himmler nodded slowly, sipping his coffee. 'Yes, I suppose you're right.'

Canaris stood up. 'Anyway, if you'll excuse me, I think I'll get a little sleep.'

He moved to another seat, covered himself with a blanket provided and made himself as comfortable as possible for the three-hour trip that lay ahead.

From the other side of the aisle Himmler watched him, eyes cold, fixed, staring. There was no expression on his face – none at all. He might have been a corpse lying there had it not been for the muscle that twitched constantly in his right cheek.

When Canaris reached the Abwehr offices at 74–76 Tirpitz Ufer in Berlin it was almost dawn. The driver who had picked him up at Tempelhof had brought the Admiral's two favourite dachshunds with him and when Canaris got out of the car, they scampered at his heels as he walked briskly past the sentries.

He went straight up to his office. Unbuttoning his naval greatcoat as he went, he handed it to the orderly who opened the door for him. 'Coffee,' the Admiral told him. 'Lots of coffee.' The orderly started to close the door and Canaris called him back. 'Do you know if Colonel Radl is in?'

'I believe he slept in his office last night, Herr Admiral.'

'Good, tell him I'd like to see him.'

The door closed. He was alone and suddenly tired and he slumped down in the chair behind the desk. Canaris's personal style was modest. The office was old-fashioned and relatively bare, with a worn carpet. There was a portrait of Franco on the wall with a dedication. On the desk was a marble paperweight with three bronze monkeys seeing, hearing and speaking no evil.

'That's me,' he said softly, tapping them on the head.

He took a deep breath to get a grip on himself: it was the very knife-edge of danger he walked in that insane world. There were things he suspected that even he should not have known. An attempt by two senior officers earlier that year to blow up Hitler's plane in flight from Smolensk to Rastenburg, for instance, and the constant threat of what might happen if von Dohnanyi and his friends cracked and talked.

The orderly appeared with a tray containing coffee pot, two cups and a small pot of real cream, something of a rarity in Berlin at that time. 'Leave it,' Canaris said. 'I'll see to it myself.'

The orderly withdrew and as Canaris poured the coffee, there was a knock at the door. The man who entered might have stepped straight off a parade ground, so immaculate was his uniform. A lieutenant-colonel of mountain troops with the ribbon for the Winter War, a silver wound badge and a Knight's Cross at his throat. Even the patch which covered his right eye had a regulation look about it, as did the black leather glove on his left hand.

'Ah, there you are, Max,' Canaris said. 'Join me for coffee and restore me to sanity. Each time I return from Rastenburg I feel increasingly that I need a keeper, or at least that someone does.'

Max Radl was thirty and looked ten or fifteen years older, depending on the day and weather. He had lost his right eye and left hand during the Winter War in 1941 and had worked for Canaris ever since being invalided home. He was at that time Head of Section Three, which was an office of Department Z, the Central Department of the Abwehr and directly under the Admiral's personal control. Section Three was a unit which was supposed to look after particularly difficult assignments and as such, Radl was authorised to poke his nose into any other Abwehr section that he wanted, an activity which made him considerably less popular amongst his colleagues.

'As bad as that?'

'Worse,' Canaris told him. 'Mussolini was like a walking automaton, Goebbels hopped as usual from one foot to the other like some ten-year-old schoolboy bursting for a pee.'

Radl winced, for it always made him feel decidedly uneasy when the admiral spoke in that way of such powerful people. Although the offices were checked daily for microphones, one could never really be sure.

Canaris carried on, 'Himmler was his usual pleasant corpse-like self and as for the Führer . . .'

Radl cut in hastily. 'More coffee, Herr Admiral?'

Canaris sat down again. 'All he could talk about was Gran Sasso and what a bloody miracle the whole thing was and why didn't the Abwehr do something as spectacular.'

He jumped up, walked to the window and peered out through the curtains into the grey morning. 'You know what he suggests we do, Max? Get Churchill for him.'

Radl started violently. 'Good God, he can't be serious.'

'Who knows? One day, yes, another day, no. He didn't actually specify whether he wanted him alive or dead. This business with Mussolini has gone to his head. Now he seems to think anything is possible. Bring the Devil from Hell if necessary, was a phrase he quoted with some feeling.'

'And the others – how did they take it?' Radl asked.

'Goebbels was his usual amiable self, the Duce looked hunted. Himmler was the difficult one. Backed the Führer all the way. Said that the least we could do was look into it. A feasibility study, that was the phrase he used.'

'I see, sir.' Radl hesitated. 'You do think the Führer is serious?'

'Of course not.' Canaris went over to the army cot in the corner, turned back the blankets, sat down and started to unlace his shoes. 'He'll have forgotten it already. I know what he's like when he's in that kind of mood. Comes out with all sorts of rubbish.' He got into the cot and covered himself with the blanket. 'No, I'd say Himmler's the only worry. He's after my blood. He'll remind him about the whole miserable affair at some future date when it suits him, if only to make it look as if I don't do as I'm told.'

'So what do you want me to do?'

'Exactly what Himmler suggested. A feasibility study. A nice, long report that will look as if we've really been trying. For example, Churchill's in Canada at the moment, isn't he? Probably coming back by boat. You can always make it look as if you've seriously considered the possibility of having a U-boat in the right place at the right time. After all, as our Führer assured me personally not six hours ago, miracles do happen, but only under the right divine inspiration. Tell Krogel to wake me in one hour and a half.'

He pulled the blanket over his head and Radl turned off the light and went out. He wasn't at all happy as he made his way back to his office and not because of the ridiculous task he'd been given. That sort of thing was commonplace. In fact, he often referred to Section Three as the

Department of Absurdities.

No, it was the way Canaris talked which worried him and as he was one of those individuals who liked to be scrupulously honest with himself, Radl was man enough to admit that he wasn't just worried about the Admiral. He was very much thinking of himself and his family.

Technically the Gestapo had no jurisdiction over men in uniform. On the other hand he had seen too many acquaintances simply disappear off the face of the earth to believe that. The infamous Night and Fog Decree in which various unfortunates were made to vanish into the mists of night in the most literal sense, was supposed to apply only to inhabitants of conquered territories, but as Radl was well aware, there were more than fifty thousand non-Jewish German citizens in concentration camps at that particular point in time. Since 1933, nearly two hundred thousand had died.

When he went into the office, Sergeant Hofer, his assistant, was going through the night mail which had just come in. He was a quiet, dark-haired man of forty-eight, an innkeeper from the Harz Mountains, a superb skier who had lied about his age to join up and had served with Radl in Russia.

Radl sat down behind his desk and gazed morosely at a picture of his wife and three daughters, safe in Bavaria in the mountains. Hofer, who knew the signs, gave him a cigarette and poured him a small brandy from a bottle of Courvoisier kept in the bottom drawer of the desk.

'As bad as that, Herr Oberst?'

'As bad as that, Karl,' Radl answered, then he swallowed his brandy and told him the worst.

And there it might have rested had it not been for an extraordinary coincidence. On the morning of the 22nd, exactly one week after his interview with Canaris, Radl was seated at his desk, fighting his way though a mass of paperwork which had accumulated during a three-day visit to Paris.

He was not in a happy mood and when the door opened and Hofer entered, he glanced up with a frown and said impatiently, 'For God's sake, Karl, I asked to be left in peace. What is it now?'

'I'm sorry, Herr Oberst. It's just that a report has come to my notice which I thought might interest you.'

'Where did it come from?'

'Abwehr One.'

Which was the department which handled espionage abroad and Radl was aware of a faint, if reluctant, stirring of interest. Hofer stood there waiting, hugging the manilla folder to his chest and Radl put down his pen with a sigh. 'All right, tell me about it.'

Hofer placed the file in front of him and opened it. 'This is the latest report from an agent in England. Code name Starling.'

Radl glanced at the front sheet as he reached for a cigarette from the box on the table. 'Mrs. Joanna Grey.'

'She's situated in the northern part of Norfolk close to the coast, Herr Oberst. A village called Studley Constable.'

'But of course,' Radl said, suddenly rather more enthusiastic. 'Isn't she the woman who got the details of the Oboe installation?' He turned over the first two or three pages briefly and frowned. 'There's a hell of a lot of it. How does she manage that?'

'She has an excellent contact at the Spanish Embassy who puts her stuff through in the diplomatic bag. It's as good as the post. We usually take delivery within three days.'

'Remarkable,' Radl said. 'How often does she report?'

'Once a month. She also has a radio link, but this is seldom used, although she follows normal procedure and keeps her channel open three times a week for one hour in case she's needed. Her link man at this end is Captain Meyer.'

'All right, Karl,' Radl said. 'Get me some coffee and I'll read it.'

'I've marked the interesting paragraph in red, Herr Oberst. You'll find it on page three. I also put in a large-scale, British ordnance survey map of the area,' Hofer told him and went out.

The report was very well put together, lucid and full of information of worth. A general description of conditions in the area, the location of two new American B17 squadrons south of the Wash, a B24 squadron near Sheringham. It was all good, useful stuff without being terribly exciting. And then he came to page three and that brief paragraph, underlined in red, and his stomach contracted in a spasm of nervous excitement.

It was simple enough. The British Prime Minister, Winston Churchill, was to inspect a station of RAF Bomber Command near the Wash on the morning of Saturday 6 November. Later on the same day, he was scheduled to visit a factory near King's Lynn and make a brief speech to the workers.

Then came the interesting part. Instead of returning to London he intended to spend the weekend at the home of Sir Henry Willoughby, Studley Grange, which was just five miles outside the village of Studley Constable. It was a purely private visit, the details supposedly secret. Certainly no one in the village was aware of the plan, but Sir Henry, a retired naval commander, had apparently been unable to resist confiding in Joanna Grey, who was, it seemed, a personal friend.

Radl sat staring at the report for a few moments, thinking about it, then he took out the ordnance survey map Hofer had provided and unfolded it. The door opened and Hofer appeared with the coffee. He placed the tray on the table, filled a cup and stood waiting, face impassive. Radl looked up. 'All right, damn you. Show me where the place is. I expect you know.'

'Certainly, Herr Oberst.' Hofer placed a finger on the Wash and ran it south along the coast. 'Studley Constable, and here are Blakeney and Cley on the coast, the whole forming a triangle. I have looked at Mrs. Grey's report on the area from before the war. An isolated place – very rural. A lonely coastline of vast beaches and salt marshes.'

Radl sat there staring at the map for a while and then came to a decision. 'Get me Hans Meyer. I'd like to have a word with him, only don't even hint what it's about.'

'Certainly, Herr Oberst.'

Hofer moved to the door. 'And Karl,' Radl added, 'every report she's ever sent. Everything we have on the entire area.'

The door closed and suddenly it seemed very quiet in the room. He reached for one of his cigarettes. As usual they were Russian, half-tobacco, half-cardboard tube. An affectation with some people who had served in the East. Radl smoked them because he liked them. They were far too strong and made him cough. That was a matter of indifference to him: the doctors had already warned of a considerably shortened lifespan due to his massive injuries.

He went and stood at the window feeling curiously deflated. It was all such a farce really. The Führer, Himmler, Canaris – like shadows behind the white sheet in a Chinese play. Nothing substantial. Nothing real and this silly business – this Churchill thing. While good men were dying on the Eastern Front in their thousands he was playing damned stupid games like this which couldn't possibly come to anything.

He was full of self-disgust, angry with himself for no known reason and then a knock at the door pulled him up short. The man who entered was of medium height and wore a Donegal tweed suit. His grey hair was untidy and the horn-rimmed spectacles made him seem curiously vague.

'Ah, there you are, Meyer. Good of you to come.'

Hans Meyer was at that time fifty years of age. During the First World War he had been a U-boat commander, one of the youngest in the German Navy. From 1922 onwards he had been wholly employed in intelligence work and was considerably sharper than he looked.

'Herr Oberst,' he said formally.

'Sit down, man, sit down.' Radl indicated a chair. 'I've been reading the latest report from one of your agents – Starling. Quite fascinating.'

'Ah, yes.' Meyer took off his spectacles and polished them with a grubby handkerchief. 'Joanna Grey. A remarkable woman.'

'Tell me about her.'

Meyer paused, a slight frown on his face. 'What would you like to know, Herr Oberst?'

'Everything!' Radl said.

Meyer hesitated for a moment, obviously on the point of asking why and then thought better of it. He replaced his spectacles and started to talk.

Joanna Grey had been born Joanna Van Oosten in March, 1875, at a small town called Vierskop in the Orange Free State. Her father was a farmer and pastor of the Dutch Reform Church and, at the age of ten, had taken part in the Great Trek, the migration of some ten thousand Boer farmers between 1836 and 1838 from Cape Colony to new lands north of the Orange River to escape British domination.

She had married, at twenty, a farmer named Dirk Jansen. She had one child, a daughter born in 1898, a year before the outbreak of hostilities with the British of the following year that became known as the Boer War.

Her father raised a mounted commando and was killed near Bloemfontein in May, 1900. From that month the war was virtually over, but the two years which followed proved to be the most tragic of the whole conflict for, like others of his countrymen, Dirk Jansen fought on, a bitter guerrilla war in small groups, relying upon outlying farms for shelter and support.

The British cavalry patrol who called at the Jansen homestead on 11 June 1901, were in search of Dirk Jansen, ironically, and unknown to his wife, already dead of wounds in a mountain camp two months earlier. There was only Joanna, her mother and the child at home. She had refused to answer the corporal's questions and had been taken into the barn for an interrogation that had involved being raped twice.

Her complaint to the local area commander was turned down and, in any case, the British were at that time attempting to combat the guerrillas by burning farms, clearing whole areas and placing the population in what soon became known as concentration camps.

The camps were badly run – more a question of poor administration than of any deliberate ill-will. Disease broke out and in fourteen months over twenty thousand people died, amongst them Joanna Jansen's mother and daughter. Greatest irony of all, she would have died herself had it not been for the careful nursing she had received from an English doctor named Charles Grey who had been brought into her camp in an attempt to improve things after a public outcry in England over the disclosure of conditions.

Her hatred of the British was now pathological in its intensity, burned into her forever. Yet she married Grey when he proposed to her. On the other hand, she was twenty-eight years of age and broken by life. She had lost husband and child, every relative she had in the world, had not a penny to her name.

That Grey loved her there can be no doubt. He was fifteen years older and made few demands, was courteous and kind. Over the years she developed a certain affection for him, mixed with the kind of constant irritation and impatience one feels for an unruly child.

He accepted work with a London Bible Society as a medical missionary and for some years held a succession of appointments in Rhodesia and Kenya and finally amongst the Zulu. She could never understand his preoccupation with what to her were kaffirs, but accepted it, just as she accepted the drudgery of the teaching she was expected to do to help his work.

In March, 1925 he died of a stroke and on the conclusion of his affairs, she was left with little more than one hundred and fifty pounds to face life at the age of fifty. Fate had struck her another bitter blow, but she fought on, accepting a post as governess to an English civil servant's family in Cape Town.

During this time she started to interest herself in Boer nationalism, attending meetings held regularly by one of the more extreme organisations engaged in the campaign to take South Africa out of the British Empire. At one of these meetings she met a German civil engineer named Hans Meyer. He was ten years her junior and yet a romance flowered briefly, the first, genuine physical attraction she had felt for anyone since her first marriage.

Meyer was in reality an agent of German Naval Intelligence, in Cape Town to obtain as much information as he could about naval installations in South Africa. By chance, Joanna Grey's employer worked for the Admiralty and she was able, at no particular risk, to take from the safe at his house certain interesting documents which Meyer had copied before she returned them.

She was happy to do it because she felt a genuine passion for him, but there was more to it than that. For the first time in her life she was striking a blow against England. Some sort of return for everything she felt had been done to her.

Meyer had gone back to Germany and continued to write to her and then, in 1929, when for most people the world was cracking into a thousand pieces as Europe nose-dived into a depression, Joanna Grey had the first piece of genuine good fortune of her entire life.

She received a letter from a firm of solicitors in Norwich, informing her that her late husband's aunt had died leaving her a cottage outside the village of Studley Constable in North Norfolk and an income of a little over four thousand pounds a year. There was only one snag. The old lady had had a sentimental regard for the house and it was a strict provision of the will that Joanna Grey would have to take up residence.

To live in England. The very idea made her flesh crawl, but what was the alternative? To continue her present life of genteel slavery, her only prospect a poverty-stricken old age? She obtained a book on Norfolk from the library and read it through thoroughly, particularly the section covering the northern coastal area.

The names bewildered her. Stiffkey, Morston, Blakeney, Cley-next-the-Sea, salt marshes, shingle beaches. None of this made any kind of sense to her so she wrote to Hans Meyer with her problem and Meyer wrote back at once, urging her to go and promising to visit her as soon as he could.

It was the best thing she had ever done in her life. The cottage turned out to be a charming five-bedroomed Georgian house set in half an acre of walled garden. Norfolk at that time was still the most rural county in England, had changed comparatively little since the nineteenth century so that in a small village like Studley Constable she was regarded as a wealthy woman, a person of some importance. And another, stranger thing happened. She found the salt marshes and the shingle beaches fascinating, fell in love with the place, was happier than at any other time in her life.

Meyer came to England in the autumn of that year and visited her several times. They went for long walks together. She showed him everything. The endless beaches stretching into infinity, the salt marshes, the dunes of Blakeney Point. He never once referred to the period in Cape Town when she had helped him obtain the information he needed, she never once asked him about his present activities.

They continued to correspond and she visited him in Berlin in 1935. He showed her what National Socialism was doing for Germany. She was intoxicated by everything she saw, the enormous rallies, uniforms everywhere, handsome boys, laughing, happy women and children. She accepted completely that this was the new order. This was how it should be.

And then, one evening as they strolled back along Unter den Linden after an evening at the opera in which she had seen the Führer himself in his box, Meyer had calmly told her that he was now with the Abwehr, had asked her if she would consider working for them as an agent in

England.

She had said yes instantly, without needing to think about it, her whole body pulsing with an excitement that she had never known in her life before. So, at sixty, she had become a spy, this upper-class English lady, for so she was considered, with the pleasant face, walking the countryside in sweater and tweed skirt with her black retriever at her heels. A pleasant, white-haired lady who had a wireless transmitter and receiver in a small cubbyhole behind the panelling in her study and a contact in the Spanish Embassy in London who passed anything of a bulky nature out to Madrid in the diplomatic bag from where it was handed on to German Intelligence.

Her results had been consistently good. Her duties as a member of the Women's Voluntary Service took her into many military installations and she had been able to pass out details of most RAF heavy bomber stations in Norfolk and a great deal of additional relevant information. Her great coup had been at the beginning of 1943 when the RAF had introduced two new blind bombing devices which were hoped to greatly increase the success of the night bombing offensive against Germany.

The most important of these, Oboe, operated by linking up with two ground stations in England. One was in Dover and known as Mouse, the other was situated in Cromer on the North Norfolk coast and rejoiced in the name of Cat.

It was amazing how much information RAF personnel were willing to give a kindly WVS lady handing out library books and cups of tea, and during half-a-dozen visits to the Oboe installation at Cromer, she was able to put one of her miniature cameras to good use. A single phone call to Señor Lorca, the clerk at the Spanish Embassy who was her contact, a trip by train to London for the day, a meeting in Green Park, was all it took.

Within twenty-four hours the information on Oboe was leaving England in the Spanish diplomatic bag. Within thirty-six, a delighted Hans Meyer was laying it on the desk of Canaris himself in his office at the Tirpitz Ufer.

When Hans Meyer had finished, Radl laid down the pen with which he had been making brief notes. 'A fascinating lady,' he said. 'Quite remarkable. Tell me one thing – how much training has she done?'

'An adequate amount, Herr Oberst,' Meyer told him. 'She holidayed in the Reich in 1936 and 1937. On each occasion she received instruction in certain obvious matters. Codes, use of radio, general camera work, basic sabotage techniques. Nothing too advanced admittedly, except for her morse code which is excellent. On the other hand, her function was never intended to be a particularly physical one.'

'No, I can see that. What about use of weapons?'

'Not much need for that. She was raised on the veld. Could shoot the eye out of a deer at a hundred yards by the time she was ten years old.'

Radl nodded, frowning into space and Meyer said tentatively, 'Is there something special involved here, Herr Oberst? Perhaps I could be of assistance?'

'Not now,' Radl told him, 'but I could well need you in the near future. I'll let you know. For the moment, it will be sufficient to pass all files on Joanna Grey to this office and no radio communication until further orders.'

Meyer was aghast and quite unable to contain himself. 'Please, Herr Oberst, if Joanna is in any kind of danger . . .'

'Not in the slightest,' Radl said. 'I understand your concern, believe me, but there is really nothing more I can say at this time. A matter of the highest security, Meyer.'

Meyer recovered himself enough to apologise. 'Of course, Herr Oberst. Forgive me, but as an old friend of the lady . . .'

He withdrew. A moment or so after he had gone, Hofer came in from the anteroom carrying several files and a couple of rolled-up maps under his arm. 'The information you wanted, Herr Oberst, and I've also brought two British Admiralty charts which cover the coastal area – numbers one hundred and eight and one hundred and six.'

'I've told Meyer to let you have everything he has on Joanna Grey and I've told him no more radio communication,' Radl said. 'You take over from now on.'

He reached for one of those eternal Russian cigarettes and Hofer produced a lighter made from a Russian 7.62 mm cartridge case. 'Do we proceed, then, Herr Oberst?'

Radl blew a cloud of smoke and looked up at the ceiling. 'Are you familiar with the works of Jung, Karl?'

'The Herr Oberst knows I sold good beer and wine before the war.'

'Jung speaks of what he calls synchronicity. Events sometimes having a coincidence in time and, because of this, the feeling that some much deeper motivation is involved.'

'Herr Oberst?' Hofer said politely.

'Take this affair. The Führer, whom heaven protect naturally, has a brainstorm and comes up with the comical and absurd suggestion that we should emulate Skorzeny's exploit at Gran Sasso by getting Churchill, although whether alive or dead has not been specified. And then synchronicity rears its ugly head in a routine Abwehr report. A brief mention that Churchill will be spending a weekend no more than seven or eight miles from the coast at a remote country house in as quiet a part of the country as one could wish. You take my meaning? At any other time that report of Mrs. Grey's would have meant nothing.'

'So we do proceed then, Herr Oberst?'

'It would appear that fate has taken a hand, Karl,' Radl said. 'How long did you say Mrs. Grey's reports take to come in through the Spanish diplomatic bag?'

'Three days, Herr Oberst, if someone is waiting in Madrid to collect. No more than a week, even if circumstances are difficult.'

'And when is her next radio contact time?'

'This evening, Herr Oberst.'

'Good – send her this message.' Radl looked up at the ceiling again, thinking hard, trying to compress his thoughts. 'Very interested in your visitor of sixth November. Like to drop some friends in to meet him in the hope they might persuade him to come back with them. Your early comments looked for by usual route with all relevant information.'

'Is that all, Herr Oberst?'

'I think so.'

That was Wednesday and it was raining in Berlin, but the following morning when Father Philip Vereker limped out through the lychgate of St. Mary's and All the Saints, Studley Constable, and walked down through the village, the sun was shining and it was that most beautiful of all things, a perfect autumn day.

At that time, Philip Vereker was a tall, gaunt young man of thirty, the gauntness emphasised even more by the black cassock. His face was strained and twisted with pain as he limped along, leaning heavily on his stick. He had only been discharged from a military hospital four months earlier.

The younger son of a Harley Street surgeon, he had been a brilliant scholar who at Cambridge had shown every sign of an outstanding future. Then, to his family's dismay, he had decided to train for the priesthood, had gone to the English College in Rome and joined the Society of Jesus.

He had entered the army as a padre in 1940 and had finally been assigned to the Parachute Regiment and had seen action only once in November, 1942, in Tunisia when he had jumped with units of the First Parachute Brigade with orders to seize the airfield at Oudna, ten miles from Tunis. In the end, they had been compelled to make a fighting retreat over fifty miles of open country, strafed from the air every yard of the way and under constant attack from ground forces.

One hundred and eighty made it to safety. Two hundred and sixty didn't. Vereker was one of the lucky ones, in spite of a bullet which had passed straight through his left ankle, chipping bone. By the time he reached a field hospital, sepsis had set in. His left foot was amputated and he was invalided out.

Vereker found it difficult to look pleasant these days. The pain was constant and would not go away, and yet he did manage a smile as he approached Park Cottage and saw Joanna Grey emerge pushing her bicycle, her retriever at her heels.

'How are you, Philip?' she said. 'I haven't seen you for several days.'

She wore a tweed skirt, polo-necked sweater underneath a yellow oilskin coat and a silk scarf was tied around her white hair. She really did look very charming with that South African tan of hers that she had never really lost.

'Oh, I'm all right,' Vereker said. 'Dying by inches of boredom more than anything else. One piece of news since I last saw you. My sister, Pamela. Remember me speaking of her? She's ten years younger than me. A corporal in the WAAF.'

'Of course I remember,' Mrs. Grey said. 'What's happened?'

'She's been posted to a bomber station only fifteen miles from here at Pangbourne, so I'll be able to see something of her. She's coming over this weekend. I'll introduce you.'

'I'll look forward to that.' Joanna Grey climbed on to her bike.

'Chess tonight?' he asked hopefully.

'Why not? Come around and have supper as well. Must go now.'

She pedalled away along the side of the stream, the retriever, Patch, loping along behind. Her face was serious now. The radio message of the previous evening had come as an enormous shock to her. In fact, she had decoded it three times to make sure she hadn't made an error.

She had hardly slept, certainly not much before five and had lain there listening to the Lancasters setting out across the sea to Europe and then, a few hours later, returning. The strange thing was that after finally dozing off, she had awakened at seven-thirty full of life and vigour.

It was as if for the first time she had a really important task to handle. This – this was so incredible. To kidnap Churchill – snatch him from under the very noses of those who were supposed to be guarding him.

She laughed out loud. Oh, the damned English wouldn't like that. They wouldn't like that one little bit, with the whole world amazed.

As she coasted down the hill to the main road, a horn sounded behind her and a small saloon car passed and drew into the side of the road. The man behind the wheel had a large white moustache and the florid complexion of one who consumes whisky in large quantities daily. He was wearing the uniform of a lieutenant-colonel in the Home Guard.

'Morning, Joanna,' he called jovially.

The meeting could not have been more fortunate. In fact it saved her a visit to Studley Grange later in the day. 'Good morning, Henry,' she said and dismounted from her bike.

He got out of the car. 'We're having a few people on Saturday night. Bridge and so on. Supper afterwards. Nothing very special. Jean thought you might like to join us.'

'That's very kind of her. I'd love to,' Joanna Grey said. 'She must have an awful lot on, getting ready for the big event at the moment.'

Sir Henry looked slightly hunted and dropped his voice a little. 'I say, you haven't mentioned that to anyone else, have you?'

Joanna Grey managed to look suitably shocked. 'Of course not. You did tell me in confidence, remember.'

'Shouldn't have mentioned it at all actually, but then I knew I could trust you, Joanna.' He slipped an arm around her waist. 'Mum's the word on Saturday night, old girl, just for me, eh. Any of that lot get a hint of what's afoot and it will be all over the county.'

'I'd do anything for you, you know that,' she said calmly.

'Would you, Joanna?' His voice thickened and she was aware of his thigh pushed against her, trembling slightly. He pulled away suddenly. 'Well, I'll have to be off. Got an area command meeting in Holt.'

'You must be very excited,' she said, 'at the prospect of having the Prime Minister.'

'Indeed I am. Very great honour.' Sir Henry beamed. 'He's hoping to do a little painting and you know how pretty the views are from the Grange.' He opened the door and got back into the car. 'Where are you off to, by the way?'

She'd been waiting for exactly that question. 'Oh, a little bird-watching, as usual. I may go down to Cley or the marsh. I haven't made up my mind yet. There are some interesting passage migrants about at the moment.'

'You damn well watch it.' His face was serious. 'And remember what I told you.'

As local Home Guard commander he had plans covering every aspect of coastal defence in the area, including details of all mined beaches and – more importantly – beaches which were only supposedly mined. On one occasion, full of solicitude for her welfare, he had spent two careful hours going over the maps with her, showing her exactly where not to go on her bird-watching expeditions.

'I know the situation changes all the time,' she said. 'Perhaps you could come round to the cottage again with those maps of yours and give me another lesson.'

His eyes were slightly glazed. 'Would you like that?'

'Of course. I'm at home this afternoon, actually.'

'After lunch,' he said. 'I'll be there about two,' and he released the handbrake and drove rapidly away.

Joanna Grey got back on her cycle and started to pedal down the hill towards the main road, Patch running behind. Poor Henry. She was really quite fond of him. Just like a child and so easy to handle.

Half-an-hour later, she turned off the coast road and cycled along the top of a dyke through desolate marshes known locally as Hobs End. It was a strange, alien world of sea creeks and mud flats and great pale barriers of reeds higher than a man's head, inhabited only by the birds, curlew and redshank and brent geese coming south from Siberia to winter on the mud flats.

Half-way along the dyke, a cottage crouched behind a mouldering flint wall, sheltered by a few sparse pine trees. It looked substantial enough with outbuildings and a large barn, but the windows were shuttered and there was a general air of desolation about it. This was the marsh warden's house and there had been no warden since 1940.

She moved on to a high ridge lined with pines. She dismounted from her bicycle and leaned it against a tree. There were sand dunes beyond and then a wide, flat beach stretching with the tide out a quarter of a mile towards the sea. In the distance she could see the Point on the other side of the estuary, curving in like a great bent forefinger, enclosing an area of channels and sandbanks and shoals that, on a rising tide, was probably as lethal as anywhere on the Norfolk coast.

She produced her camera and took a great many pictures from various angles. As she finished, the dog brought her a stick to throw, which he had laid carefully down between her feet. She crouched and fondled his ears. 'Yes, Patch,' she said softly. 'I really think this will do very well indeed.'

She tossed the stick straight over the line of barbed wire which prevented access to the beach and Patch darted past the post with the notice board that said *Beware of mines*. Thanks to Henry Willoughby, to her certain knowledge there wasn't a mine on the beach.

To her left was a concrete blockhouse and a machine-gun post, a very definite air of decay to both of them, and in the gap between the pine trees, the tank trap had filled with drifting sand. Three years earlier, after the Dunkirk debacle, there would have been soldiers here. Even a year ago, Home Guard, but not now.

In June, 1940, an area up to twenty miles inland from the Wash to the Rye was declared a Defence Area. There were no restrictions on people living there, but outsiders had to have a good reason for visiting. All that had altered considerably and now, three years later, virtually no one bothered to enforce the regulations for the plain truth was that there was no longer any need.

Joanna Grey bent down to fondle the dog's ears again. 'You know what it is, Patch? The English just don't expect to be invaded any more.'

3

It was the following Tuesday before Joanna Grey's report arrived at the Tirpitz Ufer. Hofer had put a red flag out for it. He took it straight in to Radl who opened it and examined the contents.

There were photos of the marsh at Hobs End and the beach approaches, their position indicated only by a coded map reference. Radl passed the report itself to Hofer.

'Top priority. Get that deciphered and wait while they do it.'

The Abwehr had just started using the new Sonlar coding unit that took care in a matter of minutes of a task that had previously taken hours. The machine had a normal typewriter keyboard. The operator simply copied the coded message, which was automatically deciphered and delivered in a sealed reel. Even the operator did not see the actual message involved.

Hofer was back in the office within twenty minutes and waited in silence while the colonel read the report. Radl looked up with a smile and pushed it across the desk. 'Read that, Karl, just you read that. Excellent – really excellent. What a woman.'

He lit one of his cigarettes and waited impatiently for Hofer to finish. Finally the sergeant glanced up. 'It looks quite promising.'

'Promising? Is that the best you can do? Good God, man, it's a definite possibility. A very real possibility.'

He was more excited now than he had been for months, which was bad for him, for his heart, so appalling strained by his massive injuries. The empty eye socket under the black patch throbbed, the aluminium hand inside the glove seemed to come alive, every tendon taut as a bow string. He fought for breath and slumped into his chair.

Hofer had the Courvoisier bottle out of the bottom drawer in an instant, half-filled a glass and held it to the colonel's lips. Radl swallowed most of it down, coughed heavily, then seemed to get control of himself again.

He smiled wryly. 'I can't afford to do that too often, eh, Karl? Only two more bottles left. It's like liquid gold these days.'

'The Herr Oberst shouldn't excite himself so,' Hofer said and added bluntly, 'You can't afford to.'

Radl swallowed some more of the brandy. 'I know, Karl, I know, but don't you see? It was a joke before – something the Führer threw out in an angry mood on a Wednesday, to be forgotten by Friday. A feasibility study, that was Himmler's suggestion and only because he wanted to make things awkward for the Admiral. The Admiral told me to get something down on paper. Anything, just so long as it showed we were doing our job.'

He got up and walked to the window. 'But now it's different, Karl. It isn't a joke any longer. It could be done.'

Hofer stood stolidly on the other side of the desk, showing no emotion. 'Yes, Herr Oberst, I think it could.'

'And doesn't that prospect move you in any way at all?' Radl shivered. 'God, but it frightens me. Bring me those Admiralty charts and the ordnance survey map.'

Hofer spread them on the desk and Radl found Hobs End and examined it in conjunction with the photos. 'What more could one ask for? A perfect dropping zone for parachutists and that weekend the tide comes in again by dawn and washes away any signs of activity.'

'But even quite a small force would have to be conveyed in a transport type of aircraft or a bomber,' Hofer pointed out. 'Can you imagine a Dornier or a Junkers lasting for long over the Norfolk coast these days, with so many bomber stations protected by regular night fighter patrols?'

'A problem,' Radl said, 'I agree, but hardly insurmountable. According to the Luftwaffe target chart for the area there is no low-level radar on that particular section of coast, which means an approach under six hundred feet would be undetected. But that kind of detail is immaterial at the moment. It can be handled later. A feasibility study, Karl, that's all we need at this stage. You agree that in theory it would be possible to drop a raiding party on that beach?'

Hofer said, 'I accept that as a proposition, but how do we get them out again? By U-boat?'

Radl looked down at the chart for a moment, then shook his head. 'No, not really practical. The raiding party would be too large. I know that they could all be crammed on board somehow, but the rendezvous would need to be some distance off-shore and there would be problems getting so many out there. It needs to be something simpler, more direct. An E-boat, perhaps. There's plenty of E-boat activity in that area in the coastal shipping lanes. I don't see any reason why one couldn't slip in between the beach and the Point. It would be on a rising tide and according to the report, there are no mines in that channel, which would simplify things considerably.'

'One would need Navy advice on that,' Hofer said cautiously. 'Mrs. Grey does say in her report that those are dangerous waters.'

'Which is exactly what good sailors are for. Is there anything else you're not happy with?'

'Forgive me, Herr Oberst, but it would seem to me that there is a time factor involved which could be quite crucial to the success of the entire operation and, frankly, I don't see how it could be reconciled.' Hofer pointed to Studley Grange on the ordnance survey map. 'Here is the target, approximately eight miles from the dropping zone. Considering the unfamiliar territory and the darkness, I would say it would take the raiding party two hours to reach it and however brief the visit, it would still take as long for the return journey. My estimate would be an action span of six hours. If one accepts that the drop would have to be made around midnight for security reasons, this means that the rendezvous with the E-boat would take place at dawn if not after, which would be completely unacceptable. The E-boat must have at least two hours of darkness to cover her departure.'

Radl had been lying back in the chair, face turned up to the ceiling, eyes closed. 'Very lucidly put, Karl. You're learning.' He sat up. 'You're absolutely right, which is why the drop would have to be made the night before.'

'Herr Oberst?' Hofer said, astonishment on his face. 'I don't understand.'

'It's quite simple. Churchill will arrive at Studley Grange during the afternoon or evening of the sixth and spend the night there. Our party drops in on the previous night, November fifth.'

Hofer frowned, considering the point. 'I can see the advantage, of course, Herr Oberst. The additional time would give them room to manoeuvre in case of any unlooked-for eventuality.'

'It would also mean that there would no longer be any problem with the E-boat,' Radl said. 'They could be picked up as early as ten or eleven o'clock on the Saturday.' He smiled and took another cigarette from the box. 'So, you agree that this, too, is feasible?'

'There would be a grave problem of concealment on the Saturday itself,' Hofer pointed out. 'Especially for a sizable group.'

'You're absolutely right,' Radl stood up and started to pace up and down the room again. 'But it seems to me there's a rather obvious answer. Let me ask you a question as an old forester, Karl. If you wanted to hide a pine tree, what would be the safest place on earth?'

'In a forest of pines, I suppose.'

'Exactly. In a remote and isolated area like this a stranger – any stranger – stands out like a sore thumb, especially in wartime. No holidaymakers, remember. The British, like good Germans, spend their holidays at home to help the war effort. And yet, Karl, according to Mrs. Grey's report, there are strangers constantly passing through the lanes and the villages every week who are accepted without question.' Hofer looked mystified and Radl continued. 'Soldiers, Karl, on manoeuvres, playing war-games, hunting each other through the hedgerows.' He reached for Joanna Grey's report from the desk and turned the pages. 'Here, on page three, for example, she speaks of this place Meltham House eight miles from Studley Constable. During the past year used as a training establishment for commando-type units on four occasions. Twice by British commandos, once by a similar unit composed of Poles and Czechs with English officers and once by American Rangers.'

He passed the report across and Hofer looked at it.

'All they need are British uniforms to be able to pass through the countryside with no difficulty. A Polish commando unit would do famously.'

'It would certainly take care of the language problem,' Hofer said. 'But that Polish unit Mrs. Grey mentioned had English officers, not just English-speaking. If the Herr Oberst will forgive me for saying so, there's a difference.'

'Yes, you're right,' Radl told him. 'All the difference in the world. If the officer in charge is English or apparently English, then that would make the whole thing so much tighter.'

Hofer looked at his watch. 'If I might remind the Herr Oberst, the Heads of Section weekly meeting is due to start in the Admiral's office in precisely ten minutes.'

'Thank you, Karl.' Radl tightened his belt and stood up. 'So, it would appear that our feasibility study is virtually complete. We seem to have covered everything.'

'Except for what is perhaps the most important item of all, Herr Oberst.'

Radl was half-way to the door and now he paused. 'All right, Karl, surprise me.'

'The leader of such a venture, Herr Oberst. He would have to be a man of extraordinary abilities.'

'Another Otto Skorzeny,' Radl suggested.

'Exactly,' Hofer said. 'With, in this case, one thing more. The ability to pass as an Englishman.'

Radl smiled beautifully. 'Find him for me, Karl. I'll give you forty-eight hours.' He opened the door quickly and went out.

As it happened, Radl had to go to Munich unexpectedly the following day and it was not until after lunch on Thursday that he re-appeared in his office at the Tirpitz Ufer. He was extremely tired, having slept very little in Munich the night before. The Lancaster bombers of the RAF had pressed their attentions on that city with more than usual severity.

Hofer produced coffee instantly and poured him a brandy. 'Good trip, Herr Oberst?'

'Fair,' Radl said. 'Actually, the most interesting happening was when we were landing yesterday. Our Junkers was buzzed by an American Mustang fighter. Caused more than a little panic, I can tell you. Then we saw that it had a Swastika on the tailplane. Apparently it was one which had crash-landed and the Luftwaffe had put it into working order and were flight testing.'

'Extraordinary, Herr Oberst.'

Radl nodded. 'It gave me an idea, Karl. That little problem you had about Dorniers or Junkers surviving over the Norfolk coast.' And then he noticed a fresh green manilla folder on the desk. 'What's this?'

'The assignment you gave me, Herr Oberst. The officer who could pass as an Englishman. Took some digging out, I can tell you, and there's a report of some court martial proceedings which I've indented for. They should be here this afternoon.'

'Court martial?' Radl said. 'I don't like the sound of that.' He opened the file. 'Who on earth is this man?'

'His name is Steiner. Lieutenant-Colonel Kurt Steiner,' Hofer said, 'and I'll leave you in peace to read about him. It's an interesting story.'

It was more than interesting. It was fascinating.

Steiner was the only son of Major-General Karl Steiner, at present area commander in Brittany. He had been born in 1916 when his father was a major of artillery. His mother was American, daughter of a wealthy wool merchant from Boston who had moved to London for business reasons. In the month that her son was born, her only brother had died on the Somme as a captain in a Yorkshire infantry regiment.

The boy had been educated in London, spending five years at St. Paul's during the period his father was military attaché at the German Embassy, and spoke English fluently. After his mother's tragic death in a car crash in 1931, he had returned to Germany with his father, but had continued to visit relatives in Yorkshire until 1938.

For a while, he had studied art in Paris, maintained by his father, the bargain being that if it didn't work out he would enter the Army. That was exactly what had happened. He had a brief period as a second lieutenant in the Artillery and in 1936 had answered the call for volunteers to do parachute training at Stendhal, more to relieve the boredom of military life than anything else.

It had become obvious immediately that he had a talent for that kind of freebooter soldiery. He'd seen ground action in Poland and parachuted into Narvik in the Norwegian campaign. As a full lieutenant he'd crash-landed by glider with the group that took the Albert Canal in 1940 during the big push for Belgium and had been wounded in the arm.

Greece came next – the Corinth Canal, and then a new kind of hell. May, 1941, a captain by then, in the big drop over Crete, severely wounded in savage fighting for Maleme airfield.

Afterwards, the Winter War. Radl was aware of a sudden chill in his bones at the very name. *God, will we ever forget Russia? he asked himself. Those of us who were there then?*

As an acting major Steiner had led a special assault group of three hundred volunteers, dropped by night to contact and lead out two divisions cut off during the battle for Leningrad. He had emerged from that affair with a bullet in the right leg which had left him with a slight limp, a Knight's Cross and a reputation for that kind of cutting-out operation.

He had been in charge of two further affairs of a similar nature and had been promoted lieutenant-colonel in time to go to Stalingrad where he had lost half his men, but had been ordered out several weeks before the end when there were still planes running. In January, he and the one hundred and sixty-seven survivors of his original assault group were dropped near Kiev, once again to contact and lead out two infantry divisions which had been cut off. The end product was a fighting retreat for three hundred bloodstained miles and during the last week in April Kurt Steiner had crossed into German lines with only thirty survivors of his original assault force.

There was an immediate award of the Oak Leaves to his Knight's Cross and Steiner and his men had been packed off to Germany by train as soon as possible, passing through Warsaw on the morning of the 1st of May. He had left it with his men that same evening under close arrest by order of Jurgen Stroop, SS Brigadeführer and Major-General of Police.

There had been a court martial the following week. The details were missing, only the verdict was on file. Steiner and his men had been sentenced to serve as a penal unit to work on Operation Swordfish on Alderney in the German-occupied Channel Islands. Radl sat looking at the file for a moment, then closed it and pressed the buzzer for Hofer who came in at once.

'Herr Oberst?'

'What happened in Warsaw?'

'I'm not sure, Herr Oberst. I'm hoping to have the court martial papers available later this afternoon.'

'All right,' Radl said. 'What are they doing in the Channel Islands?'

'As far as I can find out, Operation Swordfish is a kind of suicide unit, Herr Oberst. Their purpose is the destruction of allied shipping in the Channel.'

'And how do they achieve that?'

'Apparently they sit on a torpedo with the charge taken out, Herr Oberst, and a glass cupola fitted to give the operator some protection. A live torpedo is slung underneath which, during an attack, the operator is supposed to release, turning away at the last moment himself.'

'Good God Almighty,' Radl said in horror. 'No wonder they had to make it a penal unit.'

He sat there in silence for a while looking down at the file. Hofer coughed and said tentatively, 'You think he could be a possibility?'

'I don't see why not,' Radl said. 'I should imagine that anything would seem like an improvement on what he's doing now. Do you know if the Admiral is in?'

'I'll find out, Herr Oberst.'

'If he is, try and get me an appointment this afternoon. Time I showed him how far we've got. Prepare me an outline – nice and brief. One page only and type it yourself. I don't want anyone else getting wind of this thing. Not even in the Department.'

At that precise moment Lieutenant-Colonel Kurt Steiner was up to his waist in the freezing waters of the English Channel, colder than he had even been in his life before, colder even than in Russia, cold eating into his brain as he crouched behind the glass cupola on his torpedo.

His exact situation was almost two miles to the north-east of Braye Harbour on the island of Alderney, and north of the smaller off-shore island of Burhou, although he was cocooned in a sea-fog of such density that, for all he could see, he might as well have been at the end of the world. At least he was not alone. Lifelines of hemp rope disappeared into the fog on either side of him like umbilical cords connecting him with Sergeant Otto Lemke on his left and Lieutenant Ritter Neumann on his right.

Steiner had been amazed to get called out that afternoon. Even more astonishing was the evidence of a radar contact, indicating a ship so close inshore, for the main route up-Channel was much further north. As it transpired later, the vessel in question, an eight-thousand-ton Liberty ship, *Joseph Johnson*, out of Boston for Plymouth with a cargo of high explosives, had sustained damage to her steering in a bad storm near Land's End three days earlier. Her difficulties in this direction and the heavy fog had conspired to put her off course.

North of Burhou, Steiner slowed, jerking on the lifelines to alert his companions. A few moments later, they coasted out of the fog on either side to join him. Ritter Neumann's face was blue with cold in the black cowl of his rubber suit. 'We're close, Herr Oberst,' he said. 'I'm sure I can hear them.'

Sergeant Lemke drifted in to join them. The curly black beard, of which he was very proud, was a special dispensation from Steiner in view of the fact that Lemke's chin was badly deformed by a Russian high-velocity bullet. He was very excited, eyes sparkling, and obviously looked upon the whole thing as a great adventure.

'I, too, Herr Oberst.'

Steiner raised a hand to silence him and listened. The muted throbbing was quite close now for the *Joseph Johnson* was taking it very steady indeed.

'An easy one, Herr Oberst.' Lemke grinned in spite of the fact that his teeth were chattering in the cold. 'The best touch we've had yet. She won't even know what's hit her.'

'You speak for yourself, Lemke,' Ritter Neumann said. 'If there's one thing I've learned in my short and unhappy life it's never to expect anything and to be particularly suspicious of that which is apparently served up on a plate.'

As if to prove his words, a sudden flurry of wind tore a hole in the curtain of the fog. Behind them was the grey-green sweep of Alderney, the old Admiralty breakwater poking out like a granite finger for a thousand yards from Braye, the Victorian naval fortification of Fort Albert clearly visible.

No more than a hundred and fifty yards away, the *Joseph Johnson* moved on a north-westerly course for the open Channel at a steady eight or ten knots. It could only be a matter of moments before they were seen, Steiner acted instantly. 'All right, straight in, release torpedoes at fifty yards and out again and no stupid heroics, Lemke. There aren't any medals to be had in the penal regiments, remember. Only coffins.'

He increased power and surged forward, crouching behind the cupola as waves started breaking over his head. He was aware of Ritter Neumann on his right, roughly abreast of him, but Lemke had surged on and was already fifteen or twenty yards in front.

'The silly young bastard,' Steiner thought. 'What does he think this is, the Charge of the Light Brigade?'

Two of the men at the rail of the *Joseph Johnson* had rifles in their hands and an officer came out of the wheelhouse and stood on the bridge firing a Thompson sub-machine gun with a drum magazine. The ship was picking up speed now, driving through a light curtain of mist, as the blanket of fog began to settle again. Within another few moments she would have disappeared altogether. The riflemen at the rail were having difficulty in taking aim on a heaving deck at a target so low in the water and their shots were very wide of the mark. The Thompson, not too accurate at the best of times, was doing no better and making a great deal of noise about it.

Lemke reached the fifty-yard line several lengths in front of the others and kept right on going. There wasn't a thing Steiner could do about it. The riflemen started to get the range and a bullet ricocheted from the body of his torpedo in front of the cupola.

He turned and waved to Neumann. 'Now!' he cried and fired his torpedo.

The one upon which he was seated, released from the weight it had been carrying, sprang forward with new energy and he turned to starboard quickly, following Neumann round in a great sweeping curve intended to take them away from the ship as fast as possible.

Lemke was turning away now also, no more than twenty-five yards from the *Joseph Johnson*, the men at the rail firing at him for all they were worth. Presumably one of them scored a hit, although Steiner could never be sure. The only certain thing was that one moment Lemke was crouched astride his torpedo, surging away from danger. The next, he wasn't there any more.

A second later one of the three torpedoes scored a direct hit close to the stern and the stern hold contained hundreds of tons of high explosive bombs destined for use by Flying Fortresses of bombardment groups of the 1st Air Division of the American 8th Air Force in Britain. As the *Joseph Johnson* was swallowed by the fog, she exploded, the sound re-echoing from the island again and again. Steiner crouched low as the blast swept over, swerving when an enormous piece of twisted metal hurtled into the sea in front of him.

Debris cascaded down. The air was full of it and something struck Neumann a glancing blow on the head. He threw up his hands with a cry and catapulted backwards into the sea, his torpedo running away from him, plunging over the next wave and disappearing.

Although unconscious, blood on his forehead from a nasty gash, he was kept afloat by his inflatable jacket. Steiner coasted in beside him, looped one end of of a line under the lieutenant's jacket and kept on going, pushing towards the breakwater and Braye, already fading as the fog rolled in towards the island again.

The tide was ebbing fast. Steiner didn't have one chance in hell of reaching Braye Harbour and he knew it, as he wrestled vainly against a tide that must eventually sweep them far out into the Channel beyond any hope of return.

He suddenly realised that Ritter Neumann was conscious again and staring up at him. 'Let me go!' he said faintly. 'Cut me loose. You'll make it on your own.'

Steiner didn't bother to reply at first, but concentrated on turning the torpedo over towards the right. Burhou was somewhere out there in that impenetrable blanket of fog. There was a chance the ebbing tide might push them in, a slim one perhaps, but better than nothing.

He said calmly, 'How long have we been together now, Ritter?'

'You know damn well,' Ritter said. 'The first time I clapped eyes on you was over Narvik when I was afraid to jump out of the plane.'

'I remember now,' Steiner said. 'I persuaded you otherwise.'

'That's one way of putting it,' Ritter said. 'You threw me out.'

His teeth were chattering and he was very cold and Steiner reached down to check the line. 'Yes, a snotty eighteen-year-old Berliner, fresh from the University. Always with a volume of poetry in your hip pocket. The professor's son who crawled fifty yards under fire to bring me a medical kit when I was wounded at the Albert Canal.'

'I should have let you go,' Ritter said. 'Look what you got me into. Crete, then a commission I didn't want, Russia and now this. What a bargain.' He closed his eyes and added softly, 'Sorry, Kurt, but it's no good.'

Quite suddenly, they were caught in a great eddy of water that swept them in towards the rocks of L'Equet on the tip of Burhou. There was a ship there, or half one; all that was left of a French coaster that had run on the reef in a storm earlier in the year. What was left of her stern deck sloped into deep water. A wave swept them in, the torpedo high on the swell and Steiner rolled away from it, grabbing for the ship's rail with one hand and hanging on to Neumann's lifeline with the other.

The wave receded, taking the torpedo with it. Steiner got to his feet and went up the sloping deck to what was left of the wheelhouse. He wedged himself in the broken doorway and hauled his companion after him. They crouched in the roofless shell of the wheelhouse and it started to rain softly.

'What happens now?' Neumann asked weakly.

'We sit tight,' Steiner said. 'Brandt will be out with the recovery boat as soon as this fog clears a little.'

'I could do with a cigarette,' Neumann said, and then he stiffened suddenly and pointed out through the broken doorway. 'Look at that.'

Steiner went to the rail. The water was moving fast now as the tide ebbed, twisting and turning amongst the reefs and rocks, carrying with it the refuse of war, a floating carpet of wreckage that was all that was left of the *Joseph Johnson.*

'So, we got her,' Neumann said. Then he tried to get up. 'There's a man down there, Kurt, in a yellow lifejacket. Look, under the stern.'

Steiner slid down the deck into the water and turned under the stern, pushing his way through a mass of planks to the man who floated there, head back, eyes closed. He was very young with blond hair plastered to the skull. Steiner grabbed him by the lifejacket and started to tow him towards the safety of the shattered stern, and he opened his eyes and stared at him. Then he shook his head, trying to speak.

Steiner floated beside him for a moment. 'What is it?' he said in English.

'Please,' the boy whispered. 'Let me go.'

His eyes closed again and Steiner swam with him to the stern. Neumann, watching from the wheelhouse, saw Steiner start to drag him up the sloping deck. He paused for a long moment, then slid the boy gently back into the water. A current took him away and out of sight beyond the reef, and Steiner clambered wearily back up the deck again.

'What was it?' Neumann demanded weakly.

'Both legs were gone from the knees down.' Steiner sat very carefully and braced his feet agains the rail. 'What was that poem of Eliot's that you were always quoting at Stalingrad? The one I didn't like?'

'I think we are in rat's alley,' Neumann said. 'Where the dead men lost their bones.'

'Now I understand it,' Steiner told him. 'Now I see exactly what he meant.'

They sat there in silence. It was colder now, the rain increasing in force, clearing the fog rapidly. About twenty minutes later they heard an engine not too far away. Steiner took the small signalling pistol from the pouch on his right leg, charged it with a waterproof cartridge and fired a maroon.

A few moments later, the recovery launch appeared from the fog and slowed, drifting in towards them. Sergeant-Major Brandt was in the prow with a line ready to throw. He was an enormous figure of a man, well over six feet tall and broad in proportion, rather incongruously wearing a yellow oilskin coat with *Royal National Lifeboat Institution* on the back. The rest of the crew were all Steiner's men. Sergeant Sturm at the wheel, Lance-Corporal Briegel and Private Berg acting as deckhands. Brandt jumped for the sloping deck of the wreck and hitched the line about the rail as Steiner and Neumann slid down to join him.

'You made a hit, Herr Oberst. What happened to Lemke?'

'Playing heroes as usual,' Steiner told him. 'This time he went too far. Careful with Lieutenant Neumann. He's had a bad crack on the head.'

'Sergeant Altmann's out in the other boat with Riedel and Meyer. They might see some sign of him. He has the Devil's own luck, that one.' Brandt lifted Neumann up over the rail with astonishing strength. 'Get him in the cabin.'

But Neumann wouldn't have it and slumped down on the deck with his back against the stern rail. Steiner sat beside him and Brandt gave them cigarettes as the motor boat pulled away. Steiner felt tired. More tired than he had been in a very long time. *Five years of war.* Sometimes it seemed as if it was not only all there was, but all there ever had been.

They rounded the end of the Admiralty breakwater and followed the thousand yards or so of its length into Braye. There was a surprising number of ships in the harbour, French coasters mostly, carrying building supplies from the continent for the new fortifications that were being raised all over the island.

The small landing stage had been extended. An E-boat was tied up there and as the motor boat drifted in astern, the sailors on deck raised a cheer and a young, bearded lieutenant in a heavy sweater and salt-stained cap stood smartly to attention and saluted.

'Fine work, Herr Oberst.'

Steiner acknowledged the salute as he went over the rail. 'Many thanks, Koenig.'

He went up the steps to the upper landing stage, Brandt following, supporting Neumann with a strong arm. As they came out on top a large black saloon car, an old Wolseley, turned on to the landing stage and braked to a halt. The driver jumped out and opened the rear door.

The first person to emerge was the man who at that time was acting-commandant of the island, Hans Neuhoff, a full colonel of artillery. Like Steiner, a Winter War veteran, wounded in the chest at Leningrad, he had never recovered his health, his lungs damaged beyond repair, and his face had the permanently resigned look of a man who is dying by inches and knows it. His wife got out of the car after him.

Ilse Neuhoff was at that time twenty-seven years of age, a slim, aristocratic-looking blonde with a wide, generous mouth and good cheekbones. Most people turned to look at her twice and not only because she was beautiful, but because she usually seemed familiar. She had enjoyed a successful career as a film starlet working for UFA in Berlin. She was one of those odd people that everyone likes and she had been much in demand in Berlin society. She was a friend of the Goebbels. The Führer himself had admired her.

She had married Hans Neuhoff out of a genuine liking that went far beyond sexual love, something of which he was no longer capable anyway. She had nursed him back on his feet after Russia, supported him every step of the way, used all her influence to secure him his present post, had even obtained a pass to visit him by influence of Goebbels himself. They had an understanding – a warm and mutual understanding and it was because of this that she was able to go forward to Steiner and kiss him openly on the cheek.

'You had us worried, Kurt.'

Neuhoff shook hands, genuinely delighted. 'Wonderful work, Kurt. I'll get a signal off to Berlin at once.'

'Don't do that, for God's sake,' Steiner said in mock alarm. 'They might decide to send me back to Russia.'

Ilse took his arm. 'It wasn't in the cards when I last read Tarot for you, but I'll look again tonight if you like.'

There was a hail from the lower landing stage and they moved forward to the edge in time to see the second recovery boat coming in. There was a body on the stern deck covered with a blanket and Sergeant Altmann, another of Steiner's men, came out of the wheelhouse. 'Herr Oberst?' he called, awaiting orders.

Steiner nodded and Altmann raised the blanket briefly. Neumann had moved to join Steiner and now he said bitterly, 'Lemke. Crete, Leningrad, Stalingrad – all those years and this is how it ends.'

'When your name's on the bullet, that's it,' Brandt said.

Steiner turned to look into Ilse Neuhoff's troubled face. 'My poor Ilse, better to leave those cards of yours in the box. A few more afternoons like this and it won't be so much a question of *will* the worst come to pass as *when.*'

He took her arm, smiling cheerfully and led her towards the car.

Canaris had a meeting with Ribbentrop and Goebbels during the afternoon and it was six o'clock before he could see Radl. There was no sign of Steiner's court martial papers.

At five minutes to six Hofer knocked on the door and entered Radl's office. 'Have they come?' Radl demanded eagerly.

'I'm afraid not, Herr Oberst.'

'Why not, for God's sake?' Radl said angrily.

'It seems that as the original incident was concerned with a complaint from the SS, the records are at Prinz Albrechtstrasse.'

'Have you got the outline that I asked you for?'

'Herr Oberst.' Hofer handed him a neatly typed sheet of paper.

Radl examined it quickly. 'Excellent, Karl. Really excellent.' He smiled and straightened his already immaculate uniform. 'You're off duty now, aren't you?'

'I'd prefer to wait until the Herr Oberst returns,' Hofer said.

Radl smiled and clapped him on the shoulder. 'All right, let's get it over with.'

The Admiral was being served with coffee by an orderly when Radl went in. 'Ah, there you are, Max,' he said cheerfully. 'Will you join me?'

'Thank you, Herr Admiral.'

The orderly filled another cup, adjusted the blackout curtains and went out. Canaris sighed and eased himself back in the chair, reaching down to fondle the ears of one of his dachshunds. He seemed weary and there was evidence of strain in the eyes and around the mouth.

'You look tired,' Radl told him.

'So would you if you'd been closeted with Ribbentrop and Goebbels all afternoon. Those two really get more impossible every time I see them. According to Goebbels we're still winning the war, Max. Was there ever anything more absurd?' Radl didn't really know what to say but was saved by the Admiral carrying straight on. 'Anyway, what did you want to see me about?'

Radl placed Hofer's typed outline on the desk and Canaris started to read it. After a while he looked up in obvious bewilderment. 'What is it, for God's sake?'

'The feasibility study you asked for, Herr Admiral. The Churchill business. You asked me to get something down on paper.'

'Ah, yes.' There was understanding on the Admiral's face now and he looked again at the paper. After a while he smiled. 'Yes, very good, Max. Quite absurd, of course, but on paper it does have a kind of mad logic to it. Keep it handy in case Himmler reminds the Führer to ask me if we've done anything about it.'

'You mean that's all, Herr Admiral?' Radl said. 'You don't want me to take it any further?'

Canaris had opened a file and now he looked up in obvious surprise. 'My dear Max, I don't think you quite get the point. The more absurd the idea put forward by your superiors in this game, the more rapturously should you receive it, however crazy. Put all your enthusiasm – assumed, of course – into the project. Over a period of time allow the difficulties to show, so that very gradually your masters will make the discovery for themselves that it just isn't on. As nobody likes to be involved in failure if he can avoid it, the whole project will be discreetly dropped.' He laughed lightly and tapped the outline with one finger. 'Mind you, even the Führer would need to be having a very off-day indeed to see any possibilities in such a mad escapade as this.'

Radl found himself saying, 'It would work, Herr Admiral. I've even got the right man for the job.'

'I'm sure you have, Max, if you've been anything like as thorough as you usually are.' He smiled and pushed the outline across the desk. 'I can see that you've taken the whole thing too seriously. Perhaps my remarks about Himmler worried you. But there's no need, believe me. I can handle him. You've got enough on paper to satisfy them if the occasion arises. Plenty of other things you can get on with now – really important matters.'

He nodded in dismissal and picked up his pen. Radl said stubbornly, 'But surely, Herr Admiral, if the Führer wishes it . . . '

Canaris exploded angrily, throwing down his pen. 'God in heaven, man, kill Churchill when we have already lost the war? In what way is that supposed to help?'

He had jumped up and leaned across the desk, both hands braced. Radl stood rigidly to attention, staring woodenly into space a foot above the Admiral's head. Canaris flushed, aware that he had gone too far, that there had been treason implicit in his angry words and too late to retract them.

'At ease,' he said.

Radl did as he was ordered. 'Herr Admiral.'

'We've known each other a long time, Max.'

'Yes, sir.'

'So trust me now. I know what I'm doing.'

'Very well, Herr Admiral,' Radl said crisply.

He stepped back, clicked his heels, turned and went out. Canaris stayed where he was, hands braced against the desk, suddenly looking haggard and old. 'My God,' he whispered. 'How much longer?'

When he sat down and picked up his coffee, his hand was trembling so much that the cup rattled in the saucer.

When Radl went into the office, Hofer was straightening the papers on his desk. The sergeant turned eagerly and then saw the expression on Radl's face.

'The Admiral didn't like it, Herr Oberst?'

'He said it had a certain mad logic, Karl. Actually, he seemed to find it quite amusing.'

'What happens now, Herr Oberst?'

'Nothing, Karl,' Radl said wearily and sat down behind his desk. 'It's on paper, the feasibility study they wanted and may never ask for again and that's all we were required to do. We get on with something else.'

He reached for one of his Russian cigarettes and Hofer gave him a light. 'Can I get you anything, Herr Oberst?' he said, his voice sympathetic, but careful.

'No, thank you, Karl. Go home now. I'll see you in the morning.'

'Herr Oberst.' Hofer clicked his heels and hesitated.

Radl said, 'Go on, Karl, there's a good fellow and thank you.'

Hofer went out and Radl ran a hand over his face. His empty socket was burning, the invisible hand ached. Sometimes he felt as if they'd wired him up wrongly when they'd put him back together again. Amazing how disappointed he felt. A sense of real, personal loss.

'Perhaps it's as well,' he said softly. 'I was beginning to take the whole damn thing too seriously.'

He sat down, opened Joanna Grey's file and started to read it. After a while he reached for the ordnance survey map and began to unfold it. He stopped suddenly. He'd had enough of this tiny office for one day, enough of the Abwehr. He pulled his briefcase from under the desk, stuffed the files and the map inside and took his leather greatcoat down from behind the door.

It was too early for the RAF and the city seemed unnaturally quiet when he went out of the front entrance. He decided to take advantage of the brief calm and walk home to his small apartment instead of calling for a staff car. In any case his head was splitting and the light rain which was falling was really quite refreshing. He went down the steps, acknowledging the sentry's salute and passed under the shaded street light at the bottom. A car started up somewhere further along the Tirpitz Ufer and pulled in beside him.

It was a black Mercedes saloon, as black as the uniforms of the two Gestapo men who got out of the front seats and stood waiting. As Radl saw the cuff-title of the one nearest to him, his heart seemed to stop beating. RFSS Reichsführer der SS. The cuff-title of Himmler's personal staff.

The young man who got out of the rear seat wore a slouch hat and a black leather coat. His smile had the kind of ruthless charm that only the genuinely insincere possess. 'Colonel Radl?' he said. 'So glad we were able to catch you before you left. The Reichsführer presents his compliments. If you could find it convenient to spare him a little time, he'd appreciate it.' He deftly removed the briefcase from Radl's hand. 'Let me carry that for you.'

Radl moistened dry lips and managed a smile. 'But of course,' he said and got into the rear of the Mercedes.

The young man joined him, the other got into the front and they moved away. Radl noticed that the one who wasn't driving had an Erma police sub-machine-gun across his knees. He breathed deeply in an effort to control the fear that rose inside him.

'Cigarette, Herr Oberst?'

'Thank you,' Radl said. 'Where are we going, by the way?'

'Prinz Albrechtstrasse.' The young man gave him a light and smiled. 'Gestapo Headquarters.'

4

When Radl was ushered into the office on the first floor at Prinz Albrechtstrasse, he found Himmler seated behind a large desk, a stack of files in front of him. He was wearing full uniform as Reichsführer SS, a devil in black in the shaded light, and when he looked up the face behind the silver pince-nez was cold and impersonal.

The young man in the black leather coat who had brought Radl in gave the Nazi salute and placed the briefcase on the table. 'At your orders, Herr Reichsführer.'

'Thank you, Rossman,' Himmler replied. 'Wait outside. I may need you later.'

Rossman went out and Radl waited as Himmler moved the files very precisely to one side of the desk, as if clearing the decks for action. He pulled the briefcase forward and looked at it thoughtfully. Strangely enough, Radl had got back some of his nerve, and a certain black humour that had been a saving grace to him on many occasions surfaced now.

'Even the condemned man is entitled to a last cigarette, Herr Reichsführer.'

Himmler actually smiled, which was quite something considering that tobacco was one of his pet aversions. 'Why not?' He waved a hand. 'They told me you were a brave man, Herr Oberst. You earned your Knight's Cross during the Winter War?'

'That's right, Herr Reichsführer.' Radl got his cigarette case out, one-handed, and opened it deftly.

'And have worked for Admiral Canaris ever since?'

Radl waited, smoking his cigarette, trying to make it last while Himmler stared down at the briefcase again. The room was really quite pleasant in the shaded light. An open fire burned brightly and above it there was an autographed picture of the Führer in a gilt frame.

Himmler said, 'There is not much that happens at the Tirpitz Ufer these days that I don't know about. Does that surprise you? For example, I am aware that on the twenty-second of this month you were shown a routine report from an Abwehr agent in England, a Mrs. Joanna Grey, in which the magic name of Winston Churchill figured.'

'Herr Reichsführer, I don't know what to say,' Radl told him.

'Even more fascinating, you had all her files transferred from Abwehr One into your custody, and relieved Captain Meyer, who had been this lady's link man for many years, of duty. I understand he's most upset.' Himmler placed a hand on the briefcase. 'Come, Herr Oberst, we're too old to play games. You know what I'm talking about. Now, what have you got to tell me?'

Max Radl was a realist. He had no choice at all in the matter. He said, 'In the briefcase, the Reichsführer will find all that there is to know except for one item.'

'The court martial papers of Lieutenant-Colonel Kurt Steiner of the Parachute Regiment?' Himmler picked up the top file from the pile at the side of his desk and handed it over. 'A fair exchange. I suggest you read it outside.' He opened the briefcase and started to extract the contents. 'I'll send for you when I need you.'

Radl almost raised his arm, but one last stubborn grain of self-respect turned it into a smart, if conventional salute. He turned on his heel, opened the door and went out into the ante-room.

Rossman sprawled in an easy chair reading a copy of *Signal*, the Wehrmacht magazine. He glanced up in surprise. 'Leaving us already?'

'No such luck.' Radl dropped the file on to a low coffee table and started to unbuckle his belt. 'It seems I've got some reading to do.'

Rossman smiled amiably. 'I'll see if I can find us some coffee. It looks to me as if you could be with us for quite some time.'

He went out and Radl lit another cigarette, sat down and opened the file.

The date chosen for the final erasing of the Warsaw Ghetto from the face of the earth was the 19th April. Hitler's birthday was on the 20th and Himmler hoped to present him with the good news as a suitable present. Unfortunately when the commander of the operation, SS Oberführer von Sammern-Frankenegg and his men marched in, they were chased out again by the Jewish Combat Organisation, under the command of Mordechai Anielewicz.

Himmler immediately replaced him with SS Brigadeführer and Major-General of Police, Jurgen Stroop, who, aided by a mixed force of SS and renegade Poles and Ukrainians, applied himself seriously to the task in hand: to leave not one brick standing, not one Jew alive. To be able to report to Himmler personally that *The Warsaw Ghetto is no more*. It took him twenty-eight days to accomplish.

Steiner and his men arrived in Warsaw on the morning of the Thirteenth Day on a hospital train from the Eastern Front bound for Berlin. There was a stop-over time of between one to two hours, depending on how long it took to rectify a fault in the engine's cooling system, and orders were broadcast over the loudspeaker that no one was to leave the station. There were military police on the entrances to see that the order was obeyed.

Most of his men stayed inside the coach, but Steiner got out to stretch his legs and Ritter Neumann joined him. Steiner's jump boots were worn through, his leather coat had definitely seen better days and he was wearing a soiled white scarf and sidecap of a type more common amongst NCOs than officers.

The military policeman guarding the main entrance held his rifle across his chest in both hands and said roughly, 'You heard the order, didn't you? Get back in there!'

'It would seem they want to keep us under wraps for some reason, Herr Oberst,' Neumann said.

The military policeman's jaw dropped and he came to attention hurriedly. 'I ask the Herr Oberst's pardon. I didn't realise.'

There was a quick step behind them and a harsh voice demanded, 'Schulz – what's all this about?'

Steiner and Neumann ignored it and stepped outside. A pall of black smoke hung over the city, there was a crump of artillery in the distance, the rattle of small arms fire. A hand on Steiner's shoulder spun him round and he found himself facing an immaculately uniformed major. Around his neck was suspended on a chain the gleaming brass gorget plate of the military police. Steiner sighed and pulled away the white scarf at his neck exposing not only the collar patches of his rank, but also the Knight's Cross with Oak Leaves for a second award.

'Steiner,' he said, 'Parachute Regiment.'

The major saluted politely, but only because he had to. 'I'm sorry, Herr Oberst, but orders are orders.'

'What's your name?' Steiner demanded.

There was an edge to the colonel's voice now in spite of the lazy smile, that hinted at the possibility of a little unpleasantness. 'Otto Frank, Herr Oberst.'

'Good, now that we've established that, would you be kind enough to explain exactly what's going on here? I thought the Polish Army surrendered in 'thirty-nine?'

'They are razing the Warsaw Ghetto to the ground,' Frank said.

'Who is?'

'A special task force. SS and various other groups commanded by Brigadeführer Jurgen Stroop. Jewish bandits, Herr Oberst. They've been fighting from house to house, in the cellars, in the sewers, for thirteen days now. So we're burning them out. Best way to exterminate lice.'

During convalescent leave after being wounded at Leningrad, Steiner had visited his father in France and had found him considerably changed. The General had had his doubts about the new order for some considerable time. Six months earlier he had visited a concentration camp at Auschwitz in Poland.

'The commander was a swine named Rudolf Hoess, Kurt. Would you believe it, a murderer serving a life sentence and released from gaol in the amnesty of nineteen twenty-eight. He was killing Jews by the thousand in specially constructed gas chambers, disposing of their bodies in huge ovens. After extracting such minor items as gold teeth and so forth.'

The old general had been drunk by then and yet not drunk. 'Is this what we're fighting for, Kurt? To protect swine like Hoess? And what will the rest of the world say when the time comes? That we are all guilty? That Germany is guilty because we stood by? Decent and honourable men stood by and did nothing? Well, not me, by God. I couldn't live with myself.'

Standing there in the entrance to Warsaw Station, the memory of all this welling up inside, Kurt Steiner produced an expression on his face that sent the major back a couple of steps. 'That's better,' Steiner said, 'and if you could make it downwind as well I'd be obliged.'

Major Frank's look of astonishment quickly turned to anger as Steiner walked past him, Neumann at his side. 'Easy, Herr Oberst. Easy,' Neumann said.

On the platform at the other side of the track, a group of SS were herding a line of ragged and filthy human beings against a wall. It was virtually impossible to differentiate between the sexes and as Steiner watched, they all started to take their clothes off.

A military policeman stood on the edge of the platform watching and Steiner said, 'What's going on over there?'

'Jews, Herr Oberst,' the man replied. 'This morning's crop from the Ghetto. They'll be shipped out to Treblinka to finish them off later today. They make them strip like that before a search mainly because of the women. Some of them have been carrying loaded pistols inside their pants.'

There was brutal laughter from across the track and someone cried out in pain. Steiner turned to Neumann in disgust and found the lieutenant staring along the platform to the rear of the troop train. A young girl of perhaps fourteen or fifteen, with ragged hair and smoke-blackened face, wearing a cut-down man's overcoat tied with string, crouched under the coach. She had presumably slipped away from the group opposite and her intention was obviously to make a bid for freedom by riding the rods under the hospital train when it pulled out.

In the same moment the military policeman on the edge of the platform saw her and raised the alarm, jumping down on to the track and grabbing for her. She screamed, twisting from his grasp, scrambled up to the platform and ran for the entrance, straight into the arms of Major of Police Frank as he came out of his office.

He had her by the hair and shook her like a rat. 'Dirty little Jew bitch. I'll teach you some manners.'

Steiner started forward. 'No, Herr Oberst!' Neumann said, but he was too late.

Steiner got a firm grip on Frank's collar, pulling him off balance so that he almost fell down, grabbed the girl by the hand and stood her behind him.

Major Frank scrambled to his feet, his face contorted with rage. His hand went to the Walther in the holster at his belt, but Steiner produced a Luger from the pocket of his leather coat and touched him between the eyes. 'You do,' he said, 'and I'll blow your head off. Come to think of it, I'd be doing humanity a favour.'

At least a dozen military policemen ran forward, some carrying machine pistols, others rifles and paused in a semi-circle three or four yards away. A tall sergeant aimed his rifle and Steiner got a hand in Frank's tunic and held him close, screwing the barrel of the Luger in hard.

'I wouldn't advise it.'

An engine coasted through the station at five or six miles an hour hauling a line of open wagons loaded with coal. Steiner said to the girl without looking at her, 'What's your name, child?',

'Brana,' she told him. 'Brana Lezemnikof.'

'Well, Brana,' he said, 'if you're half the girl I think you are, you'll grab hold of one of those coal trucks and hang on till you're out of here. The best I can do for you.' She was gone in a flash and he raised his voice. 'Anyone takes a shot at her puts one in the major here as well.'

The girl jumped for one of the trucks, secured a grip and pulled herself up between two of them. The train coasted out of the station. There was complete silence.

Frank said, 'They'll have her off at the first station, I'll see to it personally.'

Steiner pushed him away and pocketed his Luger. Immediately the military policemen closed in and Ritter Neumann called out, 'Not today, gentlemen.'

Steiner turned and found the lieutenant holding an MP-40 machine pistol. The rest of his men were ranged behind him, all armed to the teeth.

At that point, anything might have happened, had it not been for a sudden disturbance in the main entrance. A group of SS stormed in, rifles at the ready. They took up position in a V formation and a moment later, SS Brigadeführer and Major-General of Police Jurgen Stroop entered, flanked by three or four SS officers of varying ranks, all carrying drawn pistols. He wore a field cap and service uniform and looked surprisingly nondescript.

'What's going on here, Frank?'

'Ask him, Herr Brigadeführer,' Frank said, his face twisted with rage. 'This man, an officer of the German Army, has just allowed a Jewish terrorist to escape.'

Stroop looked Steiner over, noting the rank badges and the Knight's Cross plus the Oak Leaves. 'Who are you?' he demanded.

'Kurt Steiner – Parachute Regiment,' Steiner told him. 'And who might you be?'

Jurgen Stroop was never known to lose his temper. He said calmly, 'You can't talk to me like that, Herr Oberst. I'm a Major-General as you very well know.'

'So is my father,' Steiner told him, 'so I'm not particularly impressed. However, as you've raised the matter, are you Brigadeführer Stroop, the man in charge of the slaughter out there?'

'I am in command here, yes.'

Steiner wrinkled his nose. 'I rather thought you might be. You know what you remind me of?'

'No, Herr Oberst,' Stroop said. 'Do tell me.'

'The kind of thing I occasionally pick up on my shoe in the gutter,' Steiner said. 'Very unpleasant on a hot day.'

Jurgen Stroop, still icy calm, held out his hand. Steiner sighed, took the Luger from his pocket and handed it across. He looked over his shoulder to his men. 'That's it, boys, stand down.' He turned back to Stroop. 'They feel a certain loyalty for some reason unknown to me. Is there any chance you could content yourself with me and overlook their part in this thing?'

'Not the slightest,' Brigadeführer Jurgen Stroop told him.

'That's what I thought,' Steiner said. 'I pride myself I can always tell a thoroughgoing bastard when I see one.'

Radl sat with the file on his knee for a long time after he'd finished reading the account of the court martial. Steiner had been lucky to escape execution but his father's influence would have helped and, after all, he and his men were war heroes. Bad for morale to have to shoot a holder of the Knight's Cross with Oak Leaves. And Operation Swordfish, in the Channel Islands, was just as certain in the long run for all of them. A stroke of genius on somebody's part.

Rossman sprawled in the chair opposite, apparently asleep, the black slouch hat tipped over his eyes, but when the light at the door flashed, he was on his feet. He went straight in without knocking and was back in a moment.

'He wants you.'

The Reichsführer was still seated behind the desk. He now had the ordnance survey map spread out in front of him. He looked up. 'And what did you make of friend Steiner's little escapade in Warsaw?'

'A remarkable story,' Radl said carefully. 'An – an unusual man.'

'I would say one of the bravest you are ever likely to encounter,' Himmler said calmly. 'Gifted with high intelligence, courageous, ruthless, a brilliant soldier – and a romantic fool. I can only imagine that to be the American half of him.' The Reichsführer shook his head. 'The Knight's Cross with Oak Leaves. After that Russian affair the Führer had asked to meet him personally. And what does he do? Throws it all away, career, future, everything, for the sake of a little Jewish bitch he'd never clapped eyes on in his life before.'

He looked up at Radl as if waiting for a reply and Radl said lamely, 'Extraordinary, Herr Reichsführer.'

Himmler nodded and then, as if dismissing the subject completely, rubbed his hands together and leaned over the map. 'The Grey woman's reports are really quite brilliant. An outstanding agent.' He leaned down, eyes very close to the map. 'Will it work?'

'I think so,' Radl replied without hesitation.

'And the Admiral? What does the Admiral think?'

Radl's mind raced as he tried to frame a suitable reply. 'That's a difficult question to answer.'

Himmler sat back, hands folded. For a wild moment Radl felt as if he were back in short trousers and in front of his old village schoolmaster.

'You don't need to tell me, I think I can guess. I admire loyalty, but in this case you would do well to remember that loyalty to Germany, to your Führer, comes first.'

'Naturally, Herr Reichsführer,' Radl said hastily.

'Unfortunately there are those who would not agree,' Himmler went on. 'Subversive elements at every level in our society. Even amongst the generals of the High Command itself. Does that surprise you?'

Radl, genuinely astonished, said, 'But Herr Reichsführer, I can hardly believe . . .'

'That men who have taken an oath of personal loyalty to the Führer can behave in such a dastardly fashion?' He shook his head almost sadly. 'I have every reason to believe that, in March of this year, high-ranking officers of the Wehrmacht placed a bomb on the Führer's plane, set to explode during its flight from Smolensk to Rastenburg.'

'God in heaven,' Radl said.

'The bomb failed to explode and was removed by the individuals concerned later. Of course, it makes one realise more strongly than ever that we cannot fail, that ultimate victory must be ours. That the Führer was saved by some divine intervention seems obvious. That doesn't surprise me of course. I have always believed that some higher being is behind nature, don't you agree?'

'Of course, Herr Reichsführer,' Radl said.

'Yes, if we refused to recognise that we would be no better than Marxists. I insist that all members of the SS believe in God.' He removed his pince-nez for a moment and stroked the bridge of his nose gently with one finger. 'So, traitors everywhere. In the Army and in the Navy, too, at the highest level.'

He replaced his pince-nez and looked up at Radl. 'So you see, Radl,' Himmler went on, 'I have the very best of reasons for being sure that Admiral Canaris must have vetoed this scheme of yours.'

Radl stared at him dumbly. His blood ran cold. Himmler said gently, 'It would not be in accordance with his general aim and that aim is not the victory of the German Reich in this war, I assure you.'

That the Head of the Abwehr was working against the State? The idea was monstrous. But then Radl remembered the Admiral's acid tongue. The derogatory remarks about high state officials, about the Führer himself on occasion. His reaction earlier that evening. *We have lost the war.* And that from the Head of the Abwehr.

Himmler pressed the buzzer and Rossman came in. 'I have an important phone call to make. Show the Herr Oberst around for ten minutes then bring him back.' He turned to Radl. 'You haven't seen the cellars here, have you?'

'No, Herr Reichsführer.'

He might have added that the Gestapo cellars at Prinz Albrechtstrasse were the last places on earth he wanted to see. But he knew that he was going to whether he liked it or not, knew from the slight smile on

Rossman's mouth that it was all arranged.

On the ground floor they went along a corridor that led to the rear of the building. There was an iron door guarded by two Gestapo men wearing steel helmets and armed with machine pistols. 'Are you expecting a war or something?' Radl enquired.

Rossman grinned. 'Let's say it impresses the customers.'

The door was unlocked and he led the way down. The passage at the bottom was brilliantly lit, brickwork painted white, doors opening to right and left. It was extraordinarily quiet.

'Might as well start in here,' Rossman said and opened the nearest door and switched on the light.

It was a conventional enough looking cellar painted white except for the opposite wall which had been faced with concrete in a surprisingly crude way, for the surface was uneven and badly marked. There was a beam across the ceiling near that wall, chains hanging down with coil spring stirrups on the end.

'Something they're supposed to have a lot of success with lately,' Rossman took out a packet of cigarettes and offered Radl one. 'I think it's a dead loss myself. I can't see much point in driving a man insane when you want him to talk.'

'What happens?'

'The suspect is suspended in those stirrups, then they simply turn the electricity on. They throw buckets of water on that concrete wall to improve the electrical flow or something. Extraordinary what it does to people. If you look close you'll see what I mean.'

When Radl approached the wall he saw that what he had taken to be a crudely finished surface was in fact a patina of hand prints in raw concrete where victims had clawed in agony.

'The Inquisition would have been proud of you.'

'Don't be bitter, Herr Oberst, it doesn't pay, not down here. I've seen generals on their knees down here and begging.' Rossman smiled genially. 'Still, that's neither here nor there.' He walked to the door. 'Now what can I show you next?'

'Nothing, thank you,' Radl said. 'You've made your point, wasn't that the object of the exercise? You can take me back now.'

'As you say, Herr Oberst.' Rossman shrugged and turned out the light.

When Radl went back into the office, he found Himmler busily writing in a file. He looked up and said calmly, 'Terrible the things that have to be done. It personally sickens me to my stomach. I can't abide violence of any sort. It is the curse of greatness, Herr Oberst, that it must step over dead bodies to create new life.'

'Herr Reichsführer,' Radl said. 'What do you want of me?'

Himmler actually smiled, however slightly, contriving to look even more sinister. 'Why, it's really very simple. This Churchill business. I want it seeing through.'

'But the Admiral doesn't.'

'You have considerable autonomy, is it not so? Run your own office? Travel extensively? Munich, Paris, Antwerp within the past fortnight?' Himmler shrugged. 'I see no reason why you shouldn't be able to manage without the Admiral realising what's going on. Most of what needs to be done could be handled in conjunction with other business.'

'But why, Herr Reichsführer, why is it so important that it be done this way?'

'Because, in the first place, I think the Admiral totally wrong in this affair. This scheme of yours could work if everything falls right for it, just like Skorzeny at Gran Sasso. If it succeeds, if Churchill is either killed or kidnapped – and personally, I'd sooner see him dead – then we have a world sensation. An incredible feat of arms.'

'Which if the Admiral had had his way would never have taken place,' Radl said. 'I see now. Another nail in his coffin?'

'Would you deny that he would have earned it in such circumstances?'

'What can I say?'

'Should such men be allowed to get away with it? Is that what you want, Radl, as a loyal German officer?'

'But the Herr Reichsführer must see what an impossible position this puts me in,' Radl said. 'My relations with the Admiral have always been excellent.' It occurred to him, too late, that that was hardly the point to make under the circumstances and he added hurriedly, 'Naturally my personal loyalty is beyond question, but what kind of authority would I have to carry such a project through?'

Himmler took a heavy manilla envelope from his desk drawer. He opened it and produced a letter which he handed to Radl without a word. It was headed by the German Eagle with the Iron Cross in gold.

FROM THE LEADER AND CHANCELLOR OF THE STATE

MOST SECRET

Colonel Radl is acting under my direct and personal orders in a matter of the utmost importance to the Reich. He is answerable only to me. All personnel, military and civil, without distinction of rank, will assist him in any way he sees fit.

Adolf Hitler

Radl was stunned. It was the most incredible document he had ever held in his hand. With such a key, a man could open any door in the land, be denied nothing. His flesh crawled and a strange thrill ran through him.

'As you can see, anyone who wishes to query that document would have to be prepared to take it up with the Führer himself.' Himmler rubbed his hands together briskly. 'So, it is settled. You are prepared to accept this duty your Führer places on you?'

There was really nothing to be said except the obvious thing. 'Of course, Herr Reichsführer.'

'Good.' Himmler was obviously pleased. 'To business then. You are right to think of Steiner. The very man for the job. I suggest that you go and see him without delay.'

'It occurs to me,' Radl said carefully, 'that in view of his recent history he may not be interested in such an assignment.'

'He will have no choice in the matter,' Himmler said. 'Four days ago his father was arrested on suspicion of treason against the state.'

'General Steiner?' Radl said in astonishment.

'Yes, the old fool seems to have got himself involved with entirely the wrong sort of people. He's being brought to Berlin at the moment.'

'To – to Prinz Albrechtstrasse?'

'But of course. You might point out to Steiner that not only would it be in his own best interests to serve the Reich in any way he can at the moment. Such evidence of loyalty might well affect the outcome of his father's case.' Radl was genuinely horrified, but Himmler carried straight on. 'Now, a few facts. I would like you to elaborate on this question of disguise that you mention in your outline. That interests me.'

Radl was aware of a feeling of total unreality. No one was safe – no one. He had known of people, whole families, who had disappeared after the Gestapo called. He thought of Trudi, his wife, his three cherished daughters and the same fierce courage that had brought him through the Winter War flowed through him again. For them, he thought, I've got to survive for them. Anything it takes – anything.

He started to speak, amazed at the calmness in his own voice. 'The British have many commando regiments as the Reichsführer is aware, but perhaps one of the most successful has been the unit formed by a British officer named Stirling to operate behind our lines in Africa. The Special Air Service.'

'Ah, yes, the man they called the Phantom Major. The one Rommel thought so highly of.'

'He was captured in January of this year, Herr Reichsführer. I believe he is in Colditz now, but the work he started has not only continued, but expanded. According to our present information there are due to return

to Britain soon, probably to prepare for an invasion of Europe, the First
and Second SAS Regiments and the Third and Fourth French Parachute
Battalions. They even have a Polish Independent Parachute Squadron.'

'And the point you are trying to make?'

'Little is known of such units by the more conventional branches of the
army. It is accepted that their purposes are secret, therefore less likely
that they would be challenged by anyone.'

'You would pass off our men as Polish members of this unit?'

'Exactly, Herr Reichsführer.'

'And uniforms?'

'Most of these people are now wearing camouflage smock and trousers
in action, rather similar to SS pattern. They also wear the English
parachutists' red beret with a special badge. A winged dagger with the
inscription *Who dares – wins.*'

'How dramatic,' Himmler said drily.

'The Abwehr has ample supplies of such clothing from those taken
prisoner during SAS operations in the Greek Islands, Yugoslavia and
Albania.'

'And equipment?'

'No problem. The British Special Operations Executive still do not
appreciate the extent to which we have penetrated the Dutch resistance
movement.'

'Terrorist movement,' Himmler corrected him. 'But carry on.'

'Almost nightly they drop further supplies of arms, sabotage
equipment, radios for field use, even money. They still don't realise that
all the radio messages they receive are from the Abwehr.'

'My God,' Himmler said, 'and still we continue to lose the war.' He got
up, walked to the fire and warmed his hands. 'This whole question of
wearing enemy uniform is a matter of great delicacy and it is forbidden
under the Geneva Convention. There is only one penalty. The firing
squad.'

'True, Herr Reichsführer.'

'In this case it seems to me a compromise would be in order. The
raiding party will wear normal uniform underneath these British
camouflage outfits. That way they will be fighting as German soldiers,
not gangsters. Just before the actual attack, they could remove these
disguises. You agree?'

Radl personally thought it probably the worst idea he'd ever heard of,
but realised the futility of argument. 'As you say, Herr Reichsführer.'

'Good. Everthing else seems to me simply a question of organisation.
The Luftwaffe and the Navy for transportation. No trouble there. The
Führer's Directive will open all doors for you. Is there anything you wish

to raise with me?'

'As regards Churchill himself,' Radl said. 'Is he to be taken alive?'

'If possible,' Himmler said. 'Dead if there is no other way.'

'I understand.'

'Good, then I may safely leave tne matter in your hands. Rossman will give you a special phone number on the way out. I wish to be kept in daily touch with your progress.' He replaced the reports and the map in the briefcase and pushed it across.

'As you say, Herr Reichsführer.'

Radl folded the precious letter, put it back in the manilla envelope which he slipped inside his tunic. He picked up the briefcase and his leather greatcoat and moved to the door.

Himmler, who had started writing again, said, 'Colonel Radl.'

Radl turned. 'Herr Reichsführer?'

'Your oath as a German soldier, to your Führer and the State. You remember it?'

'Of course, Herr Reichsführer.'

Himmler looked up, the face cold, enigmatic. 'Repeat it now.'

'I swear by God this holy Oath. I will render unconditional obedience to the Führer of the German Reich and People, Adolf Hitler, the Supreme Commander of the Armed Forces and will be ready, as a brave soldier, to stake my life at any time to this oath.'

His eye socket was on fire again, his dead hand ached. 'Excellent, Colonel Radl. And remember one thing. Failure is a sign of weakness.'

Himmler lowered his head and continued to write. Radl got the door open as fast as he could and stumbled outside.

He changed his mind about going home to his apartment. Instead he got Rossman to drop him at the Tirpitz Ufer, went up to his office and bedded down on the small camp bed that he kept for such emergencies. Not that he slept much. Every time he closed his eyes he saw the silver pince-nez, the cold eyes, the calm, dry voice making its monstrous statements.

One thing was certain, or so he told himself at five o'clock when he finally surrendered and reached for the bottle of Courvoisier. He had to see this thing through, not for himself, but for Trudi and the children. Gestapo surveillance was bad enough for most people. 'But me,' he said as he put the light out again. 'I have to have Himmler himself on my tail.'

After that he slept and was awakened by Hofer at eight o'clock with coffee and hot rolls. Radl got up and walked across to the window, eating one of the rolls. It was a grey morning and raining heavily.

'Was it a bad raid, Karl?'

'Not too bad. I hear eight Lancasters were shot down.'

'If you look in the inside breast pocket of my tunic you'll find an envelope,' Radl said. 'I want you to read the letter inside.'

He waited, peering out into the rain and turned after a moment or so. Hofer was staring down at the letter, obviously shaken. 'But what does this mean, Herr Oberst?'

'The Churchill affair, Karl. It proceeds. The Führer wishes it so. I had that from Himmler himself last night.'

'And the Admiral, Herr Oberst?'

'Is to know nothing.'

Hofer stared at him in honest bewilderment, the letter in one hand. Radl took it from him and held it up. 'We are little men, you and I, caught in a very large web and we must tread warily. This directive is all we need. Orders from the Führer himself. Do you follow me?'

'I think so.'

'And trust me?'

Hofer sprang to attention. 'I have never doubted you, Herr Oberst. Never.'

Radl was aware of a surge of affection. 'Good, then we proceed as I have indicated and under conditions of the strictest secrecy.'

'As you say, Herr Oberst.'

'Good, Karl, then bring me everything. Everything we have, and we'll go over it again.'

He moved to the window, opened it and took a deep breath. There was the acrid tang of smoke on the air from last night's fires. Parts of the city that he could see were a desolate ruin. Strange how excited he felt.

'She needs a man, Karl.'

'Herr Oberst?' Hofer said.

They were leaning over the desk, the reports and charts spread before them. 'Mrs Grey,' Radl explained. 'She needs a man.'

'Ah, I see now, Herr Oberst,' Hofer said. 'Someone with broad shoulders. A blunt instrument?'

'No.' Radl frowned and took one of his Russian cigarettes from the box on the table. 'Brains as well – that is essential.'

Hofer lit the cigarette for him. 'A difficult combination.'

'It always is. Who does Section One have working for them in England at the moment, who might be able to help? Someone thoroughly reliable?'

'There are perhaps seven or eight agents who may be so considered. People like Snow White, for example. He's been working in the offices at the Naval Department in Portsmouth for two years. We receive regular and valuable information on North Atlantic convoys from him.'

Radl shook his head impatiently. 'No, no one like that. Such work is too important to be jeopardised in any way. Surely to God there are others?'

'At least fifty.' Hofer shrugged. 'Unfortunately the BIA section of MI5 has had a remarkably successful run during the past eighteen months.'

Radl got up and went to the window. He stood there tapping one foot impatiently. He was not angry – worried more than anything else. Joanna Grey was sixty-eight years of age and no matter how dedicated, no matter how reliable, she needed a man. As Hofer had put it, a blunt instrument. Without him the whole enterprise could founder.

His left hand was hurting, the hand which was no longer there, a sure sign of stress, and his head was splitting. *Failure is a sign of weakness, Colonel.* Himmler had said that, the dark eyes cold. Radl shivered uncontrollably, fear almost moving his bowels as he remembered the cellars at Prinz Albrechtstrasse.

Hofer said diffidently, 'Of course, there is always the Irish Section.'

'What did you say?'

'The Irish Section, sir. The Irish Republican Army.'

'Completely useless,' Radl said. 'The whole IRA connection was aborted long ago, you know that, after that fiasco with Goertz and the other agents. A total failure, the entire enterprise.'

'Not quite, Herr Oberst.'

Hofer opened one of the filing cabinets, leafed through it quickly and produced a manilla folder which he laid on the desk. Radl sat down with a frown and opened it.

'But, of course . . . and he's still here? At the university?'

'So I understand. He also does a little translation work when needed.'

'And what does he call himself now?'

'Devlin. Liam Devlin.'

'Get him!'

'Now, Herr Oberst?'

'You heard me. I want him here within the hour. I don't care if you have to turn Berlin upside down. I don't care if you have to call in the Gestapo.'

Hofer clicked his heels and went out quickly. Radl lit another cigarette with trembling fingers and started to go through the file.

He had not been far wrong in his earlier remarks, for every German attempt to make terms with the IRA since the beginning of the war had come to nothing and the whole business was probably the biggest tale of woe in Abwehr files.

None of the German agents sent to Ireland had achieved anything worth having. Only one had remained at large for any length of time, Captain Goertz, who had been parachuted from a Heinkel over Meath in May, 1940, and who had succeeded in remaining at large for nineteen months.

Goertz found the IRA exasperatingly amateur and unwilling to take any kind of advice. As he was to comment years later, they knew how to die for Ireland, but not how to fight for her and German hopes of regular attacks on British military installations in Ulster faded away.

Radl was familiar with all this. What really interested him was the man who called himself Liam Devlin. Devlin had actually parachuted into Ireland for the Abwehr, had not only survived, but had eventually made his way back to Germany, a unique achievement.

Liam Devlin had been born in Lismore in County Down in the North of Ireland in July, 1908, the son of a small tenant farmer who had been executed in 1921 during the Anglo-Irish War for serving with an IRA flying column. The boy's mother had gone to keep house for her brother, a Catholic priest in the Falls Road area of Belfast, and he had arranged for him to attend a Jesuit boarding school in the South. From there Devlin had moved to Trinity College, Dublin, where he had taken an excellent degree in English Literature.

He'd had a little poetry published, was interested in a career in journalism, would probably have made a successful writer if it had not been for one single incident which had altered the course of his entire life. In 1931, while visiting his home in Belfast during a period of serious sectarian rioting, he had witnessed an Orange mob sack his uncle's church. The old priest had been so badly beaten that he lost an eye. From that moment Devlin had given himself completely to the Republican cause.

In a bank raid in Derry in 1932 to gather funds for the movement, he was wounded in a gun battle with the police and sentenced to ten years imprisonment. He had escaped from the Crumlin Road Gaol in 1934 and while on the run, led the defence of Catholic areas in Belfast during the rioting of 1935.

Later that year he had been sent to New York to execute an informer who had been put on a boat to America by the police for his own good after selling information which had led to the arrest and hanging of a young IRA volunteer named Michael Reilly. Devlin had accomplished this mission with an efficiency that could only enhance a reputation that was already becoming legendary. Later that year he repeated the performance. Once in London and again in America, although this time the venue was Boston.

In 1936 he had taken himself to Spain, serving in the Lincoln Washington Brigade. He had been wounded and captured by Italian troops who, instead of shooting him, had kept him intact, hoping to effect an exchange for one of their own officers. Although this had never come to anything, it meant that he survived the war, being eventually sentenced to life imprisonment by the Franco government.

He had been freed at the instigation of the Abwehr in the autumn of 1940 and brought to Berlin, where it was hoped he might prove of some use to German Intelligence. It was at this stage that things had gone sadly wrong, for according to the record, Devlin, while having little sympathy with the Communist cause, was very definitely anti-Fascist, a fact which he had made abundantly clear during his interrogation. A bad risk, then, considered fit only for minor translation duties and English tutoring at the University of Berlin.

But the position had changed drastically. The Abwehr had made several attempts to get Goertz out of Ireland. All had failed. In desperation, the Irish Section had called in Devlin and asked him to parachute into Ireland with forged travel documents, contact Goertz and get him out via a Portuguese ship or some similar neutral vessel. He was dropped over County Meath on the 18 October 1941 but some weeks later, before he could contact Goertz, the German was arrested by the Irish Special Branch.

Devlin had spent several harrowing months on the run, betrayed at every turn, for so many IRA supporters had been interned in the Curragh by the Irish Government that there were few reliable contacts left. Surrounded by police in a farmhouse in Kerry in June, 1942, he wounded two of them and was himself rendered unconscious when a bullet creased his forehead. He had escaped from a hospital bed, made his way to Dun Laoghaire and had managed to get passage on a Brazilian boat bound for Lisbon. From there he had passed through Spain via the usual channels until he once more stood in the offices at the Tirpitz Ufer.

From then on, Ireland was a dead end as far as the Abwehr was concerned and Liam Devlin was sent back to kick his heels in translation duties and occasionally, so farcical can life be, to take tutorials again in English literature at the University of Berlin.

It was just before noon when Hofer came back into the office. 'I've got him, Herr Oberst.'

Radl looked up and put down his pen. 'Devlin?' He stood up and walked to the window, straightening his tunic, trying to work out what he was going to say. This had to go right, had to work. Yet Devlin would require careful handling. He was, after all, a neutral. The door clicked open and he turned.

Liam Devlin was smaller than he had imagined. No more than five feet five or six. He had dark, wavy hair, pale face, eyes of the most vivid blue that Radl had ever seen and a slight, ironic smile that seemed to permanently lift the corner of his mouth. The look of a man who had found life a bad joke and had decided that the only thing to do was laugh about it. He was wearing a black, belted trenchcoat and the ugly puckered scar of the bullet wound that he had picked up on his last trip to Ireland showed clearly on the left side of his forehead.

'Mr. Devlin.' Radl went round the desk and held out his hand. 'My name is Radl – Max Radl. It's good of you to come.'

'That's nice,' Devlin said in excellent German. 'The impression I got was that I didn't have much choice in the matter.' He moved forward, unbuttoning his coat. 'So this is Section Three where it all happens?'

'Please, Mr. Devlin.' Radl brought a chair forward and offered him a cigarette.

Devlin leaned forward for a light. He coughed, choking as the harsh cigarette smoke pulled at the back of his throat. 'Mother Mary, Colonel, I knew things were bad, but not that bad. What's in them or shouldn't I ask?'

'Russian,' Radl said. 'I picked up the taste for them during the Winter War.'

'Don't tell me,' Devlin said. 'They were the only thing that kept you from falling asleep in the snow.'

Radl smiled, warming to the man. 'Very likely.' He produced the bottle of Courvoisier and two glasses. 'Cognac?'

'Now you're being too nice.' Devlin accepted the glass, swallowed, closing his eyes for a moment. 'It isn't Irish, but it'll do to be going on with. When do we get to the nasty bit? The last time I was at Tirpitz Ufer they asked me to jump out of a Dornier at five thousand feet over Meath in the dark and I've a terrible fear of heights.'

'All right, Mr. Devlin,' Radl said. 'We do have work for you if you're interested.'

'I've got work.'

'At the university? Come now, for a man like you that must be rather like being a thoroughbred racing horse that finds itself pulling a milk cart.'

Devlin threw back his head and laughed out loud. 'Ah, Colonel, you've found my weak spot instantly. Vanity, vanity. Stroke me any more and I'll purr like my Uncle Sean's old tomcat. Are you trying to lead up, in the nicest way possible, to the fact that you want me to go back to Ireland? Because if you are you can forget it. I wouldn't stand a chance, not for any length of time the way things are now, and I've no intention of sitting on my arse in the Curragh for five years. I've had enough of prisons to last me quite some time.'

'Ireland is still a neutral country, Mr. de Valera has made it quite clear that she will not take sides.'

'Yes, I know,' Devlin said, 'which is why a hundred thousand Irishmen are serving in the British forces. And another thing – every time an RAF plane crash-lands in Ireland, the crew are passed over the border in a matter of days. How many German pilots have they sent you back lately?' Devlin grinned. 'Mind you, with all that lovely butter and cream and the colleens, they probably think they're better off where they are.'

'No, Mr. Devlin, we don't want you to go back to Ireland,' Radl said. 'Not the way you mean.'

'Then what in the hell do you want?'

'Let me ask you something first. You are still a supporter of the IRA?'

'Soldier of,' Devlin corrected him. 'We have a saying back home, Colonel. Once in, never out.'

'So, your total aim is victory against England?'

'If you mean a united Ireland, free and standing on her own two feet, then I'll cheer for that: I'll believe it when it happens, mind you, but not before.'

Radl was mystified. 'Then why fight?'

'God save us, but don't you ask the questions?' Devlin shrugged. 'It's better than fist-fighting outside Murphy's Select Bar on Saturday nights. Or maybe it's just that I like playing the game.'

'And which game would that be?'

'You mean to tell me you're in this line of work and you don't know?'

For some reason Radl felt strangely uncomfortable so he said hurriedly, 'Then the activities of your compatriots in London, for instance, don't commend themselves to you?'

'Hanging round Bayswater making Paxo in their landlady's saucepans?' Devlin said. 'Not my idea of fun.'

'Paxo?' Radl was bewildered.

'A joke. Paxo is a well-known package gravy, so that's what the boys call the explosive they mix. Potassium chlorate, sulphuric acid and a few other assorted goodies.'

'A volatile brew.'

'Especially when it goes up in your face.'

'This bombing campaign your people started with the ultimatum they sent to the British Prime Minister in January, 1939 . . .'

Devlin laughed. 'And Hitler and Mussolini and anyone else they thought might be interested including Uncle Tom Cobley.'

'Uncle Tom Cobley?'

'Another joke,' Devlin said. 'A weakness of mine, never having been able to take anything too seriously.'

'Why, Mr. Devlin? That interests me.'

'Come now, Colonel,' Devlin said. 'The world was a bad joke dreamed up by the Almighty on an off-day. I've always felt myself that he probably had a hangover that morning. But what was your point about the bombing campaign?'

'Did you approve of it?'

'No. I don't like soft target hits. Women, kids, passers-by. If you're going to fight, if you believe in your cause and it is a just one, then stand up on your two hind legs and fight like a man.'

His face was white and very intense, the bullet scar in his head glowing like a brand. He relaxed just as suddenly and laughed. 'There you go, bringing out the best in me. Too early in the morning to be serious.'

'So, a moralist,' Radl said. 'The English would not agree with you. They bomb the heart out of the Reich every night.'

'You'll have me in tears if you keep that up. I was in Spain fighting for the Republicans remember. What in the hell do you think those German Stukas were doing flying for Franco? Ever heard of Barcelona or Guernica?'

'Strange, Mr. Devlin, you obviously resent us and I had presumed it was the English you hated.'

'The English?' Devlin laughed. 'Sure and they're just like your mother-in-law. Something you put up with. No, I don't *hate* the English – its the bloody British Empire I hate.'

'So, you wish to see Ireland free?'

'Yes.' Devlin helped himself to another of the Russian cigarettes.

'Then would you accept that from your point of view the best way of achieving that aim would be for Germany to win this war?'

'And pigs might fly one of these days,' Devlin told him, 'but I doubt it.'

'Then why stay here in Berlin?'

'I didn't realise that I had any choice?'

'But you do, Mr. Devlin,' Colonel Radl said quietly. 'You can go to England for me.'

Devlin stared at him in amazement, for once in his life stopped dead in his tracks. 'God save us, the man's mad.'

'No, Mr. Devlin, quite sane I assure you.' Radl pushed the Courvoisier bottle across the desk and placed the manilla file next to it. 'Have another drink and read that file then we'll talk again.'

He got up and walked out.

When at the end of a good half-hour there was no sign of Devlin, Radl steeled himself to open the door and go back in. Devlin was sitting with his feet on the desk, Joanna Grey's reports in one hand, a glass of Courvoisier in the other. The bottle looked considerably depleted.

He glanced up. 'So there you are? I was beginning to wonder what had happened to you.'

'Well, what do you think,' Radl demanded.

'It reminds me of a story I heard when I was a boy,' Devlin said. 'Something that happened during the war with the English back in nineteen twenty-one. May, I think. It concerned a man called Emmet Dalton. He that was a General in the Free State Army later. Did you ever hear tell of him?'

'No, I'm afraid not,' said Radl with ill-concealed impatience.

'What we Irish would call a lovely man. Served as a major in the British Army right through the war, awarded the Military Cross for bravery, then he joined the IRA.'

'Forgive me, Mr. Devlin, but is any of this relevant?'

Devlin didn't seem to have heard him. 'There was a man in Mountjoy Prison in Dublin called McEoin, another lovely man, but in spite of that he only had the gallows before him.' He helped himself to more Courvoisier. 'Emmet Dalton had other ideas. He stole a British armoured car, put on his old major's uniform, dressed a few of the boys as *Tommis*, bluffed his way into the prison and right into the governor's office. Would you believe that?'

By now Radl was interested in spite of himself. 'And did they save this McEoin?'

'By bad luck, it was the one morning his application to see the governor was refused.'

'And these men – what happened to them?'

'Oh, there was a little shooting, but they got clean away. Bloody cheek, though.' He grinned and held up Joanna Grey's report. 'Just like this.'

'You think it would work?' Radl demanded eagerly. 'You think it possible?'

'It's impudent enough.' Devlin threw the report down. 'And I thought the Irish were supposed to be the crazy ones. To tumble the great Winston Churchill out of his bed in the middle of the night and away with him.' He laughed out loud. 'Now that would be something to see. Something that would stand the whole world on its ear in amazement.'

'And you'd like that?'

'A great ploy, surely.' Devlin smiled hugely and was still smiling when he added, 'Of course, there is the point that it wouldn't have the slightest effect on the war. The English will simply promote Attlee to fill the vacancy, the course of the Lancasters will still come over by night and the Flying Fortresses by day.'

'In other words it is your considered opinion that we'll still lose the war?' Radl said.

'Fifty marks on that any time you like.' Devlin grinned. 'On the other hand, I'd hate to miss this little jaunt, if you're really serious, that is?'

'You mean you're willing to go?' Radl was by now thoroughly bewildered. 'But I don't understand. Why?'

'I know, I'm a fool,' Devlin said. 'Look what I'm giving up. A nice safe job at the University of Berlin with the RAF bombing by night, the Yanks by day, food getting shorter, the Eastern Front crumbling.'

Radl raised both hands, laughing. 'All right, no more questions, the Irish are quite obviously mad. I was told it, now I accept it.'

'The best thing for you and, of course, we mustn't forget the twenty thousand pounds you're going to deposit to a numbered account in a Geneva bank of my choosing.'

Radl was aware of a feeling of acute disappointment. 'So, Mr. Devlin, you also have your price like the rest of us?'

'The movement I serve has always been notoriously low on funds.' Devlin grinned. 'I've seen revolutions started on less than twenty thousand pounds, Colonel.'

'Very well,' Radl said. 'I will arrange it. You will receive confirmation of the deposit before you leave.'

'Fine,' Devlin said. 'So what's the score then?'

'Today is October the first. That gives us exactly five weeks.'

'And what would my part be?'

'Mrs. Grey is a first-rate agent, but she is sixty-eight years of age. She needs a man.'

'Someone to do the running around? Handle the rough stuff?'

'Exactly.'

'And how do you get me there and don't tell me you haven't been thinking about it?'

Radl smiled. 'I must admit I've given the matter considerable thought. See how this strikes you. You're an Irish citizen who has served with the British Army. Badly wounded and given a medical discharge. That scar on your forehead will help there.'

'And how does this fit in with Mrs. Grey?'

'An old family friend who has found you some sort of employment in Norfolk. We'll have to put it to her and see what she comes up with. We'll fill the story out, supply you with every possible document from an Irish passport to your army discharge papers. What do you think?'

'It sounds passable enough,' Devlin said. 'But how do I get there?'

'We'll parachute you into Southern Ireland. As close to the Ulster border as possible. I understand it to be extremely easy to walk across the border without passing through a customs post.'

'No trouble there,' Devlin said. 'Then what?'

'The night boat from Belfast to Heysham, train to Norfolk, everything straight and above board.'

Devlin pulled the ordnance survey map forward and looked down at it. 'All right, I'll buy that. When do I go?'

'A week, ten days at the most. For the moment, you will obviously observe total security. You must also resign your post at the university and vacate your present apartment. Drop completely out of sight. Hofer will arrange other accommodation for you.'

'Then what?'

'I'm going to see the man who will probably command the assault group. Tomorrow or the next day depending on how soon I can arrange flights to the Channel Islands. You might as well come too. You're going to have a lot in common. You agree?'

'And why shouldn't I, Colonel? Won't the same bad old roads all lead to hell in the end?' He poured what was left of the Courvoisier into his glass.

5

Alderney is the most northerly of the Channel Islands and the closest to the French coast. As the German Army rolled inexorably westward in the summer of 1940 the islanders had voted to evacuate. When the first Luftwaffe plane landed on the tiny grass strip on top of the cliffs on 2 July, 1940, the place was deserted, the narrow cobbled streets of St. Anne eerily quiet.

By the autumn of 1942 there was a garrison of perhaps three thousand, mixed Army, Navy and Luftwaffe personnel and several Todt camps employing slave labour from the continent to work on the massive concrete gun emplacements of the new fortifications. There was also a concentration camp staffed by members of the SS and Gestapo, the only such establishment ever to exist on British soil.

Just after noon on Sunday Radl and Devlin flew in from Jersey in a Stork spotter plane. It was only a half-hour run and as the Stork was unarmed the pilot did the entire trip at sea level only climbing up to seven hundred feet at the last moment.

As the Stork swept in over the enormous breakwater Alderney was spread out for them like a map. Braye Bay, the harbour, St. Anne, the island itself, perhaps three miles long and a mile and a half wide, vividly green, great cliffs on one side, the land sliding down into a series of sandy bays and coves on the other.

The Stork turned into the wind and dropped down on to one of the grass runways of the airfield on top of the cliffs. It was one of the smallest Radl had ever seen, hardly deserving of the name. A tiny control tower, a scattering of prefabricated buildings and no hangars.

There was a black Wolseley car parked beside the control tower and as Radl and Devlin went towards it, the driver, a sergeant of Artillery, got out and opened the rear door. He saluted. 'Colonel Radl? The commandant asks you to accept his compliments. I'm to take you straight to the Feldkommandantur.'

'Very well,' Radl said.

They got in and were driven away, soon turning into a country lane. It was a fine day, warm and sunny, more like late spring than early autumn.

'It seems a pleasant enough place,' Radl commented.

'For some.' Devlin nodded over towards the left where hundreds of Todt workers could be seen in the distance labouring on what looked like some enormous concrete fortification.

The houses in St. Anne were a mixture of French Provincial and English Georgian, streets cobbled, gardens high-walled against the constant winds. There were plenty of signs of war – concrete pillboxes, barbed wire, machine-gun posts, bomb damage in the harbour far below – but it was the Englishness of it all that fascinated Radl. The incongruity of seeing two SS men in a field car parked in Connaught Square and of a Luftwaffe private giving another a light for his cigarette under a sign that said 'Royal Mail'.

Feldkommandantur 515, the German civilian administration for the Channel Islands, had its local headquarters in the old Lloyds Bank premises in Victoria Street and as the car drew up outside, Neuhoff himself appeared in the entrance.

He came forward, hand outstretched. 'Colonel Radl? Hans Neuhoff, temporarily in command here. Good to see you.'

Radl said, 'This gentleman is a colleague of mine.'

He made no other attempt to introduce Devlin and a certain alarm showed in Neuhoff's eyes instantly, for Devlin, in civilian clothes and a black leather military greatcoat Radl had procured for him, was an obvious curiosity. The logical explanation would seem to be that he was Gestapo. During the trip from Berlin to Brittany and then on to

Guernsey, the Irishman had seen the same wary look on other faces and had derived a certain malicious satisfaction from it.

'Herr Oberst,' he said, making no attempt to shake hands.

Neuhoff, more put out than ever, said hurriedly, 'This way, gentlemen, please.'

Inside, three clerks worked at the mahogany counter. Behind them on the wall was a new Ministry of Propaganda poster showing an eagle, with a swastika in its talons, rearing proudly above the legend *Am ende steht der Sieg!* At the end stands victory.

'My God,' Devlin said softly, 'some people will believe anything.'

A military policeman guarded the door of what had presumably been the manager's office. Neuhoff led the way in. It was sparsely furnished, a workroom more than anything else. He brought two chairs forward. Radl took one, but Devlin lit a cigarette and went and stood at the window.

Neuhoff glanced at him uncertainly and tried to smile. 'Can I offer you gentlemen a drink? Schnapps or a Cognac perhaps?'

'Frankly I'd like to get straight down to business,' Radl told him.

'But of course, Herr Oberst.'

Radl unbuttoned his tunic, took the manilla envelope from his inside pocket and produced the letter. 'Please read that.'

Neuhoff picked it up, frowning slightly and ran his eyes over it. 'The Führer himself commands.' He looked up at Radl in amazement. 'But I don't understand. What is it that you wish of me?'

'Your complete co-operation, Colonel Neuhoff,' Radl said. 'And no questions. You have a penal unit here, I believe? Operation Swordfish.'

There was a new kind of wariness in Neuhoff's eyes, Devlin noticed it instantly, and the colonel seemed to stiffen. 'Yes, Herr Oberst, that is so. Under the command of Colonel Steiner of the Parachute Regiment.'

'So I understand,' Radl said. 'Colonel Steiner, a Lieutenant Neumann and twenty-nine paratroopers.'

Neuhoff corrected him. 'Colonel Steiner, Ritter Neumann and fourteen paratroopers.'

Radl stared at him in surprise. 'What are you saying? Where are the others?'

'Dead, Herr Oberst,' Neuhoff said simply. 'You know about Operation Swordfish? You know what they do, these men? They sit astride torpedoes and . . .'

'I'm aware of that.' Radl stood up, reached for the Führer Directive and replaced it in its envelope. 'Are there any operations planned for today?'

'That depends on whether there is a radar contact.'

'No more,' Radl said. 'It stops now, from this moment.' He held up the envelope. 'My first order under this directive.'

Neuhoff actually smiled. 'I am delighted to comply with such an order.'

'I see,' Radl said. 'Colonel Steiner is a friend?'

'My privilege,' Neuhoff said simply. 'If you knew the man, you'd know what I mean. There is also the point of view that someone of his extraordinary gifts is of more use to the Reich alive than dead.'

'Which is exactly why I am here,' Radl said. 'Now, where can I find him?'

'Just before you get to the harbour there's an inn. Steiner and his men use it as their headquarters. I'll take you down there.'

'No need,' Radl said. 'I'd like to see him alone. Is it far?'

'A quarter of a mile.'

'Good, then we'll walk.'

Neuhoff stood up. 'Have you any idea how long you will be staying?'

'I have arranged for the Stork to pick us up first thing in the morning,' Radl said. 'It is essential that we're at the airfield in Jersey no later than eleven. Our plane for Brittany leaves then.'

'I'll arrange accommodation for you and your – your friend.' Neuhoff glanced at Devlin. 'Also, if you would care to dine with me tonight? My wife would be delighted and perhaps Colonel Steiner could join us.'

'An excellent idea,' Radl said. 'I'll look forward to it.'

As they walked down Victoria Street past the shuttered shops and empty houses Devlin said, 'What's got into you? You were laying it on a bit strong, weren't you? Are we feeling our oats today?'

Radl laughed, looking slightly shamefaced. 'Whenever I take that damned letter out I feel strange. A feeling of – of power comes over me. Like the centurion in the Bible, who says do this and they do it, go there and they go.'

As they turned into Braye Road a fieldcar drove past them, the artillery sergeant who had brought them in from the airfield at the wheel.

'Colonel Neuhoff sending a warning of our coming,' Radl commented. 'I wondered whether he would.'

'I think he thought I was Gestapo,' Devlin said. 'He was afraid.'

'Perhaps,' Radl said. 'And you, Herr Devlin? Are you ever afraid?'

'Not that I can remember.' Devlin laughed, without mirth. 'I'll tell you something I've never told another living soul. Even at the moment of maximum danger and, God knows, I've known enough of those in my time, even when I'm staring Death right between the eyes, I get the strangest feeling. It's as if I want to reach out and take his hand. Now isn't that the funniest thing you ever heard of?'

Ritter Neumann, wearing a black rubber wet suit, was sitting astride a torpedo moored to the number one recovery boat tinkering with its engine, when the fieldcar roared along the jetty and braked to a halt. As Neumann looked up, shading his eyes against the sun, Sergeant-Major Brandt appeared.

'What's your hurry?' Neumann called. 'Is the war over?'

'Trouble, Herr Leutnant,' Brandt said. 'There's some staff officer flown in from Jersey. A Colonel Radl. He's come for the Colonel. We've just had a tip-off from Victoria Street.'

'Staff officer?' Neumann said and he pulled himself over the rail of the recovery boat and took the towel that Private Riedel handed him. 'Where's he from?'

'Berlin!' Brandt said grimly, 'And he has someone with him who looks like a civilian, but isn't.'

'Gestapo?'

'So it would appear. They're on their way down now – walking.'

Neumann pulled on his jump boots and scrambled up the ladder to the jetty. 'Do the lads know?'

Brandt nodded, a savage look on his face, 'And don't like it. If they find he's come to put the screws in the Colonel they're quite likely to push him and his pal off the end of the jetty with sixty pounds of chain apiece around their ankles.'

'Right,' said Neumann. 'Back to the pub as fast as you can and hold them. I'll take the fieldcar and get the Colonel. He went for a walk along the breakwater with Frau Neuhoff.'

Steiner and Ilse Neuhoff were at the very end of the breakwater. She was sitting above on the rampart, those long legs dangling into space, the wind off the sea ruffling the blonde hair, tugging at her skirt. She was laughing down at Steiner. He turned as the fieldcar braked to a halt.

Neumann scrambled out and Steiner took one look at his face and smiled sardonically. 'Bad news, Ritter, and on such a lovely day.'

'There's some staff officer in from Berlin looking for you, a Colonel Radl,' Neumann said grimly. 'They say he has a Gestapo man with him.'

Steiner wasn't put out in the slightest. 'That certainly adds a little interest to the day.'

He put up his hands to catch Ilse as she jumped down, and held her close for a moment. Her face was full of alarm. 'For God's sake, Kurt, can't you ever take anything seriously?'

'He's probably only here for a head count. We should all be dead by now. They must be very put out at Prinz Albrechtstrasse.'

The old inn stood at the side of the road on the approach to the harbour backing on to the sands of Braye Bay. It was strangely quiet as Radl and the Irishman approached.

'As nice a looking pub as I've seen,' Devlin said. 'Would you think it possible they might still have a drink on the premises?'

Radl tried the front door. It opened and they found themselves in a dark passageway. A door clicked open behind them. 'In here Herr Oberst,' a soft cultured voice said.

Sergeant Hans Altmann leaned against the outside door as if to bar their exit. Radl saw the Winter War ribbbon, the Iron Cross, First and Second Class, a silver wound badge which meant at least three wounds, the Air Force Ground Combat badge and, most coveted honour of all amongst paratroopers, the *Kreta* cuff title, proud mark of those who had spearheaded the invasion of Crete in May, 1941.

'Your name?' Radl said crisply.

Altmann didn't reply, but simply pushed with his foot so that the door marked 'Saloon Bar' swung open and Radl, sensing something, but uncertain what, stuck out his chin and advanced into the room.

The room was only fair-sized. There was a bar counter to the left, empty shelves behind it, a number of framed photographs of old wrecks on the walls, a piano in one corner. There were a dozen or so paratroopers scattered around the room, all remarkably unfriendly. Radl, looking them over coolly, was impressed. He'd never before seen a group of men with so many decorations between them. There wasn't a man there who didn't have the Iron Cross, First Class, and such minor items as wound badges and tank destruction badges were ten a penny.

He stood in the centre of the room, his briefcase under his arm, his hands in his pockets, coat collar still turned up. 'I'd like to point out,' he said mildly, 'that men have been shot before now for this kind of behaviour.'

There was a shout of laughter. Sergeant Sturm, who was behind the bar cleaning a Luger said, 'That really is very good, Herr Oberst. Do you want to hear something funny? When we went operational here ten weeks ago, there were thirty-one of us, including the Colonel. Fifteen now, in spite of a lot of lucky breaks. What can you and this Gestapo shit offer that's worse than that?'

'Don't go including me in this thing,' Devlin said. 'I'm neutral.'

Sturm, who had worked the Hamburg barges since the age of twelve and was inclined to be a trifle direct in his speech, went on, 'Listen to this because I'm only going to say it once. The Colonel isn't going anywhere. Not with you. Not with anyone.' He shook his head. 'You know that's a very pretty hat, Herr Oberst, but you've been polishing a chair with your backside for so long up there in Berlin that you've forgotten how real soldiers feel. You've come to the wrong place if you're hoping for a chorus from the *Horst Wessel*.'

'Excellent,' Radl said. 'However, your completely incorrect reading of the present situation argues a lack of wit which I, for one, find deplorable in someone of your rank.'

He dumped his briefcase on the counter, opened the buttons of his coat with his good hand and shrugged it off. Sturm's jaw dropped as he saw the Knight's Cross, the Winter War ribbon. Radl moved straight into the attack.

'Attention!' he barked. 'On your feet, all of you.' There was an instant burst of activity and in the same moment the door swung open and Brandt rushed in. 'And you, Sergeant-Major,' Radl snarled.

There was pin-drop silence as every man stood rigidly to attention and Devlin, thoroughly enjoying this new turn events had taken, pulled himself up on to the bar and lit a cigarette.

Radl said, 'You think you are German soldiers, a natural error in view of the uniforms you wear, but you are mistaken.' He moved from one man to another, pausing as if committing each face to memory. 'Shall I tell you what you are?'

Which he did in simple and direct terms that made Sturm look like a beginner. When he paused for breath after two or three minutes, there was a polite cough from the open doorway and he turned to find Steiner there, Ilse Neuhoff behind him.

'I couldn't have put it better myself, Colonel Radl. I can only hope that you are willing to put down anything which has happened here to misguided enthusiasm and let it go at that. Their feet won't touch the ground when I get through with them, I promise you.' He held out his hand and smiled with considerable charm. 'Kurt Steiner.'

Radl was always to remember that first meeting. Steiner possessed that strange quality to be found in the airborne troops of every country. A kind of arrogant self-sufficiency bred of the hazards of the calling. He was wearing a blue-grey flying blouse with the yellow collar patches bearing the wreath and two stylised wings of his rank, jump trousers and the kind of sidecap known as a *Schiff*, an affectation of many of the old-timers. The rest, for a man who had every conceivable decoration in the book, was extraordinary simple. The *Kreta* cuff title, the ribbon for the Winter War and the silver and gold eagle of the paratroopers' qualification badge. The Knight's Cross with Oak Leaves was concealed by a silk scarf tied loosely about his neck.

'To be honest, Colonel Steiner, I've rather enjoyed putting these rogues of yours in their place.'

Ilse Neuhoff chuckled. 'An excellent performance, Herr Oberst, if I may say so.'

Steiner made the necessary introductions and Radl kissed her hand. 'A great pleasure, Frau Neuhoff.' He frowned. 'Have we by any chance met before?'

'Undoubtedly,' Steiner said and pulled forward Ritter Neumann who had been lurking in the background in his rubber wet suit. 'And this, Herr Oberst, is not as you may imagine, a captive Atlantic seal, but Oberleutnant Ritter Neumann.'

'Lieutenant.' Radl glanced at Ritter Neumann briefly, remembering the citation for the Knight's Cross that had been quashed because of the court martial, wondering whether he knew.

'And this gentleman?' Steiner turned to Devlin who jumped down from the counter and came forward.

'Actually everyone round here seems to think I'm your friendly neighbourhood Gestapo man,' Devlin said. 'I'm not sure I find that too flattering.' He held out his hand. 'Devlin, Colonel. Liam Devlin.'

'Herr Devlin is a colleague of mine,' Radl explained quickly.

'And you?' Steiner said politely.

'From Abwehr Headquarters. And now, if it is convenient, I would like to talk to you privately on a matter of grave urgency.'

Steiner frowned and again there was that pin-drop silence in the room. He turned to Ilse. 'Ritter will see you home.'

'No, I'd rather wait until your business with Colonel Radl is over', she said.

She was desperately worried, it showed in her eyes. Steiner said gently, 'I shouldn't imagine I'll be very long. Look after her, Ritter.' He turned to Radl. 'This way, Herr Oberst.'

Radl nodded to Devlin and they went after him.

'All right, stand down,' Ritter Neumann said. 'You damned fools.'

There was a general easing of tension. Altmann sat at the piano and launched into a popular song which assured everyone that everything would get better by and by. 'Frau Neuhoff,' he called. 'What about a song?'

Ilse sat on one of the old bar stools. 'I'm not in the mood,' she said. 'You want to know something, boys? I'm sick of this damned war. All I want is a decent cigarette and a drink, but that would be too much like a miracle, I suppose.'

'Oh, I don't know, Frau Neuhoff.' Brandt vaulted clean over the bar and turned to face her. 'For you, anything is possible. Cigarettes, for example, London gin.'

His hands went beneath the counter and came up clutching a carton of Gold Flake and a bottle of Beefeater.

'Now will you sing for us, Frau Neuhoff,' Hans Altmann called.

Devlin and Radl leaned on the parapet looking down into the water, clear and deep in the pale sunshine. Steiner sat on a bollard at the end of the jetty working his way through the contents of Radl's briefcase. Across the bay, Fort Albert loomed on the headland and below, the cliffs were splashed with birdlime, seabirds wheeling in great clouds, gulls, shags, razorbills and oystercatchers.

Steiner called, 'Colonel Radl.'

Radl moved towards him and Devlin followed, stopping two or three yards away to lean on the wall. Radl said, 'You have finished?'

'Oh, yes.' Steiner put the various papers back into the briefcase. 'You're serious, I presume?'

'Of course.'

Steiner reached forward and tapped a forefinger on Radl's Winter War ribbon. 'Then all I can say is that some of that Russian cold must have got into your brain, my friend.'

Radl took the manilla envelope from his inside pocket and produced the Führer directive. 'I think you had better have a look at that.'

Steiner read it, with no evidence of emotion, and shrugged as he handed it back. 'So what?'

'But Colonel Steiner,' Radl said. 'You are a German soldier. We swore the same oath. This is a direct order from the Führer himself.'

'You seem to have forgotten one highly important thing,' Steiner told him. 'I'm in a penal unit, under suspended sentence of death, officially disgraced. In fact, I only retain my rank because of the peculiar circumstances of the job in hand.' He produced a crumpled packet of French cigarettes from his hip pocket and put one in his mouth. 'Anyway, I don't like Adolf. He has a loud voice and bad breath.'

Radl ignored this remark. 'We must fight. We have no other choice.'

'To the last man?'

'What else can we do?'

'We can't win.'

Radl's good hand was clenched into a fist, he was filled with nervous excitement. 'But we can force them to change their views. See that some sort of settlement is better than this continual slaughter.'

'And knocking off Churchill would help?' Steiner said with obvious scepticism.

'It would show them we still have teeth. Look at the furore when Skorzeny lifted Mussolini off the Gran Sasso. A sensation all over the world.'

Steiner said, 'As I heard it, General Student and a few paratroopers had a hand in that as well.'

'For God's sake,' Radl said impatiently. 'Imagine how it would look. German troops dropping into England for one thing, but with such a target. Of course, perhaps you don't think it could be done.'

'I don't see why not,' Steiner said calmly. 'If those papers I've just looked at are accurate and if you've done your homework correctly, the whole thing could go like a Swiss watch. We could really catch the *Tommis* with their pants down. In and out again before they know what's hit them, but that isn't the point.'

'What is?' demanded Radl, completely exasperated. 'Is thumbing your nose at the Führer more important because of your court martial? Because you're here? Steiner, you and your men are dead men if you stay here. Thirty-one of you eight weeks ago. How many left – fifteen? You owe it to your men, to yourself, to take this last chance to live.'

'Or die in England instead.'

Radl shrugged. 'Straight in, straight out, that's the way it could go. Just like a Swiss watch, you said that yourself.'

'And the terrible thing about those is that if anything goes wrong with even the tiniest part, the whole damn thing stops working,' Devlin put in.

Steiner said, 'Well put, Mr. Devlin. Tell me something. Why are you going?'

'Simple,' Devlin said. 'Because it's there. I'm the last of the great adventurers.'

'Excellent.' Steiner laughed delightedly. 'Now that I can accept. To play the game. The greatest game of all. But it doesn't help, you see,' he went on. 'Colonel Radl here tells me that I owe it to my men to do the thing because it is a way out from certain death here. Now, to be perfectly frank with you, I don't think I owe anything to anybody.'

'Not even your father?' Radl said.

There was a silence, only the sea washing over the rocks below. Steiner's face turned pale, the skin stretched tight on the cheekbones, eyes dark. 'All right, tell me.'

'The Gestapo have him at Prinz Albrechtstrasse. Suspicion of treason.'

And Steiner, remembering the week he had spent at his father's headquarters in France in 'forty-two, remembering what the old man had said, knew instantly that it was true.

'Ah, I see now,' he said softly. 'If I'm a good boy and do as I'm told, it would help his case.' Suddenly his face changed and he looked about as dangerous as any man could and when he reached for Radl, it was in a kind of slow motion. 'You bastard. All of you, bastards.'

He had Radl by the throat. Devlin moved in fast and found that it took all his considerable strength to pull him off. 'Not him, you fool. He's under the boot as much as you. You want to shoot somebody, shoot Himmler. He's the man you want.'

Radl fought to get his breath and leaned against the parapet, looking very ill. 'I'm sorry,' Steiner put a hand on his shoulder in genuine concern. 'I should have known.'

Radl raised his dead hand. 'See this, Steiner, and the eye? And other damage that you can't see. Two years if I'm lucky, that's what they tell me. Not for me. For my wife and daughters because I wake up at night sweating at the thought of what might happen to them. That's why I'm here.'

Steiner nodded slowly. 'Yes, of course, I understand. We're all up the same dark alley looking for a way out.' He took a deep breath. 'All right, we'll go back. I'll put it to the lads.'

'Not the target,' Radl said. 'Not at this stage.'

'The destination then. They're entitled to know that. As for the rest – I'll only discuss it with Neumann for the moment.'

He started to walk away and Radl said, 'Steiner, I must be honest with you.' Steiner turned to face him. 'In spite of everything I've said, I also think it's worth a try, this thing. All right, as Devlin says, getting Churchill, alive or dead, isn't going to win us the war, but perhaps it will give them a shake. Make them think again about a negotiated peace.'

Steiner said, 'My dear Radl, if you believe that you'll believe anything. I'll tell you what this affair, even if it's successful, will buy you from the British. Damn all!'

He turned and walked away along the jetty.

The saloon bar was full of smoke. Hans Altmann was playing the piano and the rest of the men were crowded round Ilse, who was sitting at the bar, a glass of gin in one hand, recounting a slighty unsavoury story current in high society and relevant only to Reichsmarschall Hermann Goering's love life, such as it was. There was a burst of laughter as Steiner entered the room followed by Radl and Devlin. Steiner surveyed the scene in astonishment, particularly the array of bottles on the bar counter.

'What the hell's going on here?'

The men eased away from the bar. Ritter Neumann, who was standing behind it with Brandt said, 'Altmann found a trap door under that old rush mat behind the bar this morning, sir, and a cellar below that we didn't know about. Two parcels of cigarettes not even unwrapped. Five thousand in each.' He waved a hand along the counter. 'Gordon's gin,

Beefeater, White Horse Scotch Whisky, Haig and Haig.' He picked up a bottle and spelled out the English with difficulty. 'Bushmills Irish Whiskey. Pot distilled.'

Liam Devlin gave a howl of delight and grabbed it from him. 'I'll shoot the first man that touches a drop,' he declared. 'I swear it. It's all for me.'

There was a general laugh and Steiner calmed them with a raised hand. 'Steady down, there's something to discuss. Business.' He turned to Ilse Neuhoff. 'Sorry, my love, but this is top security.'

She was enough of a soldier's wife not to argue. 'I'll wait outside. But I refuse to let that gin out of my sight.' She exited, the bottle of Beefeater in one hand, her glass in the other.

There was silence, now, in the saloon bar, everyone suddenly sober, waiting to hear what he had to say. 'It's simple,' Steiner told them. 'There's a chance to get out of here. A special mission.'

'Doing what, Herr Oberst?' Sergeant Altmann asked.

'Your old trade. What you were trained to do.'

There was an instant reaction, a buzz of excitement. Someone whispered, 'Does that mean we'll be jumping again?'

'That's exactly what I mean,' Steiner said. 'But it's volunteers only. A personal decision for every man here.'

'Russia, Herr Oberst?' Brandt asked.

Steiner shook his head. 'Somewhere no German soldier has ever fought.' The faces were full of curiosity, tight, expectant as he looked from one to the other. 'How many of you speak English?' he asked softly.

There was a stunned silence and Ritter Neumann so far forgot himself as to say in a hoarse voice, 'For God's sake, Kurt, you've got to be joking.'

Steiner shook his head. 'I've never been more serious. What I tell you now is top secret, naturally. To be brief, in approximately five weeks we'd be expected to do a night drop over a very isolated part of the English coast across the North Sea from Holland. If everything went according to plan we'd be taken off again the following night.'

'And if not?' Neumann said.

'You'd be dead, naturally, so it wouldn't matter.' He looked around the room. 'Anything else?'

'Can we be told the purpose of the mission, Herr Oberst?' Altmann asked.

'The same sort of thing Skorzeny and those lads of the Paratroop School Battalion pulled at Gran Sasso. That's all I can say.'

'Well, it's enough for me.' Brandt glared around the room. 'If we go, we might die, if we stay here we die for certain. If you go – we go.'

'I agree,' Ritter Neumann echoed and snapped to attention.

Every man in the room followed suit. Steiner stood there for a long moment, staring into some dark, secret place in his own mind and then he nodded. 'So be it. Did I hear someone mention White Horse Whisky?'

The group broke for the bar and Altmann sat down and started to play *We march against England* on the piano. Someone threw his cap at him and Sturm called, 'You can stick that load of old crap. Let's have something worth listening to.'

The door opened and Ilse Neuhoff appeared. 'Can I come in now?'

There was a roar from the whole group. In a moment she was lifted up on to the bar. 'A song!' they chorused.

'All right,' she said, laughing. 'What do you want?'

Steiner got in before everyone, his voice sharp and quick. '*Alles ist verrückt.*'

There was a sudden silence. She looked down at him, face pale. 'You're sure?'

'Highly appropriate,' he said. 'Believe me.'

Hans Altmann moved into the opening chords, giving it everything he had and Ilse paraded slowly up and down the bar, her hands on her hips, as she sang that strange melancholy song known to every man who had ever served in the Winter War.

What are we doing here? What is it all about? Alles ist verrückt. Everything's crazy. Everything's gone to hell.

There were tears in her eyes now. She spread her arms wide as if she would embrace them all and suddenly everyone was singing, slow and deep, looking up at her, Steiner, Ritter, all of them – even Radl.

Devlin looked from one face to the other in bewilderment then turned, pulled open the door and lurched outside. 'Am I crazy or are they?' he whispered.

It was dark on the terrace because of the blackout, but Radl and Steiner went out there to smoke a cigar after dinner, more for privacy than anything else. Through the thick curtains that covered the French windows they could hear Liam Devlin's voice, Ilse Neuhoff and her husband laughing gaily.

'A man of considerable charm,' Steiner said.

Radl nodded. 'He has other qualities also. Many more like him and the British would have thankfully got out of Ireland years ago. You had a mutually profitable meeting after I left you this afternoon, I trust?'

'I think that you could say that we understand each other,' Steiner said, 'and we examined the map together very closely. It will be of great assistance to have him as an advance party, believe me.'

'Anything else I should know?'

'Yes, young Werner Briegel's actually been to that area.'

'Briegel?' Radl said. 'Who's he?'

'Lance-corporal. Twenty-one. Three years service. Comes from a place called Barth on the Baltic. He says some of that coastline is rather similar to Norfolk. Enormous lonely beaches, sand dunes and lots of birds.'

'Birds?' Radl said.

Steiner smiled through the darkness. 'I should explain that birds are the passion of young Werner's life. Once, near Leningrad, we were saved from a partisan ambush because they disturbed a huge flock of starlings. Werner and I were temporarily caught in the open, under fire and flat on our faces in the mud. He filled in the time by giving me chapter and verse on how the starlings were probably migrating to England for the winter.'

'Fascinating,' Radl said ironically.

'Oh, you may laugh, but it passed a nasty thirty minutes rather quickly for us. That's what took him and his father to North Norfolk in nineteen thirty-seven, by the way. The birds. Apparently the whole coast is famous for them.'

'Ah, well,' Radl said. 'Each one to his own taste. What about this question of who speaks English? Did you get that sorted out?'

'Lieutenant Neumann, Sergeant Altmann and young Briegel all speak good English, but with accents, naturally. No hope of passing for natives. Of the rest, Brandt and Klugl both speak the broken variety. Enough to get by. Brandt, by the way, was a deck hand on cargo boats as a youngster. Hamburg to Hull.'

Radl nodded. 'It could be worse. Tell me, has Neuhoff questioned you at all?'

'No, but he's obviously very curious. And poor Ilse is beside herself with worry. I'll have to make sure she doesn't try to take the whole thing up with Ribbentrop in a misguided attempt to save me from she knows not what.'

'Good,' Radl said. 'You sit tight then and wait. You'll have movement orders within a week to ten days, depending on how quickly I can find a suitable base in Holland. Devlin, as you know, will probably go over in about a week. I think we'd better go in now.'

Steiner put a hand on his arm. 'And my father?'

Radl said, 'I would be dishonest if I led you to believe I have any influence in the matter. Himmler is personally responsible. All that I can do – and I will certainly do this – is make it plain to him how co-operative you are being.'

'And do you honestly think that will be enough?'

'Do you?' Radl said.

Steiner's laugh had no mirth in it at all. 'He has no conception of honour.'

It seemed a curiously old-fashioned remark, and Radl was intrigued. 'And you?' he said. 'You have?'

'Perhaps not. Perhaps it's too fancy a word for what I mean. Simple things like giving your word and keeping it, standing by friends whatever comes. Does the sum of these things total honour?'

'I don't know, my friend,' Radl said. 'All I can confirm with any certainty is the undoubted fact that you are too good for the Reichsführer's world, believe me.' He put an arm around Steiner's shoulders. 'And now, we'd really better go in.'

Ilse, Colonel Neuhoff and Devlin were seated at a small round table by the fire and she was busy laying out a Celtic Circle from the Tarot pack in her left hand.

'Go on, amaze me,' Devlin was saying.

'You mean you are not a believer, Mr. Devlin?' she asked him.

'A decent Catholic lad like me? Proud product of the best the Jesuits could afford, Frau Neuhoff?' He grinned, 'Now what do you think?'

'That you are an intensely superstitious man, Mr. Devlin.' His smile slipped a little. 'You see,' she went on, 'I am what is known as a sensitive. The cards are not important. They are a tool only.'

'Go on then.'

'Very well, your future on one card, Mr. Devlin. The seventh I come to.'

She counted them out quickly and turned the seventh card over. It was a skeleton carrying a scythe and the card was upside down.

'Isn't he the cheerful one?' Devlin remarked, trying to sound unconcerned and failing.

'Yes, Death,' she said, 'but reversed it doesn't mean what you imagine.' She stared down at the card for a full half-minute and then said very quickly, 'You will live long, Mr. Devlin. Soon for you begins a lengthy period of inertia, of stagnation even and then, in the closing years of your life, revolution, perhaps assassination.' She looked up calmly. 'Does that satisfy you?'

'The long life bit does,' Devlin said cheerfully. 'I'll take my chance on the rest.'

'May I join in, Frau Neuhoff,' Radl said.

'If you like.'

She counted out the cards. This time the seventh was the Star reversed. She looked at it for another long moment. 'Your health is not good, Herr Oberst.'

'That's true,' Radl said.

She looked up and said simply, 'I think you know what is here?'

'Thank you, I believe I do,' he said, smiling calmly.

There was a slightly uncomfortable atmosphere then, as if a sudden chill had fallen and Steiner said, 'All right, Ilse, what about me?'

She reached for the cards as if to gather them up. 'No, not now, Kurt, I think we've had enough for one night.'

'Nonsense,' he said. 'I insist.' He picked up the cards. 'There, I hand you the pack with my left hand, isn't that right?'

Very hesitantly she took it, looked at him in mute appeal, then started to count. She turned the seventh card over quickly, long enough to glance at it herself and put it back on top of the pack. 'Lucky in cards as well, it seems, Kurt. You drew Strength. Considerable good fortune, a trumph in adversity, sudden success.' She smiled brightly. 'And now, if you gentlemen will excuse me, I'll see to the coffee,' and she walked out of the room.

Steiner reached down and turned the card over. It was The Hanged Man. He sighed heavily. 'Women,' he said, 'can be very silly at times. Is it not so, gentlemen?'

There was fog in the morning. Neuhoff had Radl wakened just after dawn and broke the bad news to him over coffee.

'A regular problem here, I'm afraid,' he said. 'But there it is and the general forecast is lousy. Not a hope of anything getting off the ground here before evening. Can you wait that long?'

Radl shook his head. 'I have to be in Paris by this evening and to do that it's essential that I catch the transport leaving Jersey at eleven to make the necessary connection in Brittany. What else can you offer?'

'I could arrange passage by E-boat if you insist,' Neuhoff told him. 'Something of an experience, I warn you, and rather hazardous. We've more trouble with the Royal Navy than we do with the RAF in this area. But it would be essential to leave without delay if you are to make St. Helier in time.'

'Excellent,' Radl said. 'Please make all necessary arrangements at once and I'll rouse Devlin.'

Neuhoff drove them down to the harbour himself in his staff car shortly after seven, Devlin huddled in the rear seat showing every symptom of a king-size hangover. The E-boat waited at the lower jetty. When they went down the steps they found Steiner in sea boots and reefer jacket, leaning on the rail talking to a young bearded naval lieutenant in heavy sweater and salt-stained cap.

He turned to greet them. 'A nice morning for it. I've just been making sure Koenig realises he's carrying precious cargo.'

The lieutenant saluted. 'Herr Oberst.'

Devlin, the picture of misery, stood with his hands pushed deep into his pockets.

'Not too well this morning, Mr. Devlin?' Steiner enquired.

Devlin moaned. 'Wine is a mocker; strong drink is raging.'

Steiner said, 'You won't be wanting this then?' He held up a bottle. 'Brandt found another Bushmills.'

Devlin relieved him of it instantly. 'I wouldn't dream of allowing it to do to anyone else what it's done to me.' He shook hands. 'Let's hope that when you're coming down I'll be looking up,' and he clambered over the rail and sat in the stern.

Radl shook hands with Neuhoff, then turned to Steiner. 'You'll hear from me soon. As for the other matter, I'll do everything I can.'

Steiner said nothing. Did not even attempt to shake hands and Radl hesitated, then scrambled over the rail. Koenig issued orders crisply, leaning out of an open window in the wheelhouse. The lines were cast off and the E-boat slipped away into the mist of the harbour.

They rounded the end of the breakwater and picked up speed. Radl looked about him with interest. The crew were a rough-looking lot, half of them bearded, and all attired in either Guernseys or thick fishermen's sweaters, denim pants and sea boots. In fact, there was little of the Navy about them at all and the craft itself, festooned with strange aerials, was like no E-boat he had ever seen before now that he examined it thoroughly.

When he went on to the bridge he found Koenig leaning over the chart table, a large black-bearded seaman at the wheel who wore a faded reefer jacket that carried a chief petty officer's rank badges. A cigar jutted from between his teeth, something else which, it occurred to Radl, did not seem very naval.

Koenig saluted decently enough. 'Ah, there you are, Herr Oberst. Everything all right?'

'I hope so,' Radl leaned over the chart table. 'How far is it?'

'About fifty miles.'

'Will you get us there on time?'

Koenig glanced at his watch. 'I estimate we'll arrive at St. Helier just before ten, Herr Oberst, as long as the Royal Navy doesn't get in the way.'

Radl looked out of the window. 'Your crew, Lieutenant, do they always dress like fishermen? I understood the E-boats to be the pride of the Navy.'

Koenig smiled. 'But this isn't an E-boat, Herr Oberst. Only classed as one.'

'Then what in the hell is it?' Radl demanded in bewilderment.

'Actually we're not too sure, are we, Muller?' The petty officer grinned and Koenig said, 'A motor gun boat, as you can see, Herr Oberst, constructed in Britain for the Turks and commandeered by the Royal Navy.'

'What's the story?'

'Ran aground on a sandbank on an ebb tide near Morlaix in Brittany. Her captain couldn't scuttle her, so he fired a demolition charge before abandoning her.'

'And?'

'It didn't go off and before he could get back on board to rectify the error an E-boat turned up and grabbed him and his crew.'

'Poor devil,' Radl said. 'I almost feel sorry for him.'

'But the best is yet to come, Herr Oberst,' Koenig told him. 'As the captain's last message was that he was abandoning his ship and blowing her up, the British Admiralty naturally assumed that he had succeeded.'

'Which leaves you free to make the run between the islands in what is to all intents and purposes a Royal Navy boat? I see now.'

'Exactly. You were looking at the jack staff earlier and were no doubt puzzled to find that it is the White Ensign of the Royal Navy we keep ready to unfurl.'

'And it's saved you on occasion?'

'Many times. We hoist the White Ensign, make a courtesy signal and move on. No trouble at all.'

Radl was aware of that cold finger of excitement moving inside him again. 'Tell me about the boat,' he said. 'How fast is she?'

'Top speed was originally twenty-five knots, but the Navy yard at Brest did enough work on her to bring that to thirty. Still not up to an E-boat, of course, but not bad. A hundred and seventeen feet long and as for armaments, a six-pounder, a two-pounder, two twin point five machine-guns, twin twenty millimetre anti-aircraft cannon.'

'Fine,' Radl cut him off. 'A gun boat indeed. Tell me now. What about range?'

'A thousand miles at twenty-one knots. Of course, with the silencers on, she burns up much more fuel.'

'And what about that lot?' Radl pointed out to the aerials which festooned her.

'Navigational some of them. The rest are S-phone aerials. It's a micro-wave wireless set for two-way voice communication between a moving ship and an agent on land. Far better than anything we've got. Obviously used by agents to talk them in before a landing. I'm sick of singing its praises at Naval Headquarters in Jersey. Nobody takes the slightest interest. No wonder we're . . .'

He stopped himself just in time. Radl glanced at him and said calmly, 'At what range does this remarkable gadget function?'

'Up to fifteen miles on a good day; for reliability I'd only claim half that distance, but at that range it's as good as a telephone call.'

Radl stood there for a long moment, thinking about it all and then he nodded abruptly. 'Thank you, Koenig,' he said and went out.

He found Devlin in Koenig's cabin, flat on his back, eyes closed, hands folded over the bottle of Bushmills. Radl frowned, annoyance and even a certain alarm stirring inside him and then saw that the seal on the bottle was unbroken.

'It's all right, Colonel dear,' Devlin said without apparently opening his eyes. 'The Devil hasn't got me by the big toe yet.'

'Did you bring my briefcase with you?'

Devlin squirmed to pull it from underneath him. 'Guarding it with my life.'

'Good.' Radl moved back to the door. 'They've got a wireless in the wheelhouse that I'd like you to look at before we land.'

'Wireless?' Devlin grunted.

'Oh, never mind,' Radl said. 'I'll explain later.'

When he went back to the bridge Koenig was seated at the chart table in a swivel chair drinking coffee from a tin mug. Muller still had the wheel.

Koenig got up, obviously surprised, and Radl said, 'The officer commanding naval forces in Jersey – what's his name?'

'Kápitan zur See Hans Olbricht.'

'I see – can you get us to St. Helier half an hour earlier than your estimated time of arrival?'

Koenig glanced dubiously at Muller. 'I'm not sure, Herr Oberst. We could try. Is it essential?'

'Absolutely. I must have time to see Olbricht to arrange your transfer.'

Koenig looked at him in astonishment. 'Transfer, Herr Oberst? To which command?'

'My command.' Radl took the manilla envelope from his pocket and produced the Führer directive. 'Read that.'

He turned away impatiently and lit a cigarette. When he turned again, Koenig's eyes were wide. 'My God!' he whispered.

'I hardly think He enters into the matter.' Radl took the letter from him and replaced it in the envelope. He nodded at Muller. 'This big ox is to be trusted?'

'To the death, Herr Oberst.'

'Good,' Radl said. 'For a day or two you'll stay in Jersey until orders are finalised, then I want you to make your way along the coast to Boulogne where you will await my instructions. Any problems in getting there?'

Koenig shook his head. 'None that I can see. An easy enough trip for a boat like this staying inshore.' He hesitated. 'And afterwards, Herr Oberst?'

'Oh, somewhere on the North Dutch coast near Den Helder. I haven't found a suitable place yet. Do you know it?'

It was Muller who cleared his throat and said, 'Begging the Herr Oberst's pardon, but I know that coast like the back of my hand. I used to be first mate on a Dutch salvage tug out of Rotterdam.'

'Excellent. Excellent.'

He left them, then went and stood in the prow beside the six-pounder smoking a cigarette. 'It marches,' he said softly. 'It marches,' and his stomach was hollow with excitement.

6

Just before noon on Wednesday 6 October Joanna Grey took possession of a large envelope deposited inside a copy of *The Times* left on a certain bench in Green Park by her usual contact at the Spanish Embassy.

Once in possession of the package she went straight back to King's Cross station and caught the first express north, changing at Peterborough to a local train for King's Lynn where she had left her car, taking advantage of the surplus she had managed to accumulate from the petrol allocation given to her for WVS duties.

When she turned into the yard at the back of Park Cottage it was almost six o'clock and she was dog tired. She let herself in through the kitchen where she was greeted enthusiastically by Patch. He trailed at her heels when she went into the sitting-room and poured herself a large Scotch – of which, thanks to Sir Henry Willoughby, she had a plentiful supply. Then she climbed the stairs to the small study next to her bedroom.

The panelling was Jacobean and the invisible door in the corner was none of her doing, but part of the original, a common device of the period and designed to resemble a section of panelling. She took a key from a chain around her neck and unlocked the door. A short wooden stairway gave access to a cubby-hole loft under the roof. Here she had a radio receiver and transmitter. She sat down at an old deal table, opened a drawer in it, pushing a loaded Luger to one side and rummaged for a pencil, then took out her code books and got to work.

When she sat back an hour later her face was pinched with excitement. 'My God!' she said to herself in Afrikaans. 'They meant it – they actually meant it.'

Then she took a deep breath, pulled herself together and went back downstairs. Patch was waiting patiently at the door and followed at her heels all the way to the sitting-room where she picked up the telephone and dialled the number of Studley Grange. Sir Henry Willoughby himself answered.

She said, 'Henry – it's Joanna Grey.'

His voice warmed immediately. 'Hello there, my dear. I hope you're not ringing to say you won't be coming over for bridge or something. You hadn't forgotten? Eight-thirty?'

She had, but that didn't matter. She said, 'Of course not, Henry. It's just that I've got a little favour to ask and I wanted to speak to you privately about it.'

His voice deepened. 'Fire away, old girl. Anything I can do.'

'Well, I've heard from some Irish friends of my late husband and they've asked me to try and do something for their nephew. In fact, they're sending him over. He'll be arriving in the next few days.'

'Do what exactly?'

'His name is Devlin – Liam Devlin, and the thing is, Henry, the poor man was very badly wounded serving with the British Army in France. He received a medical discharge and he's been convalescing for almost a year. He's quite fit now though and ready for work, but it needs to be the outdoor variety.'

'And you thought I might be able to fix him up?' said Sir Henry jovially. 'No difficulty there, old girl. You know what it's like getting any kind of workers for the estate these days.'

'He wouldn't be able to do much at first,' she said. 'Actually I was wondering about the marsh warden's job at Hobs End. That's been vacant since young Tom King went off to the Army two years ago, hasn't it, and there's the house standing empty? It would be good to have somebody in. It's getting very run down.'

'I'll tell you what, Joanna, I think you might have something there. We'll go into the whole thing in depth. No sense in discussing it over bridge with other people there. Are you free tomorrow afternoon?'

'Of course,' she said. 'You know, it's so good of you to help in this way,

Henry. I always seem to be bothering you with my problems these days.'

'Nonsense,' he told her sternly. 'That's what I'm here for. Woman needs a man to smooth over the rough spots for her.' His voice was shaking slightly.

'I'd better go now,' she said. 'I'll see you soon.'

'Goodbye, my dear.'

She put down the receiver and patted Patch on the head and he trailed along at her heels when she went back upstairs. She sat at the transmitter and made the briefest of signals on the frequency of the Dutch beacon for onward transmission to Berlin. An acknowledgement that her instructions had been safely received and a given code word that meant that the business of Devlin's employment had been taken care of.

In Berlin it was raining, black, cold rain drifting across the city pushed by a wind so bitter that it must have come all the way from the Urals. In the ante-room outside Himmler's office at Prinz Albrechtstrasse, Max Radl and Devlin sat facing each other, as they had been sitting for more than an hour now.

'What in the hell goes on?' Devlin said. 'Does he want to see us or doesn't he?'

'Why don't you knock and ask?' Radl suggested.

Just then the outer door opened and Rossman came in, beating rain from his slouch hat, his coat dripping water. He smiled brightly, 'Still here, you two?'

Devlin said to Radl, 'He's got the great wit to him, that one, isn't it a fact?'

Rossman knocked at the door and went in. He didn't bother closing it. 'I've got him, Herr Reichsführer.'

'Good,' they heard Himmler say. 'Now I'll see Radl and this Irish fellow.'

'What in the hell is this?' Devlin muttered. 'A command performance?'

'Watch your tongue,' Radl said, 'and let me do the talking.'

He led the way into the room, Devlin at his heels, and Rossman closed the door behind them. Everything was exactly the same as on that first night. The room in half-darkness, the open fire flickering, Himmler seated behind the desk.

The Reichsführer said, 'You've done well, Radl. I'm more than pleased with the way things are progressing. And this is Herr Devlin?'

'As ever was,' Devlin said cheerfully. 'Just a poor, old Irish peasant, straight out of the bog, that's me, your honour.'

Himmler frowned in puzzlement. 'What on earth is the man talking about?' he demanded of Radl.

'The Irish, Herr Reichsführer, are not as other people,' Radl said weakly.

'It's the rain,' Devlin told him.

Himmler stared at him in astonishment, then turned to Radl. 'You are certain he is the man for this?'

'Perfectly.'

'And when does he go?'

'On Sunday.'

'And your other arrangements? They are proceeding satisfactorily?'

'So far. My trip to Alderney I combined with Abwehr business in Paris and I have perfectly legal reasons for visiting Amsterdam next week. The Admiral knows nothing. He has been preoccupied with other matters.'

'Good.' Himmler sat staring into space, obviously thinking about something.

'Was there anything else, Herr Reichsführer?' Radl asked as Devlin stirred impatiently.

'Yes, I brought you here for two reasons tonight. In the first place I wanted to see Herr Devlin for myself. But secondly, there is the question of the composition of Steiner's assault group.'

'Maybe I should leave,' Devlin suggested.

'Nonsense,' Himmler said brusquely. 'I would be obliged if you would simply sit in the corner and listen. Or are the Irish incapable of such a feat?'

'Oh, it's been known,' Devlin said. 'But not often.'

He went and sat by the fire, took out a cigarette and lit it. Himmler glared at him, seemed about to speak and obviously thought better of it. He turned back to Radl.

'You were saying, Herr Reichsführer?'

'Yes, there seems to me one weakness in the composition of Steiner's group. Four or five of the men speak English to some degree, but only Steiner can pass as a native. This isn't good enough. In my opinion he needs the backing of someone of similar ability.'

'But people with that sort of ability are rather thin on the ground.'

'I think I have a solution for you,' Himmler said. 'There is a man called Amery – John Amery. Son of a famous English politician. He ran guns for Franco. Hates the Bolsheviks. He's been working for us for some time now.'

'Is he of any use?'

'I doubt it, but he came up with the idea of founding what he called the British Legion of St. George. The idea was to recruit Englishmen from the prisoner of war camps, mainly to fight on the Eastern Front.'

'Did he get any takers?'

'A few – not many and mostly rogues. Amery has nothing to do with it now. For a while the Wehrmacht was responsible for the unit, but now the SS has taken over.'

'These volunteers – are there many?'

'Fifty or sixty as I last heard. They now rejoice in the name British Free Corps.' Himmler opened a file in front of him and took out a record card. 'Such people do have their uses on occasion. This man, for instance, Harvey Preston. When captured in Belgium he was wearing the uniform of a captain in the Coldstream Guards, and having what I am informed are the voice and mannerisms of the English aristocrat, no one doubted him for some time.'

'And he was not what he seemed?'

'Judge for yourself.'

Radl examined the card. Harvey Preston had been born in Harrogate, Yorkshire, in 1916, the son of a railway porter. He had left home at fourteen to work as a prop boy with a touring variety company. At eighteen he was acting in repertory in Southport. In 1937 he was sentenced to two years imprisonment at Winchester Assizes on four charges of fraud.

Discharged in January, 1939, he was arrested a month later and sentenced to a further nine months on a charge of impersonating an RAF officer and obtaining money by false pretences. The judge had suspended the sentence on condition that Preston joined the forces. He had gone to France as an orderly room clerk with an RASC transport company and, when captured, held the rank of acting corporal.

His prison camp record was bad or good according to which side you were on, for he had informed on no fewer than five separate escape attempts. On the last occasion this had become known to his comrades and if he had not volunteered to serve in the Free Corps, he would in any case have had to be moved for reasons of his own safety.

Radl walked across to Devlin and handed him the card, then turned to Himmler. 'And you want Steiner to take this . . . this . . .'

'Rogue,' Himmler said, 'who is quite expendable, but who simulates the English aristocrat quite well. He really does have presence, Radl. The sort of man to whom policemen touch their helmets the moment he opens his mouth. I've always understood that the English working classes know an officer and a gentleman when they see one, and Preston should do very well.'

'But Steiner and his men, Herr Reichsführer, are soldiers – real soldiers. You know their record. Can you see such a man fitting in? Taking orders?'

'He will do as he is told,' Himmler said. 'That goes without question. We'll have him in, shall we?'

He pressed the buzzer and a moment later, Rossman appeared in the doorway. 'I'll see Preston now.' Rossman went out, leaving the door open, and a moment later Preston entered the room, closed the door behind him and gave the Nazi Party salute.

He was at that time twenty-seven years of age, a tall, handsome man in a beautifully-tailored uniform of field grey. It was the uniform particularly which fascinated Radl. He had the death's head badge of the SS in his peaked cap and collar patches depicting the three leopards. Under the eagle on his left sleeve was a Union Jack shield and a black and silver cuff-title carried the legend in Gothic lettering, *Britisches Freikorps*.

'Very pretty,' Devlin said, but so softly that only Radl heard.

Himmler made the introductions. 'Untersturmführer Preston – Colonel Radl of the Abwehr and Herr Devlin. You will be familiar with the role each of these gentlemen plays in the affair at hand from the documents I gave you to study earlier today.'

Preston half-turned to Radl, inclined his head and clicked his heels. Very formal, very military, just like someone playing a Prussian officer in a play.

'So,' Himmler said. 'You have had ample opportunity to consider this matter. You understand what is required of you?'

Preston said carefully, 'Do I take it that Colonel Radl is looking for volunteers for this mission?' His German was good, although the accent could have been improved on.

Himmler removed his pince-nez, stroked the bridge of his nose gently with a forefinger and replaced them with great care. It was a gesture somehow infinitely sinister. His voice, when he spoke, was like dry leaves brushed by the wind. 'What exactly are you trying to say, Untersturmführer?'

'It's just that I find myself in rather a difficulty here. As the Reichsführer knows, members of the British Free Corps were given a guarantee that at no time would they have to wage war or take part in any armed act against Britain or the Crown or indeed to support any act detrimental to the interests of the British people.'

Radl said, 'Perhaps this gentleman would be happier serving on the Eastern Front, Herr Reichsführer? Army Group South, under Field Marshal von Manstein. Plenty of hot spots there for those who crave real action.'

Preston, realising that he had made a very bad mistake, hastily tried to make amends. 'I can assure you, Herr Reichsführer, that . . .'

Himmler didn't give him a chance. 'You talk of volunteering, where I see only an act of sacred duty. An opportunity to serve the Führer and the Reich.'

Preston snapped to attention. It was an excellent performance and Devlin, for one, was thoroughly enjoying himself. 'Of course, Herr Reichsführer. It is my total aim.'

'I am right, am I not, in assuming that you have taken an oath to this effect? A holy oath?'

'Yes, Herr Reichsführer.'

'Then nothing more need be said. You will from this moment consider yourself to be under the orders of Colonel Radl here.'

'As you say, Herr Reichsführer.'

'Colonel Radl, I'd like to have a word with you in private.' Himmler glanced at Devlin. 'Herr Devlin, if you would be kind enough to wait in the ante-room with Untersturmführer Preston.'

Preston gave him a crisp Heil Hitler, turned on heel with a precision that would not have disgraced the Grenadier Guards, and went out. Devlin followed, closing the door behind them.

There was no sign of Rossman and Preston kicked the side of one of the armchairs viciously and threw his cap down on the table. He was white with anger and when he produced a silver case and extracted a cigarette, his hand trembled slightly.

Devlin strolled across and helped himself to a cigarette before Preston could close the case. He grinned. 'By God, the old bugger's got you by the balls.'

He had spoken in English and Preston, glaring at him, replied in the same language. 'What in the hell do you mean?'

'Come on, son,' Devlin said. 'I've heard of your little lot. Legion of St. George; British Free Corps. How was it they bought you? Unlimited booze and as many women as you can handle, if you're not too choosy, that is. Now it's all got to be paid for.'

At an inch above six feet, Preston was able to look down with some contempt at the Irishman. His left nostril curled. 'My God, the people one has to deal with – straight out of the bogs, too, from the smell. Now go away and try playing nasty little Irishmen elsewhere, there's a good chap, or I might have to chastise you.'

Devlin, in the act of putting a match to his cigarette, kicked Preston with some precision under the right kneecap.

In the office Radl had just come to the end of a progress report. 'Excellent,' Himmler said, 'and the Irishman leaves on Sunday?'

'By Dornier from a Luftwaffe base outside Brest – Laville. A north-westerly course from there will take them to Ireland without the necessity of passing over English soil. At twenty-five thousand feet for most of the way they should have no trouble.'

'And the Irish Air Force?'

'What air force, Herr Reichsführer?'

'I see.' Himmler closed the file. 'So, things seem to be really moving at last. I'm very pleased with you, Radl. Continue to keep me informed.'

He picked up his pen in a dismissive gesture and Radl said, 'There is one other matter.'

Himmler looked up. 'And what is that?'

'Major-General Steiner.'

Himmler laid down his pen. 'What about him?'

Radl didn't know how to put it, but he had to make the point somehow. He owed it to Steiner. In fact, considering the circumstances, the intensity with which he wanted to keep that promise surprised him. 'It was the Reichsführer himself who suggested I make it clear to Colonel Steiner that his conduct in this affair could have a significant effect on his father's case.'

'That is so,' Himmler said calmly. 'But what is the problem?'

'I promised Colonel Steiner, Herr Reichsführer,' Radl said lamely. 'Gave him an assurance that . . . that . . .'

'Which you had no authority to offer,' Himmler said. 'However, under the circumstances, you may give Steiner that assurance in my name.' He picked up his pen again. 'You may go now and tell Preston to remain. I want another word with him. I'll have him report to you tomorrow.'

When Radl went out into the ante-room, Devlin was standing at the window peering through a chink in the curtains and Preston was sitting in one of the armchairs. 'Raining cats and dogs out there,' he said cheerfully. 'Still, it might keep the RAF at home for a change. Are we going?'

Radl nodded and said to Preston, 'You stay. He wants you. And don't come to Abwehr Headquarters tomorrow. I'll get in touch with you.'

Preston was on his feet, very military again, arm raised. 'Very well, Herr Oberst. Heil Hitler!'

Radl and Devlin moved to the door and as they went out, the Irishman raised a thumb and grinned amiably. 'Up the Republic, me old son!'

Preston dropped his arm and swore viciously. Devlin closed the door and followed Radl down the stairs. 'Where in the hell did they find him? Himmler must have lost his wits entirely.'

'God knows,' Radl said as they paused beside the SS guards in the main entrance to turn up their collars against the heavy rain. 'There is some merit in the idea of another officer who is obviously English, but this

Preston.' He shook his head. 'A badly flawed man. Second-rate actor, petty criminal. A man who has spent most of his life living some sort of private fantasy.'

'And we're stuck with him,' Devlin said. 'I wonder what Steiner will make of it?'

They ran through the rain as Radl's staff car approached and settled themselves in the back. 'Steiner will cope,' Radl said. 'Men like Steiner always do. But now to business. We fly to Paris tomorrow afternoon.'

'Then what?'

'I've important business in Holland. As I told you, the entire operation will be based on Landsvoort, which is the right kind of end-of-the-world spot. During the operational period I shall be there myself, so, my friend, if you make a transmission, you'll know who is on the other end. As I was saying, I'll leave you in Paris when I fly to Amsterdam. You, in your turn, will be ferried down to the airfield at Laville near Brest. You take off at ten o'clock on Sunday night.'

'Will you be there?' Devlin asked.

'I'll try, but it may not be possible.'

They arrived at Tirpitz Ufer a moment later and hurried through the rain to the entrance just as Hofer, in cap and heavy greatcoat, was emerging. He saluted and Radl said, 'Going off duty, Karl? Anything for me?'

'Yes, Herr Oberst, a signal from Mrs Grey.'

Radl was filled with excitement. 'What is it, man, what does she say?'

'Message received and understood, Herr Oberst and the question of Herr Devlin's employment has been taken care of.'

Radl turned triumphantly to Devlin, rain dripping from the peak of his mountain cap. 'And what do you have to say to that, my friend?'

'Up the Republic,' Devlin said morosely. 'Right up! Is that patriotic enough for you? If so, could I go in now and have a drink?'

When the office door clicked open Preston was sitting in the corner reading an English-language edition of *Signal*. He glanced up and finding Himmler there watching him, jumped to his feet. 'Your pardon, Herr Reichsführer.'

'For what?' Himmler said. 'Come with me. I want to show you something.'

Puzzled and also faintly alarmed, Preston followed him downstairs and along the ground floor corridor to the iron door guarded by two Gestapo men. One of them got the door open, they sprang to attention, Himmler nodded and started down the steps.

The white-painted corridor seemed quiet enough and then Preston became aware of a dull, rhythmic slapping, strangely remote, as if it came from a great distance. Himmler paused outside a cell door and opened a metal gate. There was a small window of armoured glass.

A grey-haired man of sixty or so in a tattered shirt and military breeches was sprawled across a bench while a couple of heavily muscled SS men beat him systematically across the back and buttocks with rubber truncheons. Rossman stood watching, smoking a cigarette, his shirt sleeves rolled up.

'I detest this sort of mindless violence,' Himmler said. 'Don't you, Herr Untersturmführer?'

Preston's mouth had gone dry and his stomach heaved. 'Yes, Herr Reichsführer. Terrible.'

'If only these fools would listen. A nasty business, but how else can one deal with treason against the State? The Reich and the Führer demand an absolute and unquestioning loyalty and those who give less than this must accept the consequences. You understand me?'

Which Preston did – perfectly. And when the Reichsführer turned and went back up the stairs he stumbled after him, a handkerchief to his mouth in an attempt to stop himself from being sick.

In the darkness of his cell below, Major-General of Artillery Karl Steiner crawled into a corner and crouched there, arms folded as if to stop himself from falling apart. 'Not one word,' he said softly through swollen lips. 'Not one word – I swear it.'

At precisely 02.20 hours on the morning of Saturday 9 October Captain Peter Gericke of Night Fighter Group 7, operating out of Grandjeim on the Dutch coast made his thirty-eighth confirmed kill. He was flying a Junkers 88 in heavy cloud, one of those apparently clumsy, black, twin-engined planes festooned with strange radar aerials, that had proved so devastating in their attacks on RAF bombing groups engaged on night raids over Europe.

Not that Gericke had had any luck earlier that night. A blocked fuel pipe in the port engine had kept him grounded for thirty minutes while the rest of the Staffel had taken off to pounce upon a large force of British bombers returning home across the Dutch coast after a raid on Hanover.

By the time Gericke reached the area most of his comrades had turned for home. And yet there were always stragglers, so he remained on patrol for a while longer.

Gericke was twenty-three years of age. A handsome, rather saturnine young man whose dark eyes seemed full of impatience, as if life itself were too slow for him. Just now he was whistling softly between his teeth the first movement of the Pastoral Symphony.

Behind him, Haupt, the radar operator, huddled over the Lichtenstein set, gave an excited gasp. 'I've got one.'

In the same moment base took over smoothly and the familiar voice of Major Hans Berger, ground controller of NJG7, crackled over Gericke's headphones. 'Wanderer Four, this is Black Knight. I have a Kurier for you. Are you receiving?'

'Loud and clear,' Gericke told him.

'Steer nought-eight-seven degrees. Target range ten kilometres.'

The Junkers burst out of cloud cover only seconds later and Bohmler, the observer, touched Gericke's arm. Gericke saw his prey instantly, a Lancaster bomber limping home in bright moonlight, a feathered plume of smoke drifting from the port outer motor.

'Black Knight, this is Wanderer Four,' Gericke said. 'I have visual sighting and require no further assistance.'

He slipped back into the clouds, descended five hundred feet then banked steeply to port, emerging a couple of miles to the rear and below the crippled Lancaster. It was a sitting target, drifting above them like a grey ghost, that plume of smoke trailing gently.

During the second half of 1943, many German night fighters began operating with a secret weapon that was known as *Schraege Musik*, a pair of twenty millimetre cannon mounted in the fuselage and arranged to fire upwards at an angle of between ten and twenty degrees. This weapon enabled night fighters to attack from below, from which position the bomber presented an enormous target and was virtually blind. As tracer rounds were not used, scores of bombers were brought down without their crews even knowing what hit them.

So it was now. For a split second, Gericke was on target, then as he turned away to port, the Lancaster banked steeply and plunged towards the sea three thousand feet below. There was one parachute, then another. A moment later, the plane itself exploded in a brilliant ball of orange fire. Fuselage dropped down towards the sea, one of the parachutes ignited and flared briefly.

'Dear God in heaven!' Bohmler said in horror.

'What God?' Gericke demanded savagely. 'Now send base a fix on that poor sod down there so someone can pick him up and let's go home.'

When Gericke and his two crewmen reported to the Intelligence Room in the Operations building it was empty except for Major Adler, the senior Intelligence officer, a jovial fifty-year old with the slightly frozen face of someone who had been badly burned. He had actually flown during the First War in von Richthofen's Staffel and wore the Blue Max at his throat.

'Ah, there you are, Peter,' he said. 'Better late than never. Your kill's been confirmed by radio from an E-boat in the area.'

'What about the man who got clear?' Gericke demanded. 'Have they found him?'

'Not yet, but they're searching. There's an air-sea rescue launch in that area, too.'

He pushed a sandalwood box across his desk. It contained very long, pencil-slim Dutch cheroots. Gericke took one.

Adler said, 'You seem concerned, Peter. I had never imagined you a humanitarian.'

'I'm not,' Gericke told him bluntly as he put a match to his cheroot, 'but tomorrow night that could be me. I like to think those air-sea rescue bastards are on their toes.'

As he turned away, Adler said, 'Prager wants to see you.'

Lieutenant-Colonel Otto Prager was Gruppenkommandeur of Grand-jeim, responsible for three Staffeln including Gericke's. He was a strict disciplinarian and an ardent National Socialist, neither of which qualities Gericke found particularly pleasing. He atoned for these minor irritations by being a first-rate pilot in his own right, totally dedicated to the welfare of the aircrew in his Gruppe.

'What does he want?'

Adler shrugged. 'I couldn't say, but when he telephoned, he made it plain it was to be at the earliest possible moment.'

'I know,' Bohmler said, 'Goering's been on the phone. Invited you to Karinhall for the weekend and about time.'

It was a well-known fact that when a Luftwaffe pilot was awarded the Knight's Cross, the Reichsmarschall, as an old flyer himself, liked to hand it over in person.

'That'll be the day,' Gericke said grudgingly. The fact was that men with fewer kills to their credit than he had received the coveted award. It was a distinctly sore point.

'Never mind, Peter,' Adler called as they went out. 'Your day will come.'

'If I live that long,' Gericke said to Bohmler as they paused on the steps of the main entrance to the Operations building. 'What about a drink?'

'No, thanks,' Bohmler said. 'A hot bath and eight hours sleep are my total requirements. I don't approve of it at this time in the morning, you know that, even if we are living backwards way round.'

Haupt was already yawning and Gericke said morosely, 'Bloody Lutheran. All right, sod both of you.'

As he started to walk away, Bohmler called, 'Don't forget Prager wants to see you.'

'Later,' Gericke said. 'I'll see him later.'

'He's really asking for it,' Haupt remarked as they watched him go. 'What's got into him lately?'

'Like the rest of us, he lands and takes off too often,' Bohmler said.

Gericke walked towards the officers' mess wearily, his flying boots drubbing on the tarmac. He felt unaccountably depressed, stale, somehow at the final end of things. It was strange how he couldn't get that *Tommi*, the sole survivor of the Lancaster, out of his mind. What he needed was a drink. A cup of coffee, very hot, and a large Schnapps or perhaps a Steinhager?

He walked into the ante-room and the first person he saw was Colonel Prager sitting in an easy chair in the far corner with another officer, their heads together as they talked in subdued tones. Gericke hesitated, debating whether to turn tail, for the Gruppenkommandeur was particularly strict on the question of flying clothes being worn in the mess. Prager looked up and saw him.

'There you are, Peter. Come and join us.'

He snapped his finger for the mess waiter who hovered nearby and ordered coffee as Gericke approached. He didn't approve of alcohol where pilots were concerned. 'Good morning, Herr Oberst,' Gericke said brightly, intrigued by the other officer, a lieutenant-colonel of Mountain Troops with a black patch over one eye and a Knight's Cross to go with it.

'Congratulations,' Prager said. 'I hear you've got another confirmed kill.'

'That's right, a Lancaster. One man got clear, I saw his chute open. They're looking for him now.'

'Colonel Radl,' Prager said.

Radl held out his good hand and Gericke shook it briefly. 'Herr Oberst.'

Prager was more subdued than he had ever known him. In fact, he was very obviously labouring under some kind of strain, easing himself in the chair as if in acute physical discomfort as the mess waiter brought a tray with a fresh pot of coffee and three cups.

'Leave it, man, leave it!' Prager ordered curtly.

There was a slight strained silence after the waiter had departed. Then the Gruppenkommandeur said abruptly, 'The Herr Oberst here is from the Abwehr. With fresh orders for you.'

'Fresh orders, Herr Oberst?'

Prager got to his feet. 'Colonel Radl can tell you more than I can, but obviously you're being given an extraordinary opportunity to serve the Reich.' Gericke stood up and Prager hesitated, then stuck out his hand.

'You've done well here, Peter. I'm proud of you. As for the other business – I've recommended you three times now so it's right out of my hands.'

'I know, Herr Oberst,' Gericke said warmly, 'and I'm grateful.'

Prager walked away and Gericke sat down. Radl said, 'This Lancaster makes thirty-eight confirmed kills, is it not so?'

'You seem remarkably well informed, Herr Oberst,' Gericke said. 'Will you join me in a drink?'

'Why not? A cognac, I think.'

Gericke called to the waiter and gave the order.

'Thirty-eight confirmed kills and no Knight's Cross,' Radl commented. 'Isn't that unusual?'

Gericke stirred uncomfortably. 'The way it goes sometimes.'

'I know,' Radl said. 'There is also the fact to be taken into consideration that during the summer of nineteen-forty, when you were flying ME one-o-nines out of a base near Calais, you told Reichsmarschall Goering, who was inspecting your Staffel, that in your opinion the Spitfire was a better aircraft.' He smiled gently. 'People of his eminence don't forget junior officers who make remarks like that.'

Gericke said, 'With all due respect, might I point out to the Herr Oberst that in my line of work I can only rely on today because tomorrow I might very possibly be dead, so some idea of what all this is about would be appreciated.'

'It's simple enough,' Radl said. 'I need a pilot for a rather special operation.'

'*You* need?'

'All right, the Reich,' Radl told him. 'Does that please you any better?'

'Not particularly.' Gericke held up his empty Schnapps glass to the waiter and signalled for another. 'As it happens, I'm perfectly happy where I am.'

'A man who consumes Schnapps in such an amount at four o'clock in the morning? I doubt that. In any case, you've no choice in the matter.'

'Is that so?' Gericke said angrily.

'You are perfectly at liberty to confirm this with the Gruppenkommandeur,' Radl said.

The waiter brought him the second glass of Schnapps, Gericke poured it down in one quick swallow and made a face. 'God, how I hate that stuff.'

'Then why drink it?' Radl asked.

'I don't know. Maybe I've been out there in the dark too much or flying too long.' He smiled sardonically. 'Or perhaps I just need a change, Herr Oberst.'

'I think I may say without any exaggeration that I can certainly offer you that.'

'Fine.' Gericke swallowed the rest of his coffee. 'What's the next move?'

'I have an appointment in Amsterdam at nine o'clock. Our destination after that is about twenty miles north of the city, on the way to Den Helder.' He glanced at his watch. 'We'll need to leave here no later than seven-thirty.'

'That gives me time for breakfast and a bath,' Gericke said, 'I can catch a little sleep in the car if that's all right with you.'

As he got up, the door opened and an orderly came in. He saluted and passed the young captain a signal flimsy. Gericke read it and smiled. 'Something important?' Radl asked.

'The *Tommi* who parachuted out of that Lancaster I shot down earlier. They've picked him up. A pilot officer navigator.'

'His luck is good,' Radl commented.

'A good omen,' Gericke said. 'Let's hope mine is.'

Landsvoort was a desolate little place about twenty miles north of Amsterdam between Schagen and the sea. Gericke slept soundly for the entire journey, only coming awake when Radl shook his arm.

There was an old farmhouse and barn, two hangars roofed with rusting corrugated iron and a single runway of crumbling concrete, grass growing between the cracks. The wire perimeter fence was nothing very special and the steel and wire swing gate, which looked new, was guarded by a sergeant with the distinctive gorget plate of the military police hanging around his neck. He was armed with a Schmeisser machine pistol and held a rather savage-looking Alsatian on the end of a steel chain.

He checked their papers impassively while the dog growled deep in its throat, full of menace. Radl drove on through the gate and pulled up in front of the hangars. 'Well, this is it.'

The landscape was incredibly flat, stretching out towards the distant sand dunes and the North Sea beyond. As Gericke opened the door and got out, rain drifted in off the sea in a fine spray and there was the tang of salt to it. He walked across to the edge of the crumbling runway and kicked with his foot until a piece of concrete broke away.

'It was built by a shipping magnate in Rotterdam for his own use ten or twelve years ago,' Radl said as he got out of the car to join him. 'What do you think?'

'All we need now are the Wright brothers.' Gericke looked out towards the sea, shivered and thrust his hands deep into the pockets of his leather coat. 'What a dump – the last place on God's list, I should imagine.'

'Therefore exactly right for our purposes,' Radl pointed out. 'Now, let's get down to business.'

He led the way across to the first hangar which was guarded by another military policeman complete with Alsatian. Radl nodded and the man pulled back one of the sliding doors.

It was damp and rather cold inside, rain drifting in through a hole in the roof. The twin-engined aircraft which stood there looked lonely and rather forlorn, and very definitely far from home. Gericke prided himself that he had long since got past being surprised at anything in this life, but not that morning.

The aircraft was a Douglas DC3, the famous Dakota, probably one of the most successful general transport planes ever built, as much a workhorse for the Allied Forces during the war as was the Junkers 52 to the German Army. The interesting thing about this one was that it carried Luftwaffe insignia on the wings and a Swastika on the tail.

Peter Gericke loved aeroplanes as some men love horses, with a deep and unswerving passion. He reached up and touched a wing gently and his voice was soft when he said, 'You old beauty.'

'You know this aircraft?' Radl said.

'Better than any woman.'

'Six months with the Landros Air Freight Company in Brazil from June to November, nineteen thirty-eight. Nine hundred and thirty flying hours. Quite something for a nineteen-year-old. That must have been hard flying.'

'So that's why I was chosen?'

'All on your records.'

'Where did you get her?'

'RAF Transport Command, dropping supplies to the Dutch Resistance four months ago. One of your night fighter friends got her. Superficial engine damage only. Something to do with the fuel pump, I understand. The observer was too badly wounded to jump so the pilot managed to bring her down in a ploughed field. Unfortunately for him he was next door to an SS barracks. By the time he got his friend out, it was too late to blow her up.'

The door was open and Gericke pulled himself inside. In the cockpit, he sat behind the controls and for a moment he was back in Brazil, green jungle below, the Amazon twisting through it like a great, silver snake from Manaus down to the sea.

Radl took the other seat. He produced a silver case and offered Gericke one of his Russian cigarettes. 'You could fly this thing, then?'

'Where to?'

'Not very far. Across the North Sea to Norfolk. Straight in, straight out.'

'To do what?'

'Drop sixteen paratroopers.'

In his astonishment, Gericke inhaled too deeply and almost choked, the harsh Russian tobacco catching at the back of his throat.

He laughed wildly. 'Operation Sealion at last. Don't you think it's a trifle late in the war for the invasion of England?'

'This particular section of the coast has no low level radar cover,' Radl said calmly. 'No difficulty at all if you go in below six hundred feet. Naturally I'll have the plane cleaned up and the RAF roundels replaced on the wings. If anyone does see you, they see an RAF aircraft presumably going about its lawful business.'

'But why?' said Gericke. 'What in the hell are they going to do when they get there?'

'None of your affair,' Radl said firmly. 'You are just a bus driver, my friend.'

He got up and went out and Gericke followed him. 'Now look here, I think you could do better than that.'

Radl walked to the Mercedes without replying. He stood looking out across the airfield to the sea. 'Too tough for you?'

'Don't be stupid,' Gericke told him angrily. 'I just like to know what I'm getting into, that's all.'

Radl opened his coat and unbuttoned his tunic. From the inside pocket he took out the stiff manilla envelope that housed the precious letter and handed it to Gericke. 'Read that,' he said crisply.

When Gericke looked up, his face was suddenly bleak. 'That important? No wonder Prager was so disturbed.'

'Exactly.'

'All right, how long have I got?'

'Approximately four weeks.'

'I'll need Bohmler, my observer, to fly with me. He's the best bloody navigator I've ever come across.'

'Anything you need. Just ask. Top secret, the whole thing, of course. I can get you a week's leave if you like. After that, you stay here, at the farm under strict security.'

'Can I test flight?'

'If you must, but only at night and preferably only once. I'll have a team of the finest aircraft mechanics the Luftwaffe can supply. Anything you need. You'll be in charge of that side. I don't want engines failing for some absurd mechanical reason when you're four hundred feet above a Norfolk marsh. We'll go back to Amsterdam now.'

At precisely two forty-five on the following morning, Seumas O'Broin, a sheep farmer of Conroy in County Monaghan was endeavouring to find his way home across a stretch of open moorland. And making a bad job of it.

Which was understandable enough for when one is seventy-six, friends have a tendency to disappear with monotonous regularity and Seumas O'Broin was on his way home from a funeral wake for one who had just departed – a wake which had lasted for seventeen hours.

He had not only, as the Irish so delightfully put it, drink taken. He had consumed quantities so vast that he was not certain whether he was in this world or the next; so that when what he took to be a large, white bird sailed out of the darkness over his head without a sound and plunged into the field beyond the next wall, he felt no fear at all, only a mild curiosity.

Devlin made an excellent landing, the supply bag dangling twenty feet below from a line clipped to his belt, hitting the ground first, warning him to be ready. He followed a split second later, rolling in springy Irish turf, scrambling to his feet instantly and unfastening his harness.

The clouds parted at that moment, exposing a quarter-moon which gave him exactly the right amount of light to do what had to be done. He opened the supply bag, took out a small trenching shovel, his dark raincoat, a tweed cap, a pair of shoes and a large, leather Gladstone bag.

There was a thorn hedge nearby, a ditch beside it and he quickly scraped a hole in the bottom with the shovel. Then he unzipped his flying overalls. Underneath he was wearing a tweed suit and he transferred the Walther which he had carried in his belt to his right-hand pocket. He pulled on his shoes and then put the overalls, the parachute and the flying boots into the bag and dropped it into the hole, raking the soil back into place quickly. He scraped a mass of dry leaves and twigs over everything, just to finish things off and tossed the spade into a nearby copse.

He pulled on his raincoat, picked up the Gladstone bag and turned to find Seumas O'Broin leaning on the wall watching him. Devlin moved fast, his hand on the butt of the Walther. But then the aroma of good Irish whiskey, the slurred speech told him all he needed to know.

'What are ye, man or divil?' the old farmer demanded, each word slow and distinct. 'Of this world or the next?'

'God save us, old man, but from the smell of you, if one of us lit a match right now we'd be in hell together soon enough. As for your question, I'm a little of both. A simple Irish boy, trying a new way of coming home after years in foreign parts.'

'Is that a fact?' O'Broin said.

'Aren't I telling you?'

The old man laughed delightedly. '*Cead mile failte sa bhaile romhat*,' he said in Irish. 'A hundred thousand welcomes home to you.'

Devlin grinned. '*Go raibh maith agat,*' he said. 'Thanks.' He picked up the Gladstone bag, vaulted over the wall and set off across the meadow briskly, whistling softly between his teeth. It was good to be home, however brief the visit.

The Ulster border, then, as now, was wide open to anyone who knew the area. Two and a half hours of brisk walking by country lanes and field paths and he was in the county of Armagh and standing on British soil. A lift in a milk truck had him in Armagh itself by six o'clock. Half-an-hour later, he was climbing into a third-class compartment on the early morning train to Belfast

7

On Wednesday it rained all day and in the afternoon mist drifted in off the North Sea across the marshes at Cley and Hobs End and Blakeney.

In spite of the weather, Joanna Grey went into the garden after lunch. She was working in the vegetable patch beside the orchard, lifting potatoes, when the garden gate creaked. Patch gave a sudden whine and was off like a flash. When she turned, a smallish, pale-faced man with good shoulders, wearing a black, belted trenchcoat and tweed cap was standing at the end of the path. He carried a Gladstone bag in his left hand and had the most startlingly blue eyes she had ever seen.

'Mrs. Grey?' he enquired in a soft, Irish voice. 'Mrs. Joanna Grey?'

'That's right.' Her stomach knotted with excitement. For a brief moment she could hardly breathe.

He smiled. 'I shall light a candle of understanding in the heart which shall not be put out.'

'*Magna est veritas et praevalet.*'

'Great is Truth and mighty above all things.' Liam Devlin smiled. 'I could do with a cup of tea, Mrs. Grey. It's been one hell of a trip.'

Devlin had been unable to secure a ticket for the night crossing from Belfast to Heysham on Monday and the situation was no better on the Glasgow route. But the advice of a friendly booking clerk had sent him up to Larne where he'd had better luck, obtaining a passage on the Tuesday morning boat on the short run to Stranraer in Scotland.

The exigencies of wartime travel by train had left him with a seemingly interminable journey from Stranraer to Carlisle, changing for

Leeds. And in that city, a lengthy wait into the small hours of Wednesday morning before making a suitable connection for Peterborough where he had made the final change to a local train for King's Lynn.

Much of this passed through his mind again when Joanna Grey turned from the stove where she was making tea and said, 'Well, how was it?'

'Not too bad,' he said. 'Surprising in some ways.'

'How do you mean?'

'Oh, the people, the general state of things. It wasn't quite as I expected.'

He thought particularly of the station restaurant at Leeds, crowded all night with travellers of every description, all hopefully waiting for a train to somewhere, the poster on the wall which had said with particular irony in his case: *It is more than ever vital to ask yourself: Is my journey really necessary?* He remembered the rough good humour, the general high spirits and contrasted it less than favourably with his last visit to the central railway station in Berlin.

'They seem to be pretty sure they're going to win the war,' he said as she brought the tea tray to the table.

'A fool's paradise,' she told him calmly. 'They never learn. They've never had the organisation, you see, the discipline that the Führer has given to Germany.'

Remembering the bomb-scarred Chancellery as he had last seen it, the considerable portions of Berlin that were simply heaps of rubble after the Allied bombing offensive, Devlin felt almost constrained to point out that things had changed rather a lot since the good old days. On the other hand, he got the distinct impression that such a remark would not be well received.

So, he drank his tea and watched her as she walked to a corner cupboard, opened it and took down a bottle of Scotch, marvelling that this pleasant-faced, white-haired woman in the neat, tweed skirt and Wellington boots could be what she was.

She poured a generous measure into two glasses and raised one in a kind of salute. 'To the English Enterprise,' she said, her eyes shining.

Devlin could have told her that the Spanish Armada had been so described, but remembering what had happened to that ill-fated venture decided, once again, to keep his mouth shut.

'To the English Enterprise,' he said solemnly.

'Good.' She put down her glass. 'Now let me see all your papers. I must make sure you have everything.'

He produced his passport, army discharge papers, a testimonial purporting to be from his old commanding officer, a similar letter from his parish priest and various documents relating to his medical condition.

'Excellent,' she said. 'These are really very good. What happens now is this. I've fixed you up with a job working for the local squire, Sir Henry Willoughby. He wants to see you as soon as you arrive so we'll get that over with today. Tomorrow morning I'll run you into Fakenham, that's a market town about ten miles from here.'

'And what do I do there?'

'Report to the local police station. They'll give you an alien's registration form which all Irish citizens have to fill in and you'll also have to provide a passport photo, but we can get that with no trouble. Then you'll need insurance cards, an identity card, ration book, clothing coupons.'

She numbered them off on the fingers of one hand and Devlin grinned. 'Heh, hold on now. It sounds like one hell of a lot of trouble to me. Three weeks on Saturday, that's all, and I'll be away from here so fast they'll think I've never been.'

'All these things are essential,' she said. 'Everyone has them, so you must. It only needs one petty clerk in Fakenham or King's Lynn to notice that you haven't applied for something and put an enquiry in hand and then where would you be?'

Devlin said cheerfully, 'All right, you're the boss. Now what about this job?'

'Warden of the marshes at Hobs End. It couldn't be more isolated. There's a cottage to go with it. Not much, but it will do.'

'And what will be expected of me?'

'Gamekeeping duties in the main and there's a system of dyke gates that needs regular checking. They haven't had a warden for two years since the last one went off to the war. And you'll be expected to keep the vermin in check. The foxes play havoc with the wild-fowl.'

'What do I do? Throw stones at them?'

'No, Sir Henry will supply you with a shotgun.'

'That's nice of him. What about transport?'

'I've done the best I can. I've managed to persuade Sir Henry to allocate you one of the estate motor-bikes. As an agricultural worker it's legitimate enough. Buses have almost ceased to exist, so most people are allowed a small monthly ration to help them get into town occasionally for essential purposes.'

A horn sounded outside. She went into the sitting-room and was back in an instant. 'It's Sir Henry. Leave the talking to me. Just act properly servile and speak only when you're spoken to. He'll like that. I'll bring him in here.'

She went out and Devlin waited. He heard the front door open and her feigned surprise. Sir Henry said, 'Just on my way to another command meeting in Holt, Joanna. Wondered if there was anything I could get you?'

She replied much more quietly so that Devlin couldn't hear what she said. Sir Henry dropped his voice in return, there was a further murmur of conversation and then they came into the kitchen.

Sir Henry was in uniform as a lieutenant-colonel in the Home Guard, medal ribbons for the First World War and India making a splash of colour above his left breast pocket. He glanced piercingly at Devlin, one hand behind his back, the other brushing the wide sweep of his moustache.

'So you're Devlin?'

Devlin lurched to his feet and stood there twisting and untwisting his tweed cap in his two hands. 'I'd like to thank you, sir,' he said, thickening the Irish accent noticeably. 'Mrs. Grey's told me how much you've done for me. It's more than kind.'

'Nonsense, man,' Sir Henry said brusquely although it was observable that he stretched to his full height and placed his feet a little further apart. 'You did your best for the old country, didn't you? Caught a packet in France, I understand?'

Devlin nodded eagerly and Sir Henry leaned forward and examined the furrow on the left side of the forehead made by an Irish Special Branch detective's bullet. 'By heavens,' he said softly. 'You're damn lucky to be here if you ask me.'

'I thought I'd settle him in for you,' Joanna Grey said. 'If that's all right, Henry? Only you're so busy, I know.'

'I say, would you, old girl?' He glanced at his watch. 'I'm due in Holt in half an hour.'

'No more to be said. I'll take him along to the cottage, show him around the marsh generally and so on.'

'Come to think of it you probably know more about what goes on at Hobs End than I do.' He forgot himself for a moment and slipped an arm about her waist, then withdrew it hastily and said to Devlin, 'Don't forget to present yourself to the police in Fakenham without delay. You know all about that?'

'Yes, sir.'

'Anything you want to ask me?'

'The gun, sir,' Devlin said. 'I understand you want me to do a little shooting.'

'Ah, yes. No trouble there. Call at the Grange tomorrow afternoon and I'll see you fixed up. You can pick the bike up at the same time, too. Mrs. Grey has told you about that, has she? Only three gallons of petrol a month, mind you, but you'll have to make out the best way you can.

We've all got to make sacrifices.' He brushed his moustache again. 'A single Lancaster, Devlin, uses two thousand gallons of petrol to reach the Ruhr. Did you know that?'

'No, sir.'

'There you are, then. We've all got to be prepared to do our best.'

Joanna Grey took his arm. 'Henry, you're going to be late.'

'Yes, of course, my dear.' He nodded to the Irishman. 'All right, Devlin, I'll see you tomorrow afternoon.'

Devlin actually touched his forelock and waited until they'd gone out of the front door before moving into the sitting-room. He watched Sir Henry drive away and was lighting a cigarette when Joanna Grey returned.

'Tell me something,' he said. 'Are he and Churchill supposed to be friends?'

'As I understand it, they've never met. Studley Grange is famous for its Elizabethan gardens. The Prime Minister fancied the idea of a quiet weekend and a little painting before returning to London.'

'With Sir Henry falling over himself to oblige? Oh, yes, I can see that.'

She shook her head. 'I thought you were going to say begorrah any minute. You're a wicked man, Mr. Devlin.'

'Liam,' he said. 'Call me Liam. It'll sound better, especially if I still call you Mrs. Grey. He fancies you, then, and at his age?'

'Autumn romance is not completely unheard of.'

'More like winter, I should have thought. On the other hand it must be damn useful.'

'More than that – essential,' she said. 'Anyway, bring your bag and I'll get the car and take you along to Hobs End.'

The rain pushed in on the wind from the sea was cold and the marsh was shrouded in mist. When Joanna Grey braked to a halt in the yard of the old marsh warden's cottage, Devlin got out and looked about him thoughtfully. It was a strange, mysterious sort of place, the kind that made the hair lift on the back of his head. Sea creeks and mud flats, the great, pale reeds merging with the mist and somewhere out there, the occasional cry of a bird, the invisible beat of wings.

'I see what you mean about being isolated.'

She took a key from under a flat stone by the front door and opened it, leading the way into a flagged passageway. There was rising damp and the whitewash was flaking from the wall. On the left a door opened into a large kitchen-cum-living room. Again, the floor was stone flags, but there was a huge open-hearth fireplace and rush mats. At the other end of the room was an iron cooking stove and a chipped, white pot sink with a single tap. A large pine table flanked by two benches and an old wing-back chair by the fire were the only furniture.

'I've news for you,' Devlin said. 'I was raised in a cottage exactly like this in County Down in the North of Ireland. All it needs is a bloody good fire to dry the place out.'

'And it has one great advantage – seclusion,' she said. 'You probably won't see a soul the whole time you're here.'

Devlin opened the Gladstone bag and took out some personal belongings, clothing and three or four books. Then he ran a finger through the lining to find a hidden catch, and removed a false bottom. In the cavity he revealed was a Walther P38, a Sten gun, the silenced version, in three parts, and a land agent's S-phone receiver and transmitter which was no more than pocket size. There was a thousand pounds in pound notes and another thousand in fivers. There was also something in a white cloth which he didn't bother to unwrap.

'Operating money,' he said.

'To obtain the vehicles?'

'That's right. I've been given the address of the right sort of people.'

'Where from?'

'The kind of thing they have on file at Abwehr Headquarters.'

'Where is it?'

'Birmingham. I thought I'd take a run over there this weekend. What do I need to know?'

She sat on the edge of the table and watched as he screwed the barrel unit of the Sten into the main body and slotted the shoulder stock in place. 'It's a fair way,' she said. 'Say three hundred miles the round trip.'

'Obviously my three gallons of petrol isn't going to get me very far. What can I do about that?'

'There's plenty of black market petrol available, at three times the normal price, if you know the right garages. The commercial variety is dyed red to make it easy for the police to detect wrongful use, but you can get rid of the dye by straining the petrol through an ordinary civilian gas mask filter.'

Devlin rammed a magazine into the Sten, checked it, then took the whole thing to pieces again and replaced it in the bottom of the bag.

'A wonderful thing, technology,' he observed. 'That thing can be fired at close quarters and the only sound you can hear is the bolt clicking. It's English, by the way. Another of the items SOE fondly imagine it's been dropping in to the Dutch underground.' He took out a cigarette and put it in his mouth. 'What else should I know when I make this trip? What are the risks?'

'Very few,' she said. 'The lights on the machine will have the regulation blackout fittings so there's no problem there. The roads, particularly in country areas, are virtually traffic free. And white lines have been painted down the centre of most of them. That helps.'

'What about the police or the security forces?'

She gazed at him blankly. 'Oh, there's nothing to worry about there. The military would only stop you if you tried to enter a restricted area. Technically this still *is* a Defence Area, but nobody bothers with the regulations these days. As for the police, they're entitled to stop you and ask for your identity card or they might stop a vehicle on the main road as part of a spot check in the campaign against misuse of petrol.'

She almost sounded indignant and, remembering what he had left, Devlin had to fight an irresistible compulsion to open her eyes a little. Instead he said, 'Is that all?'

'I think so. There's a twenty-mile-an-hour speed limit in built-up areas and of course you won't find signposts anywhere, but they started putting place names up again in many places earlier this summer.'

'So, the odds are that I shouldn't have any trouble?'

'No one's stopped me. Nobody bothers now.' She shrugged. 'There's no problem. At the local WVS aid centre we have all sorts of official forms from the old Defence Area days. There was one that allowed you to visit relatives in hospital. I'll make one out referring to some brother in hospital in Birmingham. That and those medical discharge papers from the Army should be enough to satisfy anyone. Everybody has a soft spot for a hero these days.'

Devlin grinned. 'You know something, Mrs. Grey? I think we're going to get on famously.' He went and rummaged in the cupboard under the sink and returned with a rusty hammer and a nail. 'The very thing.'

'For what?' she demanded.

He stepped inside the hearth and drove the nail partially home at the back of the smoke-blackened beam which supported the chimney breast. Then he hung the Walther up there by its trigger guard. 'What I call my ace-in-the-hole. I like to have one around, just in case. Now, show me round the rest of the place.'

There was an assortment of outbuildings, mostly in decay, and a barn in quite reasonable condition. There was another standing behind it on the very edge of the marsh, a decrepit building of considerable age, the stonework green with mildew. Devlin got one half of the large door open with difficulty. Inside it was cold and damp and obviously hadn't been used for anything for years.

'This will do just fine,' he said. 'Even if old Sir Willoughby comes poking his nose in I shouldn't think he'd go this far.'

'He's a busy man,' she said. 'County affairs, magistrate, running the local Home Guard. He still takes that very seriously. Doesn't really have much time for anything else.'

'But you,' he said. 'The randy old bastard still has enough time left for you.'

She smiled. 'Yes, I'm afraid that's only too true.' She took his arm. 'Now, I'll show you the dropping zone.'

They walked up through the marsh along the dyke road. It was raining quite hard now and the wind carried with it the damp, wet smell of rotting vegetation. Some Brent geese flew in out of the mist in formation like a bombing squadron going in for the kill and vanished into the grey curtain.

They reached the pine trees, the pill boxes, the sand-filled tank trap, the warning *Beware of Mines* so familiar to Devlin from the photographs he had seen. Joanna Grey tossed a stone out over the sands and Patch bounded through the wire to retrieve it.

'You're sure?' Devlin said.

'Absolutely.'

He grinned crookedly. 'I'm a Catholic, remember that if it goes wrong.'

'They all are here. I'll see you're put down properly.'

He stepped over the coils of wire, paused on the edge of the sand, then walked forward. He paused again, then started to run, leaving wet footprints for the tide had not long ebbed. He turned, ran back and once again negotiated the wire.

He was immensely cheerful and put an arm around her shoulders. 'You were right – from the beginning. It's going to work, this thing. You'll see.' He looked out to sea across the creeks and the sandbanks, through the mist towards the Point. 'Beautiful. The thought of leaving all this must break your heart.'

'Leave?' She looked up at him blankly. 'What do you mean?'

'But you can't stay,' he said. 'Not afterwards. Surely you must see that?'

She looked out to the Point as if for the last time. Strange, but it had never occurred to her that she would have to leave. She shivered as the wind drove rain in hard off the sea.

At twenty to eight that evening Max Radl, in his office at the Tirpitz Ufer, decided he'd had enough for the day. He'd not felt well since his return from Brittany and the doctor he'd gone to see had been horrified at his condition.

'If you carry on like this, Herr Oberst, you will kill yourself,' he had declared firmly. 'I think I can promise you that.'

Radl had paid his fee and taken the pills – three different kinds – which with any kind of luck might keep him going. As long as he could stay out of the hands of the Army medics he had a chance, but one more physical check-up with that lot and he was finished. They'd have him into a civilian suit before he knew where he was.

He opened a drawer, took out one of the pills' bottles and popped two into his mouth. They were supposed to be pain killers, but just to make sure, he half-filled a tumbler with Courvoisier to wash them down. There was a knock on the door and Hofer entered. His normally composed face was full of emotion and his eyes were bright.

'What is it, Karl, what's happened?' Radl demanded.

Hofer pushed a signal flimsy across the desk. 'It's just in, Herr Oberst. From Starling – Mrs. Grey. He's arrived safely. He's with her now.'

Radl looked down at the flimsy in a kind of awe. 'My God, Devlin,' he whispered. 'You brought it off. It worked.'

A sense of physical release surged through him. He reached inside his bottom drawer and found another glass. 'Karl, this very definitely calls for a drink.'

He stood up, full of a fierce joy, aware that he had not felt like this in years, not since that incredible euphoria when racing for the French coast at the head of his men in the summer of 1940.

He raised his glass and said to Hofer, 'I give you a toast, Karl. To Liam Devlin and "Up the Republic".'

As a staff officer in the Lincoln Washington Brigade in Spain, Devlin had found a motor-cycle the most useful way of keeping contact between the scattered units of his command in difficult mountain country. Very different from Norfolk, but there was that same sense of freedom, of being off the leash, as he rode from Studley Grange through quiet country lanes towards the village.

He'd obtained a driving licence in Holt that morning along with his other documents, without the slightest difficulty. Wherever he'd gone, from the police station to the local labour exchange, his cover story of being an ex-infantryman, discharged because of wounds, had worked like a charm. The various officials had really put themselves out to push things through for him. It was true what they said. In wartime, everyone loved a soldier, and a wounded hero even more so.

The motor-cycle was pre-war, of course, and had seen better days. A 350 c.c. BSA, but when he took a chance and opened the throttle wide on the first straight, the needle swung up to sixty with no trouble at all. He throttled back quickly once he'd established that the power was there if needed. No sense in asking for trouble. There was no village policeman in Studley Constable, Joanna Grey had warned him that one occasionally appeared from Holt on a motor-cycle.

He came down the steep hill into the village itself past the old mill with the waterwheel which didn't seem to be turning and slowed for a young girl in a pony and trap carrying three milk churns. She wore a blue beret and a very old, First-World-War trenchcoat at least two sizes too big for her. She had high cheekbones, large eyes, a mouth that was too wide and three of her fingers poked through holes in the woollen gloves she wore.

'Good day to you, *a colleen*,' he said cheerfully as he waited for her to cross his path to the bridge. 'God save the good work.'

Her eyes widened in a kind of astonishment, her mouth opened slightly. She seemed bereft of speech and clicked her tongue, urging the pony over the bridge and into a trot as they started up the hill past the church.

'A lovely, ugly little peasant,' he quoted softly, 'who turned my head not once, but twice.' He grinned. 'Oh, no, Liam, me old love. Not that. Not now.'

He swung the motor-cycle in towards the Studley Arms and became aware of a man standing in the window glaring at him. An enormous individual of thirty or so with a tangled black beard. He was wearing a tweed cap and an old reefer coat.

And what in the hell have I done to you, son? Devlin asked himself. The man's gaze travelled to the girl and the trap just breasting the hill beside the church and moved back again. It was enough. Devlin pushed the BSA up on to its stand, unstrapped the shotgun in its canvas bag which was hanging about his neck, tucked it under his arm and went inside.

There was no bar, just a large comfortable room with a low-beamed ceiling, several high-backed benches, a couple of wooden tables. A wood fire burned brightly on an open hearth.

There were only three people in the room. The man sitting beside the fire playing a mouth organ, the one with the black beard at the window and a short, stocky man in shirt sleeves who looked to be in his late twenties.

'God bless all here,' Devlin announced, playing the bog Irishman to the hilt.

He put the gun in its canvas bag on the table and the man in the shirt sleeves smiled and stuck out his hand. 'I'm George Wilde, the publican here, and you'll be Sir Henry's new warden down on the marshes. We've heard all about you.'

'What, already?' Devlin said.

'You know how it is in the country.'

'Or does he?' the big man at the window said harshly.

'Oh, I'm a farm boy from way back myself,' Devlin said.

Wilde looked troubled, but attempted the obvious introduction. 'Arthur Seymour and the old goat by the fire is Laker Armsby.'

As Devlin discovered later, Laker was in his late forties, but looked older. He was incredibly shabby, his tweed cap torn, his coat tied with string and his trousers and shoes were caked with mud.

'Would you gentlemen join me in a drink?' Devlin suggested.

'I wouldn't say no to that,' Laker Armsby told him. 'A pint of brown ale would suit me fine.'

Seymour drained his flagon and banged it down on the table. 'I buys my own.' He picked up the shotgun and hefted it in one hand. 'The Squire's really looking after you, isn't he? This and the bike. Now I wonder why you should rate that, an incomer like you, when there's those amongst us who've worked the estate for years and still must be content with less.'

'Sure and I can only put it down to my good looks,' Devlin told him.

Madness sparkled in Seymour's eyes, the Devil looked out, hot and wild. He had Devlin by the front of the coat and pulled him close. 'Don't make fun of me, little man. Don't ever do that or I'll step on you as I'd step on a slug.'

Wilde grabbed his arm. 'Now come on, Arthur,' but Seymour pushed him away.

'You walk soft round here, you keep your place and we might get on. Understand me?'

Devlin smiled anxiously. 'Sure and if I've given offence, I'm sorry.'

'That's better.' Seymour released his grip and patted his face. 'That's much better. Only in future, remember one thing. When I come in, you leave.'

He went out, the door banged behind him and Laker Armsby cackled wildly, 'He's a bad bastard is Arthur.'

George Wilde vanished into the back room and returned with a bottle of Scotch and some glasses. 'This stuff's hard to come by at the moment, but I reckon you've earned one on me, Mr. Devlin.'

'Liam,' Devlin said. 'Call me Liam.' He accepted the glass of whisky. 'Is he always like that?'

'Ever since I've known him.'

'There was a girl outside in a pony and trap as I came in. Does he have some special interest there?'

'Fancies his chances.' Laker Armsby chuckled. 'Only she won't have any of it.'

'That's Molly Prior,' Wilde said. 'She and her mother have a farm a couple of miles this side of Hobs End. Been running it between them since last year when her father died. Laker gives them a few hours when he isn't busy at the church.'

'Seymour does a bit for them as well. Some of the heavy stuff.'

'And thinks he owns the place, I suppose? Why isn't he in the Army?'

'That's another sore point. They turned him down because of a perforated eardrum.'

'Which he took as an insult to his great manhood, I suppose?' Devlin said.

Wilde said awkwardly, as if he felt some explanation was necessary, 'I picked up a packet myself with the Royal Artillery at Narvik in April, nineteen forty. Lost my right knee-cap, so it was a short war for me. You got yours in France, I understand?'

'That's right,' Devlin said calmly. 'Near Arras. Came out through Dunkirk on a stretcher and never knew a thing about it.'

'And over a year in hospitals Mrs. Grey tells me?'

Devlin nodded. 'A grand woman. I'm very grateful to her. Her husband knew my people back home years ago. If it wasn't for her I wouldn't have this job.'

'A lady,' Wilde said. 'A real lady. There's nobody better liked round here.'

Laker Armsby said, 'Now me, I copped my first packet on the Somme in nineteen sixteen. With the Welsh Guards, I was.'

'Oh, no.' Devlin took a shilling from his pocket, slapped it down on the table and winked at Wilde, 'Give him a pint, but I'm off. Got work to do.'

When he reached the coast road, Devlin took the first dyke path that he came to at the northerly end of Hobs End marsh and drove out towards the fringe of pine trees. It was a crisp, autumnal sort of day, cold but bracing, white clouds chasing each other across a blue sky. He opened the throttle and roared along the narrow dyke path. A hell of a risk, for one wrong move and he'd be into the marsh. Stupid really, but that was the kind of mood he was in, and the sense of freedom was exhilarating.

He throttled back, braking to turn into another path, working his way along the network of dykes towards the coast, when a horse and rider suddenly appeared from the reeds thirty or forty yards to his right and scrambled up on top of the dyke. It was the girl he'd last seen in the village in the pony and trap, Molly Prior. As he slowed, she leaned low over the horse's neck and urged it into a gallop, racing him on a parallel course.

Devlin responded instantly, opening the throttle and surging forward in a burst of speed, kicking dirt out in a great spray into the marsh behind him. The girl had an advantage, in that the dyke she was on ran straight to the pine trees, whereas Devlin had to work his way through a maze, turning from one path into another and he lost ground.

She was close to the trees now and as he skidded out of one path broadside on and finally found a clear run, she plunged her mount into the water and mud of the marsh, urging it through the reeds in a final short cut. The horse responded well and a few moments later, bounded free and disappeared into the pines.

Devlin left the dyke path at speed, shot up the side of the first sand dune, travelled some little distance through the air and alighted in soft white sand, going down on one knee in a long slide.

Molly Prior was sitting at the foot of a pine tree gazing out to sea, her chin on her knees. She was dressed exactly as she had been when Devlin had last seen her except that she had taken off the beret, exposing short-cropped, tawny hair. The horse grazed on a tuft of grass that pushed up through the sand.

Devlin got the bike up on its stand and threw himself down beside her. 'A fine day, thanks be to God.'

She turned and said calmly, 'What kept you?'

Devlin had taken off his cap to wipe sweat from his forehead and he looked up at her in astonishment, 'What kept me, is it? Why, you little . . .'

And then she smiled. More than that, threw back her head and laughed and Devlin laughed too. 'By God, and I'll know you till the crack of Doomsday, that's for sure.'

'And what's that supposed to mean?' She spoke with the strong and distinctive Norfolk accent that was still so new to him.

'Oh, a saying they have where I come from.' He found a packet of cigarettes and put one in his mouth. 'Do you use these things?'

'No.'

'Good for you, they'd stunt your growth and you with your green years still ahead of you.'

'I'm seventeen, I'll have you know,' she told him. 'Eighteen in February.'

Devlin put a match to his cigarette and lay back pillowing his head on his hands, the peak of his cap over his eyes. 'February what?'

'The twenty-second.'

'Ah, a little fish, is it? Pisces. We should do well together, me being a Scorpio. You should never marry a Virgo, by the way. No chance of them and Pisces hitting it off at all. Take Arthur, now. I've a terrible hunch he's a Virgo. I'd watch it there if I were you.'

'Arthur?' she said. 'You mean Arthur Seymour? Are you crazy?'

'No, but I think he is,' Devlin replied and carried on. 'Pure, clean, virtuous and not very hot, which is a terrible pity from where I'm lying.'

She had turned round to look down at him and the old coat gaped open. Her breasts were full and firm, barely contained by the cotton blouse she was wearing.

'Oh, girl dear, you'll have a terrible problem with your weight in a year or two if you don't watch your food.'

Her eyes flashed, she glanced down and instinctively pulled her coat together. 'You bastard,' she said, somehow drawing the word out. And then she saw his lips quiver and leaned down to peer under the peak of the cap. 'Why, you're laughing at me!' She pulled off his cap and threw it away.

'And what else would I do with you, Molly Prior?' He put out a hand defensively. 'No, don't answer that.'

She sat back against the tree, her hands in her pockets. 'How did you know my name?'

'George Wilde told me at the pub.'

'Oh, I see now. And Arthur – was he there?'

'You could say that. I get the impression he looks upon you as his personal property.'

'Then he can go to hell,' she said, suddenly fierce. 'I belong to no man.'

He looked up at her from where he lay, the cigarette hanging from the corner of his mouth, and smiled. 'Your nose turns up, has anyone ever told you that? And when you're angry, your mouth goes down at the corners.'

He had gone too far, touched some source of secret inner hurt. She flushed and said bitterly, 'Oh, I'm ugly enough, Mr. Devlin. I've sat all night long at dances in Holt without being asked, too often not to know my place. You wouldn't throw me out on a wet Saturday night, I know. But that's men for you. Anything's better than nothing.'

She started to get up, Devlin had her by the ankle and dragged her down, pinning her with one strong arm as she struggled. 'You know my name? How's that?'

'Don't let it go to your head. Everybody knows about you. Everything there is to know.'

'I've news for you,' he said pushing himself up on one elbow and leaning over her. 'You don't know the first thing about me because if you did, you'd know I prefer fine autumn afternoons under the pine trees to wet Saturday nights. On the other hand, the sand has a terrible way of getting where it shouldn't.' She went very still. He kissed her briefly on the mouth and rolled away. 'Now get the hell out of it before I let my mad passion run away with me.'

She grabbed her beret, jumped to her feet and reached for the horse's bridle. When she turned to glance at him her face was serious, but after she'd scrambled into the saddle and pulled her mount round to look at him again, she was smiling. 'They told me all Irishmen were mad. Now I believe them. I'll be at Mass Sunday evening. Will you?'

'Do I look as though I will?'

The horse was stamping, turning in half-circles, but she held it well. 'Yes,' she said seriously, 'I think you do,' and she gave the horse its head and galloped away.

'Oh, you idiot, Liam,' Devlin said softly as he pushed his motor-cycle off its stand and shoved it alongside the sand dune, through the trees and on to the path. 'Won't you ever learn?'

He drove back along the main dyke top, sedately this time, and ran the motor-cycle into the barn. He found the key where he'd left it under the stone by the door and let himself in. He put the shotgun in the hallstand, went into the kitchen, unbuttoning his raincoat, and paused. There was a pitcher of milk on the table, a dozen brown eggs in a white bowl.

'Mother Mary,' he said softly. 'Would you look at that now?'

He touched the bowl gently with one finger, but when he finally turned to take off his coat, his face was bleak.

8

In Birmingham a cold wind drifted across the city, hurling rain against the plate glass window of Ben Garvald's flat above the garage in Saltley. In the silk dressing gown and with a scarf at the throat, the dark, curly hair carefully combed, he made an imposing figure; the broken nose added a sort of rugged grandeur. A closer inspection was not so flattering, the fruits of dissipation showing clearly on the fleshy arrogant face.

But this morning he faced something more – a considerable annoyance with the world at large. At eleven-thirty on the previous night, one of his business ventures, a small illegal gaming club in a house in an apparently respectable street in Aston, had been turned over by the City of Birmingham Police. Not that Garvald was in any personal danger of being arrested himself. That was what the front man was paid for, and he would be taken care of. Much more serious was the three and a half thousand pounds on the gaming tables which had been confiscated by the police.

The kitchen door swung open and a young girl of seventeen or eighteen came in. She wore a pink lace dressing gown, her peroxide-blonde hair was tousled and her face was blotched, the eyes swollen from weeping. 'Can I get you anything else, Mr. Garvald?' she said in a low voice.

'Get me anything?' he said. 'That's good. That's bloody rich, that is, seeing as how you haven't bleeding well *given* me anything yet.'

He spoke without turning round. His interest had been caught by a man on a motor-cycle who had just ridden into the yard below and parked beside one of the trucks.

The girl who had found herself quite unable to cope with some of Garvald's more bizarre demands of the previous night said tearfully, 'I'm sorry, Mr. Garvald.'

The man below had walked across the yard and disappeared now. Garvald turned and said to the girl, 'Go on, get your clothes on and piss off.' She was frightened to death, shaking with fear and staring at him, mesmerised. A delicious feeling of power, almost sexual in its intensity, flooded through him. He grabbed her hair and twisted it cruelly. 'And learn to do as you're told. Understand?'

As the girl fled, the outer door opened and Reuben Garvald, Ben's younger brother, entered. He was small and sickly-looking, one shoulder slightly higher than the other, but the black eyes in the pale face were constantly on the move, missing nothing.

His eyes followed the girl disapprovingly as she disappeared into the bedroom. 'I wish you wouldn't, Ben. A dirty little cow like that. You might catch something.'

'That's what they invented penicillin for,' Garvald said. 'Anyway, what do you want?'

'There's a bloke to see you. Just came in on a motor-cycle.'

'So I noticed. What's he want?'

'Wouldn't say. Cheeky little Mick with too much off.' Reuben held out half a five pound note. 'Told me to give you that. Said you could have the other half if you'd see him.'

Garvald laughed, quite spontaneously, and plucked the torn banknote from his brother's hand. 'I like it. Yes, I very definitely go for that.' He took it to the window and examined it. 'It looks Kosher, too.' He turned, grinning. 'I wonder if he's got any more, Reuben? Let's see.'

Reuben went out and Garvald crossed to a sideboard in high good humour and poured himself a glass of Scotch. Maybe the morning was not going to turn out to be such a dead loss after all. It might even prove to be quite entertaining. He settled himself in an easy chair by the window.

The door opened and Reuben ushered Devlin into the room. He was wet through, his raincoat saturated, and he took off his tweed cap and squeezed it over a Chinese porcelain bowl filled with bulbs. 'Would you look at that now?'

'All right,' Garvald said. 'I know all you bleedin' Micks are cracked. You needn't rub it in. What's the name?'

'Murphy, Mr. Garvald,' Devlin told him. 'As in spuds.'

'And I believe that, too,' Garvald said. 'Take that coat off, for Christ's sake. You'll ruin the bloody carpet. Genuine Axminster. Costs a fortune to get hold of that these days.'

Devlin removed his dripping trenchcoat and handed it to Reuben, who looked mad but took it anyway and draped it over a chair by the window.

'All right, sweetheart,' Garvald said. 'My time's limited so let's get to it.'

Devlin rubbed his hands dry on his jacket and took out a packet of cigarettes. 'They tell me you're in the transport business,' he said. 'Amongst other things.'

'Who tells you?'

'I heard it around.'

'So?'

'I need a truck. Bedford three-tonner. Army type.'

'Is that all?' Garvald was still smiling, but his eyes were watchful.

'No, I also want a jeep, a compressor plus spray equipment and a couple of gallons of khaki-green paint. And I want both trucks to have service registration.'

Garvald laughed out loud. 'What are you going to do, start the Second Front on your own or something?'

Devlin took a large envelope from his inside breast pocket and held it out. 'There's five hundred quid on account in there, just so you know I'm not wasting your time.'

Garvald nodded to his brother who took the envelope, opened it and checked the contents. 'He's right, Ben. In brand new fivers, too.'

He pushed the money across. Garvald weighed it in his hand then dropped it on the coffee table in front of him. He leaned back. 'All right, let's talk. Who are you working for?'

'Me,' Devlin said.

Garvald didn't believe him for a moment and showed it, but he didn't argue the point. 'You must have something good lined up to be going to all this trouble. Maybe you could do with a little help.'

'I've told you what I need, Mr. Garvald,' Devlin said. 'One Bedford three-ton truck, a jeep, a compressor, and a couple of gallons of khaki-green paint. Now if you don't think you can help, I can always try elsewhere.'

Reuben said angrily, 'Who the hell do you think you are? Walking in here's one thing. Walking out again isn't always to easy.'

Devlin's face was very pale and when he turned to look at Reuben, the blue eyes seemed to be fixed on some distant point, cold and remote. 'Is that a fact, now?'

He reached for the bundle of fivers, his left hand in his pocket on the butt of the Walther. Garvald slammed a hand down across them hard. 'It'll cost you,' he said softly. 'A nice, round figure. Let's say two thousand quid.'

He held Devlin's gaze in a kind of challenge, there was a lengthy pause and then Devlin smiled. 'I bet you had a mean left hand in your prime.'

'I still do, boy.' Garvald clenched his fist. 'The best in the business.'

'All right,' Devlin said. 'Throw in fifty gallons of petrol in Army jerrycans and you're on.'

Garvald held out his hand. 'Done. We'll have a drink on it. What's your pleasure?'

'Irish if you've got it. Bushmills for preference.'

'I got everything, boy. Anything and everything.' He snapped his fingers. 'Reuben, how about some of that Bushmills for our friend here?'

Reuben hesitated, his face set and angry, and Garvald said in a low, dangerous voice, 'The Bushmills, Reuben.'

His brother went over to the sideboard and opened the cupboard, disclosing dozens of bottles underneath. 'You do all right for yourself,' Devlin observed.

'The only way.' Garvald took a cigar from a box on the coffee table. 'You want to take delivery in Birmingham or someplace else?'

'Somewhere near Peterborough on the A1 would do,' Devlin said.

Reuben handed him a glass. 'You're bloody choosy, aren't you?'

Garvald cut in. 'No, that's all right. You know Norman Cross? That's on the A1 about five miles out of Peterborough. There's a garage called Fogarty's a couple of miles down the road. It's closed at the moment.'

'I'll find it,' Devlin said.

'When do you want to take delivery?'

'Thursday the twenty-eighth and Friday the twenty-ninth. I'll take the truck and the compressor and the jerrycans the first night, the jeep on the second.'

Garvald frowned slightly. 'You mean you're handling the whole thing yourself?'

'That's right.'

'Okay – what kind of time were you thinking of?'

'After dark. Say about nine to nine-thirty.'

'And the cash?'

'You keep that five hundred on account. Seven-fifty when I take delivery of the truck, the same for the jeep and I want delivery licences for each of them.'

'That's easy enough,' Garvald said. 'But they'll need filling in with purpose and destination.'

'I'll see to that myself when I get them.'

Garvald nodded slowly, thinking about it. 'That looks all right to me. Okay, you're on. What about another snort?'

'No, thanks,' Devlin said. 'I've places to go.'

He pulled on the wet trenchcoat and buttoned it quickly. Garvald got up and went to the sideboard and came back with the freshly opened bottle of Bushmills. 'Have that on me, just to show there's no ill will.'

'The last thought in my mind,' Devlin told him. 'But thanks anyway. A little something in return.' He produced the other half of the five pound note from his breast pocket. 'Yours, I believe.'

Garvald took it and grinned. 'You've got the cheek of the Devil, you know that, Murphy?'

'It's been said before.'

'All right, we'll see you at Norman Cross on the twenty-eighth. Show him out, Reuben. Mind your manners.'

Reuben moved to the door sullenly and opened it and went out. Devlin followed him, but turned as Garvald sat down again. 'One more thing, Mr. Garvald.'

'What's that?'

'I keep my word.'

'That's nice to know.'

'See that you do.'

He wasn't smiling now, the face bleak for the moment longer that he held Garvald's gaze before turning and going out.

Garvald stood up, walked to the sideboard and poured himself another Scotch, then he went to the window and looked down into the yard. Devlin pulled his motor-cycle off the stand and kicked the engine into life. The door opened and Reuben entered the room.

He was thoroughly aroused now. 'What's got into you, Ben? I don't understand. You let a little Mick, so fresh out of the bogs he's still got mud on his boots, walk all over you. You took more from him than I've seen you take from anyone.'

Garvald watched Devlin turn into the main road and ride away through the heavy rain. 'He's on to something, Reuben, boy,' he said softly. 'Something nice and juicy.'

'But why the Army vehicles?'

'Lots of possibilities there. Could be almost anything. Look at that case

in Shropshire the other week. Some bloke dressed as a soldier drives an
Army lorry into a big NAAFI depot and out again with thirty thousand
quids' worth of Scotch on board. Imagine what that lot would be worth
on the black market.'

'And you think he could be on to something like that?'

'He's got to be,' Garvald said, 'and whatever it is, I'm in, whether he
likes it or not.' He shook his head in a kind of bewilderment. 'Do you
know, he threatened me, Reuben – me! We can't have that, now can
we?'

Although it was only mid-afternoon, the light was beginning to go as
Koenig took the E-boat in towards the low-lying coastline. Beyond,
thunderclouds towered into the sky, black and swollen and edged with
pink.

Muller, who was bending over the chart table, said, 'A bad storm soon,
Herr Leutnant.'

Koenig peered out of the window. 'Another fifteen minutes before it
breaks. We'll be well up by then.'

Thunder rumbled ominously, the sky darkened and the crew, waiting
on deck for the first glimpse of their destination, were strangely quiet.

Koenig said, 'I don't blame them. What a bloody place after St.
Helier.'

Beyond the line of sand dunes the land was flat and bare, swept clean
by the constant wind. In the distance he could see the farmhouse and the
hangars at the airstrip, black against a pale horizon. The wind brushed
across the water and Koenig reduced speed as they approached the inlet.
'You take her in, Erich.'

Muller took the wheel. Koenig pulled on an old pilot coat and went
out on deck and stood at the rail smoking a cigarette. He felt strangely
depressed. The voyage had been bad enough, but in a sense his problems
were only beginning. The people he was to work with, for example. That
was of crucial importance. In the past he'd had certain unfortunate
experiences in similar situations.

The sky seemed to split wide open and rain began to fall in torrents.
As they coasted in towards the concrete pier, a field car appeared on the
track between the dunes. Muller cut the engines and leaned out of the
window shouting orders. As the crew bustled to get a line ashore, the field
car drove on to the pier and braked to a halt. Steiner and Ritter
Neumann got out and walked to the edge.

'Hello, Koenig, so you made it?' Steiner called cheerfully. 'Welcome
to Landsvoort.'

Koenig, half-way up the ladder, was so astonished that he missed his footing and almost fell into the water. 'You, Herr Oberst, but . . .' And then as the implication struck home, he started to laugh. 'And here was I worrying like hell about who I was going to have to work with.'

He scrambled up the ladder and grabbed Steiner's hand.

It was half past four when Devlin rode down through the village past the Studley Arms. As he went over the bridge he could hear the organ playing and lights showed very dimly at the windows of the church for it was not yet dark. Joanna Grey had told him that evening Mass was held in the afternoon to avoid the blackout. As he went up the hill he remembered Molly Prior's remark. Smiling, he pulled up outside the church. She was there, he knew, because the pony stood patiently in the shafts of the trap, its nose in a feed bag. There were two cars, a flat-backed truck and several bicycles parked there also.

When Devlin opened the door, Father Vereker was on his way down the aisle with three young boys in scarlet cassocks and white cottas, one of them carrying a bucket of holy water, Vereker sprinkling the heads of the congregation as he passed, washing them clean. '*Asperges me*,' he intoned and Devlin slipped down the right-hand aisle and found a pew.

There were no more than seventeen or eighteen people in the congregation. Sir Henry and a woman who was presumably his wife and a young, dark-haired girl in her early twenties in the uniform of the Women's Auxiliary Air Force who sat with them and who was obviously Pamela Vereker. George Wilde was there with his wife. Laker Armsby sat with them, scrubbed clean in stiff white collar and an ancient, black suit.

Molly Prior was across the aisle with her mother, a pleasant, middle-aged woman with a kind face. Molly wore a straw hat decorated with some kind of fake flowers, the brim tilted over her eyes, and a flowered cotton dress with a tightly buttoned bodice and a rather short skirt. Her coat was folded neatly over the pew.

I bet she's been wearing that dress for at least three years now, he told himself. She turned suddenly and saw him. She didn't smile, simply looked at him for a second or so, then glanced away.

Vereker in his faded rose cope was up at the altar, hands together as he commenced Mass. 'I confess to Almighty God, and to you, my brothers and sisters, that I have sinned through my own fault.'

He struck his breast and Devlin, aware that Molly Prior's eyes had swivelled sideways under the brim of the straw hat to watch him, joined in out of devilment, asking Blessed Mary ever Virgin, all the Angels and Saints and the rest of the congregation to pray for him to the Lord our God.

When she went down on her knees on the hassock, she seemed to descend in slow motion, lifting her skirt perhaps six inches too high. He had to choke back his laughter at the demureness of it. But he sobered soon enough when he became aware of Arthur Seymour's mad eyes glaring from the shadows beside a pillar on the far aisle.

When the service was over, Devlin made sure he was first out. He was astride the motor-cycle and ready for off when he heard her call, 'Mr. Devlin, just a minute.' He turned as she hurried towards him, an umbrella over her head, her mother a few yards behind her. 'Don't be in such a rush to be off,' Molly said. 'Are you ashamed or something?'

'Damn glad I came,' Devlin told her.

Whether she blushed or not, it was impossible to say for the light was bad. In any case, her mother arrived at that moment. 'This is my mum,' Molly said. 'And this is Mr. Devlin.'

'I know all about you,' Mrs. Prior said. 'Anything we can do, you just ask now. Difficult for a man on his own.'

'We thought you might like to come back and have tea with us,' Molly told him.

Beyond them, he saw Arthur Seymour standing by the lychgate, glowering. Devlin said, 'It's very nice of you, but to be honest, I'm in no fit state.'

Mrs. Prior reached out to touch him. 'Lord bless us, boy, but you're soaking. Get you home and into a hot bath on the instant. You'll catch your death.'

'She's right,' Molly told him fiercely. 'You get off and mind you do as she says.'

Devlin kicked the starter. 'God protect me from this monstrous regiment of women,' he said and rode away.

The bath was an impossibility. It would have taken too long to heat the copper of water in the back scullery. He compromised by lighting an enormous, log fire on the huge stone hearth; then he stripped, towelled himself briskly and dressed again in a navy-blue flannel shirt and trousers of dark worsted.

He was hungry, but too tired to do anything much about it, so he took a glass and the bottle of Bushmills Garvald had given him and one of his books and sat in the old wing-back chair and roasted his feet and read by the light of the fire. It was perhaps an hour later that a cold wind touched the back of his neck briefly. He had not heard the latch, but she was there, he knew that.

'What kept you?' he said without turning round.

'Very clever. I'd have thought you could have done better than that after I've walked a mile and a quarter over wet fields in the dark to bring you your supper.'

She moved round to the fire. She was wearing her old raincoat, Wellington boots and a headscarf and carried a basket in one hand. 'A meat and potato pie, but then I suppose you've eaten?'

He groaned aloud. 'Don't go on. Just get it in the oven as quick as you can.'

She put the basket down and pulled off her boots and unfastened the raincoat. Underneath she was wearing the flowered dress. She pulled off the scarf, shaking her hair. 'That's better. What are you reading?'

He handed her the book. 'Poetry,' he said, 'by a blind Irishman called Raftery who lived a long time ago.'

She peered at the page in the firelight. 'But I can't understand it,' she said. 'It's in a foreign language.'

'Irish,' he said. 'The language of kings.' He took the book from her and read,

> *Anois, teacht an Earraigh, beidh an la dul chun sineadh,*
> *is tar eis feile Bride, ardochaidh me mo sheol . . .*
> . . . Now, in the springtime, the day's getting longer,
> On the feastday of Bridget, up my sail will go,
> Since my journey's decided, my step will get stronger,
> Till once more I stand in the plains of Mayo . . .

'That's beautiful,' she said. 'Really beautiful.' She dropped down on the rush mat beside him, leaning against the chair, her left hand touching his arm. 'Is that where you come from, this place Mayo?'

'No,' he said, keeping his voice steady with some difficulty. 'From rather farther north, but Raftery had the right idea.'

'Liam,' she said. 'Is that Irish, too?'

'Yes, m'am.'

'What does it mean?'

'William.'

She frowned. 'No, I think I prefer Liam. I mean, William's so ordinary.'

Devlin hung on to the book in his left hand and caught hold of her hair at the back with his right. 'Jesus, Joseph and Mary aid me.'

'And what's that supposed to mean?' she asked, all innocence.

'It means, girl dear, that if you don't get that pie out of the oven and on to the plate this instant, I won't be responsible.'

She laughed suddenly, deep in the throat, leaning over for a moment, her head on his knee. 'Oh, I do like you,' she said. 'Do you know that?

From the first moment I saw you, Mr. Devlin, sir, sitting astride that bike outside the pub, I liked you.'

He groaned, closing his eyes and she got to her feet, eased the skirt over her hips and got his pie from the oven.

When he walked her home over the fields it had stopped raining and the clouds had blown away, leaving a sky glowing with stars. The wind was cold and beat amongst the trees over their heads as they followed the field path, showering them with twigs. Devlin had the shotgun over his shoulder and she hung on to his left arm.

They hadn't talked much after the meal. She'd made him read more poetry to her, leaning against him, one knee raised. It had been infinitely worse than he could have imagined. Not in his scheme of things at all. He had three weeks, that was all, and a great deal to do in that time and no room for distraction.

They reached the farmyard wall and paused beside the gate.

'I was wondering. Wednesday afternoon if you've nothing on, I could do with some help in the barn. Some of the machinery needs moving for winter storage. It's a bit heavy for Mum and me. You could have your dinner with us.'

It would have been churlish to refuse. 'Why not?' he said.

She reached a hand up behind his neck, pulling his face down and kissed him with a fierce, passionate, inexperienced urgency that was incredibly moving. She was wearing some sort of lavender perfume, infinitely sweet, probably all she could afford. He was to remember it for the rest of his life.

She leaned against him and he said into her ear gently, 'You're seventeen and I'm a very old thirty-five. Have you thought about that?'

She looked up at him, eyes blind. 'Oh, you're lovely,' she said. 'So lovely.'

A silly, banal phrase, laughable in other circumstances, but not now. Never now. He kissed her again, very lightly on the mouth. 'Go in!'

She went without any attempt at protest, wakening only the chickens as she crossed the farmyard. Somewhere on the other side of the house, a dog barked hollowly, a door banged, Devlin turned and started back.

It began to rain again as he skirted the last meadow above the main road. He crossed to the dyke path opposite with the old wooden sign, *Hobs End Farm*, which no one had ever thought worth taking down. Devlin trudged along, head bowed against the rain. Suddenly there was a rustling in the reeds to his right and a figure bounded into his path.

In spite of the rain, the cloud cover was only sparse and in the light of the quarter moon he saw that Arthur Seymour crouched in front of him.

'I told you,' he said. 'I warned you, but you wouldn't take no notice. Now you'll have to learn the hard way.'

Devlin had the shotgun off his shoulder in a second. It wasn't loaded, but no matter. He thumbed the hammers back with a very definite double click and rammed the barrel under Seymour's chin.

'Now you be careful,' he said. 'Because I've licence to shoot vermin here from the squire himself and you're on the squire's property.'

Seymour jumped back. 'I'll get you, see if I don't. And that dirty little bitch. I'll pay you both out.'

He turned and ran into the night. Devlin shouldered his gun and moved on towards the cottage, head down as the rain increased in force. Seymour was mad – no, not quite – just not responsible. He wasn't worried about his threats in the slightest, but then he thought of Molly and his stomach went hollow.

'My God,' he said softly. 'If he harms her, I'll kill the bastard. I'll kill him.'

9

The Sten machine carbine was probably the greatest mass-produced weapon of the Second World War and the standby of most British infantrymen. Shoddy and crude it may have looked, but it could stand up to more ill-treatment than any other weapon of its type. It came to pieces in seconds and would fit into a handbag or the pockets of an overcoat – a fact which made it invaluable to the various European resistance groups to whom it was parachuted by the British. Drop it in the mud, stamp on it and it would still kill as effectively as the most expensive Thompson gun.

The MK IIS version was specially developed for use by commando units, fitted with a silencer which absorbed the noise of the bullet explosions to an amazing degree. The only sound when it fired was the clicking of the bolt and that could seldom be heard beyond a range of twenty yards.

The one which Staff Sergeant Willi Scheid held in his hands on the improvised firing range amongst the sand dunes at Landsvoort on the morning of Wednesday, 20 October, was a mint specimen. There was a row of targets at the far end, lifesize replicas of charging *Tommis*. He emptied the magazine into the first five, working from left to right. It was an eerie experience to see the bullets shredding the target and to hear only the clicking of the bolt. Steiner and the rest of his small assault force, standing in a semi-circle behind him, were suitably impressed.

'Excellent!' Steiner held out his hand and Scheid passed the Sten to him. 'Really excellent!' Steiner examined it and handed it to Neumann. Neumann cursed suddenly. 'Dammit, the barrel's hot.'

'That is so, Herr Oberleutnant,' Scheid said. 'You must be careful to hold only the canvas insulating cover. The silencer tubes heat rapidly when the weapon is fired on full automatic.'

Scheid was from the Ordnance Depot at Hamburg, a small, rather insignificant man in steel spectacles and the shabbiest uniform Steiner had ever seen. He moved across to a ground-sheet on which various weapons were displayed. 'The Sten gun, in both the silenced and normal versions, will be the machine pistol you will use. As regards a light machine-gun, the Bren. Not as good a general-purpose weapon as our own MG-forty-two, but an excellent section weapon. It fires in either single shots or bursts of four or five rounds so it's very economical and highly accurate.'

'What about rifles?' Steiner asked.

Before Scheid could reply, Neumann tapped Steiner on the shoulder and the Colonel turned in time to see the Stork come in low from the direction of the Ijsselmeer and turn for its first circuit over the airstrip.

Steiner said, 'I'll take over for a moment, Sergeant.' He turned to the men. 'From now on what Staff Sergeant Scheid says goes. You've got a couple of weeks, and by the time he's finished with you I'll expect you to be able to take these things apart and put them together again with your eyes closed.' He glanced at Brandt. 'Any assistance he wants, you see that he gets it, understand?'

Brandt sprang to attention. 'Herr Oberst.'

'Good.' Steiner's glance seemed to take in each man as an individual. 'Most of the time Oberleutnant Neumann and myself will be in there with you. And don't worry. You'll know what it's all about soon enough, I promise you.'

Brandt brought the entire group to attention. Steiner saluted, then turned and hurried across to the field car which was parked nearby, followed by Neumann. He got into the passenger seat, Neumann climbed behind the wheel and drove away. As they approached the main entrance to the airstrip the military policeman on duty opened the gate and saluted awkwardly, hanging on to his snarling guard dog with the other hand.

'One of these days that brute is going to get loose,' Neumann said, 'and frankly, I don't think it knows which side it's on.'

The Stork dropped in for an excellent landing and four or five Luftwaffe personnel raced out to meet it in a small truck. Neumann followed in the field car and pulled up a few yards away from the Stork. Steiner lit a cigarette as they waited for Radl to disembark.

Neumann said, 'He's got someone with him.'

Steiner looked up with a frown as Max Radl came towards him, a cheerful smile on his face. 'Kurt, how goes it?' he called, hand outstretched.

But Steiner was more interested in his companion, the tall, elegant young man with the deathshead of the SS in his cap. 'Who's your friend, Max?' he asked softly.

Radl's smile was awkward as he made the necessary introduction. 'Colonel Kurt Steiner – Untersturmführer Harvey Preston of the British Free Corps.'

Steiner had had the old living room of the farmhouse converted into the nerve centre for the entire operation. There were a couple of army cots at one end of the room for himself and Neumann and two large tables placed down the centre were covered with maps and photos of the Hobs End and Studley Constable general area. There was also a beautifully made three-dimensional mock-up as yet only half completed. Radl leaned over it with interest, a glass of brandy in one hand. Ritter Neumann stood on the other side of the table and Steiner paced up and down by the window, smoking furiously.

Radl said, 'This model is really superb. Who's working on it?'

'Private Klugl,' Neumann told him. 'He was an artist, I think, before the war.'

Steiner turned impatiently. 'Let's stick to the matter in hand, Max. Do you seriously expect me to take that – that object out there?'

'It's the Reichsführer's idea, not mine,' Radl said mildly. 'In matters like this, my dear Kurt, I take orders, I don't give them.'

'But he must be mad.'

Radl nodded and went to the sideboard to help himself to more cognac. 'I believe that has been suggested before.'

'All right,' Steiner said. 'Let's look at it from the purely practical angle. If this thing is to succeed it's going to need a highly disciplined body of men who can move as one, think as one, act as one and that's exactly what we've got. Those lads of mine have been to hell and back. Crete, Leningrad, Stalingrad and a few places in between and I was with them every step of the way. Max, there are times when I don't even have to give a spoken order.'

'I accept that completely.'

'Then how on earth do you expect them to function with an outsider at this stage, especially one like Preston?' He picked up the file Radl had given him and shook it. 'A petty criminal, a poseur who's acted since the day he was born, even to himself.' He threw the file down in disgust. 'He doesn't even know what real soldiering is.'

'What's more to the point at the moment, or so it seems to me,' Ritter Neumann put in, 'he's never jumped out of an aeroplane in his life.'

Radl took out one of his Russian cigarettes and Neumann lit it for him. 'I wonder, Kurt, whether you're letting your emotions run away with you in this matter.'

'All right,' Steiner said. 'So my American half hates his lousy guts because he's a traitor and a turncoat and my German half isn't too keen on him either.' He shook his head in exasperation. 'Look, Max, have you any idea what jump training is like?' He turned to Neumann. 'Tell him, Ritter.'

'Six jumps go into the paratrooper's qualification badge and after that, never less than six a year if he wants to keep it,' Neumann said. 'And that applies to everyone from private to general officer. Jump pay is sixty-five to one hundred and twenty Reichsmarks per month, according to rank.'

'So?' Radl said.

'To earn it you train on the ground for two months, make your first jump alone from six hundred feet. After that, five jumps in groups and in varying light conditions, including darkness, bringing the altitude down all the time and then the grand finale. Nine plane-loads dropping together in battle conditions at under four hundred feet.'

'Very impressive,' Radl said. 'On the other hand, Preston has to jump only once, admittedly at night, but to a large and very lonely beach. A perfect dropping zone as you have admitted yourselves. I would have thought it not beyond the bounds of possibility to train him sufficiently for that single occasion.'

Neumann turned in despair to Steiner. 'What more can I say?'

'Nothing,' Radl said, 'because he goes. He goes because the Reichsführer thinks it a good idea.'

'For God's sake,' Steiner said. 'It's impossible, Max, can't you see that?'

'I'm returning to Berlin in the morning.' Radl replied. 'Come with me and tell him yourself if that's how you feel. Or would you rather not?'

Steiner's face was pale. 'Damn you to hell, Max, you know I can't and you know why.' For a moment he seemed to have difficulty in speaking. 'My father – he's all right? You've seen him?'

'No,' Radl said, 'But the Reichsführer instructed me to tell you that you have his personal assurance in this matter.'

'And what in the hell is that supposed to mean?' Steiner took a deep breath and smiled ironically. 'I know one thing. If we can take Churchill, who I might as well tell you now is a man I've always personally admired, and not just because we both had an American mother, then we can drop in on Gestapo Headquarters in Prinz Albrechtstrasse and grab that little shit any time we want. Come to think of it, that's quite an idea.' He grinned at Neumann. 'What do you think, Ritter?'

'Then you'll take him?' Radl said eagerly. 'Preston, I mean?'

'Oh, I'll take him all right,' Steiner said, 'only by the time I've finished, he'll wish he'd never been born.' He returned to Neumann. 'All right, Ritter. Bring him in and I'll give him some idea of what hell is going to be like.'

When Harvey Preston was in repertory he'd once played a gallant young British officer in the trenches of the First World War in that great play, *Journey's End*. A brave, war-weary young veteran, old beyond his years, able to meet death with a wry smile on his face and a glass raised, at least symbolically, in his right hand. When the roof of the dug-out finally collapsed and the curtain fell, you simply picked yourself up and went back to the dressing room to wash the blood off.

But not now. This was actually happening, terrifying in its implication and quite suddenly he was sick with fear. It was not that he had lost any faith in Germany's ability to win the war. He believed in that totally. It was simply that he preferred to be alive to see the glorious day for himself.

It was cold in the garden and he paced nervously up and down, smoking a cigarette and waiting impatiently for some sign of life from the farmhouse. His nerves were jagged. Steiner appeared at the kitchen door. 'Preston!' he called in English. 'Get in here.'

He turned without another word. When Preston went into the living room, he found Steiner, Radl and Ritter Neumann grouped around the map table.

'Herr Oberst,' he began.

'Shut up!' Steiner told him coldly. He nodded to Radl. 'Give him his orders.'

Radl said formally, 'Untersturmführer Harvey Preston of the British Free Corps, from this moment you are to consider yourself under the total and absolute command of Lieutenant-Colonel Steiner of the Parachute Regiment. This by direct order of Reichsführer Heinrich Himmler himself. You understand?'

As far as Preston was concerned Radl might as well have worn a black cap for his words were like a death sentence. There was sweat on his forehead as he turned to Steiner and stammered, 'But, Herr Oberst, I've never made a parachute jump.'

'The least of your deficiencies,' Steiner told him grimly. 'But we'll take care of all of them, believe me.'

'Herr Oberst, I must protest,' Preston began and Steiner cut in on him like an axe falling.

'Shut your mouth and get your feet together. In future you speak when you're spoken to and not before.' He walked round behind Preston who was by now standing rigidly to attention. 'All you are at the moment is excess baggage. You're not even a soldier, just a pretty uniform. We'll have to see if we can change that, won't we?' There was silence and he repeated the question quite softly into Preston's left ear. 'Won't we?'

He managed to convey an infinite menace, and Preston said hurriedly, 'Yes, Herr Oberst.'

'Good. So now we understand each other.' Steiner walked round to the front of him again. 'Point number one – at the moment the only people at Landsvoort who know the purpose for which this whole affair has been put together are the four of us present in this room. If anyone else finds out before I'm ready to tell them because of a careless word from you, I'll shoot you myself. Understand?'

'Yes, Herr Oberst.'

'As regards rank, you cease to hold any for the time being. Lieutenant Neumann will see that you're provided with parachutist's overalls and a jump smock. You'll therefore be indistinguishable from the rest of your comrades with whom you will be training. Naturally there will be certain additional work necessary in your case, but we'll come to that later. Any questions?'

Preston's eyes burned, he could hardly breathe so great was his rage. Radl said gently, 'Of course, Herr Untersturmführer, you could always return to Berlin with me if dissatisfied and take up the matter personally with the Reichsführer.'

In a choked whisper, Preston said, 'No questions.'

'Good.' Steiner turned to Ritter Neumann. 'Get him kitted out, then hand him over to Brandt. I'll speak to you about his training schedule later.' He nodded to Preston. 'All right, you're dismissed.'

Preston didn't give the Nazi party salute because it suddenly occurred to him that it would very possibly not be appreciated. Instead he saluted, turned and stumbled out. Ritter Neumann grinned and went after him.

As the door closed, Steiner said, 'After that I really do need a drink,' and he moved across to the sideboard and poured a cognac.

'Will it work out, Kurt?' Radl asked.

'Who knows?' Steiner smiled wolfishly. 'With luck he might break a leg in training.' He swallowed some of his brandy. 'Anyway, to more important matters. How's Devlin doing at the moment? Any more news?'

In her small bedroom in the old farmhouse above the marsh at Hobs End, Molly Prior was trying to make herself presentable for Devlin, due to arrive for his dinner as promised at any moment. She undressed quickly and stood in front of the mirror in the old mahogany wardrobe for a moment in pants and bra and examined herself critically. The underwear was neat and clean, but showed signs of numerous repairs. Well, that was all right and the same for everybody. There were never enough clothing coupons to go round. It was what was underneath that mattered and that wasn't too bad. Nice, firm breasts, round hips, good thighs.

She placed a hand on her belly and thought of Devlin touching her like that and her stomach churned. She opened the top drawer of the dresser, took out her only pair of pre-war silk stockings, each one darned many times and rolled them on carefully. Then she got the cotton dress that she had worn on Saturday from the wardrobe.

As she pulled it over her head, there was the sound of a car horn. She peered out of the window in time to see an old Morris drive into the farmyard. Father Vereker was at the wheel. Molly cursed softly, eased the dress over her head, splitting a seam under one arm and pulled on her Sunday shoes with the two-inch heels.

As she went downstairs she ran a comb through her hair, wincing as it snagged on the tangles. Vereker was in the kitchen with her mother and he turned and greeted her with what for him was a surprisingly warm smile.

'Hello, Molly, how are you?'

'Hard pressed and hard worked, Father.' She tied an apron about her waist and said to her mother, 'That meat and tatie pie. Ready is it? He'll be here any minute.'

'Ah, you're expecting company,' Vereker stood up, leaning on his stick. 'I'm in the way. A bad time.'

'Not at all, Father,' Mrs. Prior said. 'Only Mr. Devlin, the new warden at Hobs End. He's having his dinner here, then giving us an afternoon's work. Was there anything special?'

Vereker turned to look at Molly, speculatively, noting the dress, the shoes and there was a frown on his face as if he disapproved of what he saw. Molly flared angrily. She put her left hand on her hip and faced him belligerently.

'Was it me you wanted, Father?' she asked, her voice dangerously calm.

'No, it was Arthur I wanted a word with. Arthur Seymour. He helps you up here Tuesdays and Wednesdays, doesn't he?'

He was lying, she knew that instantly. 'Arthur Seymour doesn't work here any more, Father. I'd have thought you'd have known that. Or didn't he tell you I sacked him?'

Vereker was very pale. He would not admit it, yet he was not prepared to lie to her face. Instead he said, 'Why was that, Molly?'

'Because I didn't want him round here any more.'

He turned to Mrs. Prior enquiringly. She looked uncomfortable, but shrugged. 'He's not fit company for man nor beast.'

He made a bad mistake then and said to Molly, 'The feeling in the village is that he's been hard done to. That you should have a better reason than preference for an outsider. Hard on a man who's bided his time and helped where he could, Molly.'

'Man,' she said. 'Is that what he is, Father? I never realised. You could tell 'em he was always sticking his hand up my skirt and trying to feel me.' Vereker's face was very white now, but she carried on remorsely. 'Of course, people in the village might think that all right, him having acted no different round females since he was twelve years old and no one ever did a thing about it. And you don't seem to be shaping no better.'

'Molly!' her mother cried, aghast.

'I see,' Molly said. 'One mustn't offend a priest by telling him the truth, is that what you're trying to say?' There was contempt on her face when she looked at Vereker. 'Don't tell me you don't know what he's like, Father. He never misses Mass Sundays so you must confess him often enough.'

She turned from the furious anger in his eyes as there was a knock at the door, smoothing her dress over her hips as she hurried to answer. But when she opened the door it wasn't Devlin, but Laker Armsby who stood there rolling a cigarette beside the tractor with which he'd just towed in a trailer loaded with turnips.

He grinned. 'Where you want this lot then, Molly?'

'Damn you, Laker, you choose your times, don't you? In the barn. Here, I'd better show you myself or you're bound to get it wrong.'

She started across the yard, picking her way through the mud in her good shoes and Laker trailed after her. 'Dressed up like a dog's dinner today. Now I wonder why that should be, Molly?'

'You mind your business, Laker Armsby,' she told him, 'and get this door open.'

Laker tipped the holding bar and started to open one of the great barn doors. Arthur Seymour was standing on the other side, his cap pulled low over the mad eyes, the massive shoulders straining the seams of the old reefer coat.

'Now then, Arthur,' Laker said warily.

Seymour shoved him to one side and grabbed Molly by the right wrist, pulling her towards him. 'You get in here, you bitch. I want words with you.'

Laker pawed at his arm ineffectually. 'Now look here, Arthur,' he said. 'No way to behave.'

Seymour slapped him back-handed, bringing blood from his nose in a sudden gush. 'Get out of it!' he said and shoved Laker backwards into the mud.

Molly kicked out furiously. 'You let me go!'

'Oh, no,' he said. He pushed the door closed behind him and shot the bolt. 'Never again, Molly.' He grabbed for her hair with his left hand. 'Now you be a good girl and I won't hurt you. Not so long as you give me what you've been giving that Irish bastard.'

His fingers were groping for the hem of her skirt.

'You stink,' she said. 'You know that? Like an old sow that's had a good wallow.'

She leaned down and bit his wrist savagely. He cried out in pain, releasing his grip, but clutched at her with his other hand as she turned, dress tearing, and ran for the ladder to the loft.

Devlin, on his way across the fields from Hobs End, reached the crest of the meadow above the farm in time to see Molly and Laker Armsby crossing the farmyard to the barn. A moment later Laker was propelled from the barn to fall flat on his back in the mud and the great door slammed. Devlin tossed his cigarette to one side and went down the hill on the run.

By the time he was vaulting the fence into the farmyard, Father Vereker and Mrs. Prior were at the barn. The priest hammered on the door with his stick. 'Arthur?' he shouted. 'Open the door – stop this foolishness.'

The only reply was a scream from Molly. 'What's going on?' Devlin demanded.

'It's Seymour,' Laker told him, holding a bloody handkerchief to his nose. 'Got Molly in there, he has, and he's bolted the door.'

Devlin tried a shoulder and realised at once that he was wasting his time. He glanced about him desperately as Molly cried out again and his eyes lit on the tractor where Laker had left it, engine ticking over. Devlin was across the yard in a moment, scrambled up into the high seat behind the wheel and rammed the stick into gear, accelerating so savagely that the tractor shot forward, trailer swaying, turnips scattering across the yard like cannon balls. Vereker, Mrs. Prior and Laker got out of the way just in time as the tractor collided with the doors, bursting them inwards and rolling irresistibly forward.

Devlin braked to a halt. Molly was up in the loft, Seymour down below trying to re-position the ladder which she had obviously thrown down. Devlin switched off the engine and Seymour turned and looked at him, a strange, dazed look in his eyes.

'Now then, you bastard,' Devlin said.

Vereker limped in. 'No, Devlin, leave this to me!' he called and turned to Seymour. 'Arthur, this won't do, will it?'

Seymour paid not the slightest heed to either of them. It was as if they didn't exist and he turned and started to climb the ladder. Devlin jumped down from the tractor and kicked the ladder from under him. Seymour fell heavily to the ground. He lay there for a moment or so, shaking his head. Then his eyes cleared.

As Seymour got to his feet, Father Vereker lurched forward. 'Now, Arthur, I've told you . . .'

It was as far as he got for Seymour hurled him so violently to one side that he fell down. 'I'll kill you, Devlin!'

He gave a cry of rage and rushed in, great hands outstretched to destroy. Devlin dodged to one side and the weight of Seymour's progress carried him into the tractor. Devlin gave him a left and right to the kidneys and danced away as Seymour cried out in agony.

He came in with a roar and Devlin feinted with his right and smashed his left fist into the ugly mouth, splitting the lips so that blood spurted. He followed up with a right under the ribs that sounded like an axe going into wood.

He ducked in under Seymour's next wild punch and hit him under the ribs again. 'Footwork, timing and hitting, that is the secret. The Holy Trinity, we used to call them, Father. Learn those and ye shall inherit the earth as surely as the meek. Always helped out by a little dirty work now and then, of course.'

He kicked Seymour under the right kneecap and as the big man doubled over in agony, put a knee into the descending face, lifting him back through the door into the mud of the yard. Seymour got to his feet slowly and stood there like a dazed bull in the centre of the plaza, blood on his face.

Devlin danced in, 'You don't know when to lie down, do you, Arthur, but that's hardly surprising with a brain the size of a pea?'

He advanced his right foot, slipped in the mud and went down on one knee. Seymour delivered a stunning blow to his forehead that put him flat on his back. Molly screamed and rushed in, hands clawing at Seymour's face. He threw her away from him and raised a foot to crush Devlin. But the Irishman got a hand to it and twisted, sending him staggering into the barn entrance again.

When he turned, Devlin was reaching for him, no longer smiling, the white killing face on him now. 'All right, Arthur. Let's get it over with. I'm hungry.'

Seymour tried to rush him again and Devlin circled, driving him across the yard, giving him neither quarter nor peace, evading his great swinging punches with ease, driving his knuckles into the face again and again until it was a mask of blood.

There was an old zinc water trough near the back door and Devlin pushed him towards it relentlessly. 'And now you will listen to me, you bastard!' he said. 'Touch that girl again, harm her in any way and I'll take the shears to you myself. Do you understand me?' He punched under the ribs again and Seymour groaned, his hands coming down. 'And in future, if you are in a room and I enter, you get up and walk out. Do you understand that too?'

His right connected twice with the unprotected jaw and Seymour fell across the trough and rolled on to his back.

Devlin dropped to his knees and pushed his face into the rain-water in the trough. He surfaced for air to find Molly crouched beside him, and Father Vereker bending over Seymour. 'My God, Devlin, you might have killed him,' the priest said.

'Not that one,' Devlin said. 'Unfortunately.'

As if anxious to prove him right, Seymour groaned and tried to sit up. At the same moment Mrs. Prior came out of the house with a double-barrelled shotgun in her hands. 'You get him out of here,' she told Vereker. 'And tell him from me, when his brains are unscrambled, that if he comes back here bothering my girl again, I'll shoot him like a dog and answer for it.'

Laker Armsby dipped an old enamel bucket into the trough and emptied it over Seymour. 'There you go, Arthur,' he said cheerfully. 'First bath you've had since Michaelmas, I dare say.'

Seymour groaned and grabbed for the trough to pull himself up. Father Vereker said, 'Help me, Laker,' and they took him between them across to the Morris.

Quite suddenly, the earth moved for Devlin, like the sea turning over. He closed his eyes. He was aware of Molly's cry of alarm, her strong, young shoulder under his arm and then her mother was on the other side of him and they were walking him towards the house between them.

He surfaced to find himself in the kitchen chair by the fire, his face against Molly's breasts, while she held a damp cloth to his forehead. 'You can let me go now, I'm fine,' he told her.

She looked down at him, face anxious. 'God, but I thought he'd split your skull with that one punch.'

'A weakness of mine,' Devlin told her, aware of her concern and momentarily serious. 'After periods of intense stress I sometimes keel over, go out like a light. Some psychological thing.'

'What's that?' she demanded, puzzled.

'Never mind,' he said. 'Just let me put my head back where I can see your right nipple.'

She put a hand to her torn bodice and flushed, 'You devil.'

'You see,' he said. 'Not much difference between Arthur and me when it comes right down to it.'

She tapped a finger very gently between his eyes. 'I never heard such rubbish from a grown man in all my life.'

Her mother bustled into the kitchen fastening a clean apron about her waist. 'By God, boy, but you must have a powerful hunger on you after that little bout. Are you ready for your meat and potato pie now, then?'

Devlin looked up at Molly and smiled. 'Thank you kindly, ma'am. As a matter of fact, I think I could say with some truth that I'm ready for anything.'

The girl choked back laughter, shook a clenched fist under his nose and went to help her mother.

It was late evening when Devlin returned to Hobs End. It was very still and quiet on the marsh as if rain threatened and the sky was dark and thunder rumbled uneasily on the far horizon. He took the long way round to check the dyke gates that controlled the flow into the network of waterways and when he finally turned into the yard, Joanna Grey's car was parked by the door. She was wearing WVS uniform and leaning on the wall looking out to sea, the retriever sitting beside her patiently. She turned to look at him as he joined her. There was a sizable bruise on his forehead where Seymour's fist had landed.

'Nasty,' she said. 'Do you try to commit suicide often?'

He grinned. 'You should see the other fella.'

'I have.' She shook her head. 'It's got to stop, Liam.'

He lit a cigarette, match flaring in cupped hands. 'What has?'

'Molly Prior. You're not here for that. You've got a job to do.'

'Come off it,' he said. 'I haven't a thing to lay hand to before my meeting with Garvald on the twenty-eighth.'

'Don't be silly. People in places like this are the same the world over, you know that. Distrust the stranger and look after your own. They don't like what you did to Arthur Seymour.'

'And I didn't like what he tried to do to Molly.' Devlin half-laughed in a kind of astonishment. 'God save us, woman, if only half the things

Laker Armsby told me about Seymour this afternoon are true, they should have locked him up years ago and thrown away the key. Sexual assaults of one kind or another too numerous to mention and he's crippled at least two men in his time.'

'They never use the police in places like this. They handle it themselves.' She shook her head impatiently. 'But this isn't getting us anywhere. We can't afford to alienate people so do the sensible thing. Leave Molly alone.'

'Is that an order, ma'am?'

'Don't be an idiot. I'm appealing to your good sense, that's all.'

She walked to the car, put the dog in the back and got behind the wheel. 'Any news from the Sir Henry front?' Devlin asked as she switched on the engine.

She smiled. 'I'm keeping him warm, don't worry. I'll be on the radio to Radl again on Friday night. I'll let you know what comes up.'

She drove away and Devlin unlocked the door and let himself in. Inside he hesitated for a long moment and then shot the bolt and went into the living room. He pulled the curtain, lit a small fire and sat in front of it, a glass of Garvald's Bushmills in his hand.

It was a shame – one hell of a shame, but perhaps Joanna Grey was right. It would be silly to go looking for trouble. He thought of Molly for one brief moment, then resolutely selected a copy of *The Midnight Court* in Irish from his small stock of books and forced himself to concentrate.

It started to rain, brushing the window pane. It was about seven-thirty when the handle of the front door rattled vainly. After a while, there was a tap at the window on the other side of the curtain and she called his name softly. He kept on reading, straining to follow the words in the failing light of the small fire and after a while, she went away.

He swore softly, black rage in his heart and threw the book at the wall, resisting with every fibre of his being the impulse to run to the door, unlock it and go after her. He poured himself another large whiskey and stood at the window, feeling suddenly lonelier than he had ever felt in his life before, as rain hurtled in across the marsh in a sudden fury.

And at Landsvoort there was a gale blowing in off the sea, with the kind of bitter drenching rain that cut to the bone like a surgeon's knife. Harvey Preston, on guard duty at the garden gate of the old farmhouse, huddled against the wall, cursing Steiner, cursing Radl, cursing Himmler and whatever else had combined to reduce him to this, the lowest and most miserable level of his entire life.

10

During the Second World War, the German paratrooper differed from his British counterpart in one highly important aspect – the type of parachute used.

The German version, unlike that issued to Luftwaffe pilots and aircrew, did not have straps, known as lift webs, fastening the shroud lines to the harness. Instead, the shroud lines connected directly to the pack itself. It made the whole process of jumping entirely different and because of that, on Sunday morning at Landsvoort, Steiner arranged for a demonstration of the standard British parachute in the old barn at the back of the farmhouse.

The men stood in front of him in a semi-circle, Harvey Preston in the centre, dressed, like the others, in jump boots and overalls. Steiner faced them, Ritter Neumann and Brandt on either side of him.

Steiner said, 'The whole point of this operation, as I've already explained, is that we pass ourselves off as a Polish unit of the Special Air Service. Because of this, not only will all your equipment be British – you'll jump using the standard parachute used by British airborne forces.' He turned to Ritter Neumann. 'All yours.'

Brandt picked up a parachute pack and held it aloft. Neumann said, 'X Type parachute as used by British Airborne forces. Weighs around twenty-eight pounds and, as the Herr Oberst says, very different from ours.'

Brandt pulled the ripcord, the pack opened, disgorging the khaki chute. Neumann said, 'Note the way the shroud lines are fastened to the harness by shoulder straps, just like the Luftwaffe.'

'The point being,' Steiner put in, 'that you can manipulate the chute, change direction, have the kind of control over your own destiny that you just don't get with the one you're used to.'

'Another thing,' Ritter said, 'With our parachute the centre of gravity is high which means you get snagged up in the shroud lines unless you exit in a partially face-down position, as you all know. With the X type, you can go out in the standing posture and that's what we're going to practise now.'

He nodded to Brandt, who said, 'All right, let's have you all down here.'

There was a loft perhaps fifteen feet high at the far end of the barn. A rope had been looped over a beam above it, an X type parachute harness fastened to one end. 'A trifle primitive,' Brandt announced jovially, 'but good enough. You jump off the loft and there'll be half a dozen of us on the other end to make sure you don't hit the dirt too hard. Who's first?'

Steiner said, 'I'd better claim that honour, mainly because I've things to do elsewhere.'

Ritter helped him into the harness, then Brandt and four others got on the other end of the rope and hauled him up to the loft. He paused on the edge for a moment or so, Ritter signalled and Steiner swung out into space. The other end of the rope went up, taking three of the men with it, but Brandt and Sergeant Sturm hung on, cursing. Steiner hit the dirt, rolled over in a perfect fall and sprang to his feet.

'All right,' he told Ritter. 'Usual stick formation. I've time to see everyone do it once. Then I must go.'

He moved to the rear of the group and lit a cigarette as Neumann buckled himself into the harness. From the back of the barn it looked reasonably hair-raising as the Oberleutnant was hoisted up to the loft, but there was a roar of laughter when Ritter made a mess of his landing and ended up flat on his back.

'See?' Private Klugl said to Werner Briegel. 'That's what riding those damn torpedoes does for you. The Herr Leutnant's forgotten everything he ever knew.'

Brandt went next and Steiner observed Preston closely. The Englishman was very pale, sweat on his face – obviously terrified. The group worked through with varying success, the men on the end of the rope in one unfortunate lapse mistaking the signal and leaving go at the wrong moment so that Private Hagl descended the full fifteen feet under his own power with all the grace of a sack of potatoes. But he picked himself up, none the worse for his experience.

Finally, it was Preston's turn. The good humour faded abruptly.

Steiner nodded to Brandt. 'Up with him.'

The five men on the end of the rope hauled with a will and Preston shot up, banging against the loft on the way, finishing just below the roof. They lowered him till he stood on the edge, gazing down at them wildly.

'All right, English,' Brandt called. 'Remember what I told you. Jump when I signal.'

He turned to instruct the men on the rope, and there was a cry of alarm from Briegel as Preston simply fell forward into space. Ritter Neumann jumped for the rope. Preston came to rest three feet above the ground, swinging like a pendulum, arms hanging at his side, head down.

Brandt put a hand under the chin and looked into the Englishman's face. 'He's fainted.'

'So it would appear,' Steiner said.

'What do we do with him, Herr Oberst?' Ritter Neumann demanded.

'Bring him round,' Steiner said calmly. 'Then put him up again. As many times as it takes until he can do it satisfactorily – or breaks a leg.' He saluted. 'Carry on, please,' turned and went out.

There were at least a dozen men in the tap room of the Studley Arms when Devlin went in. Laker Armsby in his usual place by the fire with his mouth organ, the rest seated around the two large tables playing dominoes. Arthur Seymour was staring out of the window, a pint in his hand.

'God save all here!' Devlin announced cheerfully. There was complete silence, every face in the room turned towards him except for Seymour's. 'God save you kindly, was the answer to that one,' Devlin said. 'Ah, well.'

There was a step behind him and he turned to find George Wilde emerging from the back room, wiping his hands on a butcher's apron. His face was grave and steady, no emotion there at all. 'I was just closing, Mr. Devlin,' he said politely.

'Time for a jar, surely.'

'I'm afraid not. You'll have to leave, sir.'

The room was very quiet. Devlin put his hands in his pockets and hunched his shoulders, head down. And when he looked up, Wilde took an involuntary step back, for the Irishman's face had turned very pale, the skin stretched tight over the cheek bones, blue eyes glittering.

'There is one man here who will leave,' Devlin said quietly, 'and it is not me.'

Seymour turned from the window. One eye was still completely closed, his lips scabbed and swollen. His entire face seemed lopsided and was covered with purple and green bruises. He stared at Devlin dully, then put down his half-finished pint of ale and shuffled out.

Devlin turned back to Wilde, 'I'll have that drink, now, Mr. Wilde. A drop of Scotch, Irish being something you'll never have heard of here at the edge of your own little world, and don't try to tell me you don't have a bottle or two under the counter for favoured customers.'

Wilde opened his mouth as if to speak and obviously thought better of it. He went into the back and returned with a bottle of White Horse and a small glass. He poured out a single measure and placed the glass on the shelf next to Devlin's head.

Devlin produced a handful of change. 'One shilling and sixpence,' he said cheerfully, counting it out on the nearest table. 'The going price for a nip. I'm taking it for granted, of course, that such a fine, upstanding pillar of the church as yourself wouldn't be dealing in black market booze.'

Wilde made no reply. The whole room waited. Devlin picked up the glass, held it to the light, then emptied it in a golden stream to the floor. He put the glass down carefully on the table. 'Lovely,' he said. 'I enjoyed that.'

Laker Armsby broke into a wild cackle of laughter, Devlin grinned. 'Thank you, Laker, my old son. I love you too,' he said and walked out.

It was raining hard at Landsvoort as Steiner drove across the airstrip in his field car. He braked to a halt outside the first hangar and ran for its shelter. The starboard engine of the Dakota was laid bare and Peter Gericke, in a pair of old overalls, grease up to his elbows, worked with a Luftwaffe sergeant and three mechanics. 'Peter?' Steiner called. 'Have you got a moment? I'd like a progress report.'

'Oh, things are going well enough.'

'No problems with the engines?'

'None at all. They're nine-hundred horsepower Wright Cyclones. Really first class and as far as I can judge, they've done very little time. We're only stripping as a precaution.'

'Do you usually work on your own engines?'

'Whenever I'm allowed.' Gericke smiled. 'When I flew these things in South America you had to service your own engines, because there was nobody else who could.'

'No problems?'

'Not as far as I can see. She's scheduled to have her new paint job some time next week. No rush on that and Bohmler's fitting a Lichtenstein set so we'll have good radar coverage. A milk run. An hour across the North Sea, an hour back. Nothing to it.'

'In an aircraft whose maximum speed is half that of most RAF or Luftwaffe fighters.'

Gericke shrugged. 'It's all in how you fly them, not in how fast they go.'

'You want a test flight, don't you?'

'That's right.'

'I've been thinking,' Steiner said. 'It might be a good idea to combine it with a practice drop. Preferably one night when the tide is well out. We could use the beach north of the sand pier. It will give the lads a chance to try out these British parachutes.'

'What altitude are you thinking of?'

'Probably four hundred feet. I want them down fast and from that height fifteen seconds is all it takes.'

'Rather them than me. I've only had to hit the silk three times in my career and it was a lot higher than that.' The wind howled across the airstrip, driving rain before it, and he shivered. 'What a bloody awful place.'

'It serves its purpose.'

'And what's that?'

Steiner grinned. 'You ask me that at least five times a day. Don't you ever give up?'

'I'd like to know what it's all about, that's all.'

'Maybe you will, one day, that's up to Radl, but for the moment we're here because we're here.'

'And Preston?' Gericke said. 'I wonder what his reason is? What makes a man do what he's done.'

'All sorts of things,' Steiner said. 'In his case, he's got a pretty uniform, officer status. He's somebody for the first time in his life, that means a lot when you've been nothing. As regards the rest – well, he's here as a result of a direct order from Himmler himself.'

'What about you?' Gericke asked. 'The greater good of the Third Reich? A life for the Führer?'

Steiner smiled. 'God knows. War is only a matter of perspective. After all, if it had been my father who was American and my mother German, I'd have been on the other side. As for the Parachute Regiment – I joined that because it seemed like a good idea at the time. After a while, of course, it grows on you.'

'I do it because I'd rather fly anything than nothing,' Gericke said, 'and I suppose it's much the same for most of those RAF lads on the other side of the North Sea. But you . . .' He shook his head. 'I don't really see it. Is it a game to you, then, just that and nothing more?'

Steiner said wearily, 'I used to know, now I'm not so sure. My father was a soldier of the old school. Prussian blue. Plenty of blood and iron, but honour, too.'

'And this task they've given you to do,' Gericke said, 'this – this English business, whatever it is. You have no doubts?'

'None at all. A perfectly proper military venture, believe me. Churchill himself couldn't fault it, in principle, at least.' Gericke tried to smile and failed and Steiner put a hand on his shoulder. 'I know, there are days when I could weep myself – for all of us,' and he turned and walked away through the rain.

In the Reichsführer's private office, Radl stood in front of the great man's desk while Himmler read through his report. 'Excellent, Herr Oberst,' he said finally. 'Really quite excellent.' He laid the report down. 'Everything would appear to be progressing more than satisfactorily. You have heard from the Irishman?'

'No, only from Mrs. Grey, that is the arrangement. Devlin has an excellent radio-telephone set. Something which we picked up from the British SOE, which will keep him in touch with the E-boat on its way in. That is the part of the operation he will handle as regards communication.'

'The Admiral has not become suspicious in any way? Has picked up no hint of what is happening? You're sure of that?'

'Perfectly, Herr Reichsführer. My visits to France and Holland, I've been able to handle in conjunction with Abwehr business in Paris and Antwerp or Rotterdam. As the Reichsführer is aware, I have always had considerable latitude from the Admiral as regards running my own section.'

'And when do you go to Landsvoort again?'

'Next weekend. By a fortunate turn of events, the Admiral goes to Italy on the first or second of November. This means I can afford to stay at Landsvoort myself during the final crucial days and, indeed, for the period of the operation itself.'

'No coincidence, the Admiral's visit to Italy, I can assure you.' Himmler smiled thinly. 'I suggested it to the Führer at exactly the right moment. Within five minutes he'd quite decided he'd thought of it himself.' He picked up his pen. 'So, it progresses, Radl. Two weeks from today and it will all be over. Keep me informed.'

He bent over his work and Radl licked dry lips and yet it had to be said. 'Herr Reichsführer.'

Himmler sighed heavily. 'I'm really very busy, Radl. What is it now?'

'General Steiner, Herr Reichsführer. He is – he is well?'

'Of course,' Himmler said calmly. 'Why do you ask?'

'Colonel Steiner,' Radl explained, his stomach churning. 'He is naturally extremely anxious . . .'

'There is no need to be,' Himmler said gravely. 'I gave you my personal assurance, is that not so?'

'Of course.' Radl backed to the door. 'Thank you again,' and he turned and got out as fast as he could.

Himmler shook his head, sighed in a kind of exasperation and returned to his writing.

When Devlin went into the church, Mass was almost over. He slipped down the right-hand aisle and eased into a pew. Molly was on her knees beside her mother dressed exactly as she had been on the previous Sunday. Her dress showed no evidence of the rough treatment it had received from Arthur Seymour. He was present also, in the same position he usually occupied and he saw Devlin instantly. He showed no emotion at all, but simply got to his feet and slipped down the aisle in the shadows and went out.

Devlin waited, watching Molly at prayer, all innocence kneeling there in the candlelight. After a while, she opened her eyes and turned very slowly as if physically aware of his presence. Her eyes widened, she looked at him for a long moment, then turned away again.

Devlin left just before the end of the service and went out quickly. By the time the first of the congregation exited, he was already at his motor-cycle. It was raining slightly and he turned up the collar of his trenchcoat and sat astride the bike and waited. When Molly finally came down the path with her mother she ignored him completely. They got into the trap, her mother took the reins and they drove away.

'Ah, well, now,' Devlin told himself softly. 'And who would blame her?'

He kicked the engine into life, heard his name called and found Joanna Grey bearing down on him. She said in a low voice, 'I had Philip Vereker at me for two hours this afternoon. He wanted to complain to Sir Henry about you.'

'I don't blame him.'

She said, 'Can't you ever be serious for more than five minutes at any one time?'

'Too much of a strain,' he said and she was prevented from continuing the conversation by the arrival of the Willoughbys.

Sir Henry was in uniform. 'Now then, Devlin, how's it working out?'

'Fine, sir,' Devlin rolled out the Irish. 'I can't thank you enough for this wonderful opportunity to make good.'

He was aware of Joanna Grey standing back, tight-lipped, but Sir Henry liked it well enough. 'Good show, Devlin. Getting excellent reports on you. Excellent. Keep up the good work.'

He turned to speak to Joanna Grey and Devlin, seizing his opportunity, rode away.

It was raining very heavily by the time he reached the cottage, so he put the motor-cycle in the first barn, changed into waders and an oilskin coat, got his shotgun and started out into the marsh. The dyke gates needed checking in such heavy rain and trudging round in such conditions was a nice negative sort of occupation to take his mind off things.

It didn't work. He couldn't get Molly Prior out of his thoughts. The image recurred constantly of her dropping to her knees in prayer the previous Sunday in a kind of slow motion, the skirt sliding up her thighs. Would not go away.

'Holy Mary and all the Saints,' he said softly. 'If this is what love is really like, Liam my boy, you've taken one hell of a long time finding out about it.'

As he came back along the main dyke towards the cottage he smelt woodsmoke heavy on the damp air. There was a light at the window in the evening gloom, the tiniest chink where the blackout curtains had failed to come together. When he opened the door he could smell cooking. He put the shotgun in the corner, hung the oilskin coat up to dry and went into the living room.

She was on one knee at the fire, putting on another log. She turned to look over her shoulder gravely. 'You'll be wet through.'

'Half an hour in front of that fire and a couple of whiskies inside me and I'll be fine.'

She went to the cupboard, got the bottle of Bushmills and a glass. 'Don't pour it on the floor,' she said. 'Try drinking it this time.'

'So you know about that?'

'Not much you don't hear in a place like this. Irish stew on the go. That all right?'

'Fine.'

'Half an hour, I'd say.' She crossed to the sink and reached for a glass dish. 'What went wrong, Liam? Why did you keep out of the way?'

He sat down in the old wing-back chair, legs wide to the fire, steam rising from his trousers. 'I thought it best at first.'

'Why?'

'I had my reasons.'

'And what went wrong today?'

'Sunday, bloody Sunday. You know how it is.'

'Damn your eyes.' She crossed the room, drying her hands on her apron and looked down at the steam rising from Devlin's trousers. 'You'll catch your death if you don't change those. Rheumatism at least.'

'Not worth it,' he said. 'I'll go to bed soon. I'm tired.'

She reached out hesitantly and touched his hair. He seized her hand and kissed it. 'I love you, you know that?'

It was as if a lamp had been switched on inside her. She glowed, seemed to expand and take on an entirely new dimension. 'Well, thank God for that. At least it means I can go to bed now with a clear conscience.'

'I'm bad for you, girl dear, there's nothing in it. No future, I warn you. There should be a notice above that bedroom door. Abandon hope all ye who enter here.'

'We'll see about that,' she said. 'I'll get your stew,' and she moved across to the stove.

Later, lying in the old brass bed, an arm about her, watching the shadow patterns on the ceiling from the fire, he felt more content, more at peace with himself than he had done for years.

There was a radio on a small table at her side of the bed. She switched

it on, then turned her stomach against his thigh and sighed, eyes closed.
'Oh, that was lovely. Can we do it again some time?'
    'Would you give a fella time to catch his breath?'
She smiled and ran a hand across his belly. 'The poor old man. Just
listen to him.'
A record was playing on the radio.

> When that man is dead and gone . . .
> Some fine day the news will flash,
> Satan with a small moustache
> Is asleep beneath the tomb.

'I'll be glad when that happens,' she said drowsily.
'What?' he asked.
'Satan with a small moustache asleep beneath the tomb. Hitler. I
mean, it'll all be over then, won't it?' She snuggled closer. 'What's going
to happen to us, Liam? When the war's over?'
    'God knows.'
He lay there staring at the fire. After a while her breathing steadied
and she was asleep. *After the war was over.* Which war? He'd been on the
barricades one way or another for twelve years now. How could he tell
her that? It was a nice little farm, too, and they needed a man. God, the
pity of it. He held her close and the wind moaned about the old house,
rattling the windows.

And in Berlin, at Prinz Albrechtstrasse, Himmler still sat at his desk,
methodically working his way through dozens of reports and sheets of
statistics, mainly those relating to the extermination squads who, in the
occupied lands of Eastern Europe and Russia, liquidated Jews, gypsies,
the mentally and physically handicapped and any others who did not fit
into the Reichsführer's plan for a Greater Europe.
    There was a polite knock at the door and Karl Rossman entered.
Himmler looked up. 'How did you get on?'
    'I'm sorry, Herr Reichsführer, he won't budge and we really have
tried just about everything. I'm beginning to think he might be innocent
after all.'
    'Not possible.' Himmler produced a sheet of paper. 'I received this
document earlier this evening. A signed confession from an artillery
sergeant who was his batman for two years and who during that time
engaged in work prejudicial to State Security on Major-General Karl
Steiner's direct order.'
    'So what now, Herr Reichsführer?'

'I'd still prefer a signed confession from General Steiner himself. It makes everything that much tighter.' Himmler frowned slightly. 'Let's try a little more psychology. Clean him up, get an SS doctor to him, plenty of food. You know the drill. The whole thing has been a shocking mistake on somebody's part. Sorry you have still to detain him, but one or two points still remain to be cleared up.'

'And then?'

'When he's had, say, ten days of that, go to work on him again. Right out of the blue. No warning. The shock might do it.'

'I'll do as you suggest, Herr Reichsführer,' Rossman said.

11

At four o'clock on the afternoon of Thursday, the twenty-eighth October, Joanna Grey drove into the yard of the cottage at Hobs End and found Devlin in the barn working on the motor-cycle.

'I've been trying to get hold of you all week,' she said. 'Where have you been?'

'Around,' he told her cheerfully, wiping grease from his hands on an old rag. 'Out and about. I told you there was nothing for me to do till my meeting with Garvald so I've been having a look at the countryside.'

'So I've heard,' she said grimly. 'Riding around on that motor-cycle with Molly Prior on the pillion. You were seen in Holt at a dance on Tuesday night.'

'A very worthy cause,' he said. 'Wings for Victory. Actually your friend Vereker turned up and made an impassioned speech about how God would help us crush the bloody Hun. I found that ironic in view of the fact that everywhere I went in Germany I used to see signs saying *God with us.*'

'I told you to leave her alone.'

'I tried that, it didn't work. Anyway, what did you want? I'm busy. I'm having a certain amount of magneto trouble and I want this thing to be in perfect working order for my run to Peterborough tonight.'

'Troops have moved into Meltham House,' she said. 'They arrived on Tuesday night.'

He frowned. 'Meltham House – isn't that the place where Special Force outfits train?'

'That's right. It's about eight miles up the coast road from Studley Constable.'

'Who are they?'

'American Rangers.'

'I see. Should it make any difference, their being here?'

'Not really. They usually stay up at that end, the units who use the facilities. There's a heavily wooded area, a salt marsh and a good beach. It's a factor to be considered, that's all.'

Devlin nodded. 'Fair enough. Let Radl know about it in your next broadcast and there's your duty done. And now, I must get on.'

She turned to go to the car and hesitated. 'I don't like the sound of this man Garvald.'

'Neither do I, but don't worry, my love. If he's going to turn nasty, it won't be tonight. It will be tomorrow.'

She got to the car and drove away and he returned to his work on the motor-cycle. Twenty minutes later Molly rode up out of the marsh, a basket hanging from her saddle. She slipped to the ground and tied the horse to a hitching ring in the wall above the trough. 'I've brought you a shepherd's pie.'

'Yours or your mother's?' She threw a stick at him and he ducked. 'It'll have to wait. I've got to go out tonight. Put it in the oven for me and I'll heat it up when I get in.'

'Can I go with you?'

'Not a chance. Too far. And besides, it's business.' He slapped her behind. 'A cup of tea is what I crave, woman of the house, or maybe two, so off with you and put the kettle on.'

He reached for her again, she dodged him, grabbed her basket and ran for the cottage. Devlin let her go. She went into the living room and put the basket on the table. The Gladstone bag was at the other end and as she turned to go to the stove, she caught it with her left arm, knocking it to the floor. It fell open disgorging packets of banknotes and the Sten gun parts.

She knelt there, stunned for the moment, suddenly icy cold, as if aware by some kind of precognition that nothing ever would be the same again.

There was a step in the doorway and Devlin said quietly, 'Would you put them back, now, like a good girl?'

She looked up, white-faced, but her voice was fierce. 'What is it? What does it mean?'

'Nothing,' he said, 'for little girls.'

'But all this money.'

She held up a packet of fivers. Devlin took the bag from her, stuffed the money and the weapons back inside and replaced the bottom. Then he opened the cupboard under the window, took out a large envelope and tossed it to her.

'Size ten. Was I right?'

She opened the envelope, peered inside and there was an immediate look of awe on her face. 'Silk stockings. Real silk and two pairs. Where on earth did you get these?'

'Oh, a man I met in a pub in Fakenham. You can get anything you want if you know where to look.'

'The black market,' she said. 'That's what you're mixed up in, isn't it?'

There was a certain amount of relief in her eyes and he grinned. 'The right colour for me. Now would you kindly get the tea on and hurry? I want to be away by six and I've still got work to do on the bike.'

She hesitated, clutching the stockings and moved close. 'Liam, it's all right, isn't it?'

'And why wouldn't it be?' He kissed her briefly, turned and went out, cursing his own stupidity.

And yet as he walked towards the barn, he knew in his heart that there was more to it than that. For the first time he had been brought face to face with what he was doing to this girl. Within little more than a week, her entire world was going to be turned upside down. That was absolutely inevitable and nothing he could do about it except leave her, as he must, to bear the hurt of it alone.

Suddenly, he felt physically sick and kicked out at a packing case savagely. 'Oh, you bastard,' he said. 'You dirty bastard, Liam.'

Reuben Garvald opened the judas in the main gate of the workshop of Fogarty's garage and peered outside. Rain swept across the cracked concrete of the forecourt where the two rusting petrol pumps stood forlornly. He closed the judas hurriedly and stepped back inside.

The workshop had once been a barn and was surprisingly spacious. A flight of wooden steps led up to a loft, but in spite of a wrecked saloon car in one corner, there was still plenty of room for the three-ton Bedford truck and the van in which Garvald and his brother had travelled from Birmingham. Ben Garvald himself walked up and down impatiently, occasionally beating his arms together. In spite of the heavy overcoat and scarf he wore, he was bitterly cold.

'Christ, what a dump,' he said. 'Isn't there any sign of that little Irish sod?'

'It's only a quarter to nine, Ben,' Reuben told him.

'I don't care what bleeding time it is.' Garvald turned on a large, hefty young man in a sheepskin flying jacket who leaned against the truck reading a newspaper. 'You get me some heat in here tomorrow night, Sammy boy, or I'll have your balls. Understand?'

Sammy, who had long dark sideburns and a cold, rather dangerous-looking face seemed completely unperturbed. 'Okay, Mr. Garvald. I'll see to it.'

'You'd better, sweetheart, or I'll send you back to the Army.' Garvald patted his face. 'And you wouldn't like that, would you?'

He took out a packet of Gold Flake, selected one and Sammy gave him a light with a fixed smile. 'You're a card, Mr. Garvald. A real card.'

Reuben called urgently from the door. 'He's just turned on to the forecourt.'

Garvald tugged at Sammy's arm. 'Get the door open and let's have the bastard in.'

Devlin entered in a flurry of rain and wind. He wore oilskin leggings with his trenchcoat, an old leather flying helmet and goggles which he'd bought in a secondhand shop in Fakenham. His face was filthy and when he switched off and pushed up his goggles, there were great white circles round his eyes.

'A dirty night for it, Mr. Garvald,' he said as he shoved the BSA on its stand.

'It always is, son,' Garvald replied cheerfully. 'Nice to see you.' He shook hands warmly. 'Reuben you know and this is Sammy Jackson, one of my lads. He drove the Bedford over for you.'

There was an implication that Jackson had somehow done him a great personal favour and Devlin responded in kind, putting on the Irish as usual. 'Sure and I appreciate that. It was damn good of you.' he said, wringing Sammy's hand.

Jackson looked him over contemptuously but managed a smile and Garvald said, 'All right then, I've got business elsewhere and I don't expect you want to hang around. Here's your truck. What do you think?'

The Bedford had definitely seen better days, the paintwork badly fading and chipped, but the tyres weren't too bad and the canvas tilt was almost new. Devlin heaved himself over the tailboard and noted the Army jerrycans, the compressor and the drum of paint he'd asked for.

'It's all there, just like you said.' Garvald offered him a cigarette. 'Check the petrol if you want.'

'No need, I'll take your word for it.'

Garvald wouldn't have tried any nonsense with the petrol, he was sure of that. After all, he wanted him to return on the following evening. He went round to the front and lifted the bonnet. The engine seemed sound enough.

'Try it,' Garvald invited.

He switched on and tapped the accelerator, and the engine broke into a healthy enough roar as he had expected. Garvald would be much too interested in finding out exactly what he was up to to spoil things by trying to push second-class goods at this stage.

Devlin jumped down and looked at the truck again, noting the military registration. 'All right?' Garvald asked.

'I suppose so.' Devlin nodded slowly. 'From the state of it, it looks as if it's been having a hard time in Tobruk or somewhere.'

'Very probably, old son.' Garvald kicked a wheel. 'But these things are built to take it.'

'Have you got the delivery licence I asked for?'

'Sure thing.' Garvald snapped a finger. 'Let's have that form, Reuben.'

Reuben produced it from his wallet and said sullenly, 'When do we see the colour of his money?'

'Don't be like that, Reuben. Mr. Murphy here is as sound as a bell.'

'No, he's right enough, a fair exchange.' Devlin took a fat manilla envelope from his breast pocket and passed it to Reuben. 'You'll find seven hundred and fifty in there in fivers, as agreed.'

He pocketed the form Reuben had given him after glancing at it briefly and Ben Garvald said, 'Aren't you going to fill that thing in?'

Devlin tapped his nose and tried to assume an expression of low cunning. 'And let you see where I'm going? Not bloody likely, Mr. Garvald.'

Garvald laughed delightedly. He put an arm about Devlin's shoulder. The Irishman said, 'If someone could give me a hand to put my bike in the back I'll be off.'

Garvald nodded to Jackson who dropped the tailboard of the Bedford and found an old plank. He and Devlin ran the BSA up and laid it on its side. Devlin clipped the tailboard in place and turned to Garvald. 'That's it then, Mr. Garvald, same time tomorrow.'

'Pleasure to do business with you, old son,' Garvald told him, wringing his hand again. 'Get the door open, Sammy.'

Devlin climbed behind the wheel and started the engine. He leaned out of the window. 'One thing, Mr. Garvald. I'm not likely to find the military police on my tail, now am I?'

'Would I do that to you, son?' Garvald beamed. 'I ask you.' He banged the side of the truck with the flat of his hand. 'See you tomorrow night. Repeat performance. Same time, same place and I'll bring you another bottle of Bushmills.'

Devlin drove out into the night and Sammy Jackson and Reuben got the doors closed. Garvald's smile disappeared. 'It's up to Freddy now.'

'What if he loses him?' Reuben asked.

'Then there's tomorrow night, isn't there?' Garvald patted him on the face. 'Where's that half of brandy you brought?'

'Lose him?' Jackson said. 'That little squirt?' He laughed harshly.

'Christ, he couldn't even find the way to the men's room unless you showed him.'

Devlin, a quarter of a mile down the road, was aware of the dim lights behind him indicating the vehicle which had pulled out of a lay-by a minute or so earlier as he passed, exactly as he expected.

An old ruined windmill loomed out of the night on his left and a flat stretch of cleared ground in front of it. He switched off all his lights suddenly, swung the wheel and drove into the cleared area blind, and braked. The other vehicle carried straight on, increasing its speed and Devlin jumped to the ground, went to the back of the Bedford and removed the bulb from the rear light. Then he got back behind the wheel, turned the truck in a circle on to the road and only switched on his lights when he was driving back towards Norman Cross.

A quarter of a mile this side of Fogarty's he turned right into a side road, the B660, driving through Holme, stopping fifteen minutes later outside Doddington to replace the bulb. When he returned to the cab, he got out the delivery licence form and filled it in in the light of a torch. There was the official stamp of a Service Corps unit near Birmingham at the bottom and the signature of the commanding officer, a Major Thrush. Garvald had thought of everything. Well, not quite everything. Devlin grinned and filled in his destination as the RAF radar station at Sheringham ten miles further along the coast road from Hobs End.

He got back behind the wheel and drove away again. Swaffham first, then Fakenham. He'd worked it all out very carefully on the map and he sat back and took it steadily because the blackout visors on his headlamps didn't give him a great deal of light to work by. Not that it mattered. He'd all the time in the world. He lit a cigarette and wondered how Garvald was getting on.

It was just after midnight when he turned into the yard outside the cottage at Hobs End. The journey had proved to be completely uneventful and in spite of the fact that he had boldly used the main roads for most of the way, he had passed no more than a handful of vehicles during the entire trip. He coasted round to the old barn on the very edge of the marsh, jumped out into the heavy rain and unlocked the padlock. He got the doors open and drove inside.

There were only a couple of round loft windows and it had been easy enough to black those out. He primed two Tilley lamps, pumped them until he had plenty of light, went outside to check that nothing showed, then he went back in and got his coat off.

Within half an hour, he had the truck unloaded, running the BSA out on an old plank and sliding the compressor to the ground the same way. The jerrycans he stacked in a corner, covering them with an old tarpaulin. Then he washed down the truck. When he was satisfied that it was as clean as he was going to get it he brought newspapers and tape which he had laid by earlier and proceeded to mask the windows. He did this very methodically, concentrating all the time and when he was finished went across to the cottage and had some of Molly's shepherds pie and a glass of milk.

It was still raining very hard when he ran back to the barn, hissing angrily into the waters of the marsh, filling the night with sound. Conditions were really quite perfect. He filled the compressor, primed the pump and turned its motor over, then he put the spraying equipment together and mixed some paint. He started on the tailboard first, taking his time, but it really worked very well indeed and within five minutes he had covered it with a glistening new coat of khaki green.

'God save us,' he said to himself softly. 'It's a good thing I haven't a criminal turn of mind for I could be making a living at this sort of thing and that's a fact.'

He moved round to the left and started on the side panels.

After lunch on Friday, he was touching up the numbers on the truck with white paint when he heard a car drive up. He wiped his hands and let himself out of the barn quickly, but when he went round the corner of the cottage it was only Joanna Grey. She was trying the front door, a trim and surprisingly youthful figure in the green WVS uniform.

'You always look your best in that outfit,' he said. 'I bet it has old Sir Henry crawling up the wall.'

She smiled. 'You're on form, anyway. Things must have gone well.'

'See for yourself?'

He opened the barn door and led her in. The Bedford, in its fresh coat of khaki green paint, really looked very well indeed. 'As my information has it, Special Force vehicles don't usually carry divisional flashes or insignia. Is that so?'

'That's true,' she said. 'The stuff I've seen operating out of Meltham House in the past have never advertised who they are.' She was obviously very impressed. 'This is really good, Liam. Did you have any trouble?'

'He had someone try to follow me, but I soon shook him off. The big confrontation should be tonight.'

'Can you handle it?'

'This can.' He picked up a cloth bundle lying on the packing case beside his brushes and tins of paint, unwrapped it and took out a Mauser with a rather strange bulbous barrel. 'Ever seen one of these before?'

'I can't say I have.' She weighed it in her left hand with professional interest and took aim.

'Some of the SS security people use them,' he said, 'but there just aren't enough to go round. Only really efficient silenced handgun I've ever come across.'

She said dubiously, 'You'll be on your own.'

'I've been on my own before.' He wrapped the Mauser in the cloth again and went to the door with her. 'If everything goes according to plan I should be back with the jeep around midnight. I'll check with you first thing in the morning.'

'I don't think I can wait that long.'

Her face was tense and anxious. She put out her hand impulsively and he held it tight for a moment. 'Don't worry. It'll work. I have the sight, or so my old grannie used to say. I know about these things.'

'You rogue,' she said and leaned forward and kissed him on the cheek in genuine affection. 'I sometimes wonder how you've survived so long.'

'That's easy,' he said. 'Because I've never particularly cared whether I do or not.'

'You say that as if you mean it?'

'Tomorrow.' He smiled gently. 'I'll be round first thing. You'll see.'

He watched her drive away, then kicked the door of the barn shut behind him and stuck a cigarette in his mouth. 'You can come out now,' he called.

There was a moment's delay and then Molly emerged from the rushes on the far side of the yard. Too far to have heard anything which was why he had let it go. He padlocked the door, then walked towards her. He stopped a yard away, hands pushed into his pockets. 'Molly, my own sweet girl,' he said gently. 'I love you dearly, but any more games like this and I'll give you the thrashing of your young life.'

She flung her arms about his neck. 'Is that a promise?'

'You're entirely shameless.'

She looked up at him, hanging on. 'Can I come over tonight?'

'You can't,' he said, 'because I won't be here,' and he added a half-truth. 'I'm going to Peterborough on private business and I won't be back until the small hours.' He tapped the end of her nose with a finger. 'And that's between us. No advertising.'

'More silk stockings?' she said. 'Or is it Scotch whisky this time.'

'Five quid a bottle the Yanks will pay, so they tell me.'

'I wish you wouldn't.' Her face was troubled. 'Why can't you be nice and normal like everyone else?'

'Would you have me in my grave so early?' He turned her round. 'Go and put the kettle on the stove and if you're a good girl, I'll let you make my dinner – or something.'

She smiled briefly over her shoulder, looking suddenly quite enchanting, then ran across to the cottage. Devlin put the cigarette back into his mouth, but didn't bother to light it. Thunder rumbled far out on the horizon, heralding more rain. *Another wet ride.* He sighed and went after her across the yard.

In the workshop at Fogarty's garage it was even colder than it had been on the previous night, in spite of Sammy Jackson's attempts to warm things up by punching holes in an old oil drum and lighting a coke fire. The fumes it gave off were quite something.

Ben Garvald, standing beside it, a half-bottle of brandy in one hand, a plastic cup in the other, retreated hastily. 'What in the hell are you trying to do, poison me?'

Jackson, who was sitting on a packing case on the opposite side of the fire nursing a sawn-off, double-barrelled shotgun across his knees, put it down and stood up. 'Sorry, Mr. Garvald. It's the coke – that's the trouble. Too bloody wet.'

Reuben, at the judas, called suddenly, 'Here, I think he's coming.'

'Get that thing out of the way,' Garvald said quickly, 'and remember you don't make your move till I tell you.' He poured some more brandy into the plastic cup and grinned. 'I want to enjoy this, Sammy boy. See that I do.'

Sammy put the shotgun under a piece of sacking beside him on the packing case and hurriedly lit a cigarette. They waited as the sound of the approaching engine grew louder, then moved past and died away into the night.

'For Christ's sake,' Garvald said in disgust. 'It wasn't him. What time is it?'

Reuben checked his watch. 'Just on nine. He should be here any moment.'

If they had but known it Devlin was, in fact, already there, standing in the rain at the broken rear window which had been roughly boarded up with planks. His vision, through a crack, was limited, but at least covered Garvald and Jackson beside the fire. And he'd certainly heard every word spoken during the past five minutes.

Garvald said, 'Here, you might as well do something useful while we're waiting, Sammy. Top up the jeep's tank with a couple of those jerrycans so you're ready for the run back to Brum.'

Devlin withdrew, worked his way through the yard, negotiating with caution the wrecks of several cars, regained the main road and ran back along the verge to the lay-by, a quarter of a mile away where he had left the BSA.

He unbuttoned the front flap of his trenchcoat, took out the Mauser and checked it in the light of the headlamp. Satisfied, he pushed it back inside, but left the flap unbuttoned, then he got back in the saddle. He wasn't afraid, not in the slightest. A little excited, true, but only enough to put an edge to him. He kicked the starter and turned into the road.

Inside the workshop, Jackson had just finished filling the jeep's tank when Reuben turned from the judas again excitedly. 'It's him. Definitely this time. He's just turned on to the forecourt.'

'Okay, get the doors open and let's have him in,' Garvald said.

The wind was so strong it caused a massive draught when Devlin entered that had the coke crackling like dried wood. Devlin switched off and shoved the bike up on its stand. His face was in an even worse state than it had been in the night before, plastered with mud. But when he pushed up his goggles he was smiling cheerfully.

'Hello there, Mr. Garvald.'

'Here we are again.' Garvald passed him the half of brandy. 'You look as if you could do with a nip.'

'Did you remember my Bushmills?'

'Course I did. Get those two bottles of Irish out of the van for Mr. Murphy, Reuben.'

Devlin took a quick pull at the brandy bottle while Reuben went to the van and returned with the two bottles of Bushmills. His brother took them from him. 'There you are, boy, just like I promised.' He went across to the jeep and put the bottles down on the passenger seat. 'Everything went off all right last night, then?'

'No problems at all,' Devlin said.

He approached the jeep. Like the Bedford, its coachwork was badly in need of a fresh coat of paint, but otherwise it was fine. It had a strip canvas roof with open sides and a mounting point for a machine gun. The registration, in contrast to the rest of the vehicle, had been freshly painted and when Devlin looked closely he could see traces of another underneath.

'There's a thing now, Mr. Garvald,' he said. 'Would some Yank airbase be missing one of these?'

'Now, look here, you,' Reuben put in angrily.

Devlin cut him off. 'Come to think of it, Mr. Garvald, there was a moment last night when I thought someone was trying to follow me. Nerves, I suppose. Nothing came of it.'

He turned back to the jeep and had another quick pull at the bottle. Garvald's anger, contained with considerable difficulty, overflowed now.

'You know what you need?'

'And what would that be?' Devlin enquired softly. He turned, still holding the half of brandy, clutching one lapel of his trenchcoat with his right hand.

'A lesson in manners, sweetheart,' Garvald said. 'You need putting in place and I'm just the man to do it.' He shook his head. 'You should have stayed back home in the bogs.'

He started to unbutton his overcoat and Devlin said, 'Is that a fact now? Well, before you start, I'd just like to ask Sammy boy, here, if that shotgun he's got under the sacking is cocked or not, because if it isn't, he's in big trouble.'

In that single, frozen moment in time, Ben Garvald suddenly knew beyond any shadow of a doubt that he'd just made the worst mistake of his life. 'Take him, Sammy!' he cried.

Jackson was way ahead of him, had already grabbed for the shotgun under the sacking – already too late. As he frantically thumbed back the hammers, Devlin's hand was inside his trenchcoat and out again. The silenced Mauser coughed once, the bullet smashed into Jackson's left arm, turning him in a circle. The second shot shattered his spine, driving him headfirst into the wrecked car in the corner. In death his finger tightened convulsively on the triggers of the shotgun, discharging both barrels into the ground.

The Garvald brothers backed away slowly, inching towards the door. Reuben was shaking with fear, Garvald watchful, waiting for any kind of chance to seize on.

Devlin said, 'That's far enough.'

In spite of his size, the old flying helmet and goggles, the soaking-wet coat, he seemed a figure of infinite menace as he faced them from the other side of the fire, the Mauser with the bulbous silencer in his hand.

Garvald said, 'All right, I made a mistake.'

'Worse than that, you broke your word,' Devlin said. 'And where I come from, we have an excellent specific for people who let us down.'

'For God's sake, Murphy . . .'

He didn't get any further because there was a dull thud as Devlin fired again. The bullet splintered Garvald's right kneecap. He went back against the door with a stifled cry and fell to the ground. He rolled over, clutching at his knee with both hands, blood pumping between his fingers.

Reuben crouched, hands raised in futile protection, head down. He spent two or three of the worst moments of his life in that position and when he finally had the courage to look up, discovered Devlin positioning an old plank at the side of the jeep. As Reuben watched, the Irishman ran the BSA up and into the rear.

He came forward and opened one half of the garage doors. Then he snapped his fingers at Reuben. 'The delivery licence.'

Reuben produced it from his wallet with shaking fingers and handed it over. Devlin checked it briefly, then took out an envelope which he dropped at Garvald's feet. 'Seven hundred and fifty quid, just to keep the books straight. I told you, I'm a man of my word. You should try it some time.' He got into the jeep, pressed the starter and drove out into the night.

'The door,' Garvald said to his brother through clenched teeth. 'Get the bloody door closed or you'll have every copper for miles turning up to see what the light is.'

Reuben did as he was told, then turned to survey the scene. The air was full of hazy blue smoke and the stench of cordite.

Reuben shuddered. 'Who was that bastard, Ben?'

'I don't know and I don't really care.' Garvald pulled free the white silk scarf he wore around his neck. 'Use this to bandage this bloody knee.'

Reuben looked at the wound in fascinated horror. The 7.63 mm cartridge had gone in one side and out the other, and the kneecap had fragmented, splinters of white bone protruding through the flesh and blood.

'Christ, it's bad, Ben. You need a hospital.'

'Like hell I do. You carry me into any casualty department in this country with a gunshot wound and they'll shout for the coppers so fast you'll think you're standing still.' There was sweat on his face. 'Go on, bandage it for Christ's sake.'

Reuben started to wind the scarf round the shattered knee. He was almost in tears. 'What about Sammy, Ben?'

'Leave him where he is. Just cover him with one of the tarpaulins for the moment. You can get some of the boys over here tomorrow to get rid of him.' He cursed as Reuben tightened the scarf. 'Hurry up, and let's get out of here.'

'Where to, Ben?'.

'We'll go straight to Birmingham. You can take me to that nursing home in Aston. The one that Indian doctor runs. What's his name?'

'You mean Das?' Reuben shook his head. 'He's in the abortion racket, Ben. No good to you.'

'He's a doctor, isn't he?' Ben said. 'Now give me a hand up and let's get out of here.'

Devlin drove into the yard at Hobs End half an hour after midnight. It was a dreadful night with gale-force winds, torrential rain and when he had unlocked the doors of the barn and driven inside, he had a hard tussle to get them closed again.

He lit the Tilley lamps and manoeuvred the BSA out of the back of the jeep. He was tired and bitterly cold, but not tired enough to sleep. He lit a cigarette and walked up and down, strangely restless.

It was quiet in the barn, only the rain drumming against the roof, the quiet hissing of the Tilley lamps. The door opened in a flurry of wind and Molly entered, closing it behind her. She wore her old trenchcoat, wellington boots and a headscarf and was soaked to the skin so that she shook with cold, but it didn't seem to matter. She walked to the jeep, a puzzled frown on her face.

She gazed at Devlin dumbly. 'Liam?' she said.

'You promised,' he told her. 'No more prying. It's useful to know how you keep your word.'

'I'm sorry, but I was so frightened, and then all this.' She gestured at the vehicles. 'What does it mean?'

'None of your business,' he told her brutally. 'As far as I'm concerned you can clear off right now. If you want to report me to the police – well, you must do as you see fit.'

She stood staring at him, eyes very wide, mouth working. 'Go on!' he said. 'If that's what you want. Get out of it!'

She ran into his arms, bursting into tears. 'Oh, no, Liam, don't send me away. No more questions, I promise, and from now on I'll mind my own business, only don't send me away.'

It was the lowest point in his life and the self-contempt he felt as he held her in his arms was almost physical in its intensity. But it had worked. She would cause him no more trouble, of that he was certain.

He kissed her on the forehead. 'You're freezing. Get on over to the house with you and build up the fire. I'll be with you in a few minutes.'

She gazed up at him searchingly, then turned and went out. Devlin sighed and went over to the jeep and picked up one of the bottles of Bushmills. He eased out the cork and took a long swallow.

'Here's to you, Liam, old son,' he said with infinite sadness.

In the tiny operating theatre in the nursing home at Aston, Ben Garvald lay back on the padded table, eyes closed. Reuben stood beside him while Das, a tall, cadaverous Indian in an immaculate white coat, cut away the trouser leg with surgical scissors.

'Is it bad?' Reuben asked him, his voice shaking.

'Yes, very bad,' Das replied calmly. 'He needs a first-rate surgeon, if he is not to be crippled. There is also the question of sepsis.'

'Listen, you bleeding wog bastard,' Ben Garvald said, eyes opening.

'It says physician and surgeon on the fancy brass plate of yours by the door, doesn't it?'

'True, Mr. Garvald,' Das told him calmly. 'I have degrees of the Universities of Bombay and London, but that is not the point. You need specialist assistance in this instance.'

Garvald pushed himself up on one elbow. He was in considerable pain and sweat was pouring down his face. 'You listen to me and listen good. A girl died in here three months ago. What the law would call an illegal operation. I know about that and a lot more. Enough to put you away for seven years at least, so if you don't want the coppers in here, get moving on this leg.'

Das seemed quite unperturbed. 'Very well, Mr. Garvald, on your own head be it. I'll have to give you an anaesthetic. You understand this?'

'Give me anything you bleeding well like, only get on with it.'

Garvald closed his eyes. Das opened a cupboard, took out a gauze face mask and a bottle of chloroform. He said to Reuben, 'You'll have to help. Add chloroform to the pad as I tell you, drop by drop. Can you manage it?'

Reuben nodded, too full to speak.

12

It was raining on the following morning when Devlin rode over to Joanna Grey. He parked his bike by the garage and went to the back door. She opened it instantly and drew him inside. She was still in her dressing gown and her face was strained and anxious.

'Thank God, Liam.' She took his face between her two hands and shook him. 'I hardly slept a wink. I've been up since five o'clock drinking whisky and tea alternately. A hell of a mixture at this time in the morning.' She kissed him warmly. 'You rogue, it's good to see you.'

The retriever swung its hindquarters frantically from side-to-side, anxious to be included. Joanna Grey busied herself at the stove and Devlin stood in front of the fire.

'How was it?' she asked.

'All right.'

He was deliberately non-committal, for it seemed likely she might not be too happy about the way he had handled things.

She turned, surprise on her face. 'They didn't try anything?'

'Oh, yes,' he said. 'But I persuaded them otherwise.'

'Any shooting?'

'No need,' he said calmly. 'One look at that Mauser of mine was enough. They're not used to guns, the English criminal fraternity. Razors are more their style.'

She carried the tea things on a tray across to the table. 'God, the English. Sometimes I despair of them.'

'I'll drink to that in spite of the hour. Where's the whisky?'

She went and got the bottle and a couple of glasses. 'This is disgraceful at this time of day, but I'll join you. What do we do now?'

'Wait,' he said. 'I've got the jeep to fix up, but that's all. You'll need to squeeze old Sir Henry dry right up to the last moment, but other than that, all we can do is bite our nails for the next six days.'

'Oh, I don't know,' she said. 'We can always wish ourselves luck.' She raised her glass. 'God bless you, Liam, and long life.'

'And you, my love.'

She raised her glass and drank. Suddenly something moved inside Devlin like a knife in his bowels. In that moment he knew, beyond any shadow of a doubt, that the whole bloody thing was going to go about as wrong as it could do.

Pamela Vereker had a thirty-six-hour pass that weekend, coming off duty at seven a.m., and her brother had driven over to Pangbourne to pick her up. Once at the presbytery, she couldn't wait to get out of uniform and into a pair of jodhpurs and a sweater.

In spite of this symbolic turning away, however temporarily, from the dreadful facts of daily life on a heavy bomber station, she still felt edgy and extremely tired. After lunch she cycled six miles along the coast road to Meltham Vale Farm where the tenant, a parishioner of Vereker's, had a three-year-old stallion badly in need of exercise.

Once over the dunes behind the farm, she gave the stallion his head and galloped along the winding track through the tangled gorse, climbing towards the wooded ridge above. It was completely exhilarating, with the rain beating in her face, and for a while she was back in another, safer place, the world of her childhood that had ended at four forty-five on the morning of 1 September 1939 when General Gerd von Rundsted's Army Group South had invaded Poland.

She entered the trees, following the old forestry commission track and the stallion slowed as it approached the crest of the hill. There was a pine tree across the track a yard or two further on, a windfall. It was no more than three feet high and the stallion took it in its stride. As it landed on the other side, a figure stood up in the undergrowth on the right. The stallion swerved. Pamela Vereker lost her stirrups and was tossed to one side. A rhododendron bush broke her fall, but for a moment she was winded and lay there fighting for breath, aware of voices all around.

'You stupid bastard, Krukowski,' someone said. 'What were you trying to do, kill her?'

The voices were American. She opened her eyes and found a ring of soldiers in combat jackets and steel helmets surrounding her, faces daubed with camouflage cream, all heavily armed. Kneeling beside her was a large rugged Negro with a master sergeant's stripes on his arm. 'You all right, miss?' he asked anxiously.

She frowned and shook her head, and suddenly felt rather better. 'Who are you?'

He touched his helmet in a kind of half-salute. 'Name's Garvey. Master Sergeant. Twenty-first Specialist Raiding Force. We're based at Meltham House for a couple of weeks for field training.'

A jeep arrived at that moment, skidding to a halt in the mud. The driver was an officer, she could tell that, although not sure of his rank, having had little to do with American forces during her service career. He wore a forage cap and normal uniform and was certainly not dressed for manoeuvres.

'What in the hell is going on here?' he demanded.

'Lady got thrown from her horse, Major,' Garvey replied. 'Krukowski jumped out of the bushes at the wrong moment.'

Major, she thought, surprised at his youth. She scrambled to her feet. 'I'm all right, really I am.'

She swayed and the major took her arm. 'I don't think so. Do you live far, ma'am?'

'Studley Constable. My brother is parish priest there.'

He guided her firmly towards the jeep. 'I think you'd better come with me. We've got a medical officer down at Meltham House. I'd like him to make sure you're still in one piece.'

The flash on his shoulder said *Rangers* and she remembered having read somewhere that they were the equivalent of the British Commandos. 'Meltham House?'

'I'm sorry, I should introduce myself. Major Harry Kane, attached to the Twenty-first Specialist Raiding Force under the command of Colonel Robert E. Shafto. We're here for field training.'

'Oh, yes,' she said. 'My brother was telling me that Meltham was being used for some such purpose these days.' She closed her eyes. 'Sorry, I feel a little faint.'

'You just relax. I'll have you there in no time.'

It was a nice voice. Most definitely. For some absurd reason it made her feel quite breathless. She lay back and did exactly as she was told.

The five acres of garden at Meltham House were surrounded by a typical Norfolk flint wall, some eight feet in height. It had been spiked with barbed wire at the top for extra security. Meltham itself was of modest size, a small manor house dating from the early part of the seventeenth century. Like the wall, a great deal of split flint had been used, the construction of the building, particularly the design of the gable ends, showed the Dutch influence typical of the period.

Harry Kane and Pamela strolled through the shrubbery towards the house. He had spent a good hour showing her over the estate and she had enjoyed every minute of it. 'How many of you are there?'

'At the present time, about ninety. Most of the men are under canvas, of course, in the camp area I pointed out on the other side of the spinney.'

'Why wouldn't you take me down there? Secret training or something?'

'Good God, no.' He chuckled. 'You're entirely too good-looking, it's as simple as that.'

A young soldier hurried down the steps of the terrace and came towards them. He saluted smartly. 'Colonel's back, sir. Master Sergeant Garvey is with him now.'

'Very well, Appleby.'

The boy returned Kane's salute, turned and doubled away.

'I thought Americans were supposed to take things terribly easy,' Pamela said.

Kane grinned. 'You don't know Shafto. I think they must have coined the term martinet especially for him.'

As they went up the steps to the terrace, an officer came out through the french windows. He stood facing them, slapping a riding crop against his knee, full of a restless animal vitality. Pamela did not need to be told who he was. Kane saluted. 'Colonel Shafto, allow me to present Miss Vereker.'

Robert Shafto was at that time forty-four years of age, a handsome, arrogant-looking man; a flamboyant figure in polished top boots and riding breeches. He wore a forage cap slanted to his left eye and the two rows of medal ribbons above his left pocket made a bright splash of colour. Perhaps the most extraordinary thing about him was the pearl handled Colt .45 he carried in an open holster on his left hip.

He touched his riding crop to his brow and said gravely, 'I was distressed to hear of your accident, Miss Vereker. If there is anything I can do to make up for the clumsiness of my men . . .'

'That's most kind of you,' she said. 'However, Major Kane here has very kindly offered to run me back to Studley Constable, if you can spare him, that is. My brother is priest there.'

'The least we can do.'

She wanted to see Kane again and there seemed to be only one sure way she could accomplish that. She said, 'We're having a little party at the presbytery tomorrow night. Nothing very special. Just a few friends for drinks and sandwiches. I was wondering whether you and Major Kane would care to join us.' Shafto hesitated. It seemed obvious that he was going to make some excuse and she carried on hurriedly, 'Sir Henry Willoughby will be there, the local squire. Have you met yet?'

Shafto's eyes lit up. 'No, I haven't had that pleasure.'

'Miss Vereker's brother was a padre with the First Parachute Brigade,' Kane said. 'Dropped with them at Oudna in Tunisia last year. You remember that one, Colonel?'

'I certainly do,' Shafto said. 'That was one hell of an affair. Your brother must be quite a man to have survived that, young lady.'

'He was awarded the Military Cross,' she said. 'I'm very proud of him.'

'And so you should be. I'll be happy to attend your little soirée tomorrow night and have the pleasure of meeting him. You make the necessary arrangements, Harry.' He saluted again with the riding crop. 'And now you must excuse me. I have work to do.'

'Were you impressed?' Kane asked her as they drove back along the coast road in his jeep.

'I'm not sure,' she said. 'He's rather a flamboyant figure, you must admit.'

'The understatement of this or any other year,' he said. 'Shafto is what is known in the trade as a fighting soldier. The kind of guy who used to lead his men over the top of some trench in Flanders in the old days armed with a swagger stick. Like that French general said at Balaclava, magnificent, but it isn't war.'

'In other words he doesn't use his head?'

'Well, he does have one hell of a fault from the Army's point of view. He can't take orders – from anybody. Fighting Bobby Shafto, the pride of the infantry. Got himself out of Bataan back in April last year when the Japs overran the place. Only trouble was, he left an infantry regiment behind. That didn't sit too well at the Pentagon. Nobody wanted him so they shipped him over to London to work on the staff at Combined Operations.'

'Which he didn't like?'

'Naturally. Used it as a stepping stone to further glory. He discovered the British had their Small Scale Raiding Force slipping over the Channel by night playing Boy Scouts and decided the American Army should have the same. Unfortunately some imbecile at Combined

Operations thought it was a good idea.'

'Don't you?' she said.

He seemed to evade the question. 'During the past nine months, men from the Twenty-first have raided across the Channel on no fewer than fourteen separate occasions.'

'But that's incredible.'

'Which includes', he carried on, 'the destruction of an empty lighthouse in Normandy and several landings on uninhabited French islands.'

'You don't think much of him, it seems?'

'The great American public certainly does. Three months ago some war reporter, in London and short of a story, heard how Shafto had captured the crew of a lightship off the Belgian coast. There were six of them and as they happened to be German soldiers, it looked pretty good, especially the photos of the landing craft coming into Dover in the grey dawn, Shafto and his boys, one helmet strap dangling, the prisoners looking suitably cowed. Straight off Stage Ten at MGM.' He shook his head. 'How the folks back home bought that one. Shafto's Raiders. *Life, Colliers, Saturday Evening Post.* You name it, he was in there someplace. The people's hero. Two DSCs, Silver Star with Oak Leaf clusters. Everything but the Congressional Medal of Honour and he'll have that before he's through, even if he has to kill the lot of us doing it.'

She said stiffly, 'Why did you join this unit, Major Kane?'

'Stuck behind a desk,' he said. 'That about sums it up. Guess I'd have done just about anything to get out – and did.'

'So you weren't on any of the raids you mention?'

'No, ma'am.'

'Then I suggest you think twice in future before dismissing so lightly the actions of a brave man, especially from the vantage point of a desk.'

He pulled into the side of the road and braked to a halt. He turned to her, smiling cheerfully. 'Heh, I like that. Mind if I write it down to use in that great novel we journalists are always going to write?'

'Damn you, Harry Kane.'

She raised a hand as if to strike him, and he pulled out a pack of Camels and shook one out. 'Have a cigarette instead. Soothes the nerves.'

She took it and the light which followed and inhaled deeply, staring out over the salt marsh towards the sea. 'Sorry, I suppose I am reacting too strongly, but this war has become very personal for me.'

'Your brother?'

'Not only that. My job. When I was on duty yesterday afternoon, I got a fighter pilot on the RT. Badly shot up in a dogfight over the North Sea. His Hurricane was on fire and he was trapped in the cockpit. He screamed all the way down.'

'It started out by being a nice day,' Kane said. 'Suddenly it isn't.'

He reached for the steering wheel and she put her hand on his impulsively. 'I'm sorry – really I am.'

'That's okay.'

Her expression changed to one of puzzlement and she raised his hand. 'What's wrong with your fingers? Several of them are crooked. Your nails . . . Good God, Harry, what happened to your nails?'

'Oh, that?' he said. 'Somebody pulled them out for me.'

She stared at him in horror. 'Was it – was it the Germans, Harry?' she whispered.

'No.' He switched on the engine. 'As a matter of fact they were French, but working for the other side, of course. It's one of life's more distressing discoveries, or so I've found, that it very definitely takes all sorts to make a world.'

He smiled crookedly and drove away.

On the evening of the same day in his private room in the nursing home at Aston, Ben Garvald took a decided turn for the worse. He lost consciousness at six o'clock. His condition was not discovered for another hour. It was eight before Doctor Das arrived in answer to the nurse's urgent phone call, ten past when Reuben walked in and discovered the situation.

He had been back to Fogarty's on Ben's instructions, with a hearse and a coffin obtained from the funeral firm which was another of the Garvald brothers' many business ventures. The unfortunate Jackson had just been disposed of at a local private crematorium in which they also had an interest – not the first time, by any means, that they had got rid of an inconvenient corpse in this way.

Ben's face was bathed in sweat and he groaned, moving from side to side. There was a faint unpleasant odour like rotten meat. Reuben caught a glimpse of the knee as Das lifted the dressing. He turned away, fear rising into his mouth like bile.

'Ben?' he said.

Garvald opened his eyes. For a moment he didn't seem to recognize his brother and then he smiled. 'You get it done, Reuben boy? Did you get rid of him?'

'Ashes to ashes, Ben.'

Garvald closed his eyes and Reuben turned to Das. 'How bad is it?'

'Very bad. There is a chance of gangrene here. I warned him.'

'Oh, my God,' Reuben said. 'I knew he should have gone to hospital.'

Ben Garvald's eyes opened and he glared feverishly. He reached for his brother's wrist. 'No hospital, you hear me? What do you want to do?

Give those bleeding coppers the opening they've been looking for for
years?'

He fell back, eyes closed again. Das said, 'There is one chance. There
is a drug called penicillin. You have heard of it?'

'Sure I have. They say it'll cure anything. Fetches a fortune on the
black market.'

'Yes, it has quite miraculous results in cases like this. Can you get hold
of some? Now – tonight?'

'If it's in Birmingham,you'll have it within an hour.' Reuben walked
to the door and turned. 'But if he dies, then you go with him, son. That's
a promise.'

He went out and the door swung behind him.

At the same moment in Landsvoort the Dakota lifted off the runway and
turned out to sea. Gericke didn't waste any time. Simply took her straight
up to a thousand feet, banked to starboard and dropped down towards
the coast. Inside, Steiner and his men made ready. They were all dressed
in full British paratroop gear, all weapons and equipment stowed in
suspension bags in the British manner. 'All right,' Steiner called.

They all stood and clipped their lines to the anchor line cable, each
man checking the comrade in front of him, Steiner seeing to Harvey
Preston who was last in line. The Englishman was trembling, Steiner
could feel it as he tightened his straps for him.

'Fifteen seconds,' he said 'So you haven't got long – understand? And
get this straight, all of you. If you're going to break a leg, do it here. Not
in Norfolk.'

There was general laugh and he walked to the front of the line where
Ritter Neumann checked his straps. Steiner slid back the door as the red
light blinked above his head and there was the sudden roaring of the
wind.

In the cockpit, Gericke throttled back and went in low. The tide was
out, the wide, wet lonely beaches pale in the moonlight, stretching into
infinity. Bohmler, beside him, was concentrating on the altimeter. 'Now!'
Gericke cried and Bohmler was ready for him.

The green light flared above Steiner's head, he slapped Ritter on the
shoulder. The young Oberleutnant went out followed by the entire stick,
very fast, ending with Brandt. As for Preston, he stood there, mouth
gaping, staring out into the night.

'Go on!' Steiner cried and grabbed for his shoulder.

Preston pulled away, holding on to a steel strut to support himself. He
shook his head, mouth working. 'Can't!' he finally managed to say. 'Can't
do it!'

Steiner struck him across the face back-handed, grabbed him by the right arm and slung him towards the open door. Preston hung there, bracing himself with both hands. Steiner put a foot in his rear and shoved him out into space. Then he clipped on to the anchor line and went after him.

When you jump at four hundred feet there isn't really time to be frightened. Preston was aware of himself somersaulting, the sudden jerk, the slap of the 'chute catching air and then he was swinging beneath the dark khaki umbrella.

It was fantastic. The moon pale on the horizon, the flat wet sands, the creamy line of the surf. He could see the E-boat by the sand pier quite clearly, men watching and further along the beach a line of collapsed parachutes as the others gathered them in. He glanced up and caught a glimpse of Steiner above him and to the left and then seemed to be going in very fast.

The supply bag, swinging twenty feet below at the end of a line clipped to his waist, hit the sand with a solid thump warning him to get ready. He went in hard, too hard, or so it seemed, rolled and miraculously found himself on his feet, the parachute billowing up like some pale flower in the moonlight.

He moved in quickly to deflate it as he had been taught and suddenly paused there on his hands and knees, a sense of overwhelming joy, of personal power sweeping through him of a kind he had never known in his life before.

'I did it!' he cried aloud. 'I showed the bastards. I did it! I did it! I did it!'

In the bed at the nursing home in Aston Ben Garvald lay very still. Reuben stood at the end and waited as Doctor Das probed for a heartbeat with his stethoscope.

'How is he?' Reuben demanded.

'Still alive, but only just.'

Reuben made his decision and acted on it. He grabbed Das by the shoulder and shoved him at the door. 'You get an ambulance round here quick as you like. I'm having him in hospital.'

'But that will mean the police, Mr. Garvald,' Das pointed out.

'Do you think I care?' Reuben said hoarsely. 'I want him alive, understand? He's my brother. Now get moving!'

He opened the door and pushed Das out. When he turned back to the bed there were tears in his eyes. 'I promise you one thing, Ben,' he said brokenly. 'I'll have that little Irish bastard for this if it's the last thing I do.'

13

At forty-five, Jack Rogan had been a policeman for nearly a quarter of a century – a long time to work a three-shift system and be disliked by the neighbours. But that was the policeman's lot, and only to be expected, as he frequently pointed out to his wife.

It was nine-thirty on Tuesday 2 November when he entered his office at Scotland Yard. By rights, he shouldn't have been there at all. Having spent a lengthy night at Muswell Hill interrogating members of an Irish club, he was entitled to a few hours in bed, but there was a little paperwork to clear up first.

He'd just settled down at his desk when there was a knock at the door and his assistant, Detective Inspector Fergus Grant, entered. Grant was the younger son of a retired Indian Army colonel. Winchester and Hendon Police College. One of the new breed who were supposed to revolutionise the Force. In spite of this, he and Rogan got on well together.

Rogan put up a hand defensively. 'Fergus, all I want to do is sign a few letters, have a cup of tea and go home to bed. Last night was hell.'

'I know, sir,' Grant said. 'It's just that we've had a rather unusual report in from the City of Birmingham Police. I thought it might interest you.'

'You mean me in particular or the Irish Section?'

'Both.'

'All right.' Rogan pushed back his chair and started to fill his pipe from a worn, leather pouch. 'I'm not in the mood for reading so tell me about it.'

'Ever hear of a man called Garvald, sir?'

Rogan paused. 'You mean Ben Garvald? He's been bad news for years. Biggest villain in the Midlands.'

'He died early this morning. Gangrene as the result of a gunshot wound. The hospital got their hands on him too late.'

Rogan struck a match. 'There are people I know who might say that was the best bit of news they'd heard in years, but how does it affect us?'

'He was shot in the right kneecap, by an Irishman.'

Rogan stared at him. 'That *is* interesting. The statutory IRA punishment when someone tries to cross you.' He cursed as the match in his left hand burned down to his fingers and dropped it. 'What was his name, this Irishman?'

'Murphy, sir.'

'It would be. Is there more?'

'You could say that,' Grant told him. 'Garvald had a brother who's so cut up about his death that he's singing like a bird. He wants friend Murphy nailing to the door.'

Rogan nodded. 'We'll have to see if we can oblige him. What was it all about?'

Grant told him in some detail and by the time he had finished, Rogan was frowning. 'An Army truck, a jeep, khaki-green paint? What would he want with that little lot?'

'Maybe they're going to try a raid on some army camp, sir, to get arms.'

Rogan got up and walked to the window. 'No, I can't buy that, not without firm evidence. They're just not active enough at the moment. Not capable of that kind of ploy, you know that.' He came back to the desk. 'We've broken the back of the IRA here in England, and in Ireland de Valera's put most of them in internment at the Curragh.' He shook his head. 'It wouldn't make sense that kind of operation at this stage. What did Garvald's brother make of it?'

'He seemed to think Murphy was organising a raid on a NAAFI depot or something like that. You know the sort of thing? Drive in dressed as soldiers in an army truck.'

'And drive out again with fifty thousand quids' worth of scotch and cigarettes. It's been done before,' Rogan said.

'So Murphy's just another thief on the take, sir? Is that your hunch?'

'I'd accept that if it wasn't for the bullet in the kneecap. That's pure IRA. No, my left ear's twitching about this one, Fergus. I think we could be on to something.'

'All right, sir, what's the next move?'

Rogan walked over to the window thinking about it. Outside it was typical autumn weather, fog drifting across the rooftops from the Thames, rain dripping from the sycamore trees.

He turned. 'I know one thing. I'm not having Birmingham cock this up for us. You handle it personally. Book a car from the pool and get up there today. Take the files with you, photos, the lot. Every known IRA man not under wrappers. Maybe Garvald can pick him out for us.'

'And if not, sir?'

'Then we start asking questions at this end. All the usual channels. Special Branch in Dublin will help all they can. They hate the IRA worse than ever since they shot Detective Sergeant O'Brien last year. You always feel worse when it's one of your own.'

'Right, sir,' Grant said. 'I'll get moving.'

It was eight that evening when General Karl Steiner finished the meal which had been served to him in his room on the second floor at Prinz Albrechtstrasse. A chicken leg, potatoes fried in oil, just as he liked them, a tossed salad and a half-bottle of Riesling, served ice-cold. Quite incredible. And real coffee to follow.

Things had certainly changed since the final terrible night when he had collapsed after the electrical treatment. The following morning he had awakened to find himself lying between clean sheets in a comfortable bed. No sign of that bastard Rossman and his Gestapo bully boys. Just an Obersturmbannführer named Zeidler, a thoroughly decent type, even if he was SS. A gentleman.

He had been full of apologies. A dreadful mistake had been made. False information had been laid with malicious intent. The Reichsführer himself had ordered the fullest possible enquiry. Those responsible would undoubtedly be apprehended and punished. In the meantime, he regretted the fact that the Herr General still had to be kept under lock and key, but this would only be for a matter of a few days. He was sure he understood the situation.

Which Steiner did perfectly. All they had ever had against him was innuendo, nothing concrete, and he hadn't said a word in spite of everything Rossman had done, so the whole thing was going to look like one God-Almighty foul-up on someone's part. They were hanging on to him now to make sure he looked good for when they released him. Already, the bruises had almost faded. Except for the rings around his eyes he looked fine. They'd even given him a new uniform.

The coffee was really quite excellent. He started to pour another cup and the key rattled in the lock and the door opened behind him. There was an uncanny silence. The hair seemed to lift on the back of his head.

He turned slowly and found Karl Rossman standing in the doorway. He was wearing his slouch hat, the leather coat over his shoulders and a cigarette dangled from the corner of his mouth. Two Gestapo men in full uniform stood on either side of him.

'Hello, there, Herr General,' Rossman said. 'Did you think we'd forgotten you?'

Something seemed to break inside Steiner. The whole thing became dreadfully clear. 'You bastard!' he said and threw the cup of coffee at Rossman's head.

'Very naughty,' Rossman said. 'You shouldn't have done that.'

One of the Gestapo men moved in quickly. He rammed the end of his baton into Steiner's groin, who dropped to his knees with a scream of agony. A further blow to the side of the head put him down completely.

'The cellars,' Rossman said simply, and went out.

The two Gestapo men got an ankle apiece and followed, dragging the General behind them face-down, keeping in step with a military precision that didn't even falter when they reached the stairs.

Max Radl knocked at the door of the Reichsführer's office and went in. Himmler was standing in front of the fire, drinking coffee. He put down his cup and crossed to the desk. 'I had hoped that you would have been on your way by now.'

'I leave on the overnight flight for Paris,' Radl told him. 'As the Herr Reichsführer is aware, Admiral Canaris only flew to Italy this morning.'

'Unfortunate,' Himmler said. 'However, it should still leave you plenty of time.' He removed his pince-nez and polished them as meticulously as usual. 'I've read the report you gave Rossman this morning. What about these American Rangers who have appeared in the area? Show me.'

He unfolded the ordnance survey map in front of him and Radl put a finger on Meltham House. 'As you can see, Herr Reichsführer, Meltham House is eight miles to the north along the coast from Studley Constable. Twelve or thirteen from Hobs End. Mrs. Grey anticipates no trouble whatsoever in that direction in her latest radio message.'

Himmler nodded. 'Your Irishman seems to have earned his wages. The rest is up to Steiner.'

'I don't think he'll let us down.'

'Yes, I was forgetting,' Himmler said dryly. 'He has, after all, a personal stake in this.'

Radl said, 'May I be permitted to enquire after Major-General Steiner's health?'

'I last saw him yesterday evening,' Himmler replied with perfect truth, 'although I must confess he did not see me. At that time he was working his way through a meal consisting of roast potatoes, mixed vegetables and a rather large rump steak.' He sighed. 'If only these meat eaters realised the effect on the system of such a diet. Do you eat meat, Herr Oberst?'

'I'm afraid so.'

'And smoke sixty or seventy of those vile Russian cigarettes a day and drink. What is your brandy consumption now?' He shook his head as he shuffled his papers into a neat pile in front of him. 'Ah, well, in your case I don't suppose it really matters.'

Is there anything the swine doesn't know? Radl thought. 'No, Herr Reichsführer.'

'What time do they leave on Friday?'

'Just before midnight. A one-hour flight, weather permitting.'

Himmler looked up instantly, eyes cold. 'Colonel Radl, let me make one thing perfectly plain. Steiner and his men go in as arranged, weather or no weather. This is not something that can be postponed until another night. This is a once in a lifetime opportunity. There will be a line kept open to these headquarters at all times. From Friday morning you will communicate with me each hour on the hour and continue so doing until the operation is successfully concluded.'

'I will, Herr Reichsführer.'

Radl turned for the door and Himmler said, 'One more thing. I have not kept the Führer informed of our progress in this affair for many reasons. These are hard times, Radl, the destiny of Germany rests on his shoulders. I would like this to be – how can I put it? – a surprise for him.'

For a moment, Radl thought he must be going out of his mind. Then realised that Himmler was serious. 'It is essential that we don't disappoint him,' Himmler went on. 'We are all in Steiner's hands now. Please impress that on him.'

'I will, Herr Reichsführer.' Radl choked back an insane desire to laugh.

Himmler flipped up his right arm in a rather negligent party salute. 'Heil Hitler!'

Radl, in what he afterwards swore to his wife was the bravest action of his entire life, gave him a punctilious military salute, turned to the door and got out as fast as he could.

When he went into his office at the Tirpitz Ufer, Hofer was packing an overnight bag for him. Radl got out the Courvoisier and poured himself a large one. 'Is the Herr Oberst all right?' Hofer enquired anxiously.

'You know what our esteemed Reichsführer has just let slip, Karl? He hasn't told the Führer about how far along the road we are with this thing. He wants to surprise him. Now isn't that sweet?'

'Herr Oberst, for God's sake.'

Radl raised his glass. 'To our comrades, Karl, the three hundred and ten of the regiment who died in the Winter War, I'm not sure what for. If you find out, let me know.' Hofer stared at him and Radl smiled. 'All right, Karl, I'll be good. Did you check the time of my Paris flight?'

'Ten-thirty from Tempelhof. I've ordered a car for nine-fifteen. You have plenty of time.'

'And the onward flight to Amsterdam?'

'Some time tomorrow morning. Probably about eleven, but they couldn't be sure.'

'That's cutting it fine. All I need is a little dirty weather and I won't get to Landvoort till Thursday. What's the met. report?'

'Not good. A cold front coming in from Russia.'

'There always is,' Radl told him bleakly. He opened the desk drawer and took out a sealed envelope. 'That's for my wife. See that she gets it. Sorry you can't come with me, but you must hold the fort here, you understand that?'

Hofer looked down at the letter and there was fear in his eyes. 'Surely the Herr Oberst doesn't think . . .'

'My dear, good Karl,' Radl told him. 'I think nothing. I simply prepare for any unpleasant eventuality. If this thing goes wrong then it seems to me that those connected with it might not be considered – how shall I put it? – persona grata at court. In any such eventuality your own line should be to deny all knowlege of the affair. Anything I've done, I've done alone.'

'Herr Oberst, please,' Hofer said hoarsely. There were tears in his eyes.

Radl took out another glass, filled it and handed it to him. 'Come now, a toast. What shall we drink to?'

'God knows, Herr Oberst.'

'Then I shall tell you. To life, Karl, and love and friendship and hope.' He smiled wryly. 'You know, it's just occurred to me that the Reichsführer very probably doesn't know the first thing about any one of these items. Ah, well . . .'

He threw back his head and emptied his glass at a single swallow.

Like most senior officers at Scotland Yard, Jack Rogan had a small camp bed in his office for use on those occasions when air raids made travelling home a problem. When he came back from the Assistant Commissioner, Special Branch's, weekly co-ordinating meeting with section heads on Wednesday morning just before noon, he found Grant asleep on it, eyes closed.

Rogan stuck his head out of the door and told the duty constable to make some tea. Then he gave Grant a friendly kick and went and stood at the window filling his pipe. The fog was worse than ever. A real London particular, as Dickens has once aptly phrased it.

Grant got up, adjusting his tie. His suit was crumpled and he needed a shave. 'Hell of a journey back. The fog was really quite something.'

'Did you get anywhere?'

Grant opened his briefcase, took out a file and produced a card which he laid on Rogan's desk. A photo of Liam Devlin was clipped to it. Strangely enough he looked older. There were several different names typed underneath. 'That's Murphy, sir.'

Rogan whistled softly. 'Him? Are you sure?'

'Reuben Garvald is.'

'But this doesn't make sense.' Rogan said. 'Last I heard, he was in trouble in Spain, fighting for the wrong side. Serving a life sentence on some penal farm.'

'Evidently not, sir.'

Rogan jumped up and walked to the window. He stood there, hands in pockets, for a moment. 'You know, he's one of the few top-liners in the movement I've never met. Always the mystery man. All those bloody aliases for one thing.'

'Went to Trinity College according to his file, which is unusual for a Catholic,' Grant said. 'Good degree in English Literature. There's irony, considering he's in the IRA.'

'That's the bloody Irish for you.' Rogan turned, prodding a finger into his skull. 'Puddled from birth. Round the twist. I mean his uncle's a priest, he has a university degree and what is he? The most cold-blooded executioner the movement's had since Collins and his Murder Squad.'

'All right, sir,' Grant said. 'How do we handle it?'

'First of all get in touch with the Special Branch in Dublin. See what they've got.'

'And next?'

'If he's here legally he must have registered with his local police, wherever that is. Alien's registration form plus photograph.'

'Which are then passed on to the headquarters of the force concerned.'

'Exactly.' Rogan kicked the desk. 'I've been arguing for two years now that we should have them on a central file, but with nearly three-quarters of a million micks working over here nobody wants to know.'

'That means circulating copies of this photo to all city and county forces and asking for someone to go through every registration on file.' Grant picked up the card. 'It'll take time.'

'What else can we do, stick it in the paper and say: *Has anybody seen this man?* I want to know what he's up to, Fergus, I want to catch him at it, not frighten him off.'

'Of course, sir.'

'Just get on with it. Top Priority. Give it a National Security Red File rating. That will make the buggers jump to it.'

Grant went out and Rogan picked up Devlin's file, leaned back in the chair and started to read it.

In Paris, all aircraft were grounded and the fog was so thick that when Radl walked out of the entrance of the departure lounge at Orly he couldn't see his hand in front of his face. He went back inside and spoke to the Duty Officer. 'What do you think?'

'I'm sorry, Herr Oberst, but on the basis of the latest met. report, nothing before morning. To be honest with you, there could be further

delays even then. They seem to think this fog could last for some days.'
He smiled amiably. 'It keeps the *tommis* at home, anyway.'

Radl made his decision and reached for his bag. 'Absolutely essential
that I'm in Rotterdam no later than tomorrow afternoon. Where's the
motor pool?'

Ten minutes later he was holding the Führer directive under the nose
of a middle-aged transport captain and twenty minutes after that was
being driven out of the main gate of Orly Airport in a large, black
Citroën saloon.

At the same moment in the sitting room of Joanna Grey's cottage at
Studley Constable, Sir Henry Willoughby was playing bezique with
Father Vereker and Joanna Grey. He had had more to drink than was
perhaps good for him and was in high good humour.

'Let me see now, I had a Royal Marriage – forty points and now a
sequence in trumps.'

'How many is that?' Vereker demanded.

'Two hundred and fifty,' Joanna Grey said. 'Two-ninety with his
Royal Marriage.'

'Just a minute,' Vereker said. 'He's got a ten above the Queen.'

'But I explained that earlier,' Joanna told him. 'In bezique, the ten *does*
come before the Queen.'

Philip Vereker shook his head in disgust. 'It's no good. I'll never
understand this damned game.'

Sir Henry laughed delightedly. 'A gentleman's game, my boy. The
aristocrat of card games.' He jumped up, knocking his chair over and
righted it. 'Mind if I help myself, Joanna?'

'Of course not, my dear,' she said brightly.

'You seem pleased with yourself tonight,' Vereker remarked.

Sir Henry, warming his backside in front of the fire, grinned. 'I am,
Philip, I am and good cause to be.' It all came flowing out of him in a
sudden burst. 'Don't see why I shouldn't tell you. You'll know soon
enough now.'

God, the old fool. Joanna Grey's alarm was genuine as she said hastily,
'Henry, do you think you should?'

'Why not?' he said. 'If I can't trust you and Philip, who can I trust.' He
turned to Vereker. 'Fact is, the Prime Minister is coming to stay the
weekend on Saturday.'

'Good heavens. I'd heard he was speaking at King's Lynn, of course.'
Vereker was astounded. 'To be honest, sir, I didn't realise you knew Mr.
Churchill.'

'I don't,' Sir Henry said. 'Thing is he fancied a quiet weekend and a little painting before going back to town. Naturally he'd heard about the gardens at Studley, I mean who hasn't? Laid down in the Armada year. When Downing Street got in touch to ask if he could stay, I was only too delighted.'

'Naturally,' Vereker said.

'Now you must keep it to yourselves, I'm afraid.' Sir Henry said. 'Villagers can't know till he's gone. They're most insistent about that. Security, you know. Can't be too careful.'

He was very drunk now, slurring his words. Vereker said, 'I suppose he'll be quite heavily guarded.'

'Not at all,' Sir Henry said. 'Wants as little fuss as possible. He'll only have three or four people with him. I've arranged for a platoon of my Home Guard chaps to guard the perimeter of the Grange while he's there. Even they don't know what it's all about. Think it's an exercise.'

'Is that so?' Joanna said.

'Yes, I'm to go up to King's Lynn on Saturday to meet him. We'll come back by car.' He belched and put down his glass. 'I say, would you excuse me? Don't feel too good.'

'Of course,' Joanna Grey said.

He walked to the door, turned and put a finger to his nose. 'Mum's the word now.'

After he'd gone, Vereker said, 'That is a turn-up for the book.'

'He's really very naughty,' Joanna said. 'He isn't supposed to say a word and yet he told me in exactly similar circumstances when he'd had too much to drink. Naturally I felt bound to keep quiet about it.'

'Of course,' he said. 'You were absolutely right.' He stood up, groping for his stick. 'I'd better run him home. He's not fit to drive.'

'Nonsense.' She took his arm and steered him to the door. 'That would mean you having to walk up to the presbytery to get your own car out. There's no need. I'll take him.'

She helped him into his coat. 'If you're sure, then?'

'Of course.' She kissed his cheek. 'I'm looking forward to seeing Pamela on Saturday.'

He limped away into the night. She stood at the door listening as the sound of his progress faded. It was so still and quiet, almost as quiet as the veldt when she was a young girl. Strange, but she hadn't thought of that for years.

She went back inside and closed the door. Sir Henry appeared from the downstairs cloakroom and weaved an unsteady path to his chair by the fire. 'Must go, old girl.'

'Nonsense,' she said. 'Always time for another one.' She poured two fingers of Scotch into his glass and sat on one arm of the chair, gently stroking his neck. 'You know, Henry, I'd love to meet the Prime Minister. I think I'd like that more than anything else in the world.'

'Would you, old girl?' He gazed up at her foolishly.

She smiled and gently brushed her lips along his forehead. 'Well, almost anything.'

It was very quiet in the cellars at Prinz Albrechtstrasse as Himmler went down the stairs. Rossman was waiting at the bottom. His sleeves were rolled up to the elbows and he was very pale.

'Well?' Himmler demanded.

'He's dead, I'm afraid, Herr Reichsführer.'

Himmler was not pleased and showed it. 'That seems singularly careless of you, Rossman. I told you to take care.'

'With all due respect, Herr Reichsführer, it was his heart which gave out. Dr. Prager will confirm this. I sent for him at once. He's still in there.'

He opened the nearest door. Rossman's two Gestapo assistants stood at one side, still wearing rubber gloves and aprons. A small, brisk-looking man in a tweed suit was leaning over the body on the iron cot in the corner, probing the naked chest with a stethoscope.

He turned as Himmler entered and gave the party salute. 'Herr Reichsführer.'

Himmler stood looking down at Steiner for a while. The General was stripped to the waist and his feet were bare. His eyes were partly open, fixed, staring into eternity.

'Well?' Himmler demanded.

'His heart, Herr Reichsführer. No doubt about it.'

Himmler removed his pince-nez and gently rubbed between his eyes. He'd had a headache all afternoon and it simply would not go away. 'Very well, Rossman,' he said. 'He was guilty of treason against the State, of plotting against the life of the Führer himself. As you know, the Führer has decreed a statutory punishment for this offence and Major-General Steiner cannot evade this, even in death.'

'Of course, Herr Reichsführer.'

'See that the sentence is carried out. I won't stay myself, I am summoned to Rastenburg but take photographs and dispose of the body in the usual way.'

They all clicked their heels in the party salute and left.

He was arrested where?' Rogan said in astonishment. It was just before five and already dark enough for the blackout curtains to be drawn.

'At a farmhouse near Caragh Lake in Kerry in June last year, after a gunfight in which he shot two policemen and was wounded himself. He escaped from the local hospital the following day and dropped out of sight.'

'Dear God and they call themselves policemen,' Rogan said in despair.

'The thing is, Special Branch, Dublin, weren't involved in any of this, sir. They only identified him later by the prints on the revolver. The arrest was made by a patrol from the local *Garda* barracks checking for an illicit still. One other point, sir. Dublin say they checked with the Spanish Foreign Office, our friend supposedly being in gaol over there. They were reluctant to come across, you know how difficult they can be about this kind of thing. They finally admitted that he'd escaped from a penal farm in Granada in the autumn of 1940. Their information was that he'd made it to Lisbon and taken passage to the States.'

'And now he's back,' Rogan said. 'But what for? That's the thing. Have you heard from any of the provincial forces yet?'

'Seven, sir – all negative, I'm afraid.'

'All right. There's nothing more we can do at the moment except hope. The moment you have anything, contact me instantly. Day or night, no matter where I am.'

'Very well, sir.'

14

It was precisely eleven-fifteen on Friday morning at Meltham Grange when Harry Kane, who was supervising a squad's progess over the assault course, received an urgent summons to report to Shafto at once. When he reached his commanding officer's outer office he found things in something of a turmoil. The clerks looked frightened and Master-Sergeant Garvey paced up and down, smoking a cigarette nervously.

'What's happened?' Kane demanded.

'God knows, Major. All I know is he blew his stack about fifteen minutes ago after receiving an urgent despatch from Headquarters. Kicked young Jones clean out of the office. And I mean kicked.'

Kane knocked at the door and went in. Shafto was standing at the window, his riding crop in one hand, a glass in the other. He turned angrily and then his expression changed. 'Oh, it's you, Harry.'

'What is it, sir?'

'It's simple. Those bastards up at Combined Operations who've been trying to get me out of the way have finally managed it. When we finish here next weekend, I hand over command to Sam Williams.'

'And you, sir?'

'I'm to go back Stateside. Chief Instructor in Fieldcraft at Fort Benning.'

He kicked a wastepaper bin clean across the room and Kane said, 'Isn't there anything you can do about it, sir?'

Shafto turned on him like a madman. 'Do about it?' He picked up the order and pushed it into Kane's face. 'See the signature on that? Eisenhower himself.' He crumpled it into a ball and threw it away. 'And you know something, Kane? He's never been in action. Not once in his entire career.'

At Hobs End Devlin was lying in bed writing in his personal notebook. It was raining hard and outside mist draped itself over the marsh in a damp, clinging shroud. The door was pushed open and Molly came in. She was wearing Devlin's trenchcoat and carried a tray which she put down on the table beside the bed.

'There you are, O lord and master. Tea and toast, two boiled eggs, four and a half minutes as you suggested, and cheese sandwiches.'

Devlin stopped writing and looked at the tray appreciatively. 'Keep up this standard and I might be tempted to take you on permanently.'

She took off the trenchcoat. Underneath she was only wearing pants and a bra and she picked up her sweater from the end of the bed and pulled it over her head. 'I'll have to get moving. I told Mum I'd be in for my dinner.'

He poured himself a cup of tea and she picked up the notebook. 'What's this?' She opened it. 'Poetry?'

He grinned. 'A matter of opinion in some quarters.'

'Yours?' she said and there was genuine wonder on her face. She opened it at the place where he had been writing that morning. 'There is no certain knowledge of my passing, where I have walked in woodland after dark.' She looked up. 'Why, that's beautiful, Liam.'

'I know,' he said. 'Like you keep telling me, I'm a lovely boy.'

'I know one thing, I could eat you up.' She flung herself on top of him and kissed him fiercely. 'You know what today is? The fifth of November only we can't have no bonfire because of rotten old Adolf.'

'What a shame,' he jeered.

'Never you mind.' She wriggled into a comfortable position, her legs straddling him. 'I'll come round tonight and cook you supper and we'll have a nice little bonfire all our own.'

'No, you won't,' he said. 'Because I shan't be here.'

Her face clouded. 'Business?'

He kissed her lightly. 'Now you know what you promised.'

All right,' she said. 'I'll be good. I'll see you in the morning.'

'No. I probably won't get back till tomorrow afternoon. Far better to leave it that I'll call for you – all right?'

She nodded reluctantly. 'If you say so.'

'I do.'

He kissed her and there was the sound of a horn outside. Molly darted to the window and came back in a hurry, grabbing for her denim trousers. 'My God, it's Mrs. Grey.'

'That's what's called being caught with your pants down,' Devlin told her, laughing.

He pulled on a sweater. Molly reached for her coat. 'I'm off. I'll see you tomorrow, beautiful. Can I take this? I'd like to read the others.'

She held up his notebook of poetry. 'God, but you must like punishment,' he said.

She kissed him hard and he followed her out, opening the back door for her, standing watching her run through the reeds to the dyke, knowing that this could well be the end. 'Ah, well,' he said softly. 'The best thing for her.'

He turned and went to open the door in answer to Joanna Grey's repeated knocking. She surveyed him grimly as he tucked his shirt into his trousers. 'I caught a glimpse of Molly on the dyke path a second ago.' She walked past him. 'You really should be ashamed of yourself.'

'I know,' he said as he followed her into the sitting room. 'I'm a terrible bad lot. Well, the big day. I'd say that warrants a little nip. Will you join me?'

'Quarter of an inch in the bottom of the glass and no more,' she said sternly.

He brought the Bushmills and two glasses and poured a couple of drinks. 'Up the Republic!' he told her. 'Both the Irish and South African varieties. Now, what's the news?'

'I switched to the new wavelength last night as ordered, transmitting directly to Landsvoort. Radl himself is there now.'

'And it's still on?' Devlin said. 'In spite of the weather?'

Her eyes were shining. 'Come hell or high water, Steiner and his men will be here at approximately one o'clock.'

Steiner was addressing the assault group in his quarters. The only person present other than those actually making the drop was Max Radl. Even Gericke had been excluded. They all stood around the map table. There was an atmosphere of nervous excitement as Steiner turned from the window where he had been talking to Radl in a low voice and faced them. He indicated Gerhard Klugl's model, the photos, the maps.

'All right. You all know where you're going. Every stick, every stone of it, which has been the object of the exercise for the past few weeks. What you don't know is what we're supposed to do when we get there.'

He paused, glancing at each face in turn, tense, expectant. Even Preston, who, after all, had known for some time, seemed caught by the drama of the occasion.

So Steiner told them.

Peter Gericke could hear the roar from as far away as the hangar.

'Now what's happening, for God's sake?' Bohmler said.

'Don't ask me,' Gericke replied sourly. 'Nobody tells me anything around here.' The bitterness suddenly overflowed. 'If we're good enough to risk our necks flying the sods in, you'd think we might at least be told what it's all about.'

'If it's as important as that,' Bohmler said, 'I'm not sure I want to know. I'm going to check the Lichtenstein set.'

He climbed into the plane and Gericke lit a cigarette and moved a little further away, looking the Dakota over again. Sergeant Witt had done a lovely job on the RAF roundels. He turned and saw the field car moving across the airstrip towards him, Ritter Neumann at the wheel, Steiner beside him, Radl in the rear. It braked to a halt a yard or two away. No one got out.

Steiner said, 'You don't look too pleased with life, Peter.'

'Why should I?' Gericke said. 'A whole month I've spent in this dump, worked all the hours God sends on that plane in there and for what?' His gesture took in the mist, the rain, the entire sky. 'In this kind of shit I'll never even get off the ground.'

'Oh, we have every confidence that a man of your very special calibre will be able to accomplish that.'

They started to get out of the field wagon and Ritter particularly was having the greatest difficulty in holding back his laughter. 'Look, what's going on here?' Gericke said truculently. 'What's it all about?'

'Why, it's really quite simple, you poor, miserable, hard-done-to son of a bitch,' Radl said. 'I have the honour to inform you that you have just been awarded the Knight's Cross.'

Gericke stared at him, open-mouthed and Steiner said gently, 'So, you see, my dear Peter, you get your weekend at Karinhall after all.'

Koenig leaned over the chart table with Steiner and Radl and Chief Petty Officer Muller stood at a respectful distance, but missing nothing.

The young lieutenant said, 'Four months ago a British armed trawler was torpedoed off the Hebrides by a U-boat under the command of Horst

Wengel, an old friend of mine. There were only fifteen in the crew so he took them all prisoner. Unfortunately for them, they hadn't managed to get rid of their documents, which included some interesting charts of the British coastal minefields.'

'That was a break for somebody,' Steiner said.

'For all of us, Herr Oberst, as these latest charts from Wilhemshaven prove. See, here, east of the Wash where the minefield runs parallel to the coast to protect the inshore shipping lane? There is a route through quite clearly marked. The British Navy made it for their own purposes, but units of the Eighth E-boat Flotilla out of Rotterdam have used it with perfect safety for some time now. In fact, as long as navigation is accurate enough, one may proceed at speed.'

'There would seem to be an argument for saying that the minefield itself in such circumstances will afford you considerable protection,' Radl said.

'Exactly, Herr Oberst.'

'And what about the estuary approach behind the Point to Hobs End?'

'Difficult certainly, but Muller and I have studied the Admiralty Charts until we know them by heart. Every sounding, every sandbank. We will be going in on a rising tide, remember, if we are to make the pick-up at ten.'

'You estimate eight hours for the passage which would mean your leaving here at what – one o'clock?'

'If we are to have a margin at the other end in which to operate. Of course, this is a unique craft as you know. She could do the trip in seven hours if it comes to that. I'm just playing safe.'

'Very sensible,' Radl said, 'because Colonel Steiner and I have decided to modify your orders. I want you off the Point and ready to go in for the pick-up at *any* time between nine and ten. You'll get your final run-in orders from Devlin on the S-phone. Be guided by him.'

'Very well, Herr Oberst.'

'You shouldn't be in any particular danger under cover of darkness,' Steiner said and smiled. 'After all, this is a British ship.'

Koenig grinned, opened a cupboard under the chart table and took out a British Navy White Ensign. 'And we'll be flying this, remember.'

Radl nodded. 'Radio silence from the moment you leave. Under no circumstances must you break it until you hear from Devlin. You know the code sign, of course.'

'Naturally, Herr Oberst.'

Koenig was being polite and Radl clapped him on the shoulder. 'Yes, I know, to you I am a nervous old man. I'll see you tomorrow before you leave. You'd better say goodbye to Colonel Steiner now.'

Steiner shook hands with both of them. 'I don't quite know what to say except: Be on time for God's sake.'

Koenig gave him a perfect naval salute. 'I'll see you on that beach, Herr Oberst, I promise you.'

Steiner smiled wryly. 'I damn well hope so.' He turned and followed Radl outside.

As they walked along the sand pier towards the field car Radl said, 'Well, is it going to work, Kurt?'

At that moment Werner Briegel and Gerhard Klugl came over the sand dunes. They were wearing ponchos and Briegel's Zeiss fieldglasses were slung around his neck.

'Let's seek their opinion,' Steiner suggested and called out in English, 'Private Kunicki! Private Moczar! Over here, please!' Briegel and Klugl doubled across without hesitation. Steiner looked them over calmly and continued in English, 'Who am I?'

'Lieutenant-Colonel Howard Carter, in command of the Polish Independent Parachute Squadron, Special Air Service Regiment,' Briegel replied promptly in good English.

Radl turned to Steiner with a smile, 'I'm impressed.'

Steiner said, 'What are you doing here?'

'Sergeant-Major Brandt,' Briegel began and hastily corrected himself. 'Sergeant-Major Kruczek told us to relax.' He hesitated then added in German, 'We're looking for shorelarks, Herr Oberst.'

'Shorelarks?' Steiner said.

'Yes, they're quite easy to distinguish. A most striking black and yellow pattern on face and throat.'

Steiner exploded into laughter. 'You see, my dear Max? Shorelarks. How can we possibly fail?'

But the elements seemed determined to make sure that they did. As darkness, fell, fog still blanketed most of Western Europe. At Landsvoort, Gericke inspected the airstrip constantly from six o'clock onwards, but in spite of the heavy rain the fog was as thick as ever.

'There's no wind, you see,' he informed Steiner and Radl at eight o'clock. 'That's what we need now to clear this damn stuff away. Lots of wind.'

Across the North Sea in Norfolk things were no better. In the secret cubbyhole in the loft of her cottage, Joanna Grey sat by the radio receiver in her headphones and filled in the time reading a book Vereker had lent her in which Winston Churchill described how he had escaped from a prison camp during the Boer War. It was really quite enthralling and she was conscious of a rather reluctant admiration.

Devlin, at Hobs End, had been out to check on the weather as frequently as Gericke, but nothing changed and the fog seemed as impenetrable as ever. At ten o'clock he went along the dyke to the beach for the fourth time that night, but conditions didn't seem to have altered.

He flashed his torch into the gloom then shook his head and said softly to himself, 'A good night for dirty work, that's about all you can say for it.'

It seemed obvious that the whole thing was a washout and it was hard to escape that conclusion at Landsvoort, too. 'Are you trying to say you can't take off?' Radl demanded when the young Hauptmann came back inside the hangar from another inspection.

'No problem there,' Gericke told him. 'I can take off blind. Not particularly hazardous in country as flat as this. The difficulty's going to be at the other end. I can't just drop those men and hope for the best. We could be a mile out to sea. I need to see the target, however briefly.'

Bohmler opened the judas in one of the big hangar doors and peered in. 'Herr Hauptmann.'

Gericke moved to join him. 'What is it?'

'See for yourself.'

Gericke stepped through, Bohmler had switched on the outside light and in spite of its dimness, Gericke could see the fog swirling in strange patterns. Something touched his cheek coldly. 'Wind!' he said. 'My God, we've got wind.'

There was a sudden gap torn in the curtain and he could see the farmhouse for a moment. Dimly, but it was there. 'Do we go?' Bohmler demanded.

'Yes,' Gericke said. 'But it's got to be now,' and he turned and plunged back through the judas to tell Steiner and Radl.

Twenty minutes later, at exactly eleven o'clock, Joanna Grey straightened abruptly as her earphones started to buzz. She dropped her book, reached for a pencil and wrote on the pad in front of her. It was a very brief message, decoded in seconds. She sat staring at it, momentarily spellbound, then she made an acknowledgement.

She went downstairs quickly and took her sheepskin coat from behind the door. The retriever sniffed at her heels. 'No, Patch, not this time,' she said.

She had to drive carefully because of the fog and it was twenty minutes later before she turned into the yard at Hobs End. Devlin was getting his gear together on the kitchen table when he heard the car. He reached for the Mauser quickly and went out into the passageway.

'It's me, Liam,' she called.

He opened the door and she slipped in. 'What's all this?'

'I've just received a message from Landsvoort, timed eleven o'clock exactly,' she said. 'The eagle has flown.'

He stared at her, astonished. 'They must be crazy. It's like pea soup up there on the beach.'

'It seemed a little clearer to me as I turned along the dyke.'

He went out quickly and opened the front door. He was back in a moment, face pale with excitement. 'There's a wind coming in off the sea, not much, but it could get stronger.'

'Don't you think it will last?' she said.

'God knows.' The silenced Sten gun was assembled on the table and he handed it to her. 'You know how to work these?'

'Of course.'

He picked up a bulging rucksack and slung it over his shoulders. 'Right then, let's you and me get to it. We've got work to do. If your timing's right, they'll be over that beach in forty minutes.' As they moved into the passage, he laughed harshly. 'By God, but they mean business, I'll say that for them.'

He opened the door and they plunged out into the fog.

'I'd close my eyes if I were you,' Gericke told Bohmler cheerfully, above the rumblings of the engines warming up as he made his final check before take-off. 'This one's going to be pretty hair-raising.'

The flares to mark the take-off run had been lit, but only the first few could be seen. Visibility was still no more than forty or fifty yards. The door behind them opened and Steiner poked his head into the cockpit.

'Everything strapped down back there?' Gericke asked him.

'Everything and everybody. We're ready when you are.'

'Good, I don't want to be an alarmist, but I should point out that anything could happen and very probably will.'

He increased his engine revs and Steiner grinned, shouting to make himself heard above the roaring. 'We have every faith in you.'

He closed the door and retired. Gericke boosted power instantly and let the Dakota go. To plunge headlong into that grey wall was probably the most terrifying thing he had ever done in his life. He needed a run of several hundred yards, a speed of around eighty miles an hour for lift-off.

'My God,' he thought. 'Is this it? Is this finally it?'

The vibrations as he gave her more power seemed unbearable. Up came the tail as he pushed the column forward. Just a touch. She yawed to starboard in a slight crosswind and he applied a little rudder correction.

The roar of the engines seemed to fill the night. At eighty, he eased back slightly, but held on. And then, as that feeling flowed through him, that strange sense, the product of several thousand hours of flying that told you when things were just right, he hauled back on the column.

'Now!' he cried.

Bohmler, who had been waiting tensely, his hand on the undercarriage lever, responded frantically, winding up the wheels. Suddenly they were flying. Gericke kept her going, straight into that grey wall, refusing to sacrifice power for height, hanging on till the last possible moment, before pulling the column right back. At five hundred feet they burst out of the fog, he stamped on the right rudder and turned out to sea.

Outside the hangar, Max Radl sat in the passenger seat of the field car staring up into the fog, a kind of awe on his face. 'Great God in heaven!' he whispered. 'He did it!'

He sat there for a moment longer, listening as the sound of the engines faded into the night, then nodded to Witt behind the wheel. 'Back to the farmhouse as quickly as you like, Sergeant. I've got things to do.'

In the Dakota there was no easing of tension. There had been none in the first place. They talked amongst themselves in low tones with all the calm of veterans who had done this sort of thing so many times that it was second nature. As nobody had been allowed to have German cigarettes on his person, Ritter Neumann and Steiner moved amongst them handing them out singly.

Altmann said, 'He's a flyer, that Hauptmann, I'll say that for him. A real ace to take off in that fog.'

Steiner turned to Preston sitting at the end of the stick. 'A cigarette, Lieutenant?' he said in English.

'Thanks very much, sir, I think I will.' Preston replied in a beautifully clipped voice that suggested he was playing the Coldstream Guards Captain again.

'How do you feel?' Steiner asked in a low voice.

'In excellent spirits, sir,' Preston told him calmly. 'Can't wait to get stuck in.'

Steiner gave up and retreated to the cockpit where he found Bohmler passing Gericke coffee from a Thermos flask. They were flying at two thousand feet. Through occasional gaps in the clouds, stars could be seen and a pale sickle moon. Below, fog covered the sea like smoke in a valley, a spectacular sight.

'How are we doing?' Steiner asked.

'Fine. Another thirty minutes. Not much of a wind though. I'd say about five knots.'

Steiner nodded down into the cauldron below. 'What do you think? Will it clear enough when you go down?'

'Who knows?' Gericke grinned. 'Maybe I'll end up on that beach with you.'

At that moment Bohmler, huddled over the Lichtenstein set, gave an excited gasp. 'I've got something, Peter.'

They entered a short stretch of cloud. Steiner said, 'What's it likely to be?'

'Probably a night fighter, as he's on his own,' Gericke said. 'Better pray it isn't one of ours. He'll blow us out of the sky.'

They emerged from the clouds into clear air and Bohmler tapped Gericke's arm. 'Coming in like a bat out of hell on the starboard quarter.'

Steiner turned his head and after a few moments, could plainly see a twin-engined aircraft levelling out to starboard.

'Mosquito,' Gericke said and added calmly, 'Let's hope he knows a friend when he sees one.'

The Mosquito held course with them for only a few more moments, then waggled its wingtips and swung away to starboard at great speed, disappearing into heavy cloud.

'See.' Gericke smiled up at Steiner. 'All you have to do is live right. Better get back to your lads and make sure they're ready to go. If everything works, we should pick up Devlin on the S-phone twenty miles out. I'll call you when we do. Now get the hell out of here. Bohmler's got some fancy navigating to do.'

Steiner returned to the main cabin and sat down beside Ritter Neumann. 'Not long now.' He passed him a cigarette.

'Thanks very much,' Steiner said. 'Just what I needed.'

It was cold on the beach and the tide was about two-thirds of the way in. Devlin walked up and down restlessly to keep warm, holding the receiver in his right hand, the channel open. It was almost ten to twelve and Joanna Grey, who had been sheltering from the light rain in the trees, came towards him.

'They must be close now.'

As if in direct answer, the S-phone crackled and Peter Gericke said with astonishly clarity, 'This is Eagle, are you receiving me, Wanderer?'

Joanna Grey grabbed Devlin's arm. He shook her off and spoke into the S-phone. 'Loud and clear.'

'Please report conditions over nest.'

'Visibility poor,' Devlin said. 'One hundred to one hundred and fifty yards, wind freshening.'

'Thank you, Wanderer. Estimated time of arrival, six minutes.'

Devlin shoved the S-phone into Joanna Grey's hand. 'Hang on to that while I lay out the markers.'

Inside his rucksack he had a dozen cycle lamps. He hurried along the beach, putting them down at intervals of fifteen yards in a line following the direction of the wind, switching each one on. Then he turned and went back in a parallel line at a distance of twenty yards.

When he rejoined Joanna Grey he was slightly breathless. He took out a large and powerful spotlight and ran a hand over his forehead to wipe sweat from his eyes.

'Oh, this damn fog.' she said. 'They'll never see us. I know they won't.'

It was the first time he'd seen her crack in any way and he put a hand on her arm. 'Be still, girl.'

Faintly, in the distance, there was the rumble of engines.

The Dakota was down to a thousand feet and descending through intermittent fog. Gericke said over his shoulder, 'One pass, that's all I'll get, so make it good.'

'We will,' Steiner told him.

'Luck, Herr Oberst. I've got a bottle of Dom Perignon back there at Landsvoort on ice, remember. We'll drink it together, Sunday morning.'

Steiner clapped him on the shoulder and went out. He nodded to Ritter who gave the order. Everyone stood and clipped his static line to the anchor cable. Brandt slid back the Exit door and as fog and cold air billowed in, Steiner moved down the line checking each man personally.

Gericke went in very low, so low that Bohmler could see the white of waves breaking in the gloom. Ahead was only fog and more darkness. 'Come on!' Bohmler whispered, hammering his clenched fist on his knee. 'Come on, damn you!'

As if some unseen power had decided to take a hand, a sudden gust of wind tore a hole in the grey curtain and revealed Devlin's parallel lines of cycle lamps, clear in the night, a little to starboard.

Gericke nodded. Bohmler pressed the switch and the red light in the cabin flashed above Steiner's head. 'Ready!' he cried.

Gericke banked to starboard, throttled back until his airspeed indicator stood at a hundred and made his pass along the beach at three hundred and fifty feet. The green light flashed, Ritter Neumann jumped into darkness, Brandt followed, the rest of the men tumbled after them. Steiner could feel the wind on his face, smell the salt tang of the sea and waited for Preston to falter. The Englishman stepped into space without a second's hesitation. It was a good omen. Steiner clipped on to the anchor line and went after him.

Bohmler, peering out through the open door of the cockpit, tapped Gericke on the arm. 'All gone, Peter. I'll go and close the door.'

Gericke nodded and swung out towards the sea again. It was no more than five minutes later that the S-phone receiver crackled and Devlin said clearly, 'All fledglings safe and secure in the nest.'

Gericke reached for the mike. 'Thank you, Wanderer. Good luck.'

He said to Bohmler, 'Pass that on the Landsvoort at once. Radl must have been walking on hot bricks for the past hour.'

In his office at Prinz Albrechtstrasse, Himmler worked alone in the light of the desk lamp. The fire was low, the room rather cold, but he seemed oblivious of both those facts and wrote on steadily. There was a discreet knock at the door and Rossman entered.

Himmler looked up. 'What is it?'

'We've just heard from Radl at Landsvoort, Herr Reichsführer. The Eagle has landed.'

Himmler's face showed no emotion whatsoever. 'Thank you, Rossman,' he said. 'Keep me informed.'

'Yes, Herr Reichsführer.'

Rossman withdrew and Himmler returned to his work, the only sound in the room the steady scratching of his pen.

Devlin, Steiner and Joanna Grey stood together at the table examining a large-scale map of the area. 'See here, behind St Mary's,' Devlin was saying, 'Old Woman's Meadow. It belongs to the church and the barn with it which is empty at the moment.'

'You move in there tomorrow,' Joanna Grey said. 'See Father Vereker and tell him you're on exercises and wish to spend the night in the barn.'

'And you're certain he'll agree?' Steiner said.

Joanna Grey nodded. 'No question of it. That sort of thing happens all the time. Soldiers appear either on exercises or forced marches, disappear again. No one ever really knows who they are. Nine months ago we had a Czechoslovakian unit through here and even their officers could only speak a few words of English.'

'Another thing, Vereker was a paratrooper padre in Tunisia,' Devlin added, 'so he'll be leaning over backwards to assist when he sees those red berets.'

'There's an even stronger point in our favour where Vereker's concerned,' Joanna Grey said. 'He knows the Prime Minister is spending the weekend at Studley Grange which is going to work on our behalf very nicely. Sir Henry let it slip the other night at my house when he'd been drinking a little bit too much. Of course Vereker was sworn to secrecy. Can't even tell his own sister until after the great man's gone.'

'And how will this help us?' Steiner asked.

'It's simple,' Devlin said. 'You tell Vereker you're here for the weekend on some exercise or other and ordinarily he would accept that at face value. But this time, remember, he knows that Churchill is visiting the area incognito, so what interpretation does he put on the presence of a crack outfit like the SAS?'

'Of course,' Steiner said. 'Special security.'

'Exactly.' Joanna Grey nodded. 'Another point in our favour. Sir Henry is giving a small dinner party for the Prime Minister tomorrow night.' She smiled and corrected herself. 'Sorry, I mean tonight. Seven-thirty for eight and I'm invited. I'll go only to make my excuses. Say that I've had a call to turn out on night duty for the WVS emergency service. It's happened before, so Sir Henry and Lady Willoughby will accept it completely. It means, of course, that if we make contact in the vicinity of the Grange, I'll be able to give you a very exact discription of the immediate situation there.'

'Excellent,' Steiner said. 'The whole thing seems more plausible by the minute.'

Joanna Grey said, 'I must go.'

Devlin brought her coat and Steiner took it from him and held it open for her courteously. 'Is there no danger for you in driving round the countryside alone at this hour of the morning?'

'Good heavens no.' She smiled. 'I'm a member of the WVS motor pool. That's why I'm allowed the privilege of running a car at all, but it means that I'm required to provide an emergency service in the village and surrounding area. I often have to turn out in the early hours to take people to hospital. My neighbours are perfectly used to it.'

The door opened and Ritter Neumann entered. He was wearing a camouflaged jump jacket and trousers and there was an SAS winged dagger badge in his red beret.

'Everything all right out there?' Steiner asked.

Ritter nodded. 'Everyone bedded down snugly for the night. Only one grumble. No cigarettes.'

'Of course. I knew there was something I'd forgotten. I left them in the car.' Joanna Grey hurried out.

She was back in a few moments and put two cartons of Players on the table, five hundred in each in packets of twenty.

'Holy Mother,' Devlin said in awe 'Did you ever see the like? They're like gold, those things. Where did they come from?'

'WVS stores. You see, now I've added theft to my accomplishments.'

She smiled. 'And now, gentlemen, I must leave you. We'll meet again, by accident, of course, tomorrow when you are in the village.'

Steiner and Ritter Neumann saluted and Devlin took her out to her car. When he returned, the two Germans had opened one of the cartons and were smoking by the fire.

'I'll have a couple of packets of these myself,' Devlin said.

Steiner gave him a light. 'Mrs. Grey is a remarkable woman. Who did you leave in charge out there, Ritter? Preston or Brandt?'

'I know who thinks he is.'

There was a light tap on the door and Preston entered. The camouflaged jump jacket, the holstered revolver at his waist, the red beret slanted at just the right angle towards the left eye, made him seem more handsome than ever.

'Oh, yes,' Devlin said. 'I like it. Very dashing. And how are you, me old son? Happy to be treading your native soil again, I dare say?'

The expression on Preston's face suggested that Devlin reminded him of something that needed scraping off his shoe. 'I didn't find you particularly entertaining in Berlin, Devlin. Even less so now. I'd be pleased if you would transfer your attentions elsewhere.'

'God save us,' Devlin said, amazed. 'Who in the hell does the lad think he's playing now?'

Preston said to Steiner, 'Any further orders, sir?'

Steiner picked up the two cartons of cigarettes and handed them to him. 'I'd be obliged if you'd give these out to the men,' he said gravely.

'They'll love you for that,' Devlin put in.

Preston ignored him, put the cartons under his left arm and saluted smartly. 'Very well, sir.'

In the Dakota, the atmosphere was positively euphoric. The return trip had passed completely without incident. They were thirty miles out from the Dutch coast and Bohmler opened the Thermos and passed Gericke another cup of coffee. 'Home and dry,' he said.

Gericke nodded cheerfully. Then the smile vanished abruptly. Over his headphones he heard a familiar voice. Hans Berger, the controller at his old unit, NJG7.

Bohmler touched his shoulder. 'That's Berger, isn't it?'

'Who else?' Gericke said. 'You've listened to him often enough.'

'Steer o-eight-three degrees.' Berger's voice crackled through the static.

'Sounds as if he's leading a night fighter in for the kill,' Bohmler said. 'On our heading.'

'Target five kilometres.'

Suddenly Berger's voice seemed like the hammer on the last nail in a coffin, crisp, clear, final. Gericke's stomach knotted in a cramp that was almost sexual in its intensity. And he was not afraid. It was as if after years of looking for Death, he was now gazing upon his face with a kind of yearning.

Bohmler grabbed his arm convulsively, 'It's us, Peter!' he screamed. 'We're the target!'

The Dakota rocked violently from side to side as cannon shell punched through the floor of the cockpit, tearing the instrument panel apart, shattering the windscreen. Shrapnel ripped into Gericke's right thigh and a heavy blow shattered his left arm. Another part of his brain told him exactly what was happening. *Schraege Musik*, delivered from below by one of his own comrades – only this time he was on the receiving end.

He wrestled with the control column, heaving it back with all his strength as the Dakota started to go down. Bohmler was struggling to rise to his feet, blood on his face.

'Get out!' Gericke shouted above the roaring of the wind through the shattered windscreen. 'I can't hold her for long.'

Bohmler was on his feet now and trying to speak. Gericke lashed out wildly with his left arm, catching him across the face. The pain was excruciating and he screamed again, 'Get out! That's an order.'

Bohmler turned and moved back along the Dakota to the exit. The plane was in a hell of a state, great holes ripped in the body, pieces of fuselage rattling in the turbulence. He could smell smoke and burning oil. Panic gave him new strength, as he wrestled with the release handles on the hatch.

'Dear God, don't let me burn,' he thought, 'Anything but that.' Then the hatch eased back and he poised for a moment and tumbled into the night.

The Dakota corkscrewed and the port wing lifted. Bohmler somersaulted, his head caught the tailplane a violent blow even as his right hand fastened convulsively on the metal ring. He pulled his ripcord in the very moment of dying. The parachute opened like a strange, pale flower and carried him gently down into darkness.

The Dakota flew on, descending now, the port engine in fire, flames spreading along the wing, reaching for the main body of the plane. Gericke sat at the controls, still fighting to hold her, unaware that his left arm was broken in two places.

There was blood in his eyes. He laughed weakly as he strained to peer through the smoke. *What a way to go.* No visit to Karinhall now, no Knight's Cross. His father would be disappointed about that. Though they'd simply award the damn thing posthumously.

Suddenly, the smoke cleared and he could see the sea through intermittent fog. The Dutch coast couldn't be far away. There were ships down there, at least two. A line of tracer arched up towards him. Some bloody E-boat showing it had teeth. It was really very funny.

He tried to move in his seat and found that his left foot was trapped by a piece of twisted fuselage. Not that it mattered, for by now he was too far down to jump. He was only three hundred feet above the sea, aware of the E-boat to starboard racing him like a greyhound, firing with everything it had got, cannon shells ripping into the Dakota.

'Bastards!' Gericke shouted. 'Stupid bastards!' He laughed weakly again and said softly, as if Bohmler was still there on his left. 'Who in the hell am I supposed to be fighting, anyway?'

Quite suddenly, the smoke was torn away in a violent crosswind and he saw the sea no more than a hundred feet below and coming up to meet him fast.

At that moment he became a great pilot for the only time in his life when it really mattered. Every instinct for survival surged up to give him new strength. He pulled on the column and in spite of the agony in his left arm throttled back and dropped what was left of his flaps.

The Dakota almost stalled, the tail started to fall. He gave a final burst of power to straighten her up as she dropped into the waves and pulled hard on the column again. She bounced three times, skimming the water like a gigantic surfboard and came to a halt, the burning engine hissing angrily as a wave slopped across it.

Gericke sat there for a moment. Everything wrong, nothing by the book and yet he had done it and against every conceivable odds. There was water around his ankles. He tried to get up, but his left foot was securely held. He pulled the fire axe on his right from its holding clip and smashed at the crumpled fuselage, and his foot, breaking the ankle in the process. By then he was beyond reason.

It came as no surprise to find himself standing, the foot free. He got the hatch open – no trouble at all, and fell out into the water, bumping against the wing clumsily, pulling at the quick release ring on his life-jacket. It inflated satisfactorily and he kicked out at the wing, pushing himself away as the Dakota started to go under.

When the E-boat arrived behind him he didn't even bother to turn, but floated there watching the Dakota slide under the surface.

'You did all right, old girl. All right,' he said.

A rope splashed into the water beside him and someone called in English with a heavy German accent, 'Catch hold, *Tommi*, and we'll haul you in. You're safe now.'

Gericke turned and looked up at the young German naval lieutenant and half a dozen sailors who leaned over the rail above him.

'Safe, is it?' he demanded in German. 'You stupid bastards – I'm on your side.'

<h2 style="text-align:center">15</h2>

It was just after ten on Saturday morning when Molly rode down through the fields towards Hobs End. The heavy rain of the previous night had slackened into a light drizzle, but the marsh itself was still blanketed in fog.

She'd risen early and worked hard all morning, had fed the livestock and seen to the milking herself, for Laker Armsby had a grave to dig. Her decision to ride down to the marsh had been a sudden impulse for, in spite of the fact that she had promised Devlin to wait until he called for her, she was terrified that something might happen to him. Conviction of those involved in black market activities usually meant a heavy prison sentence.

She took the horse down into the marsh and came to the cottage from the rear through the reed barrier, letting the animal choose its own way. The muddy water came up to its belly and some slopped inside her wellington boots. She paid no heed and leaned over the horse's neck, peering through the fog. She was sure she could smell woodsmoke. Then the barn and the cottage gradually materialised from the fog, and there *was* smoke ascending from the chimney.

She hesitated, momentarily undecided. Liam was at home, obviously back earlier than he had intended, but if she went in now he would think she had been snooping again. She dug her heels into her horse's flanks and started to turn it away.

In the barn the men were getting their equipment ready for the move out. Brandt and Sergeant Altmann were supervising the mounting of a Browning M2 heavy machine-gun on the jeep. Preston stood watching, hands clasped behind his back, giving the impression of being somehow in charge of the whole thing.

Werner Briegel and Klugl had partially opened one of the rear shutters and Werner surveyed what he could of the marsh through his Zeiss fieldglasses. There were birds in the *suaeda* bushes, the reedy dykes. Enough to content even him. Grebes and moorhens, curlew, widgeon, Brent geese.

'There's a good one,' he said to Klugl. 'A green sandpiper. Passage migrant, usually in the autumn, but they've been known to winter here,' He continued his trajectory and Molly jumped into view. 'Christ, we're being watched.'

In a moment Brandt and Preston were at his side. Preston said, 'I'll get her,' and he turned and ran for the door.

Brandt grabbed at him, too late, and Preston was across the yard and into the reeds in a matter of moments. Molly turned, reining in. Her first thought that it was Devlin. Preston grabbed for the reins and she looked down at him in astonishment.

'All right, let's have you.'

He reached for her and she tried to back her mount away. 'Here, you leave me be. I haven't done anything.'

He grabbed her right wrist and pulled her out of the saddle, catching her as she fell. 'We'll see about that, shall we?'

She started to struggle and he tightened his grip. He slung her over his shoulder and carried her kicking and shouting through the reeds to the barn.

Devlin had been up to the beach at first light to make certain that the tide had covered all traces of the previous night's activities. He had gone up again with Steiner after breakfast to show him as much of the general pick-up area of the estuary and the Point as could be seen in the fog. They were on their way back, only thirty yards from the cottage when Preston emerged from the marsh with the girl on his shoulder.

'What is it?' Steiner demanded.

'It's Molly Prior, the girl I told you about.'

He started to run, entering the yard as Preston reached the entrance. 'Put her down, damn you!' Devlin shouted.

Preston turned. 'I don't take orders from you.'

But Steiner, hard on Devlin's heel into the yard, took a hand. 'Lieutenant Preston,' he called in a voice like iron. 'You will release the lady now.'

Preston hesitated, then set Molly down reluctantly. She promptly slapped his face. 'And you keep your hands to yourself, you bugger,' she stormed at him.

There was immediate laughter from inside the barn and she turned to see through the open door a line of grinning faces, the truck beyond, the jeep with the Browning machine-gun mounted.

Devlin arrived and shoved Preston out of the way. 'Are you all right, Molly?'

'Liam,' she said in bewilderment. 'What is it? What's going on?'

But it was Steiner who handled it, smooth as silk. 'Lieutenant Preston,' he said coldly. 'You will apologise to this young lady at once.' Preston hesitated and Steiner really laid it on. 'At once, Lieutenant!'

Preston got his feet together. 'Humble apologies, ma'am. My mistake,' he said with some irony, turned and went inside the barn.

Steiner saluted gravely. 'I can't tell you how sorry I am about this whole unfortunate incident.'

'This is Colonel Carter, Molly,' Devlin explained.

'Of the Polish Independent Parachute Squadron,' Steiner said. 'We're here in this area for tactical field training and I'm afraid Lieutenant Preston gets rather carried away when it comes to a question of security.'

She was more bewildered than ever now. 'But, Liam,' she began.

Devlin took her by the arm. 'Come on now, let's catch that horse and get you back into the saddle.' He pushed her towards the edge of the marsh where her mount nibbled peacefully at the tussocks of grass. 'Now look what you've done,' he scolded her. 'Didn't I tell you to wait for me to call this afternoon? When will you learn to stop sticking your nose into things that don't concern you?'

'But I don't understand,' she said. 'Paratroopers – here, and that truck and the jeep you painted?'

He gripped her arm fiercely. 'Security, Molly, for God's sake. Didn't you get the drift of what the Colonel was saying? Sure and why do you think that lieutenant reacted like he did? They've a very special reason for being here. You'll find out when they've gone, but for the moment it's top secret and you mustn't mention seeing them here to a living soul. As you love me, promise me that.'

She stared up at him and there was a kind of understanding in her eyes. 'I see the way of it now,' she said. 'All these things you've been doing, the trips at night and so on. I thought it was something to do with the black market and you let me think it. But I was wrong. You're still in the army, that's it, isn't it?'

'Yes,' he said with some truth. 'I'm afraid I am.'

Her eyes were shining. 'Oh, Liam, can you ever forgive me thinking you some cheap spiv peddling silk stockings and whisky round the pubs?'

Devlin took a very deep breath, but managed a smile. 'I'll think about it. Now go home like a good girl and wait until I call, no matter how long.'

'I will, Liam. I will.'

She kissed him, one hand behind his neck and swung up into the saddle. Devlin said, 'Mind now, not a word.'

'You can rely on me.' She kicked her heels into the horse's belly and moved away through the reeds.

Devlin went back across the yard walking very fast, Ritter had joined Steiner from the cottage and the Colonel said, 'Is it all right?'

Devlin brushed past him and plunged into the barn. The men were talking together in small groups and Preston was in the act of lighting a cigarette, the match flaring in his cupped hands. He looked up with a slight, mocking smile. 'And we all know what you've been getting up to during the past few weeks. Was it nice, Devlin?'

Devlin got in one beautiful right hand that landed high on Preston's cheekbone and sent the Englishman sprawling over someone's outstretched foot. Then Steiner had him by the arm.

'I'll kill the bastard!' Devlin said.

Steiner got in front of him, both hands on the Irishman's shoulders and Devlin was astonished at the strength. 'Go up to the cottage,' he said calmly. 'I'll handle it.'

Devlin glared at him, that bone-white killing face on him again and then the eyes dulled a little. He turned and went out, breaking into a run across the yard. Preston got to his feet, a hand to his face. There was total silence.

Steiner said, 'There is a man who will kill you if he can, Preston. Be warned. Step out of line once more and if he doesn't I'll shoot you myself.' He nodded to Ritter, 'Take command!'

When he went into the cottage, Devlin was at the Bushmills. The Irishman turned with a shaky grin. 'God, but I would have killed him. I must be going to pieces.'

'What about the girl?'

'No worries there. She's convinced I'm still in the army and up to my neck in official secrets.' The self-disgust was plain on his face. 'Her lovely boy, that's what she called me. I'm that all right.' He started to pour another whiskey, hesitated then corked the bottle firmly. 'All right,' he said to Steiner. 'What now?'

'We'll move up to the village around noon and go through the motions. My own feeling is that you should keep completely out of the way for the time being. We can meet up again this evening, after dark, when we're closer to making the assault.'

'All right.' Devlin said. 'Joanna Grey is certain to contact you at the village somehow during the afternoon. Tell her I'll be at her place by six-thirty. The E-boat should be available any time between nine and ten. I'll bring the S-phone with me so that you can contact Koenig direct from the scene of operations and fix a pick-up time to fit the circumstances.'

'Fine,' Steiner said and appeared to hesitate. 'There's one thing.'

'What's that?'

'My orders regarding Churchill. They're quite explicit. They'd like to have him alive, but if that isn't possible . . .'

'You've got to put a bullet in him. So what's the problem?'

'I wasn't sure whether there might be one for you?'

'Not in the slightest,' Devlin said. 'This time everyone's a soldier, and takes a soldier's chances. That includes old Churchill.'

In London, Rogan was clearing his desk, thoughts of lunch in his mind, when the door opened with no preliminary knock and Grant entered. His face was tense with excitement. 'Just in over the teleprinter, sir.' He slapped the message down in front of Rogan. 'We've got him.'

'Norfolk Constabulary, Norwich,' Rogan said.

'That's where his registration particulars ended up, but he's some distance from there, right up on the North Norfolk coast near Studley Constable and Blakeney. Very isolated sort of place.'

'Do you know the area?' Rogan asked as he read the message.

'Two holidays in Sheringham when I was a nipper, sir.'

'So, he's calling himself Devlin and he's working as a marsh warden for Sir Henry Willoughby, the local squire. He's certainly due for shock. How far is this place?'

'I'd say about a couple of hundred miles.' Grant shook his head. 'What in the hell could he be up to?'

'We'll find that out soon enough,' Rogan looked up from the report.

'What's the next move, sir? Shall I get the Norfolk Constabulary to pick him up?'

'Are you mad?' Rogan said in amazement. 'You know what these country police are like? Turnip heads. No, we'll handle this one ourselves, Fergus. You and me. It's a while since I've had a weekend in the country. It'll make a nice change.'

'You've got an appointment at the Attorney General's office after lunch,' Grant reminded him. 'Evidence for the Halloran case.'

'I'll be out of there by three o'clock. Three-thirty at the latest. You get a car from the pool and be ready and waiting and we can get straight off.'

'Should I clear it with the Assistant Commissioner, sir?'

Rogan flared in irritation. 'For Christ's sake, Fergus, what's wrong with you? He's in Portsmouth, isn't he? Now get moving.'

Unable to explain his strange reluctance to himself, Grant made an effort. 'Very well, sir.'

He had a hand on the door when Rogan added, 'And Fergus.'

'Yes, sir?'

'Call in at the armoury and draw a couple of Browning Hi-Powers. This character shoots first and asks what you wanted afterwards.'

Grant swallowed hard. 'I'll see to that, sir,' he said, his voice shaking slightly and went out.

Rogan pushed back his chair and went to the window. He flexed the fingers of both hands, full of tension. 'Right, you bastard,' he said softly. 'Let's see if you're as good as they say you are.'

It was just before noon Philip Vereker opened the door at the end of the presbytery hall under the back stairs and went down to the cellar. His foot was giving him hell and he had hardly slept at all during the night. That was his own fault. The doctor had offered a plentiful supply of morphine tablets, but Vereker had a morbid fear of becoming addicted.

So he suffered. At least Pamela was coming for the weekend. She'd telephoned early that morning, not only to confirm it, but to tell him that Harry Kane had offered to pick her up from Pangbourne. At least it saved Vereker a gallon of petrol, and that was something. And he liked Kane. Had done instinctively, which was rare for him. It was nice to see Pamela taking an interest in someone at last.

A large torch hung from a nail at the bottom of the cellar steps. Vereker took it down, then opened an ancient, black, oak cupboard opposite, stepped inside and closed the door. He switched on the torch, felt for a hidden catch and the back of the cupboard swung open to reveal a long, dark tunnel with Norfolk flint walls that glistened with moisture.

It was one of the finest remaining examples of such a structure in the country, a priest's tunnel linking the presbytery with the church, a relic of the days of Roman Catholic persecution under Elizabeth Tudor. The secret of it was handed on from one incumbent to the next. From Vereker's point of view it was simply a very great convenience.

At the end of the tunnel, he mounted a flight of stone steps and paused in surprise, listening carefully. Yes, there could be no mistake. Someone was playing the organ, and very well indeed. He went up the rest of the stairs, opened the door at the top (which was in fact a section of the oak-panelled wall in the sacristy), closed it behind him, opened the other door and moved into the church.

When Vereker went up the aisle he saw to his astonishment that a paratrooper sergeant in camouflaged jump jacket was sitting at the organ, his red beret on the seat beside him. He was playing a Bach choral prelude, one highly appropriate to the season, for it was usually sung to the old Advent hymn *Gottes Sohn ist kommen.*

Hans Altmann was thoroughly enjoying himself. A superb instrument, a lovely church. Then he glanced up and in the organist's mirror saw Vereker at the bottom of the chancel steps. He stopped playing abruptly and turned.

'I'm sorry, Father, but I just couldn't help myself.' He spread his hands. 'One doesn't often get the chance in my – my present occupation.' His

English was excellent but with a definite accent.

Vereker said, 'Who are you?'

'Sergeant Emil Janowski, Father.'

'Polish?'

'That's right.' Altmann nodded. 'Came in here looking for you with my C.O. You were not here, of course, so he told me to wait on while he tried the presbytery.'

Vereker said, 'You play very well indeed. Bach needs to be played well, a fact I constantly remember with bitterness each time I take that seat.'

'Ah, you play yourself?' Altmann said.

'Yes,' Vereker said. 'I'm very fond of the piece you were playing.'

Altmann said. 'A favourite of mine.' He started to play, singing at the same time, *Gott, durch deine Güte, wolst uns arme Leute . . .*'

'But that's a Trinity Sunday hymn,' Vereker said.

'Not in Thuringia, Father.' At that moment the great oak door creaked open and Steiner entered.

He moved down the aisle, a leather swagger stick in one hand, his beret in the other. His boots rang on the flagstones and as he came towards them, the shafts of light, slanting down through the gloom from the clerestory windows above, touched with fire his pale, fair hair.

'Father Vereker?'

'That's right.'

'Howard Carter, in command Independent Polish Parachute squadron of the Special Air Service Regiment.' He turned to Altmann. 'You been behaving yourself, Janowski?'

'As the Colonel knows, the organ is my principal weakness.'

Steiner grinned. 'Go on, cut along and wait outside with the others.' Altmann departed and Steiner looked up into the nave. 'This is really quite beautiful.'

Vereker looked him over curiously, noting the crown and pip of a lieutenant-colonel on the epaulettes of the jump jacket. 'Yes, we're rather proud of it. SAS. Aren't you and your chaps rather a long way from your usual haunts? I thought the Greek Islands and Yugoslavia were your stamping ground?'

'Yes, well so did I until a month or so ago and then the powers-that-be in their wisdom decided to bring us home for special training, although perhaps home isn't exactly the right word to use, my lads all being Polish.'

'Like Janowski?'

'Not at all. He speaks really very good English. Most of the others manage *Hello* or *Will you come out with me tonight* and that's it. They don't seem to think they need any more.' Steiner smiled. 'Paratroopers can be a pretty arrogant lot, Father. Always the trouble with elite units.'

'I know,' Vereker said. 'I was one myself. Padre to the First Parachute Brigade.'

'Were you, by God?' Steiner said. 'You served in Tunisia then?'

'Yes, at Oudna, which was where I got this.' Vereker tapped his stick against his aluminium foot. 'And now I'm here.'

Steiner reached for his hand and shook it. 'It's a pleasure to meet you. Never expected anything like this.'

Vereker managed one of his rare smiles. 'What can I do for you?'

'Put us up for the night, if you will. You've a barn in the field next door that's had similar use before, I believe.'

'You're on exercise?'

Steiner smiled lightly. 'Yes, you could call it that. I've only got a handful of men with me here. The rest are scattered all over North Norfolk. At a given time tomorrow everyone's supposed to race like hell for a certain map reference, just to see how fast we can come together.'

'So you'll only be here this afternoon and tonight?'

'That's it. We'll try not to be a nuisance, of course. I'll probably give the lads a few tactical exercises round the village and so on, just to keep them occupied. You don't think anyone will mind?'

It worked, exactly as Devlin had predicted. Philip Vereker smiled. 'Studley Constable has been used for military manoeuvres of one kind or another many times before, Colonel. We'll all be only too happy to help in any way we can.'

When Altmann came out of the church he went down the road to where the Bedford stood beside the five-barred gate at the entrance to the track which gave access to the barn in Old Woman's Meadow. The jeep waited beside the lychgate, Klugl at the wheel, Werner Briegel behind the Browning M2.

Werner had his Zeiss fieldglasses trained on the rookery in the beech trees. 'Very interesting,' he said to Klugl. 'I think I'll take a closer look. Are you coming?'

He'd spoken in German as there was no one around and Klugl answered in the same language. 'Do you think we should?'

'What harm?' Werner said.

He got out, went in through the lychgate and Klugl followed him reluctantly. Laker Armsby was digging a grave up at the west end of the church. They threaded their way between the tombstones and Laker, seeing them coming, stopped work and took a half-smoked cigarette from behind his ear.

'Hello, there,' Werner said.

Laker squinted up at them. 'Foreigners, eh? Thought you was British boys in them uniforms.'

'Poles,' Werner told him, 'so you'll have to excuse my friend. He doesn't speak English.' Laker fiddled ostentatiously with the dog-end and the young German took the hint and produced a packet of Players. 'Have one of these.'

'Don't mind if I do.' Laker's eyes sparkled.

'Take another.'

Laker needed no second bidding. He put one cigarette behind his ear and lit the other. 'What's your name, then?'

'Werner.' There was a nasty pause as he realised his mistake and added, 'Kunicki.'

'Oh, aye,' Laker said, 'Always thought Werner was a German name. I took a prisoner once in France in nineteen-fifteen. He was called Werner. Werner Schmidt.'

'My mother was German,' Werner explained.

'Not your fault that,' Laker replied. 'We can't choose who brings us into this world.'

'The rookery,' Werner said. 'Can I ask you how long it has been here?'

Laker looked at him in puzzlement, then stared up at the trees. 'Since I were a lad, that is a fact. Are you interested in birds or something?'

'Certainly,' Werner told him. 'The most fascinating of living creatures. Unlike man, they seldom fight with each other, they know no boundaries, the whole world is their home.'

Laker looked at him as if he was mad and laughed. 'Go on. Who'd want to get worked up over a few tatty old rooks?'

'But are they, my friend?' Werner said. 'Rooks are an abundant and widespread resident of Norfolk, true, but many arrive during the late autumn and winter from as far afield as Russia.'

'Get away,' Laker told him.

'No, it's true. Many rooks in this area before the war were found to have been ringed around Leningrad, for example.'

'You mean some of these old ragbags sitting above my head could have come from there?' Laker demanded.

'Most certainly.'

'Well, I never did.'

'So, my friend, in future you must treat them with the respect they deserve as much-travelled ladies and gentlemen, these rooks from Leningrad,' Werner told him.

There was a shout, 'Kunicki – Moczar,' and they turned and found Steiner and the priest standing outside the church porch. 'We're leaving,' Steiner called and Werner and Klugl doubled back through the cemetery to the jeep.

Steiner and Father Vereker started to walk down the path together. A horn sounded and another jeep came up the hill from the direction of the village and pulled in at the opposite side of the road. Pamela Vereker got out in WAAF uniform. Werner and Klugl eyed her appreciatively and then they stiffened as Harry Kane came round from the other side. He was wearing a side cap, combat jacket and jump boots.

As Steiner and Vereker reached the gate, Pamela joined them and reached up to kiss her brother on the cheek. 'Sorry I'm late, but Harry wanted to see a little more of Norfolk than he's been able to manage so far.'

'And you took him the long way round?' Vereker said affectionately.

'At least I got her here, Father,' Kane said.

'I'd like you both to meet Colonel Carter of the Polish Independent Parachute Squadron,' Vereker said. 'He and his men are on exercise in this district. They'll be using the barn in Old Woman's Meadow. My sister Pamela, Colonel, and Major Harry Kane.'

'Twenty-first Specialist Raiding Force.' Kane shook hands. 'We're up the road at Meltham House. I noticed your boys on the way up, Colonel. You guys have sure got it made with those crazy red berets. I bet the girls go wild.'

'It's been known to happen,' Steiner said.

'Polish, eh? We've one or two Polish guys in our outfit. Krukowski for instance. He's from Chicago. Born and raised there and yet his Polish is as good as his English. Funny people. Maybe we can have some sort of get together.'

'I'm afraid not,' Steiner said. 'I'm under special orders. Exercises this afternoon and this evening, move on to join up with other units under my command tomorrow. You know how it is.'

'I certainly do,' Kane said, 'being in exactly the same position myself.' He glanced at his watch. 'In fact, if I'm not back at Meltham House within twenty minutes the Colonel will have me shot.'

Steiner said pleasantly, 'Nice to have met you anyway. Miss Vereker. Father.' He nodded into the jeep and nodded to Klugl who released the brake and moved away.

'Try to remember it's the left-hand side of the road you drive on here, Klugl,' Steiner said calmly.

The walls of the barn were three feet thick in places. Tradition had it that during the Middle Ages it had been part of a manor house. It was certainly adequate enough for their purposes. There was the usual smell of old hay and mice. A broken wagon stood in one corner and a large loft with round, glassless windows let in light.

They left the Bedford outside with a man on guard, but took the jeep inside. Steiner stood in it and addressed them all.

'So far, so good. From now on we've got to make the whole thing look as natural as possible. First, get the field stoves out and cook a meal.' He looked at his watch. 'That should take us somewhere up towards three o'clock. Afterwards, some field training. That's what we're here for and that's what people will expect to see. Basic infantry tactics across the fields, by the stream, amongst the houses. Another thing – be careful at all times about speaking German. Keep your voices low. Use hand signals wherever possible during the field exercises. The only spoken orders to be in English naturally. The field telephones are for emergency only and I mean emergency. Oberleutnant Neumann will give section leaders the necessary call signs.'

Brandt said, 'What's the drill if people try to speak to us?'

'Pretend you don't understand, even if you've got good English. I'd rather you did that than get involved.'

Steiner turned to Ritter. 'I'll leave the field training organisation to you. Make sure each group has at least one person who speaks good English. You should be able to manage that.' He turned back to the men. 'Remember it will be dark by six to six-thirty. We have only to look busy until then.'

He jumped down and went outside. He walked down the track and leaned on the gate. Joanna Grey was toiling up the hill on her bicycle, a large bunch of flowers in the basket which hung from her handlebars, Patch running along behind.

'Good afternoon, ma'am.' Steiner saluted.

She dismounted and came forward, pushing the machine. 'How's everything progressing?'

'Fine.'

She held out her hand as if introducing herself formally. At a distance it must have looked very natural. 'And Philip Vereker?'

'Couldn't be more helpful. Devlin was right. I think he's decided we're here to keep an eye on the great man.'

'What happens now?'

'You'll see us playing soldiers round the village. Devlin said he'll be up to see you at six-thirty.'

'Good.' She held out her hand again. 'I'll see you later.'

Steiner saluted, turned and went back to the barn and Joanna remounted and continued up the hill to the church. Vereker was standing in the porch waiting for her and she leaned her cycle against the wall and went towards him with the flowers.

'They're nice,' he said. 'Where on earth did you get them?'

'Oh, a friend in Holt. Iris. Raised under glass, of course. Dreadfully unpatriotic. I suppose she should have put the time in on potatoes or cabbages.'

'Nonsense, man does not live by bread alone.' Strange how pompous he could sound. 'Did you see Sir Henry before he left?'

'Yes, he called in on his way. Full uniform, too. He really looked very splendid.'

'And he'll be back with the great man himself before nightfall,' Vereker said. 'A brief line in some biography of him one of these days. *Spent the night at Studley Grange.* The villagers don't know a thing about it and yet a little piece of history is being made here.'

'Yes, I suppose you're right if you look at it that way.' She smiled beautifully. 'Now, shall we arrange these flowers on the altar.'

He opened the door for her and they went inside.

16

In London, as Big Ben struck three, Rogan came out of the Royal Courts of Justice and hurried along the pavement to where Fergus Grant waited at the wheel of a Humber saloon. In spite of the heavy rain the Chief Inspector was in high good humour as he opened the door.

'Everything go off all right, sir?' Fergus asked him.

Rogan grinned smugly. 'If friend Halloran draws less than ten years I'm a monkey's uncle. Did you get them?'

'Glove compartment, sir.'

Rogan opened it and found a Browning Hi-Power automatic. He checked the clip, rammed it back into the butt. Strange how good it felt in his hand. How right. He hefted it for a moment, then slipped it into his inside breast pocket.

'All right, Fergus, now for friend Devlin.'

At the same moment Molly was approaching St. Mary and All the Saints on horseback by way of the field paths. Because of the light drizzle she wore her old trenchcoat and a scarf around her hair and carried a rucksack on her back covered with a piece of sacking.

She tethered her horse under the trees at the back of the presbytery and went through the back gate into the graveyard. As she went round to the porch, a shouted command drifted up the hill and she paused and looked down towards the village. The paratroops were advancing in skirmishing order towards the old mill by the stream, their red berets very clear against the green of the meadow. She could see Father Vereker, George Wilde's boy, Graham, and little Susan Turner standing on the footbridge above the weir watching. There was another shouted command and the paratroopers flung themselves down.

When she went inside the church she found Pamela Vereker on her knees at the altar polishing the brass rails. 'Hello, Molly,' she said. 'Come to help?'

'Well, it is my mum's weekend for the altar,' Molly said, slipping her arms out of the rucksack, 'only she has a bad cold and thought she'd spend the day in bed.'

Another shouted order echoed faintly from the village. 'Are they still out there?' Pamela asked. 'Wouldn't you think there was enough war to get on with and still they have to play their stupid games. Is my brother down there?'

'He was when I came in.'

A shadow crossed Pamela Vereker's face, 'I wonder about that sometimes. Wonder if he somehow resents being out of it all now.' She shook her head. 'Men are strange creatures.'

There were no obvious signs of life in the village except for smoke here and there from a chimney. For most people it was a working day. Ritter Neumann had split the assault group into three sections of five, all linked to each other by field telephone. He and Harvey Preston were deployed amongst the cottages with one section each. Preston was rather enjoying himself. He crouched by the wall at the side of the Studley Arms, revolver in hand and gave his section a hand signal to come forward. George Wilde leaned on the wall watching and his wife, Betty, appeared in the doorway, wiping her hands on her apron.

'Wish you was back in action then?'

Wilde, shrugged. 'Maybe.'

'Men,' she said in disgust. 'I'll never understand you.'

The group in the meadow consisted of Brandt, Sergeant Sturm, Corporal Becker and Privates Jansen and Hagl. They were deployed opposite the old mill. It had not been in use for thirty years or more and there were holes in the roof where slates were missing.

Usually the massive waterwheel stood still, but during the night the rushing water of the stream, flooded by many days of heavy rain, had exerted such pressure that the locking bar, already eaten away by rust, had snapped. Now the wheel was moving round again with an unearthly creaking and groaning, churning the water into foam.

Steiner, who had been sitting in the jeep examining the wheel with interest, turned to watch Brandt correcting young Jansen's technique in the prone firing position. Higher up the stream above the weir, Father Vereker and the two children also watched. George Wilde's son, Graham, was eleven and considerably excited by the activities of the paratroops.

'What are they doing now, Father?' he asked Vereker.

'Well, Graham, it's a question of having the elbows in the right position,' Vereker said. 'Otherwise he won't be able to get a steady aim. See, now he's demonstrating the leopard crawl.'

Susan Turner was bored with the entire proceedings and, hardly surprising in a five-year-old girl, was more interested in the wooden doll her grandfather had made for her the evening before. She was a pretty, fair-haired child, an evacuee from Birmingham. Her grandparents, Ted and Agnes Turner, ran the village Post Office and general store and small telephone exchange. She'd been with them for a year now.

She crossed to the other side of the footbridge, ducked under the rail and squatted at the edge. The floodwaters rushed past not more than two feet below, brown and foam-flecked. She dangled the doll by one of its movable arms just above the surface, chuckling as water splashed across its feet. She leaned still lower, clutching the rail above her head, dipping the doll's legs right into the water now. The rail snapped and with a scream she went head first into the water.

Vereker and the boy turned in time to see her disappear. Before the priest could move she was swept under the bridge. Graham, more by instinct than courage, jumped in after her. At that point the water was usually no more than a couple of feet deep. During the summer he had fished there for tadpoles. But now all was changed. He grabbed the tail of Susan's coat and hung on tight. His feet were scrabbling for the bottom, but there was no bottom and he cried out in fear as the current swept them towards the weir above the bridge.

Vereker, frozen with horror, had not uttered a sound, but Graham's cry alerted Steiner and his men instantly. As they all turned to see what the trouble was the two children went over the edge of the weir and slid down the concrete apron into the mill pool.

Sergeant Sturm was on his feet and running for the edge of the pool, tearing off his equipment. He had no time to unzip his jump jacket. The children, with Graham still hanging on to Susan, were being carried relentlessly by the current into the path of the water wheel.

Sturm plunged in without hesitation and struck out towards them. He grabbed Graham by the arm. Brandt plunged waist deep into the water behind him. As Sturm pulled Graham in, the boy's head dipped momentarily under the water. He panicked, kicking and struggling, releasing his grip on the girl. Sturm swung him round in an arc so that Brandt could catch hold of him, then plunged on after Susan.

She had been saved by the enormous force of the current, which had kept her on the surface. She was screaming as Sturm's hand fastened on her coat. He pulled her into his arms and tried to stand. But he went right under and when he surfaced again, he felt himself being drawn inexorably into the path of the water wheel.

He was aware of a cry above the roaring, turned and saw that his comrades on the bank had the boy, that Brandt was back in the water again and pushing towards him. Walter Sturm summoned up everything he had, every ounce of strength and hurled the child bodily through the air to the safety of Brandt's arms. A moment later and the current took him in a giant hand and swept him in. The wheel thundered down and he went under.

George Wilde had gone into the pub to get a bucket of water to swill the front step. He came out again in time to see the children go over the weir. He dropped the bucket, called out to his wife and ran across the road to the bridge. Harvey Preston and his section, who had also witnessed the mishap, followed.

Except for being soaked to the skin, Graham Wilde seemed none the worse for his experience. The same held true for Susan, though she was crying hysterically. Brandt thrust the child into George Wilde's arms and ran along the bank to join Steiner and the others, searching beyond the water wheel for Sturm. Suddenly he floated to the surface in calm water. Brandt plunged in and reached for him.

Except for a slight bruise on the forehead there wasn't a mark on him, but his eyes were closed, his lips slightly parted. Brandt waded out of the water holding him in his arms, and everyone seemed to arrive at once. Vereker, then Harvey Preston and his men and finally, Mrs. Wilde, who took Susan from her husband.

'Is he all right?' Vereker demanded.

Brandt ripped the front of the jump jacket open and got a hand inside the blouse, feeling for the heart. He touched the small bruise on the forehead and the skin was immediately suffused with blood, the flesh and bone soft as jelly. In spite of this Brandt remained sufficiently in control to remember where he was.

He looked up at Steiner and said in fair English, 'I'm sorry, sir, but his skull is crushed.'

For a moment, the only sound was the mill wheel's eerie creaking. It was Graham Wilde who broke the silence, saying loudly, 'Look at his uniform, Dad. Is that what the Poles wear?'

Brandt, in his haste, had committed an irretrievable blunder. Beneath the open jump jacket was revealed Paul Sturm's *Fliegerbluse*, with the Luftwaffe eagle badge on the right breast. The blouse had been pierced to take the red, white and black ribbon of the Iron Cross 2nd Class. On the left breast was the Iron Cross 1st Class, the ribbon for the Winter War, the paratrooper's qualification badge, the silver wound badge. Under the jump jacket, full uniform, as Himmler himself had insisted.

'Oh, my God,' Vereker whispered.

The Germans closed round in a circle. Steiner said in German to Brandt, 'Put Sturm in the jeep.' He snapped his fingers at Jansen who was carrying one of the field telephones. 'Let me have that. Eagle One to Eagle Two,' he called. 'Come in please.'

Ritter Neumann and his section were at work out of sight on the far side of the cottages. He replied almost instantly. 'Eagle Two, I hear you.'

'The Eagle is blown,' Steiner said. 'Meet me at the bridge now.'

He passed the phone back to Jansen. Betty Wilde said in bewilderment, 'What is it, George? I don't understand?'

'They're Germans,' Wilde said. 'I've seen uniforms like that before, when I was in Norway.'

'Yes,' Steiner said. 'Some of us were there.'

'But what do you want?' Wilde said. 'It doesn't make sense. There's nothing for you here.'

'You poor stupid bastard,' Preston jeered. 'Don't you know who's staying at Studley Grange tonight? Mr. Lord-God-Almighty-Winston-bloody-Churchill himself.'

Wilde stared at him in astonishment and then he actually laughed. 'You must be bloody cracked. I never heard such nonsense in all my life. Isn't that so, Father?'

'I'm afraid he's right.' Vereker got the words out slowly and with enormous difficulty. 'Very well, Colonel. Do you mind telling me what happens now? To start with, these children must be chilled to the bone.'

Steiner turned to Betty Wilde. 'Mrs. Wilde, you may take your son and the little girl home now. When the boy has changed, take Susan in to her grandparents. They run the Post Office and general store, is this not so?'

She glanced wildly at her husband, still bemused by the whole thing. 'Yes, that's right.'

Steiner said to Preston. 'There are only six telephones in the general village area. All calls come through a switchboard at the Post Office and are connected by either Mr. Turner or his wife.'

'Shall we rip it out?' Preston suggested.

'No, that might attract unnecessary attention. Someone might send a repair man. When the child is suitably changed, send her and her grandmother up to the church. Keep Turner himself on the switchboard. If there are any incoming calls, he's to say that whoever they want isn't in or something like that. It should do for the moment. Now get to it and try not to be melodramatic about it.'

Preston turned to Betty Wilde. Susan had stopped crying and he held out his hands and said with a dazzling smile. 'Come on, beautiful, I'll give you a piggyback.' The child responded instinctively with a delighted smile. 'This way, Mrs. Wilde, if you'd be so kind.'

Betty Wilde, after a desperate glance at her husband, went after him, holding her son by the hand. The rest of Preston's section, Dinter, Meyer, Riedel and Berg followed a yard or two behind.

Wilde said hoarsely, 'If anything happens to my wife . . .'

Steiner ignored him. He said to Brandt, 'Take Father Vereker and Mr. Wilde up to the church and hold them there. Becker and Jansen can go with you. Hagl, you come with me.'

Ritter Neumann and his section had arrived at the bridge. Preston had just reached them and was obviously telling the Oberleutnant what had happened.

Philip Vereker said, 'Colonel, I've a good mind to call your bluff. If I walk off now you can't afford to shoot me out of hand. You'll arouse the whole village.'

Steiner turned to face him. 'There are sixteen houses or cottages in Studley Constable, Father. Forty-seven people in all and most of the men aren't even here. They are working on any one of a dozen farms within a radius of five miles from here. Apart from that . . .' He turned to Brandt. 'Give him a demonstration.'

Brandt took Corporal Becker's Mk IIS Sten from him, turned and fired from the hip, spraying the surface of the mill pool. Fountains of water spurted high into the air, but the only sound was the metallic chattering as the bolt reciprocated.

'Remarkable, you must admit,' Steiner said. 'And a British invention. But there's an even surer way, Father. Brandt puts a knife under your ribs in just the right way to kill you instantly and without a sound. He knows how, believe me. He's done it many times. Then we walk you to the jeep between us, set you up in the passenger seat and drive off with you. Is that ruthless enough for you?'

'It will do to be going on with, I fancy,' Vereker said.

'Excellent.' Steiner nodded to Brandt. 'Get going, I'll be up in a few minutes.'

He turned and hurried towards the bridge, walking very fast so that Hagl had to trot to keep up with him. Ritter came to meet them. 'Not so good. What happens now?'

'We take over the village. You know what Preston's orders are?'

'Yes, he told me. What do you want us to do?'

'Send a man up for the truck, then start at one end of the village and work your way through house by house. I don't care how you do it, but I want everybody out and up in that church within fifteen to twenty minutes.'

'And afterwards?'

'A road block at each end of the village. We'll make it look nice and official, but anyone who comes in stays.'

'Shall I tell Mrs. Grey?'

'No, leave her for the time being. She needs to stay free to use the radio. I don't want anyone to know she's on our side until it's absolutely necessary. I'll see her myself later.' He grinned. 'A tight one, Ritter.'

'We've known them before, Herr Oberst.'

'Good.' Steiner saluted formally. 'Get to it then.' He turned and started up the hill to the church.

In the living room of the Post Office and General Stores Agnes Turner wept as she changed her granddaughter's clothes. Betty Wilde sat beside her, hanging on tightly to Graham. Privates Dinter and Berg stood on either side of the door waiting for them.

'I'm that feared, Betty,' Mrs. Turner said. 'I've read such terrible things about them. Murdering and killing. What are they going to do to us?'

In the tiny room behind the Post Office counter that held the switchboard, Ted Turner said in some agitation, 'What's wrong with my missus?'

'Nothing,' Harvey Preston said, 'and there isn't likely to be as long as you do exactly as you're told. If you try shouting a message into the phone when someone rings through. Any tricks at all.' He took the revolver from his webbing holster. 'I won't shoot you – I'll shoot your wife and that's a promise.'

'You swine,' the old man said. 'Call yourself an Englishman?'

'A better one than you, old man.' Harvey struck him across the face with the back of his hand. 'Remember that.'

He sat back in the corner, lit a cigarette and picked up a magazine.

Molly and Pamela Vereker had finished at the altar and used up what remained of the reeds and marsh grasses Molly had brought to create a display by the font. Pamela said, 'I know what it needs. Ivy leaves. I'll get some.'

She opened the door, went out through the porch and plucked two or three handfuls of leaves from the vine which climbed the tower at that spot. As she was about to go into the church again, there was a squeal of brakes and she turned to see the jeep draw up. She watched them get out, her brother and Wilde, and at first concluded that the paratroopers had merely given them a lift. Then it occurred to her that the huge sergeant-major was covering her brother and Wilde with the rifle he held braced against his hip. She would have laughed at the absurdity of it had it not been for Becker and Jansen who followed the others through the lychgate carrying Sturm's body.

Pamela retreated through the partly opened door, bumping into Molly. 'What is it?' Molly demanded.

Pamela hushed her. 'I don't know, but something's wrong – very wrong.'

Half-way along the path, George Wilde attempted to make a break for it, but Brandt, who had been expecting such a move, deftly tripped him. He leaned over Wilde, prodding him under the chin with the muzzle of the M1. 'All right, *Tommi*, you're a brave man. I salute you. But try anything like that again and I blow your head off.'

Wilde, helped by Vereker, scrambled to his feet and the party moved on towards the porch. Inside Molly looked at Pamela in consternation. 'What's it mean?'

Pamela hushed her again. 'Quick, in here,' she said and opened the sacristy door. They slipped inside, she closed it and slid home the bolt. A moment later they heard voices clearly.

Vereker said, 'All right, now what?'

'You wait for the Colonel,' Brandt told him. 'On the other hand, I don't see why you shouldn't fill in the time by doing what's right for poor old Sturm. As it happens, he was a Lutheran, but I don't suppose it matters. Catholic or Protestant, German or English. It's all the same to the worms.'

'Bring him to the Lady Chapel,' Vereker said.

The footsteps died away and Molly and Pamela crouched against the door, looked at each other. 'Did he say German?' Molly said. 'That's crazy.'

Footsteps echoed hollowly on the flags of the porch and the outer door creaked open. Pamela put a finger to her lips and they waited.

Steiner paused by the font and looked around him, tapping his swagger stick against his thigh. He hadn't bothered to remove his beret this time. 'Father Vereker,' he called. 'Down here, please.' He moved to the sacristy door and tried the handle. On the other side the two girls eased back in alarm. As Vereker limped down the aisle, Steiner said, 'This seems to be locked. Why? What's in there?'

The door had never been locked to Vereker's knowledge because the key had been lost for years. That could only mean that someone had bolted it from the inside. Then he remembered that he had left Pamela working on the altar when he had gone to watch the paratroopers. The conclusion was obvious.

He said clearly. 'It is the sacristy, Herr Oberst. Church registers, my vestments, things such as that. I'm afraid the key is over at the presbytery. Sorry for such inefficiency. I suppose you order things better in Germany?

'You mean we Germans have a passion for order, Father?' Steiner said. 'True. I, on the other hand, had an American mother although I went to school in London. In fact, lived there for many years. Now, what does that mixture signify?'

'That it is highly unlikely that your name is Carter.'

'Steiner, actually. Kurt Steiner.'

'What of, the SS?'

'It seems to have a rather morbid fascination for your people. Do you imagine all German soldiers serve in Himmler's private army?'

'No, perhaps it is just that they behave as if they do.'

'Like Sergeant Sturm, I suppose.' Vereker could find nothing to say to that. Steiner added, 'For the record, we are not SS. We are Fallschirmjäger. The best in the business, with all due respect to your Red Devils.'

Vereker said, 'So, you intend to assassinate Mr. Churchill at Studley Grange tonight?'

'Only if we have to,' Steiner said. 'I'd much prefer to keep him in one piece.'

'And now the planning's gone slightly awry? The best laid schemes and so on . . .'

'Because one of my men sacrificed himself to save the lives of two children of this village, or perhaps you don't wish to know about that? Why should that be, I wonder? Because it destroys this pitiful delusion that all German soldiers are savages whose sole occupation is murder and rape? Or is it something deeper? Do you hate all of us because it was a German bullet that crippled you?'

'Go to hell!' Vereker said.

'The Pope, Father, would not be at all pleased with such a sentiment. To answer your original question. Yes, the plan has gone a little awry, but improvisation is the essence of our kind of soldiering. As a paratrooper yourself, you must know that.'

'For heavens sakes, man, you've had it,' Vereker said. 'No element of surprise.'

'There still will be,' Steiner told him calmly. 'If we hold the entire village incommunicado, so to speak, for the required period.'

Vereker was, for the moment, rendered speechless by the audacity of this suggestion. 'But that is impossible.'

'Not at all. My men are at this very moment rounding up everyone at present in Studley Constable. They'll be up here within the next fifteen or twenty minutes. We control the telephone system, the roads, so that anyone entering will be immediately apprehended.'

'But you'll never get away with it.'

'Sir Henry Willoughby left the Grange at eleven this morning to travel to King's Lynn where he was to have lunch with the Prime Minister. They were due to leave in two cars with an escort of four Royal Military Police motor-cyclists at three-thirty.' Steiner looked at his watch. 'Which, give or take a minute or two, is right now. The Prime Minister has expressed a particular desire to pass through Walsingham, by the way, but forgive me, I must be boring you with all this.'

'You seem to be very well informed?'

'Oh, I am. So, you see, all we have to do is to hang on until this evening as arranged, and the prize will still be ours. Your people, by the way, have nothing to fear as long as they do as they are told.'

'You won't get away with it,' Vereker said stubbornly.

'Oh, I don't know. It's been done before. Otto Skorzeny got Mussolini out of an apparently impossible situation. Quite a feat of arms as Mr. Churchill himself conceded in a speech at Westminster.'

'Or what's left of it after your damned bombs,' Vereker said.

'Berlin isn't looking too good either these days,' Steiner pointed out, 'and if your friend Wilde is interested, tell him that the five-year-old daughter and the wife of the man who died to save his son, were killed by RAF bombs four months ago.' Steiner held out his hand. 'I'll have the keys of your car. It might come in useful.'

'I haven't got them with me,' Vereker began.

'Don't waste my time, Father. I'll have my lads strip you if I have to.'

Vereker reluctantly produced his keys and Steiner slipped them into his pocket. 'Right, I have things to do.' He raised his voice. 'Brandt, hold the fort here. I'll send Preston to relieve you, then report to me in the village.'

He went out, and Private Jansen came and stood against the door with his M1. Vereker walked up the aisle slowly, past Brandt and Wilde who was sitting in one of the pews, shoulders hunched. Sturm was lying in front of the altar in the Lady Chapel. The priest stood looking down at him for a moment, then knelt, folded his hands and in a firm, confident voice, began to recite the prayers for the dying.

'So now we know,' Pamela Vereker said as the door banged behind Steiner.

'What are we going to do?' Molly said dully.

'Get out of here, that's the first thing.'

'But how?'

Pamela moved to the other side of the room, found the concealed catch and a section of the panelling swung back to reveal the entrance to the priest's tunnel. She picked up the torch her brother had left on the table. Molly was gaping in amazement. 'Come on,' Pamela said impatiently. 'We must get moving.'

Once inside, she closed the door and led the way quickly along the tunnel. They exited through the oak cupboard in the presbytery cellar and went up the stairs to the hall. Pamela put the torch on the table beside the telephone and when she turned, saw that Molly was crying bitterly.

'Molly, what is it?' she said, taking the girl's hands in hers.

'Liam Devlin,' Molly said. 'He's one of them. Must be. They were at his place, you see. I saw them.'

'When was this?'

'Earlier today. He let me think he was still in the army. Some kind of secret job.' Molly pulled her hands free and clenched them into fists. 'He used me. All the time he was using me. God help me, but I hope they hang him.'

'Molly, I'm sorry,' Pamela said. 'Truly I am. If what you say is true then he'll be taken care of. But we've got to get out of here.' She looked down at the telephone. 'No use trying to get through to the police or somebody on that, not if they control the village exchange. And I haven't got the keys of my brother's car.'

'Mrs. Grey has a car,' Molly said.

'Of course.' Pamela's eyes glinted with excitement. 'Now if I could only get down to her house.'

'Then what would you do? There isn't a phone for miles.'

'I'd go straight to Meltham House,' Pamela said. 'There are American Rangers down there. A crack outfit. They'd show Steiner and his bunch a thing or two. How did you get here?'

'Horseback. He's tied up in the woods behind the presbytery.'

'All right, leave him. We'll take the field path back of Hawks Wood and see if we can get to Mrs. Grey's without being seen.'

Molly didn't argue. Pamela tugged her sleeve, they darted across the road into the shelter of Hawks Wood.

The path was centuries old and cut deep into the earth, giving complete concealment. Pamela led the way, running very fast, not stopping until they came out into the trees on the opposite side of the stream from Joanna Grey's cottage. There was a narrow footbridge and the road seemed deserted.

Pamela said, 'All right, let's go. Straight across.'

Molly grabbed her arm. 'Not me, I've changed my mind.'

'But why?'

'You try this way. I'll go back for my horse and try another. Two bites of the apple.'

Pamela nodded. 'That makes sense. All right then, Molly.' She kissed her on the cheek impulsively. 'Only watch it! They mean business, this lot.'

Molly gave her a little push and Pamela darted across the road and disappeared round the corner of the garden wall. Molly turned and started to run back up the track through Hawks Wood. *Oh, Devlin, you bastard*, she thought, *I hope they crucify you.*

By the time she reached the top, the tears, slow, sad and incredibly painful were oozing from her eyes. She didn't even bother to see if the road was clear, but simply dashed across and followed the line of the garden wall round to the wood at the back. Her horse was waiting patiently where she'd tethered him, cropping the grass. She untied him quickly, scrambled into the saddle and galloped away.

When Pamela went into the yard at the rear of the cottage the Morris saloon was standing outside the garage. When she opened the car door the keys were in the ignition. She started to get behind the wheel and an indignant voice called, 'Pamela, what on earth are you doing?'

Joanna Grey was standing at the back door. Pamela ran towards her. 'I'm sorry, Mrs. Grey, but something absolutely terrible has happened. This Colonel Carter and his men who are exercising in the village. They're not SAS at all. His name is Steiner and they're German paratroopers here to kidnap the Prime Minister.'

Joanna Grey drew her into the kitchen and closed the door. Patch fawned about her knees. 'Now calm down,' Joanna said. 'This really is a most incredible story. The Prime Minister isn't even here.'

She turned to her coat hanging behind the door and fumbled in the pocket. 'Yes, but he will be this evening,' Pamela said. 'Sir Henry is bringing him back from King's Lynn.'

Joanna turned, a Walther automatic in her hand. 'You have been busy, haven't you?' She reached behind and got the cellar door open. 'Down you go.'

Pamela was thunderstruck. 'Mrs. Grey, I don't understand.'

'And I don't have time to explain. Let's just say we're on different sides in this affair and leave it at that. Now get down those stairs. I won't hesitate to shoot if I have to.'

Pamela went down, Patch scampering in front of her, and Joanna Grey followed. She switched on a light at the bottom and opened a door opposite. Inside was a dark windowless storeroom filled with junk. 'In you go.'

Patch, circling his mistress, managed to get between her feet. She stumbled against the wall. Pamela gave her a violent push through the doorway. As she fell back, Joanna Grey fired at point-blank range. Pamela was aware of the explosion that half-blinded her, the sudden touch of a white-hot poker against the side of her head, but she managed to slam the door in Joanna Grey's face and ram home the bolt.

The shock of a gunshot wound is so great that it numbs the entire central nervous system for a while. There was a desperate air of unreality to everything as Pamela stumbled upstairs to the kitchen. She leaned on a chest of drawers to stop herself from falling, and looked in the mirror above it. A narrow strip of flesh had been gouged out of the left side of her forehead and bone showed through. There was surprisingly little blood and, when she touched it gently with a fingertip, no pain. *That would come later.*

'I must get to Harry,' she said aloud. 'I must get to Harry.'

Then, like something in a dream, she found herself behind the wheel of the Morris driving out of the yard, as if in slow motion.

As he walked down the road Steiner saw her go and made the natural assumption that Joanna Grey was at the wheel. He swore softly, turned and went back to the bridge where he had left the jeep with Werner Briegel manning the machine-gun and Klugl at the wheel. As he arrived, the Bedford came back down the hill from the church, Ritter Neumann standing on the running-board and hanging on to the door. He jumped down.

'Twenty-seven people up at the church now, Herr Oberst, including the two children. Five men, nineteen women.'

'Ten children at harvest camp,' Steiner said. 'Devlin estimated a present population of forty-seven. If we allow for Turner in the exchange, and Mrs. Grey, that leaves eight people who are certain to turn up at some time. Mostly men, I would imagine. Did you find Vereker's sister?'

'No sign of her at the presbytery and when I asked him where she was, he told me to go to hell. Some of the women were more forthcoming. It seems she goes riding on Saturday afternoons when she's at home.'

'You'll have to keep an eye out for her as well, then,' Steiner said.

'Have you seen Mrs. Grey?'

'I'm afraid not.' Steiner explained what had happened. 'I made a bad mistake there. I should have allowed you to go and see her when you suggested it. I can only hope she returns soon.'

'Perhaps she's gone to see Devlin?'

'That's a point. Worth checking on. We'll have to let him know what's happening anyway.' He slapped the swagger stick agains his palm.

There was a crash of breaking glass and a chair came through the window of Turner's shop. Steiner and Ritter Neumann drew their Brownings and ran across the road.

For most of the day Arthur Seymour had been felling the trees of a small plantation on a farm to the east of Studley Constable. He sold the logs to his own benefit in and around the village. Mrs. Turner had given him an order only that morning. When he was finished at the plantation, he filled a couple of sacks, put them on his handcart and went down to the village across the field tracks, coming into the yard at the back of the Turner's shop from the rear.

He kicked open the kitchen door without knocking and walked in, a sack of logs on his shoulder – and came face to face with Dinter and Berg who were sitting on the edge of the table drinking coffee. If anything they were more surprised than Seymour.

'Here, what's going on?' he demanded.

Dinter, who had his Sten slung across his chest, moved it on target and Berg picked up his M1. At the same moment Harvey Preston appeared in the door. He stood there, hands on hips, looking Seymour over. 'My God,' he said. 'The original walking ape.'

Something stirred in Seymour's dark mad eyes. 'You watch your mouth, soldier boy.'

'It can talk as well,' Preston said. 'Wonders will never cease. All right, put him with the others.'

He turned to go back into the exchange and Seymour tossed the sack of logs at Dinter and Berg and jumped on him, one arm clamping around Preston's throat, a knee in his back. He snarled like an animal. Berg got to his feet and slammed the butt of his M1 into Seymour's kidneys. The big man cried out in pain, released his hold on Preston and launched himself at Berg with such force that they went through the open door behind into the shop, a display cabinet collapsing beneath them.

Berg lost his rifle but managed to get to his feet and back away. Seymour advanced on him, sweeping the counter clear of the pyramids of tinned goods and packages, growling deep in his throat. Berg picked up the chair Mrs. Turner habitually sat on behind the counter. Seymour knocked it aside in mid-flight and it went out through the shop window. Berg drew his bayonet and Seymour crouched.

Preston took a hand then, moving in from behind, Berg's M1 in his hands. He raised it high and drove the butt into the back of Seymour's skull. Seymour cried out and swung round. 'You bloody great ape,' Preston cried. 'We'll have to teach you your manners, won't we?'

He smashed the butt into Seymour's stomach and as the big man started to fold, hit him again in the side of the neck. Seymour fell back, grabbed for support and only succeeded in bringing a shelf and its contents down on top of him as he slid to the floor.

Steiner and Ritter Neumann burst in through the shop doorway at that moment, guns ready. The place was a shambles, cans of various descriptions, sugar, flour, scattered everywhere. Harvey Preston handed Berg his rifle. Dinter appeared in the doorway, swaying slightly, a streak of blood on his forehead.

'Find some rope,' Preston said, 'and tie him up or next time you might not be so lucky.'

Old Mr. Turner was hovering in the door of the exchange. There were tears in his eyes as he surveyed the shambles. 'And who's going to pay for that lot.'

'Try sending the bill to Winston Churchill, you never know your luck,' Preston said brutally. 'I'll have a word with him for you if you like. Press your case.'

The old man slumped down in a chair in the small exchange, the picture of misery and Steiner said, 'All right, Preston, I won't need you down here any more. Get on up to the church and take that specimen behind the counter with you. Relieve Brandt. Tell him to report to Oberleutnant Neumann.'

'What about the switchboard?'

'I'll send Altmann in. He speaks good English. Dinter and Berg can keep an eye on things until then.'

Seymour was stirring, pushing himself up on his knees and making the discovery that his hands were lashed behind his back. 'Comfortable, are we?' Preston kicked him in the backside and hauled him to his feet. 'Come on, ape, start putting one foot in front of the other.'

At the church, the villagers sat in pews as instructed and awaited their fate, talking to each other in low voices. Most of the women were plainly terrified. Vereker moved amongst them, bringing what comfort he could. Corporal Becker stood guard near the chancel steps, a Sten gun in his hands, Private Jansen at the door. Neither spoke English.

After Brandt had departed, Harvey Preston found a length of rope in the bell room at the bottom of the tower, lashed Seymour's ankles together, then turned him over and dragged him on his face to the Lady Chapel where he dumped him beside Sturm. There was blood on Seymour's cheek where the skin had rubbed away and there were gasps of horror, particularly from the women.

Preston ignored them and kicked Seymour in the ribs. 'I'll cool you down before I'm through, I promise you.'

Vereker limped forward and grabbed him by the shoulder, turning him round. 'Leave that man alone.'

'Man?' Preston laughed in his face. 'That isn't a man, it's a thing.' Vereker reached down to touch Seymour and Preston knocked him away and drew his revolver. 'You just won't do as you're told, will you?'

One of the women choked back a scream. There was a terrible silence as Preston thumbed back the hammer. A moment in time. Vereker crossed himself and Preston laughed again and lowered the revolver. 'A lot of good that will do you.'

'What kind of man are you?' Vereker demanded. 'What moves you to act like this?'

'What kind of man?' Preston said. 'That's simple. A special breed. The finest fighting men that ever walked the face of the earth. The Waffen SS in which I have the honour to hold the rank of Untersturmführer.'

He walked up the aisle, turned at the chancel steps, unzipped his jump jacket and took it off, revealing the tunic underneath, the collar patches with the three leopards, the eagle on his left arm, the Union Jack shield beneath and the black and silver cuff-title.

It was Laker Armsby sitting beside George Wilde who said, 'Here, he's got a Union Jack on his sleeve.'

Vereker moved forward, a frown on his face and Preston held out his arm. 'Yes, he's right. Now read the cuff-title.'

'Britisches Freikorps,' Vereker said aloud and glanced up sharply. 'British Free Corps?'

'Yes, you damned fool. Don't you realise? Don't any of you realise? I'm English, like you, only I'm on the right side. The only side.'

Susan Turner started to cry. George Wilde came out of his pew, walked up the aisle slowly and deliberately and stood looking up at Preston. 'The Jerries must be damned hard up, because the only place they could have found you was under a stone.'

Preston shot him at point-blank range. As Wilde fell back across the steps below the roodscreen, blood on his face, there was pandemonium. Women were screaming hysterically. Preston fired another shot into the air. 'Stay where you are!'

There was the kind of frozen silence produced by complete panic. Vereker got down on one knee awkwardly and examined Wilde as he groaned and moved his head from side to side. Betty Wilde ran up the aisle, followed by her son, and dropped to her knees beside her husband.

'He'll be all right, Betty, his luck is good,' Vereker told her. 'See, the bullet has just gouged his cheek.'

At that moment the door at the other end of the church crashed open and Ritter Neumann rushed in, his Browning in his hand. He ran up the centre aisle and paused. 'What's going on here?'

'Ask your colleague from the SS,' Vereker suggested.

Ritter glanced at Preston, then dropped to one knee and examined Wilde. 'Don't you touch him, you – you bloody German swine,' Betty said.

Ritter took a field dressing from one of his breast pockets and gave it to her. 'Bandage him with that. He'll be fine.' He stood up and said to Vereker, 'We are Fallschirmjäger, Father, and proud of our name. This gentleman, on the other hand . . .' He turned in an almost casual gesture and struck Preston a heavy blow across the face with the Browning. The Englishman cried out and crumpled to the floor.

The door opened again and Joanna Grey ran in. 'Herr Oberleutnant,' she called in German. 'Where's Colonel Steiner? I must speak with him.'

Her face was streaked with dirt and her hands were filthy. Neumann went down the aisle to meet her. 'He isn't here. He's gone to see Devlin. Why?'

Vereker said, 'Joanna?' There was a question in his voice, but more than that, a kind of dread as if he was afraid to know for certain what he feared.

She ignored him and said to Ritter, 'I don't know what's been going on here, but about forty-five minutes ago, Pamela Vereker turned up at the cottage and she knew everything. Wanted my car to go to Meltham House to get the Rangers.'

'What happened?'

'I tried to stop her and ended up locked in the cellar. I only managed to break out five minutes ago. What are we going to do?'

Vereker put a hand on her arm and pulled her round to face him. 'Are you saying you're one of them?'

'Yes,' she said impatiently, 'Now will you leave me alone? I've work to do.' She turned back to Ritter.

'But why?' Vereker said. 'I don't understand. You're British . . .'

She rounded on him then. 'British?' she shouted. 'Boer, damn you! Boer! How could I be British? You insult me with that name.'

There was a genuine horror on virtually every face there. The agony in Philip Vereker's eyes was plain for all to see. 'Oh, my God,' he whispered.

Ritter took her by the arm. 'Back to your house fast. Contact Landsvoort on the radio. Let Radl know the position. Keep the channel open.'

She nodded and hurried out. Ritter stood there, for the first time in his military career totally at a loss. *What in the hell are we going to do?* he thought. But there was no answer. Couldn't be without Steiner.

He said to Corporal Becker. 'You and Jansen stay here,' and he hurried outside.

There was silence in the church. Vereker walked up the aisle, feeling inexpressibly weary. He mounted the chancel steps and turned to face them. 'At times like these there is little left but prayer,' he said. 'And it frequently helps. If you would all please kneel.'

He crossed himself, folded his hands and began to pray aloud in a firm and remarkably steady voice.

17

Harry Kane was supervising a course in field tactics in the wood behind Meltham Farm when he received Shafto's urgent summons to report to the house and bring the training squad with him. Kane left the sergeant, a Texan named Hustler from Fort Worth, to follow with the men and went on ahead.

As he arrived, sections which had been training on various parts of the estate were all coming in together. He could hear the revving of engines from the motor pool in the stabling block at the rear. Several jeeps turned into the gravel drive in front of the house and drew up line abreast.

The crews started to check their machine guns and equipment. An officer jumped out of the lead vehicle, a captain named Mallory.

'What gives, for Christ's sake?' Kane demanded.

'I haven't the slightest idea,' Mallory said. 'I get the orders, I follow them through. He wants you in a hurry, I know that.' He grinned. 'Maybe it's the Second Front.'

Kane went up the steps on the run. The outer office was a scene of frenzied activity. Master Sergeant Garvey paced up and down outside Shafto's door, nervously smoking a cigarette. His face brightened as Kane entered.

'What in the hell is going on?' Kane demanded. 'Have we orders to move out or something?'

'Don't ask me, Major. All I know is that lady friend of yours arrived in one hell of a state about fifteen minutes ago and nothing's been the same since.'

Kane opened the door and went in. Shafto, in breeches and riding boots, was standing at the desk with his back to him. When he swung round Kane saw that he was loading the pearl-handled Colt. The change in him was extraordinary. He seemed to crackle with electricity, his eyes sparkled as if he was in a high fever, his face was pale with excitement.

'Fast action, Major, that's what I like.'

He reached for belt and holster and Kane said, 'What is it, sir? Where's Miss Vereker?'

'In my bedroom. Under sedation and badly shocked.'

'But what happened?'

'She took a bullet in the side of the head.' Shafto buckled his belt quickly, easing the holster low down on his right hip. 'And the finger on the trigger was that friend of her brother's, Mrs. Grey. Ask her yourself. I can only spare you three minutes.'

Kane opened the bedroom door. Shafto followed him in. The curtains had been partially drawn and Pamela was in bed, the blankets up to her chin. She looked pale and very ill and there was a bandage around her head, a little blood soaking through.

As Kane approached, her eyes opened and she stared up at him fixedly. 'Harry?'

'It's all right.' He sat on the edge of the bed.

'No, listen to me.' She pushed herself up and tugged at his sleeve and when she spoke, her voice was remote, far-away. 'Mr. Churchill leaves King's Lynn at three-thirty for Studley Grange with Sir Henry Willoughby. They'll be coming by way of Walsingham. You must stop him.'

'Why must I?' Kane said gently.

'Because Colonel Steiner and his men will get him if you don't. They're waiting at the village now. They're holding everyone prisoner at the church.'

'Steiner?'

'The man you know as Colonel Carter. And his men, Harry. They aren't Poles. They're German paratroops.'

'But Pamela,' Kane said. 'I met Carter. He's as English as you are.'

'No, his mother was American and he went to school in London. Don't you see? That explains it.' There was a kind of exasperation in her voice now. 'I overheard them talking in the church, Steiner and my brother. I was hiding with Molly Prior. After we got away, we split up and I went to Joanna's only she's one of them. She shot me and I – I locked her in the cellar.' She frowned, trying hard. 'Then I took her car and came here.'

There was a sudden release that was almost physical in its intensity. It was as if she had been holding herself together by willpower alone and now it didn't matter. She lay back against the pillow and closed her eyes. Kane said, 'But how did you get away from the church, Pamela?'

She opened her eyes and stared at him, dazed, uncomprehending. 'The church? Oh, the – the usual way.' Her voice was the merest whisper. 'And then I went to Joanna's and she shot me.' She closed her eyes again. 'I'm so tired, Harry.'

Kane stood up and Shafto led the way back into the other room. He adjusted his sidecap in the mirror. 'Well, what do you think? That Grey woman for a start. She must be the great original bitch of all time.'

'Who have we notified? The War Office and GOC East Anglia for a start and . . .'

Shafto cut right in. 'Have you any idea how long I'd be on the phone while those chair-bound bastards at Staff try to decide whether I've got it right or not?' He slammed a fist down on the table. 'No, by Godfrey. I'm going to nail these Krauts myself, here and now, and I've got the men to do it. Action this day!' He laughed harshly. 'Churchill's personal motto. I'd say that's rather appropriate.'

Kane saw it all then. To Shafto it must have seemed like a dispensation from the gods themselves. Not only the salvaging of his career, but the making of it. The man who had saved Churchill. A feat of arms that would take its place in the history books. Let the Pentagon try to keep that general's star from him after this and there would be rioting in the streets.

'Look, sir,' Kane said stubbornly. 'If what Pamela said is true, this must be just about the hottest potato of all time. If I might respectfully suggest, the British War Office won't take too kindly . . .'

Shafto's fist slammed down on the desk again. 'What's got into you? Maybe those Gestapo boys did a better job than they knew?' He turned to the window restlessly, then swung back as quickly, smiling like a contrite schoolboy. 'Sorry, Harry, that was uncalled for. You're right, of course.'

'Okay, sir, what do we do?'

Shafto looked at his watch. 'Four-fifteen. That means the Prime Minister must be getting close. We know the road he's coming on. I think it might be a good idea if you took a jeep and headed him off. From what the girl said you should be able to catch him this side of Walsingham.'

'I agree, sir. At least we can offer him one hundred and ten per cent security here.'

'Exactly.' Shafto sat down behind the desk and picked up the telephone. 'Now get moving and take Garvey with you.'

'Colonel.'

As Kane opened the door he heard Shafto say, 'Get me the General Officer commanding East Anglia District and I want him personally – no one else.'

When the door closed Shafto removed his left index finger from the telephone rest. The operator's voice crackled in his ear. 'Did you want something, Colonel?'

'Yes, get Captain Mallory in here on the double.'

Mallory was with him in about forty-five seconds. 'You wanted me, Colonel?'

'That's right, plus a detail of forty men ready to move out five minutes from now. Eight jeeps should do it. Cram 'em in.'

'Very well, sir.' Mallory hesitated, breaking one of his strictest rules. 'Is it permitted to ask what the Colonel intends?'

'Well, let's put it this way,' Shafto said. 'You'll be a major by nightfall – or dead.'

Mallory went out, his heart pumping and Shafto went to the cupboard in the corner and took out a bottle of Bourbon and half-filled a glass. Rain beat against the window and he stood there, drinking his Bourbon, taking his time. Within twenty-four hours he would probably have the best-known name in America. His day had come, he knew that with absolute conviction.

When he went outside three minutes later the jeeps were drawn up in line, the crews on board. Mallory was standing in front talking to the unit's youngest officer, a second lieutenant named Chalmers. They sprang to attention and Shafto paused at the top of the steps.

'You're wondering what all this is about. I'll tell you. There's a village named Studley Constable about eight miles from here. You'll find it marked plainly enough on your maps. Most of you will have heard that Winston Churchill was visiting a RAF station near King's Lynn today. What you don't know is that he's spending tonight at Studley Grange. This is where it gets interesting. There are sixteen men from the Polish Independent Parachute Squadron of the SAS training in Studley Constable. You can't miss them in those pretty red berets and camouflage uniforms.' Somebody laughed and Shafto paused until there was complete silence again. 'I've got news for you. Those guys are Krauts. German paratroops here to get Churchill and we're going to nail them to the wall.' The silence was total and he nodded slowly. 'One thing I can promise you boys. Handle this right and by tomorrow your names will ring from California to Maine. Now get ready to move out.'

There was an instant burst of activity as engines roared into life. Shafto went down the steps and said to Mallory, 'Make sure they go over those maps on the way. No time for any fancy briefing when we get there.' Mallory hurried away and Shafto turned to Chalmers. 'Hold the fort, boy, until Major Kane gets back.' He slapped him on the shoulder. 'Don't look too disappointed. He'll have Mr. Churchill with him. You see he gets the hospitality of the house.' He jumped into the lead jeep and nodded to the driver. 'Okay, son, let's move out.'

They roared down the drive, the sentries on the massive front gate had got it open fast and the convoy turned into the road. A couple of hundred yards farther on, Shafto waved them to a halt and told his driver to pull in close to the nearest telephone pole. He turned to Sergeant Hustler in the rear seat. 'Give me that Thompson gun.'

Hustler handed it over. Shafto cocked it, took aim and sprayed the top of the pole, reducing the crossbars to matchwood. The telephone lines parted, springing wildly through the air.

Shafto handed the Thompson back to Hustler. 'I guess that takes care of any unauthorised phone calls for a while.' He slapped the side of the vehicle. 'Okay, let's go, let's go, let's go!'

Garvey handled the jeep like a man possessed, roaring along the narrow country lanes at the kind of speed which assumed that nothing was coming the other way. Even then, they almost missed their target, for as they drove along the final stretch to join the Walsingham road, the small convoy flashed past at the end of the lane. Two military policemen on motor-cycles leading the way, two Humber saloon cars, two more policemen bringing up the rear.

'It's him!' Kane cried.

The jeep skidded into the main road, Garvey rammed his foot down hard. It was only a matter of moments before they caught up the convoy. As they roared up behind, the two military policemen at the rear glanced over their shoulders. One waved them back.

Kane said, 'Sergeant, pull out and overtake and if you can't stop them any other way you have my permission to ram that front car.'

Dexter Garvey grinned. 'Major, I'm going to tell you something. If this goes wrong we'll end up in that Leavenworth stockade so fast you won't know which day it is.'

He swerved out to the right past the motor-cyclists and pulled alongside the rear Humber. Kane couldn't see much of the man in the back seat because the side curtains were pulled forward just sufficiently to ensure privacy. The driver, who was in dark blue chauffeur's uniform, glanced sideways in alarm and the man in the grey suit in the front passenger seat drew a revolver.

'Try the next one,' Kane ordered and Garvey pulled alongside the front saloon, blaring his horn.

There were four men in there, two in army uniform, both colonels, one with the red tabs of a staff officer. The other turned in alarm and Kane found himself looking at Sir Henry Willoughby. There was instant recognition and Kane shouted to Garvey, 'Okay, pull out in front. I think they'll stop now.'

Garvey accelerated, overtaking the military policemen at the head of the small convoy. A horn blared three times behind them, obviously some pre-arranged signal. When Kane looked over his shoulder they were pulling in at the side of the road. Garvey braked and Kane jumped out and ran back.

The military policemen had a Sten gun apiece trained on him before he was anywhere close and the man in the grey suit, presumably the Prime Minister's personal detective, was already out of the rear car, revolver in hand.

The staff colonel with the red tabs got out of the first car, Sir Henry in Home Guard uniform at his heels. 'Major Kane,' Sir Henry said in bewilderment. 'What on earth are you doing here?'

The staff colonel said curtly, 'My name is Corcoran, Chief Intelligence Officer to the GOC, East Anglia District. Will you kindly explain yourself, sir?'

'The Prime Minister mustn't go to Studley Grange,' Kane told him. 'The village has been taken over by German paratroops and . . .'

'Good God,' Sir Henry interrupted. 'I've never heard such nonsense . . .'

Corcoran waved him to silence. 'Can you substantiate this statement, Major?'

'Dear God Almighty,' Kane shouted. 'They're here to get Churchill like Skorzeny dropped in for Mussolini, don't you understand? What in the hell does it take to convince you guys? Won't anybody listen?'

A voice from behind, a voice that was entirely familiar to him said, 'I will, young man. Tell your story to me.'

Harry Kane turned slowly, leaned down at the rear window and was finally face-to-face with the great man himself.

When Steiner tried the door of the cottage at Hobs End it was locked. He went round to the barn, but there was no sign of the Irishman there either. Briegel shouted, 'Herr Oberst, he's coming.'

Devlin was riding the BSA across the network of narrow dyke paths. He turned into the yard, shoved the bike up on its stand and pushed up his goggles. 'A bit public, Colonel.'

Steiner took him by the arm and led him across to the wall where, in a few brief sentences, he filled him in on the situation. 'Well,' he said when he was finished. 'What do you think?'

'Are you sure your mother wasn't Irish?'

'*Her* mother was.'

Devlin nodded. 'I might have known. Still, who knows? We might get away with it.' He smiled. 'I know one thing. My fingernails will be down to the quick by nine tonight.'

Steiner jumped into the jeep and nodded to Klugl. 'I'll keep in touch.'

From the wood on the hill on the other side of the road Molly stood beside her horse and watched Devlin take out his key and unlock the front door. She had intended to confront him, filled with the desperate hope that even now she might be mistaken, but the sight of Steiner and his two men in the jeep was the ultimate truth of things.

A half mile outside Studley Constable Shafto waved the column to a halt and gave his orders. 'No time for any nonsense now. We've got to hit them and hit them hard before they know what's happening. Captain Mallory, you take three jeeps and fifteen men, cross the fields to the east of the village using those farm tracks marked on the map. Circle round till you come out on the Studley Grange road north of the watermill. Sergeant Hustler, the moment we reach the edge of the village, you dismount and take a dozen men on foot and make your way up this sunken track through Hawks Wood to the church. The remaining men stay with me. We'll plug the road by the Grey woman's house.'

'So we've got them completely bottled up, Colonel,' Mallory said.

'Bottled up hell. When everyone's in position and I give the signal on field telephone, we go in and finish this thing fast.'

There was silence. It was Sergeant Hustler who finally broke it. 'Begging the Colonel's pardon, but wouldn't some sort of reconnaisance be in order?' He tried to smile. 'I mean, from what we hear, these Kraut paratroopers ain't exactly Chesterfields.'

'Hustler,' Shafto said coldly. 'You ever query an order of mine again and I'll have you down to private so fast you won't know your own first name.' A muscle twitched in his right cheek as his glance took in the assembled NCOs one by one. 'Hasn't anybody got any guts here?'

'Of course, sir,' Mallory answered. 'We're right behind you, Colonel.'

'Well you'd better be,' Shafto said, 'Because I'm going in there now on my own with a white flag.'

'You mean you're going to invite them to surrender, sir?'

'Surrender, my backside, Captain. While I do some talking, the rest of you will be getting into position and you've got exactly ten minutes from the moment I enter that dump so let's get to it.'

Devlin was hungry. He heated a little soup, fried an egg and made a sandwich of it with two thick slices of bread, Molly's own baking. He was eating it in the chair by the fire when a cold draught on his left cheek told him that the door had opened. When he looked up, she was standing there.

'So there you are?' he said cheerfully. 'I was having a bite before coming looking for you.' He held up the sandwich. 'Did you know these things were invented by a belted earl, no less?'

'You bastard!' she said. 'You dirty swine! You used me.'

She flung herself on him, hands clawing at his face. He grabbed her wrists and fought to control her. 'What is it?' he demanded. Yet in his heart, he knew.

'I know all about it. Carter isn't his name – it's Steiner and he and his men are bloody Germans come for Mr. Churchill. And what's your name? Not Devlin, I'll be bound.'

He pushed her away from him, went and got the Bushmills and a glass. 'No, Molly, it isn't.' He shook his head. 'You weren't meant to be any part of this, my love. You just happened.'

'You bloody traitor!'

He said in a kind of exasperation. 'Molly, I'm Irish, that means I'm as different from you as a German is from a Frenchman. I'm a foreigner. We're not the same just because we both speak English with different accents. When will you learn, you people?'

There was uncertainty in her eyes now, but she still persisted. 'Traitor!'

His face was bleak then, the eyes very blue, the chin tilted. 'No traitor, Molly. I am a soldier of the Irish Republican Army. I serve a cause as dear to me as yours.'

She needed to hurt him then, to wound and had the weapon to do it. 'Well, much good may it do you and your friend Steiner. He's finished or soon will be. You next.'

'What are you talking about?'

'Pamela Vereker was with me at the church when he and his men took her brother and George Wilde up there. We overheard enough to send her flying off to Meltham to get those Yankee Rangers.'

He grabbed her by the arms. 'How long ago?'

'You go to hell!'

'Tell me, damn you!' he shook her roughly.

'I'd say they must be there by now. If the wind was in the right direction you could probably hear the shooting, so there isn't a bloody thing you can do about it except run while you have the chance.'

He released her and said wryly. 'Sure and it would be the sensible thing to do, but I was never one for that.'

He pulled on his cap and goggles, his trenchcoat, and belted it around his waist. He crossed to the fireplace and felt under a pile of old newspapers behind the log basket. There were two hand grenades there which Ritter Neumann had given him. He primed them and placed them carefully inside the front flap of his trenchcoat. He put the Mauser into his right pocket and lengthened the sling to his Sten, suspending it around his neck almost to waist level so that he could fire it one-handed if necessary.

Molly said, 'What are you going to do?'

'Into the valley of death, Molly, my love, rode the six hundred and all that sort of good old British rubbish.' He poured himself a glass of Bushmills and saw the look of amazement on her face. 'Did you think I'd run for the hills and leave Steiner in the lurch?' He shook his head. 'God, girl, and I thought you knew something about me.'

'You can't go up there.' There was panic in her voice now. 'Liam, you won't stand a chance.' She caught hold of him by the arm.

'Oh, but I must, my pet.' He kissed her on the mouth and pushed her firmly to one side. He turned at the door. 'For what it's worth, I wrote you a letter. No much, I'm afraid, but if you're interested, it's on the mantelpiece.'

The door banged, she stood there rigid, frozen. Somewhere in another world the engine roared into life and moved away.

She found the letter and opened it feverishly. It said: *Molly, my own true love. As a great man once said, I have suffered a sea-change and nothing can ever be the same again. I came to Norfolk to do a job, not to fall in love for the first and last time in my life with an ugly little peasant girl that should have known better. By now you'll know the worst of me, but try not to think it. To leave you is punishment enough. Let it end there. As they say in Ireland, we knew the two days. Liam.*

The words blurred, there were tears in her eyes. She stuffed the letter into her pocket and stumbled outside. Her horse was at the hitching ring. She untied him quickly, scrambled up on his back and urged him into a gallop, beating her clenched fist against his neck. At the end of the dyke she took him straight across the road, jumped the hedge and galloped for the village, taking the shortest route across the fields.

Otto Brandt sat on the parapet of the bridge and lit a cigarette as if he didn't have a care in the world. 'So what do we do, run for it?'

'Where to?' Ritter looked at his watch. 'Twenty to five. It should be dark by six-thirty at the latest. If we can hang on until then, we could fade away in twos and threes and make for Hobs End across country. Maybe some of us could catch that boat.'

'The Colonel could have other ideas,' Sergeant Altmann said.

Brandt nodded. 'Exactly, only he isn't here, so for the moment it seems to me we'd better get ready to do a little fighting.'

'Which raises an important point,' Ritter said. 'We fight only as German soldiers. That was made clear from the beginning. It seems to me that the time has come to drop the pretence.'

He took off his red beret and jump jacket, revealing his *Fliegerbluse*. From his hip pocket he produced a Luftwaffe sidecap or *Schiff* and adjusted it to the correct angle.

'All right,' he said to Brandt and Altmann. 'The same for everybody, so you'd better get moving.'

Joanna Grey had witnessed the entire scene from her bedroom window and the sight of Ritter's uniform brought a chill to her heart. She watched Altmann go in to the Post Office. A moment later Mr. Turner emerged. He crossed the bridge and started up the hill to the church.

Ritter was in an extraordinary dilemma. Ordinarily in such circumstances he would have ordered an immediate withdrawal, but as he had said to Brandt, where to? Including himself, he had twelve men to guard the prisoners and hold the village. An impossible situation. *But so was the Albert Canal and Eban Emael*, that's what Steiner would have said. It occurred to him, and not for the first time, how much he had come to depend on Steiner over the years.

He tried to raise him again on the field telephone. 'Come in Eagle One,' he said in English. 'This is Eagle Two.'

There was no reply. He handed the phone back to Private Hagl who lay in the shelter of the bridge wall, the barrel of his Bren protruding through a drainage hole giving him a fair field of fire. A supply of magazines was neatly stacked beside him. He, too, had divested himself of the red beret and jump jacket and wore *Schiff* and *Fliegerbluse* while still retaining his camouflaged trousers.

'No luck, Herr Oberleutnant?' he said and then stiffened. 'I think that's a jeep I hear now.'

'Yes, but from the wrong direction entirely,' Ritter told him grimly.

He vaulted over the wall beside Hagl, turned and saw a jeep come round the corner by Joanna Grey's cottage. A white handkerchief fluttered at the end of the radio aerial. There was one occupant only, the man at the wheel. Ritter stepped from behind the wall and waited, hands on hips.

Shafto hadn't bothered swopping to a tin hat and still wore his sidecap. He took a cigar from one of his shirt pockets, and put it between his teeth purely for effect. He took his time over lighting it, then got out of the jeep and came forward. He stopped a yard or two away from Ritter and stood, legs apart, looking him over.

Ritter noted the collar tabs and saluted formally. 'Colonel.'

Shafto returned the salute. His glance took in the two Iron Crosses, the Winter War ribbon, the wound badge in silver, the combat badge for distinguished service in ground battles, the paratrooper's qualification badge, and knew that in this fresh-faced young man he was looking on a hardened veteran.

'So, no more pretence, Herr Oberleutnant? Where's Steiner? Tell him Colonel Robert E. Shafto, in command Twenty-first Specialist Raiding Force, would like to speak with him.'

'I am in charge here, Herr Oberst. You must deal with me.'

Shafto's eyes took in the barrel of the Bren poking through the drainage hole in the bridge parapet, swivelled to the Post Office, the first floor of the Studley Arms where two bedroom windows stood open. Ritter said politely, 'Is there anything else, Colonel, or have you seen enough?'

'What happened to Steiner? Has he run out on you or something?' Ritter made no reply and Shafto went on, 'Okay, son, I know how many men you have under your command and if I have to bring my boys in here you won't last ten minutes. Why not be practical and throw in the towel?'

'So sorry,' Ritter said, 'But the fact is I left in such a hurry that I forgot to put one in my overnight bag.'

Shafto tapped ash from his cigar. 'Ten minutes, that's all I'll give you, then we come in.'

'And I'll give you two, Colonel,' Ritter said. 'To get to hell out of here before my men open fire.'

There was the metallic click of weapons being cocked. Shafto looked up at the windows and said grimly, 'Okay, sonny, you asked for it.'

He dropped the cigar, stamped it very deliberately into the ground, walked back to the jeep and got behind the wheel. As he drove away he reached for the mike on the field radio. 'This is Sugar One. Twenty seconds and counting. Nineteen, eighteen, seventeen . . .'

He was passing Joanna Grey's cottage at twelve, disappeared round the bend in the road on ten.

She watched him go from the bedroom window, turned and went into the study. She opened the secret door to the cubbyhole loft, closed it behind her and locked it. She went upstairs, sat down at the radio, took the Luger from the drawer and laid it down on the table where she could reach it quickly. Strange, but now that it had come to this she wasn't in the least afraid. She reached for a bottle of Scotch and as she poured a large one, firing started outside.

The lead jeep in Shafto's section roared round the corner into the straight. There were four men inside and the two in the rear were standing up working a Browning machine-gun. As they passed the garden of the cottage next to Joanna Grey's, Dinter and Berg stood up together, Dinter supporting the barrel of a Bren gun across his shoulder while Berg did the firing. He loosed one long continuous burst that knocked the two men at the Browning off their feet. The jeep bounced over the verge and rolled over, coming to rest upside down in the stream.

The next jeep in line swerved away wildly, the driver taking it round in a circle over the grass bank that almost had it into the stream with the other. Berg swung the barrel of the Bren, continuing to fire in short bursts, driving one of the jeep's machine gun crew over the side of the vehicle and smashing its windscreen before it scrambled round the corner to safety.

In the rubble of Stalingrad, Dinter and Berg had learned that the essence of success in such situations was to make your hit, then get out fast. They exited immediately through a wrought-iron gate in the wall and worked their way back to the Post Office, using the cover of the back garden hedges at the rear of the cottages.

Shafto, who had witnessed the entire debacle from a rise in the woods further down the road, ground his teeth with rage. It had suddenly become all too obvious that Ritter had let him see exactly what he had wanted him to see. 'Why, that little bastard was setting me up,' he said softly.

The jeep which had just been shot-up pulled in at the side of the road in front of number three. Its driver had a bad cut on the face. A sergeant named Thomas was putting a field dressing on it. Shafto shouted down, 'For Christ's sake, Sergeant, what are you playing at? There's a machine-gun behind the wall of the garden of the second cottage along. Go forward with three men on foot now and take care of it.'

Krukowski, who waited behind him with the field telephone, winced. *Five minutes ago we were thirteen. Now it's nine. What in the hell does he think he's playing at?*

There was heavy firing from the other side of the village. Shafto raised his fieldglasses, but could see little except for a piece of the road curving beyond the bridge and the roof of the mill standing up beyond the end houses. He snapped a finger and Krukowski passed him the phone. 'Mallory, do you read me?'

Mallory answered instantly. 'Affirmative, Colonel.'

'What in the hell goes on up there? I expected you with bells on by now.'

'They've got a strong point set up in the mill on the first floor. Commands one hell of a field of fire. They knocked out the lead jeep. It's blocking the road now. I've already lost four men.'

'Then lose some more,' Shafto yelled into the phone. 'Get in there, Mallory. Burn them out. Whatever it takes.'

The firing was very heavy now as Shafto tried the other section. 'You there, Hustler?'

'Colonel, this is Hustler.' His voice sounded rather faint.

'I expected to see you up on the hill at that church by now.'

'It's been tough going, Colonel. We just started across the fields like you said and got tangled up in a bog. Just approaching the south end of Hawks Wood now.'

'Well, get the lead out, for Christ's sake!'

He handed the phone back to Krukowski. 'Christ Jesus!' he said bitterly. 'You can't rely on anybody: when it comes right down to it, anything I need doing right, I've got to see to myself.'

He slid down the bank into the ditch as Sergeant Thomas and the three men he'd taken with him returned. 'Nothing to report, Colonel.'

'What do you mean, nothing to report?'

'No one there, sir, just these.' Thomas held out a handful of .303 cartridge cases.

Shafto struck his hand violently, spilling them to the ground. 'Okay, I want both jeeps out in front, two men to each Browning. I want that bridge plastering. I want you to lay down such a field of fire that even a blade of grass won't be able to stand up.'

'But Colonel,' Thomas began.

'And you take four men and work your way on foot back of the cottages. Hit that Post Office by the bridge from the rear. Krukowski stays with me.' He slammed his hand hard down on the bonnet of the jeep. 'Now move it!'

Otto Brandt had Corporal Walther, Meyer and Riedel with him in the mill. From a defence point of view it was perfect: the ancient stone walls were about three feet thick and downstairs the oak doors were bolted and barred. The windows of the first floor commanded an excellent field of fire and Brandt had a Bren gun set up there.

Down below a jeep burned steadily, blocking the road. One man was still inside, two more sprawled in the ditch. Brandt had disposed of the jeep personally, making no sign at first, letting Mallory and his men come roaring in, only lobbing down a couple of grenades from the loft door at the last moment. The effect had been catastrophic. From behind the hedges further up the road the Americans poured in a considerable amount of fire to little effect because of those massive stone walls.

'I don't know who's in charge down there, but he doesn't know his business,' Walther observed as he reloaded his M1.

'Well, what would you have done?' Brandt asked him, squinting along the barrel of the Bren as he loosed off a quick burst.

'There's the stream, isn't there? No windows on that side. They should be moving in from the rear . . .'

Brandt held up his hand. 'Everyone stop firing.'

'Why?' Walther demanded.

'Because they have, or hadn't you noticed?'

There was a deathly silence and Brandt said softly, 'I'm not sure I really believe this, but get ready.'

A moment later, with a rousing battlecry, Mallory and eight or nine men emerged from shelter and ran for the next ditch, firing from the hip. In spite of the fact that they were getting covering fire from the Brownings of the two remaining jeeps on the other side of the hedge, it was an incredible act of folly.

'My God!' Brandt said. 'Where do they think they are? The Somme?'

He put a long, almost leisurely burst into Mallory and killed him instantly. Three more went down as the Germans all fired at once. One of them picked himself up and staggered back to the safety of the first hedge as the survivors retreated.

In the quiet which followed, Brandt reached for a cigarette. 'I make that seven. Eight if you count the one who dragged himself back.'

'Crazy,' Walther said. 'Suicide. I mean, why are they in such a hurry? All they have to do is wait.'

Kane and Colonel Corcoran sat in a jeep two hundred yards down the road from the main gate at Meltham House and looked up at the shattered telephone pole. 'Good God!' Corcoran said. 'It's really quite incredible. What on earth was he thinking of?'

Kane could have told him, but refrained. He said, 'I don't know, Colonel. Maybe some notion he had about security. He sure was anxious to get to grips with those paratroopers.'

A jeep turned out of the main gate and moved towards them. Garvey was at the wheel and when he braked, his face was serious. 'We just got a message in the radio room.'

'From Shafto?'

Garvey shook his head. 'Krukowski, of all people. He asked for you, Major, personally. It's a mess down there. He says they walked right into it. Dead men all over the place.'

'And Shafto?'

'Krukowski was pretty hysterical. Kept saying the Colonel was acting like a crazy man. Some of it didn't make much sense.'

Dear God, Kane thought, *he's gone riding straight in, guidons fluttering in the breeze.* He said to Corcoran, 'I think I should get down there, Colonel.'

'So do I,' Corcoran said. 'Naturally, you'll leave adequate protection for the Prime Minister.'

Kane turned to Garvey. 'What have we got left in the motor pool?'

'A White Scout car and three jeeps.'

'All right, we'll take them plus a detail of twenty men. Ready to move out in five minutes if you please, Sergeant.'

Garvey swung the jeep in a tight circle and drove away fast. 'That leaves twenty-five for you, sir,' Kane told Corcoran. 'Will that be all right?'

'Twenty-six with me,' Corcoran said. 'Perfectly adequate, especially as I shall naturally assume command. Time someone licked you colonials into shape.'

'I know, sir,' Harvey Kane said as he switched on the engine. 'Nothing but a mass of complexes since Bunker Hill.' He let in the clutch and drove away.

18

The village was still a good mile and a half away when Steiner first became aware of the persistent electronic buzz from the Grauman field phone. Someone was on channel, but too far away to be heard. 'Put your foot down,' he told Klugl. 'Something's wrong.'

When they were a mile away, the rattle of small arms fire in the distance confirmed his worst fears. He cocked his Sten gun and looked up at Werner. 'Be ready to use that thing. You might have to.'

Klugl had the jeep pushed right up to its limit, his foot flat on the boards. 'Come on, damn you! Come on!' Steiner cried.

The Grauman had ceased the buzz and as they drew closer to the village, he tried to make voice contact. 'This is Eagle One. Come in, Eagle Two.'

There was no reply. He tried again, but with no better success. Klugl said, 'Maybe they're too busy, Herr Oberst.'

A moment later they topped the rise at Garrowby Heath three

hundred yards west of the church at the top of the hill and the whole panorama was spread below. Steiner raised his field glasses, took in the mill and Mallory's detail in the field beyond. He moved on, noting the Rangers behind the hedges at the rear of the Post Office and the Studley Arms and Ritter, young Hagl beside him, pinned down behind the bridge by the heavy concentration of machine-gun fire from the Brownings of Shafto's two remaining jeeps. One of them had been sited alongside Joanna Grey's garden wall from where the gun crew were able to fire over the top and yet remain in good cover. The other employed the same technique against the wall of the next cottage.

Steiner tried the Grauman again. 'This is Eagle One. Do you read me?'

On the first floor of the mill, his voice crackled in the ear of Riedel, who had just switched on during a lull in the fighting. 'It's the Colonel,' he cried to Brandt and said into the phone. 'This is Eagle Three, in the water mill. Where are you?'

'On the hill above the church,' Steiner said. 'What is your situation?'

Several bullets passed through the glassless windows and ricocheted from the wall. 'Give it to me!' Brandt called from his position flat on the floor behind the Bren.

'He's on the hill,' Riedel said. 'Trust Steiner to turn up to pull us out of the shit.' He crawled along to the loft door above the waterwheel and kicked it open.

'Come back here,' Brandt called.

Riedel crouched to peer outside. He laughed excitedly and raised the Grauman to his mouth. 'I can see you, Herr Oberst, we're . . .'

There was a heavy burst of automatic fire from outside, blood and brains sprayed across the wall as the back of Riedel's skull disintegrated and he went head-first out of the loft, still clutching the field phone.

Brandt flung himself across the room and peered over the edge. Riedel had fallen on top of the waterwheel. It kept on turning, carrying him with it, down into the churning waters. When it came round again, he was gone.

On the hill, Werner tapped Steiner on the shoulder. 'Below, Herr Oberst, in the wood on the right. Soldiers.'

Steiner swung his field glasses. With the height advantage the hill gave him it was just possible to see down into one section of the sunken track through Hawks Wood about half-way along. Sergeant Hustler and his men were passing through.

Steiner made his decision and acted on it. 'It seems we're Fallschirm-jäger again, boys.'

He tossed his red beret away, unbuckled his webbing belt and the Browning in its holster and took off his jump jacket. Underneath he was wearing his *Fliegerbluse*, the Knight's Cross with Oak Leaves at his throat. He took a *Schiff* from his pocket and jammed it down on his head. Klugl and Werner followed his example.

Steiner said, 'Right, boys, the grand tour. Straight down that track through the wood, across the footbridge for a few words with those jeeps. I think you can make it, Klugl, if you go fast enough, then on to Oberleutnant Neumann.' He looked up at Werner. 'And don't stop firing. Not for anything.'

The jeep was doing fifty as they went down the final stretch towards the church. Corporal Becker was outside the porch. He crouched in alarm, Steiner waved, then Klugl swung the wheel and turned the jeep into the Hawks Wood track.

They bounced over a slight rise, hurtled round a bend between the steep walls and there was Hustler with his men, no more than twenty yards away, strung out on either side of the track. Werner started to fire at point blank range, had no more than a few seconds in which to take aim because, by then, the jeep was into them. Men were jumping for their lives, trying to scramble up the steep banks. The offside front wheel bounced over a body and then they were through, leaving Sergeant Horace Hustler and seven of his men dead or dying behind them.

The jeep emerged from the end of the track like a thunderbolt. Klugl kept right on going as ordered, straight across the four-foot wide footbridge over the stream, snapping the rustic pole handrails like matchsticks, and shot up the bank to the road, all four wheels clear of the ground as they bounced over the rise.

The two men comprising the machine-gun crew of the jeep sheltering behind Joanna Grey's garden wall swung their Browning frantically, already too late as Werner raked the wall with a sustained burst that knocked them both off their feet.

But the fact of their dying gave the crew of the second jeep, positioned at the side of the next garden wall, the two or three precious seconds to react – the seconds that meant the difference between life and death. They had their Browning round and were already firing as Klugl swung the wheel and drove back towards the bridge.

It was the Rangers' turn now. Werner got in a quick burst as they flashed past that caught one of the machine-gun crew, but the other kept firing his Browning, bullets hammering into the Germans' jeep, shattering the windscreen. Klugl gave a sudden sharp cry and fell towards the steering wheel, the jeep swerved wildly and smashed into the parapet at the end of the bridge. It seemed to hang there for a moment, then tipped over on to its side very slowly.

Klugl lay huddled in the shelter of the jeep and Werner crouched over him, blood on his face where flying glass had cut him. He looked up at Steiner. 'He's dead, Herr Oberst,' he said and his eyes were wild.

He reached for a Sten gun and started to stand. Steiner dragged him down. 'Pull yourself together, boy. He's dead, you're alive.'

Werner nodded dully. 'Yes, Herr Oberst.'

'Now get this Browning set up and keep them busy down there.'

As Steiner turned, Ritter Neumann crawled out from behind the parapet carrying a Bren gun. 'You certainly created hell back there.'

'They had a section moving up through the wood to the church,' Steiner said. 'We didn't do them any good either. What about Hagl?'

'Done for, I'm afraid.' Neumann nodded to where Hagl's boots protruded from behind the parapet.

Werner had the Browning set up at the side of the jeep now and started to fire in short bursts. Steiner said, 'All right, Herr Oberleutnant, and what exactly did you have in mind?'

'It should be dark in an hour,' Ritter said. 'I thought if we could hold on till then and slip away in twos and threes. We could lie low in the marsh at Hobs End under cover of darkness. Still make that boat if Koenig arrives as arranged. After all, we'll never get near the old man now.' He hesitated and added rather awkwardly, 'It gives us some sort of chance.'

'The only one,' Steiner said. 'But not here. I think it's time we re-grouped again. Where is everybody?'

Ritter gave him a quick run-down on the general situation and when he was finished, Steiner nodded. 'I managed to raise them in the mill on the way in. Got Riedel on the Grauman plus a lot of machine-gun fire. You get Altmann and his boys and I'll see if I can get through to Brandt.'

Werner gave Ritter covering fire as the Oberleutnant darted across the road and Steiner tried to raise Brandt on the Grauman. He had no success at all and as Neumann emerged from the door of the Post Office with Altmann, Dinter and Berg, there was an outbreak of heavy firing up at the mill.

They all crouched behind the parapet and Steiner said, 'I can't raise Brandt. God knows what's happening. I want the rest of you to make a run for it to the church. You've good cover for most of the way if you keep to the hedge. You're in charge, Ritter.'

'What about you?'

'I'll keep them occupied with the Browning for a while then I'll follow on.'

'But Herr Oberst,' Ritter began.

Steiner cut him off short. 'No buts about it. Today's my day for playing hero. Now get to hell out of it, all of you and that's an order.'

Ritter hesitated, but only fractionally. He nodded to Altmann then slipped past the jeep and ran across the bridge, crouching behind the parapet. Steiner got down to the Browning and started to fire.

At the other end of the bridge there was a stretch of open ground, no more than twenty-five feet before the safety of the hedge. Ritter, crouching on one knee, said, 'Taking it one by one is no good because after he's seen the first, that joker on the machine-gun will be ready and waiting for whoever comes next. When I give the word, we all go together.'

A moment later he was out of cover and dashing across the road, vaulting the stile and dropping into the safety of the hedge, Altmann right on his heels and followed by the others. The Ranger on the Browning at the other end of the village was a corporal named Bleeker, a Cape Cod fisherman in happier times. Just now, he was nearly out of his mind with pain, a piece of glass having buried itself just beneath his right eye. More than anything else in the world he hated Shafto for bringing him to this, but right now any target would do. He saw the Germans crossing the road and swung the Browning, too late. In his rage and frustration he raked the hedge anyway.

On the other side Berg tripped and fell and Dinter turned to help him. 'Give me your hand, you daft bastard,' he said. 'Two left feet as usual.'

Berg stood up to die with him as bullets shredded the hedge, hammering into them, driving them back across the meadow in a last frenzied dance. Werner turned with a cry and Altmann grabbed him by the shoulder and pushed him after Ritter.

From the loft entrance above the waterwheel, Brandt and Meyer saw what had happened in the meadow. 'So now we know,' Meyer said. 'From the look of things I'd say we've taken up permanent residence here.'

Brandt watched Ritter, Altmann and Briegel toil up the long run of the hedge and scramble over the wall into the churchyard. 'They made it,' he said. 'Wonders will never cease.'

He moved across to Meyer, who was propped against a box in the middle of the floor. He'd been shot in the stomach. His blouse was open and there was an obscene hole with swollen purple lips just below his navel. 'Look at that,' he said, sweat on his face. 'At least I'm not losing any blood. My mother always did say I had the luck of the Devil.'

'So I've observed.' Brandt put a cigarette in Meyer's mouth, but before he could light it, heavy firing started again from outside.

Shafto crouched in the shelter of the wall in Joanna Grey's front garden, stunned by the enormity of the news one of the survivors of Hustler's section had just brought him. The catastrophe seemed complete. In little over half-an-hour he had lost at least twenty-two men dead or wounded. More than half his command. The consequences now were too appalling to contemplate.

Krukowski, crouching behind him with the field telephone, said, 'What are you going to do, Colonel?'

'What do you mean, what am *I* going to do?' Shafto demanded. 'It's always me when it comes right down to it. Leave things to other people, people with no conception of discipline or duty, and see what happens.'

He slumped against the wall and looked up. At that exact moment Joanna Grey peered from behind the bedroom curtain. She drew back instantly, too late. Shafto growled deep in his throat. 'My God, Krukowski, that Goddamned, double-dealing bitch is still in the house.'

He pointed up at the window as he scrambled to his feet. Krukowski said, 'I can't see anyone, sir.'

'You soon will, boy!' Shafto cried, drawing his pearl-handled Colt. 'Come on!' and he ran up the path to the front door.

Joanna Grey locked the secret door and went up the stairs quickly to the cubbyhole loft. She sat down at the radio and started to transmit on the Landsvoort channel. She could hear noise downstairs. Doors were flung open and furniture knocked over as Shafto ransacked the house. He was very close now, stamping about in the study. She heard his cry of rage quite clearly as he went out on the stairs.

'She's got to be in here someplace.'

A voice echoed up the stairs. 'Heh, Colonel, there was this dog locked in the cellar. He's on his way up to you now like a bat out of hell.'

Joanna Grey reached for the Luger and cocked it, continuing to transmit without faltering. On the landing, Shafto stood to one side as Patch scurried past him. He followed the retriever into the study and found him scratching at the panelling in the corner.

Shafto examined it quickly and found the tiny keyhole almost at once. 'She's here, Krukowski!' There was a savage, almost insane joy in his voice. 'I've got her!'

He fired three shots point blank in the general area of the keyhole. The wood splintered as the lock disintegrated and the door swung open of its own accord, just as Krukowski entered the room, his M1 ready.

'Take it easy, sir.'

'Like hell I will.' Shafto started up the stairs, the Colt held out in front of him as Patch flashed past. 'Come down out of there, you bitch!'

As his head rose above floor level, Joanna Grey shot him between the eyes. He tumbled back down into the study. Krukowski poked the barrel of his M1 round the corner and loosed off a fifteen-round clip so fast that it sounded like one continuous burst. The dog howled, there was the sound of a body falling, and then silence.

Devlin arrived outside the church as Ritter, Altmann and Werner Briegel ran through the tombstones towards the porch. They veered towards him as Devlin braked to a halt at the lychgate. 'It's a mess,' Ritter said. 'And the Colonel's still down there by the bridge.'

Devlin looked down to the village where Steiner continued to fire the Browning from behind the damaged jeep and Ritter grabbed his arm and pointed. 'My God, look what's coming!'

Devlin turned and saw, on the other side of the bend in the road beyond Joanna Grey's cottage, a White Scout Car and three jeeps. He revved his motor and grinned. 'Sure and if I don't go now I might think better of it and that would never do.'

He went straight down the hill and skidded broadside on into the entrance to Old Woman's Meadow, leaving the track within a few yards and taking the direct route straight across the field to the footbridge above the weir. He seemed to take off again and again as the machine bounced over the tussocky grass and Ritter watched from the lychgate, marvelling that he remained in the saddle.

The Oberleutnant ducked suddenly as a bullet chipped the woodwork beside his head. He dropped into the shelter of the wall with Werner and Altmann and started to return the fire as the survivors of Hustler's section, finally re-grouped, reached the fringe of the wood opposite the church.

Devlin shot across the footbridge and followed the track through the wood on the other side. There were men up there by the road, he was sure of it. He pulled one of the grenades from inside his coat and yanked the pin with his teeth. And then he was through the trees and there was a jeep on the grass verge, men turning in alarm.

He simply dropped the grenade behind him. He took out the other. There were more Rangers behind the hedge on his left and he tossed the second grenade over towards them as the first exploded. He kept right on going, down the road past the mill and round the corner, skidding to a halt behind the bridge where Steiner still crouched with the machine-gun.

Steiner didn't say a word. He simply stood up, holding the Browning in both hands and emptied it in a long burst of such savagery that it sent Corporal Bleeker diving for cover behind the garden wall. In the same moment, Steiner tossed the Browning to one side and swung a leg over the pillion. Devlin gunned the motor, swerved across the bridge and went straight up the hill as the White Scout Car nosed round the corner of Joanna Grey's cottage. Harry Kane stood to watch them go.

'And what in the hell was *that*?' Garvey demanded.

Corporal Bleeker fell out of his jeep and stumbled towards them, blood on his face. 'Is there a medic there, sir? I think maybe I lost my right eye. I can't see a thing.'

Someone jumped down to hold him and Kane surveyed the shambles of the village. 'The crazy, stupid bastard,' he whispered.

Krukowski came out of the front gate and saluted. 'Where's the Colonel?' Kane asked.

'Dead, sir, upstairs in the house. The lady in there – she shot him.'

Kane got down in a hurry. 'Where is she?'

'I – I killed her, Major,' Krukowski said, and there were tears in his eyes.

Kane couldn't think of a single damn thing to say. He patted Krukowski on the shoulder and went up the path to the cottage.

At the top of the hill, Ritter and his two comrades were still firing from behind the wall at the Rangers in the wood when Devlin and Steiner arrived on the scene. The Irishman changed gear, got his foot down and let the bike drift, turning at just the right moment for a clear run through the lychgate and up the path to the porch. Ritter, Altmann and Werner retreated steadily using the tombstones for cover and finally made the safety of the porch without further casualties.

Corporal Becker had the door open, they all passed inside and he slammed it shut and bolted it. The firing resumed outside with renewed intensity. The villagers huddled together, tense and anxious. Philip Vereker limped down the aisle to confront Devlin, his face white with anger. 'Another damned traitor!'

Devlin grinned. 'Ah, well,' he said. 'It's nice to be back amongst friends.'

In the mill everything was quiet. 'I don't like it,' Walther commented.

'You never do,' Brandt said and frowned. 'What's that?'

There was the sound of a vehicle approaching. Brandt tried to peer out of the loft entrance over the road and immediately came under fire. He drew back. 'How's Meyer?'

'I think he's dead.'

Brandt reached for a cigarette as the noise of the approaching vehicle drew close. 'Just think,' he said. 'The Albert Canal, Crete, Stalingrad and where does the end of the road turn out to be? Studley Constable.' He put a light to his cigarette.

The White Scout Car was doing at least forty when Garvey swung the wheel and smashed it straight through the mill doors. Kane stood in the back behind a Browning anti-aircraft machine-gun and was already firing up through the wooden floor above, the enormous .50 calibre rounds smashing their way through with ease, ripping the planking to pieces. He was aware of the cries of agony, but kept on firing, working the gun from side to side, only stopping when there were great gaping holes in the floor.

A bloodstained hand showed at one of them. It was very quiet. Garvey took a Thompson gun from one of the men, jumped down and went up the flight of wooden steps in the corner. He came down again almost instantly.

'That's it, Major.'

Harry Kane's face was pale, but he was completely in command of himself. 'All right,' he said. 'Now for the church.'

Molly arrived on Garrowby Heath in time to see a jeep drive up the hill, a white handkerchief fluttering from its radio aerial. It pulled up at the lychgate and Kane and Dexter Garvey got out. As they went up the path through the churchyard Kane said softly, 'Use your eyes, Sergeant. Make sure you'd know this place again if you saw it.'

'Affirmative, Major.'

The church door opened and Steiner moved out of the porch and Devlin leaned against the wall behind him smoking a cigarette. Harry Kane saluted formally. 'We've met before, Colonel.'

Before Steiner could reply, Philip Vereker pushed past Becker at the door and limped forward. 'Kane, where's Pamela? Is she all right?'

'She's fine, Father,' Kane told him. 'I left her back at Meltham House.'

Vereker turned to Steiner, face pinched and very white. There was a glitter of triumph in his eyes. 'She fixed you beautifully, didn't she, Steiner? Without her you might actually have got away with it.'

Steiner said calmly, 'Strange how the perspective changes with the point of view. I thought we failed because a man called Karl Sturm sacrificed himself to save two children's lives.' He didn't wait for an answer, but turned to Kane. 'What can I do for you?'

'Surely that's obvious. Surrender. There's no point in further useless bloodshed. The men you left down in the mill are all dead. So is Mrs. Grey.'

Vereker caught him by the arm. 'Mrs. Grey is dead? How?'

'She killed Colonel Shafto when he tried to arrest her, died herself in the exchange of gunfire which followed.' Vereker turned away, a look of utter desolation on his face and Kane said to Steiner. 'You are quite alone now. The Prime Minister is safe at Meltham House under as heavy a guard as he's likely to see in his lifetime. It's all over.'

Steiner thought of Brandt and Walther and Meyer, Gerhard Klugl, Dinter and Berg and nodded, his face very pale. 'Honourable terms?'

'No terms!' Vereker shouted it aloud like a cry to heaven. 'These men came here in British uniform, must I remind you of that, Major?'

'But did not fight in them,' Steiner cut in. 'We fought only as German soldiers, in German uniforms. As Fallschirmjäger. The other was a legitimate *ruse de guerre*.'

'And a direct contravention of the Geneva Convention,' Vereker answered. 'Which not only expressly forbids the wearing of an enemy's uniform in time of war, but also prescribes the death penalty for offenders.'

Steiner saw the look on Kane's face and smiled gently. 'Don't worry, Major, not your fault. The rules of the game and all that.' He turned to Vereker. 'Well now, Father, your God is a God of Wrath indeed. You would dance on my grave, it seems.'

'Damn you, Steiner!' Vereker lurched forward, raising his stick to strike, stumbled over the long skirts of his cassock and fell, striking his head on the edge of a tombstone.

Garvey dropped to one knee beside him and made a quick examination. 'Out for the count.' He looked up. 'Somebody should check him out, though. We've got a good medic down in the village.'

'Take him by all means,' Steiner said. 'Take all of them.'

Garvey glanced at Kane, then picked Vereker up and carried him to the jeep. Kane said, 'You'll let the villagers go?'

'The obvious thing to do since a further outbreak of hostilities seems imminent.' Steiner looked faintly amused. 'Why, did you think we'd hold the entire village hostage or come out fighting, driving the women in front of us? The brutal Hun? Sorry I can't oblige.' He turned. 'Send them out, Becker, all of them.'

The door swung open with a crash and the villagers started to pour through, led by Laker Armsby. Most of the women were crying hysterically as they rushed past. Betty Wilde came last with Graham and Ritter Neumann supported her husband, who looked dazed and ill. Garvey hurried back up the path and got an arm round him and Betty Wilde reached for Graham's hand and turned to Ritter.

'He'll be all right, Mrs. Wilde,' the young Oberleutnant said. 'I'm sorry about what happened in there, believe me.'

'That's all right,' she said. 'It wasn't your fault. Would you do something for me? Would you tell me your name?'

'Neumann,' he said. 'Ritter Neumann.'

'Thank you,' she said simply. 'I'm sorry I said the things I did.' She turned to Steiner. 'And I want to thank you and your men for Graham.'

'He's a brave boy,' Steiner said. 'He didn't even hesitate. He jumped straight in. That takes courage and courage is something that never goes out of fashion.'

The boy stared up at him. 'Why are you a German?' he demanded. 'Why aren't you on our side?'

Steiner laughed out loud. 'Go on, get him out of here,' he said to Betty Wilde. 'Before he completely corrupts me.'

She took the boy by the hand and hurried away. Beyond the wall the women streamed down the hill. At that moment the White Scout Car emerged from the Hawks Wood track and stopped, its anti-aircraft gun and heavy machine-gun traversing on to the porch.

Steiner nodded wryly. 'So, Major, the final act. Let battle commence then.' He saluted and went back into the porch where Devlin had been standing throughout the entire conversation without saying a word.

'I don't think I've ever heard you silent for so long before,' Steiner said.

Devlin grinned. 'To tell you the truth I couldn't think of a single damned thing to say except *Help*. Can I go in now and pray?'

From her vantage point on the heath Molly watched Devlin disappear inside the porch with Steiner and her heart sank like a stone. *Oh, God,* she thought, *I must do something*. She got to her feet and at the same moment, a dozen Rangers, headed by the big black sergeant, cut across the road from the wood well up from the church where they couldn't be seen. They ran back along the wall and entered the presbytery garden through the wicket gate.

But they didn't go into the house. They slipped over the wall into the cemetery, approaching the church from the tower end and worked their way round to the porch. The big sergeant had a coil of rope over his shoulder and as she watched, he jumped for the porch guttering and pulled himself over, then scrambled fifteen feet up the ivy vine to the lower leads. Once there, he uncoiled the rope and tossed the end down and the other Rangers began to follow.

Seized by a sudden new determination, Molly swung into the saddle and urged her horse across the heath, turning down to the woods at the rear of the presbytery.

It was very cold inside the church, a place of shadows, only the flickering candles, the ruby light of the sanctuary lamp. There were eight of them now including Devlin. Steiner and Ritter, Werner Briegel, Altmann, Jansen, Corporal Becker and Preston. There was also, unknown to any of them, Arthur Seymour who, overlooked in the stampede to get out, still lay beside Sturm in the darkness of the Lady Chapel, his hands and feet bound. He had managed to push himself into a sitting position against the wall and was working on his wrists, his strange mad eyes fixed on Preston.

Steiner tried the tower door and the sacristy, both of which appeared to be locked behind the curtain at the foot of the tower where ropes soared through holes in the wooden floor thirty feet up to bells which hadn't rung since 1939.

He turned and walked up the aisle to face them. 'Well, all I can offer you is another fight.'

Preston said, 'It's a ludicrous situation. How can we fight? They've got the men, the equipment. We couldn't hold this place for ten minutes once they really start.'

'It's quite simple,' Steiner said. 'We don't have any other choice. As you heard, under the terms of the Geneva Convention we have put ourselves gravely at risk by wearing British uniforms.'

'We fought as German soldiers,' Preston insisted. 'In German uniforms. You said that yourself.'

'A neat point,' Steiner said. 'I'd hate to stake my life on it, even with a good lawyer. If it's to be a bullet, rather now than from a firing squad later.'

'I don't know what you're getting so worked up about anyway, Preston,' Ritter said. 'It's the Tower of London for you without a doubt. The English, I'm afraid, have never held traitors in particularly high regard. They'll hang you so high the crows won't be able to get at you.'

Preston sank down in a pew, head in hands.

The organ rumbled into life and Hans Altmann, sitting high above the choir stalls, called, 'A choral prelude of Johann Sebastian Bach, particularly appropriate to our situation as it is entitled *For the Dying.*'

His voice echoed up into the nave as the music swelled. *Ach wie nichtig, ach wie fluchtig. O how cheating, O how fleeting are our days departing . . .*

One of the clerestory windows high up in the nave smashed. A burst of automatic fire knocked Altmann off the seat into the choir stalls. Werner turned, crouching, firing his Sten. A Ranger pitched headlong through the window and landed between two pews. In the same moment, several more clerestory windows crashed in and heavy fire was poured down into the church. Werner was hit in the head as he ran along the south aisle and fell on his face without a cry. Someone was using a Thompson gun up there now, spraying it back and forth.

Steiner crawled to Werner, turned him over, then moved on, dodging up the chancel steps to check on Altmann. He returned by way of the south aisle, keeping down behind the pews as intermittent firing continued.

Devlin crawled to meet him. 'What's the situation up there?'

'Altmann and Briegel both gone.'

'It's a bloodbath,' the Irishman said. 'We don't stand a chance. Ritter's been hit in the legs and Jansen's dead.'

Steiner crawled back with him to the rear of the church and found Ritter on his back behind the pews binding a field dressing round one thigh. Preston and Corporal Becker crouched beside him.

'Are you all right, Ritter?' Steiner asked.

'They'll run out of wound badges, Herr Oberst.' Ritter grinned, but was obviously in great pain.

They were still firing from above and Steiner nodded towards the sacristy door, barely visible now in the shadows and said to Becker, 'See if you can shoot your way through that door. We can't last long out here, that's for certain.'

Becker nodded and slipped through the shadows behind the font, keeping low. There was that strange metallic clicking of the bolt reciprocating as he fired the silenced Sten, he stamped against the sacristy door, it swung open.

All firing stopped and Garvey called from high above. 'You had enough yet, Colonel? This is like shooting fish in a barrel and I'd rather not, but we'll carry you out on a plank if we have to.'

Preston cracked then, jumped to his feet and ran out into the open by the font. 'Yes, I'll come! I've had enough!'

'Bastard!' Becker cried and he ran out of the shadows by the sacristy door and rammed the butt of his rifle against the side of Preston's skull. The Thompson gun rattled, a short burst only, but it caught Becker full in the back, driving him headlong through the curtains at the base of the tower. He grabbed at the ropes in dying as if trying to hang on to life itself and somewhere overhead, a bell tolled sonorously for the first time in years.

There was silence again and Garvey called, 'Five minutes, Colonel.'

'We'd better get moving,' Steiner said to Devlin in a low voice. 'We'll do better inside that sacristy than out here.'

'How long for?' Devlin asked.

There was a slight eerie creaking and straining his eyes, Devlin saw that someone was standing in the entrance to the sacristy where the broken door swung crazily. A familiar voice whispered, 'Liam?'

'My God,' he said to Steiner. 'It's Molly. Where in the hell did she spring from?' He crawled across the floor to join her and was back in a moment. 'Come on!' he said, getting a hand under Ritter's left arm. 'The little darling's got a way out for us. Now let's have this one on his feet and get moving while those lads up on the leads are still waiting.'

They slipped though the shadows, Ritter between them, and moved into the sacristy. Molly waited by the secret panel. Once they were inside she closed it and led the way down the stairs and along the tunnel.

It was very quiet when they came out into the hall at the presbytery. 'Now what?' Devlin said. 'We'll not get far with Ritter like this.'

'Father Vereker's car is in the yard at the back,' Molly said.

And Steiner, remembering, put a hand in his pocket. 'And I've got his keys.'

'Don't be silly,' Ritter told him. 'The moment you start the motor you'll have Rangers swarming all over you.'

'There's a gate at the back,' Molly said. 'A track over the fields beside the hedge. We can push that little Morris Eight of his between us for a couple of hundred yards. Nothing to it.'

They were at the bottom of the first meadow and a hundred and fifty yards away, when shooting began again at the church. Only then did Steiner start the engine and drive away, following Molly's directions, sticking to farm tracks across the fields, all the way down the coast road.

After the tiny click of the panel door in the sacristy closing, there was a stirring in the Lady Chapel and Arthur Seymour stood up, hands free. He padded down the north aisle without a sound, holding in his left hand the coil of rope with which Preston had bound his feet.

It was totally dark now, the only light the candles at the altar and the sanctuary lamp. He leaned down to satisfy himself that Preston was still breathing, picked him up and slung him over one massive shoulder. Then he turned and walked straight up the centre aisle towards the altar.

On the leads, Garvey was beginning to worry. It was so dark down there that you couldn't see a damn thing. He snapped his fingers for the field telephone and spoke to Kane who was at the gate with the White Scout Car. 'Silent as the grave in here, Major. I don't like it.'

'Try a burst. See what happens,' Kane told him.

Garvey pushed the barrel of his Thompson through the clerestory window and fired. There was no response and then the man on his right grabbed his arm. 'Down there, Sergeant, near the pulpit. Isn't someone moving?'

Garvey took a chance and flashed his torch. The young private on his right gave a cry of horror. Garvey ran the torch quickly along the south aisle, then said into the field phone, 'I don't know what's happening, Major, but you'd better get in there.'

A moment later, a burst from a Thompson gun shattered the lock on the main door, it crashed back and Harry Kane and a dozen Rangers moved in fast, ready for action. But there was no Steiner and no Devlin. Only Arthur Seymour kneeling in the front pew in the guttering candlelight, staring up into the hideously swollen face of Harvey Preston hanging by his neck from the centre pole of the rood screen.

19

The Prime Minister had taken the library overlooking the rear terrace at Meltham House for his personal use. When Harry Kane came out at seven-thirty Corcoran was waiting. 'How was he?'

'Very interested,' Kane said. 'Wanted chapter and verse on the whole battle. He seems fascinated by Steiner.'

'Aren't we all. What I'd like to know is where the damn man is now and that Irish scoundrel.'

'Nowhere near the cottage he's been living in, that's for sure. I had a report over the radio from Garvey just before I went in. It seems that when they went to check out this cottage of Devlin's they found two inspectors from Special Branch waiting for him.'

'Good God,' Corcoran said. 'How on earth did they get on to him?'

'Some police investigation or other. Anyway, he's highly unlikely to turn up there now. Garvey is staying in the area and setting up a couple of road blocks on the coast road, but we can't do much more till we get more men.'

'They're coming in, my boy, believe me,' Corcoran said. 'Since your chaps got the telephones working again, I've had several lengthy discussions with London. Another couple of hours should see the whole of North Norfolk sealed up tight. By morning most of this area will be, to all intents and purposes, under martial law. And it will certainly stay that way until Steiner is caught.'

Kane nodded. 'There's no question that he could get anywhere near the Prime Minister. I've got men on his door, on the terrace outside and at least two dozen prowling out there in the garden, with blackened faces and Thompson guns. I've given it to them straight. They shoot first. Accidents we can argue about afterwards.'

The door opened and a young corporal entered, a couple of typewritten sheets in his hand. 'I've got the final lists if you'd like to see them, Major.'

He went out and Kane looked at the first sheet. 'They've had Father Vereker and some of the villagers look at the German bodies.'

'How is he?' Corcoran asked.

'Concussed, but otherwise he seems okay. From what they say everyone is accounted for except for Steiner, his second in command, Neumann, and the Irishman, of course. The other fourteen are all dead.'

'But how the hell did they get away, that's what I'd like to know?'

'Well, they blasted their way into the sacristy to get out of the line of fire from Garvey and his men up on the leads. My theory is that when Pamela and the Prior girl got out through this priest's tunnel, they were in such a hurry they didn't close the secret door properly.'

Corcoran said, 'I understand the young Prior girl was rather sweet on this scoundrel Devlin. You don't think she could be involved in any way?'

'I wouldn't have thought so. According to Pamela the kid was really bitter about the whole thing.'

'I suppose so,' Corcoran said. 'Anyway, what about casualties on your side?'

Kane glanced at the second list. 'Including Shafto and Captain Mallory, twenty-one dead, eight wounded.' He shook his head. 'Out of forty. There's going to be one God Almighty rumpus when this gets out.'

'*If* it gets out.'

'What do you mean?'

'London is already making it clear they want a very low profile on this one. They don't want to alarm the people for one thing. I ask you, German Fallschirmjäger dropping into Norfolk to seize the Prime Minister. And coming too damn close for comfort. And what about this British Free Corps? Englishmen in the SS. Can you imagine how *that* would look in the papers?' He shuddered. 'I'd have hung the damn man myself.'

'I see what you mean.'

'And look at it from the Pentagon's point of view. A crack American unit, the elite of the elite, takes on a handful of German paratroops and sustains a seventy per cent casualty rate.'

'I don't know,' Kane shook his head. 'It's expecting a hell of a lot of people to keep quiet.'

'There's a war on, Kane,' Corcoran said. 'And in wartime, people can be made to do as they are told, it's as simple as that.'

The door opened, the young corporal looked in. 'London on the phone again, Colonel.'

Corcoran went out in a hurry, and Kane followed. He lit a cigarette which he held in the palm of his hand when he went out of the front door and down the steps past the sentries. It was raining hard and very dark, but he could smell fog on the air as he walked across the front terrace. Maybe Corcoran was right? It could happen that way. A world at war was crazy enough for anything to be believable.

He went down the steps and in a moment had an arm about his throat, a knee in his back. A knife gleamed dully. Someone said, 'Identify yourself.'

'Major Kane.'

A torch flicked on and off. 'Sorry, sir. Corporal Bleeker.'

'You should be in bed, Bleeker. How's that eye?'

'Five stitches in it, Major, but it's going to be fine. I'll move on now, sir, with your permission.'

He faded away and Kane stared into the darkness. 'I will never,' he said softly, 'to the end of my days even begin to understand my fellow human beings.'

In the North Sea area generally, as the weather report had it, the winds were three to four with rain squalls and some sea fog persisting till morning. The E-boat had made good time and by eight o'clock they were through the minefields and into the main coastal shipping lane.

Muller was at the wheel and Koenig looked up from the chart table where he had been laying off their final course with great care. 'Ten miles due east of Blakeney Point, Erich.'

Muller nodded, straining his eyes into the murk ahead. 'This fog isn't helping.'

'Oh, I don't know,' Koenig said. 'You might be glad of it before we're through.'

The door banged open and Teusen, the leading telegraphist, entered. He held out a signal flimsy. 'Message from Landsvoort, Herr Leutnant.'

He held out the flimsy, Koenig took it from him and read it in the light of the chart table. He looked down at it for a long moment, then crumpled it into a ball in his right hand.

'What is it?' Muller asked.

'The Eagle is blown. The rest is just words.'

There was a short pause. Rain pattered against the window. Muller said, 'And our orders?'

'To proceed as I see fit.' Koenig shook his head. 'Just think of it. Colonel Steiner, Ritter Neumann – all those fine men.'

For the first time since childhood he felt like crying. He opened the door and stared out into the darkness, rain beating against his face. Muller said carefully, 'Of course, it's always possible some of them might make it. Just one or two. You know how these things go?'

Koenig slammed the door. 'You mean you'd still be willing to go in there?' Muller didn't bother to reply and Koenig turned to Teusen. 'You, too?'

Teusen said, 'We've been together a long time, Herr Leutnant. I've never asked where we were going before.'

Koenig was filled with a wild elation. He slapped him on the back. 'All right, then send this signal.'

Radl's condition had deteriorated steadily during the late afternoon and evening, but he had refused to remain in bed in spite of Witt's pleadings. Since Joanna Grey's final message he had insisted on staying in the radio room, lying back in an old armchair Witt had brought in while the operator tried to raise Koenig. The pain in his chest was not only worse, but had spread to his left arm. He was no fool. He knew what that meant. Not that it mattered. Not that anything mattered now.

At five minutes to eight, the operator turned, a smile of triumph on his face. 'I've got them, Herr Oberst. Message received and understood.'

'Thank God,' Radl said and fumbled open his cigarette case, but suddenly his fingers seemed too stiff and Witt had to do it for him.

'Only one left, Herr Oberst,' he said as he took out the distinctive Russian cigarette and put it in Radl's mouth.

The operator was writing feverishly on his pad. He tore off the sheet and turned, 'Reply, Herr Oberst.'

Radl felt strangely dizzy and his vision wasn't good. He said, 'Read it, Witt.'

'Will still visit nest. Some fledglings may need assistance. Good luck.' Witt looked bewildered. 'Why does he add that, Herr Oberst?'

'Because he is a very perceptive young man who suspects I'm going to need it as much as he does.' He shook his head slowly. 'Where do we get them from, these boys? To dare so much, sacrifice everything and for what?'

Witt looked troubled. 'Herr Oberst, please.'

Radl smiled. 'Like this last of my Russian cigarettes, my friend, all good things come to an end sooner or later.' He turned to the radio operator and braced himself to do what should have been done at least two hours earlier. 'Now you can get me Berlin.'

There was a decaying farm cottage on the eastern boundary of Prior Farm, at the back of the wood on the opposite side of the main road above Hobs End. It provided some sort of shelter for the Morris.

It was seven-fifteen when Devlin and Steiner left Molly to look after Ritter and went down through the trees to make a cautious reconnaissance. They were just in time to see Garvey and his men go up the dyke round to the cottage. They retreated through the trees and crouched in the lee of a wall to consider the situation.

'Not so good,' Devlin said.

'You don't need to go to the cottage. You can cut through the marsh on foot and still reach that beach in time,' Steiner pointed out.

'For what?' Devlin sighed. 'I've a terrible confession to make, Colonel. I went off in such a devil of a hurry that I left the S-phone at the bottom of a carrier-bag filled with spuds that's hanging behind the kitchen door.'

Steiner laughed softly. 'My friend, you are truly yourself alone. God must have broken the mould after turning you out.'

'I know,' Devlin said. 'A hell of a thing to live with, but staying with the present situation, I can't call Koenig without it.'

'You don't think he'll come in without a signal?'

'That was the arrangement. Any time between nine and ten as ordered. Another thing. Whatever happened to Joanna Grey, it's likely she got some sort of message off to Landsvoort. If Radl has passed it on to Koenig, he and his boys could be already on their way back.'

'No,' Steiner said. 'I don't think so. Koenig will come. Even if he fails to get your signal, he will come in to that beach.'

'Why should he?'

'Because he told me he would,' Steiner said simply. 'So you see, you can manage without the S-phone. Even if the Rangers search the area, they won't bother with the beach because the signs say it is mined. If you get there in good time you can walk along the estuary for at least a quarter of a mile with the tide as it is.'

'With Ritter in his state of health?'

'All he needs is a stick and a shoulder to lean on. Once in Russia he walked eighty miles in three days through snow with a bullet in his right foot. When a man knows he'll die if he stays where he is, it concentrates his mind wonderfully on moving somewhere else. You'll save a considerable amount of time. Meet Koenig on his way in.'

'You're not going with us.' It was a statement of fact, not a question.

'I think you know where I must go, my friend.'

Devlin sighed. 'I was always the great believer in letting a man go to hell his own way, but I'm willing to make an exception in your case. You won't even get close. They'll have more guards round him than there are flies on a jam jar on a hot summer day.'

'In spite of that I must try.'

'Why, because you think it might help your father's case back home? That's an illusion. Face up to it. Nothing you do can help him if that old sod at Prinz Albrechtstrasse decides otherwise.'

'Yes, you're very probably right. I think I've always known that.'

'Then why?'

'Because I find it impossible to do anything else.'

'I don't understand.'

'I think you do. This game you play. Trumpets on the wind, the tricolour fluttering bravely in the grey morning. Up the Republic. Remember Easter nineteen-sixteen. But tell me this, my friend. In the end, do you control the game, or does the game possess you? Can you stop, if you want, or must it always be the same? Trenchcoats and Thompson guns, my life for Ireland until the day you lie in the gutter with a bullet in your back?'

Devlin said hoarsely, 'God knows, I don't.'

'But I do, my friend. And now, I think, we should rejoin the others. You will naturally say nothing about my personal plans. Ritter could prove difficult.'

'All right,' Devlin said reluctantly.

They moved back through the night to the ruined cottage where they found Molly rebandaging one of Ritter's thighs. 'How are you doing?' Steiner asked him.

'Fine,' Ritter answered, but when Steiner put a hand on his forehead it was damp with sweat.

Molly joined Devlin in the angle of the two walls where he sheltered from the rain, smoking a cigarette. 'He's not good,' she said. 'Needs a doctor if you ask me.'

'You might as well send for an undertaker,' Devlin said. 'But never mind him. It's you I'm worried about now. You could be in serious trouble from this night's work.'

She was curiously indifferent. 'Nobody saw me get you out of the church, nobody can prove I did. As far as they're concerned I've been sitting on the heath in the rain crying my heart out at finding the truth about my lover.'

'For God's sake, Molly.'

'Poor, silly little bitch, they'll say. Got her fingers burned and serves her right for trusting a stranger.'

He said awkwardly, 'I haven't thanked you.'

'It doesn't matter. I didn't do it for you. I did it for me.' She was a simple girl in many ways and content to be so and yet now, more than at any other time in her life, she wanted to be able to express herself with complete certainty. 'I love you. That doesn't mean I like what you are or what you've done or even understand it. That's something different. The love is a separate issue. It's in a compartment of its own. That's why I got you out of that church tonight. Not because it was right or wrong, but because I couldn't have lived with myself if I'd stood by and let you die.' She pulled herself free. 'I'd better check on how the lieutenant is getting on.'

She walked over to the car and Devlin swallowed hard. Wasn't it the strange thing? The bravest speech he'd ever heard in his life, a girl to cheer from the rooftops and here he felt more like crying at the tragic waste of it all.

At twenty past eight, Devlin and Steiner went down through the trees again. The cottage out there in the marsh was in darkness but on the main road there were subdued voices, the dim shape of a vehicle. 'Let's move a little closer,' Steiner whispered.

They got to the boundary wall between the wood and the road and peered over. It was raining hard now. There were two jeeps, one on either side of the road and several Rangers were sheltering under the trees. A match flared in Garvey's cupped hands, lighting his face for a brief moment.

Steiner and Devlin retreated. 'The big negro,' Steiner said. 'The Master Sergeant who was with Kane, waiting to see if you show up.'

'Why not at the cottage?'

'He probably has men out there, too. This way he covers the road as well.'

'It doesn't matter,' Devlin said. 'We can cross the road further down. Make it to the beach on foot as you said.'

'Easier if you had a diversion.'

'Such as?'

'Me in a stolen car passing through that road block. I could do with your trenchcoat, by the way, if you'd consider a permanent loan.'

Devlin couldn't see his face in the darkness and suddenly didn't want to. 'Damn you, Steiner, go to hell your own way,' he said wearily. He unslung his Sten gun, took off the trenchcoat and handed it over. 'You'll find a silenced Mauser in the right-hand pocket and two extra magazines.'

'Thank you,' Steiner took off his *Schiff* and pushed it inside his *Fliegerbluse*. He pulled on the trenchcoat and belted it. 'So, the final end of things. We'll say goodbye here, I think.'

'Tell me one thing,' Devlin said. 'Has it been worth it? Any of it?'

'Oh, no.' Steiner laughed lightly. 'No more philosophy, please.' He held out his hand. 'May you find what you are searching for, my friend.'

'I already have and lost it in the finding,' Devlin told him.

'Then from now on, nothing really matters,' Steiner said. 'A dangerous situation. You will have to take care,' and he turned and went back to the ruined cottage.

They got Ritter out of the car and pushed it to where the track started to slope to a five-barred gate, the road on the other side. Steiner ran down and opened it, pulling a six-foot length of rail off the fence which he gave to Ritter when he got back.

'How's that?' he asked.

'Fine,' Ritter said bravely. 'Do we go now?'

'You, not me. There are Rangers down there on the road. I thought I might arrange a small diversion while you get across. I'll catch you up later.'

Ritter grabbed his arm and there was panic in his voice. 'No, Kurt, I can't let you do this.'

Steiner said, 'Oberleutnant Neumann, you are undoubtedly the finest soldier I've ever known. From Narvik to Stalingrad, you've never shirked your duty or disobeyed an order of mine and I haven't the slightest intention of letting you start now.'

Ritter tried to straighten up, bracing himself against the rail. 'As the Herr Oberst wishes,' he said formally.

'Good,' Steiner said. 'Go now, please, Mr. Devlin, and good luck.'

He opened the car door and Ritter called softly, 'Herr Oberst.'

'Yes?'

'A privilege to serve with you, sir.'

'Thank you, Herr Oberleutnant.'

Steiner got into the Morris, released the brake and the car started to roll down the track.

Devlin and Molly went through the trees, Ritter between them and paused at the side of the low wall. Devlin whispered, 'Time for you to go, girl.'

'I'll see you to the beach, Liam,' she said firmly.

He had no chance to argue because the car engine started forty yards up the road and the Morris's slotted headlights were turned on. One of the Rangers took a red lamp from under his cape and waved it. Devlin had expected the German to drive straight on, but to his astonishment, he slowed. Steiner was taking a coldly calculated risk, something designed to draw every last men there. There was only one way he could do that.

He waited for Garvey's approach, his left hand on the wheel, his right holding the Mauser.

Garvey said as he approached, 'Sorry, but you'll have to identify yourself.'

He switched on the torch in his left hand, picking Steiner's face out of the darkness. The Mauser coughed once as Steiner fired, apparently at point blank range, but a good two inches to one side, the wheels skidded as he stamped on the accelerator and was away.

'That was Steiner himself, Goddammit!' Garvey cried. 'Get after him!'

There was a mad scramble as everyone jumped to get on board. Garvey's jeep was away first, the other hard behind. The sound dwindled into the night.

Devlin said, 'Right, let's get out of it then,' and he and Molly helped Ritter over the wall and started across the road.

Built in 1933, the Morris was still on the road only because of the wartime shortage of new cars. Her engine was virtually worn out and although she suited Vereker's requirements adequately enough, they were not those of Steiner that night. With his foot flat on the boards, the needle hovered on forty and obstinately refused to move beyond that point.

He had minutes only, not even that, for as he debated the merits of stopping suddenly and taking to the woods on foot, Garvey, in the lead jeep, started to fire its Browning. Steiner ducked over the wheel, bullets hammered through the body, the windscreen dissolved in a snowstorm of flying glass.

The Morris swerved to the right, smashed through some wooden railings and lumbered down a slope of young firs. The braking effect of these was such that the speed was not very great. Steiner got the car door open and tumbled out. He was on his feet in a moment, moving away through the trees into the darkness as the Morris went into the flooded waters of the marsh below and started to sink.

The jeeps skidded to a halt on the road above. Garvey was first out, going down the bank fast, the torch ready in his hand. As he reached the bank, the muddy waters of the marsh closed over the roof of the Morris.

He took off his helmet and started to unbuckle his belt and Krukowski, sliding down after him, grabbed him by the arm. 'Don't even think it. That isn't just water down there. The mud in some of these places is deep enough to swallow a man whole.'

Garvey nodded slowly. 'Yes, I suppose you're right.' He played his torch on the surface of the muddy pool where bubbles broke through, then turned and went back up the slope to radio in.

Kane and Corcoran were having supper in the ornate front drawing room, when the corporal from the radio room rushed in with the signal. Kane looked at it briefly then slid it across the polished surface of the table.

'My God, and he was pointing in this direction, you realise that?' Corcoran frowned in distaste. 'What a way for such a man to go.'

Kane nodded. He should have been pleased and felt curiously depressed. He said to the corporal, 'Tell Garvey to stay where he is, then get the motor pool to send some sort of recovery vehicle out to him. I want Colonel Steiner's body out of there.'

The corporal went out and Corcoran said, 'What about the other one and the Irishman?'

'I don't think we need worry. They'll turn up, but not here.' Kane sighed. 'No, in the end it was Steiner on his own, I think. The sort of man who never knows when to give up.'

Corcoran went to the sideboard and poured two large whiskies. He handed one to Kane. 'I won't say cheers because I think I know how you feel. A strange sense of personal loss.'

'Exactly.'

'I've been at this game far too long, I think.' Corcoran shivered and downed his whisky. 'Will you tell the Prime Minister or shall I?'

'Your privilege, I fancy, sir.' Kane managed a smile. 'I'd better let the men know.'

When he went out of the front door it was pouring with rain and he stood at the top of the steps in the porch and shouted, 'Corporal Bleeker?'

Bleeker ran out of the darkness within a few moments and came up the steps. His combat jacket was soaked, his helmet shiny with rain and the dark camouflage cream on his face had streaked.

Kane said, 'Garvey and his boys got Steiner back along the coast road. Spread the word.'

Bleeker said, 'That's it then. Do we stand down, sir?'

'No, but you can phase the guard system now. Work it so you get some time off in turns for a hot meal and so on.'

Bleeker started down the steps and vanished into the darkness. The Major stayed there for quite some time, staring out into the rain and then finally turned and went back inside.

The cottage at Hobs End was in total darkness as Devlin, Molly and Ritter Neumann approached. They paused by the wall and Devlin whispered, 'It looks quiet enough to me.'

'Not worth the risk,' Ritter whispered.

But Devlin, thinking of the S-phone, said stubbornly, 'And bloody daft we'd be and no one in the place. You two keep moving along the dyke. I'll catch you up.'

He slipped away before either of them could protest, and went across the yard cautiously and listened at the window. All was quiet, only the rain falling, not a chink of light anywhere. The front door opened to his touch with a slight creak and he moved into the hall, the Sten gun ready.

The living door stood ajar, a few embers from the dying fire glowing redly on the hearth. He stepped inside and knew instantly that he had made a very bad mistake. The door slammed behind him, the muzzle of a Browning was rammed into the side of his neck and the Sten plucked from his hand.

'Hold it right there,' Jack Rogan said. 'All right, Fergus, let's have a little light on the situation.'

A match flared as Fergus Grant touched the wick of the oil lamp and replaced the glass chimney. Rogan put his knee into Devlin's back and sent him staggering across the room. 'Let's have a look at you.'

Devlin half-turned, a foot on the hearth. He put a hand on the mantelpiece. 'I haven't had the honour.'

'Chief Inspector Rogan, Inspector Grant, Special Branch.'

'The Irish Section, is it?'

'That's right, son, and don't ask for my warrant card or I'll belt you.' Rogan sat on the edge of the table, holding his Browning against his thigh. 'You know, you've been a very naughty boy from what I hear.'

'Do you tell me?' Devlin said, leaning a little further into the hearth, knowing that even if he got to the Walther his chances were of the slimmest. Whatever Rogan might be doing, Grant was taking no chances and had him covered.

'Yes, you really give me a pain, you people,' Rogan said. 'Why can't you stay back there in the bogs where you belong?'

'It's a thought,' Devlin said.

Rogan took a pair of handcuffs out of his coat pocket. 'Get over here.'

A stone crashed through the window on the other side of the blackout curtain and both policemen turned in alarm. Devlin's hand reached for the Walther hanging on the nail at the back of the beam that supported the chimney breast. He shot Rogan in the head, knocking him back off the table, but Grant was already turning. He got off one wild shot that caught the Irishman in the right shoulder and Devlin fell back in the easy chair, still firing, shattering the young inspector's left arm, putting another bullet into the shoulder on the same side.

Grant fell back against the wall and slid down to the floor. He seemed in deep shock and gazed across the room uncomprehendingly at Rogan lying on the other side of the table. Devlin picked up the Browning and stuffed it in his waistband, then went to the door, took down the carrier back and emptied the potatoes on the floor. The small canvas bag at the bottom contained the S-phone and a few other odds and ends and he slung it over his shoulder.

'Why don't you kill me as well?' Fergus Grant asked weakly.

'You're nicer than he was,' Devlin said. 'I'd find a better class of work, son, if I was you.'

He went out quickly. When he opened the front door, Molly was standing against the wall. 'Thank God!' she said, but he put a hand to her mouth and hurried her away. They reached the wall where Ritter waited. Molly said, 'What happened?'

'I killed a man, wounded another, that's what happened,' Devlin told her. 'Two Special Branch detectives.'

'I helped you do that?'

'Yes,' he said. 'Will you go now, Molly, while you still can?'

She turned from him suddenly and started to run back along the dyke. Devlin hesitated and then, unable to contain himself, went after her. He caught her within a few yards and pulled her into his arms. Her hands went to his neck, she kissed him with a passion that was all-consuming. He pushed her away. 'Go now, girl, and God go with you.'

She turned without a word and ran into the night and Devlin went back to Ritter Neumann. 'A very remarkable young woman,' the Oberleutnant said.

'Yes, you could say that,' Devlin told him, 'And you'd be making the understatement of the age.' He got the S-phone out of the bag and switched on to channel. 'Eagle to Wanderer. Eagle to Wanderer. Come in, please.'

On the bridge of the E-boat where the S-phone receiver had been situated, his voice sounded as clearly as if he was just outside the door. Koenig reached for the mike quickly, his heart beating. 'Eagle, this is Wanderer. What is your situation?'

'Two fledglings still in the nest,' Devlin said. 'Can you come immediately?'

'We're on our way,' Koenig told him. 'Over and out.' He put the mike back on its hook and turned to Muller. 'Right, Erich, switch to silencers and break out the White Ensign. We're going in.'

As Devlin and Neumann reached the trees, the Irishman glanced back and saw car headlights turn out of the main road and move along the dyke path. Ritter said, 'Who do you think it is?'

'God knows,' Devlin told him.

Garvey, waiting a couple of miles along the road for the recovery vehicle, had decided to send the other jeep back to check on the two Special Branch men.

Devlin got a hand under Ritter's arm. 'Come on, son, we'd better get out of this.' He cursed suddenly at the searing pain in his shoulder now that the shock was beginning to wear off.

'Are you all right?' Ritter asked.

'Bleeding like Mrs. O'Grady's pig. I stopped one in the shoulder back there, but never mind that now. Nothing like a sea voyage to cure what ails you.'

They went past the warning notice, picked their way gingerly through the barbed wire and started across the beach. Ritter was gasping with pain at every step. He leaned heavily on the rail Steiner had given him, yet he never faltered. The sands stretched wide and flat before them, fog rolling in on the wind, and then they were walking in water, only an inch or two at first, rather more in the depressions.

They paused to take stock and Devlin looked back and saw lights moving in the trees. 'Christ almighty,' he said, 'don't they ever give up?'

They stumbled on towards the estuary across the sands and as the tide flowed in, the water grew deeper. At first knee-deep and then it was up to their thighs. They were well out into the estuary now and Ritter groaned suddenly and fell to one knee, dropping his rail. 'It's no good, Devlin. I've had it. I've never known such pain.'

Devlin crouched beside him and raised the S-phone to his mouth again. 'Wanderer, this is Eagle. We are waiting for you in the estuary a quarter of a mile off-shore. Signalling now.'

From the canvas bag he took out a luminous signal ball, another gift from the Abwehr by courtesy of SOE, and held it up in the palm of his right hand. He glanced round towards the shore, but the fog had rolled in now, blanketing everything back there.

Twenty minutes later, the water was up to his chest. He had never been so cold in his life before. He stood on the sandbank, legs apart, his left arm supporting Ritter, his right hand holding the luminous signalling ball high, the tide flowing around them.

'It's no good,' Ritter whispered. 'I can't feel a thing. 'I'm finished. I can't take any more.'

'As Mrs. O'Flynn said to the Bishop,' Devlin said. 'Come on, boy, don't give in now. What would Steiner say?'

'Steiner?' Ritter coughed, choking a little as salt water slopped over his chin and into his mouth. 'He'd have swum across.'

Devlin forced a laugh. 'That's the way, son, keep smiling.' He started to sing at the top of his voice, 'And down the glen rode Sarsfield's men all in their jackets green.'

A wave passed right over his head and they went under. Oh, Christ, he thought, this is it, but when it had rolled on, still managed to find his feet, his right hand holding the signalling ball high, although by now, the water was up to his chin.

It was Teusen who caught sight of the light to port and ran to the bridge instantly. Three minutes later, the E-boat slid out of the darkness and someone shone a torch down on the two men. A net was thrown over, four seamen clambered down and willing hands reached for Ritter Neumann.

'Watch him,' Devlin urged. 'He's in a bad way.'

When he went over the rail himself a couple of moments later and collapsed, it was Koenig who knelt beside him with a blanket. 'Mr. Devlin, drink some of this.' He passed him a bottle.

'Cead mile Failte,' Devlin said.

Koenig leaned close. 'I'm sorry, I don't understand.'

'And how should you? It's Irish, the language of kings. I simply said, a hundred thousand welcomes.'

Koenig smiled through the darkness. 'I am glad to see you, Mr. Devlin. A miracle.'

'The only one you're likely to get this night.'

'You are certain?'

'As the coffin lid closing.'

Koenig stood up. 'Then we will go now. Please excuse me.'

A moment later, the E-boat swung round and surged forward. Devlin got the cork out of the bottle and sniffed at the contents. *Rum.* Not one of his favourites, but he swallowed deep and huddled against the stern rail looking back towards the land.

In her bedroom at the farm, Molly sat up suddenly, then moved across the room and drew the curtains. She threw the windows open and leaned out into the rain, a tremendous feeling of elation, of release filling her and at that very moment, the E-boat moved from behind the Point and turned out towards the open sea.

In his office at Prinz Albrechtstrasse, Himmler worked at his eternal files in the light of the desk lamp. There was a knock at the door and Rossman entered.

'Well?' Himmler said.

'I'm sorry to disturb you, Herr Reichsführer, but we've had a signal from Landsvoort. The Eagle is blown.'

Himmler showed no emotion whatsoever. He laid down his pen

carefully and held out his hand. 'Let me see.' Rossman gave him the signal and Himmler read it through. After a while, he looked up. 'I have an errand for you.'

'Herr Reichsführer.'

'Take two of your most trusted men. Fly to Landsvoort at once and arrest Colonel Radl. I will see that you have all necessary authorisation before you leave.'

'Of course, Herr Reichsführer. And the charge?'

'Treason against the state. That should do for a start. Report to me as soon as you get back.' Himmler picked up his pen and started to write again and Rossman withdrew.

Just before nine o'clock Corporal George Watson of the Military Police ran his motor-cycle into the side of the road a couple of miles south from Meltham House and pushed it up on its stand. Having ridden from Norwich with almost torrential rain the whole way, he was soaked to the skin, in spite of his long dispatch rider's coat – bitterly cold and very hungry. He was also lost.

He opened his map case in the light of his headlamp and leaned down to check it. A slight movement to his right made him look up. A man in a trenchcoat was standing there. 'Hello,' he said. 'Lost, are you?'

'I'm trying to find Meltham House,' Watson told him. 'All the way from Norwich in this bloody rain. These country districts all look the same with the damned signposts missing.'

'Here, let me show you,' Steiner said.

Watson leaned down to examine the map again in the light from the headlamp, the Mauser rose and fell across the back of his neck. He lay in a puddle of water and Steiner pulled his dispatch case over his head and examined the contents quickly. There was only one letter, heavily sealed and marked *Urgent*. It was addressed to Colonel William Corcoran, Meltham House.

Steiner got hold of Watson under the armpits and dragged him into the shadows. When he re-appeared a few moments later, he was wearing the dispatch rider's long raincoat, helmet and goggles and leather gauntlets. He pulled the sling of the dispatch case over his head, pushed the motor-cycle off its stand, kicked the engine into life and rode away.

At the side of the road they had a spotlight set up and as the Scammell recovery truck's winch started to revolve, the Morris came up out of the marsh on to the bank. Garvey stayed up on the road, waiting.

The corporal in charge had the door open. He peered inside and looked up. 'There's nothing here.'

'What in the hell are you talking about?' Garvey demanded and he moved down through the trees quickly.

He looked inside the Morris, but the corporal was right. Lots of stinking mud, a certain amount of water, but no Steiner. 'Oh, my God,' Garvey said as the full implication hit him and he turned, scrambled up the bank, and grabbed for the mike on his jeep's radio.

Steiner turned in at the gate of Meltham House, which was closed, and halted. The Ranger on the other side shone a torch on him and called, 'Sergeant of the Guard.'

Sergeant Thomas came out of the lodge and approached the gate. Steiner sat there, anonymous in helmet and goggles. 'What is it?' Thomas demanded.

Steiner opened his dispatch case, took out the letter and held it close to to the bars. 'Dispatch from Norwich for Colonel Corcoran.'

Thomas nodded, the Ranger next to him unbolted the gate. 'Straight up to the front of the house. One of the sentries will take you in.'

Steiner rode up the drive and turned away from the front door, following a branch that finally brought him to the motor pool at the rear of the building. He stopped beside a parked truck, switched off and pushed the motor-cycle up on its stand, then turned and followed the path round towards the garden. When he'd gone a few yards, he stepped into the shelter of the rhododendrons.

He removed the crash helmet, the raincoat and gauntlets, took his *Schiff* from inside his *Fliegerbluse* and put it on. He adjusted the Knight's Cross at his throat and moved off, the Mauser ready.

He paused on the edge of a sunken garden below the terrace to get his bearings. The blackout wasn't too good, chinks of light showing at several windows. He took a step forward and someone said, 'That you, Bleeker?'

Steiner grunted. A dim shape moved forward. The Mauser coughed in his right hand, there was a startled gasp as the Ranger slumped to the ground. In the same moment, a curtain was pulled back and light fell across the terrace above.

When Steiner looked up, he saw the Prime Minister standing at the balustrade smoking a cigar.

When Corcoran came out of the Prime Minister's room he found Kane waiting. 'How is he?' Kane asked.

'Fine. Just gone out on the terrace for a last cigar and then he's going to bed.'

They moved into the hall. 'He probably wouldn't sleep too well if he heard my news, so I'll keep it till morning,' Kane told him. 'They hauled that Morris out of the marsh and no Steiner.'

Corcoran said. 'Are you suggesting he got away? How do you know he isn't still down there? He might have been thrown out or something.'

'It's possible,' Kane said, 'but I'm doubling the guard anyway.'

The front door opened and Sergeant Thomas came in. He unbuttoned his coat to shake the rain from it. 'You wanted me, Major?'

'Yes,' Kane said. 'When they got the car out, Steiner was missing. We're taking no chances and doubling the guard. Nothing to report from the gate?'

'Not a damn thing since the recovery Scammell went out. Only that military policeman from Norwich with the dispatch for Colonel Corcoran.'

Corcoran stared at him, frowning. 'That's the first I've heard of it. When was this?'

'Maybe ten minutes ago, sir.'

'Oh, my God!' Kane said. 'He's here! The bastard's here!' And he turned, tugging at the Colt automatic in the holster at his waist and ran for the library door.

Steiner went up the steps to the terrace slowly. The scent of the good Havana cigar perfumed the night. As he put foot on the top step it crunched in gravel. The Prime Minister turned sharply and looked at him.

He removed the cigar from his mouth, that implacable face showing no kind of reaction, and said, 'Oberstleutnant Kurt Steiner of the Fallschirmjäger, I presume?'

'Mr. Churchill.' Steiner hesitated. 'I regret this, but I must do my duty, sir.'

'Then what are you waiting for?' the Prime Minister said calmly.

Steiner raised the Mauser, the curtains at the french windows billowed and Harry Kane stumbled through, firing wildly. His first bullet hit Steiner in the right shoulder spinning him round, the second caught him in the heart, killing him instantly, pushing him back over the balustrade.

Corcoran arrived on the terrace a moment later, revolver in hand, and below in the sunken garden, Rangers appeared from the darkness on the run, to pause and stand in a semi-circle. Steiner lay in the pool of light from the open window, the Knight's Cross at his throat, the Mauser still gripped firmly in his right hand.

'Strange,' the Prime Minister said. 'With his finger on the trigger, he hesitated. I wonder why?'

'Perhaps that was his American half speaking, sir?' Harry Kane said.

The Prime Minister had the final word, 'Whatever else may be said, he was a fine soldier and a brave man. See to him, Major.' He turned and went back inside.

20

It was almost a year to the day since I had made that astonishing discovery in the churchyard at St. Mary and All the Saints when I returned to Studley Constable, this time by direct invitation of Father Philip Vereker. I was admitted by a young priest with an Irish accent.

Vereker was sitting in a wing-back chair in front of a huge fire in the study, a rug about his knees, a dying man if ever I've seen one. The skin seemed to have shrunk on his face, exposing every bone and the eyes were full of pain. 'It was good of you to come.'

'I'm sorry to see you so ill,' I said.

'I have a cancer of the stomach. Nothing to be done. The Bishop has been very good in allowing me to end it here, arranging for Father Damian to assist with parish duties, but that isn't why I sent for you. I hear you've had a busy year.'

'I don't understand,' I said. 'When I was here before you wouldn't say a word. Drove me out, in fact.'

'It's really very simple. For years I've only known half the story myself. I suddenly discover that I have an insatiable curiosity to know the rest before it is too late.'

So I told him because there didn't really seem any reason why I shouldn't. By the time I had finished, the shadows were falling across the grass outside and the room was half in darkness.

'Remarkable,' he said. 'How on earth did you find it all out?'

'Not from any official source, believe me. Just from talking to people, those who are still alive and who are willing to talk. The biggest stroke of luck was in being privileged to read a very comprehensive diary kept by the man responsible for the organisation of the whole thing, Colonel Max Radl. His widow is still alive in Bavaria. What I'd like to know is what happened here afterwards.'

'There was a complete security clampdown. Every single villager involved was interviewed by the intelligence and security people. The Official Secrets Act invoked. Not that it was really necessary. These are a peculiar people. Drawing together in adversity, hostile to strangers, as you have seen. They looked upon it as their business and no one else's.'

'And there was Seymour.'

THE EAGLE HAS LANDED

'Exactly. Did you know that he was killed last February?'

'No.'

'Driving back from Holt one night drunk. He ran his van off the coast road into the marsh and was drowned.'

'What happened to him after the other business?'

'He was quietly certified. Spent eighteen years in an institution before he managed to obtain his release when the mental health laws were relaxed.'

'But how could people stand having him around?'

'He was related by blood to at least half the families in the district. George Wilde's wife, Betty, was his sister.'

'Good God,' I said. 'I didn't realise.'

'In a sense, the silence of the years was also a kind of protection for Seymour.'

'There is another possibility,' I said. 'That the terrible thing he did that night was seen as a reflection on all of them. Something to hide rather than reveal.'

'That, too.'

'And the tombstone?'

'The military engineers who were sent here to clean up the village, repair damage and so on, placed all the bodies in a mass grave in the churchyard. Unmarked, of course and we were told it was to remain so.'

'But you thought differently?'

'Not just me. All of us. Wartime propaganda was a pernicious thing then, however necessary. Every war picture we saw at the cinema, every book we read, every newspaper, portrayed the average German soldier as a ruthless and savage barbarian, but these men were not like that. Graham Wilde is alive today, Susan Turner married with three children because one of Steiner's men gave his life to save them. And at the church, remember, he let the people go.'

'So, a secret monument was decided on?'

'That's right. It was easy enough to arrange. Old Ted Turner was a retired monumental mason. It was laid, dedicated by me at a private service, then concealed from the casual observer as you know. The man Preston is down there, too, but was not included on the monument.'

'And you all agreed with this?'

He managed one of his rare, wintry smiles. 'As some kind of personal penance if you like. Dancing on his grave was the term Steiner used and he was right. I hated him that day. Could have killed him myself.'

'Why?' I said. 'Because it was a German bullet that crippled you?'

'So I pretended until the day I got down on my knees and asked God to help me face the truth.'

'Joanna Grey?' I said gently.

His face was completely in shadow. I found it impossible to see his expression. 'I am more used to hearing confessions than making them, but yes, you are right. I worshipped Joanna Grey. Oh, not in any silly superficial sexual way. To me she was the most wonderful woman I'd ever known. I can't even begin to describe the shock I experienced on discovering her true role.'

'So in a sense, you blamed Steiner?'

'I think it was the psychology of it.' He sighed. 'So long ago. How old were you in nineteen forty-three? Twelve, thirteen? Can you remember what it was like?'

'Not really – not in the way you mean.'

'People were tired because the war seemed to have gone on for ever. Can you possibly imagine the terrible blow to national morale if the story of Steiner and his men and what took place here, had got out? That German paratroopers could land in England and come within an ace of snatching the Prime Minister himself?'

'Could come as close as the pull of a finger on the trigger to blowing his head off.'

He nodded. 'Do you still intend to publish?'

'I don't see why not.'

'It didn't happen, you know. No stone any more and who is to say it ever existed? And have you found one single official document to substantiate any of it?'

'Not really,' I said cheerfully. 'But I've spoken to a lot of people and together they've told me what adds up to a pretty convincing story.'

'It could have been.' He smiled faintly. 'If you hadn't missed out on one very important point.'

'And what would that be?'

'Look up any one of two dozen history books on the last war and check what Winston Churchill was doing during the weekend in question. But perhaps that was too simple, too obvious.'

'All right,' I said. 'You tell me.'

'Getting ready to leave in HMS *Renown* for the Teheran conference. Called at Algiers on the way, where he invested Generals Eisenhower and Alexander with special versions of the North Africa ribbon and arrived at Malta, as I remember, on the seventeenth November.'

It was suddenly very quiet. I said, 'Who was he?'

'His name was George Howard Foster, known in the profession as the Great Foster.'

'The profession?'

'The stage, Mr. Higgins. Foster was a music hall act, an impressionist.

The war was his salvation.'

'How was that?'

'He not only did a more than passable imitation of the Prime Minister. He even looked like him. After Dunkirk, he started doing a special act, a kind of grand finale to the show. *I have nothing to offer but blood, sweat and tears. We will fight them on the beaches.* The audiences loved it.'

'And Intelligence pulled him in?'

'On special occasions. If you intend to send the Prime Minister to sea at the height of the U-boat peril, it's useful to have him publicly appearing elsewhere.' He smiled. 'He gave the performance of his life that night. They all believed it was him, of course. Only Corcoran knew the truth.'

'All right,' I said. 'Where's Foster now?'

'Killed, along with a hundred and eight other people when a flying bomb hit a little theatre in Islington in February, nineteen forty-four. So you see, it's all been for nothing. It never happened. Much better for all concerned.'

He went into a bout of coughing that racked his entire body. The door opened and the nun entered. She leaned over him and whispered. He said, 'I'm sorry, it's been a long afternoon. I think I should rest. Thank you for coming and filling in the gaps.'

He started to cough again so I left as quickly as I could and was ushered politely to the door by young Father Damian. On the step I gave him my card. 'If he gets worse.' I hesitated. 'You know what I mean? I'd appreciate hearing from you.'

I lit a cigarette and leaned on the flint wall of the churchyard beside the lychgate. I would check the facts, of course, but Vereker was telling the truth, I knew that beyond any shadow of a doubt and did it really change anything? I looked towards the porch where Steiner had stood that evening so long ago in confrontation with Harry Kane, thought of him on the terrace at Meltham House, the final, and for him, fatal hesitation. *And even if he had pulled that trigger it would still all have been for nothing.*

There's irony for you, as Devlin would have said. I could almost hear his laughter. Ah, well, in the final analysis there was nothing I could find that would be any improvement on the words of a man who had played his own part so well on that fatal night.

Whatever else may be said, he was a fine soldier and a brave man. Let it end there. I turned and walked away through the rain.

The Tightrope Men

Desmond Bagley

1

Giles Denison lay asleep. He lay on his back with his right arm held crooked across his forehead with the hand lightly clenched into a fist, giving him a curiously defensive appearance as of one who wards off a blow. His breathing was even and shallow but it deepened a little as he came into consciousness in that everyday miracle of the reintegration of the psyche after the little death of sleep.

There was a movement of eyes behind closed lids and he sighed, bringing his arm down and turning over on to his side to snuggle deeper into the bedclothes. After a few moments the eyelids flickered and drew back and he stared uncomprehendingly at the blank wall next to the bed. He sighed again, filling his lungs with air, and then leisurely drew forth his arm and looked at his wristwatch.

It was exactly twelve o'clock.

He frowned and shook the watch, then held it to his ear. A steady tick told him it was working and another glance at the dial showed the sweep second hand jerking smoothly on its circular course.

Suddenly – convulsively – he sat up in bed and stared at the watch. It was not the time – midday or midnight – that now perturbed him, but the realization that this was not his watch. He normally wore a fifteen-year-old Omega, a present from his father on his twenty-first birthday, but this was a sleek Patek Philippe, gleaming gold, with a plain leather strap instead of the flexible metal band he was accustomed to.

A furrow creased his forehead as he stroked the dial of the watch with his forefinger and then, as he raised his eyes to look about the room, he received another shock. He had never been in the room before.

He became aware that his heart thumped in his chest and he raised his hand to feel the coolness of silk against his fingers. He looked down and saw the pyjamas. Habitually he slept peeled to the skin; pyjamas constricted him and he had once said that he never saw the sense in getting dressed to go to bed.

Denison was still half asleep and his first impulse was to lie down and wait for the dream to be over so that he could wake up again in his own bed, but a pressing necessity of nature was suddenly upon him and he had to go to the bathroom. He shook his head irritably and threw aside the bedclothes – not the sheets and blankets to which he was accustomed but one of those new-fangled quilt objects which fashion had recently imported from the Continent.

He swung his legs out of the bed and sat up, looking down at the pyjamas again. *I'm in hospital*, he thought suddenly; *I must have had an accident.* Recollection told him otherwise. He had gone to bed in his own flat in Hampstead in the normal way, after perhaps a couple of drinks too many the previous evening. Those extra couple of drinks had become a habit after Beth died.

His fingers caressed the softness of the silk. Not a hospital, he decided; these were not National Health issue – not with an embroidered monogram on the pocket. He twisted his head to see the letters but the embroidery was complex and the monogram upside down and he could not make it out.

He stood up and looked about the room and knew immediately he was in a hotel. There were expensive-looking suitcases and in no other place but a hotel room could you find special racks on which to put them. He walked three paces and stroked the fine-grained leather which had hardly a scuff mark. The initials on the side of the suitcase were plain and unmonogrammed – H.F.M.

His head throbbed with the beginning of a headache – the legacy of those extra couple of drinks – and his mouth was parched. He glanced around the room and noted the unrumpled companion bed, the jacket hanging tidily on the back of a chair and the scatter of personal possessions on the dressing-table. He was about to cross to the dressing-table when the pressure in his bladder became intolerable and he knew he had to find a bathroom.

He turned and stumbled into the small hall off the bedroom. One side was panelled in wood and he swung a door open to find a wardrobe full of hung clothes. He turned again and found a door on the other side which opened into darkness. He fumbled for a switch, found it, and light sprang up in a white-tiled bathroom.

While he was relieving himself his mind worried about the electric switch, wondering what was strange about it, and then he realised that it was reversed – an upward movement to turn on the light instead of the more normal down pressure.

He flushed the toilet and turned to the hand basin seeking water. Two glasses stood on a shelf, wrapped in translucent paper. He took one down, ripped off the paper and, filling it with water from the green-topped tap, he drank thirstily. Up to this moment he had been awake for, perhaps, three minutes.

He put down the glass and rubbed his left eye which was sore. Then he looked into the mirror above the basin and, for the first time in his life, experienced sheer terror.

2

When Alice went through the Looking Glass the flowers talked to her and she evinced nothing but a mild surprise; but a psychologist once observed, 'If a flower spoke to a man, that man would know terror.'

So it was with Giles Denison. After seeing the impossible in the bathroom mirror he turned and vomited into the toilet bowl, but his laboured retchings brought up nothing but a thin mucus. Panting with his efforts, he looked into the mirror again – and reason left him.

When he became self-aware he found himself prone on the bed, his hands shaped into claws which dug into the pillow. A single sentence was drumming through his mind with mechanical persistence. '*I am Giles Denison! I* am *Giles Denison! I* AM *Giles Denison! I am* GILES DENISON!'

Presently his heavy breathing quieted and he was able to think beyond that reiterated statement of identity. With his head sideways on the pillow he spoke aloud, gathering reassurance from the familiar sound of his own voice. In a slurred tone which gradually became firmer he said, 'I am Giles Denison. I am thirty-six years old. I went to bed last night in my own home. I was a bit cut, that's true, but not so drunk as to be incapable. I *remember* going to bed – it was just after midnight.'

He frowned, then said, 'I've been hammering the bottle a bit lately, but I'm *not* an alcoholic – so this isn't the D.T.s. Then what is it?' His left hand moved up to stroke his cheek. 'What the hell is *this*?'

He arose slowly and sat on the edge of the bed, screwing up his nerve to go back into the bathroom as he knew he must. When he stood up he found his whole body trembling and he waited a while until the fit had passed. Then he walked with slow paces into the bathroom to face again the stranger in the mirror.

The face that looked back at him was older – he judged the man to be in his mid-forties. Giles Denison had worn a moustache and a neatly clipped beard – the stranger was clean shaven. Giles Denison had a full head of hair – the stranger's hair receded at the temples. Denison had no distinguishing marks as called for in passport descriptions – the stranger had an old scar on the left side of his face which passed from the temple across the cheekbone to the corner of the mouth; the left eyelid drooped, whether as a result of the scar or not it was impossible to say. There was also a small portwine birthmark on the angle of the right jaw.

If that had been all perhaps Denison would not have been so frightened, but the fact was that the face was *different*. Denison had been proud in a non-committal way of his aquiline good looks. Aquiline was the last word to describe the face of the stranger. The face was pudgy, the nose a round, featureless blob, and there was an incipient but perceptible double chin.

Denison opened his mouth to look at the stranger's teeth and caught the flash of a gold capping on a back molar. He closed both his mouth and his eyes and stood there for a while because the trembling had begun again. When he opened his eyes he kept them averted from the mirror and looked down at his hands which were gripping the edge of the basin. They were different, too; the skin looked older and the nails were shortened to the quick as though the stranger bit them. There was another old cicatrice on the back of the right thumb, and the backs of the forefinger and middle finger were stained with nicotine.

Denison did not smoke.

He turned blindly from the mirror and went back into the bedroom where he sat on the edge of the bed and stared at the blank wall. His mind threatened to retreat to the mere insistence of identity and yammered at him. 'I AM GILES DENISON!' and the trembling began again, but with an effort of will he dragged himself back from the edge of that mental precipice and forced himself to think as coherently as he could.

Presently he stood up and went to the window because the street noises forced themselves on his attention in an odd way. He heard an impossible sound, a sound that brought back memories of his childhood. He drew back the curtain and looked into the street to find its origin.

The tramcar was passing just below with the accompanying clangour of a past era of transport. Beyond it, in a dazzle of bright sunshine, were gardens and a bandstand and an array of bright umbrellas over tables where people sat eating and drinking. Beyond the gardens was another street filled with moving traffic.

Another tramcar passed and Denison caught a glimpse of the destination board. It made no sense to him because it seemed to be in a foreign language. There was something else odd about the tramcar and his eyes narrowed as he saw there were two single-deck coaches coupled together. He looked across the street at the fascia boards of the shops and found the words totally meaningless.

His head was aching worse than ever so he dropped the curtain to avoid the bright wash of sunlight and turned into the dimness of the room. He crossed to the dressing-table and looked down at the scatter of objects – a cigarette case, apparently of gold, a smoothly modelled cigarette lighter, a wallet and a note-case, and a handful of loose change.

Denison sat down, switched on the table lamp, and picked up one of the silver coins. The head depicted in profile was that of a fleshy man with a prow of a nose; there was something of the air of a Roman emperor about him. The wording was simple: OLAV.V.R. Denison turned the coin over to find a prancing horse and the inscription: I KRONE. NORGE.

Norway!

Denison began to feel his mind spin again and he bent forward as a sudden stomach cramp hit him. He laid down the coin and held his head in his hands until he felt better. Not a lot better, but marginally so.

When he had recovered enough he took the wallet and went through the pockets quickly, tossing the contents into a heap on the table top. The wallet emptied, he put it aside after noting its fine quality and began to examine the papers. There was an English driving licence in the name of Harold Feltham Meyrick of Lippscott House, near Brackley, Buckinghamshire. Hair prickled at the nape of Denison's neck as he looked at the signature. It was in his own handwriting. It was not his name but it was his penmanship – of that he was certain.

He stretched out his hand and took a pen, one of a matched set of fountain pen and ballpoint. He looked around for something on which to write, saw nothing, and opened the drawer in front of him where he found a folder containing writing paper and envelopes. He paused for a moment when he saw the letter heading – HOTEL CONTINENTAL, STORTINGS GATA, OSLO.

His hand trembled as the pen approached the paper but he scribbled his signature firmly enough – Giles Denison. He looked at the familiar loops and curlicues and felt immeasurably better, then he wrote another signature – H. F. Meyrick. He took the driving licence and compared it with what he had just written. It confirmed what he already knew; the signature in the driving licence was in his own handwriting.

So were the signatures in a fat book of Cook's traveller's cheques. He counted the cheques – nineteen of them at £50 each – £950 in all. If he was indeed Meyrick he was pretty well breeched. His headache grew worse.

There were a dozen engraved visiting cards with Meyrick's name and address and a fat sheaf of Norwegian currency in the note-case which he did not bother to count. He dropped it on to the desk and held his throbbing head in his hands. In spite of the fact that he had just woken up he felt tired and light-headed. He knew he was in danger of going into psychological retreat again; it would be so easy to curl up on the bed and reject this crazy, impossible thing that had happened to him, taking refuge in sleep with the hope that it would prove to be a dream and that when he woke he would be back in bed in his own flat in Hampstead, a thousand miles away.

He opened the drawer a fraction, put his fingers inside, and then smashed the drawer closed with the heel of his other hand. He gasped with the pain and when he drew his hand from the drawer there were flaring red marks on the backs of his fingers. The pain caused tears to come to his eyes and, as he nursed his hand, he knew this was too real to be a dream.

So if it was not a dream, what was it? He had gone to bed as one person and woken up, in another country, as another. But wait! That was not quite accurate. He had woken up knowing he was Giles Denison – the persona of Harold Feltham Meyrick was all on the exterior – inside he was still Giles Denison.

He was about to pursue this line of thought when he had another spasm of stomach cramp and suddenly he realised why he felt so weak and tired. He was ravenously hungry. Painfully he stood up and went into the bathroom where he stared down into the toilet bowl. He had been violently sick but his stomach had been so empty that there was hardly anything to be brought up but a thin, acid digestive juice. And yet the previous evening he had had a full meal. Surely there was something wrong there.

He went back into the bedroom and paused irresolutely by the telephone and then, with a sudden access of determination, picked it up. 'Give me room service,' he said. His voice was hoarse and strange to his own ears.

The telephone crackled. 'Room service,' it said in accented English.

'I'd like something to eat,' said Denison. He glanced at his watch – it was nearly two o'clock. 'A light lunch.'

'Open sandwiches?' suggested the telephone.

'Something like that,' said Denison. 'And a pot of coffee.'

'Yes, sir. The room number is . . .?'

Denison did not know. He looked around hastily and saw what must be the room key on a low coffee-table by the window. It was attached to about five pounds of brass on which a number was stamped. 'Three-sixty,' he said.

'Very good, sir.'

Denison was inspired. 'Can you send up a newspaper?'

'English or Norwegian, sir?'

'One of each.'

'*The Times*?'

'That and an equivalent local paper. And I may be in the bathroom when you come up – just leave everything on the table.'

'Very good, sir.'

Denison put down the telephone with a feeling of relief. He would have to face people some time but he did not feel eager to do so immediately. Certainly he would have to ask a lot of questions, but he

wanted time to compose himself. He could not help feeling there would
be a lot of trip wires to avoid in the taking over of another personality.

He took the silk Paisley dressing-gown which he found draped over a
chair and went into the bathroom, where he was coward enough to hang
a towel over the mirror. After fumbling for a moment with unfamiliar
plumbing, he drew a bath of hot water, then stripped off the pyjamas. He
became aware of the sticking-plaster on his left arm and was about to
take it off but he thought better of it, wondering if he really wanted to
know what was underneath.

He got into the bath and soaked in the hot water, feeling the heat ease
his suddenly aching limbs, and again, he drowsily wondered why he felt
so tired after being up only two hours. Presently he heard the door of the
suite open and there was a clatter of crockery. The door banged closed
and everything was quiet again so he got out of the bath and began to
rub himself down.

While sitting on the cork-topped stool he suddenly bent forward and
examined his left shin. There was a blue-white scar there, about the size
and shape of an orange pip. He remembered when that had happened;
it was when he was eight years old and had fallen off his first bicycle.

He raised his head and laughed aloud, feeling much better. He had
remembered that as Giles Denison and that little scar was a part of his
body that did not belong to Mr. Harold Blasted Feltham Bloody
Meyrick.

3

The Norwegian idea of a light lunch was an enormous tray filled with a
variety of edible goodies which Denison surveyed with satisfaction before
plunging in. The discovery of the scar had cheered him immensely and
had even emboldened him to shave Meyrick's face. Meyrick was old-
fashioned enough to use a safety-razor and a silver-mounted badger-hair
brush instead of an electric shaver and Denison had had some difficulty
in guiding the blade over unfamiliar contours and had cut himself – or
Meyrick – twice. And so, when he picked up the newspapers, his face was
adorned with two bloody patches of toilet paper.

The London *Times* and the Norwegian *Aftenposten* both had the same
date – July 9 – and Denison went very still, a piece of herring on rye
bread poised in mid-air. His last memory as Giles Denison had been
going to bed just after midnight on July 1 – no, it would be July 2 if it was

after midnight.

Somewhere he had lost a week.

He put his hand to his arm and felt the sticking-plaster. Someone had been doing things to him. He did not know who and he did not know why but, by God, he was going to find out and someone was going to pay dearly. While shaving he had examined his face closely. The scar on his left cheek was there all right, the remnant of an old wound, but it did not feel like a scar when he touched it. Still, no matter how hard he rubbed it would not come off, so it was not merely an example of clever theatrical make-up. The same applied to the birthmark on the right jaw.

There was something else odd about his nose and his cheeks and that double chin. They had a rubbery feel about them. Not ever having had any excess fat on his body he did not know whether this was normal or not. And, again, Meyrick's face had grown a light stubble of hair which he had shaved off, but the bald temples were smooth which meant that whoever had lifted his hairline had not done it by shaving.

The only part of his face Denison recognised were his eyes – those had not changed; they were still the same grey-green eyes he had seen every morning in the mirror. But the expression was different because of the droop of the left eyelid. There was a slight soreness in the outer corner of that eye which aroused his suspicions but he could see nothing but a tiny inflamed spot which could have been natural.

As he ate voraciously he glanced through *The Times*. The world still seemed to be wobbling on its political axis as unsteadily as ever and nothing had changed, so he tossed the newspaper aside and gave himself up to thought over a steaming cup of black coffee. What could be the motive for spiriting a man from his own bed, transforming him bodily, giving him a new personality and dumping him in a luxury hotel in the capital of Norway?

No answer.

The meal had invigorated him and he felt like moving and not sitting. He did not yet feel up to encountering people so he compromised by going through Meyrick's possessions. He opened the wardrobe and in one of the drawers, underneath a pile of underwear, he found a large travelling wallet. Taking it to the dressing-table he unzipped it and went through the contents.

The first thing to catch his eyes was a British passport. He opened it to find the description of the holder was filled out in his own handwriting as was Meyrick's signature underneath. The face that looked out of the photograph on the opposite page was that of Meyrick, who was described as a civil servant. Whoever had thought up this lark had been thorough about it.

He flipped through the pages and found only one stamped entry and his brow wrinkled as he studied it. *Sverige?* Would that be Sweden? If so he had arrived at a place called Arlanda in Sweden on a date he could not tell because the stamping was blurred. Turning to the back of the passport he found that the sum of £1,500 had been issued a month earlier. Since the maximum travel allowance for a tourist was £300 it would seem that H. F. Meyrick was operating on a businessman's allowance.

At the bottom of a pocket in the wallet he found an American Express credit card, complete with the ubiquitous fake signature. He looked at it pensively, flicking it with his fingernail. With this he could draw money or traveller's cheques anywhere; he could use it to buy an airline ticket to Australia if he felt the urge to emigrate suddenly. It represented complete and unlicensed freedom unless and until someone put a stopper on it at head office.

He transferred it to the small personal wallet along with the driving licence. It would be better to keep that little bit of plastic available in case of need.

Meyrick had an extensive wardrobe; casual clothing, lounge suits and even a dinner-jacket with accessories. Denison investigated a small box and found it contained personal jewellery – studs, tiepins and a couple of rings – and he realised he probably held a thousand pounds' worth of gold in his hand. The Patek Philippe watch on his wrist would cost £500 if it cost a penny. H. F. Meyrick was a wealthy man, so what kind of a civil servant did that make him?

Denison decided to get dressed. It was a sunny day so he chose casual trousers and a sports coat. The clothing fitted him as though made to measure. He looked at himself in the full-length mirror built into the wardrobe door, studiously ignoring the face on top of the body, and thought crazily that it, too, had probably been made to measure. The world began to spin again, but he remembered the small scar on his shin that belonged to Denison and that helped him to recover.

He put his personal possessions into his pockets and headed for the door, key in hand. As the door swung open a card which had been hung on the outer handle fell to the floor. He picked it up and read: VENNLIGST IKKE FORSTYRR – PLEASE DO NOT DISTURB. He was thoughtful as he hung it on the hook inside the door before locking the room; he would give a lot to know who had hung out that sign.

He went down in the lift with a couple of American blue-rinsed matrons who chattered to each other in a mid-West twang. 'Say, have you been out to Vigeland Park? All those statues – I didn't know where to look.' The lift stopped and the doors slid open with a soft hiss, and the

American ladies bustled out intent on sightseeing.

Denison followed them diffidently into the hotel lobby and stood by the lifts for a while, trying to get his bearings, doing his best to appear nonchalantly casual while he took in the scene.

'Mr. Meyrick . . . Mr. Meyrick, sir!'

He turned his head and saw the porter at the desk smiling at him. Licking lips that had suddenly gone dry he walked over. 'Yes?'

'Would you mind signing this, sir? The check for the meal in your room. Just a formality.'

Denison looked at the proffered pen and laid down the room key. He took the pen and scribbled firmly 'H. F. Meyrick' and pushed the slip across the counter. The porter was hanging the key on the rack but he turned and spoke to Denison before he could slip away. 'The night porter put your car away, sir. Here is the key.'

He held out a key with a tag on it and Denison extended his hand to take it. He glanced at the tag and saw the name, Hertz, and a car number. He cleared his throat. 'Thank you.'

'You sound as though you have a cold coming on,' said the porter.

Denison took a chance. 'Why do you think that?'

'Your voice sounds different.'

'Yes, I do feel a bit chesty,' said Denison.

The porter smiled. 'Too much night air, perhaps.'

Denison took another chance. 'What time *did* I get in last night?'

'This morning, sir. The night porter said it was about three o'clock.' The porter offered Denison a man-of-the-world smile. 'I wasn't surprised when you slept in this morning.'

No, thought Denison; *but I was!* He was growing bolder as he gained confidence. 'Can you tell me something? I was having a discussion with a friend about how long I've been here in Oslo and, for the life of me, I can't remember the exact day I booked in here. Could you check it for me?'

'Certainly, sir.' The porter moved away and began to run through cards in a file. Denison looked at the car key. It was thoughtful of Hertz to put the car number on the tag; he might even be able to recognise it when he saw it. It was also thoughtful of the night porter to put the car away – but where the hell had he put it?

The porter returned. 'You checked in on the eighteenth of June, sir. Exactly three weeks ago.'

The butterflies in Denison's stomach collided. 'Thank you,' he said mechanically, and moved away from the desk and across the lobby. An arrow pointed the direction to the bar and he glanced sideways and saw a dark, cool cavern with a few drinkers, solitary or in couples. It looked quiet and he desperately wanted to think, so he went in.

When the barman came up, he said, 'A beer, please.'

'Export, sir?'

Denison nodded absently. *June 18.* He had reckoned he had lost a week so how the devil could he have booked into the Hotel Continental in Oslo three weeks earlier? How the hell could he have been in two places at the same time?

The barman returned, poured the beer into a glass, and went away. Denison tried to figure where he had been on June 18 and found it difficult. Three weeks was a long time. *Where were you at 6.17 on the evening of June 18?* No wonder people found it difficult to establish alibis. He found it extraordinarily difficult to focus his thoughts; they flicked about, skittering here and there wildly out of control. *When did you last see your father?* Nuts!

A vagrant thought popped to the surface of his consciousness. *Edinburgh!* He had been to Edinburgh on the 17th and the 18th he had taken off as a reward for hard work. There had been a leisurely morning and he had played golf in the afternoon; he had gone to the cinema in the evening and had dined late in Soho, getting back to Hampstead fairly late.

He – as Giles Denison – had dined in Soho at about the same time as he – as Harold Feltham Meyrick – had dined in Oslo. Where was the sense of that?

He was aware that he was looking at bubbles rising in amber liquid and that he had not touched his beer. He lifted the glass and drank; it was cold and refreshing.

He had two things going for him – two things that kept him sane. One – Giles Denison's scar on H. F. Meyrick's shin – and two – the change in the timbre of Meyrick's voice as recognised by the hotel porter. And what did that imply? Obviously that there were *two* Meyricks; one who had booked in on June 18, and another – himself – who had just been planted. Never mind why and never mind how. Just accept the fact that it was done.

He drank some more beer and rested his chin in his hand, feeling the unaccustomed flab of his jowl. He had lost a week of his life. Could so much plastic surgery be done in a week? He added that to the list of things to be checked on.

And what to do? He could go to the British Embassy and tell his story. Mentally he ran through the scenario.

'What can we do for you, Mr. Meyrick?'

'Well, the fact is I'm not Meyrick – whoever he is. My name is Giles Denison and I've been kidnapped from London, my face changed, and dumped into an Oslo hotel with a hell of a lot of money and an unlimited credit account. Can you help me?'

'Certainly, Mr. Meyrick. Miss Smith, will you ring for a doctor?'

'My God!' said Denison aloud. 'I'd end up in the loony-bin.'

The barman cocked his head and came over. 'You wish something, sir?'

'Just to pay,' said Denison, finishing his beer.

He paid from the loose change in his pocket and left the bar. In the lobby he spotted a sign saying GARAGE, so he went through a door and down a flight of stairs to emerge into a basement car park. He checked the number on the Hertz key and walked along the first row of cars. It was right at the end – a big black Mercedes. He unlocked the door.

The first thing he saw was the doll on the driver's seat, a most curious object made of crudely carved wood and rope. The body was formed of rope twisted into a spiral and coming out in the form of a tail. The feet were but roughly indicated and the head was a round knob with a peg nose. The eyes and a mouth twisted to one side had been inked on to the wood, and the hair was of rope teased out into separate strands. It was a strange and somehow repulsive little figure.

He picked it up and discovered a piece of paper underneath it. He unfolded the deckle-edged note-paper and read the scrawled handwriting: *Your Drammen Dolly awaits you at Spiraltoppen. Early morning, July 10.*

He frowned. July 10 was next day, but where was Spiraltoppen and who – or what – was a Drammen Dolly? He looked at the ugly little doll. It had been lying on the driver's seat as though it had been deliberately left for him to find. He tossed it in his hand a couple of times and then thrust it into his pocket. It made an unsightly bulge, but what did he care? It was not his jacket. The note he put into his wallet.

The car was almost new, with just over 500 kilometres on the clock. He found a sheaf of papers relating to the car hire; it had been rented five days earlier, a fact which was singularly devoid of informative content. There was nothing else to be found.

He got out of the car, locked it, and left the garage by the car entrance, emerging on to a street behind the hotel. It was a little bewildering for him; the traffic drove on the wrong side of the road, the street and shop signs were indecipherable and his command of Norwegian was minimal, being restricted to one word – *skål* – which, while being useful in a cheery sort of way, was not going to be of much use for the more practical things of life.

What he needed was information and he found it on the corner of the street in the form of a bookshop. He went inside and found an array of maps from which he selected a map of central Oslo, one of Greater Oslo, and a motoring map of Southern Norway. To these he added a guide to the city and paid out of the slab of Norwegian currency in Meyrick's wallet. He made a mental note to count that money as soon as he had privacy.

He left the shop intending to go back to the hotel where he could study the maps and orient himself. He paused on the pavement and rubbernecked at the corner of a building where one would normally expect to find a street name – and there it was – *Roald Amundsens Gata*.

'Harry!'

He turned to go in the direction of the hotel but paused as he felt a hand on his arm. 'Harry Meyrick!' There was a note of anger in the voice. She was a green-eyed redhead of about thirty and she was flying alarm flags – her lips were compressed and pink spots glowed in her cheeks. 'I'm not used to being stood up,' she said. 'Where were you this morning?'

Momentarily he was nonplussed but remembered in time what the hotel porter had thought about his voice. 'I wasn't feeling well,' he managed to get out. 'I was in bed.'

'There's a thing called a telephone,' she said angrily. 'Alexander Graham Bell invented it – remember?'

'I was knocked out by sleeping pills,' he protested. With a small portion of his mind he noted that this was probably a true statement. 'Perhaps I overdid it.'

Her expression changed. 'You do sound a bit glued-up,' she admitted. 'Maybe I'll forgive you.' There was a faint American undertone to her English. 'It will cost you a drink, darling.'

'In the hotel?' he suggested.

'It's too nice a day to be inside. We'll go into the *Studenterlunden*.' She waved her arm past a passing articulated tramcar towards the gay umbrellas in the gardens on the other side of the street.

Denison felt trapped as he escorted her across the street, but he also realised that if he was to learn anything about Meyrick then this was too good a chance to pass up. He had once been accosted in the street by a woman who obviously knew him but he did not have the faintest idea of who she was. There is a point of no return in that type of conversation after which one cannot, in decency, admit ignorance. On that occasion Denison had fumbled it, had suffered half an hour of devious conversation, and they had parted amicably without him finding out who she was. He still did not know. Grimly he thought that it was good practice for today's exercise.

As they crossed the street she said. 'I saw Jack Kidder this morning. He was asking about you.'

'How is he?'

She laughed. 'Fine, as always. You know Jack.'

'Of course,' said Denison deadpan. 'Good old Jack.'

They went into the outdoor café and found an empty table with difficulty. Under other circumstances Denison would have found it pleasant to have a drink with a pretty woman in surroundings like this, but his mind was beleaguered by his present problems. They sat down and he put his parcel of maps on the table.

One of them slipped out of the packet and his main problem prodded at it with a well-manicured forefinger. 'What are these?'

'Maps,' said Denison succinctly.

'Maps of where?'

'Of the city.'

'Oslo!' She seemed amused. 'Why do you want maps of Oslo? Isn't it your boast that you know Oslo better than London?'

'They're for a friend.'

Denison chalked up a mental note. *Meyrick knows Oslo well; probably a frequent visitor. Steer clear of local conditions or gossip. Might run into more problems like this.*

'Oh!' She appeared to lose interest.

Denison realised he was faced with a peculiar difficulty. He did not know this woman's name and, as people do not commonly refer to themselves by name in conversation, he did not see how he was going to get it, short of somehow prying into her handbag and looking for identification.

'Give me a cigarette, darling,' she said.

He patted his pockets and found he had left the cigarette case and lighter in the room. Not being a smoker it had not occurred to him to put them in his pocket along with the rest of Meyrick's personal gear. 'I'm sorry,' he said. 'I don't have any with me.'

'My!' she said. 'Don't tell me the great Professor Meyrick has stopped smoking. Now I *will* believe in cancer.'

Professor!

He used the pretext of illness again. 'The one I tried this morning tasted like straw. Maybe I will stop smoking.' He held his hand over the table. 'Look at those nicotine stains. Imagine what my lungs must be like.'

She shook her head in mock sorrow. 'It's like pulling down a national monument. To imagine Harry Meyrick without a cigarette is like trying to imagine Paris without the Eiffel Tower.'

A Nordic waitress came to the table; she looked rather like Jeanette MacDonald dressed for an appearance in *White Horse Inn*. Denison raised his eyebrows at his companion. 'What will you have?'

'The usual,' she said indifferently, delving into her handbag.

He took refuge in a paroxysm of coughing, pulling out his handkerchief and only emerging when he heard her giving the order. He waited until the waitress left before putting away the handkerchief. The woman opposite him said, 'Harry, that's a really bad cough. I'm not surprised you're thinking of giving up the cancer sticks. Are you feeling all right, darling? Maybe you'd be better off in bed, after all.'

'I'm all right,' he said.

'Are you sure?' she asked solicitously.

'Perfectly sure.'

'Spoken like the old Professor Meyrick,' she said mockingly. 'Always sure of everything.'

'Don't call me Professor,' he said testily. It was a safe enough thing to say regardless of whether Meyrick was really a professor or whether she was pulling his leg in a heavy-handed manner. The British have never been keen on the over-use of professional titles. And it might provoke her into dropping useful information.

All he got was a light and inconsequential, 'When on the Continent do as the Continentals do.'

He went on the attack. 'I don't like it.'

'You're so British, Harry.' He thought he detected a cutting edge to her voice. 'But then, of course, you would be.'

'What do you mean by that?'

'Oh, come off it. There's nobody more British than an outsider who has bored his way in. Where were you born, Harry? Somewhere in Mittel Europa?' She suddenly looked a little ashamed. 'I'm sorry; I shouldn't have said that. I'm being bitchy, but you're behaving a bit oddly, too.'

'The effect of the pills. Barbiturates have never agreed with me. I have a headache.'

She opened her handbag. 'I have aspirin.'

The waitress, Valkyrie-like, bore down on them. Denison looked at the bottles on the tray, and said, 'I doubt if aspirin goes with beer.' That was the last thing he would have thought of as 'the usual'; she did not look the beery type.

She shrugged and closed the bag with a click. 'Please yourself.'

The waitress put down two glasses, two bottles of beer and a packet of cigarettes, said something rapid and incomprehensible, and waited expectantly. Denison took out his wallet and selected a 100-kroner note. Surely two beers and a packet of cigarettes could not cost more than a hundred kroner. My God, he did not even know the value of the currency! This was like walking through a minefield blindfolded.

He was relieved when the waitress made no comment but made change from a leather bag concealed under her apron. He laid the money on the table intending to check it surreptitiously. The redhead said, 'You've no need to buy my cigarettes, Harry.'

He smiled at her. 'Be my guest,' he said, and stretched out his hand to pour her beer.

'You've given it up yourself but you're quite prepared to pay for other people's poison.' She laughed. 'Not a very moral attitude.'

'I'm not a moral philosopher,' he said, hoping it was true.

'No, you're not,' she agreed. 'I've always wondered where you stood in that general direction. What would you call yourself, Harry? Atheist? Agnostic? Humanist?'

At last he was getting something of the quality of Meyrick. Those were questions but they were leading questions, and he was quite prepared to discuss philosophy with her – a nice safe subject. 'Not an atheist,' he said. 'It's always seemed to me that to believe in the non-existence of something is somewhat harder than to believe in its existence. I'd put myself down as an agnostic – one of the "don't know" majority. And that doesn't conflict with humanism.'

He fingered the notes and coins on the table, counted them mentally, subtracted the price of two beers based on what he had paid for a beer in the hotel, and arrived at the price of a packet of cigarettes. Roughly, that is. He had an idea that the price of a beer in a luxury hotel would be far higher than in an open-air café.

'I went to church last Sunday,' she said pensively. 'To the English church – you know – the one on Møllergata.' He nodded as though he did know. 'I didn't get much out of it. I think next time I'll try the American church.' She frowned. 'Where is the American church, Harry?'

He had to say *something*, so he took a chance. 'Isn't it near the Embassy?'

Her brow cleared. 'Of course. Between Bygdøy Alle and Drammens Veien. It's funny, isn't it? The American church being practically next door to the British Embassy. You'd expect it to be near the American Embassy.'

He gulped. 'Yes, you would,' he said, and forbore to mention that that was what he had meant. Even a quasitheological conversation was strewn with pitfalls. He had to get out of this before he really dropped a clanger.

And an alarming suspicion had just sprung to mind, fully armed and spiky. Whoever had planted him in that hotel room and provided him with money and the means to provide all the necessities of life – and a lot of the luxuries, too – was unlikely to leave him unobserved. Someone would be keeping tabs on him, otherwise the whole operation was a nonsense. Could it be this redhead who apparently had qualms about her immortal soul? What could be better than to plant someone right next to him for closer observation?

She opened the packet of cigarettes and offered him one. 'You're sure you won't?'

He shook his head. 'Quite sure.'

'It must be marvellous to have will power.'

He wanted peace and not this continuous exploration of a maze where every corner turned could be more dangerous than the last. He started to cough again, and dragged his handkerchief from his pocket. 'I'm sorry,' he said in a muffled voice. 'I think you're right; I'd be better off in bed. Do you mind if I leave you?'

'Of course not.' Her voice was filled with concern. 'Do you want a doctor?'

'That's not necessary,' he said. 'I'll be all right tomorrow – I know how these turns take me.' He stood up and she also rose. 'Don't bother to come with me. The hotel is only across the road.'

He picked up the packet and thrust the maps back into it, and put the handkerchief into his pocket. She looked down at his feet. 'You've dropped something,' she said, and stooped to pick it up. 'Why, it's a Spiralen Doll.'

'A what?' he asked incautiously. It must have been pulled from his pocket when he took out the handkerchief.

She regarded him oddly. 'You pointed these out at the Spiralen when we were there last week. You laughed at them and called them tourist junk. Don't you remember?'

'Of course,' he said. 'It's just this damned headache.'

She laughed. 'I didn't expect to see you carrying one. You didn't buy this when we were there – where did you get it?'

He told the truth. 'I found it in the car I hired.'

'You can't trust anyone to do a good job these days,' she said, smiling. 'Those cars are supposed to be cleaned and checked.' She held it out. 'Do you want it?'

'I may be a bit light-headed,' he said, 'but I think I do.' He took it from her. 'I'll be going now.'

'Have a hot toddy and a good night's sleep,' she advised. 'And ring me as soon as you're better.'

That would be difficult, to say the least, with neither telephone number nor name. 'Why don't you give me a ring tomorrow,' he said. 'I think I'll be well enough to have dinner. I promise not to stand you up again.'

'I'll ring you tomorrow afternoon.'

'Promise,' he insisted, not wanting to lose her.

'Promise.'

He put the rope doll into his pocket and left her with a wave, and went out of the garden, across the road and into the hotel, feeling relieved that he was well out of a difficult situation. *Information,* he thought, as he walked across the hotel lobby; *that's what I need – I'm hamstrung without it.*

He paused at the porter's desk and the porter looked up with a quick smile. 'Your key, sir?' He swung around and unhooked it.

On impulse Denison held out the doll. 'What's that?'

The porter's smile broadened. 'That's a Spiralen Doll, sir.'

'Where does it come from?'

'From the Spiralen, sir – in Drammen. If you're interested, I have a pamphlet.'

'I'm very much interested,' said Denison.

The porter looked through papers on a shelf and came up with a leaflet printed in blue ink. 'You must be an engineer, sir.'

Denison did not know what the hell Meyrick was. 'It's in my general field of interest,' he said guardedly, took the key and the leaflet, and walked towards the lifts. He did not notice the man who had been hovering behind him and who regarded him speculatively until the lift door closed.

Once in his room Denison tossed the maps and the leaflet on to the dressing-table and picked up the telephone. 'I'd like to make a long distance call, please – to England.' He took out his wallet. 'What is the number, sir?'

'There's a little difficulty about that. I don't have a number – only an address.' He opened the wallet with one hand and extracted one of Meyrick's cards.

The telephonist was dubious. 'That may take some time, sir.'

'It doesn't matter – I'll be in my room for the rest of the day.'

'What is the address, sir?'

Denison said clearly, 'Lippscott House, near Brackley, Buckinghamshire, England.' He repeated it three times to make sure it had got across.

'And the name?'

Denison opened his mouth and then closed it, having suddenly acquired a dazed look. He would appear to be a damned fool if he gave the name of Meyrick – no one in his right mind rings up himself, especially after having admitted he did not know his own telephone number. He swallowed, and said shortly, 'The name is not known.'

The telephone sighed in his ear. 'I'll do my best, sir.'

Denison put down the telephone and settled in a chair to find out about the Spiralen. The front of the leaflet was headed: DRAMMEN. There was an illustration of a Spiralen Doll which did not look any the better for being printed in blue. The leaflet was in four languages.

The Spiralen was described as being 'a truly unique attraction, as well as a superb piece of engineering'. Apparently there had been a quarry at the foot of Bragernesåsen, a hill near Drammen, which had become an eyesore until the City Fathers decided to do something about it. Instead of quarrying the face of the hill the operation had been extended into the interior.

A tunnel had been driven into the hill, thirty feet wide, fifteen feet high and a mile long. But not in a straight line. It turned back on itself six complete times in a spiral drilled into the mountain, climbing five hundred feet until it came out on top of Bragernesåsen where the Spiraltoppen Restaurant was open all the year round. The views were said to be excellent.

Denison picked up the doll; its body was formed of six complete turns of rope. He grinned weakly.

Consultation of the maps revealed that Drammen was a small town forty kilometres west of Oslo. That would be a nice morning drive, and he could get back in the afternoon well in time for any call from the redhead. It was not much to go on, but it was all he had.

He spent the rest of the afternoon searching through Meyrick's possessions but found nothing that could be said to be a clue. He ordered dinner to be sent to his room because he suspected that the hotel restaurant might be full of unexploded human mines like the redhead he had met, and there was a limit to what he could get away with.

The telephone call came when he was half-way through dinner. There were clicks and crackles and a distant voice said, 'Dr. Meyrick's residence.'

Doctor!

'I'd like to speak to Dr. Meyrick.'

'I'm sorry, sir; but Dr. Meyrick is not at home.'

'Have you any idea where I can find him?'

'He is out of the country at the moment, sir.'

'Oh! Have you any idea where?'

There was a pause. 'I believe he is travelling in Scandinavia, sir.'

This was not getting anywhere at all. 'Who am I speaking to?'

'This is Andrews – Dr. Meyrick's personal servant. Would you like to leave a message, sir?'

'Do you recognise my voice, Andrews?' asked Denison.

A pause. 'It's a bad line.' Another pause. 'I don't believe in guessing games on the telephone, sir.'

'All right,' said Denison. 'When you see Dr. Meyrick will you tell him that Giles Denison called, and I'll be getting in touch with him as soon as possible. Got that?'

'Giles Denison. Yes, Mr. Denison.'

'When is Dr. Meyrick expected home?'

'I really couldn't say, Mr. Denison.'

'Thank you, Mr. Andrews.'

Denison put down the telephone. He felt depressed.

4

He slept poorly that night. His sleep was plagued with dreams which he did not remember clearly during the few times he was jerked into wakefulness but which he knew were full of monstrous and fearful figures which threatened him. In the early hours of the morning he fell into a heavy sleep with deadened senses and when he woke he felt heavy and listless.

He got up tiredly and twitched aside the window curtain to find that the weather had changed; the sky was a dull grey and the pavements were wet and a fine drizzle filled the air. The outdoor café in the gardens opposite would not be doing much business that day.

He rang down for breakfast and then had a shower, finishing with needle jets of cold water in an attempt to whip some enthusiasm into his suddenly heavy body and, to a degree, he succeeded. When the floor waitress came in with his breakfast he had dressed in trousers and white polo-necked sweater and was combing his hair before the bathroom mirror. Incredibly enough, he was whistling in spite of having Meyrick's face before him.

The food helped, too, although it was unfamiliar and a long way from an English breakfast. He rejected the raw, marinated herring and settled for a boiled egg, bread and marmalade and coffee. After breakfast he checked the weather again and then selected a jacket and a short topcoat from the wardrobe. He also found a thin, zippered leather satchel into which he put the maps and the Spiralen leaflet which had a street plan of Drammen on the back. Then he went down to the car. It was exactly nine o'clock.

It was not easy getting out of town. The car was bigger and more powerful than those he had been accustomed to driving and he had to keep to what was to him the wrong side of the road in a strange city in early rush-hour traffic. Three times he missed signs and took wrong turnings. The first time he did this he cruised on and got hopelessly lost and had to retrace his path laboriously. Thereafter when he missed a turn he reversed immediately so as not to lose his way again.

He was quite unaware of the man following him in the Swedish Volvo. Denison's erratic course across the city of Oslo was causing him a lot of trouble, especially when Denison did his quick and unexpected reversals. The man, whose name was Armstrong, swore freely and frequently, and his language became indescribable when the drizzle intensified into a downpour of heavy driving rain.

Denison eventually got out of the centre of the city and on to a six-lane highway, three lanes each way. The windscreen wipers had to work hard to cope with the rain, but it was better when he fiddled with a switch and discovered they had two speeds. Resolutely he stuck to the centre lane, reassured from time to time by the name DRAMMEN which appeared on overhead gantries.

To his left was the sea, the deeply penetrating arm of Oslofjord, but then the road veered away and headed inland. Presently the rain stopped, although no sun appeared, and he even began to enjoy himself, having got command of the unfamiliar car. And suddenly he was in Drammen, where he parked and studied the plan on the back of the leaflet.

In spite of the plan he missed the narrow turning to the right and had to carry on for some way before he found an opportunity to reverse the car, but eventually he drove up to the entrance of the tunnel where he stopped to pay the two kroner charge.

He put the car into gear and moved forward slowly. At first the tunnel was straight, and then it began to climb, turning to the left. There was dim illumination but he switched on his headlights in the dipped position and saw the reflection from the wetness of the rough stone wall. The gradient was regular, as was the radius of the spiral, and by the time he came to a board marked 1 he had got the hang of it. All he had to do was to keep the wheel at a fixed lock to correspond with the radius of the spiral and grind upwards in low gear.

All the same, it was quite an experience – driving upwards through the middle of a mountain. Just after he passed level 3 a car passed him going downwards and momentarily blinded him, but that was all the trouble he had. He took the precaution of steering nearer to the outer curve and closer to the wall.

Soon after passing level 6 he came out of the tunnel into a dazzle of light and on to level ground. To his left there was a large car park, empty of cars, and beyond it was the roof of a large wooden building constructed in chalet style. He parked as close to the building as he could, and got out of the car and locked it.

The chalet was obviously the Spiraltoppen Restaurant, but it was barely in business. He looked through a glass door and saw two women mopping the floor. It was still very early in the morning. He retreated a few steps and saw a giant Spiralen Doll outside the entrance, a leering figure nearly as big as a man.

He looked about him and saw steps leading down towards the edge of a cliff where there was a low stone wall and a coin-in-the-slot telescope. He walked down the path to where he could get a view of the Drammen Valley. The clouds were lifting and the sun broke through and illuminated the river so far below. The air was crystal clear.

Very pretty, he thought sourly; *but what the hell am I doing here? What do I expect to find? Drammen Dolly, where are you?*

Perhaps the answer lay in the restaurant. He looked at the view for a long time, made nothing of it from his personal point of view, and then returned to the restaurant where the floor mopping operation had been completed.

He went inside and sat down, looking around hopefully. It was a curiously *ad hoc* building, all odd angles and discrepancies as though the architect – if there had been an architect – had radically changed his mind during construction. Presently a waitress came and took his order without displaying much interest in him, and later returned with his coffee. She went away without giving him the secret password, so he sat and sipped the coffee gloomily.

After a while he pulled out the leaflet and studied it. He was on the top of Bragernesåsen which was 'the threshold of the unspoilt country of Drammensmarka, an eldorado for hikers in summer, and skiers in winter, who have the benefit of floodlit trails.' There might be something there, he thought; so he paid for his coffee and left.

Another car had arrived and stood on the other side of the car park. A man sat behind the wheel reading a newspaper. He glanced across incuriously as the restaurant door slammed behind Denison and then returned to his reading. Denison pulled the topcoat closer about him against the suddenly cold wind and walked away from the cliff towards the unspoilt country of Drammensmarka.

It was a wooded area with tall conifers and equally tall deciduous trees with whitish trunks which he assumed to be birches, although he could have been wrong, botany not being his subject. There was a trail leading away from the car park which appeared to be well trodden. Soon the trees closed around him and, on looking back, the restaurant was out of sight. The trail forked and, tossing a mental coin, he took the route to the right. After walking for a further ten minutes he stopped and again wondered what the hell he was doing. Just because he had found a crude doll in a car he was walking through a forest on a mountain in Norway. It was bloody ridiculous.

It had been the redhead's casual theory that the doll had been left in the car by a previous hirer. But what previous hirer? The car was obviously new. The doll had been left in a prominent position and there was the note to go with it with the significant reference to the 'Drammen Dolly'.

Early morning – that's what the note had said. But how early was early? *Come out, come out, wherever you are, my little Drammen Dolly. Wave your magic wand and take me back to Hampstead.*

He turned around and trudged back to the fork in the path and this time took the route to the left. The air was fresh and clean after the rain. Drops of water sparkled prismatically on the leaves as the sun struck them and occasionally, as he passed under a tree, a miniature shower would sprinkle him.

And he saw nothing but trees.

He came to another fork in the trail and stopped, wondering what to do. There was a sound behind him as of a twig breaking and he swung around and stared back along the trail but saw nothing as he peered into the dappled forest, shading his eyes from the sun. He turned away but heard another sound to his right and out of the corner of his eye saw something dark moving very fast among the trees.

Behind him he heard footsteps and whirled around to find himself under savage attack. Almost upon him was a big man, a six-footer with broad shoulders, his right hand uplifted and holding what appeared to be a short club.

Denison was thirty-six, which is no age to indulge in serious fisticuffs. He also led a sedentary life which meant that his wind was not too good, although it was better than it might have been because he did not smoke. Yet his reflexes were fast enough. What really saved him, though, was that in his time he had been a middling-good middleweight boxer who had won most of his amateur fights by sheer driving aggression.

The last two days had been frustrating for a man of his aggressive tendencies. He had been in a mist with nothing visible to fight and this had gnawed at him. Now that he had something to fight – someone to fight – his instincts took over.

Which is why, instead of jumping back under the attack, unexpectedly he went in low, blocked the descending arm with his own left arm and sank in his right fist into his attacker's belly just below the sternum. The man's breath came out of him with a gasp and he doubled up on the ground wheezing and making retching noises.

Denison wasted no time, but ran for it back to the car park, aware that his were not the only feet that made those thudding noises on the trail. He did not waste time by looking back but just put his head down and ran. To his left he was aware of a man bounding down the hill dodging trees and doing his best to cut him off – what was worse, he seemed to be succeeding.

Denison put on an extra burst of speed but it was no use – the man leaped on to the trail about fifteen yards ahead. Denison heard his pursuer pounding behind and knew that if he stopped he would be trapped, so he bored on up the trail without slackening pace.

When the man ahead realised that Denison did not intend to stop a look of surprise came over his face and his hand plucked at his waist and he dropped into a crouch. Sun gleamed off the blade of the knife he held in his right hand. Denison ran full tilt at him and made as to break to the man's left – the safe side – but at the last minute he sold him the dummy and broke away on the knife side.

He nearly got through unscathed because the man bought it. But at the last moment he lashed out with the knife and Denison felt a hot pain across his flank. Yet he had got past and plunged along the trail with undiminished speed, hoping to God he would not trip over an exposed tree root. There is nothing like being chased by a man with a knife to put wings on the feet.

There were three of them. The big man he had laid out with a blow to the solar plexus would not be good for anything for at least two minutes and probably longer. That left the knifer and the other man who had chased him. Behind he heard cries but ahead he saw the roof of the restaurant just coming in sight over the rise.

His wind was going fast and he knew he could not keep up this sprint for long. He burst out into the car park and headed for his car, thankful there was now firm footing. A car door slammed and he risked a glance to the left and saw the man who had been reading the newspaper in the parked car beginning to run towards him.

He fumbled hastily for his car key and thanked God when it slipped smoothly into the lock. He dived behind the wheel and slammed the door with one hand while stabbing the key at the ignition lock with the other – this time he missed and had to fumble again. The man outside hammered on the window and then tugged at the door handle. Denison held the door closed with straining muscles and brought over his other hand quickly to snap down the door catch.

He had dropped the car key on the floor and groped for it. His lungs were hurting and he gasped for breath, and the pain in his side suddenly sharpened, but somewhere at the back of his mind cool logic told him that he was reasonably safe, that no one could get into a locked car before he took off – always provided he could find that damned key.

His fingers brushed against it and he grabbed it, brought it up, and rammed it into the ignition lock. Cool logic evaporated fast when he saw the man stand back and produce an automatic pistol. Denison frantically pumped his foot on the clutch, slammed into first gear, and took off in a tyre-burning squeal even before he had a finger on the wheel. The car weaved drunkenly across the car park than straightened out and dived into the Spiralen tunnel like a rabbit down a hole.

Denison's last glimpse of daylight in the rear-view mirror showed him the other car beginning to move with two doors open and his pursuers piling in. That would be the ferret after the rabbit.

It took him about ten seconds, after he hit the curve, to know he was going too fast. The gradient was one in ten and the curve radius only a hundred and fifteen feet, turning away to the right so that he was on the inside. His speed was such that centrifugal force tended to throw the car sideways over the centre line, and if anything was coming up he would surely hit it.

He could be compared to a man on a bobsled going down the Cresta Run – with some important differences. The Cresta Run is designed so that the walls can be climbed; here the walls were of jagged, untrimmed rock and one touch at speed would surely wreck the car. The Cresta Run does not have two-way traffic with a continuous blind corner a mile long, and the competitors are not pursued by men with guns – if they were, more records might be broken.

So Denison reluctantly eased his foot on the accelerator and risked a glance in his mirror. The driver of the car behind was more foolhardy than he and was not worrying about up-traffic. He was barrelling down the centre line and catching up fast. Denison fed more fuel to the engine, twisted the wheel and wondered if he could sustain a sideways drift a mile long.

The walls of the tunnel were a blur and the lights flicked by and he caught sight of an illuminated number 5. Four more circuits to go before the bottom. The car jolted and pitched suddenly and he fought the wheel which had taken on a life of its own. It did it again and he heard a nasty sound from the rear. He was being rammed. There was another sound as sheet metal ripped and the car slewed across the whole width of the tunnel.

He heard – and felt – the crunch as the rear off-side of the car slammed into the opposite wall, but Denison was not particularly worried about the property of the Hertz Company at that moment because he saw the dipped headlights of a vehicle coming up the Spiralen towards him. He juggled madly with wheel, clutch and accelerator and shot off to the other side of the tunnel again, scraping across the front of the tour bus that was coming up. There was a brief vignette of the driver of the bus, his mouth open and his eyes staring, and then he was gone.

The front fender scraped along the nearside tunnel wall in a shower of sparks and Denison wrenched the wheel over and nearly clipped the rear of the bus as it went by. He wobbled crazily from side to side of the tunnel for about a hundred and fifty yards before he had proper control, and it was only by the grace of God that the bus had not been the first in a procession of vehicles.

Level 2 passed in a flash and a flicker of light in Denison's eyes, reflected from the rear-view mirror, told him that the car behind had also avoided the bus and was catching up again. He increased speed again and the tyres protested noisily with a rending squeal; the whole of the Spiralen would be filled with the stench of burning rubber.

Level 1. A brightness ahead warned of the approach of another vehicle and Denison tensed his muscles, but the tunnel straightened and he saw it was the daylight of the exit. He rammed down his foot and the car surged forward and came out of the tunnel like a shell from a gun. The fee-collector threw up his arms and jumped aside as the car shot past him. Denison screwed up his eyes against the sudden bright glare of sunlight and hurtled down the hill towards the main street of Drammen at top speed.

At the bottom of the hill he jammed on his brakes and wrenched the wheel sideways. The car heeled violently as it turned the corner and the tyres screamed again, leaving black rubber on the road. Then he literally stood on the brake pedal, rising in his seat, to avoid ploughing into a file of the good people of Drammen crossing the street at a traffic light. The car's nose sank and the rear came up as it juddered to a halt, just grazing the thigh of a policeman who stood in the middle of the road with his back to Denison.

The policeman turned, his face expressionless. Denison sagged back into his seat and twisted his head to look back along the road. He saw the pursuing car break the other way and head down the road at high speed out of Drammen.

The policeman knocked on the car window and Denison wound it down to be met by a blast of hot Norwegian. He shook his head, and said loudly. 'I have no Norwegian. Do you speak English?'

The policeman halted in mid-spate with his mouth open. He shut it firmly, took a deep breath, and said, 'What you think you do?'

Denison pointed back. 'It was those damn fools. I might have been killed.'

The policeman stood back and did a slow circumnavigation of the car, inspecting it carefully. Then he tapped on the window of the passenger side and Denison opened the door. The policeman got in. 'Drive!' he said.

When Denison pulled up outside the building marked POLISI and switched off the engine the policeman firmly took the car key from him and waved towards the door of the building. 'Inside!'

It was a long wait for Denison. He sat in a bare room under the cool eye of a Norwegian policeman, junior grade, and meditated on his story. If he told the truth then the question would arise: *Who would want to attack an Englishman called Meyrick?* That would naturally lead to: *Who is this Meyrick?* Denison did not think he could survive long under questions like that. It would all come out and the consensus of opinion would be that they had a right nut-case on their hands, and probably homicidal at that. They would have to be told something other than the strict truth.

He waited an hour and then the telephone rang. The young policeman answered briefly, put down the telephone, and said to Denison, 'Come!'

He was taken to an office where a senior policeman sat behind a desk. He picked up a pen and levelled it at a chair. 'Sit!'

Denison sat, wondering if the English conversation of the Norwegian police was limited to one word at a time. The officer poised his pen above a printed form. 'Name?'

'Meyrick?' said Denison. 'Harold Feltham Meyrick.'

'Nationality?'

'British.'

The officer extended his hand, palm upwards. 'Passport.' It was not a question.

Denison took out his passport and put it on the outstretched palm. The officer flicked through the pages, then put it down and stared at Denison with eyes like chips of granite. 'You drove through the streets of Drammen at an estimated speed of 140 kilometres an hour. I don't have to tell you that is in excess of the speed limit. You drove through the Spiralen at an unknown speed – certainly less than 140 kilometres otherwise we would have the distasteful task of scraping you off the walls. What is your explanation?'

Denison now knew what a Norwegian policeman sounded like in an extended speech in the English language, and he did not particularly relish it. The man's tone was scathing. He said, 'There was a car behind me. The driver was playing silly buggers.' The officer raised his eyebrows, and Denison said, 'I think they were teenage hooligans out to throw a scare into someone – you know how they are. They succeeded with me. They rammed me a couple of times and I had to go faster. It all led on from that.'

He stopped and the officer stared at him with hard, grey eyes but said nothing. Denison let the silence lengthen, then said slowly and clearly, 'I would like to get in touch with the British Embassy immediately.'

The officer lowered his eyes and consulted a typewritten form. 'The condition of the rear of your car is consistent with your story. There was another car. It has been found abandoned. The condition of the front of that car is also consistent with your story. The car we found had been stolen last night in Oslo.' He looked up. 'Do you want to make any changes in your statement?'

'No,' said Denison.

'Are you sure?'

'Quite sure.'

The officer stood up, the passport in his hand. 'Wait here.' He walked out.

Denison waited another hour before the officer came back. He said, 'An official from your Embassy is coming to be present while you prepare your written statement.'

'I see,' said Denison. 'What about my passport?'

'That will be handed to the embassy official. Your car we will keep here for spectrographic tests of the paintwork. If there has been transfer of paint from one car to another it will tend to support your statement. In any event, the car cannot be driven in its present condition; both indicator lights are smashed – you would be breaking the law.'

Denison nodded. 'How long before the Embassy man gets here?'

'I cannot say. You may wait here.' The officer went away.

Denison waited for two hours. On complaining of hunger, food and coffee were brought to him on a tray. Otherwise he was left alone except for the doctor who came in to dress an abrasion on the left side of his forehead. He dimly remembered being struck by a tree branch on the chase along the trail, but did not correct the doctor who assumed it had occurred in the Spiralen. What with one thing and another, the left side of Meyrick's face was taking quite a beating; any photographs had better be of the right profile.

He said nothing about the wound in his side. While alone in the office he had checked it quickly. That knife must have been razor sharp; it had sliced through his topcoat, his jacket, the sweater and into his side, fortunately not deeply. The white sweater was red with blood but the wound, which appeared clean, had stopped bleeding although it hurt if he moved suddenly. He left it alone.

At last someone came – a dapper young man with a fresh face who advanced on Denison with an outstretched hand. 'Dr. Meyrick – I'm George McCready, I've come to help you get out of this spot of trouble.'

Behind McCready came the police officer, who drew up another chair and they got down to the business of the written statement. The officer wanted it amplified much more than in Denison's bald, verbal statement so he obligingly told all that had happened from the moment he had entered the Spiralen tunnel on top of Bragernesåsen. He had no need to lie about anything. His written statement was taken away and typed up in quadruplicate and he signed all four copies, McCready countersigning as witness.

McCready cocked his eye at the officer. 'I think that's all.'

The officer nodded. 'That's all – for the moment. Dr. Meyrick may be required at another time. I trust he will be available.'

'Of course,' said McCready easily. He turned to Denison. 'Let's get you back to the hotel. You must be tired.'

They went out to McCready's car. As McCready drove out of Drammen Denison was preoccupied with a problem. How did McCready know to address him as 'Doctor'? The designation on his passport was just plain 'Mister'. He stirred and said, 'If we're going to the hotel I'd like to have my passport. I don't like to be separated from it.'

'You're not going to the hotel,' said McCready. 'That was for the benefit of the copper. I'm taking you to the Embassy. Carey flew in from London this morning and he wants to see you.' He laughed shortly. '*How* he wants to see you.'

Denison felt the water deepening. 'Carey,' he said in a neutral tone, hoping to stimulate conversation along those lines. McCready had dropped Carey's name casually as though Meyrick was supposed to know him. Who the devil was Carey?

McCready did not bite. 'That explanation of yours wasn't quite candid, was it?' He waited for a reaction but Denison kept his mouth shut. 'There's a witness – a waitress from the Spiraltoppen – who said something about a fight up there. It seems there was a man with a gun. The police are properly suspicious.'

When Denison would not be drawn McCready glanced sideways at him, and laughed. 'Never mind, you did the right thing under the circumstances. Never talk about guns to a copper – it makes them nervous. Mind you, the circumstances should never have arisen. Carey's bloody wild about that.' He sighed. 'I can't say that I blame him.'

It was gibberish to Denison and he judged that the less he said the better. He leaned back, favouring his injured side, and said, 'I'm tired.'

'Yes,' said McCready. 'I suppose you must be.'

5

Denison was kept kicking his heels in an ante-room in the Embassy while McCready went off, presumably to report. After fifteen minutes he came back. 'This way, Dr. Meyrick.'

Denison followed him along a corridor until McCready stopped and politely held open a door for him. 'You've already met Mr. Carey, of course.'

The man sitting behind the desk could only be described as square. He was a big, chunky man with a square head topped with close-cut grizzled grey hair. He was broad-chested and squared off at the shoulders, and his hands were big with blunt fingers. 'Come in, Dr. Meyrick.' He nodded at McCready. 'All right, George; be about your business.'

McCready closed the door. 'Sit down, Doctor,' said Carey. It was an invitation, not a command. Denison sat in the chair on the other side of the desk and waited for a long time while Carey inspected him with an inscrutable face.

After a long time Carey sighed. 'Dr. Meyrick, you were asked not to stray too far from your hotel and to keep strictly to central Oslo. If you wanted to go farther afield you were asked to let us know so that we could make the necessary arrangements. You see, our manpower isn't infinite.'

His voice rose. 'Maybe you shouldn't have been *asked*; maybe you should have been *told*.' He seemed to hold himself in with an effort, and lowered his voice again. 'So I fly in this morning to hear that you're missing, and then I'm told that you isolated yourself on a mountain top – for what reason only you know.'

He raised his hand to intercept interruption. Denison did not mind; he was not going to say anything, anyway.

'All right,' said Carey. 'I know the story you told the local coppers. It was a good improvisation and maybe they'll buy it and maybe they won't.' He put his hands flat on the desk. 'Now what really happened?'

'I was up there walking through the woods,' said Denison, 'when suddenly a man attacked me.'

'Description?'

'Tall. Broad. Not unlike you in build, but younger. He had black hair. His nose was broken. He had something in his hand – he was going to hit me with it. Some sort of cosh, I suppose.'

'So what did you do?'

'I laid him out,' said Denison.

'*You* laid him out,' said Carey in a flat voice. There was disbelief in his eye.

'I laid him out,' said Denison evenly. He paused. 'I was a useful boxer at one time.'

Carey frowned and drummed his fingers. 'Then what happened?'

'Another man was coming at me from behind, so I ran for it.'

'Wise man – some of the time, anyway. And . . . ?'

'Another man intercepted me from the front.'

'Describe him.'

'Shortish – about five foot seven – with a rat-face and a long nose. Dressed in jeans and a blue jersey. He had a knife.'

'He had a knife, did he?' said Carey. 'So what did you do about that?'

'Well, the other chap was coming up behind fast – I didn't have much time to think – so I charged the joker with the knife and sold him the dummy at the last moment.'

'You *what?*'

'I sold him the dummy. It's a rugby expression meaning . . .'

'I know what it means,' snapped Carey. 'I suppose you were a useful rugby player at one time, too.'

'That's right,' said Denison.

Carey bent his head and put his hand to his brow so that his face was hidden. He seemed to be suppressing some strong emotion. 'What happened next?' he asked in a muffled voice.

'By that time I'd got back to the car park – and there was another man.'

'*Another* man,' said Carey tiredly. 'Description.'

'Not much. I think he wore a grey suit. He had a gun.'

'Escalating on you, weren't they?' said Carey. His voice was savage. 'So what did you do then?'

'I was in the car by the time I saw the gun and I got out of there fast and . . .'

'And did a Steve McQueen through the Spiralen, roared through Drammen like an express train and butted a copper in the arse.'

'Yes,' said Denison simply. 'That about wraps it up.'

'I should think it does,' said Carey. He was silent for a while, then he said, 'Regardless of the improbability of all this, I'd still like to know why you went to Drammen in the first place, and why you took the trouble to shake off any followers before leaving Oslo.'

'Shake off followers,' said Denison blankly. 'I didn't know I was being followed.'

'You know now. It was for your own protection. But my man says he's never seen such an expert job of shaking a tail in his life. You were up to all the tricks. You nearly succeeded twice, and you did succeed the third time.'

'I don't know what you're talking about,' said Denison. 'I lost my way a couple of times, that's all.'

Carey took a deep breath and looked at the ceiling. 'You lost your way,' he breathed. His voice became deep and solemn. 'Dr. Meyrick: can you tell me why you lost your way when you know this area better than your own county of Buckinghamshire? You showed no signs of losing your way when you went to Drammen last week.'

Denison took the plunge. 'Perhaps it's because I'm not Dr. Meyrick.'

Carey whispered, *'What did you say?'*

6

Denison told all of it.

When he had finished Carey's expression was a mixture of perturbation and harassment. He heard everything Denison had to say but made no comment; instead, he lifted the telephone, dialled a number, and said, 'George? Ask Ian to come in here for a minute.'

He came from behind the desk and patted Denison on the shoulder. 'I hope you don't mind waiting for a few minutes.' He strode away to intercept the man who had just come in and they held a whispered colloquy before Carey left the room.

He closed the door on the other side and stood for a moment in thought, then he shook his head irritably and went into McCready's office. McCready looked up, saw Carey's expression, and said, 'What's the matter?'

'Our boy has rolled clean off his tiny little rocker,' snapped Carey. 'That's what's the matter. He started off by telling cock-and-bull stories, but then it got worse – much worse.'

'What did he say?'

Carey told him – in gruesome detail.

Ten minutes later he said, 'Discounting a lot of balls about mysterious attackers, *something* happened up there on top of the Spiralen which knocked Meyrick off his perch.' He rubbed his forehead. 'When they wish these eggheads on us you'd think they'd test them for mental stability. What we need now is an alienist.'

McCready suppressed a smile. 'Isn't that rather an old-fashioned term?'

Carey glared at him. 'Old-fashioned and accurate.' He stabbed his finger at the office wall. 'That . . . that *thing* in there isn't human any more. I tell you, my flesh crawled when I heard what he was saying.'

'There isn't a chance that he's right, is there?' asked McCready diffidently.

'No chance at all. I was facing Meyrick at the original briefing in London for two bloody days until I got to hate the sight of his fat face. It's Meyrick, all right.'

'There is one point that puzzles me,' said McCready. 'When I was with him at the police station in Drammen he didn't speak a word of Norwegian, and yet I understand he knows the language.'

'He speaks it fluently,' said Carey.

'And yet I'm told that his first words were to the effect that he spoke no Norwegian.'

'For God's sake!' said Carey. 'You know the man's history. He was born in Finland and lived there until he was seventeen, when he came to live here in Oslo. When he was twenty-four he moved to England where he's been ever since. That's twenty-two years. He didn't see a rugby ball until he arrived in England, and I've studied his dossier and know for a fact that he never boxed in his life.'

'Then it all fits in with his story that he's not Meyrick.' McCready paused for thought. 'There *was* a witness at Spiraltoppen who said she saw a gun.',

'A hysterical waitress,' sneered Carey. 'Wait a minute – did you tell Meyrick about that?'

'I did mention it.'

'It fits,' said Carey. 'You know, I wouldn't be surprised if the story Meyrick gave to the police wasn't the absolute truth. He was razzled by a few kids out for a joyride in a stolen car and the experience knocked him off his spindle.'

'And the gun?'

'*You* told him about the gun. He seized that and wove it into his fairy tale, and added a few other trimmings such as the knife and the cosh. I think that in the Spiralen he felt so bloody helpless that he's invented this story to retain what he thinks is his superiority. At the briefing I assessed him as an arrogant bastard, utterly convinced of his superiority to us lesser mortals. But he wasn't very superior in the Spiralen, was he?'

'Interesting theory,' said McCready. 'You'd make a good alienist – except for one thing. You lack empathy.'

'I can't stand the man,' said Carey bluntly. 'He's an over-weening, overbearing, supercilious son-of-a-bitch who thinks the sun shines out of his arse. Mr. Know-it-all in person and too bloody toplofty by half.' He shrugged. 'But I can't pick and choose the people I work with. It's not in my contract.'

'What did you say he called himself?'

'Giles Denison from Hampstead. Hampstead, for Christ's sake!'

'I'll be back in a minute,' said McCready. He left the room.

Carey loosened his tie with a jerk and sat biting his thumbnail. He looked up as McCready came back holding a book. 'What have you got there?'

'London telephone directory.'

'Give me that,' said Carey, and grabbed it. 'Let's see – Dennis, Dennis, Dennis . . . Dennison. There's a George and two plain Gs – neither in Hampstead.' He sat back, looking pleased.

McCready took the book and flipped the pages. After a minute he said, 'Denison, Giles . . . Hampstead. He spells it with one "n".'

'Oh, Christ!' said Carey, looking stricken. He recovered. 'Doesn't mean a thing. He picked the name of someone he knows. His daughter's boy-friend, perhaps.'

'Perhaps,' said McCarthy non-committally.

Carey drummed his fingers on the desk. 'I'll stake my life that this is Meyrick; anything else would be too ridiculous.' His fingers were suddenly stilled. 'Mrs. Hansen,' he said. 'She's been closer to him than anybody. Did she have anything to say?'

'She reported last night that she'd met him. He'd broken a date with her in the morning and excused it by pleading illness. Said he'd been in bed all morning.'

'Had he?'

'Yes.'

'Did she notice anything about him – anything odd or unusual?'

'Only that he had a cold and that he'd stopped smoking. He said cigarettes tasted like straw.'

Carey, a pipe-smoker, grunted. 'They taste like straw to me without a cold. But he recognised her.'

'They had a drink and a conversation – about morals and religion, she said.'

'That does it,' said Carey. 'Meyrick is ready to pontificate about anything at the drop of a hat, whether he knows anything about it or not.' He rubbed his chin and said grudgingly, 'Trouble is, he usually talks sense – he has a good brain. No, this is Meyrick, and Meyrick is as flabby as a bladder of lard – that's why we have to coddle him on this operation. Do you really think Meyrick could stand up against four men with guns and knives and coshes? The man could hardly break the skin on the top of a custard. He's gone out of his tiny, scientific mind and his tale of improbable violence is just to save his precious superiority, as I said before.'

'And what about the operation?'

'As far as Meyrick is concerned the operation is definitely off,' said Carey decisively. 'And, right now, I don't see how it can be done without him. I'll cable London to that effect as soon as I've had another talk with him.' He paused. 'You'd better come along, George. I'm going to need a witness on this one or else London will have *me* certified.'

They left the office and walked along the corridor. Outside the room where Meyrick was held Carey put his hand on McCready's arm. 'Hold yourself in, George. This might be rough.'

They found Meyrick still sitting at the desk in brooding silence, ignoring the man he knew only as Ian who sat opposite. Ian looked up at Carey and shrugged eloquently.

Carey stepped forward. 'Dr. Meyrick, I'm sorry to . . .'

'My name is Denison. I told you that.' His voice was cold.

Carey softened his tone. 'All right, Mr. Denison; if you prefer it that way. I really think you ought to see a doctor. I'm arranging for it.'

'And about time,' said Denison. 'This is hurting like hell.'

'What is?'

Denison was pulling his sweater from his trousers. 'This bloody knife wound. Look at it.'

Carey and McCready bent to look at the quarter-inch deep slash along Denison's side. It would, Carey estimated, take sixteen stitches to sew it up.

Their heads came up together and they looked at each other with a wild surmise.

7

Carey paced restlessly up and down McCready's office. His tie was awry and his hair would have been tousled had it not been so close-cropped because he kept running his hand through it. 'I still don't believe it,' he said. 'It's too bloody incredible.'

He swung on McCready. 'George, supposing you went to bed tonight, here in Oslo, and woke up tomorrow, say, in a New York hotel, wearing someone else's face. What would be your reaction?'

'I think I'd go crazy,' said McCready soberly. He smiled slightly. 'If I woke up with your face I would go crazy.'

Carey ignored the wisecrack. 'But Denison didn't go crazy,' he said meditatively. 'All things considered, he kept his cool remarkably well.'

'If he is Denison,' remarked McCready. 'He could be Meyrick and quite insane.'

Carey exploded into a rage. 'For God's sake! All along you've been arguing that he's Denison; now you turn around and say he could be Meyrick.'

McCready eyed him coolly. 'The role of devil's advocate suits me, don't you think?' He tapped the desk. 'Either way, the operation is shot to hell.'

Carey sat down heavily. 'You're right, of course. But if this is a man called Denison then there are a lot of questions to be answered. But first, what the devil do we do with him?'

'We can't keep him here,' said McCready. 'For the same reason we didn't keep Meyrick here. The Embassy is like a fishbowl.'

Carey cocked his head. 'He's been here for over two hours. That's about normal for a citizen being hauled over the coals for a serious driving offence. You suggest we send him back to the hotel?'

'Under surveillance.' McCready smiled. 'He says he has a date with a redhead for dinner.'

'Mrs. Hansen,' said Carey. 'Does he know about her?'

'No.'

'Keep it that way. She's to stick close to him. Give her a briefing and ask her to guard him from interference. He could run into some odd situations. And talk to him like a Dutch uncle. Put the fear of God into him so that he stays in the hotel. I don't want him wandering around loose.'

Carey drew a sheet of paper towards him and scribbled on it. 'The next thing we want are doctors – tame ones who will ask the questions we want asked and no others. A plastic surgeon and –' he smiled at McCready bleakly – 'and an alienist. The problem must be decided one way or the other.'

'We can't wait until they arrive,' said McCready.

'Agreed,' said Carey. 'We'll work on the assumption that a substitution has been made – that this man is Denison. We know when the substitution was made – in the early hours of yesterday morning, Denison was brought in – how?'

'On a stretcher – he must have been unconscious.'

'Right!' said Carey. 'A hospital patient in transit under the supervision of a trained nurse and probably a doctor. And they'd have taken a room on the same floor as Meyrick. The switch was made and Meyrick taken out yesterday morning – probably in an ambulance at the back entrance of the hotel by arrangement with the management. Hotels don't like stretchers being paraded through the front lobby.'

'I'll get on to it,' said McCready. 'It might be an idea to check on all the people who booked in on the previous day, regardless of the floor they stayed on. I don't think this was a two man job.'

'I don't, either. And you check the comings and goings for the past week – somebody must have been watching Meyrick for a long time.'

'That's a hell of a big job,' objected McCready. 'Do we get the co-operation of the Norwegians?'

Carey pondered. 'At this time – no. We keep it under wraps.'

McCready's face took on a sad look at the thought of all the legwork he was going to have to do. Carey tilted his chair back. 'And then there's the other end to be checked – the London end. Why Giles Denison of Hampstead?' His chair came down with a thump. 'Hasn't it struck you that Denison has been very unforthcoming?'

McCready shrugged. 'I haven't talked to him all that much.'

'Well, look,' said Carey. 'Here we have this man in this bloody odd situation in which he finds himself. After recovering from the first shock, he not only manages to deceive Mrs. Hansen as to his real identity but he has the wit to ring Meyrick's home. But why only Meyrick? Why didn't he check back on himself?'

'How do you mean?'

Carey sighed. 'There's a man called Giles Denison missing from Hampstead. Surely he'd be missed by someone? Even if Denison is an unmarried orphan he must have friends – a job. Why didn't he ring back to reassure people that he was all right and still alive and now living it up in Oslo?'

'I hadn't thought of that,' admitted McCready. 'That's a pointer to his being Meyrick, after all. Suffering from delusions but unable to flesh them out properly.'

Carey gave a depressed nod. 'All I've had from him is that he's Giles Denison from Hampstead – nothing more.'

'Why not put it to him now?' suggested McCready.

Carey thought about it and shook his head. 'No, I'll leave that to the psychiatrist. If this is really Meyrick, the wrong sort of questions could push him over the edge entirely.' He pulled the note pad towards him again. 'We'll have someone check on Denison in Hampstead and find out the score.' He ripped off the sheet. 'Let's get cracking. I want those cables sent to London immediately – top priority and coded. I want those quacks here as fast as possible.'

8

Giles Denison stirred his coffee and smiled across the table at Diana Hansen. His smile was steady, which was remarkable because a thought had suddenly struck him like a bolt of lightning and left him with a churning stomach. Was the delectable Diana Hansen who faced him Meyrick's mistress?

The very thought put him into a dilemma. Should he make a pass or not? Whatever he did – or did not – do, he had a fifty per cent chance of being wrong. The uncertainty of it spoiled his evening which had so far been relaxing and pleasant.

He had been driven back to the hotel in an Embassy car after dire warnings from George McCready of what would happen to him if he did not obey instructions. 'You'll have realised by now that you've dropped right into the middle of something awkward,' said McCready. 'We're doing our best to sort it out but, for the next couple of days, you'd do well to stay in the hotel.' He drove it home by asking pointedly, 'How's your side feeling now?'

'Better,' said Denison. 'But I could have done with a doctor.' He had been strapped up by McCready, who had produced a first-aid box and displayed a competence which suggested he was no stranger to knife wounds.

'You'll get a doctor,' assured McCready. 'Tomorrow.'

'I have a dinner date,' said Denison. 'With that redhead I told you about. What should I do about that? If she goes on like she did yesterday I'm sure to put my foot in it.'

'I don't see why you should,' said McCready judiciously.

'For God's sake! I don't even know her name.'

McCready patted him on the shoulder, and said soothingly, 'You'll be all right.'

Denison was plaintive. 'It's all very well you wanting me to go on being Meyrick but surely you can tell me *something*. Who *is* Meyrick, for instance?'

'It will all be explained tomorrow,' said McCready, hoping that he was right. 'In the meantime, go back to the hotel like a good chap, and don't leave it until I call for you. Just have a quiet dinner with . . . with your redhead and then go to bed.'

Denison had a last try. 'Are you in Intelligence or something? A spy?'

But to that McCready made no answer.

So Denison was delivered to the hotel and he had not been in the room more than ten minutes when the telephone rang. He regarded it warily and let it ring several times before he put out his hand as though about to pick up a snake. 'Yes?' he said uncommunicatively.

'Diana here.'

'Who?' he asked cautiously.

'Diana Hansen, who else? We have a dinner date, remember? How are you?'

Again he caught the faint hint of America behind the English voice. 'Better,' he said, thinking it was convenient of her to announce her name.

'That's good,' she said warmly. 'Are you fit enough for dinner?'

'I think so.'

'Mmm,' she murmured doubtfully. 'But I still don't think you should go out; there's quite a cold wind. What about dinner in the hotel restaurant?'

Even more convenient; he had just been about to suggest that himself. In a more confident voice he said, 'That'll be fine.'

'Meet you in the bar at half past seven,' she said.

'All right.'

She rang off and he put down the telephone slowly. He hoped that McCready was right; that he could manage a sustained conversation with this woman in the guise of Meyrick. He sat in the armchair and winced as pain stabbed in his side. He held his breath until the pain eased and then relaxed and looked at his watch. Half past five. He had two hours before meeting the Hansen woman.

What a mess! What a stinking mess! Lost behind another man's face, he had apparently dropped into the middle of an intrigue which involved the British government. That man, Carey, had been damned patronising about what had happened on top of the Spiralen and had not bothered to hide his disbelief. It had been that, more than anything else, that had driven Denison into disclosing who he was. It had certainly taken the smile off Carey's face.

But who was Carey? To begin with, he was obviously McCready's boss – but that did not get him very far because who was McCready? A tight little group in the British Embassy in Oslo dedicated to what? Trade relations? That did not sound likely.

Carey had made it clear that he had warned Meyrick not to move far from the hotel. Judging by what had happened on the Spiralen the warning was justified. But who the hell was Meyrick that he was so important? The man with the title of Doctor or perhaps Professor, and who was described on his passport as a civil servant.

Denison's head began to ache again. *Christ!* he thought; *I'll be bloody glad to get back to Hampstead, back to my job and the people I . . .*

The thought tailed off to a deadly emptiness and he felt his stomach lurch. A despairing wail rose in his mind – *God help me!* he cried silently as he realised his mind was a blank, that he did not know what his job was, that he could not put a name to a single friend or acquaintance, and that all he knew of himself was that he was Giles Denison and that he came from Hampstead.

Bile rose in his throat. He struggled to his feet and staggered to the bathroom where he was violently sick. Again there was that insistent beat in his mind; I AM GILES DENISON. But there was nothing more – no link with a past life.

He left the bathroom and lay on the bed, staring at the ceiling. *You must remember!* he commanded himself. *You must!* But there was nothing – just Giles Denison of Hampstead and a vague mind picture of a house as in a half-forgotten memory.

Think!

The scar on his shin – he remembered that. He saw himself on the small child-size bicycle going down a hill too fast, and the inevitable tumble at the bottom – then the quick tears and the comfort of his mother. I remember that, he told himself in triumph.

What else? Beth – he remembered Beth who had been his wife, but she had died. How many years ago was it? Three years. And then there was the whisky, too much whisky. He remembered the whisky.

Denison lay on the bed and fought to extract memories from a suddenly recalcitrant mind. There was a slick sheen of sweat on his brow and his fists were clenched, the nails digging into his palms.

Something else he had remembered before. He had come back from Edinburgh on June 17, but what had he been doing there? Working, of course; but what was his work? Try as he might he could not penetrate the blank haze which cloaked his mind.

On June 18 he had played golf in the afternoon. With whom? Of course it was possible for a man to play a round of golf alone, and also to go to the cinema alone and to dine in Soho alone, but it was hardly likely that he would forget everything else. Where had he played golf? Which cinema did he go to? Which restaurant in Soho?

A blazing thought struck him, an illumination of the mind so clear that he knew certainly it was the truth. He cried aloud, 'But I've never played golf in my life!'

There was a whirling spiral of darkness in his mind and, mercifully, he slept.

9

Denison walked into the bar at a quarter to eight and saw the woman who called herself Diana Hansen sitting at a table. He walked over and said, 'Sorry I'm late.'

She smiled and said lightly, 'I was beginning to think I was being stood up again.'

He sat down. 'I fell asleep.'

'You look pale. Are you all right?'

'I'm fine.' There was a vague memory at the back of his mind which disturbed him; something had happened just before he had fallen asleep. He was reluctant to probe into it because he caught a hint of terror and madness which frightened him. He shivered.

'Cold?' Her voice was sympathetic.

'Nothing that a stiff drink won't cure.' He beckoned to a passing waiter, and raised his eyebrows at her.

'A dry martini, please.'

He turned to the hovering waiter. 'A dry martini and . . . do you have a scotch malt?' Normally he bought the cheapest blend he could buy in the cut-price supermarkets but with Meyrick's finances behind him he could afford the best.

'Yes, sir. Glenfiddich?'

'That will do fine. Thank you.'

Diana Hansen said, 'Food may be better than drink. Have you eaten today?'

'Not much.' Just the meal in the police station at Drammen, taken for fuel rather than pleasure.

'You men!' she said with scorn. 'No better than children when left on your own. You'll feel better after dinner.'

He leaned back in his chair. 'Let's see – how long have we known each other, Diana?'

She smiled. 'Counting the days, Harry? Nearly three weeks.'

So he had met her in Oslo – or, rather, Meyrick had. 'I was just trying to find out how long it takes a woman to become maternal. Less than three weeks, I see.'

'Is that the scientific mind at work?'

'One aspect of it.' Could that mean anything? Was Dr. Meyrick a scientist – a government boffin?

She looked across the room and a shadow seemed to darken her face momentarily. 'There's Jack Kidder and his wife.'

Denison paused before he turned round. 'Oh! Where?'

'Just coming in.' She put out her hand and covered his. 'Do you want to be bothered by them, darling? He's a bit of a bore, really.'

Denison looked at the tall, fleshy man who was escorting a petite woman. Jack Kidder was the name Diana Hansen had mentioned when he had bumped into her outside the bookshop. If she did not want to mix with the Kidders it was all right with him; he had enough to cope with already. He said, 'You're right. I don't think I could cope with a bore tonight.'

She laughed, 'Thanks for the compliment – hidden though it was. I'll put him off tactfully if he comes across.' She sighed theatrically. 'But if he says that damned slogan of his again I'll scream.'

'What's that?'

'You must have heard it, It's when he pulls off one of his dreadful jokes.' She burlesqued an American accent. ' "You know me – Kidder by name and kidder by nature." '

'Jack was always the life and soul of the party,' said Denison drily.

'I don't know how Lucy puts up with him,' said Diana. 'If you can talk about a hen-pecked husband, can you refer to a cock-pecked wife?'

Denison grinned. 'It sounds rude.' Diana Hansen was making things very easy for him. She had just given him a thumbnail sketch of the Kidders, including names and temperaments. It could not have been better if done deliberately.

The waiter put the drinks on the table and Denison found he had a scotch on the rocks, a desecration of good malt. He did not feel like making a fuss about it so he raised his glass. '*Sköl!*' He sipped the whisky and reflected that this was the first real drink he had had since his transformation into Meyrick.

The familiar taste bit at his tongue and somehow released a wave of memories which washed through him tumultuously, tantalisingly close to the surface of his mind. And with the memories, unrealised though they were, came the fear and the terror which set his heart thumping in his chest. Hastily he set down the glass, knowing he was close to panic.

Diana Hansen looked at his shaking fingers. 'What's the matter, Harry?'

Denison covered up. 'I don't think a drink is a good idea, after all. I've just remembered I'm stuffed full of pills.' He managed a smile. 'If you shook me I'd rattle. I don't think they'd mix with alcohol.'

She put down her glass. 'Then let's have dinner before the Kidders catch up with us.' She stood up and took her handbag from the table. Denison arose and they moved towards the entrance, but then she turned her head and murmured, 'Too late, I'm afraid.'

Kidder was also standing up, his big body blocking the way. 'Hey,

Lucy, look who's here. It's Diana and Harry.'

'Hallo, Jack,' said Denison. 'Had a good day?'

'We've been up to Holmenkollen; you know – the big ski-jump you can see from all over the city. It's quite a thing when you get up to it close. Can you imagine, it's only used once a year?'

'I can't imagine,' said Denison blandly.

Lucy Kidder said, 'And we went to the Henie-Onstad Art Centre, too.'

'Yeah, modern art,' said Kidder disparagingly. 'Harry, can you make any sense out of Jackson Pollock?'

'Not much,' said Denison.

Kidder turned on his wife. 'Anyway, why the hell do we have to come to Norway to see an American artist?'

'But he's internationally famous, Jack. Aren't you proud of that?'

'I guess so,' he said gloomily. 'But the locals aren't much better. Take the guy with the name like a breakfast food.' Everyone looked at Kidder with blank faces and he snapped his fingers impatiently. 'You know who I mean – the local Scowegian we saw yesterday.'

Lucy Kidder sighed. 'Edvard Munch,' she said resignedly.

'That's the guy. Too gloomy for me even if you can see the people in his pictures,' said Kidder.

Diana cut in quickly. 'Harry's not been feeling too well lately. I'm taking him in to an early dinner and sending him right to bed.'

'Gee, I'm sorry to hear that,' said Kidder. He sounded sincere.

'There's a lot of this two-day flu about,' said his wife. 'And it can be nasty while it lasts. You look after yourself – hear?'

'I don't think it's too serious,' said Denison.

'But we'd better go in to dinner,' said Diana. 'Harry hasn't eaten a thing all day.'

'Sure,' said Kidder, standing aside. 'I hope you feel better real soon. You look after him, Diana.'

Over dinner they talked in generalities, much to Denison's relief, and he was able to hold his own without much effort. There was not a single thing to trouble him until the coffee was served and that startling thought about the possible relationship between Diana and Meyrick came into his head. He looked at her speculatively and wondered what to do. For all he knew, Meyrick was an old ram.

He held the smile on his face and stirred his coffee mechanically. A waiter came to the table. 'Mrs. Hansen?'

Diana looked up. 'Yes?'

'A telephone call.'

'Thank you.' She looked at Denison apologetically. 'I told someone I'd be here. Do you mind?'

'Not at all.' She stood up and left the restaurant, going into the lobby. He watched her until she was out of sight and then stopped stirring his coffee and put the spoon in the saucer with a clink. Thoughtfully he looked at the handbag on the other side of the table.

Mrs. Hansen! He could bear to know more about that. He stretched out his hand slowly and picked up the handbag, which was curiously heavy. Holding it on his lap, below the level of the table, he snapped open the catch and bent his head to look inside.

When Diana came back the bag was back in its place. She sat down, picked it up, and took out a packet of cigarettes. 'Still not smoking, Harry?'

He shook his head. 'They still taste foul.'

Soon thereafter he signed the bill and they left, parting in the lobby, he to go to bed and she to go to wherever she lived. He had decided against making a pass at Mrs. Diana Hansen because it was most unlikely that Dr. Harold Felthem Meyrick would be having an affaire with a woman who carried a gun – even if it was only a small gun.

10

The next day was boring. He obeyed instructions and stayed in the hotel waiting to hear from McCready. He breakfasted in his room and ordered English newspapers. Nothing had changed – the news was as bad as ever.

At mid-morning he left the room to allow the maid to clean up, and went down to the lobby where he saw the Kidders at the porter's desk. He hung back, taking an inordinate interest in a showcase full of Norwegian silver, while Kidder discussed in a loud voice the possibilities of different bus tours. Finally they left the hotel and he came out of cover.

He discovered that the bookshop on the corner of the street had a convenient entrance inside the hotel, so he bought a stack of English paperbacks and took them to his room. He read for the rest of the day, gutting the books, his mind in low gear. He had a curious reluctance to think about his present predicament and, once, when he put a book aside and tried to think coherently, his mind skittered about and he felt the unreasoning panic come over him. When he picked up the book again his head was aching.

At ten that night no contact had been made and he thought of ringing the Embassy and asking for McCready but the strange disinclination to thought had spread to action and he was irresolute. He looked at the telephone for a while, and then slowly undressed and went to bed.

He was almost asleep when there was a tap at his door. He sat up and listened and it came again, a discreet double knock. He switched on the light and put on Meyrick's bath robe, then went to the door. It was McCready, who came in quickly and closed the door behind him. 'Ready for the doctor?' he asked.

Denison frowned. 'At this time of night?'

'Why not?' asked McCready lightly.

Denison sighed. It was just one more mystery to add to the others. He reached for his underwear and took off the bath robe. McCready picked up the pyjamas which were lying neatly folded on top of the suitcase. 'You don't wear these?'

'Meyrick did.' Denison sat on the edge of the bed to put on his socks. 'I don't.'

'Oh!' McCready thoughtfully tugged at his ear.

When Denison picked up his jacket he turned to McCready. 'There's something you ought to know, I suppose. Diana Hansen carries . . .'

'Who?' asked McCready.

'The redhead I took to dinner – her name is Diana Hansen. She carries a gun.'

McCready went still. 'She does? How do you know?'

'I looked in her handbag.'

'Enterprising of you. I'll tell Carey – he'll be interested.' McCready took Denison by the arm. 'Let's go.'

McCready's car was in the garage and when he drove out into the street he turned left which Denison knew was away from the Embasssy. 'Where are we going?'

'Not far,' said McCready. 'Five minutes. Possess your soul in patience.'

Within two minutes Denison was lost. The car twisted and turned in the strange streets until his sense of direction deserted him. Whether McCready was deliberately confusing him he did not know, but he thought it likely. Another possibility was that McCready was intent on shaking off any possible followers.

After a few minutes the car pulled up outside a large building which could have been a block of flats. They went inside and into a lift which took them to the fifth floor. McCready unlocked a door and motioned Denison inside. He found himself in a hall with doors on each side. McCready opened one of them, and said, 'This is Mr. Iredale. He'll fix up your side for you.'

Iredale was a sallow, middle-age man, balding and with deep grooves cut from the base of his nose to the corners of his mouth. He said pleasantly, 'Come in, Mr. Denison; let me have a look at you.'

Denison heard the door close behind him and turned to find that McCready had already gone. He whirled around to confront Iredale. 'I thought I was being taken to a doctor.'

'I am a doctor,' said Iredale. 'I'm also a surgeon. We surgeons have a strange inverted snobbery – we're called "mister" and not "doctor". I've never known why. Take off your coat, Mr. Denison, and let me see the damage.'

Denison hesitated and slowly took off his jacket and then his shirt. 'If you'll lie on the couch?' suggested Iredale, and opened a black bag which could only have been the property of a doctor. Somewhat reassured, Denison lay down.

Iredale snipped away the bandages with a small pair of scissors and examined the slash. 'Nasty,' he said. 'But clean. It will need a local anaesthetic. Are you allergic to anaesthetic, Mr. Denison?'

'I don't know – I don't think so.'

'You'll just feel three small pricks – no more.' Iredale took out a hypodermic syringe and filled it from a phial. 'Lie still.'

Denison felt the pricks, and Iredale said, 'While we're waiting for that to take effect you can sit up.' He took an ophthalmoscope from his bag. 'I'd just like to look at your eyes.' He flashed a light into Denison's right eye. 'Had any alcohol lately?'

'No.'

Iredale switched to the left eye upon which he spent more time. 'That seems to be all right,' he said.

'I was stabbed in the side, not hit on the head,' said Denison. 'I don't have concussion.'

Iredale put away the ophthalmoscope. 'So you have a little medical knowledge.' He put his hands to Denison face and palpated the flesh under the chin. 'You know what they say about a little knowledge.' He stood up and looked down at the top of Denison's head, and then his fingers explored the hairline. 'Don't knock the experts, Mr. Denison – they know what they're doing.'

'What sort of a doctor are you?' asked Denison suspiciously.

Iredale ignored that. 'Ever had scalp trouble? Dandruff, for instance?'

'No.'

'I see. Right.' He touched Denison's side. 'Feel anything?'

'It's numb but I can feel pressure.'

'Good,' said Iredale. 'I'm going to stitch the wound closed. You won't feel anything – but if you do then shout like hell.' He put on rubber gloves which he took out of a sealed plastic bag and then took some fine thread out of another small packet. 'I'd turn your head away,' he advised.

'Lie down.'

He worked on Denison's side for about fifteen minutes and Denison felt nothing but the pressure of his fingers. At last he said, 'All right, Mr. Denison; I've finished.'

Denison sat up and looked at his side. The wound was neatly closed and held by a row of minute stitches. 'I've always been good at needlework,' said Iredale conversationally. 'When the stitches are out there'll be but a hairline. In a year you won't be able to see it.'

Denison said, 'This isn't a doctor's surgery. Who are you?'

Iredale packed his bag rapidly and stood up. 'There'll be another doctor to see you in a moment.' He walked to the door and closed it behind him.

There was something about the way the door closed that vaguely alarmed Denison. He stood up and walked to the door and found it locked. Frowning, he turned away and looked about the room. There was the settee on which he had been lying, a table, two armchairs and a bookcase against the wall. He went over to the bookcase to inspect it and tripped over a wire which threatened to topple a telephone from a small table. He rescued the telephone and then stood looking down at it.

Iredale walked along the corridor and into a room at the end. Carey glanced up at him expectantly, breaking off his conversation with McCready. Harding, the psychiatrist, sat in an armchair, his long legs outstretched and his fingertips pressed together. There was also another man whom Iredale did not know. Carey saw Iredale looking at him, and said, 'Ian Armstrong of my staff. Well?' He could not suppress his eagerness.

Iredale put down his case. 'He's not Meyrick.' He paused. 'Not unless Meyrick has had plastic surgery recently.'

Carey blew out his breath in a long gasp. 'Are you sure?'

'Of course I'm sure,' said Iredale, a little testily.

'That's it, then.' Carey looked across at Harding. 'It's your turn, Dr. Harding. Try to get out of him as much as you can.'

Harding nodded and uncoiled himself from the chair. He walked out of the room without speaking. As the door closed Carey said, 'You understand that, to the best of our knowledge, this alteration was made in the space of a week – not more.' He took a thin, cardboard file from the table. 'We've just received a lengthy cable from London about Denison – and a photo came over the wire.' He took the photograph and handed it to Iredale. 'That's Denison as he was quite recently. It hardly seems possible.'

Iredale studied the photograph. 'Very interesting,' he commented.

'Could this thing be done in a week?' Carey persisted.

Iredale put down the photograph. 'As far as I could ascertain there was only one lesion,' he said precisely. 'That was at the outside corner of the left eyelid. A very small cut which was possibly held together by one stitch while it healed. It would certainly heal in a week although there might have been a residual soreness. I detected a minute inflammation.'

McCready said in disbelief, 'You mean that was the only cut that was made?'

'Yes,' said Iredale. 'The purpose was to draw down the left eyelid. Have you got that photograph of Meyrick?'

'Here,' said Carey.

Iredale put down his forefinger. 'There – you see? The eyelid was drawn down due to the skin contraction caused by this scar.' He paused and said sniffily, 'A bit of a butcher's job, if you ask me. That should never have happened.'

'It was a war wound when Meyrick was a boy,' said Carey. He tapped the photograph of Meyrick. 'But how the devil did they reproduce this scar on Denison without cutting?'

'That was very cleverly done,' said Iredale with sudden enthusiasm. 'As expert a job of tattooing as I've ever seen, as also was the birthmark on the right jaw.' He leaned back in his chair. 'In my field, of course, I come across a lot of tattooing but I specialise in removal rather than application.' He leaned forward again and traced a line on the photograph. 'The hairline was adjusted by depilation; nothing as crude as mere shaving and leaving the hair to grow out. I'm afraid Mr. Denison has lost his hair permanently.'

'That's all very well,' said McCready, coming forward. He leaned over the table, comparing the two photographs. 'But just look at these two men. Denison is thin in the face, and he'd look thinner without the beard. Meyrick is fat-jowled. And look at the differences in the noses.'

'That was done by liquid silicone injection,' said Iredale. 'Some of my more light-minded colleagues aid film stars in their mammary development by the same means.' His tone was distasteful. 'I palpated his cheeks and felt it. It was quite unmistakable.'

'I'll be damned!' said Carey.

'You say that Denison lost a week of objective time?' asked Iredale.

'He said he'd lost a week out of his life – if that's what you mean.'

'Then I can hazard a guess as to how it was done,' said Iredale. 'He was drugged, of course, and kept unconscious for the whole week. I noticed a dressing on his left arm. I didn't investigate it, but that was where the intravenous drip feed was inserted to keep him alive.'

He paused, and Carey said in a fascinated voice, 'Go on!'

'The cut would be made at the corner of the eye, giving it a full week to heal. Any competent surgeon could do that in five minutes. Then I suppose they'd do the tattooing. Normally there'd be a residual soreness from that, but it would certainly clear up in a week. Everthing else could be done at leisure.'

He picked up the two photographs. 'You see, the underlying bone structure of these two men, as far as the heads go, is remarkably similar. I rather think that if you had a photograph of Meyrick taken fifteen to twenty years ago he would look not unlike Denison or, rather, as Denison used to look. I take it that Meyrick has been used to expensive living?'

'He's rich enough,' said Carey.

'It shows on his face,' said Iredale, and tossed down the photographs. 'Denison, however, looks a shade undernourished.'

'Interesting you should say that,' said Carey, opening the folder. 'From what we have here it seems that Denison, if not an alcoholic, was on the verge. He'd just lost his job – fired for incompetence on June 24.'

Iredale nodded. 'Symptomatic. Alcoholics reject food – they get their calories from the booze.' He stood up. 'That's all I can do tonight, gentlemen. I should like to see Denison tomorrow with a view to restoring him to his former appearance, which won't be easy – that silicone polymer will be the devil to get out. Is there any more?'

'Nothing, Mr. Iredale,' said Carey.

'Then if you'll excuse me, I'll go to bed. It's been a long day.'

'You know where your room is,' said Carey, and Iredale nodded and left the room.

Carey and McCready looked at each other in silence for some time, and then Carey stirred and said over his shoulder, 'What did you make of all that, Ian?'

'I'm damned if I know,' said Armstrong.

Carey grunted. 'I'm damned, too. I've been involved in some bizarre episodes in this game, but this takes the prize for looniness. Now we'll have to see what Harding comes up with, and I suspect he's going to be a long time. I think somebody had better make coffee. It's going to be a long night.'

Carey was right because more than two hours elapsed before Harding returned. His face was troubled, and he said abruptly, 'I don't think Denison should be left alone.'

'Ian!' said Carey.

Armstrong got up, and Harding said, 'If he wants to talk let him. Join in but steer clear of specifics. Stick to generalities. Understand?'

Armstrong nodded and went out. Harding sat down and Carey studied him. Finally Carey said, 'You look as though you could do with a drink, Doctor. Whisky?'

Harding nodded. 'Thanks.' He rubbed his forehead. 'Denison is in a bad way.'

Carey poured two ounces of whisky into a glass. 'How?'

'He's been tampered with,' said Harding flatly.

Carey handed him the glass. 'His mind?'

Harding sank half the whisky and choked a little. He held out the glass. 'I'll have water in the other half. Yes. Someone has been bloody ruthless about it. He has a week missing, and whatever was done to him was done in that week.'

Carey frowned. 'Iredale suggested he'd been unconscious all that week.'

'It's not incompatible,' said Harding. 'He was probably kept in a mentally depressed state by drugs during the whole week.'

'Are you talking about brain-washing?' asked McCready sceptically.

'In a manner of speaking.' Harding accepted his refilled glass. 'Whoever did this to Denison has a problem. The ideal would have been to get Denison into such a condition that he thought he *was* Meyrick – but that couldn't be done.' Harding paused for consideration. 'At least, not in a week.'

'You mean the possibility of such a thing is there?' asked Carey incredulously.

'Oh, yes,' said Harding calmly. 'It could be done. But this crowd didn't have the time for that, so they had to go about it another way. As I see it, their problem was to put Denison in the hotel as Meyrick and to make sure he didn't fly off the handle. They didn't want him to take the next plane to London, for instance. So they *treated* him.' From Harding's mouth the emphasis was an obscenity.

'How?' said Carey.

'Do you know anything about hypnosis?'

McCready snorted and Harding, staring at him with suddenly flinty eyes, said coldly, 'No, it is *not* witchcraft, Mr. McCready. Denison was kept in a drug-induced hypnogogic state for a long time, and in that period his psyche was deliberately broken down.' He made a suddenly disarming gesture. 'I suspect Denison was already neurotically inclined and no doubt there were many ready-made tools to hand – irrational fears, half-healed traumas and so on – to aid in the process.'

'What do you mean by neurotically inclined?' asked Carey.

'It's hard to say, but I suspect that he was already a disturbed man before this was done to him.'

'Off his head?' interjected McCready.

Harding gave him a look of dislike. 'No more than yourself, Mr. McCready,' he said tartly. 'But I think something had happened which threw him off balance.'

'Something did happen,' said Carey. 'He lost his job.' He took a thin sheaf of papers from the file. 'I didn't have time to discuss this with you before, but this is what we have on Denison. There'll be more coming but this is what we've got now.'

Harding studied the typed sheets, reading slowly and carefully. He said, 'I wish I'd seen this before I went in to Denison; it would have saved a lot of trouble.'

'He was a film director for a small specialist outfit making documentary and advertising films,' said Carey. 'Apparently he went off the rails and cost the firm a packet of money. They thought his drinking had got out of hand, so they fired him.'

Harding shook his head. 'That wasn't what threw him off balance. The drinking must have been a symptom, not a cause.' He turned back a page. 'I see that his wife died three years ago. She must have been quite young. Have you any idea how she died?'

'Not yet,' said Carey. 'But I can find out.'

'It would be advisable. I wonder if it was about that time he started to drink heavily.'

'That isn't the present point at issue,' said Carey.

Harding's voice took on an edge. 'It is for me,' he said curtly. 'I have to treat the man.'

Carey's voice was soothing. 'I know, Doctor; and you shall have all the relevant information as soon as we get it ourselves. But my present interest is in what was done to Denison and how it was done.'

Harding was placated. 'Very well. Denison was literally dismantled. All he retained was a name and a location – and the location wasn't very exact. Giles Denison of Hampstead. They could, of course, have induced complete amnesia, but that wouldn't do because Denison had to substitute for Meyrick and he would need enough active personality to carry out the role. Why Denison had to act as Meyrick I don't know.'

'I have ideas on that,' said Carey. 'Go on, Doctor.'

'At the same time Denison must not retain too much personality, certainly not enough for him to reject the persona that had been thrust upon him. He had to be kept in a sort of limbo. There were some very strong blocks inserted into his mind to the effect that he should not question his origins. In addition, to confuse the issue, he has been given selective false memories. For instance, he distinctly remembers playing a game of golf, but at the same time he knows that he has never played a game of golf in his life. So he is a very confused man and this leads to a paralysis of the will, enough to make him stay in one place – a hotel in Oslo – while he tries to sort things out.'

McCready stirred restlessly. 'Is all this possible?'

'Quite possible. If I draw an imaginary square on the floor of this room I could hypnotise you into avoiding it by a post-hypnotic suggestion. You could spend the rest of your life coming in and out of this room but you would never walk on that imaginary square. More to the point, you would not be aware of the irrationality of your behaviour.'

McCready looked sceptical, and Harding said, 'I'm willing to give you a demonstration at any time.'

'No!' said McCready hurriedly. 'I believe you.'

Carey smiled grimly. 'Carry on, Doctor.'

'The mind is a self-stabilising organism,' said Harding. 'If it wasn't we'd all go crazy. And to inquire is basic. When Denison did try to delve into his past life he encountered the blocks and was so shocked at the impossibility of what he found in his own mind that he took refuge in a fugue.' He saw the incomprehension on Carey's face, and said simply, 'He fell asleep. A typical hysterical symptom. He did it twice when he was talking to me. I let him sleep for a quarter of an hour each time, and when he woke up he'd forgotten the reason for it – wiped it out of his mind. It's a self-protective mechanism against insanity, and I rather think it's happened to him before.'

'I don't think I've got this straight,' said Carey. 'You're saying that Denison is half out of his mind and likely to fall asleep – or unconscious – at any time. How do you square that with the fact that he pulled the wool over one of my people's eyes very successfully, and that he encountered a very tricky situation which might have been the death of him and coped with it very well?'

'Oh, he's quite competent,' said Harding. 'It's only when he tries to question his own past that he faces the impossible and goes into a fugue. Judging by what you told me of the manner in which he was wounded I'd say that he's more competent than I would have expected under the circumstances.'

'He's bloody competent,' said McCready suddenly, and Carey turned to look at him. 'I haven't told you this, but he's tagged Mrs. Hansen.'

'He's *what*?'

'He knows she carries a gun – he told me so. He said he thought I ought to know.'

Harding wore an I-told-you-so expression and Carey's face was a study in bafflement. 'Another thing,' said McCready. 'Alcoholic or not, he's on the wagon now. Mrs. Hansen said he tried a whisky last night and he gave the impression that he'd swallowed prussic acid.'

'Interesting,' said Harding. 'The man's mind has been stirred like porridge. It would be remarkable if it has cured his alcoholism. However, I'm afraid the cure is much worse than the complaint. He'll have to be hospitalised, of course. I can make the arrangements for that.'

Carey stood up. 'Thank you, Dr. Harding.'

Harding also arose. 'I'd like to see him again tomorrow. What's going to happen to him now?'

'I'll take good care of him,' said Carey smoothly.

'You'd better,' warned Harding. 'If he doesn't get skilled attention he's quite likely to go insane.' He yawned. 'Well, I'm off to bed.'

He left the room and Carey sat down again. He picked up the two photographs and brooded over them. McCready said, 'That's it, then; the whole thing's a bust. No Meyrick – no operation.'

Carey did not say anything, and McCready asked, 'What are you thinking?'

Carey said slowly, 'I'm thinking that, while we may not have Meyrick, we've got a bloody good substitute.'

McCready's jaw dropped. 'You mean you want to hang on to him? You heard what Harding just said – the man's likely to go crazy. It's not what I'd call ethical.'

'Don't talk to me about ethics,' said Carey harshly. 'I have a job to do.' He threw down the photographs. 'Iredale wants to give Denison his face back, and Harding wants to restore his past. If we let Harding at him tomorrow with his tricky bloody hypnotism then Denison is going to pick up his marbles and go home.'

He frowned and came to a decision. 'Take him back to the hotel,' he said abruptly.

'For Christ's sake!' said McCready. 'Do you know what you're doing?'

'I know,' said Carey. 'But just work this one out while you're taking Denison back. When the attempt was being made on Denison's life at the Spiralen who was being attacked – Denison or Meyrick?'

McCready opened his mouth slowly while his mind spun. Carey said, 'Denison must be watched. The guard on his room stays and I want somebody outside keeping an eye on his window. And I want that whole bloody hotel sewn up tight. Now get cracking.'

McCready dropped Denison off in the garage of the hotel. 'I won't come up,' he said. 'But I'll see you tomorrow.' He looked at his watch. 'Which is today. God, it's nearly five o'clock in the morning. You get to bed.'

They had both been silent during the short drive. Now Denison said, 'What was all that about? I understood the first doctor, but the second was a psychiatrist, wasn't he?'

McCready said, 'Carey will be seeing you tomorrow. He'll explain everything.' He paused, biting his lip. 'I promise you.'

'All right,' said Denison. 'I'm too tired to argue now. But Carey had better come up with something good.' He nodded to McCready and walked towards the stairs. He did not look back, but if he had and if he had been able to interpret the look in McCready's eyes he might have recognised compassion.

Denison opened the door leading into the hotel lobby and saw suitcases stacked into a pile. There was a peal of laughter from the group of early arrivals, a crowd of young people who adorned the lobby like butterflies. He walked towards the porter's desk and stood waiting while the overworked night porter did his best to deal with the rush.

At last, Denison caught his eye, and said, 'Three-sixty, please.'

'Yes, Mr. Meyrick.' The porter unhooked the key.

Denison did not see the girl who stared at him in surprise, but heard the cool voice behind him saying, 'Daddy!' He turned leisurely and was suddenly and horrifying aware that the young woman was addressing him.

11

It was greatly to Denison's credit that he did not panic. His first impulse was to step back and deny he was Meyrick – that it was a question of mistaken identity. Hard on that decision came the realisation that it would not do; the night porter knew his name and was within earshot, and, in any case, a disclaimer in the hotel lobby was sure to create a fuss. He cancelled the impulse.

She was kissing him and felt his own lips hard and unresponsive. Perhaps it was his lack of reaction that caused her to step back, the smile fading from her face. She said, 'I was hoping to find you here, but I hardly expected to run into you in the same hotel – and at five in the morning. What are you doing up so early – or so late?'

She was young – not much more than twenty – and had the clear eyes and clear skin of youth. Her eyes were grey and her mouth wide and generous, perhaps too wide for perfect beauty. To the untutored male eye she wore no make-up but perhaps that was a tribute to skill.

He swallowed. 'I was visiting a friend; the talk tended to go on a bit.'

'Oh.' She thrust her hands deep into the pockets of her motoring coat and turned her head to look at the harassed porter. 'It's going to take hours before I get my room. Can I freshen up in yours? I must look a sight.'

His mouth was dry and, for a moment, he could not speak. She looked at him curiously. 'You *are* staying here?' Then she laughed. 'Of course you are; you have the key in your hand.'

'I just have to make a telephone call,' he said, and stepped away slightly, disengaging himself.

'Why not from the room?'

'It's just as easy from down here.' He walked away to the public telephones, fumbling in his pockets for coins.

The public telephones were not in booths but were surrounded by large transparent plastic hoods which theoretically would keep conversations private. He was aware that the girl had followed him and was standing close by. He took out his wallet, extracted a slip of paper, and dialled the number. The ringing sound buzzed in his ear six times, and then a voice said, 'Yes?'

He kept his voice low. 'I want Carey.'

'You'll have to speak up. I can't hear you.'

He raised his voice a little. 'I want to talk to Carey.'

Doubtfully: 'I don't think that's possible. He's in bed.'

'I don't care if he's in his coffin. Get him up. This is Denison.'

There was a sharp intake of breath. 'Right!'

In a remarkably short time Carey came on the line. 'Denison?'

'It's trouble. Meyrick's . . .'

Carey cut in with a voice like gravel. 'How did you know to ring this number?'

'For God's sake! That can wait.'

'How did you know?' insisted Carey.

'There was a telephone in the room where I saw the doctors,' said Denison. 'I took the number off that.'

'Oh!' said Carey. Then with grudging respect, 'Harding said you were competent; now I believe him. All right; what's your problem?'

'Meyrick's daughter has just pitched up at the hotel.'

The telephone blasted in his ear. '*What!*'

'What the hell am I to do?' said Denison desperately. 'I don't even know her bloody name.'

'Jesus H. Christ!' said Carey. 'Wait a minute.' There was a confused murmur and then Carey said, 'Her name is Lyn – L-Y-N.'

'Do you know anything else about her?'

'How the devil would I?' demanded Carey. 'Not off the top of my head.'

'Damn you!' said Denison violently. 'I have to talk to this girl. I must know something about her. She's my *daughter*.'

'Is she there now?'

Denison looked sideways through the plastic hood. 'She's standing within ten feet of me. I'm in the hotel lobby and I don't know how soundproof this canopy is. She wants to come to my room.'

'I'll do what I can,' said Carey. 'Hold on.'

'Make it quick.' Out of the corner of his eye he saw the girl walking towards him. He put his head around the edge of the hood, and said, 'I won't be a minute, Lyn. Is there anything you want to take up to the room?'

'Oh, yes; my little travelling bag. I'll go and get it.'

He watched her walk across the lobby with a bouncing stride, and felt the sweat break out on his forehead. Carey came back on the line. 'Margaret Lyn Meyrick – but she prefers Lyn; Meyrick's daughter by his first wife.'

Denison digested that, and said quickly, 'Is her mother still alive?'

'Yes – divorced and remarried.'

'Name?'

'Patricia Joan Metford – her husband is John Howard Metford; he's something in the City.'

'What about Meyrick's present wife?'

'There isn't one. Also divorced three years ago. Her name was Janet Meyrick, née Austin.'

'About the girl – what does she do? Her work? Her hobbies?'

'I don't know,' said Carey. 'All this stuff is from Meyrick's dossier. We didn't delve into the daughter.'

'You'd better get something fast,' said Denison. 'Look, Carey; I don't know why I'm doing this for you. My impulse right now is to blow the whole thing.'

'Don't do that,' said Carey quickly. 'I'll get as much information on the Meyrick girl as I can and I'll let you have it as soon as possible.'

'How?'

'I'll send it in a sealed envelope by special messenger; she doesn't have to know what's on the sheet of paper you're reading. And if things get too tough I'll find a way of separating her from you. But, Denison – don't blow your cover, whatever you do.'

There was a pleading quality in Carey's voice and Carey, in Denison's brief experience of him, was not a man who was used to pleading. Denison thought it was a good opportunity to turn the screw. 'I've been given the fast run around by you ever since this . . . this indecent thing was done to me. Now I want an explanation – a full explanation – and it had better be good.' He was aware that his voice had risen and that he was in danger of becoming hysterical.

'You'll get your explanation today,' promised Carey. 'Now do your best to handle that girl.'

'I don't know if I can. It's one thing fooling a stranger and another to try it on a member of Meyrick's family.'

'We may be lucky,' said Carey. 'I don't think they were too close. I think she was brought up by her mother.'

Denison turned to face the lobby. 'I'll have to go now – the girl's coming.' He put down the telephone and heard a faint squawking noise just before the connection was broken. It sounded as though Carey had said, 'Good luck!'

He walked away from the telephone as she approached. 'All finished.'

She fell into step with him. 'You looked as if you were having an argument.'

'Did I?'

'I know you're an argumentative type, but I wondered who you'd found to argue with at five o'clock in the morning in the middle of Oslo.'

They stopped in front of the lifts and Denison pressed the button. 'Where have you just come from?'

'Bergen. I hired a car and drove over. Most of yesterday and all night.' She sighed. 'I feel a bit pooped.'

He kept his voice neutral. 'Travelling alone?'

'Yes.' She smiled, and said, 'Wondering about a boyfriend?'

He nodded towards the thinning group in the lobby. 'I just thought you were with that lot.' The lift arrived and they stepped inside. 'No wonder you're tired if you did all that driving. What it is to be young.'

'Right now I feel as old as Methuselah,' she said glumly. 'It's the hunger that does it. I'll feel better after breakfast, I dare say.'

He risked a probe. 'How old are you, Lyn? I tend to lose track.'

'Yes, you do, don't you? You even forgot my twenty-first – or did you forget?' There was an unexpected bitterness in her voice. 'Any father who could do that . . .' She stopped and bit her lip. 'I'm sorry, Daddy. It's my birthday next week.'

'That's all right.' There was an undercurrent of antagonism Denison did not understand. He hesitated, and said, 'Anyway, you're old enough to stop calling me Daddy. What's wrong with Harry?'

She looked at him in surprise and then impulsively squeezed his hand.

They had arrived at the room door and he unlocked it. 'Bedroom straight ahead – bathroom to the left.'

She walked ahead of him into the bedroom and put down the travelling bag. 'The bathroom for me,' she said. 'I want to wash off some of the grime.' She opened the bag, picked out a couple of small articles, and disappeared into the bathroom.

He heard the sound of water as she turned on a tap and then he picked up the telephone. 'This is room three-sixty. If there are any messages for Meyrick – or anything at all – I want to know immediately.' He put down the telephone and looked contemplatively at the travelling bag.

The bathroom noises continued so he crossed the room quickly and looked into the bag. It was more neatly packed than he had expected which made it easier to search. He saw the blue cover of a British passport and took it out and turned the pages. It was Lyn Meyrick's birthday on July 21, and she would be twenty-two. Her occupation was given as teacher.

He put the passport back and took out a book of traveller's cheques. As he flicked through them he whistled softly; the Meyrick family did not believe in stinting themselves. There was a wallet fitted with acetate envelopes which contained credit cards and photographs. He had no time to examine these in detail because he thought she might come out of the bathroom at any moment.

He thrust back the wallet and zipped open a small interior pocket in the bag. It contained the key for a rented car and a bunch of smaller keys. As he zipped it closed he heard all sound cease in the bathroom and, when she emerged, he was standing by the armchair taking off his jacket.

'That's much better,' she said. She had taken off the motoring coat and, in lime green sweater and stretch pants, she looked very trim. 'When is the earliest I can order breakfast?'

He checked his watch. 'Not much before half past six, I think. Perhaps the night porter can rustle up sandwiches and coffee.'

She frowned and sat on the bed. 'No, I'll wait and have a proper breakfast.' Blinking her eyes, she said, 'I still feel as though I'm driving.'

'You shouldn't push so hard.'

'That isn't what you told me the last time we met.'

Denison did not know what to make of that, so he said neutrally, 'No.' The silence lengthened. 'How's your mother?' he asked.

'She's all right,' said Lyn indifferently. 'But, my God, he's such a bore.'

'In what way?'

'Well, he just sits in an office and makes money. Oh, I know you're rich, but you made money by making *things*. He just makes money.'

Denison presumed that 'he' was John Howard Metford who was 'something in the City'. 'Metford isn't such a bad chap,' he said.

'He's a bore,' she said definitely. 'And it isn't what you said about him last time.'

Denison decided against making gratuitous judgements. 'How did you know I was here?' he asked.

'I got it out of Andrews,' she said. 'When he told me you were in Scandinavia I knew you'd be here or in Helsinki.' She seemed suddenly nervous. 'Now I'm not sure I should have come.'

Denison realised he was standing over her. He sat in the armchair and, perhaps in response, she stretched out on the bed. 'Why not?' he asked.

'You can't be serious when you ask that.' Her voice was bitter. 'I still remember the flaming row we had two years ago – and when you didn't remember my twenty-first birthday I knew *you* hadn't forgotten. But, of course, you didn't forget my birthday – you never forget anything.'

He was getting into deep water. 'Two years is a long time,' he said platitudinously. He would have to learn how to speak like a politician – saying a lot and meaning nothing.

'You've changed,' she said. 'You're . . . you're milder.'

That would never do. 'I can still be acid when I want to be.' He smiled. 'Perhaps I'm just becoming older and, maybe, wiser.'

'You always were wise,' said Lyn. 'If only you weren't so bloody right *all* the time. Anyway, I wanted to tell you something to your face. I was disappointed when I found you weren't in England, so I rushed over here.' She hesitated. 'Give me a cigarette.'

'I've stopped smoking.'

She stared at him. 'You *have* changed.'

'Temporarily,' he said, and stretched out his hand to open a drawer in the dressing-table. He took out the gold cigarette case and the lighter and offered her a cigarette. 'I've had a bad head cold.'

She took a cigarette and he lit it. 'That never stopped you before.' She drew on the cigarette nervously and blew a plume of smoke. 'I suppose you're surprised I'm not smoking a joint.'

Denison suspected that he was encountering something of which hitherto he had only heard – the generation gap. He said, 'Stop talking nonsense, Lyn. What's on your mind?'

'Direct and to the point as usual. All right – I've taken my degree.'

She looked at him expectantly and he was aware that she had dropped a bombshell. How he was supposed to react to it he did not know, but the damned thing had better be defused carefully. However, taking a degree was usually a matter for congratulation, so he said, 'That's good news, Lyn.'

She regarded him warily. 'You mean it?'

'It's the best news I've heard for a long time.'

She seemed relieved. 'Mother thought it was silly. She said that with all the money I'm going to have why should I worry about working – especially with a lot of snotty-nosed East End kids. You know what she's like. And the Bore didn't care one way or another.' For a moment she sounded pathetic. 'Do you really mean it?'

'Of course I do.' He found he was really glad for her and that put sincerity into his voice.

'Oh, Daddy; I'm so glad!' She scrambled off the bed and went to her bag. 'Look what it says in here. I had to get a new passport, anyway.' She opened the passport and displayed it. 'Occupation – teacher!' she said proudly.

He looked up. 'Was it a good degree?'

She made a wry face. 'Middling-good.' There was no smile on her face now. 'I suppose you think a Meyrick should have passed with honours.'

Mentally he damned Meyrick who, apparently, set a superhuman standard. This girl was set on a hair trigger and his slightest word could cause an explosion in which somebody would get hurt – probably Lyn. 'I'm very glad you've got your degree,' he said evenly. 'Where are you going to teach?'

The tension eased from her and she lay on the bed again. 'First I need experience,' she said seriously. 'General experience. Then I want to specialise. After that, if I'm going to have a lot of money I might as well put it to use.'

'How?'

'I'll have to know more about what I'm doing before I can tell you that.'

Denison wondered how this youthful idealism would stand up to the battering of the world. Still, a lot could be done with enthusiasm and money. He smiled, and said, 'You seem to have settled on a lifetime plan. Is there room in the programme for marriage and a family?'

'Of course; but he'll have to be the right man – he'll have to want what I want.' She shrugged. 'So far no one like that has come my way. The men at university could be divided into two classes; the stodges who are happy with the present system, and the idealists who aren't. The stodges are already working out their retirement pensions before they get a job, and the idealists are so damned naive and impractical. Neither of them suit me.'

'Someone will come along who will,' predicted Denison.

'How can you be sure?'

He laughed. 'How do you suppose the population explosion came about? Men and women usually get together somehow. It's in the nature of the animal.'

She put out her cigarette and lay back and closed her eyes. 'I'm prepared to wait.'

'My guess is that you won't have to wait long.' She did not respond and he regarded her intently. She had fallen asleep as readily as a puppy might, which was not surprising considering she had been up all night. So had he, but sleep was the last thing he could afford.

He put on his jacket and took the keys from the zippered compartment of her bag. In the lobby he saw two suitcases standing before the desk and, after checking to make sure they were Lyn's, he said to the porter, 'I'd like these taken to my daughter's room. What's the number?'

'Did she have a reservation, Mr. Meyrick?'

'It's possible.'

The porter checked and took down a key. 'Room four-thirty. I'll take the bags up.'

In Lyn's room Denison tipped the porter and put the two cases on the bed as soon as the door closed. He took out the keys and unlocked them and searched them quickly, trying not to disturb the contents too much. There was little that was of value to him directly, but there were one or two items which cast a light on Lyn Meyrick. There was a photograph of himself – or, rather, of Harry Meyrick – in a leather case. The opposing frame was empty. In a corner of one suitcase was a small Teddy-bear, tattered with much childish loving and presumably retained as a mascot. In the other suitcase he found two textbooks, one on the theory and practice of teaching, the other on child psychology; both heavyweights, the pages sprinkled with diagrams and graphs.

He closed and locked the suitcases and put them on the rack, then went down to his own room. As the lift door opened on the third floor he saw Armstrong just stepping out of the other lift. Armstrong held out an envelope. 'Mr. Carey told me to give you this.'

Denison ripped open the envelope and scanned the sparse typescript on the single sheet. The only thing it told him that he had not learned already was that Lyn Meyrick's sport was gymnastics. 'Carey will have to do better than this,' he said curtly.

'We're doing the best we can,' said Armstrong. 'We'll get more later in the day when people have woken up in England.'

'Keep it coming.' said Denison. 'And don't forget to remind Carey that I'm waiting for an explanation.'

'I'll tell him,' said Armstrong.

'Another thing,' said Denison. 'She said she'd find me either here in Oslo or in Helsinki in Finland. That baffled me until I realised I don't know a bloody thing about Meyrick. Carey mentioned a dossier on Meyrick – I want to see it.'

'I don't think that will be possible,' said Armstrong hesitantly. 'You're not cleared for security.'

Denison speared him with a cold eye. 'You bloody fool!' he said quietly. 'Right now *I* am your security – and don't forget to tell Carey that, too.' He walked past Armstrong and up the corridor to his room.

12

Carey walked past the Oslo City Hall in the warm mid-afternoon sunshine and inspected the statuary with a sardonic eye. Each figure represented a different trade and the whole, no doubt, was supposed to represent the Dignity of Labour. He concluded that the Oslo City Fathers must have been socialist at one time.

He sat on a bench and looked out over the harbour and Oslofjord. A ship slid quietly by – the ferry bound for Copenhagen – and there was a constant coming and going of smaller, local ferries bound for Bygdøy, Ingierstrand and other places on the fjord. Camera-hung tourists strolled by and a tour bus stopped, disgorging more of them.

McCready walked up and sat on the bench. Carey did not look at him but said dreamily, 'Once my job was easy – just simple eyeball stuff. That was back in the days when Joshua sent his spies into the land of Caanan. Then the bloody scientists got busy and ballsed the whole thing up.'

McCready said nothing; he had encountered Carey in this mood before and knew there was nothing to do but wait until Carey got it off his chest.

'Do you realise the state we've got ourselves into now?' asked Carey rhetorically. 'I think you're George McCready, but I could be wrong. What's more, *you* could think you're George McCready and, if Harding is to be believed, still be wrong. How the hell am I supposed to cope with a situation like that?'

He disregarded McCready's opening mouth. 'The bloody boffins are lousing up the whole damned world,' he said violently, and pointed towards the line of statuary. 'Look at that crowd of working stiffs. There's not a trade represented there that isn't obsolete or obsolescent. Pretty soon they'll put up a statue of me; there'll be a plaque saying "Intelligence agent, Mark II" and my job'll be farmed out to a hot-shot computer. Where's Denison?'

'Asleep in the hotel.'

'And the girl?'

'Also asleep – in her own room.'

'If he's had five minutes' sleep that's five minutes more than I've had. Let's go and wake the poor bastard up. Mrs. Hansen will join us at the hotel.'

He stood up, and McCready said, 'How much are you going to tell him?'

'As much as I have to and no more,' said Carey shortly. 'Which may be more than I want to tell him. He's already putting the screws on me through young Ian. He wants to see Meyrick's dossier.'

'You can't expect him to carry out an impersonation without knowing something of Meyrick,' said McCready reasonably.

'Why did that damned girl have to turn up?' grumbled Carey. 'As though we don't have enough trouble. I had a row with Harding this morning.'

'I'm not surprised.'

'George – I have no option. With Meyrick gone I have to use Denison. I'll play fair; I'll tell him the truth – maybe not all of it, but what I tell him will be true – let him make up his own mind. And if he wants out that's my hard luck.'

McCready noticed the reservation and shook his head. The truth, in Carey's hands, could take on a chameleon-like quality. Denison did not stand a chance.

Carey said, 'Something Iredale told me gave me the shudders. This silicone stuff that was rammed into Denison's face is polymer; it's injected in liquid form and then it hardens in the tissues to the consistency of fat – and it's permanent. If Denison wants to get his own face back it will be a major surgical operation – they'll have to take his face apart to scrape the stuff out.'

McCready grimaced. 'I take it that's a part of the truth you're not going to tell him.'

'That – and a few other titbits from Harding.' Carey stopped. 'Well, here's the hotel. Let's get it over with.'

Denison woke from a deep sleep to hear hammering on his door. He got up groggily, put on the bath robe, and opened the door. Carey said, 'Sorry to waken you, but it's about time we had a talk.'

Denison blinked at him. 'Come in.' He turned and went into the bathroom, and Carey, McCready and Mrs. Hansen walked through into the bedroom. When Denison reappeared he was wiping his face with a towel. He stared at Diana Hansen. 'I might have known.'

'You two know each other,' said Carey. 'Mrs. Hansen was keeping tabs on Meyrick.' He drew back the curtain, letting sunlight spill into the room, and tossed an envelope on the the dressing-table. 'Some more stuff on the girl. We have quite a few people in England running about in circles on your behalf.'

'Not mine,' corrected Denison. 'Yours!' He put down the towel. 'Any moment from now she's going to start playing "Do you remember when?" No information you can give me will help in that sort of guessing game.'

'You'll just have to develop a bad memory,' said McCready.

'I need to know more about Meyrick,' insisted Denison.

'And I'm here to tell you.' Carey pulled the armchair forward. 'Sit down and get comfortable. This is going to take a while.' He sat in the other chair and pulled out a stubby pipe which he started to fill. McCready and Diana Hansen sat on the spare bed.

Carey struck a match and puffed at his pipe. 'Before we start on Meyrick you ought to know that we discovered how, and when, the switch was made. We figured how we'd do a thing like that ourselves and then checked on it. You were brought in on a stretcher on June 8 and put in room three-sixty-three, just across the corridor. Meyrick was probably knocked out by a Mickey Finn in his nightly Ovaltine or something like that, and the switch was made in the wee, small hours.'

'Meyrick was taken out next morning before you woke up,' said McCready. 'He was put into an ambulance, the hotel management co-operating, and driven to Pier Two at Vippetangen where he was put aboard a ship sailing to Copenhagen. Another ambulance was waiting there which took him God knows where.'

Carey said, 'If you'd contacted the Embassy as soon as it happened we'd have been able to work all that out so damned fast that *we* could have been waiting at Copenhagen.'

'For God's sake!' said Denison. 'Would you have believed me any the quicker? It took you long enough to check anyway with your doctor and your tame psychiatrist.'

'He's right,' said McCready.

'Do you think that's why it was done this way? To buy time?'

'Could be,' said McCready. 'It worked, didn't it?'

'Oh, it worked all right. What puzzles me is what happened at the Spiralen the next day.' Carey turned to Denison. 'Have you got the doll and the note?'

Denison opened a drawer and handed them to Carey. He unfolded the single deckle-edged sheet and read the note aloud. '"Your Drammen Dolly awaits you at Spiraltoppen. Early morning June 10."' He lifted the paper and sniffed delicately. 'Scented, too. I thought that went out in the nineteen twenties.'

Diana Hansen said, 'This is the first I've heard of a note. I know about the doll, but not the note.'

'It's what took Denison to the Spiralen,' said McCready.

'Could I see it?' said Diana, and Carey passed it to her. She read it and said pensively, 'It could have been . . .'

'What is it, Mrs. Hansen?' said Carey sharply.

'Well, when Meyrick and I went to Drammen last week we lunched at the Spiraltoppen Restaurant.' She looked a little embarrassed. 'I had to go to the lavatory and I was away rather a long time. I had stomach trouble – some kind of diarrhoea.'

McCready grinned. 'Even Intelligence agents are human,' he said kindly.

'When I got back Meyrick was talking to a woman and they seemed to be getting on well together. When I came up she went away.'

'That all?' asked Carey.

'That's all.'

He regarded her thoughtfully. 'I think there's something you're not telling us, Mrs. Hansen.'

'Well, it's something about Meyrick. I was with him quite a lot during the last few weeks and he gave me the impression of being something of a womaniser – perhaps even a sexual athlete.'

A chuckle escaped from McCready. 'Did he proposition you?'

'He had as many arms as an octopus,' she said. 'I thought I wasn't going to last out this operation without being raped. I think he'd go for anything on two legs that wore skirts, with the possible exception of Scotsmen – and I wouldn't be too sure of that.'

'Well, well,' said Carey. 'How little we know of our fellow men.'

Denison said, 'He was divorced twice.'

'So you think this note was to set up an assignation.'

'Yes,' said Diana.

'But Meyrick wouldn't have fallen for that, no matter how horny he was,' said Carey. 'He was too intelligent a man. When you and he went to Drammen last week he checked with me according to instructions. Since you were going with him I gave him the okay.'

'Did Meyrick know Diana was working for you?' asked Denison.

Carey shook his head. 'No – we like to play loose. But Meyrick didn't find the note.' He pointed his pipe stem at Denison. 'You did – and you went to the Spiralen. Tell me, did the men who attacked you give the impression that they wanted to capture or to kill you?'

'I didn't stop to ask them,' said Denison acidly.

'Um,' said Carey, and lapsed into thought, his pipe working overtime. After a while he stirred, and said, 'All right, Mrs. Hansen; I think that's all.'

She nodded briefly and left the room, and Carey glanced at McCready. 'I suppose we must tell him about Meyrick.'

McCready grinned. 'I don't see how you can get out of it.'

'I have to know,' said Denison. 'if I'm going to carry on with this impersonation.'

'I trust Mrs. Hansen and she doesn't know,' said Carey. 'Not the whole story. I work on the "need to know" principle.' He sighed. 'I suppose you need to know, so here goes. The first thing to know about Meyrick is that he's a Finn.'

'With a name like that?'

'Oddly enough, it's his own name. In 1609 the English sent a diplomat to the court of Michael, the first Romanov Czar, to negotiate a trade treaty and to open up the fur trade. The courtiers of James I had to get their bloody ermine somewhere. The name of the diplomat was John Merick – or Meyrick – and he was highly philoprogenitive. He left by-blows all over the Baltic and Harry Meyrick is the end result of that.'

'It seems that Harry takes after his ancestor,' commented McCready.

Carey ignored him. 'Of course, Meyrick's name was a bit different in Finnish, but when he went to England he reverted to the family name. But that's by the way.' He laid down his pipe. 'More to the point, Meyrick is a Karelian Finn; to be pedantic, if he'd stayed at home in the town where he was born he'd now be a Russian. How good is your modern history?'

'Average I suppose,' said Denison.

'And that means bloody awful,' observed Carey. 'All right; in 1939 Russia attacked Finland and the Finns held them off in what was known as the Winter War. In 1941 Germany attacked Russia and the Finns thought it a good opportunity to have another go at the Russkies, which was a pity because that put them on the losing side. Still, it's difficult to see what else they could have done.

'At the end of this war, which the Finns know as the Continuation War, there was a peace treaty and the frontier was withdrawn. The old frontier was too close to Leningrad, which had the Russians edgy. An artilleryman could stand in Finland and lob shells right into the middle of Leningrad, so the Russians took over the whole of the Karelian Isthmus, together with a few other bits and pieces. This put Meyrick's home town, Enso, on the Russian side, and the Russians renamed it Svetogorsk.'

Carey sucked on his pipe which had gone out. It gurgled unpleasantly. 'Am I making myself clear?'

'You're clear enough,' said Denison. 'But I want more than a history lesson.'

'We're getting there,' said Carey. 'Meyrick was seventeen at the end of the war. Finland was in a hell of a mess; all the Karelian Finns cleared out of the isthmus because they didn't want to live under the Russians and this put the pressure on the rest of Finland because there was nowhere for them to go. The Finns had to work so bloody hard producing the reparations the Russians demanded that there was no money or men or time left over to build housing. So they turned to the Swedes and asked calmly if they'd take 100,000 immigrants.' Carey snapped his fingers. 'Just like that – and the Swedes agreed.'

Denison said, 'Noble of them.'

Carey nodded. 'So young Meyrick went to Sweden. He didn't stay long because he came here, to Oslo, where he lived until he was twenty-four. Then he went to England. He was quite alone all this time – his family had been killed during the war – but as soon as he arrived in England he married his first wife. She had what he needed, which was money.'

'Who doesn't need money?' asked McCready cynically.

'We'll get on faster if you stop asking silly questions,' said Carey. 'The second thing you have to know about Meyrick is that he's a bright boy. He has a flair for invention, particularly in electronics, and he has something else which the run-of-the-mill inventor doesn't have – the ability to turn his inventions into money. The first Mrs. Meyrick had a few thousand quid which was all he needed to get started. When they got divorced he'd turned her into a millionairess and he'd made as much for himself. And he went on making it.'

Carey struck a match and applied it to his pipe. 'By this time he was a big boy as well as a bright boy. He owned a couple of factories and was deep in defence contracts. There's a lot of his electronics in the Anglo-French Jaguar fighter as well as in Concorde. He also did some bits and pieces for the Chieftain main battle tank. He's now at the stage where he heads special committees on technical matters concerning defence, and the Prime Minister has pulled him into a Think Tank. He's a hell of a big boy but the man-in-the-street knows nothing about him. Got the picture?'

'I think so,' said Denison. 'But it doesn't help me a damn.'

Carey blew a plume of smoke into the air. 'I think Meyrick inherited his brains from his father, so let's take a look at the old boy.'

Denison sighed. 'Must we?'

'It's relevant,' said Carey flatly. 'Hannu Merikken was a physicist and, by all accounts, a good one. The way the story runs is that if he hadn't been killed during the war he'd have been in line for the Nobel Prize. The war put a stop to his immediate researches and he went to work for the Finnish government in Viipuri, which was then the second biggest city in Finland. But it's in Karelia and it's now a Russian city and the Russians call it Vyborg.' He looked at Denison's closed eyes, and said sharply, 'I trust I'm not boring you.'

'Go on,' said Denison. 'I'm just trying to sort out all these names.'

'Viipuri was pretty well smashed up during the war, including the laboratory Merikken was working in. So he got the hell out of there and went home to Enso which is about thirty miles north of Viipuri. He knew by this time that no one was going to stop the Russians and he wanted to see to the safety of his papers. He'd done a lot of work before the war which hadn't been published and he didn't want to lose it.'

'So what did he do?' asked Denison. He was becoming interested.

'He put all the papers into a metal trunk, sealed it, and buried it in the garden of his house. Young Harri Merikken – that's our Harry Meyrick – helped him. The next day Hannu Merikken, his wife and his younger son, were killed by the same bomb, and if Harri had been in the house at the same time he'd have been killed, too.'

'And the papers are important?' said Denison.

'They are,' said Carey soberly. 'Last year Meyrick was in Sweden and he bumped into a woman who had given him a temporary home when he'd been evacuated from Finland. She said she'd been rummaging about in the attic or whatever and had come across a box he'd left behind. She gave it to him. He opened it in his hotel that night and looked through it. Mostly he was amused by the things he found – the remnants of the enthusiasms of a seventeen-year-old. There were the schematics of a ham radio he'd designed – he was interested in electronics even then – some other drawings of a radio-controlled model aircraft, and things like that. But in the pages of an old radio magazine he found a paper in his father's handwriting, and that suddenly made the papers buried in Merikken's garden very important indeed.'

'What are they about?' asked Denison.

Carey ignored the question. 'At first, Meyrick didn't realise what he'd got hold of and he talked about it to a couple of scientists in Sweden. Then the penny dropped and he bolted back to England and began to talk to the right people – we're lucky he was big enough to know who to talk to. The people he talked to got interested and, as an end result of a lot of quiet confabulation, I was brought in.'

'The idea being to go and dig up the garden?'

'That's right. The only snag is that the garden is in Russia.' Carey knocked out his pipe in the ashtray. 'I have a couple of men scouting the Russian border right now. The idea was that as soon as they report Meyrick and I would pop across and dig up the papers.'

McCready snapped his fingers. 'As easy as walking down Piccadilly.'

'But Meyrick was snatched,' said Carey. 'And you were substituted.'

'Yes,' said Denison heavily. 'Why me?'

'I don't think we need to go too deeply into that,' said Carey delicately. He did not want Denison to ruminate about his past life and go off into a fugue. 'I think it could have been anybody who looked enough like Meyrick to need the least possible surgery.'

There was a whole list of other qualifications – someone who would not be missed too easily, someone who had the right psychological make-up, someone very easily accessible. It had been a job which had been carefully set up in England and back in London there was a team of ten men sifting through the minutiae of Denison's life in the hope of coming up with a clue to his kidnapping. It was a pity that Denison could not be directly questioned but Harding was dead against it, and Carey had a need for Denison – he did not want an insane man on his hands.

'Which brings us to the next step,' said Carey. 'Someone – call them Crowd X – has pinched Meyrick, but they're not going to broadcast the fact. They don't know if we've tumbled to the substitution or not – and we're not going to tell them.' He looked steadily at Denison. 'Which is why we need your co-operation, Mr. Denison.'

'In what way?' asked Denison cautiously.

'We want you to carry on being Meyrick, and we want you to go to Finland.'

Denison's jaw dropped. 'But that's impossible,' he said. 'I'd never get away with it. I can't speak Finnish.'

'You've got away with it up to now,' pointed out Carey. 'You fooled Mrs. Hansen and you're doing very well with Meyrick's daughter. It's quite true what Harding said – you're very competent.'

'But the language! Meyrick speaks Finnish.'

'He speaks Finnish, Swedish, Norwegian and English fluently and idiomatically,' said Carey easily. 'His French passes but his Italian and Spanish aren't too hot.'

'Then how the hell can I get away with it?' demanded Denison. 'All I have is English and schoolboy French.'

'Take it easy. Let me tell you a story.' Carey began to fill his pipe again. 'At the end of the First World War quite a number of the British troops married French wives and stayed in France. A lot of them were given jobs by the War Graves Commission – looking after the war cemeteries. Twenty years after, there came another war and another British Expeditionary Force. The new young soldiers found that the old soldiers had completely lost their English – their mother tongue – and could speak only French.'

He struck a match. 'And that's what's going to happen to Meyrick. He hasn't been back to Finland since he was seventeen; I don't think it's unreasonable to suppose he'd lose the language.'

'But why do you want me? I can't lead you to the papers – only Meyrick can do that.'

Carey said, 'When this happened my first impulse was to abandon the operation, but then I started to think about it. Firstly, we don't know that Meyrick was snatched because of this operation – it might have been for a different reason. In that case the papers are reasonably safe. Secondly, it occurred to me that you could be a good distracting influence – we could use you to confuse the opposition as much as they've confused us. If you go to Finland as Meyrick they won't know what the hell to think. In the ensuing brouhaha we might get a chance at the papers. What do you think?'

'I think you're crazy,' said Denison.

Carey shrugged. 'Mine is a crazy profession – I've seen crazier ploys come off. Look at Major Martin – the man who never was.'

'He didn't have to stand up to questioning,' said Denison. 'The whole thing is bloody ridiculous.'

'You'd be paid, of course.' said Carey casually. 'Well paid, as a matter of fact. You'd also get a compensatory grant for the injuries that have been done to you, and Mr. Iredale is ready and willing to bring you back to normality.'

'Dr. Harding, too?'

'Dr. Harding, too,' confirmed Carey. He wondered to what extent Denison knew his mental processes to be abnormal.

'Suppose I turn you down,' said Denison. 'Do I still get the services of Iredale and Harding?'

McCready tensed, wondering what Carey would say. Carey placidly blew a smoke ring. 'Of course.'

'So it's not a matter of blackmail,' said Denison.

The unshockable Carey arranged his features in an expression of shock. 'There is no question of blackmail,' he said stiffly.

'Why are Merikken's papers so important? What's in them?'

'I can't tell you that, Mr. Denison,' said Carey deliberately.

'Can't or won't?'

Carey shrugged. 'All right, then – won't.'

'Then I'm turning you down,' said Denison.

Carey put down his pipe. 'This is a question of state security, Denison; and we work on the principle of "need to know". Mrs. Hansen doesn't need to know. Ian Armstrong doesn't need to know. You don't need to know.'

'I've been kidnapped and stabbed,' said Denison. 'My face has been altered and my mind has been jiggered with.' He raised this hand. 'Oh, I know that – Harding got that much across – and I'm scared to the marrow about thinking of who I once was. Now you're asking me to go on with this charade, to go to Finland and put myself in danger again.' His voice was shaking. 'And when I ask why you have the gall to tell me I don't need to know.'

'I'm sorry,' said Carey.

'I don't care how sorry you are. You can book me on a flight to London.'

'Now who is using blackmail?' said Carey ironically.

'It's a reasonable request,' said McCready.

'I know it is, damn it!' Carey looked at Denison with cold eyes. 'If you breathe a word of what I'm going to tell you you'll be behind bars for the rest of your life. I'll see to that personally. Understand?'

Denison nodded. 'I've still got to know,' he said stubbornly.

Carey forced the words through reluctant lips. He said slowly, 'It seems that in 1937 or 1938 Hannu Merikken discovered a way of reflecting X-rays.'

Denison looked at him blankly. 'Is that all?'

'That's all,' said Carey curtly. He stood up and stretched.

'It isn't enough,' said Denison. 'What's so bloody important about that?

'You've been told what you want to know. Be satisfied.'

'It isn't enough. I must know the significance.'

Carey sighed. 'All right, George; tell him.'

'I felt like that at first,' said McCready. 'Like you, I didn't see what all the fuss was about. Merikken was doing a bit of pure research when he came across this effect before the war and in those days there wasn't much use for it. All the uses of X-rays depended upon their penetrative power and who'd want to reflect them. So Merikken filed it away as curious but useless and he didn't publish a paper on it.'

He grinned. 'The joke is that now every defence laboratory in the world is working on how to reflect X-rays, but no one has figured out a way to do it.'

'What happened to make it important?' asked Denison.

'The laser happened,' said Carey in a voice of iron.

'Do you know how a laser works?' When Denison shook his head, McCready said, 'Let's have a look at the very first laser as it was invented in 1960. It was a rod of synthetic ruby about four inches long and less than half an inch in diameter. One end was silvered to form a reflective surface, and the other end was half-silvered. Coiled around the rod was a spiral gas discharge lamp something like the flash used in photography. Got that?'

'All clear so far.'

'There's a lot more power in these electronic flashes than people imagine,' said McCready. 'For instance, an ordinary flash, as used by a professional photographer, develops about 4,000 horse power in the brief fraction of a second when the condensers discharge. The flash used in the early lasers was more powerful than that – let's call it 20,000 horse power. When the flash is used the light enters the ruby rod and something peculiar happens; the light goes up and down the rod, reflected from the silvered ends, and all the light photons are brought in step with each other. The boffins call that coherent light, unlike ordinary light where all the photons are out of step.

'Now, because the photons are in step the light pressure builds up. If you can imagine a crowd of men trying to batter down a door, they're more likely to succeed if they charge at once than if they try singly. The photons are all charging at once and they burst out of the half-silvered end of the rod as a pulse of light – and that light pulse has nearly all the 20,000 horse power of energy that was put into the rod.'

McCready grinned. 'The boffins had great fun with that. They discovered that it was possible to drill a hole through a razor blade at a range of six feet. At one time it was suggested that the power of a laser should be measured in Gillettes.'

'Stick to the point,' said Carey irritably.

'The military possibilities were easily seen,' said McCready. 'You could use a laser as a range-finder, for instance. Fire it at a target and measure the light bouncing back and you could tell the range to an inch. There were other uses – but there was one dispiriting fact. The laser used light and light can be stopped quite easily. It doesn't take much cloud to stop a beam of light, no matter how powerful it is.'

'But X-rays are different,' said Denison thoughtfully.

'Right! It's theoretically possible to make an X-ray laser, but for one snag. X-rays penetrate and don't reflect. No one has found a way of doing it except Merikken who did it before the war – and the working of a laser depends entirely upon multiple reflection.'

Denison rubbed his chin, feeling the flabbiness. Already he was becoming used to it. 'What would be the use of a gadget like that?'

'Take a missile coming in at umpteen thousand miles an hour and loaded with an atomic warhead. You've got to knock it down so you use another missile like the American Sprint. But you don't shoot your missile directly at the enemy missile – you aim it at where the enemy will be when your missile gets up there. That takes time to work out and a hell of a lot of computing power. With an X-ray laser you aim directly at the enemy missile because it operates with the speed of light – 186,000 miles a second – and you'll drill a hole right through it.'

'Balls,' said Carey. 'You'd cut the damned thing in two.'

'My God!' said Denison. 'That's a death ray.' He frowned. 'Could it be made powerful enough?'

'Lasers have come a long way since the first one,'said McCready soberly. 'They don't use the flash any more on the big ones – they pour in the power with a rocket engine. Already they're up to millions of horse power – but it's still ordinary light. With X-rays you could knock a satellite out of orbit from the ground.'

'Now do you understand the significance?' asked Carey. When Denison nodded, he said, 'So what are you going to do about it?'

There was a long silence while Denison thought. Carey stood up and went to the window where he looked across to the *Studenterlunden*, his fingers drumming on the window sill. McCready lay back on the bed with his hands behind his head, and inspected the ceiling closely.

Denison stirred and unclasped his fingers. He straightened in his chair and stretched his arms, then he sighed deeply. 'My name is Harry Meyrick,' he said.

13

Three days later Denison, descending for breakfast, bought a newspaper at the kiosk in the lobby and scanned it over coffee. Diana Hansen joined him, and said, 'What's new?'

He shrugged. 'The world is still going to hell in a handcart. Listen to this. Item one. Two more skyjackings, one successful and one not. In the *unsuccessful* one – God save the mark – two passengers were killed. Item two – pollution. A tanker collision in the Baltic and a fifteen mile oil slick is drifting on to Gotland; the Swedes are understandably acid. Item three. There are strikes in Britain, France and Italy, with consequent riots in London, Paris and Milan. Item four . . .' He raised his head. '. . . 'Do you want me to go on?'

She sipped her coffee. 'You sound a bit acid yourself.'

'Just how would you feel in my circumstances?' he asked a little grimly.

Diana shrugged. 'Where's Lyn?'

'The young sleep late.'

'I have a feeling she's sharpening her claws, getting ready to scratch my eyes out,' said Diana meditatively. 'She's made one or two odd remarks lately.' She stretched over and patted Denison's hand. 'She thinks her daddy is getting into bad company.'

'How right the child is.'

'Child!' Diana raised her eyebrows. 'She's only eight years younger than I am. She's no child – she's a healthy young woman with all her wits about her – so watch your step.'

Denison put his head on one side. 'Of course!' he said, somewhat surprised. Privately he thought that Diana was drawing the longbow a bit. He put her age at thirty-two which probably meant she was thirty-four; that would give her twelve years on Lyn, not much less that the fourteen years he had himself.

'Carey wants to see you,' said Diana. 'If you leave the hotel, turn left and walk about three hundred yards, you'll come to a place where they're building a memorial or something. Be around there at ten o'clock.'

'All right,' said Denison.

'And here's your darling daughter.' Diana raised her voice. 'Good morning, Lyn.'

Denison turned and smiled appreciatively at Lyn's *chic* appearance. It's the money that makes the difference, he thought; the grand ideas of the rulers of the fashion world are apt to look tatty when filtered through the salary of a junior London typist. 'Did you have a good night?'

'Fine,' said Lyn lightly, and sat down. 'I didn't expect to see you at breakfast, Mrs. Hansen.' She glanced sideways at Denison. 'Did you sleep in the hotel last night?'

'No, darling,' said Diana sweetly. 'I brought a message for your father.'

Lyn poured coffee. 'What are we doing today?'

'I have a business appointment this morning,' said Denison. 'Why don't you two go shopping?'

A shadow briefly crossed Lyn's face, but she said, 'All right.' Diana's answering smile was sickly in its sweetness.

Denison found Carey with his rump buttressed by a coping stone and his back to the Royal Palace. He looked up at Denison's approach and said brusquely, 'We're ready to move. Are you fit?'

'As fit as I'll ever be.'

Carey nodded. 'How are you getting on with the girl?'

'I'm tired of being Daddy,' said Denison bitterly. 'I'm only getting through by the skin of my teeth. She asks the damnedest questions.'

'What's she like?'

'A nice kid in danger of being spoiled rotten – but for one thing.'

'What's that?'

'Her parents were divorced and it's messed up her life. I'm beginning to realise what an unmitigated bastard Harry Meyrick is.' He paused.

'Or was.' He looked at Carey. 'Any news?'

Carey flapped his hand in negation. 'Tell me more.'

'Well, the mother is a rich bitch who ignores the girl. I don't think Lyn would care if she dropped dead tomorrow. But Lyn has always had a respect for her father; she doesn't like him but she respects him. She looks up to him like a . . . like a sort of God.' Denison rubbed his chin and said meditatively, 'I suppose people respect God, but do they really *like* him? Anyway, every time she tries to get near Meyrick he slaps her down hard. That's no way to bring up a daughter and it's been breaking her up.'

'I never did like his arrogance myself,' said Carey. 'It's the one thing that would have given you away in the end. You're not bloody-minded enough to be Meyrick.'

'Thank God for that,' said Denison.

'But you get on with her all right? As Meyrick?'

Denison nodded. 'So far – but no future guarantees.'

'I've been thinking about her,' said Carey. 'Suppose we took her to Finland – what would the opposition think?'

'For God's sake!' said Denison disgustedly.

'Think about it, man,' Carey urged. 'They'd check on her, and when they find out who she is they'd be bloody flummoxed. They might think that if you're good enough to deceive Meyrick's daughter you're good enough to deceive me.'

Denison was acid. 'That's not far short of the mark. I had to *tell* you who I was.'

'You can do it,' said Carey. 'It adds a bit of confusion, and there's nothing like confusion for creating opportunity. Right now we need all the luck we can create for ourselves. Will you ask her if she'll go with you to Helsinki tomorrow?'

Denison was troubled. 'It's all right for me,' he said. 'I'm going into this with my eyes open – but she's being conned. Will you guarantee her safety?'

'Of course I will. She'll be as safe as though she were in England.'

It was a long time before Denison made his decision. 'All right,' he said resignedly. 'I'll ask her.'

Carey slapped him lightly on the arm. 'Which brings us back to Meyrick's character. As you said – he's a right bastard. Bear that in mind when you're handling her.'

'You want her in Finland,' said Denison. 'I don't. If I really act like her father she's going to run and hide like she always has. Do you want that?'

'I can't say I do,' said Carey. 'But lean too far the other way and she'll know you're not Meyrick.'

Denison thought of the many ways in which he had hurt Lyn by his apparent forgetfulness. As in the case of her mascot, for instance; he had idly picked it up and asked what it was. 'But you *know*,' said Lyn in astonishment. He had incautiously shaken his head, and she burst out, 'But you *named* him.' There was a hurt look in her eyes. 'You called him Thread-Bear.'

He laughed sourly. 'Don't worry; I'm hurting her enough just by being myself.'

'It's settled then,' said Carey. 'You have an appointment at Helsinki University tomorrow afternoon with Professor Pentti Kääriänen. Your secretary arranged it.'

'Who the devil is he?'

'He was one of Hannu Merikken's assistants before the war. You are to introduce yourself as Merikken's son and pump him about what Merikken was doing in his laboratory from 1937 to 1939. I want to find out if there's been any other leakage about his X-ray researches.' He paused. 'Take the girl with you; it adds to your cover.'

'All right.' Denison gave Carey a level look. 'And her name is Lyn. She's not a bloody puppet; she's a human being.'

Carey's answering stare was equally unblinking. 'That's what I'm afraid of,' he said.

Carey watched Denison walk away and waited until he was joined by McCready. He sighed. 'Sometimes I have moments of quiet desperation.'

McCready suppressed a smile. 'What is it this time?'

'See those buildings over there?'

McCready looked across the road. 'That scrubby lot?'

'That's Victoria Terrace – there's a police station in there now. The authorities wanted to pull it down but the conservationists objected and won their case on architectural grounds.'

'I don't see the point.'

'Well, you see, it was Gestapo Headquarters during the war and it still smells to a lot of Norwegians.' He paused. 'I had a session in there once, with a man called Dieter Brun. Not a nice chap. He was killed towards the end of the war. Someone ran him down with a car.'

McCready was quiet because Carey rarely spoke of his past service. 'I've been running around Scandinavia for nearly forty years – Spitzbergen to the Danish-German border, Bergen to the Russo-Finnish border. I'll be sixty next month,' said Carey. 'And the bloody world hasn't changed, after all.' There was a note of quiet melancholy in his voice.

Next morning they all flew to Finland.

Lyn Meyrick was worried about her father, which was a new and unwanted experience. Her previous worries in that direction had always been for herself in relation to her father. To worry for her father was something new which gave her an odd feeling in the pit of her stomach.

She had been delighted when he suggested that she accompany him to Finland; a delight compounded by the fact that for the first time he was treating her like a grown-up person. He now asked her opinion and deferred to her wishes in a way he had never done before. Diffidently she had fallen in with his wish that she call him by his given name and she was becoming accustomed to it.

However, the delight had been qualified by the presence of Diana Hansen who somehow destroyed that adult feeling and made her feel young and gawky like a schoolgirl. The relationship between Diana and her father puzzled her. At first she had thought they were lovers and had been neither surprised nor shocked. Well, not *too* shocked. Her father was a man and not all that old, and her mother had not been reticent about the reasons for the divorce. And, yet, she had not thought that Diana Hansen would have been the type to appeal to her father and the relationship seemed oddly cold and almost businesslike.

And there were other things about him that were strange. He would become abstract and remote. This was nothing new because he had always had that ability to switch off in the middle of a conversation which made her feel as though he had dropped a barrier to cut her off. What was new was that he would snap out of these abstracted moments and smile at her in a way he never had before, which made her heart turn over. And he seemed deliberately to put himself out to please her.

And he was losing his memory, too. Not about anything big or important, but about minor things like . . . like Thread-Bear, for instance. How could a man forget a pun which had caused so much excitement in a little girl? If there was anything about her father that had annoyed her in the past it was his memory for detail – he usually remembered too much for her comfort. It was all very odd.

Anyway, she was glad he had invited her to go to the University to meet the man with the unpronounceable name. He had been hesitant about it, and she said, 'Why are you going?'

'It's just that I want to find out something about my father.'

'But that's my grandfather,' she said. 'Of course I'm coming.'

It seemed strange to have a grandfather called Hannu Merikken. She sat before the mirror and contemplated herself, making sure that all was in order. I'm not bad-looking, she thought, as she regarded the straight black eyebrows and the grey eyes. Mouth too big, of course. I'm no raving beauty, but I'll do.

She snatched up her bag and went to the door on the way to meet her father. Then she stopped in mid pace and thought, *What am I thinking of? It's my father . . . not . . . not . . .* She shook the thought from her and opened the door.

Professor Kääriänen was a jolly, chubby-faced man of about sixty, not at all the dry professorial stick Lyn had imagined. He rose from his desk to greet Denison, and shot out a spate of Finnish. Denison held up his hand in protest: 'I'm sorry; I have no Finnish.'

Kääriänen raised his eyebrows and said in English, 'Remarkable!'

Denison shrugged. 'Is it? I left when I was seventeen. I suppose I spoke Finnish for fifteen years – and I haven't spoken it for nearly thirty.' He smiled. 'You might say my Finnish language muscle has atrophied.'

Kääriänen nodded understandingly. 'Yes, yes; my own German was once quite fluent – but now?' He spread his hands. 'So you are Hannu Merikken's son.'

'Allow me to introduce my daughter, Lyn.'

Kääriänen came forward, his hands outstretched. 'And his granddaughter – a great honour. But sit down, please. Would you like coffee?'

'Thank you; that would be very nice.'

Kääriänen went to the door, spoke to the girl in the other office, and then came back. 'Your father was a great man, Dr. . . . er . . . Meyrick.'

Denison nodded. 'That is my name now. I reverted to the old family name.'

The professor laughed. 'Ah, yes; I well remember Hannu telling me the story. He made it sound so romantic. And what are you doing here in Finland, Dr. Meyrick?'

'I don't really know,' said Denison cautiously. 'Perhaps it's a need to get back to my origins. A delayed homesickness, if you like.'

'I understand,' said Kääriänen. 'And you want to know something about your father – that's why you've come to me?'

'I understand you worked with him – before the war.'

'I did, much to my own profit. Your father was not only a great research worker – he was also a great teacher. But I was not the only one. There were four of us, as I remember. You should remember that.'

'I was very young before the war,' said Denison defensively. 'Not even into my teens.'

'And you don't remember me,' said Kääriänen, his eyes twinkling. His hand patted his plump belly. 'I'm not surprised; I've changed quite a lot.'

But I remember you. You were a young rascal – you upset one of my experiments.'

Denison smiled. 'If guilty I plead sorrow.'

'Yes,' said Kääriänen reminiscently. 'There were four of us with your father in those days. We made a good team.' He frowned. 'You know; I think I am the only one left.' He ticked them off on his fingers. 'Olavi Koivisto joined the army and was killed. Liisa Linnankivi – she was also killed in the bombing of Viipuri; that was just before your father died, of course. Kaj Salojärvi survived the war; he died three years ago – cancer, poor fellow. Yes, there is only me left of the old team.'

'Did you all work together on the same projects?'

'Sometimes yes, sometimes no.' Kääriänen leaned forward. 'Sometimes we worked on our own projects with Hannu giving advice. As a scientist yourself, Dr. Meyrick, you will understand the work of the laboratory.'

Denison nodded. 'What was the main trend of my father's thought in those days before the war?'

Kääriänen spread his hands. 'What else but the atom? We were *all* thinking about the atom. Those were the great pioneering days, you know; it was very exciting.' He paused, and added drily, 'Not long after that, of course, it became too exciting, but by that time no one in Finland had time to think about the atom.'

He clasped his hands across his belly. 'I well remember the time Hannu showed me a paper written by Meitner and Frisch interpreting Hahn's experiments. The paper showed clearly that a chain reaction could take place and that the generation of atomic energy was clearly possible. We were all excited – you cannot imagine the excitement – and all our work was put aside to concentrate on this new thing.' He shrugged heavily. 'But that was 1939 – the year of the Winter War. No time for frivolities like atoms.' His tone was sardonic.

'What was my father working on when this happened?'

'Ah – here is the coffee,' said Kääriänen. He fussed about with the coffee, and offered small cakes to Lyn. 'And what do you do, young lady? Are you a scientist like your father and your grandfather?'

'I'm afraid not,' said Lyn politely. 'I'm a teacher.'

'We must have the teachers, too,' said Kääriänen. 'What was that you asked, Doctor?'

'I was wondering what my father was working on at the time he read the paper on atomic fission.'

'Ah, yes,' the professor said vaguely, and waved his hand a little helplessly. 'It was a long time ago, you know; so much has happened since – it is difficult to remember.' He picked up a cake and was about to bite into it when he said, 'I remember – it was something to do with some aspects of the properties of X-rays.'

'Did you work on that project?'

'No – that would be Liisa – or was it Olavi?'

'So you don't know the nature of the work he was doing?'

'No.' Kääriänen's face broke into a smile, and he shook with laughter. 'But, knowing your father, I can tell you it had no practical application. He was very proud of being a pure research physicist. We were all like that in those days – proud of being uncontaminated by the world.' He shook his head sadly. 'A pity we're not like that now.'

The next hour and a half was spent in reminiscences from Kääriänen interspersed with Denison's desperate ploys to fend off his inquiries into Meyrick's work. After allowing what he thought was a decent time he excused himself and he and Lyn took their leave of the professor with assurances that they would keep in professional contact.

They came out into Senate Square and made their way back to the hotel along Aleksanterinkatu, Helsinki's equivalent of Bond Street. Lyn was thoughtful and quiet, and Denison said, 'A penny for your thoughts.'

'I was just thinking,' she said. 'It seemed at one time as though you were pumping Professor Kääriänen.'

Did it, by God! thought Denison. *You're too bloody smart by half.* Aloud he said, 'I just wanted to know about my father, the work he did and so on.'

'You didn't give much back,' said Lyn tartly. 'Every time *he* asked a question you evaded it.'

'I had to,' said Denison. 'Most of my work is in defence. I can't babble about that in a foreign country.'

'Of course,' said Lyn colourlessly.

They were outside a jeweller's shop and Denison pointed. 'What do you think of that?'

She caught her breath. 'Oh, it's beautiful!'

It was a necklace – chunky, rough-hewn gold of an intricate and yet natural shape. He felt reckless and took her arm. 'Come on,' he said. 'Inside.'

The necklace cost him £215 of Meyrick's money which he paid by credit card. Apart from the fact that he thought that Meyrick ought to pay more attention to his daughter he thought it would take her mind off other things.

'Your birthday present,' he said.

Lyn was breathless with excitement. 'Oh, thank you, Da . . . Harry.' Impulsively she kissed him. 'But I have nothing to wear with it.'

'Then you'll have to buy something, won't you? Let's go back to the hotel.'

'Yes, let's.' She slipped her fingers into his. 'I have a surprise for you, too – at the hotel.'

'Oh? What is it?'

'Well, I thought that now you're back in Finland you ought to become reacquainted with the sauna.'

He laughed, and said cheerfully, 'I've never been to a sauna in my life.'

She stopped dead on the pavement and stared at him. 'But you must have. When you were a boy.'

'Oh, yes; I went then.' He cursed himself for the slip. Carey had given him books to read about Finland; language was one thing but there was a minimum any Finn would know, expatriate or not. The sauna definitely fitted into that category. 'I tend to regard my years in Finland as another life.' It was lame but it would have to do.

'It's about time you were reintroduced to the sauna,' she said firmly. 'I go often in London – it's great fun. I've booked for us both in the hotel sauna for six o'clock.'

'Great!' he said hollowly.

15

In the hotel he escaped to his room and rang the number he had been given. When Carey answered he gave a report on his interview with Kääriänen, and Carey said, 'So it all comes to this: Merikken *was* working on X-rays at the time but no one can remember exactly what he was doing. Those who would know are dead. That's encouraging.'

'Yes,' said Denison.

'You don't sound pleased,' said Carey.

'It's not that. I have something else on my mind.'

'Out with it.'

'Lyn has booked me in for the sauna this evening.'

'So?'

'She's booked us both in.'

'So?' There was a pause before Carey chuckled. 'My boy; I can see you have a wrong impression or an evil mind. This is not Hamburg nor is it the lower reaches of Soho; you're in Helsinki and the Finns are a decent people. I think you'll find there is one sauna for gentlemen and another for ladies.'

'Oh!' said Denison weakly. 'It's just that I don't know much about it. One gets the wrong impression.'

'Didn't you read the books I gave you?'

'I must have missed that one.'

'In any case, there's nothing wrong with a father joining his daughter in the sauna,' said Carey judicially. 'It may be done in your own home but not, I think, in an international hotel.' He paused. 'You'd better read up on it. Meyrick wouldn't have forgotten the sauna – no Finn would.'

'I'll do that.'

'Have fun,' said Carey, and rang off.

Denison put down the telephone and rummaged in his suitcase where he found a slim book on the sauna written for the benefit of English-speaking visitors to Finland. On studying it he was relieved to find that the sauna appeared to be little more than a Turkish bath in essence – with differences.

He turned back the pages and read the introduction. There was, apparently, one sauna for every six Finns which, he reflected, was probably a greater incidence than bathrooms in Britain. A clean people, the Finns – *mens sana in corpore sauna.* Stones were heated by birch logs or, in modern times, by electric elements. Humidity was introduced by *löyly* – tossing water on the stones. The booklet managed to convey an air of mystic ritual about what was essentially a prosaic activity, and Denison came to the conclusion that the sauna was the Finnish equivalent of the Japanese tea ceremony.

At quarter to six Lyn rang him. 'Are you ready?'

'Yes, of course.'

'I'll meet you afterwards in the swimming pool. Have you got your trunks?'

Denison mentally ran down a checklist of Meyrick's clothing. 'Yes.'

'At half past six, then.' She rang off.

He went up to the top floor of the hotel, found the sauna for men, and went into the change room where he took his time, taking his cue from the others who were there. He stripped and went into the ante-chamber to the sauna where he showered and then took a square of towelling from a pile and went into the sauna itself.

It was hot.

Out of the corner of his eye he saw a man lay his towel on a slatted, wooden bench and sit on it, so he followed suit. The wood beneath his feet was almost unbearably hot and sweat was already beginning to start from his skin. A man left the sauna and another took a bucket of water and sluiced it along the wood on which his feet were resting. Tendrils of steam arose but his feet were cooler.

Another man left the sauna and Denison turned and found a thermometer on the wall by his head. It registered 115 degrees. Not too bad, he thought; I can stand that. Then he looked again and saw that the thermometer was calibrated in degrees Celsius. Christ Almighty! Water *boils* at 100°C.

He blinked the sweat out of his eyes and turned his head to find that there was just himself and another man left – a broad-shouldered, deep-chested man, shaggy with hair. The man picked up a wooden dipper and filled it with water from a bucket. He paused with it in his hand, and said interrogatively, '*Löyly?*'

Denison answered with one of the few Finnish words he had picked up. '*Kiitos.*'

The man tossed the dipperful of water on to the square tub of hot stones in the corner. A blast of heat hit Denison like a physical blow and he gasped involuntarily. The man shot a sudden spate of Finnish at him, and Denison shook his head. 'I'm sorry; I have no Finnish.'

'Ah; first time in Finland?'

'Yes,' said Denison, and added, 'Since I was a boy.'

The man nodded. A sheen of sweat covered his hairy torso. He grinned. 'First time in sauna?'

Sweat dripped from Denison's nose. 'For a long time – many years.'

The man nodded and rose. He picked up the dipper again and, turning away from Denison, he filled it from the bucket. Denison gritted his teeth. Anything a bloody Finn can stand, I can; he thought.

With a casual flick of the wrist the man tossed the water on to the hot stones, then quickly went out of the sauna, slamming the door behind him. Again the wave of heat hit Denison, rising to an almost intolerable level so that he gasped and spluttered. A bloody practical joker – baiting a beginner!

He felt his head swim and tried to stand up but found that his legs had gone rubbery beneath him. He rolled off the top bench and tried to crawl to the door and felt the hot wood burning his hands. Darkness closed in on him and the last thing he saw was his own hand groping for the door handle before he collapsed and passed out.

He did not see the door open, nor did he feel himself being lifted up and carried out.

16

He awoke to darkness.

For a long time he just lay there, unable to think because of the throbbing pain in his head. Then his head cleared a little and he stirred and knew he was lying on a bed. When he moved he heard a metallic clinking noise. He moved again and became aware that he was naked, and a recollection of the sauna came back.

His first thought was that he had collapsed of heat prostration and had been taken to his own room, but when he lifted his hand that theory disintegrated quickly. There was a tug on both wrists and he felt cold metal, and when he twisted his hands around he heard that chinking sound again and felt the handcuffs.

He lay quiet for a while before he levered himself up on one elbow to stare into the blackness, then he swung his legs over the side of the bed and sat up. Tentatively he moved his feet apart; at least they were not manacled and he could walk. But walk where? He held his arms out before him and moved them sideways, first to the left and then to the right, until he encountered an object. It was flat with square edges and he concluded it was a bedside table. Exploring the top brought no joy; there was nothing on it.

Although his headache had eased he felt as weak as a kitten and he sat for a few moments to conserve his strength. Whether his weakness was a natural result of the heat of the sauna was debatable. He reasoned that if the sauna did that to everyone then it would not be so popular in Finland. Apart from that, he had no idea of how long he had been unconscious. He felt his skin and found it cool and with no moisture.

After a while he stood up with his arms out in front of him and began to shuffle forward. He had gone only a few feet when he stubbed his toe on something and the pain was agonising. 'Damn!' he said viciously, and stepped back until he felt the bed behind his legs. He sat down and nursed his foot.

A sound came from the other side of the room and he saw a patch of greyness, quickly obscured and vanishing. A light suddenly stabbed at him and he blinked and screwed up his eyes against the sudden glare. A voice said in accented English, 'So Dr. Meyrick is awake – and up, too.'

Denison brought up his hands before his eyes. The voice said sharply, 'Don't move, Meyrick. Stay on the bed.' Then, more coolly, 'Do you know what this is?'

The lamp dipped a little so that he could see the vague outline of a man in back-reflected light. He saw the glint of metal in an out-thrust hand. 'Well?' said the voice impatiently. 'What is it, Meyrick?'

Denison's voice was hoarse. 'A pistol.' He cleared his throat. 'I'd like to know what the hell this is all about.'

The voice was amused. 'No doubt you would.' As Denison tried to sort out the accent the light played over him. 'I see you've hurt your side, Dr. Meyrick. How did that happen?'

'A pack of maniacs attacked me in Norway. They seem to have the same breed in Finland, too.'

'Poor Dr. Meyrick,' mocked the voice. 'You seem to be continually in trouble. Did you report it to the police?'

'Of course I did. What else would you expect me to do? And to the British Embassy in Oslo.' He remembered what Carey had said about Meyrick's bloody-mindedness, and added irascibly, 'Bloody incompetents – the lot of them.'

'Who did you see at the Embassy?'

'A man called McCready picked me up at the police station and took me to the Embassy. Look, I've had enough of this. I'm answering no more questions. None at all.'

The pistol moved languidly. 'Yes, you will. Did you meet Carey?'

'No.'

'You're a liar.'

'If you think you know the answers, why ask me the questions? I don't know anyone called Carey.'

A sigh came out of the darkness. 'Meyrick, I think you ought to know that we have your daughter.'

Denison tensed, but sat quietly. After a moment he said, 'Prove it.'

'Nothing easier.' The pistol withdrew slowly. 'Tape recorders are made conveniently small these days, are they not?' There was a click and a slight hissing noise in the darkness beyond the flashlight, then a man spoke:

'Now tell me; what's your father doing here in Finland?'

'He's on holiday.'

That was Lyn's clear voice. Denison recognised it in spite of the slight distortion which was far less than that of a telephone.

'Did he tell you that?'

'Who else would tell me?' She sounded amused.

'But he went to see Professor Kääriänen this afternoon. That sounds more like business than pleasure.'

'He wanted to find out something about his father – my grandfather.'

'What did he want to find out?'

There was a raw silence, then the man said, *'Come now, Miss Meyrick; nothing will happen, either to you or to your father, if you answer my questions, I assure you that you will be released unharmed.'*

A switch snapped and the voices stopped. From the darkness: 'You see, Dr. Meyrick! Of course, I cannot guarantee the truthfulness of my friend regarding his last statement.' The pistol reappeared, glinting in the light. 'Now, to return to Mr. Carey – what did he have to say?'

'He hauled me over the coals for being in a road accident,' said

Denison.

The voice sharpened. 'You can do better than that. Now, having put you and Carey together, I want to know just what you're doing here in Finland. I want it truthfully, and I want it quickly. And you'd better start thinking seriously of your daughter's health.' The gun jerked. 'Talk!'

Denison was never more conscious of the disadvantages of being naked; it took the pith out of a man. 'All right,' he said. 'We're here to see the Finnish government.'

'What about?'

'A defence project.'

'Who in the government?'

'Not really the government,' said Denison inventively. 'Someone in the army – in military intelligence.'

'The name?' When Denison was silent the gun jerked impatiently. 'The name, Meyrick.'

Denison was hastily trying to slap together a name that sounded even remotely Finnish. 'Saarinen.'

'He's an architect.'

'Not this one – this one's a colonel,' said Denison, hoping it was a rank in the Finnish army. He was listening intently but heard no sound other than an occasional rustle of clothing from the other side of the bright light.

'What's the project?'

'Electronic espionage – equipment for monitoring Russian broadcasts, especially on military wavelengths.'

There was a long silence. 'I suppose you know that this is already done.'

'Not the way I do it,' said Denison.

'All right; how do you do it? And let's not have me extract answers like pulling teeth or that girl of yours might have some of her teeth pulled.'

'I invented an automatic decoder,' said Denison. A barrier broke in his mind and a wave of panic and terror swept over him. He felt sweat trickle down his chest and then deliberately pushed the panic back where it had come from – but he retained the words that had come with it.

'It's a stochastic process,' he said, not even knowing what the word meant. 'A development of the Monte Carlo method. The Russian output is repeatedly sampled and put through a series of transformations at random. Each transformation is compared with a store held in a computer memory – if a match is made a tree branching takes place leading to a further set of transformations. There are a lot of dead ends and it needs a big, fast computer – very powerful.'

The sweat poured off him. He had not understood a word of what he had said.

'I got most of that,' said the voice, and Denison thought he detected a touch of awe. 'You invented this thing?'

'I developed the circuits and helped with the programming,' said Denison sullenly.

'There's one thing I don't understand – and this I really have to know. Why give it to the Finns?'

'We didn't,' said Denison. 'They gave it to us. They developed the basics. They didn't have the resources to follow up, so they gave it to us.'

'Professor Kääriänen?'

'Look,' said Denison. 'Let me hear that tape again.'

'Why?'

'I'm not saying another bloody word until I hear it,' said Denison stubbornly.

A pause. 'All right; here's a re-run.'

The gun vanished and there was a click.

'Now tell me; what's your father doing here in Finland?'

'He's on holiday.'

Denison strained his ears as he listened to the conversation and evaluated the voices. He raised his hands and slowly parted them so that the link of the handcuffs tightened.

'He wanted to find out something about his father – my grandfather.'

'What did he want to find out?' A pause. *'Come now, Miss Meyrick; nothing will happen, either to you or to your father, if you ans . . .'*

Denison lunged, moving fast. He had moved his legs under the bed, so that when he moved he was on the balls of his feet and utilising the maximum thrust of his thighs. His hands were as wide apart as he could spread them and he rammed them forward as though to grab the man by the ears. The link between the handcuffs caught the man right across the larynx.

Both tape recorder and flashlight dropped to the floor; the flashlight rolled, sending grotesque shadows about the room, and the recorder babbled. Denison kept up his pressure on the man's throat and was aware of cloth as he pressed his hands to his opponent's face. In the shifting light he saw the glint of metal as the man raised the pistol from his pocket and he twisted his hand frantically and managed to grab the wrist as it came up.

With his left hand holding firmly on to his opponent's right wrist he thrust firmly so that the steel link cut into the man's throat. The gun was thus held close to the man's right ear, and when it went off with a blinding flare and a deafening explosion the man reeled away and dropped it.

Denison dived for it and came up again quickly. The door banged closed and the recorder chattered insanely. He made for the door and opened it, to find himself in a narrow corridor with another door at the end. As he ran for it he heard Diana Hansen say, from behind him, '*Lyn, if you take this attitude it will be the worse for you.*'

He heard the words but they made little sense and he had no time to evaluate them. He burst through the door and found himself in the brightly lit hotel corridor. There was no one to be seen, so he ran to the corner where the corridor turned and came to the lifts, and skidded to a halt in front of an astonished couple in evening dress. One lift was going down.

He made for the stairs, hearing a startled scream from behind him, and ran down two flights of stairs, causing quite a commotion as he emerged into the lobby yelling for the police and wearing nothing but a pair of handcuffs and an automatic pistol.

17

'Incredible!' said Carey. His voice was dead as though he, himself, did not believe what he was saying, and the single word made no echo in the quiet room.

'That's what happened,' said Denison simply.

McCready stirred. 'It would seem that more than water was thrown on to the hot stones in the sauna.'

'Yes,' said Carey. 'I have heard that some Finns, in an experimental mood, have used koskenkorva as *löyly.*'

'What's that?' asked Denison.

'A sort of Finnish vodka.' Carey put down his dead pipe. 'I dare say some smart chemist could come up with a vaporising knock-out mixture. I accept that.' He frowned and shook his head. 'Could you repeat what you told this fellow about your bloody decoder?'

'It's engraved on my memory,' said Denison bitterly. 'I said, "It's a stochastic process – a development of the Monte Carlo method. The Russian output is repeatedly sampled and put through a series of transformations at random. Each transformation is compared with a store held in a computer memory – if a match is made a tree branching takes place leading to a further set of transformations. There are a lot of dead ends and it needs a big, fast computer – very powerful."'

'It would,' said Carey drily.

'I don't even know what stochastic means,' said Denison helplessly.

Carey took a smoker's compendium from his pocket and began to clean his pipe, making a dry scraping sound. 'I know what it means. A stochastic process has an element of probability in it. The Monte Carlo method was first devised as a means of predicting the rate of diffusion of uranium hexafluoride through a porous barrier – it's been put to other uses since.'

'But I don't know anything about that,' expostulated Denison.

'Apparently you do,' said Carey. 'If you thought you were talking gobbledegook you were wrong. It would make sense to a mathematician or a computer man. And you were right about something else; you'd need a bloody powerful computer to handle it – the transformations would run into millions for even a short message. In fact, I don't think there is that kind of a computer, unless the programming method is equally powerful.'

Denison developed the shakes. 'Was I a mathematician? Did I work on computers?' he whispered.

'No,' said Carey levelly. 'What did you think you were doing when you reeled off all that stuff?'

'I was spinning a yarn – I couldn't tell him why we were really here.'

McCready leaned forward. 'What did you feel like when you were spouting like that?'

'I was scared to death,' confessed Denison.

'Of the man?'

There was violence in Denison's headshake. 'Not of the man – of myself. What was in *me*.' His hands began to quiver again.

Carey caught McCready's eye and shook his head slightly; that line of questioning was too dangerous for Denison. He said, 'We'll leave that for a moment and move on. You say this chap accepted you as Meyrick?'

'He didn't question it.'

'What made you go for him? That was a brave thing to do when he had a gun.'

'He wasn't holding the gun,' said Denison. 'He was holding the recorder. I suddenly tumbled to it that the recording was a fake. The threatening bit at the end had a different quality – a dead sound. All the other stuff was just ordinary conversation and could have happened quite naturally. It followed that this chap couldn't have Lyn, and that left me free to act.'

'Quite logical,' said Carey. 'And quite right.' There was a bemused look on his face as he muttered to himself, '*Competent!*'

McCready said, 'Lyn was in the hotel lounge yesterday afternoon and a chap sat at the table and began to pump her. Either the flower pot or the ashtray was bugged and the conversation recorded. Diana Hansen was around and caught on to what was happening and butted in, spoiling the game. Of course, she didn't know about the bug at the time.'

A look of comprehension came over Denison's face. 'I heard Diana's voice on the tape. She was threatening Lyn, too.'

McCready grinned. 'When this character was foiled he went away, and Diana and Lyn had a row. The bug was still there so that, too, was picked up on the tape. It seems that your daughter is trying to protect her father against the wiles of a wicked woman of the world.'

'Oh, no!' moaned Denison.

'You'll have to come the heavy father,' McCready advised.

'Does Lyn know what happened?'

Carey grunted and glanced at his watch. 'Six in the morning – she'll still be asleep. When you went missing I had Mrs. Hansen tell her that the two of you were going on the town and you'd be late back. I didn't want her alarmed.'

'She's certain to find out,' said McCready. 'This is too good a story to suppress – the eminent Dr. Meyrick capering in the lobby of the city's best hotel as naked as the day he was born and waving a gun. Impossible to keep out of the papers.'

'Why in hell did you do it?' demanded Carey. 'You were bawling for the police, too.'

'I thought I could catch the chap,' said Denison. 'When I didn't I thought of what Meyrick would have done – the real Meyrick. If an innocent man is threatened with a gun the first thing he does is to yell for the coppers. An innocent Meyrick would be bloody outraged – so I blew my top in the hotel lobby.'

'Still logical,' muttered Carey. He raised his voice. 'All right; the man in the sauna. Description?'

'He was hairy – he had a pelt like a bear.'

'I don't care if he was as hairy as Esau,' said Carey caustically. 'We can't go stripping the clothes off suspects to find how hairy they are. His face, man!'

'Brown eyes,' said Denison tiredly. 'Square face – a bit battered. Nose on one side. Dimple in chin.'

'That's the bloke who was quizzing Lyn Meyrick,' said McCready.

'The other man – the one with the gun.'

'I never saw him,' said Denison. 'The room was darkened and when I got my hands on him I found he was wearing some kind of a mask. But I . . .' He stopped on a doubtful note.

'Carry on,' said Carey encouragingly.

'He spoke English but with an accent.'

'What sort of accent?'

'I don't know,' said Denison desperately. 'Call it a generalized middle-European accent. The thing is that I think I've heard the voice before.'

At that, Carey proceeded to put Denison through the wringer. Fifteen minutes later Denison yelled, 'I tell you I don't know.' He put his head in his hands. 'I'm tired.'

Carey stood up. 'All right; you can go to bed. We'll let you sleep, but I can't answer for the local cops – they'll want to see you again. Got your story ready?'

'Just the truth.'

'I'd leave out that bit about the decoder you invented,' advised Carey. 'It's a bit too much.' He jerked his head at McCready. 'Come on, George.'

They left Denison to his bed. In the lift Carey passed his hand over his face. 'I didn't think this job would call for so many sleepless nights.'

'Let's find some coffee,' proposed McCready. 'There's sure to be an early morning place open by now.'

They left the hotel in silence and walked along Mannerheimintie. The street was quiet with only the occasional taxi and the odd cyclist on his way to an early start at work. Carey said suddenly, 'Denison worries me.'

'You mean that stuff he came out with?'

'What the hell else?' The corners of Carey's mouth turned down. 'And more – but principally that. A man like Meyrick might design just such a contraption – but where did Denison get it from?'

'I've been thinking about it,' said McCready. His voice was careful. 'Have you considered the possibility of a double shuffle?'

Carey broke stride. 'Speak plainly.'

'Well, here we have a man whom we think is Denison. His past is blocked out and every time he tries to probe it he breaks into a muck sweat. You saw that.'

'Well?'

'But supposing he really is Meyrick – also with the past blocked out – who only thinks he's Denison. Harding said it was possible. Then anything brought out of the past in an emergency would be pure Meyrick.'

Carey groaned. 'What a bloody roundabout to be on.' He shook his head decisively. 'That won't wear. Iredale said he wasn't Meyrick.'

'No, he didn't,' said McCready softly. 'I can quote his exact words. Iredale said, "He's not Meyrick – not unless Meyrick has had plastic surgery recently."'

Carey thought that out. 'Stop trying to confuse me. That would mean

that the man we had in the hotel in Oslo for three weeks was *not* Meyrick
– that the ringer was the other way round.'

He stopped dead on the pavement. 'Look, George; let's get one thing
quite clear.' He stabbed a finger back at the hotel. 'That man there is *not*
Meyrick. I *know* Meyrick – he fights with his tongue and uses sarcasm as
a weapon, but if you put him in a real fight he'd collapse. Denison is a
quiet-spoken, civil man who, in an emergency, seems to have the instincts
of a born killer. He's the antithesis of Meyrick. Ram that into your mind
and hold on to it fast.'

McCready shrugged. 'It leaves a lot to be explained.'

'It will be explained. I want Giles Denison sorted out once and for all
back in London. I want his life sifted day by day and minute by minute,
if necessary, to find out how he knows that mathematical jargon. And I
want Harding brought here *tout de suite*.'

'He'll like that,' said McCready sardonically. 'I'll pass the word on.'

They walked for another hundred yards and McCready said, 'Denison
is quite a boy. Who else would think of handcuffs as a weapon?' He
chuckled. 'I think he's neither Meyrick nor Denison – I think he's Clark
Kent.'

Carey's jaw dropped. 'And who the blazes is that?'

'Superman,' said McCready blandly.

18

Denison slept, was interviewed by the police, and slept again. He got up
at four, bathed and dressed, and went downstairs. Crossing the lobby he
saw the receptionist stare at him, then turn and say something to the
porter with a smile. Dr. H. F. Meyrick was evidently the hotel celebrity.

He looked into the lounge, saw no one he knew, and then investigated
the bar where he found Diana Hansen sitting at a table and reading a
paperback. She looked up as he stood over her. 'I was wondering when
you'd show.'

'I had to get some sleep. Yesterday was a bit wearing.' He sat down
and picked up the ashtray to inspect its underside.

Diana laughed. 'No bugs – I checked.'

He put it down. 'Where's Lyn?'

'Out.' At his raised eyebrows she elaborated slightly. 'Sightseeing.'

A waiter came up. '*Mitä otatte?*'

'*Olut E, oikaa hyvä,*' said Denison. He looked at Diana. 'And you?'

'Nothing for me,' she said. 'Your Finnish is improving.'

'Only enough to order the necessities of life. Has Carey come to any conclusions about yesterday?'

'Carey isn't here,' she said. 'I'm to tell you to sit tight until he comes back.'

'Where is he?'

'He's gone to Sweden.'

'Sweden!' His eyes were blank. 'Why has he gone there?'

'He didn't tell me.' She stood up and picked up her book. 'Now that I've passed on the word I'll get about my business.' Her lips quirked. 'Don't take any wooden saunas.'

'Never again,' he said fervently. He bit his lip. 'But they might take another crack at me.'

'Not to worry,' she said. 'You're under Ian Armstrong's eye, and he's well named. He's sitting at the bar now. Don't acknowledge him – and don't move so fast he can't keep up with you.'

She went away as the waiter came up with his beer. He drank it moodily and ordered another bottle. Over at the bar Armstrong was making a single beer stretch a long way. Why Sweden? What could possibly have happened there to drag Carey away? No answer came.

He was half-way through the second bottle when Lyn entered the bar. She sat at his table and looked at his beer. 'You look dissipated.'

He grinned at her. 'I feel dissipated. I was up late.'

'So I'm told,' she said unsmilingly. 'I heard a strange story this morning – about you.'

He regarded her warily and decided to riposte. 'And I've heard something pretty odd about you. Why did you quarrel with Diana?'

Pink spots came into her cheeks. 'So she told you.'

'She didn't say anything about it,' said Denison truthfully.

Lyn flared up. 'Then who did if she didn't? We were alone.' She tugged viciously at the strap of her bag and looked down at the table. 'It doesn't feel nice to be ashamed of one's own father. I never really believed everything Mother said about you, but now I can see she was telling the truth.'

'Calm down,' he said. 'Have a drink. What will you have? A Coca-Cola?'

Her chin came up. 'A dry martini.'

He signalled to the waiter, suppressing a smile, and gave the order. When the waiter had gone, she said, 'It was disgusting of you.'

'What's so disgusting about Diana Hansen?'

'You know what I mean. I've heard the jet set gets up to some queer things but, my God, I didn't expect it of you. Not my own father.' Her eyes were unnaturally bright.

'No, I don't know what you mean. What am I supposed to have done?' he asked plaintively.

A hurt look came into her eyes. 'I know you went out with that woman last night because she told me so. And I know how you came back, too. You must have been disgustingly drunk to do that. Did *she* have any clothes on? No wonder they had to send for the police.'

'Oh, my God!' said Denison, appalled. 'Lyn, it wasn't like that.'

'Then why is everyone talking about it? I heard it at breakfast this morning. There were some Americans at the next table – you ought to have heard them. It was . . . dirty!' She broke into tears.

Denison hastily looked about the bar and then put his hand on Lyn's. 'It wasn't like that; I'll tell you.'

So he told her, leaving out everything important which would only complicate the issue. He was interrupted once by the waiter bringing the martini, and then he bore in again to finish his story.

She dabbed at her eyes with a small handkerchief and sniffed. 'A likely tale!'

'If you don't believe me, would you believe the police?' he said exasperatedly. 'They've been on my neck all morning.'

'Then why did Diana tell me you were going out with her?'

'It was the best thing she could have done,' said Denison. 'She didn't want you worried. And about your quarrel – I heard a bit of it on the tape.' He explained about that, and said, 'The police have the tape now.'

Lyn was horrified. 'You mean everyone is listening to that quarrel?'

'Everyone except me,' said Denison drily. 'Have your martini.'

Something else occurred to her. 'But you might have been hurt – he might have *killed* you!'

'But he didn't – and all's well.'

'Who could it have been?'

'I suppose I'm a fairly important man in some respects,' said Denison tiredly. 'I told you yesterday that I don't babble about my work. Some-one wanted information and took direct action.'

She straightened her shoulders and looked at him with shining eyes. 'And didn't get it.'

He brutally chopped the props from under the hero worship. 'As for Diana Hansen, there's nothing in it – not the way you think. But even if there were it's got nothing to do with you. You're behaving more like an affronted wife than a daughter.'

The glow died. Lyn hunched her shoulders a little and looked down at the martini glass. Suddenly she picked it up and drained the contents at a swallow. It took her breath away and she choked a little before putting down the empty glass. Denison grinned. 'Does that make you feel better?'

'I'm sorry,' she said miserably.

'That's all right,' he said. 'No harm done. Let's go for a walk.' He signalled to the waiter and paid the bill and, as he got up from the table, he glanced over at the bar and saw Armstrong doing the same. It was comforting to have a bodyguard.

They left the bar and went into the lobby. As they approached the entrance a porter came in loaded with baggage, and a burly figure followed. 'Hey, Lucy; look who's here,' boomed a voice. 'It's Harry Meyrick.'

'Oh, hell!' said Denison, but there was no escape.

'Who is it?' asked Lyn.

'I'll introduce you,' said Denison grimly.

'Hi, Harry!' shouted Kidder, advancing across the lobby with outstretched hand. 'It's great to see you, it sure is.'

'Hallo, Jack,' said Denison without enthusiasm, and allowed his hand to be pulped.

'It's a small world,' said Kidder predictably. 'I was only saying that to Lucy the other day when we bumped into the Williamsons in Stockholm. You remember the Williamsons?'

'Of course,' said Denison.

'I guess we're all on the same Scandinavian round, eh? I wouldn't be surprised if the Williamsons don't turn up here, too. Wouldn't it be great if they did?'

'Great!' said Denison.

Lucy Kidder popped out from behind her husband. 'Why, Harry, how nice to see you. Did Jack tell you we saw the Williamsons in Stockholm?'

'Yes, he did.'

'It's a small world,' said Lucy Kidder.

'It sure is,' said Jack. 'If the Williamsons get here – and that nice friend of yours, Diana Hansen – we could get down to some poker. That gal is a mean player.'

Lyn said, 'Diana Hansen? Why, she's here.'

Surprise and pleasure beamed from Kidder's face. 'Now, isn't that just great? Maybe I'll be able to win some of my dough back, Lucy.'

'Lose it, more likely,' she said tartly. 'Jack really believes he can play poker.'

'Now then, Momma,' he said good-humouredly. 'Don't knock the old man.' He looked down at Lyn. 'And who's the little lady?'

'Excuse me,' said Denison. 'Jack Kidder – my daughter, Lyn – Lucy Kidder.'

They shook hands and Kidder said, 'You didn't tell me you had a daughter, Harry. You certainly didn't tell me you had a beautiful daughter. Where you been hiding her?'

'Lyn's been at University,' said Denison. 'She's now on vacation.'

Lucy said, 'I don't want to break things up, Jack, but I guess we gotta register. The desk clerk's waiting.'

'Sure,' said Kidder. 'I'll be seeing you around, Harry. Tell Diana to break out that deck of cards – we'll be playing poker.'

'I'll do that,' said Denison and, taking Lyn by the arm, he steered her out of the hotel. Under his breath he said, 'Over my dead body.'

'Who was that?' asked Lyn.

'The biggest bore from the North American continent,' said Denison. 'With his long-suffering wife.'

19

Carey and McCready were being violently seasick. They clung to the rail of the small boat as it pitched in the summer gale which had blown up from the south and whistled up the narrow channel between the Swedish mainland and the island of Öland. There was but one significant difference between them – while Carey thought he was dying McCready *knew* he was dying.

They both felt better when they set foot ashore at Borgholm. There a car awaited them, and a police officer who introduced himself with a jerky bow as 'Hoglund, Olof.'

'I'm Carey and this is McCready.' The wind blew off the sea and ruffled his short grey hair. 'Shall we get on with it?'

'Certainly. This way.' As Hoglund ushered them to the car he said, 'Your Mr. Thornton arrived an hour ago.'

Carey stopped dead in his tracks. 'Has he, indeed?' He glanced sideways at McCready, and muttered, 'What the hell does he want?'

'He won't tell us,' prophesied McCready.

They were silent as they drove through the streets of Borgholm. It was not the time yet for talk; that would come later after they had seen what they had come to see. Carey's mind was busy with speculations arising from the presence of Thornton, and even if he wanted to discuss it with McCready he could not do so in the presence of Hoglund.

The car pulled up in front of a two-storey building and they went inside, Hoglund leading the way. He took them into a back room where there was a trestle table set up. On the table was a long shape covered with a white cloth. Behind the table stood a short man with a neat vandyke beard, who wore a white coat. Hoglund introduced him as Dr. Carlson. 'You already know Mr. Thornton.'

Thornton was a tall, dark man of cadaverous features, smooth unlined skin and indecipherable expression. He was a young-looking sixty or an aged forty – it was hard to determine which and Thornton was not going to tell anybody. It was not his habit to tell anyone anything that did not concern him and he was chary of doing even that. He could have been Carey's boss but he was not; Carey was proud and pleased to be in another department.

He lifted yellowed, dyspeptic eyes as Carey and McCready entered the room. Carey nodded to him curtly, and turned to Carlson. 'Good afternoon, Doctor,' he said in a weary voice. He was very tired. 'May I see it?'

Carlson nodded without speaking and drew back the cloth. Carey looked down with an expressionless face and motioned for the cloth to be drawn back farther. 'This is how he was found?'

'The body has been cleaned externally,' said Carlson. 'It was covered with oil. And the manacles have been removed, of course.'

Carey nodded. 'Of course. There was no clothing?'

'The man was naked.'

McCready looked at Carey and raised his eyebrows. 'The same as . . .'

Carey was unaccountably clumsy. He turned and trod heavily on McCready's foot. 'Sorry, George.' He turned to Carlson. 'What was the cause of death, Doctor?'

Carlson frowned. 'That will have to await the autopsy,' he said cautiously. 'At the moment it is a question of whether he was drowned or poisoned.'

Thornton stepped forward. 'Did you say poisoned?' Carey analysed the tone of voice. In spite of Thornton's habitual flatness of expression he thought he detected a note of genuine surprise.

'I'll show you,' said Carlson. He opened the jaws of the corpse and took a long spatula and thrust it down the throat. McCready winced and turned away. Carlson withdrew the spatula and held it out. 'A scraping from the inside of the throat.'

Carey inspected the blackened end of the spatula. 'Oil?'

When Carlson nodded Thornton said, 'I don't think it really matters if he drowned in oil or if it poisoned him.' His attitude was relaxed.

'I agree,' said Hoglund. 'Do you make the identification, Mr. Carey?'

Carey hesitated. 'At this moment – no.' He nodded at Thornton. 'What about you?'

'I've never seen the man before in my life,' said Thornton.

A grim expression settled on Carey's face. 'The body will have to be . . . preserved. Do you have facilities?'

'Not on Oland,' said Carlson.

'We can take it to the mainland as soon as Dr. Carlson has completed the autopsy,' said Hoglund.

'No,' said Carey forcibly. 'I need a positive identification before the body is touched. That means the body must go to England or someone must come to Sweden. In any case, I want one of our own pathologists to assist at the autopsy.'

'This comes within our jurisdiction,' said Hoglund sharply.

Carey rubbed his eyes tiredly; the inside of his eyelids seemed to be covered in sand. This would have to be handled carefully considering the Swedish tradition of neutrality. He said slowly, 'As far as we are concerned this has now become a matter of State. I am going to push the question upstairs, and I suggest you also consult your superiors. Let our masters argue the question of jurisdiction, my friend; it will be safer for both of us.' As Hoglund considered the suggestion Carey added, 'In any case, the incident took place in international waters.'

'Perhaps that would be best,' said Hoglund. His manner was stiff. 'I will do as you suggest. Would you like to see the manacles?' When Carey nodded he strode to a shelf and took down a pair of handcuffs.

Carey examined them. 'British,' he commented. He handed them to Thornton. 'Wouldn't you think so?'

Thornton shrugged. 'It means little.' He turned to Hoglund. 'Is it established he did not come from the tanker?'

'The crew of the tanker are all accounted for,' said Hoglund. 'One man was killed but the body was recovered.' Carlson was replacing the sheet over the body as Hoglund gestured at it. 'This man probably came from the other boat. The captain of the tanker says it must have been running without lights.'

'He would say that,' said Carey cynically. 'He could be right, though. It has not been identified yet?'

'Not yet. No boat has been reported missing; no insurance claim has been made. We are making inquiries, naturally.' Hoglund frowned. 'Apart from the body there is the matter of the oil. It will cost a lot to clean the coasts of Gotland and someone must pay.'

'That's something I don't understand,' said McCready. 'If the oil is drifting on to Gotland how is it that the body turned up here on Öland? They are a long way apart.'

'The body was taken from the sea south of Gotland,' said Hoglund. 'But the ship was coming here.'

Carey cleared his throat. 'What have you got to go on in your inquiries?'

'Not a great deal. The captain of the tanker was not on the bridge at the time, and the boat sank within minutes. The captain estimated it as something between three hundred and four hundred tons. He derives this figure from the damage done to the bows of the tanker and its speed at the time of impact.'

'A small coaster,' said Carey thoughtfully. 'Or a biggish fisherman.'

Hoglund shrugged. 'We will soon find out.'

I wouldn't hold your breath, my friend, thought Carey. He turned to Carlson. 'There is no reflection on your ability as a pathologist, Dr. Carlson. I hope you understand that. Will you begin preparations for the preservation of the body?'

Carlson looked warily at Hoglund, who nodded. 'I understand. I will do as you ask.'

'Then there's nothing more we can do here,' said Carey. 'Unless Mr. Thornton has anything further to add.'

'Nothing,' said Thornton. 'I'll leave the details of the identification to you.'

They left the room. At the entrance of the building Carey paused to button up his coat, and turned to Thornton. 'Your arrival was unexpected. What brought you here?'

'I happened to be at the Embassy in Stockholm,' said Thornton easily. 'About another matter, of course. They're a bit short-handed so when this thing blew up I volunteered to come here and look after the British interest.'

Carey turned up his collar. 'How did you know there *was* a British interest?' he asked blandly.

Thornton was equally bland. 'The handcuffs, of course.' He nodded back towards the room they had come from. 'Who was he?'

'We'll know that when he's been identified.'

Thornton smiled. 'Your department has a vested interest in mysteries, I know – but you shouldn't let it become an obsession.' He pointed. 'Hoglund is waiting for you at the car.'

'Aren't you coming?'

'I came by helicopter,' said Thornton. 'Sorry I can't offer you a lift back, but I don't know where you came from, do I?' His smile was malicious.

Carey grunted and walked towards the car. Again there was silence in the car because Hoglund was there but, as they drew up to the quay side, Carey said abruptly, 'Was the British Embassy informed of the country of origin of those handcuffs?'

Hoglund furrowed his brow. 'I don't think so. Not by me.'

'I see. Thank you.'

The wind had moderated and the passage back to the mainland of Sweden was easier. Carey and McCready stayed on deck where it was possible to talk with some privacy. 'I didn't expect to see Thornton,' said McCready. 'What's he up to?'

'I don't know,' said Carey broodingly. 'He tried to spin me a yarn. Can you imagine a Whitehall mandarin like Thornton volunteering for an errand boy's job which any Embassy whippersnapper could do? The mind boggles.' He thumped the rail with his fist. 'Damn these interdepartmental rivalries! We're all supposed to be on the same side, but I spend more time guarding my back against people like Thornton than I do on my job.'

'Do you suppose he knows about the switch on Meyrick?'

'I don't know. Accordingly to what he said back there he doesn't even know Meyrick.' Carey looked down at the grey sea. 'Somebody's luck ran out.'

'Meyrick's certainly did.'

'I was thinking of the people who snatched him. They got him to Copenhagen and put him on a boat to take him . . . where? And the boat was run down by a tanker travelling westwards.'

'So it was probably going east,' said McCready. 'Suggestive – to say the least.'

'Let's not jump to any fast conclusions,' said Carey irritably.

'I agree,' said McCready. 'Especially let's not jump to the conclusion that this oil-poisoned stiff is Meyrick. We've been had before.'

Carey gave him a withering look, and said abruptly, 'I want Iredale present at the autopsy to check for any signs of plastic surgery. I want the fingerprints of the corpse taken and a check made at Meyrick's home for matching prints. For legal identification I suggest one of Meyrick's ex-wives.'

'What's wrong with his daughter?'

'I'm trying to work that one out,' said Carey with a sigh. 'If I can do it before we get to the plane then maybe I can get some sleep on the flight back to Helsinki.' He did not sound too sanguine.

Carey sat in the Café Hildén on Aleksanterinkatu and sank a beer while waiting for Harding. After twelve hours' sleep he felt refreshed and no longer as depressed as he had been. He knew his depression had been caused by tiredness. All the same, rested and clear-headed though he was, the coming decision was not going to be easy to make.

He saw Harding come around the corner so he held up his hand. When Harding came over, he asked, 'You've seen Denison?' On Harding's nod, he said, 'Have a beer.'

Harding sat down. 'That'll be welcome. I didn't think it got as hot as this in the frozen north.'

Carey went to the counter and returned with two more beers. 'What's the verdict?'

Harding had his head on one side, apparently watching the foam rise in his glass. 'Oddly enough, he's improved since I last saw him. He's better integrated. What are his drinking habits like now?'

Carey tapped the side of his glass. 'He just has the odd beer.'

'In an odd sort of way this experience might have been therapeutic for him.' Harding smiled wryly. 'Although I wouldn't recommend it as a well-judged treatment. Now that we know more of his past history I'm better equipped to assess his present state.' He took a notebook from his pocket. 'Denison was something of a car enthusiast and ran a Lotus Elan. Three years ago he was driving with his wife, there was an accident for which he was partly – and only partly – to blame, and his wife was killed. They had been married eighteen months. She was pregnant at the time.'

'That's bad,' said Carey.

'He took *all* the blame on himself,' said Harding. 'And one thing led to another. He began to drink heavily and was on the verge of alcoholism when he lost his job for incompetence.'

'That baffles me,' said Carey. 'Because he's bloody competent at what he's doing now.' He grinned. 'I'm thinking of offering him a permanent job.'

Harding sampled his beer. 'He can't remember his wife in any meaningful way because of what's been done to him. He remembers her and he remembers her death but it's as though it happened to someone else. Of course, that's just as it should be after three years. In a normal person the sharpness of grief is blunted by the passage of time and, in that respect, Denison is now normal.'

'I'm glad to hear it,' said Carey.

Harding gave him a sharp look. He mistrusted Carey's reasons for being glad. He said, 'Consequently he has lost his irrational guilt feelings and has no need to anaesthetise himself with booze. Hence the return to competency. I rather think that, with a little expert treatment, he can be made into a much better man than he was immediately prior to his kidnapping.'

'How long would that take?'

'Three to six months – that's just a guess.'

Carey shook his head. 'Too long; I want him now. Is he fit to carry on?'

Harding pondered for a moment. 'You know, I think he's actually enjoying himself right now. He likes the cut and thrust of this business – the opportunity to exercise his wits seems to be good for him.'

'So he's fit,' said Carey in satisfaction.

'I didn't say that,' said Harding testily. 'I'm not thinking of your damned operation – I'm thinking of Denison.' He thought for a while. 'The present pressures don't seem to worry him. I'd say the only danger is if his past is revealed to him in a traumatic manner.'

'That won't happen,' said Carey definitely. 'Not where I'm sending him.'

'All right,' said Harding. 'Then he's as fit as a man in his position can be – which isn't saying a hell of a lot.'

'Which brings me to another problem,' said Carey. 'Meyrick is dead.' He inspected that statement, found it wanting, and amended it. 'Probably dead. We have a body but once bitten, twice shy.'

'I see your difficulty,' said Harding with a half smile.

'I can't tell the girl her father's dead – not with Denison around. She'd blow up like a volcano and bang goes his cover as Meyrick – and I need him as Meyrick. The point is – do I tell Denison?'

'I wouldn't,' said Harding. 'Handling Lyn Meyrick is tricky enough for him as it is. If he knows her father is dead it might put him into a moral dilemma, assuming he's a moral man which I think he is.' He sighed. 'God knows we're not.'

'We represent the higher morality,' said Carey sardonically. 'The greatest good for the greatest number. I've always been a Benthamite at heart; it's the only way to keep my job bearable.' He drained his glass. 'That's it, then. Where is Denison now?'

'Sightseeing,' said Harding. 'He took his daughter to see the Sibelius Memorial.'

21

'It looks like an organ,' said Lyn judiciously. 'If it had a keyboard you could play it. A bit funny, that, come to think of it. Sibelius was an orchestra man, wasn't he?'

'I think so,' said Denison. He consulted his guide book. 'It weighs twenty-eight tons and was made by a woman. I suppose you could call it an early example of Women's Lib – the hand that rocks the cradle can also wield the welding torch. Let's sit and watch the passing parade.'

They sat on a bench and watched a tour group debark from a bus; transatlantic accents twanged the air. Denison saw Armstrong stroll along the path below the monument, then he lifted his eyes to look at the sea. The white sails of yachts dotted the deep blue which echoed the lighter blue of the cloudless sky. He wondered when Carey was going to make his move.

Lyn sighed comfortably. 'Isn't this beautiful? I didn't think Finland would be like this – it's more like the Mediterranean, like Ibiza. Remember when we went there?'

'Mmm,' said Denison neutrally.

Lyn laughed. 'That funny little hotel where there was no hot water and you couldn't have a hot bath. I've never heard you complain so angrily. What was the name of the owner – that little fat man?'

'I don't remember,' said Denison. That was safe enough; a man was not expected to remember every casual encounter.

'And then the seafood was bad and they took you off to hospital and pumped out your stomach.'

'I always had a delicate stomach,' said Denison. He pointed out to sea. 'I think they're racing out there.' He wanted to divert her mind to the present.

'Yes, they are,' she said. 'That reminds me – I suppose *Hesperia* is still laid up if you've not been sailing her this summer. The reason I ask is that if you're not going to sail her I'd like to. I sort of half promised Janice and Kitty – friends of mine – that we'd sail together.'

Denison was silent, not knowing what to say.

Lyn said, 'Don't be a spoilsport. Billy Brooks will put her in the water and I can rig her myself.'

'All right,' he said. 'But don't get into trouble. English waters aren't as calm as the Baltic. When are you intending going back?'

'I haven't made up my mind yet. I have to write to the girls and make plans, then I'll drop a line to Billy at the yard. You were going to get a new suit of sails two years ago – did you?'

'Yes.' He stood up quickly. 'Let's press on – it's quite late and I have to see someone at the hotel.'

'All very mysterious,' she said. 'What's the sudden appointment?' She grinned at him. 'It sounds rather like Wilde's excuse – "I must decline your invitation owing to a subsequent engagement."'

Had he been as transparent as that? He forced a smile, and said, 'It's just that I promised to have a drink before dinner with the Kidders, that's all.'

'Oh,' she said lightly. 'Then let's go. We mustn't keep the Kidders waiting.'

As they walked away Denison saw Armstrong rise from his bench and follow them. *What's the use of a bodyguard?* he thought. *The enemy is by my side and stabs with a sharp tongue.* More and more he was conscious of the injustice of the fraud he was perpetrating on Lyn Meyrick and he determined to see Carey and ask him to find a way of separation.

They got back to the hotel, and Lyn said, 'Do you mind if I come to your room?' She looked about the hotel lobby. 'There's something I want to talk to you about.'

'What?'

She pointed to the hotel entrance. 'Him, for one thing.' Denison looked around and saw Armstrong just coming in. 'He's been following us for the last two days.'

'He's supposed to,' said Denison. 'You might call him a bodyguard. If I go into the sauna again – which God forbid – he'll be in there with me.'

She said quietly, 'I think you'd better tell me what it's all about. There's a lot you're keeping from me. In your room?'

'All right,' he said resignedly. They went up in the lift with three other people and Denison used the time to sort out what he was going to tell her – no lies but withholding most of the truth. He decided that a lot could be hidden behind the Official Secrets Act.

He unlocked the door and followed her in. 'What do you want to know, Lyn?'

'There's a big secret, isn't there?' she sat on the bed.

'Which I can't tell,' he answered. 'It's part of my work. Somebody had a go at me the other day so the Embassy sent that young fellow – he's called Armstrong, incidentally – to look after me. That's all.'

'No more?'

'Nothing you're entitled to know, Lyn. I'm sorry.' He spread his hands. 'I'm bound by the Official Secrets Act.'

Her face was drawn. 'I'm sorry, too, because it isn't enough.'

'My, God, I *can't* tell you anything more. If I tattle about what I'm doing they'll assume I'm a bad security risk.' He laughed shortly. 'I'd never be allowed into my own factories – and that's the best that could happen. At the worst I could go to prison.' He sat on the bed next to her. 'It isn't that I don't trust you, Lyn; it's that if you knew what I know you'd be vulnerable. I don't want to put you in danger.'

She was silent for a while. Her face was troubled and her fingers plucked at the coverlet. She moistened her lips. 'I've been worried.'

'I know you have, but there's nothing to worry about. It's over, and Armstrong will see that it doesn't happen again.'

'It's not that I've been worrying about.'

'What, then?'

'Me,' she said. 'And you – principally you. There's something wrong somewhere.'

Denison felt his stomach churn. He said, 'There's nothing wrong with me. It's your imagination.'

It was as though she had not heard him. 'Nothing big – the big things were all right. It's the little things. Thread-Bear, for instance; how could you have forgotten Thread-Bear? And then there are the Kidders.'

'What about the Kidders?'

'Two years ago you'd have cut a man like that down to size in five words.' She looked at him steadily. 'You've changed. You've changed too much.'

'For the better, I hope,' said Denison, fighting a valiant rearguard action.

'I'd say so.' There was a slight waver in her voice. 'You're not nearly as hard to get on with.'

'I'm sorry if I gave you a bad time in the past,' said Denison soberly. 'As I said before: perhaps as I grow older I grow wiser.'

'It confused me,' she said. 'And I'm no different from anyone else; I don't like being confused. And I had a crazy idea – it was so crazy I thought I must be losing my mind.'

Denison opened his mouth but she covered it with her hand. 'No, don't speak. Let me sort it out myself. I don't want to be confused again.'

She took her hand away, and Denison said quietly, 'Go on, Lyn.'

'I found myself having strange thoughts about you.' She swallowed. 'The kind of thoughts a girl shouldn't have about her own father, and I felt ashamed. You were so *different*, you see; not like my father at all – and the change was too much. I tried to see how you'd changed and the only conclusion I could come to was that suddenly you'd become human.'

'Thanks,' said Denison.

'There's a bit of my old daddy come back,' she said vehemently. 'Oh, you could use irony and sarcasm like knife blades.'

'No irony intended,' said Denison sincerely.

'Then I saw the other things like Thread-Bear and the Kidders and the fact that you've stopped smoking. Look at your hands now – no nicotine at all. Then I got this wild idea.'

Denison stood up. 'Lyn, I think we'd better stop this now,' he said coldly. 'You're becoming hysterical.'

'No, we won't stop,' she shouted, and stood to face him. 'You knew all the works of Sibelius backwards and sideways, and why wouldn't you? You're a Finn! But this morning you only *thought* his work was for the orchestra. And I don't know about you – we've been parted for many years – but I've never been to Ibiza in my life and, to the best of my knowledge, you've never been to hospital with food poisoning.'

Denison was appalled. 'Lyn!'

She was merciless. 'There is no yacht called *Hesperia*. You always said that sailing is the most inefficient means of locomotion known to man, and everyone knows that efficiency is your god. And Billy Brooks doesn't exist – I invented him. And you said you'd bought a suit of sails for a non-existent yacht.'

Her face was white and her eyes brimmed with tears and Denison knew she was deathly frightened. 'You *can't* be my father,' she whispered. 'You're *not* my father. *Who are you?*'

22

'Where the hell is Denison?' said Carey irritably.

McCready was soothing. 'He'll be along. He's not very late.'

Carey was on edge. 'He could have been jumped again.'

'It's you that's jumpy. Armstrong's looking after him.'

Carey said nothing. He bent his head to re-read the lengthy cable. Presently he said, 'Well, that's cleared up. It was a hell of a problem while it lasted.'

'What was?' asked Harding interestedly.

'When Denison was lifted from the sauna he came out with a string of mathematical stuff to confuse the opposition. He didn't know what it meant himself but it was the jargon Meyrick might have used.' He tossed the cable on to the table. 'We couldn't see how Denison could possibly have known it.'

Harding said, 'It must have come out of his past somewhere.'

'Precisely,' said Carey. 'But he didn't have that kind of past.'

'Of course not.' Harding wrinkled his brow. 'He was a film director.'

'Of a special kind,' said McCready. 'He made documentaries. We found he'd done a series of educational films on mathematics for the public relations department of one of the big computer firms. I suppose a film director must have a working knowledge of his subject although, judging by some of the movies I've seen, you wouldn't think so. Anyway, somebody talked to the computer people and we find that not only did he have a ready grasp but a keen interest. The films were largely in cartoon style and the subject was probability theory. He knew the jargon, all right.'

'But it gave me a shudder at the time,' said Carey. 'Mrs. Hansen, ring the hotel and find what's keeping Denison.'

Diana Hansen got up and crossed the room. She was about to pick up the telephone when it rang shrilly. She put it to her ear, then beckoned to Carey. 'For you – it's Armstrong.'

Carey took the telephone. 'Ian, what's the hold-up?'

'I was in my room,' said Armstrong. 'I had my door open so I could see the door of Denison's room. About twenty minutes ago Miss Meyrick busted out of there fast so I went into the corridor to find what was happening. She grabbed me and said Denison had had some kind of attack. I went into the room and found him on the floor, out cold. He came round about five minutes ago.'

'Is he all right now?'

'He says he is.'

'Then you'd better bring him along here,' said Carey. 'I'll have Harding have a look at him.'

There was a pause. 'Miss Meyrick says she's coming, too.'

'Nothing doing,' said Carey. 'Ditch her.'

'I don't think you understand,' said Armstrong. 'When she spoke to me in the corridor she said *Denison* had had an attack – not Meyrick.'

Carey's eyebrows crawled up his forehead. 'She *knows*?'

'Apparently so.'

'Bring her along and don't take your eyes off the pair of them. And be discreet.' He put down the telephone. 'The girl has caught on – and your patient is coming home to roost, Harding. He's had another of his thingummy attacks.'

'A fugue,' said Harding. 'It must have been the Meyrick girl.'

'She called him Denison,' said Carey flatly.

They waited for twenty minutes in silence. Carey produced his pipe and filled it, and then smoked jerkily. Harding stretched out his long legs and contemplated the tips of his shoes with an all-consuming interest. His forehead was creased into a frown. Diana Hansen smoked cigarettes one after the other, stubbing each out half-way down its length. McCready paced back and forward, wearing a groove in the carpet.

There was a tap at the door and everyone jerked to attention. McCready opened it, letting in Lyn and Denison, with Armstrong close behind. Carey stared at Denison. 'Harding would like a word with you in the other room. Do you mind?'

'No,' said Denison quietly, and followed Harding.

When the door closed behind them Carey stood up and said to Lyn, 'Miss Meyrick, my name is Carey and I'm from the British Embassy here. This is Mr. McCready. Mrs. Hansen you already know, and you've already met Mr. Armstrong.'

Lyn Meyrick's face was pale but two pink spots deepened in her cheeks when she saw Diana Hansen. Then she flung out her arm at the door through which Denison had gone. 'Who is that man? And where is my father?'

'Please sit down,' said Carey, and nodded to McCready who brought up a chair.

'I don't understand,' said Lyn. 'He said his name was Denison and he told me an unbelievable story . . .'

'. . . which happens to be true,' said Carey. 'I wish it wasn't so.'

Lyn's voice rose. 'Then what's happened to my father?'

Carey wagged his eyebrows at Diana Hansen who stood up and went close to Lyn. He said, 'Miss Meyrick, I'm sorry to tell you this . . .'

'He's dead, isn't he?'

Carey nodded. 'We believe it to be an accident. His body was recovered from the Baltic three days ago. There had been a collision between an oil tanker and another ship.'

'Then what this man, Denison, said is correct?'

'What did he tell you?'

They listened as Lyn spoke and finally Carey nodded. 'He seems to have given you all that's relevant.' He noted that Denison had not told her of the contents of Merikken's papers; he had just said they were important. 'I'm sorry about your father.'

'Yes,' she said coldly. 'I suppose you are.'

Carey thought that she found no difficulty in holding back her grief but that might be understandable in the circumstances. He said deliberately, 'Miss Meyrick; after Denison had told you his story did you try to probe into his past?'

'Why, yes; I wanted to know who he was – who he is.'

'You must never do that again,' said Carey solemnly. 'It could be most dangerous for him.'

She flared up. 'If only a quarter of what he told me is true, what you're doing to that man is despicable. He ought to have psychiatric treatment.'

'He's getting that now,' said Carey. 'Dr. Harding is a psychiatrist. How did Denison give himself away?' She told him and he nodded. 'We couldn't hope to get away with it for ever,' he said philosophically. 'But I did hope for another day. I was going to separate you tomorrow.'

'My God!' she said. 'Who the hell do you think you are? We're not chess pieces.'

'Denison is a volunteer,' said Carey. 'It's his own choice.'

'Some choice!' she said cuttingly.

The door behind Carey opened. He swung around in his chair and saw Harding alone. 'Ian, go and sit with Denison.'

'It won't be necessary,' said Harding. 'He'll be out in a minute. I've just given him something to think about.'

'How is he?'

'He'll be all right.'

'Does he remember spilling the beans to Miss Meyrick?'

'Oh, yes,' said Harding. 'It's just that he can't remember what Miss Meyrick was asking him just before he passed out.' He looked at Lyn with interest. 'What was it?'

'I wanted to know who he was,' Lyn said.

He shook his head. 'Don't try that again. I think I'll have to have a talk with you, young lady.'

'Don't bother,' said Carey grimly. 'She's going back to England.'

Lyn inspected Harding with a cold eye. 'Are you a doctor?'

Harding paused as he lit a cigarette. 'Among other things.'

'I think you must have been confused when you took the oath,' she said. 'You took the hypocritic oath instead of the Hippocratic oath.' Harding coloured but before he could answer she had rounded on Carey. 'As for going to England, I most certainly am. A lot of people will be very interested in what I have to tell them.'

'Oh, I wouldn't try that,' said Carey quietly.

'Try to stop me,' she challenged.

Carey leaned back in his chair and glanced at McCready. 'It looks as though we'll have to keep her here, George. Arrange the necessary – booking her out of the hotel and so on.'

'And then what?' she asked. 'You can't keep me here for ever. I'll be back in England some time and I'll make sure the story gets around about what's been happening to this man. It will make interesting reading.'

McCready smiled. 'The papers won't print it. There's a thing called a "D" notice.'

She looked at him contemptuously. 'Do you think twenty universities full of students will take any account of your stupid "D" notices?' she asked in scorn.

'My God!' said McCready. 'She's right. You know what students are like.'

'So what are you going to do?' she asked interestedly. 'Kill me?'

'They're going to do nothing,' said Denison from behind Carey. He closed the door behind him. 'Or they'll have to get themselves another boy.'

Carey did not turn round. He merely said, 'Draw up a chair, Denison. We have a problem to solve.'

Denison sat next to Carey. 'Coercion won't solve it.'

'So I'm finding out,' said Carey caustically. 'So maybe we'll try persuasion. What exactly is it you want, Miss Meyrick?'

She was suddenly nervous. 'I want you to stop whatever it is you're doing to . . . to him.' Her hand trembled as she pointed at Denison.

'We're not doing anything to him. He's a volunteer – and he'll confirm it.'

She flared. 'How can he be a volunteer when he doesn't know who he is? Any court of law would toss out that argument.'

'Careful,' said Harding suddenly, watching Denison.

'He needs help,' she pleaded.

'He's getting it,' said Carey, and indicated Harding.

'You already know what I think of that.'

'Tell me something,' said Carey. 'Why are you so agitated about Denison? He is, after all, a stranger.'

She looked down at the table. 'Not any more,' she said in a low voice. She raised her head and regarded Carey with clear eyes. 'And aren't we supposed to care for strangers? Have you never heard of the parable of the Good Samaritan, Mr. Carey?'

Carey sighed, and said dispiritedly, 'See what you can do, Giles.'

Denison opened his mouth and then closed it again. It was the first time Carey had addressed him by his Christian name, as he normally did with Armstrong and McCready. Was he now accepted as a member of the team, or was it just that the cunning old devil had decided to use psychology?

He looked across the table at the girl. 'I know what I'm doing, Lyn – and this operation is very important.'

'How can you know what you're doing?' she demanded. 'You're not competent to judge.'

'That's just what he is,' interjected Carey. 'Sorry, Giles; carry on.'

'That's not the point,' said Denison. 'It wasn't of my own free will that I was pitched into the middle of all this, but now that I'm in it I agree with Carey. If the operation is to be a success then I must continue to be

Meyrick – to be your father. And that I'm going to do, regardless of what you think. I appreciate your concern, but this is too important for considerations like that.'

She was silent, biting her lip. She said, 'All right, Har . . . Giles. But on one condition.'

'What's that?'

'That I come with you – as Lyn Meyrick with her father.' There was a dead silence around the table. 'Well, isn't that what you wanted – for the masquerade to go on? You've used me unknowingly – now you can use me knowingly.'

Carey said softly, 'It might be dangerous.'

'So is having a father like Harry Meyrick,' she said bitterly. 'But that's my condition – take it or leave it.'

'Taken,' said Carey promptly.

'No!' said Denison simultaneously.

They stopped and looked at each other. 'She's stubborn,' said Carey. 'And she's got us by the short hairs. It's the answer.'

'Are you sure?' asked Denison. He might have been replying to Carey but he looked at Lyn.

'I'm sure,' she said.

'Well, that's it,' said Carey briskly. 'Now we can get on with the planning. Thank you, Dr. Harding; I don't think we'll need you on this. I'll keep in touch with you.'

Harding stood up and nodded. He was walking to the door when Lyn said, 'No!' Her voice was sharp.

Harding stopped. 'No *what?*' said Carey exasperatedly.

'Dr. Harding stays with Giles,' she said. 'The three of us stay together.'

'For Christ's sake!' said Carey, and a suppressed snort came from McCready.

Harding had a white smile. 'My dear Miss Meyrick; I'm hardly . . . I'm no . . . no . . .'

'No gunman, like the rest of them probably are? Well, let me tell you something. You won't be worth a damn as a psychiatrist unless you stay with your patient.'

Harding flushed again. Carey said, 'Impossible!'

'What's so impossible about it?' Lyn looked at Harding speculatively. 'But I'm willing to leave it to the doctor – and his conscience, if he has one. What about it, Dr. Harding?'

Harding rubbed his lean jaw. 'Insofar as it will help Denison I'm willing to stay. But I warn you – I'm no man of action.'

'That's it, then,' said Lyn, parodying Carey.

Carey looked at her helplessly, and McCready said, 'It might not be a bad idea if the doctor is willing, as he seems to be.'

Carey gave up. 'Sit down, Harding,' he said ungraciously.

As he picked up his briefcase Denison murmured, 'You did say by the short hairs, didn't you?'

Carey ignored him and opened the briefcase. 'I have reason to believe that quite a lot of people are interested in the movements of Dr. Meyrick. We're going to give them some movements to watch.'

He spread out a large map of Finland. 'George will fly to Ivalo in Northern Lapland – ' his finger stabbed down – 'here. That's as far north as you can fly in Finland. There'll be a car waiting and he'll drive still farther north to this place up by the Norwegian border – *Kevon Tutkimusasema* – that's a station for the exploration of the Kevo Nature Preserve, the jumping off place, as you might call it.'

He looked up at McCready. 'Your job is to cover the party from the outside. You'll inspect Kevo Camp, make sure it's clean – and I don't mean in the hygienic sense – and you'll keep an eye on the party all the time it's up there. But you won't acknowledge it – you'll be a stranger. Understand?'

'Got it,' said McCready.

'Denison and Mrs. Hansen – and now, of course, Miss Meyrick and Dr. Harding – will travel by car from Helsinki. You will leave early tomorrow and it will take you two days to get to the camp at Kevo. George will already be there but you *don't* recognise him. He's your trump card should you get into trouble.' Carey's finger moved slightly south. 'You will then explore the Kevo Nature Park. It's rough country and you'll need packs and tents.' He wagged a finger at McCready. 'We'll need extra gear; see to it, George.'

'What's the point of all this?' asked Denison.

Carey straightened. 'From my reading of Meyrick's dossier and from what I know of his character he never did take an interest in natural history. Is that correct, Miss Meyrick?'

'He was a pure technologist,' she said. 'If he ever thought of natural history – which I doubt – it would be with contempt.'

'As I thought,' said Carey. 'So if Meyrick becomes interested now it will be out of character. The people who are watching him – as I am certain they are – will be mystified and will suspect an ulterior motive, which I will be careful to provide.' He tapped Denison's arm. 'You'll take some simple instruments – a theodolite and so on – and you'll act out a charade as though you're looking for something. Got the idea?'

'A red herring,' said Denison.

'Right. You'll spend three days at Kevo and then you'll move south to another Nature Park at Sompio. There you will put on the same act until you're recalled.'

'How will that be done?' asked McCready.

'There's a little village called Vuotso just outside. I'll send you a telegram to *poste restante* – "Come home, all is forgiven." It would be useful to have webbed feet at Sompio – it's very marshy.'

'Then there'll be wildfowl,' said Harding with sudden enthusiasm.

'Very likely,' said Carey uninterestedly.

'Let me get this straight,' said Denison. 'Meyrick is supposed to be looking for something – let's say buried – in a Nature Park, but he doesn't know which one. And all he has to go on are landmarks, hence the theodolite for measuring angles.'

'Just like in a treasure hunt,' said Lyn.

'Precisely,' said Carey. 'But the treasure doesn't exist – at least, not up there. I've even got a map for you. It's as phoney as hell but very impressive.'

Denison said, 'And what will you be doing while we're wandering all over the Arctic?'

Carey grinned. 'Young Ian and I will nip into Svetogorsk to dig up the loot while, hopefully, all eyes are on you.' He turned to Mrs. Hansen. 'You're very quiet.'

She shrugged. 'What's there to say?'

'You'll be bodyguarding this lot from the inside. I had hoped you'd have but one person to worry about but, as you see, there are now three. Can you manage?'

'If they'll do as they're told.'

'They'd better,' said Carey. 'I'll give you something a bit bigger than the popgun you so incautiously let Denison see.' He looked about. 'Can anyone else here shoot?'

'I'm not bad with a shotgun,' said Harding.

'I doubt if a shotgun in a Nature Preserve would be appreciated,' said Carey ironically. 'But at least you'll know one end of a gun from the other. I'll let you have a pistol. What about you, Giles?'

Denison shrugged. 'I suppose I can pull the trigger and make the thing go bang.'

'That might be all that's needed.' Carey looked at Lyn, appeared to be about to say something, and changed his mind.

'Are you expecting shooting?' asked Harding. He looked worried.

'Let me put it this way,' said Carey. 'I don't know if there'll be shooting or not, but if there is, I hope you'll be on the receiving end and not me, because that's the object of this bloody exercise.' He put the map back into his briefcase. 'That's all. Early start tomorrow. George, I'd like a word with you before you go.'

The group at the table broke up. Denison went across to Lyn. 'Harding told me about your father. I'm sorry.'

'No need,' she said. 'I ought to feel sorry, too, but I can't.' She looked up at him. 'Carey said you are a stranger, but it's my father who was the stranger. I hadn't seen him for two years and when I thought I'd found him again, and he was different and nicer, I hadn't found him at all. So then I lost him again and it made no difference, after all. Don't you see what I mean?'

Denison followed this incoherent speech, and said, 'I think so.' He took her by the shoulders. 'I don't think you should come on this jaunt, Lyn.'

Her chin came up. 'I'm coming.'

He sighed. 'I hope you know what you've got yourself into.'

Carey filled his pipe. 'What do you think, George?'

'The girl's a bit of a handful.'

'Yes. Look after them as best you can.'

McCready leaned forward. 'It's you I'm worried about. I've been thinking about Meyrick. If the people who snatched him were the Russkies, and if he talked, you're in dead trouble. You're likely to find a reception committee awaiting you in Svetogorsk.'

Carey nodded. 'It's a calculated risk. There were no signs of physical coercion on Meyrick's body – burn marks or anything like that – and I doubt if he'd talk voluntarily. I don't think they had time to make him talk; they were too busy smuggling him around the Baltic. In any case, we don't know who snatched him.'

He struck a match. 'It's my back I'm worried about right now. I had a talk to Lyng last night on the Embassy scrambler. I told him that Thornton was nosing about. He said he'd do something about it.'

'What?'

Carey shrugged. 'They don't use guns in Whitehall but I believe they have weapons that are equally effective. It's no concern of yours, George; you won't have to worry about the Whitehall War until you get up to my level.'

'I'm not so worried about Whitehall as I am about Svetogorsk,' said McCready. 'I think it ought to be swapped around. Armstrong can go north and I'll come with you across the border.'

'He doesn't have the experience for what might happen up there. He's yet to be blooded, but he'll be all right with an old dog like me.'

'He'd be all right with me,' said McCready. 'He and I could cross the border and you could go up north.'

'Sorry,' said Carey regretfully. 'But I'm pushing sixty and I don't have the puff for that wilderness lark. And I don't have the reflexes for the fast action you might get. The plan stands, George.' His voice took on a meditative note. 'This is likely to be my last field operation. I'd like it to be a good one.'

23

The car slowed as it came to the corner. Harding, who was driving, said, 'This might be the turn-off. Check it on the map, will you?'

Denison, in the back of the car, lifted the map from his knee. 'That's it; we've just passed Kaamanen. The Kevo Camp is eighty kilometres up this side road and there's damn-all else.' He checked his watch. 'We ought to arrive before eleven.'

Harding turned on to the side road and the car lurched and bumped. After a few minutes he said, 'Make that midnight. We're not going to move fast on this road.'

Diana laughed. 'The Finns are the only people who could coin a word like *kelirikko*. It's a word Humpty-Dumpty would be proud of.'

Harding notched down a gear. 'What does it mean?'

'It means, "the bad state of the roads after the spring thaw".'

'Much in little,' said Harding. 'There's one thing I'm glad of.'

'What's that?'

'This midnight sun. I'd hate to drive along here in the dark.'

Denison glanced at Lyn who sat by his side. She was apparently asleep. It had been two days of hard driving, very tiring, and he was looking forward to his bed. He wound the window down to clear the dust from the outside surface, then looked at the countryside covered with scrub birch. Something suddenly caught him in the pit of the stomach. *What the hell am I doing here? Hundreds of miles north of the Arctic Circle in the Finnish wilderness?* It seemed preposterously improbable.

They had left Helsinki very early the previous morning and headed north out of the heavily populated southern coastal rim. Then they had left the rich farmlands very quickly and entered a region of forests and lakes, of towering pine and spruce, of white-trunked, green-leaved birch and the ever-present blue waters.

They took it in turns driving in two-hour shifts and made good time, sleeping that night in Oulu. After Oulu the land changed. There were fewer lakes and the trees were not as tall. A birch that in the south towered a hundred feet now had hardly the strength to grow to twenty, and the lakes gave way to marshes. As they passed through Ivalo, where there was the northernmost airstrip, they encountered their first Lapps, garish in red and blue, but there were really very few people of any kind in this country. Denison, under the prodding of Carey, had done his homework on Finland and he knew that in this most remote area of the country, Inari Commune, there were fewer than 8,000 people in a province the size of Yorkshire.

And there would be fewer still around Kevo.

Diana stretched, and said, 'Stop at the top of the next rise, Doctor; I'll spell you.'

'I'm all right,' said Harding.

'Stop anyway.'

He drove up the hill and was about to pull up when Diana said, 'Just a few yards more – over the crest.' Harding obligingly let the car roll and then braked to a halt. 'That's fine,' she said, taking binoculars from a case. 'I won't be a minute.'

Denison watched her leave the car and then opened his own door. He followed her back along the road and then into a growth of stunted birches. When he caught up with her she was looking back the way they had come through the glasses. 'Anything in sight?'

'No,' she said curtly.

'You've done this every hour,' he said. 'And you've still seen nothing. Nobody's following us.'

'They might be ahead,' she said without taking the glasses from her eyes.

'How would anyone know where we were going?'

'There are ways and means.' She lowered the glasses and looked at him. 'You don't know much about this business.'

'No, I don't,' Denison said reflectively. 'What's a nice girl like you doing in it? You're American, aren't you?'

She slung the binocular strap over her shoulder. 'Canadian. And it's just a job.'

'Just a civil servant,' he said ironically. 'Like any nine-to-five typist in Whitehall.' He remembered the occupation given in Meyrick's passport. 'Or like Dr. Meyrick.'

She faced him. 'Let's get one thing straight. From now on you do not refer to Meyrick in the third person – not even in private.' She tapped him on the chest with her forefinger. 'You are Harry Meyrick.'

'You've made your point, teacher.'

'I hope so.' She looked around. 'This seems a quiet spot. How long is it since you've seen anyone?'

He frowned. 'About an hour. Why?'

'I want to find out how much you lot know about guns. Target practice time.' As they went back to the car, she said, 'Go easy on Lyn Meyrick. She's a very confused girl.'

'I know,' said Denison. 'She has every reason to be confused.'

Diana looked at him sideways. 'Yes,' she agreed. 'You could call it confusion – of a sort. It's not easy to fall in love with a man who looks like the father you hate, but she's managed it.'

Denison stopped dead. 'Don't be idiotic.'

'Me!' She laughed. 'You do a bit of thinking and then figure who's the idiot around here.'

Harding pulled the car off the road and into the trees. Diana loaded a pistol from a packet of cartridges and set an empty beer can on a fallen tree trunk. 'All right; let's see who can do this.' Almost casually she lifted her arm and fired. The beer can jumped and spun away.

They took it in turns to fire three shots each. Denison missed every time, Harding hit the can once and Lyn, much to her own surprise, hit it twice. Diana said to Denison caustically, 'You were right; you can make the gun go bang.'

To Lyn she said, 'Not bad – but what would you be like shooting at a man instead of a beer can?'

'I . . . I don't know,' said Lyn nervously.

'What about you, Doctor?'

Harding hefted the gun in his hand. 'If I was being shot at I think I'd shoot back.'

'I suppose that's as much as I could expect,' said Diana resignedly. 'Let's go back to the car.'

She gave them each a pistol and watched them load. 'Don't forget to put on the safety catch. More important, don't forget to release it when you shoot. You'll put those in your bedrolls now. When we move off on foot tomorrow you'll need a more accessible place for them. Let's go.'

24

Carey lit his pipe and said, 'Slow down.'

Armstrong eased his foot on the accelerator and hastily wound down his side window. He wished Carey would not smoke at all in the car or, at least, change his brand of horse manure.

'See that tower over there?' asked Carey. 'To the right.'

Armstrong looked past him. 'A water tower?' he hazarded.

Carey grunted in amusement. 'A Russian observation tower. That's

Mother Russia.'

'We're *that* close to the frontier! It can't be more than a kilometre away.'

'That's right,' said Carey. 'You can turn round now; we'll go back to Imatra and book into the hotel.'

Armstrong came to a wide part of the road and slowed to a halt. As he turned the car, he said, 'Are there many of those towers around here?'

'All along the frontier. I suspect they're linked with electronic detection devices. The boys in those towers can record every footfall.' He looked at the spindly tower with a critical eye. 'The Russians have a suspicious nature – always trying to look over other people's walls. They're a funny crowd.'

Armstrong was silent, but his mind was busy with speculation. The trouble with Carey was that he was uncommunicative about his plans until the last moment, an idiosyncrasy apt to unnerve his subordinates. He wondered how they were going to cross the border.

He drove back into Imatra under Carey's direction and pulled up outside the entrance to the hotel. It was a big, rambling building constructed of stone with turrets and cupolas and towers. He thought it looked like a fairy tale castle as designed by Walt Disney had he been a more controlled artist. 'Some place!'

'The Valtionhotelli,' said Carey. 'Built at the turn of the century and genuine Art Nouveau. Come on.'

The hotel foyer was elaborately luxurious in an old-fashioned style. The stonework of the entrance was carved with grotesque mythological beasts and was panelled in dark wood. They registered and entered a lift accompanied by a porter carrying the bags.

The porter unlocked a door and stood back deferentially. Carey strode in, followed by Armstrong. He led the way along a wood-panelled corridor into a very large circular bedroom. 'I'll take the bed on the left,' he said as he tipped the porter.

Armstrong looked about him. 'Not bad. Not bad at all.'

'Nothing but the best for us civil servants,' said Carey. 'Let's go upstairs and have a drink.'

'There's an upstairs?'

They climbed a broad winding staircase leading off the corridor. Carey said, 'This hotel was built back in 1902 when Finland was still part of Russia. The Finns will give you arguments that it was never a part of Russia, but facts are facts. Imatra was a playground for the St. Petersburg aristocracy. The Czar stayed in the hotel – probably in this apartment.'

They emerged into another large circular room with windows all around. It was furnished with half a dozen easy-chairs and a long, low table of highly polished wood. A bear skin decorated the wall. Carey strode over to a built-in refrigerator while Armstrong looked through one of the windows. 'We must be at the top of the main tower.'

'That's right.' Carey pulled out a bottle. 'Skåne – that's Swedish; Linie – it's funny the Norwegians think that shipping their booze to Australia and back improves it. Koskenkorva – that's local. Stolichnaya – what the hell is that doing here? I call it damned unpatriotic. Ah, here's the beer.'

Armstrong turned and looked at the array of *snaps* bottles. 'Are we expected to be poured into Russia?'

Carey winked. 'The perquisites of the job. Besides, we might have to do a little entertaining.'

'Oh!' He held out field glasses he had found on a window ledge. 'Someone must have left these behind.'

Carey shook his head as he uncapped a beer bottle. 'Part of the room fittings. This apartment is where they bring the V.I.P.s to give them a little thrill.' He picked up a glass and joined Armstrong at the window. 'See those chimneys?'

Armstrong looked out of the window at the smoking factory chimneys. 'Yes?'

'That's Stalin's Finger,' said Carey. 'Svetogorsk!'

Armstrong put the binoculars to his eyes. The chimneys jumped closer and he could almost distinguish the separate bricks. 'My God!' he said. 'It's nearly part of Imatra.' He stared for a long time then slowly lowered the glasses. 'What did you say about Stalin?'

'Stalin's Finger – that's the local name. After the war the Russians wanted the frontier pushed back so there was the usual conference. Svetogorsk – or Enso, as it was then – is quite a nice little industrial town making paper. One of the Russians was drawing the revised frontier with a pen on the map but when he got to Enso he found that Stalin had put his finger in the way. He looked up at Stalin and Stalin smiled down on him, so he shrugged and drew the line around Stalin's finger. That put Enso in Russia.'

'The old bastard!' said Armstrong.

'Sit down and have a beer,' said Carey. 'I want to talk to you about procedure. I'll just nip down and get my briefcase.'

Armstrong took a beer from the refrigerator. When Carey came back he indicated the bear skin on the wall. 'Could that be a Russian bear with its hide nailed to the wall?'

'It could,' said Carey with a grim smile. 'That's part of what I want to talk to you about.' He put the briefcase on the table and sat down. 'As far as I'm concerned Svetogorsk is Svetogorsk – I'm a realist. But we'll be talking to some Finns and we'll refer to the town throughout as Enso.

They're a mite sensitive about it.'

'I can understand that,' said Armstrong.

'You don't know the half of it,' said Carey flatly. 'This has been my stamping ground all the time I've been in the service, so listen to some words of wisdom from the old man. Back in 1835 a man called Lönrot gathered together a lot of folk tales and issued them in verse form – that was the Kalevela, the Finnish national epic. It was the first major literary work the Finns ever had of their own, and it formed the basis of the new Finnish culture.'

'Interesting,' said Armstrong. 'But what the hell?'

'Just listen,' said Carey sharply. 'The heartland of the Kalevela is Karelia – which is now in Russia. The village of Kalevela itself is now Russian.' He rubbed the side of his nose. 'There's no exact English parallel, but it's as though the French had occupied Cornwall and Nottinghamshire and taken over all the King Arthur and Robin Hood legends. Of course, it runs deeper than that here, and some Finns are bitter about it.'

'They think the Russians pinched their national heritage?'

'Something like that.' Carey drained his glass. 'Now to politics. After the war President Paasikivi adopted a foreign policy that was new to Finland, and the idea was to remain strictly neutral, rather like Sweden. In actual practice it's a neutrality in favour of Russia – at all costs no offence must be given to Big Brother in the east. This is known as the Paasikivi Line, and it's followed by the current President, Kekkonen. It's like walking a tightrope but it's difficult to see what else Finland can do. They already have the example of what happened to Estonia and the other Baltic States.'

He got himself another beer. 'We're going to meet some Finns tonight who don't agree with the Paasikivi Line. They're Right Wingers and, personally, I'd call them bloody reactionaries, but they're the boys who are going to get us into Enso. If Kekkonen knew what we were doing here, what little hair he has left would turn white. He's getting on with the Russians reasonably well and he wants it to stay that way. He doesn't want any incident on the frontier that could cause a diplomatic breach and give Moscow an excuse for making demands. Neither do we – so to the Finns we meet tonight we talk softly, and when we're in Enso we walk softly.'

He fixed Armstrong with a firm eye. 'And if we're caught over there we've done it on our own hook – no Finns were involved. That's bloody important, so keep it in mind.'

'I understand,' said Armstrong soberly.

'Of course, the whole idea is *not* to get caught.' Carey unzipped his briefcase. 'Here is a street plan of Enso, dated 1939.' He unfolded it and spread it on the table. His finger wandered over the surface and then went down. 'This is the house in which Hannu Merikken lived. He buried his box full of papers in the garden which is something under half an acre – but not much under.'

Armstrong bent his head over the plan. 'That's quite an area. How big is the box?'

'Meyrick described it as two feet by one-and-a-half by one.'

Armstrong did some mental arithmetic. 'If we dug a hole at random the chances against hitting it would be over eight hundred to one.'

'We can do better than that,' said Carey. 'The original idea was to have Meyrick point out the spot – he was present when the box was buried. But after all these years his memory had slipped a few cogs.' He dipped into the briefcase again. 'All he could come up with was this.'

Armstrong examined the large-scale plan which was drawn meticulously in Indian ink. Carey said, 'There are four trees and the box is buried under one of them but he couldn't remember which one.'

'At least that's cutting it down to a maximum of four holes.'

'1944 is a long time ago,' said Carey. 'Three of the trees are no longer there. Look at these.' He produced some photographs. 'These were taken by our Finnish friends about three weeks ago.' As Armstrong looked at them, Carey said, 'I had hoped that taking Meyrick back would jog his memory, but we don't have Meyrick any more, so what we're left with is half an acre of ground and one tree.' He peered over Armstrong's shoulder and pointed. 'I think that's the one, but I'm not sure.'

'So we dig,' said Armstrong. 'It will have to be done under cover of darkness.'

Carey stared at him. 'What darkness? I know we're not in the Arctic Circle, but even so, there's precious little darkness at this time of year. The most we'll get is a deep twilight.'

'Do we have to jump in now?' asked Armstrong. 'Why not wait until later in the year?'

Carey sighed. 'Apart from the fact that these papers are of overwhelming importance, there's one very good reason why we have to go in now.' He tapped the street plan. 'When Merikken was living in this house it was in a good class suburb. But Enso has been expanding, the area has become run-down, and it's due for redevelopment. The bulldozers will be moving in before the autumn. We've got to get in first.'

'A pity Meyrick didn't make his great discovery a year earlier,' commented Armstrong. 'Anyone living in the house?'

'Yes; a Russian called Kunayev – he's a foreman in one of the paper mills. A wife and three children; one cat – no dogs.'

'So we just go along and start to dig holes all over his garden in broad daylight. He's going to like that!' Armstrong tossed down the photograph. 'It's impossible!'

Carey was unperturbed. 'Nothing is impossible, my lad. To begin with, the papers are in a tin trunk. That's a misnomer – a tin trunk is made of sheet steel and I have a natty metal detector, small but efficient.'

'Like a mine detector?'

'Something like that, but smaller. Small enough for us to take over the border without much risk. I had it specially made up. According to Meyrick's dicey memory there's not much more than two feet of earth on top of the box. I've tested this gadget with a similar box and even three feet under it gives a signal that blasts your eardrums.'

'So we get the signal and start to dig. What's Kunayev going to be doing while this is happening?'

Carey grinned. 'With a bit of luck he won't be there. The comrade will be toiling like a Stakhanovite in his bloody mill, reeling up the toilet paper, or whatever it is he does.'

'His wife will be there,' objected Armstrong. 'And his kids – and probably the next-door neighbours.'

'It won't matter. We'll take them all by the hand and lead them right up that bloody garden path.'

25

The meeting with the Finns took place that night in a house on the outskirts of Imatra. 'There are three of them,' said Carey, as they drove towards the rendezvous. 'Lassi Virtanen and his son, Tarmo, and Heikki Huovinen.'

Armstrong giggled, perhaps more out of nervous tension than anything else. 'I never thought I'd meet the Son of Lassie.'

'If you have any more remarks like that left in your system bottle them up until this operation is over,' said Carey grittily. 'This particular crowd doesn't have a strong sense of humour. Old Virtanen was a fighter pilot during the war and he still reckons it's a bad thing the Germans lost. I still don't know which is topmost in him – the Nazi sympathiser or the Russian-hater – probably a fifty-fifty mixture of both. He's brought up his son in his own image. Huovinen is a shade more liberal, but still well to the right of Attila the Hun. These are the tools we have to work with and I don't want them turning in my hand. Remember that.'

'I'll remember,' said Armstrong. He felt as though Carey had suddenly thrown a bucket of ice water over him. 'What's the scheme?'

'The Finns are expert paper makers,' said Carey. 'And the Russians are quite willing to take advantage of their expertise. They're building a new paper mill in Enso; all the machinery is Finnish and the installation is done by Finns, most of whom live in Imatra. They go over the border every day.'

A great light broke on Armstrong. 'And we go with them. How convenient.'

Carey grunted. 'Don't shout too soon. It won't be as easy as all that.' He pointed. 'There's the house.'

Armstrong drew the car to a halt. 'Do these three go over to Enso?'

'That's it.'

Armstrong thought for a moment. 'If the Virtanens hate the Russians so much why do they help them build paper factories?'

'They belong to a half-baked secret society – very right wing, of course. They fondly believe they're spying and preparing for *Der Tag*.' Carey shrugged. 'It's my belief they're at the end of their rope and the government is going to hang them with it. One of the troubles with the Paasikivi Line is keeping to the middle ground between right and left. The government can't crack down too hard on the communists because of Russian pressure, but who the hell cares what happens to a lot of neo-Nazis? They're only left loose as a makeweight on the other end of the political see-saw, but if they get out of line they get the chop. So let's use them while we can.'

Lassi Virtanen was a hard-faced man in his middle-fifties who walked with a limp. His son, Tarmo, was about thirty and did not look much like his father; he was fresh-faced and his eyes sparkled with excitement. Armstrong measured him carefully and thought he would be too excitable to be relied on for anything important. Heikki Huovinen was dark with a blue chin. To look respectable he would have to shave twice a day but, to Armstrong's eye, he seemed not to have shaved for two days.

They sat around a table on which there was an array of dishes, the open sandwiches of Scandinavia. There were also a dozen bottles of beer and two bottles of a colourless spirit. They sampled the herring and then the elder Virtanen filled small glasses with the spirit, and raised his glass slightly. '*Kippis!*' His arm went up and he threw the contents of his glass down his throat.

Armstrong took his cue from Carey and did the same. The fierce spirit bit the back of his throat and burned in his belly. Carey put down his empty glass. 'Not bad,' he said. 'Not bad at all.' He spoke in Swedish for the benefit of Armstrong. Finding Finnish speakers for the Service was

the very devil and it was fortunate that Swedish was the second language
of Finland.

Tarmo Virtanen laughed. 'It's from the other side.'

'Their vodka is the only good thing about the Russians,' said Lassi
Virtanen grudgingly. He refilled the glasses. 'Heikki is worried.'

'Oh!' Carey looked at Huovinen. 'What about?'

'It's not going to be easy,' said Huovinen.

'Of course it'll be easy,' said Lassi. 'Nothing to it.'

'It's all right for you,' said Huovinen. 'You won't be there. It's me who
has to come up with all the explanations and excuses.' He turned to
Carey. 'It can't be done for three days.'

'Why not?'

'You and your friend, here, are taking the place of the Virtanens –
right? Well, the Virtanens have got work to do over there – I know, I'm
their damned foreman. Tomorrow Lassi is working on the screening
plates, but Tarmo hasn't much to do and he wouldn't be missed. The day
after that Tarmo will be busy. The only time I can spare them both
without too many questions being asked will be the day after, and even
then I'll have to tell a lot of lies.'

Carey thought Huovinen was getting cold feet but not by any sign did
he show it. He said, 'What about it, Lassi?'

'It's true enough – as far as it goes – but it doesn't have to be that way.
Heikki, you could fix things so that no one works on the screens
tomorrow. A little bit of sabotage?'

'Not with that Georgian bastard, Dzotenidze, breathing down my
neck,' said Huovinen heatedly.

'Who's he?' asked Carey.

'The Chief Engineer for the Russians. He'll be Chief Engineer of the
mill when it gets working, and he wants everything right. He watches
me like a hawk.'

'No sabotage,' said Carey flatly. 'I want things to go right, too.'

Huovinen nodded vigorously. 'In three days,' he said. 'Then I can
conveniently lose the Virtanens.'

Carey said, 'We'll come here in the evening the day after tomorrow.
We'll spend the night here and we'll leave in the morning just as the
Virtanens would. Won't the rest of the crew be surprised at a couple of
strangers joining in?'

'That's taken care of. They may be surprised, but they won't talk.'
Huovinen drew himself up. 'They're Finns,' he said proudly. 'They're
Karelians.'

'And you're a foreman.'

Huovinen smiled. 'That's got something to do with it, too.'

Carey regarded Lassi and Tarmo Virtanen. 'And you two will stay in the house that day and you won't go out. We don't want anyone asking questions about how in hell can you be in Imatra and Enso at the same time.'

Young Virtanen laughed and tapped the bottle of vodka. 'Leave us plenty of this and we won't go out.'

Carey frowned, and Lassi said, 'We'll stay in the house.'

'Very well. Did you get the clothing?'

'It's all here.'

Carey took two folded cards from his pocket. 'These are our passes – will you check them?'

Huovinen picked them up and studied them. He took out his own pass for comparison, then said, 'These are very good; very good, indeed. But they look new – they're too clean.'

'We'll dirty them,' said Carey.

Huovinen shrugged. 'It doesn't really matter. The frontier guards have got tired of looking at passes. You'll be all right.'

'I hope so,' said Carey drily.

Lassi Virtanen picked up his glass. 'That's settled. I don't know exactly what you're doing over there, Mr. Englishman, but I know it will do *Ryssä* no good. *Kippis!*' He knocked back his vodka.

Carey and Armstrong both drank and immediately Virtanen replenished their glasses. Armstrong looked about the room and saw a photograph on the sideboard. He tipped his chair back to get a closer look and Lassi, following his gaze, laughed and got up. 'That's from the Continuation War,' he said. 'I had fire in my belly in those days.'

He passed the photograph over to Armstrong. It showed a much younger Lassi Virtanen standing next to a fighter aircraft decorated with the swastika insignia. 'My Messerschmitt,' said Virtanen proudly. 'I shot down six Russian bastards in that plane.'

'Did you?' said Armstrong politely.

'Those were the good days,' said Virtanen. 'But what an air force we had. Any aircraft that had been built anywhere in the world – we had it. American Brewsters and Curtis Hawks, British Blenheims and Gladiators, German Fokkers and Dorniers, Italian Fiats, French Morane-Saulniers – even Russian Polikarpovs. The Germans captured some of those in the Ukraine and sent them to us. Unreliable bastards they were, too. What a crazy, mixed-up air force we had – but we still held the Russians off until the end.'

He slapped his leg. 'I got mine in '44 – shot down near Räisälä and it took four of them to do it. That was behind the lines but I walked out with a bullet in my leg, dodging those damned Russian patrols. Good days those were. Drink up!'

It was late before Carey and Armstrong were able to leave because they had to listen to a monologue from Virtanen about his war experiences, interspersed with glasses of vodka. But at last they got away. Armstrong got behind the wheel of the car and looked eloquently at Carey. 'I know,' said Carey heavily. 'Drunken and unreliable. I'm not surprised they're getting nowhere.'

'That man lives in the past,' said Armstrong.

'There's a lot like him in England – men who've never really lived since the war. Never mind the Virtanens – they're staying here. It's Huovinen we have to rely on to get to the other side.'

'He was packing the stuff away as though he wanted to start a drought in vodka,' said Armstrong dispiritedly.

'I know – but they're all we've got.' Carey took out his pipe. 'I wonder how McCready and company are doing up north. They can't be doing worse than we are.'

26

'I'm tired,' said Harding. 'But I don't think I'll sleep.'

Denison inspected the narrow patch of ground for stones before he unrolled his sleeping bag. He flicked an offender aside and said, 'Why not?'

'I can't get used to broad daylight in the middle of the night.'

Denison grinned. 'Why don't you prescribe yourself a sleeping pill?'

'I might do that.' Harding picked a blade of grass and chewed it. 'How are you sleeping these days?'

'Not bad.'

'Dream much?'

'Not that I can remember. Why?'

Harding smiled. 'I'm your resident head-watcher – appointed by that chit over there.' He nodded towards Lyn who was peering dubiously into a camp kettle.

Denison unrolled his sleeping bag and sat on it. 'What do you think of her?'

'Personally or professionally?'

'Maybe a bit of both.'

'She seems to be a well-balanced young woman.' There was amusement in Harding's voice. 'She certainly knew how to handle Carey – she caught him coming and going. And she jabbed me in a sore spot. She's very capable, I'd say.'

'She took her father's death pretty coolly.'

Harding threw away the blade of grass and lit a cigarette. 'She lived with her mother and stepfather and didn't have much to do with Meyrick apart from quarrelling. I'd say her attitude to her father's death was perfectly normal. She had other things to think about at the time.'

'Yes,' said Denison pensively.

'I don't think you need worry about Lyn Meyrick,' said Harding. 'She's used to making up her own mind – and the minds of others, come to that.'

Diana Hansen came down the hill looking trim and efficient in the neat shirt and the drab trousers which she wore tucked into the tops of field boots – a world removed from the cool sophisticate Denison had met in Oslo. She cast a look at Lyn and walked over to the two men. 'Time to do your bit with the theodolite, Giles.'

Denison scrambled to his feet. 'Are they still with us?'

'So I'm told,' said Diana. 'And there's another party. We're becoming popular. I'd go up on that ridge there – and stay in sight.'

'All right.' Denison took the theodolite out of its case, picked up the lightweight tripod, and walked up the hill in the direction Diana had indicated.

Harding smiled as he watched Denison's retreating figure. He thought that Lyn Meyrick would make up Denison's mind were she allowed to. From a psychiatric point of view it was most interesting – but he would have to have a word with the girl first. He got up and walked over to where Lyn was pumping the pressure stove.

Denison stopped on top of the ridge and set up the theodolite. He took the sheet of paper from his pocket, now much creased, and studied it before looking around at the view. This was the bit of fakery Carey had given him to make the deception look good. It had been written with a broad-nibbed pen – 'No ballpoints in 1944,' Carey had said – and artificially aged. Across the top was scrawled the single word, *Iuonnonpuisto,* and below that was a rough sketch of three lines radiating from a single point with the angles carefully marked in degrees. At the end of each line was again a single word – *Järvi, Kukkula* and *Aukko* – going around clockwise. Lake, hill and gap.

'Not much to go on,' Carey had said. 'But it explains why you're wandering around nature preserves with a theodolite. If anyone wants to rob you of that bit of paper you can let him. Maybe we can start a trade in theodolites.'

Denison looked around. Below ran the thread of a small river, the

Kevojoki, and in the distance was the blue water of a lake pent in a narrow valley. He bent his head and sighted the theodolite at the head of the lake. Every time he did this he had a curious sense of *déjà vu* as though he had been accustomed to doing this all his life. Had he been a surveyor?

He checked the reading on the bezel and sighted again on the hill across the valley and took another reading. He took a notebook from his pocket and worked out the angle between the lake and the hill, then he swept the horizon looking for a possible gap. All this nonsense had to look good because he knew he was under observation – Carey's red herring appeared to be swimming well.

It had been at lunchtime on the first day that Diana had said casually, 'We're being watched.'

'How do you know?' asked Denison. 'I've seen nobody.'

'McCready told me.'

McCready had not been in evidence at Kevo Camp and Denison had not seen him since Helsinki. 'Have you been talking to him? Where is he?'

Diana nodded across the lake. 'On the other side of the valley. He says that a party of three men is trailing us.'

Denison was sceptical. 'I suppose you have a walkie-talkie tucked away in your pack.'

She shook her head. 'Just this.' From the pocket of her anorak she took a small plate of stainless steel, three inches in diameter; it had a small hole in the middle. 'Heliograph,' she said. 'Simpler than radio and less detectable.'

He examined the double-sided mirror – that is what it amounted to – and said, 'How can you aim it?'

'I know where George McCready is now,' she said. 'He's just been signalling to me. If I want to answer I hold this up and sight on his position through the hole. Then I look at my own reflection and see a circle of light on my cheek where the sun comes through the hole. If I tilt the mirror so that the circle of light goes into the hole, then the mirror on the other side flashes right into George's eyes. From then on it's simply a matter of Morse code.'

Denison was about to experiment when she took the gadget from him. 'I told you we're being watched. I can get away with it by pretending to make up my face – you can't.'

'Has McCready any idea of who is watching us?'

She shrugged. 'He hasn't got near enough to find out. I think it's about time you started your act with the theodolite.'

So he had set up the theodolite and fiddled about checking angles, and had repeated the charade several times during the past two days.

Now he found what might, by a stretch of imagination, be called a gap and took the third reading. He calculated the angle, wrote it into his notebook, and put the notebook and the fake paper back into his pocket. He was dismantling the theodolite when Lyn came up the hill. 'Supper's ready.'

'Thanks,' he said. 'Hold this.' He gave her the theodolite. 'Did Diana say anything about another group following us?'

Lynn nodded. 'They're coming up from behind very fast, she says.'

'Where's the first group?'

'Gone on ahead.'

'We're like the meat in a sandwich,' Denison said gloomily. 'Unless it's all a product of Diana's imagination. I haven't seen anyone around – and I certainly haven't seen George McCready.'

'I saw him signalling this morning,' said Lyn. 'He was on the other side of the valley. I was standing next to Diana and saw the flash, too.'

Denison collapsed the tripod and they both set off down the hill. 'You and Harding have had your heads together lately. What do you find so interesting to talk about?'

She gave him a sideways glance. 'You,' she said quietly. 'I've been finding out about you; since I can't ask you I've been asking him.'

'Nothing bad, I hope.'

She smiled at him. 'Nothing bad.'

'That's a relief,' he said. 'What's for supper?'

'Bully beef stew.'

He sighed. 'I can't wait.'

27

McCready was desperately tired. He lay on a hillside in a grove of dwarf birch and watched the group of four men making their way up the valley on the other side of the river. He had had very little sleep in the last two days and his eyes were sore and gritty. He had long since come to the conclusion that it needed two men to do this job.

He lowered the binoculars and blinked, then rubbed his eyes before checking on the camp on the top of the bluff across the river. There was a new figure on the rock above the camp which looked like Denison. At three in the morning there was quite enough light to see; the sun had skimmed the horizon at midnight and was already high in the sky. it seemed that Diana had insisted that a watch be kept.

He shifted his elbows and checked on the higher reaches of the valley and his mouth tightened as he saw a movement. The three men of the first party were coming down, keeping close to the river. Earlier he had crossed the river to scout their camp and, although he had not got close enough to hear clearly what they had been talking about, he had heard enough to know they were not Finns. Their tones had Slavic cadences and he had seen that they were very lightly equipped with no tents or even sleeping bags.

He switched his attention to the group of four who were coming up the valley. The two groups could not see each other because of a bend in the river where the water swirled around the bluff. He judged that if both groups kept up the same pace they would meet under the bluff and just below Denison.

McCready frowned as he watched. If the first group was under-equipped the second was well-outfitted to the point of decadent luxury. He had watched them stop for a meal and had seen what seemed to be a collapsible barbecue. Two of the men carried coils of rope as though they might expect rock climbing. Maybe Finns, he had thought, but now he was not so certain; not even Finns made route marches at three a.m.

At the time he had first seen the second group he had been too far away to distinguish faces, but now the men were nearer and he had a better chance. As he waited patiently he pondered over the differences between the two parties and came to the conclusion that they were indeed quite separate. Two minutes later he was sure of it when he saw the face of the leading man of the four.

It was Jack Kidder, the big loud-mouthed American who had cropped up in Oslo and, later, in Helsinki.

Whatever the first group had been speaking it had been neither Finnish or English. It was reasonable to assume that not only were the two parties quite distinct but also that neither knew of the existence of the other. Even more interesting, they were going to run into each other within twenty minutes.

McCready put down the binoculars and twisted around to open the pack which lay beside him. He took out what appeared to be the stock of a rifle and slapped open the butt plate which was hinged. From inside the hollow glassfibre stock he took out a barrel and a breech action and, within thirty seconds, he had assembled the rifle.

He patted the stock affectionately. This was the Armalite AR-7, originally designed as a survival rifle for the American Air Force. It weighed less than three pounds and was guaranteed to float in water whether knocked down or ready to fire, but what made it suitable for his purpose was the fact that, stripped down, it measured less than seventeen inches in length and so could be smuggled about unobtrusively in a back pack.

He inserted a magazine containing eight rounds of long rifle and put another clip in his pocket, then he crawled backwards out of the grove of trees and began to make his way down to the river along a ravine he had previously chosen for the eventuality. He came out to the river's edge opposite the bluff and right on the bend of the river, and took shelter behind boulders which a long-gone glacier had left in its passage.

From his position on the outside bend of the river he could see both groups although neither, as yet, was aware of the other. He looked at the bluff and could not see Denison who was farther back up the hill. Nothing like adding confusion, he thought, as he raised the rifle to firing position.

As both groups were about to round the bend he fired, not at Kidder but just in front of him, and the sand spurted at Kidder's feet. Kidder yelled and rolled sideways and, as if by magic, all four men disappeared.

McCready did not see that sudden transformation of the scene; he had already turned and slammed another shot at the leading man of the trio which ricocheted off a rock by his head. The man ducked instinctively and went to ground fast, but not so fast that McCready did not see the pistol that suddenly appeared in his hand.

McCready withdrew into his niche like a tortoise drawing its head into its shell and waited to see what would happen next.

Denison heard the shot from below and jerked to attention. Even before he took the second quick pace back to the camp he heard the flat report of the second shot which echoed from the hill behind him. Then there was no sound but the thudding of his boots on the rock.

He stooped to Diana's sleeping bag and found her already awake. 'Someone's shooting.'

'I heard. Wake the others.'

He roused Lyn and then went to Harding who, in spite of his pessimism, was fast asleep. 'Wassamatter?' he said drowsily, but came awake with a jerk as two more shots broke the early morning silence. 'What the hell?'

Diana was gesturing vigorously. 'Over the ridge,' she called. 'Away from the river.'

Harding hastily thrust his feet into his boots and cursed freely. Denison ran over to Diana who was helping Lyn. 'What about the gear?'

'Leave it. Leave everything except your gun. Get moving.'

He hauled Lyn to her feet and they ran for it, up the hill and over the top of the ridge, a matter of some three hundred yards. There they waited, breathless, until Diana and Harding caught up. Three more shots were fired in rapid succession, and Denison said, 'It sounds like a bloody battle.'

'We've got to get lost,' said Diana. 'There's cover over there.'

They ran for it.

On the other side of the river, at the water's edge, McCready watched and smiled. As he had figured, neither of the groups had time to find out where the shots had come from. They had taken cover immediately in the manner of professionals, and now they were dodging about on each side of the bluff in skirmish lines, ready for defence or attack. Kidder, on the left, caught a glimpse of a man on the right, and fired. He missed but, in firing, he exposed himself and someone took a shot at him. Another miss.

Kidder pulled back and unslung his pack which was hampering him. As the others did the same McCready smiled. A typical battle situation was developing in miniature. Kidder, to improve mobility, was divesting himself of supplies, which might be a good idea considering he outnumbered the opposition – although he could not know that. But if he lost and was overrun and had to retreat then his supplies would be lost.

McCready patted his rifle again and withdrew, to worm himself up the ravine and back into his original position in the stand of stunted trees. On the way he heard three more shots fired. He picked up the glasses and studied the situation. Denison was gone from the rock and the camp was deserted, so it was likely that they had pulled back over the hill and gone to ground, which was the sensible thing to do.

He looked down at the river. The narrow strip of sand between the bluff and the water's edge was held at each end by two men, and both sides were engaged in a classic out-flanking action. Kidder and another man were climbing the bluff on the left, obviously intending to come out on top. There they would have the advantage of height and dropping fire as well as greater numbers.

The only snag was that the opposition was doing the same with one man and he had got the idea first. McCready, enjoying his grandstand seat, watched their progress with interest and estimated that the deserted camp on top of the bluff would be the next battleground. If the single man on the right could get himself established on top of the bluff before Kidder and his friend arrived he would stand a good chance despite the two to one odds.

Meanwhile the holding action at the bottom of the bluff continued with a desultory exchange of shots more to indicate the presence of opposition than to press an attack. McCready stroked his rifle, and thought, *How to Start a War in One Easy Lesson.* He hoped no small nation got the idea – using atomic missiles instead of rifle bullets.

The man on the right made it to the top while Kidder and his man still had twenty yards to go. He came up slowly, looked at the deserted camp, and then ducked for cover behind a rock. Kidder came up to the top and also surveyed the camp from cover, then gestured to the other man to crawl farther along.

He shouted – a thin cry that came to McCready across the river – and they both broke into the open, running across the top of the bluff. The man in cover fired and Kidder's companion spun away and fell among the rocks. Kidder dropped into cover and simultaneously there was a renewed outburst of fire from the base of the bluff to which McCready transferred his attention.

There had been a casualty on the other side and from the way the man nursed his arm McCready judged it to be broken. He heard a confused and distant shouting; Kidder was worming his way among the rocks in the direction of his wounded friend, and suddenly the other man on the bluff broke away and retreated.

Within fifteen minutes both sides were retreating in opposite directions, Kidder's group going down-river, one man limping heavily with a bullet in his leg, and the others heading up-river. Honours were even in an inconclusive engagement, and McCready thought that neither party knew just exactly what had happened.

Diana Hansen waited an hour after the last shot before making a move, then she said, 'I'll go and see what's happening.'

'I'll come with you,' said Denison.

She hesitated. 'All right. I'll go to the left, you go to the right. We move alternately, one covering the other.' She looked back at the others. 'You two give us general cover. If anyone shoots at us you start banging away fast; it doesn't matter if you don't hit anything – just make a lot of noise.'

She went first and Denison watched her as she zigzagged forward up to the top of the ridge. Half-way up she stopped and waved him forward and he did his best to imitate what she had done. He flopped down when he was parallel with her and wondered how she had learned a trade like this.

She was on the move again and this time she got to the top of the ridge where she could look down on the camp. At her hand signal he also went forward and peered cautiously around a rock. The camp was deserted and nothing appeared to have been touched; he could even see a gleam from the open theodolite case where he had left it, forgetting to close the top.

She wriggled over to him. 'I'll go around to the left – you to the right – we'll come in on the camp from two sides. Don't be in too much of a hurry, and don't shoot at the first thing that moves – it might be me.'

He nodded. She was just going away when he took another look at the camp and saw a movement. He grabbed her ankle as he ducked back. 'Someone down there,' he whispered.

She turned. 'Where?'

'By the rock where we kept watch.'

After a while Diana said, 'I don't see anyone.'

'I saw it,' said Denison. 'A movement by that rock.'

Again they waited and watched until Diana said, 'Must have been your imagination.'

Denison sighed. 'I suppose so.' His hand suddenly tightened on hers. 'No – look! On the other side now.'

The figure of a man came over the edge of the bluff, paused a little wearily, and then walked slowly towards the camp. When he got there he stared about him and unslung his pack.

Diana clicked with her tongue. 'It's George McCready,' she said, and stood up.

McCready looked as though he was ready to drop on his feet. His clothing was soaked and his boots squelched when he walked. He saw them coming but made no move to advance. Instead he sat down and began to unlace his boots. 'That bloody river,' he said. 'That's the third time I've crossed it.'

'What was all the shooting?' demanded Diana.

McCready described what had happened. 'One crowd was American; I don't know who the others were. The language sounded vaguely Slav.'

'Russian?'

'Could be,' said McCready. 'I hope so. If they're chasing us up here there's a good chance they won't be on to Carey.' He wrung out his socks. 'When I'm sixty I'll be an arthritic cripple.'

'So you set them fighting each other,' said Denison. 'I don't know if that was a good idea. They might think it was us, and next time they'll come shooting.'

McCready nodded. 'Now's the time to lose them. The best way of doing that is to cross the river and go back on the other side. That will give us the three days that Carey wanted us here.'

'But we don't want to lose them,' objected Diana. 'That isn't the object.'

'I know,' said McCready. 'But I'd like to get back to the cars and away while they're still licking their wounds. We can leave plenty of signs to indicate where we've gone. They'll beat around here for a while – if we're lucky they'll have another shooting match – and then they'll follow. It's still gaining time for Carey and it's less risk for us.'

Diana thought about it. 'All right.'

McCready cocked his head on one side and regarded Denison. 'The leader of the American mob was your old pal, Kidder.'

'Kidder!' said Denison incredulously.

'I thought he turned up a bit too opportunely in Helsinki,' said Diana. 'But the man sounded such a fool I discounted him.'

'If it's any consolation, so did I,' said McCready. 'But you know what it means – our cousins of the C.I.A. are muscling in.' He took a pair of dry socks from a plastic bag. 'Unless he's a renegade or a double agent. I fancy the C.I.A. myself.' He looked up at Denison who was deep in thought. 'What's the matter with you? You look as though you've just been sandbagged.'

'For God's sake!' said Denison. 'It was *Kidder!*' He shook his head in a bewildered manner. 'The man who questioned me after I was knocked out in the sauna. I thought I recognised the voice but I couldn't place it because the American accent had gone.'

'Are you sure?' Diana's voice was sharp.

'I'm certain. I didn't associate the man with Kidder because we'd left him behind in Oslo. He hadn't appeared in Helsinki at that time. Is it important?'

'Could be,' said McCready. 'There's one bunch who knows you're *not* Meyrick – the crowd who snatched you from Hampstead. But the man who questioned you assumed you were Meyrick. If it was Kidder then the C.I.A. weren't responsible for the resculpturing of that unlovely face of yours. All these bits of jigsaw come in handy.'

'Dr. Harding and Lyn will be wondering what happened to us,' said Diana.

Denison turned. 'I'll bring them back.' He started to walk up to the top of the ridge but then veered over to the rock where he had kept watch. Something niggled at the back of his mind – he wondered how McCready could have got from one side of the camp to the other. The first movement he had seen from the top of the ridge had been by the rock, but McCready had come up the other side from the river.

Denison walked around the rock keeping his eyes on the ground. When McCready had come up his boots had been wet – waterfilled – and he had left a line of damp footprints over a smooth rock outcrop. Here there was also an outcrop but no footprints. He went to the other side of the rock and out of sight of Diana and McCready.

Something struck him on the back of the head and he felt a blinding pain and was driven to his knees. His vision swam and there was a roaring in his ears. The second thump on the head he did not feel but plunged headlong into darkness.

28

The bus rocked as it rolled along the narrow country road in the early morning. It was cold and Carey drew his coat closer about him. Armstrong, next to him, looked out of the window at the tall observation tower. It was drawing nearer.

The bus was full of Finns, most of whom were quiet at that early pre-work hour. Two seats ahead of Carey, on the aisle, sat Huovinen. He turned his head and looked back; his eyes were expressionless but Carey thought he could detect worry. Huovinen had been drinking again the previous night and Carey hoped his hangover did not get in the way of his efficiency.

Brakes squealed as the bus drew to a halt and Carey craned his neck to look through the forward windows. A soldier in Finnish uniform walked up and exchanged a few words with the driver, than he smiled and waved the bus on. It jerked into motion again.

Carey took out his pipe and filled it with steady hands. He nudged Armstrong, and said in Swedish, 'Why don't you have a cigarette? Have you stopped smoking?'

Armstrong looked at him in surprise, then shrugged. If Carey wanted him to smoke a cigarette then he would smoke a cigarette. He felt in his pocket and took out a half-empty packet of Finnish cigarettes as the bus stopped again.

The bus driver leaned out of the cab and called to the advancing Russian soldier, '*Kolmekymmentäkuusi.*' The soldier nodded and climbed into the bus by way of the passenger door and surveyed the work party. He looked as though he was doing a head count.

Carey struck a match and lit his pipe, cupping his hands about the bowl and shrouding the lower part of his face. He seemed to be doing his best to make a smokescreen. Armstrong caught on fast and flicked on his cigarette lighter, guarding the flame with his hand as though the draught from up front was about to blow it out.

The Russian left the bus and waved it on and it lurched forward with a clash of gears and rolled past the frontier post. Armstrong averted his face from the window as the bus passed an officer, a square man with broad Slavic features. He felt a sudden tightening in his belly as he realised he was in Russia. He had been in Russia many times before, but not as an illegal entry – and that had been the subject of a discussion with Carey.

Armstrong had argued for going into Russia quite legitimately through Leningrad. 'Why do we have to be illegal about it?' he asked.

'Because we'd have to be illegal anyway,' said Carey. 'We couldn't get to Enso legally – the Russkies don't like foreigners wandering loose about their frontier areas. And they keep a watch on foreigners in Leningrad; if you're not back at the Europa Hotel they start looking for you. No, this is the best way. Over the border and back – short and sharp – without them even knowing we've been there.'

Black smoke streamed overhead from the factory chimneys as the bus trundled through Enso. It traversed the streets for some minutes and then went through a gateway and halted outside a very long, low building. The passengers gathered up their belongings and stood up. Carey looked at Huovinen who nodded, so he nudged Armstrong and they got up and joined the file behind Huovinen.

They went into the building through an uncompleted wall and emerged into an immense hall. At first Armstrong could not take in what he was seeing; not only was the sight unfamiliar but he had to follow Huovinen who veered abruptly to the right and out of the main stream. He led them around the end of a great machine and stopped where there was no one in sight. He was sweating slightly. 'I should be getting twice what you're paying me,' he said.

'Take it easy,' counselled Carey. 'What now?'

'I have to be around for the next hour,' said Huovinen. 'Laying out the work and a fifteen-minute conference with Dzotenidze. I have to put up with that every morning.' He coughed and spat on the floor. 'I can't lead you out before then.'

'So we wait an hour,' said Carey. 'Where?'

Huovinen pointed. 'In the machine – where else?'

Carey turned and looked at the half-constructed machine. Designed for continuous paper-making it was over three hundred yards long and about fifty feet wide. 'Get in the middle of there and take your coats off,' said Huovinen. 'I'll bring you some tools in about ten minutes. If anyone looks in at you be tightening bolts or something.'

Carey looked up at a crane from which a big steel roller hung. 'Just see that you don't drop that on my head,' he said. 'And don't be longer than an hour. Come on, Ivan.'

Armstrong followed Carey as he climbed inside the machine. When he looked back Huovinen had gone. They found a place where there was headroom and Carey took off his coat and looked around. 'In this snug situation a British working man would be playing cards,' he said. 'I don't know about the Finns.'

Armstrong bent and peered through a tangle of complexity. 'They're working,' he reported.

Carey grunted. 'Then let's look busy even if we're not.'

Presently a man walked by and stooped. There was a clatter of metal on concrete and footsteps hastened away. 'The tools,' said Carey. Get them.'

Armstrong crawled out and came back with a selection of spanners and a hammer. Carey inspected them and tried a spanner on the nearest bolt. 'What we do now,' he announced, 'is to take off this girder and then put it back – and we keep on doing that until it's time to go.' He applied the spanner to a nut and heaved, then paused with a thoughtful look on his face. 'Just pop your head up there and see what happens when we remove this bit of iron. I don't want the whole bloody machine to collapse.'

An hour and a half later they were walking through the streets of Enso. Armstrong still wore his overalls and carried a spade over his shoulder, but Carey removed his and was now more nattily dressed. He wore, he assured Armstrong, the regulation rig of a local water distribution inspector. In his hand he carried, quite openly, the metal detection gadget. To Armstrong's approval it had a metal plate attached to it which announced in Russian that it was manufactured by Sovelectro Laboratories of Dnepropetrovsk.

As they walked they talked – discreetly and in Russian. Armstrong noted the old-fashioned atmosphere of the streets of Enso. It was, he thought, occasioned by the Russian style of dress and he could be in the nineteen-thirties. He always had that feeling when he was in Russia. 'I nearly had a heart attack when that bloody man wanted to know where Virtanen was,' he said.

It had been a tricky moment. The Chief Engineer, Dzotenidze, had stood by the machine quite close to them while he interrogated Huovinen as to the whereabouts of Lassi Virtanen. 'Those screens aren't right,' he said in Russian. 'Virtanen isn't doing his work properly.'

An interpreter transmitted this to Huovinen, who said, 'Virtanen hasn't been feeling too well lately. An old war wound. In fact, he's not here today – he's at home in bed.'

Dzotenidze had been scathing but there was nothing he could do about it. 'See that he's back on the job as soon as possible,' he said, and stalked away.

Armstrong said, 'I could have stretched out my hand and touched him.'

'Huovinen could have come up with a better story,' said Carey grimly. 'What happens if that engineer checks back and finds that the bus came in with a full crew? Still, there's nothing we can do about it.'

They walked on for five minutes in silence. Armstrong said, 'How much farther?'

'Not far – just around the corner.' Carey tapped him on the arm. 'Now, Ivan, my lad; you're a common working man, so let your betters do the talking. If you have to talk you're slow and half-witted and as thick as two planks as befits a man who wields an idiot stick.' He indicated the spade.

'The heroic worker, in fact.'

'Precisely. And I'm the technician controlling the magic of modern science and haughty to boot.' They turned the corner. 'There's the house.' Carey regarded it critically. 'It looks pretty run-down.'

'That's why it's being demolished.'

'Just so.' Carey surveyed the street. 'We'll start on the outside just for the sake of appearances – right here in the street.' He took a pair of earphones from his pocket and plugged the lead wire into a socket on the metal detector. 'Do I look technical enough?'

'Quite sweet,' said Armstrong.

Carey snorted and switched on the detector, then adjusted a control. Holding the detector close to the ground like a vacuum cleaner he walked along the pavement. Armstrong leaned on his spade and looked on with an expression of boredom. Carey went for about fifty yards and then came back slowly. There was a worried look on his face. 'I'm getting quite a few readings. This street must be littered with metal.'

'Maybe you've struck gold,' suggested Armstrong.

Carey glared at him. 'I'm not being funny,' he snarled. 'I hope to hell the garden of that house isn't the same.'

'You're arousing interest,' said Armstrong. 'The curtain just twitched.'

'I'll give it another run,' said Carey. He went through his act again and paused in front of the house, than took a notebook from his pocket and scribbled in it.

Armstrong lounged after him just as a small boy came out of the house. 'What's he doing?'

'Looking for a water pipe,' said Armstrong.

'What's that thing?'

'The thing that tells him when he's found a water pipe,' said Armstrong patiently. 'A new invention.' He looked down at the boy. 'Is your father at home?'

'No, he's at work.' The boy looked at Carey who was peering over the garden fence. 'What's he doing now?'

'I don't know,' said Armstrong. 'He's the expert, not me. Is your mother at home?'

'She's doing the wash. Do you want to see her?'

Carey straightened up. 'I think it runs through here,' he called.

'Yes,' said Armstrong. 'I think we do want to see her. Run inside and tell her, will you?' The boy dashed into the house and Armstrong went up to Carey. 'Kunayev is at work; Mrs. K. is doing the wash.'

'Right; let's get to it.' Carey walked up to the front door of the house just as it opened. A rather thin and tired-looking woman stepped out. 'This is the . . . er –' Carey took out his notebook and checked the pages – 'the Kunayev household?'

'Yes, but my husband's not here.'

'Then you'll be Grazhdanke Kunayova?'

The woman was faintly alarmed. 'Yes?'

Carey beamed. 'Nothing to worry about, Grazhdanke Kunayova. This is merely a technicality concerning the forthcoming demolition of this area. You know about that?'

'Yes,' she said. 'I do.' The faint alarm turned to faint aggression. 'We're having to move just when I've redecorated the house.'

'I'm sorry about that,' said Carey. 'Well, under the ground there are a lot of pipes – gas, water, electricity and so on. My own concern is with the water pipes. When the demolition men come in there'll be bulldozers coming through here, and we don't want them breaking the water pipes or the whole area will turn into a quagmire.'

'Why don't you turn off the water before you start?' she asked practically.

Carey was embarrassed. 'That's not as easy as it sounds, Grazhdanke Kunayova,' he said, hunting for a plausible answer. 'As you know, this is one of the older areas of Svetogorsk, built by the Finns just after the First World War. A lot of the records were destroyed twenty-five years ago and we don't even know where some of the pipes are, or even if they connect into our present water system.' He leaned forward and said confidentially, 'It's even possible that some of our water still comes from over the border – from Imatra.'

'You mean we get it free from the Finns?'

'I'm not concerned with the economics of it,' said Carey stiffly. 'I just have to find the pipes.'

She looked over Carey's shoulder at Armstrong who was leaning on his spade. 'And you want to come into the garden,' she said. 'Is he going to dig holes all over our garden?'

'Not at all,' said Carey reassuringly. He lifted the detector. 'I have this – a new invention that can trace pipes without digging. It might be necessary to dig a small hole if we find a junction, but I don't think it will happen.'

'Very well,' she said unwillingly. 'But try not to step on the flower beds. I know we're being pushed out of the house this year but the flowers are at their best just now, and my husband does try to make a nice display.'

'We'll try not to disturb the flowers,' said Carey. 'We'll just go around to the back.'

He jerked his head at Armstrong and they walked around the house followed by the small boy. Armstrong said in a low voice, 'We've got to get rid of the audience.'

'No trouble; just be boring.' Carey stopped as he rounded the corner of the house and saw the garden shed at the bottom of the garden; it was large and stoutly constructed of birch logs. 'That's not on the plan,' he said. 'I hope what we're looking for isn't under there.'

Armstrong stuck his spade upright in the soil at the edge of a flower bed, and Carey unfolded a plan of the garden. 'That's the remaining tree there,' he said. 'One of the four Meyrick picked out. I'll have a go at that first.' He donned the earphones, switched on the detector, and made a slow run up to the tree. He spent some time exploring the area about the tree, much hampered by the small boy, then called, 'Nothing here.'

'Perhaps the pipe runs down the middle,' said Armstrong.

'It's possible. I really think I'll have to search the whole area.'

Which he proceeded to do. For the benefit of the small boy every so often he would call out a number and Armstrong would dutifully record it on the plan. After half an hour of this the boy became bored and went away. Carey winked at Armstrong and carried on, and it took him well over an hour to search the garden thoroughly.

He glanced at his watch and went back to Armstrong. 'We have two possibilities. A strong reading – very strong – on the edge of the lawn there, and a weaker reading in the middle of that flower bed. I suggest we have a go at the lawn first.'

Armstrong looked past him. 'Mrs. K. is coming.'

The woman was just coming out of the house. As she approached she said, 'Have you found anything?'

'We may have found a junction,' said Carey, and pointed. 'Just there. We'll have to dig – just a small hole, Grazhdanke Kunayova, you understand. And we'll be tidy and replace the turf.'

She looked down at the straggly lawn. 'I don't suppose it matters,' she said dispiritedly. 'My husband says the grass doesn't grow as well here as down south where we come from. Would you like something to eat?'

'We brought our own sandwiches,' said Carey gravely.

'I'll make you tea,' she said decisively, and went back to the house.

'Nice woman,' commented Carey. 'It's midday, when all good workers down tools for half an hour.'

They ate their sandwiches sitting on the lawn, and drank the glasses of lemon tea which the woman brought to them. She did not stay to make small talk, for which Carey was thankful. He bit into a sandwich and said meditatively, 'I suppose this is where Merikken and his family were killed – with the exception of young Harri.' He pointed to the house. 'That end looks newer than the rest.'

'Was there much bombing here?' asked Armstrong.

'My God; this place was in the front line for a time – the sky must have been full of bombers.'

Armstrong sipped the hot tea. 'How do we know the trunk is still here? Any keen gardener might have dug it up. What about Kunayev himself?'

'Let's not be depressing,' said Carey. 'It's time you started to dig. I'll give you a reading and then let you do the work, as befits my station in life.' He walked across the lawn, searched the area briefly with the detector, and stuck a pencil upright in the ground. 'That's it. Take out the turves neatly.'

So Armstrong began to dig. He laid the turves on one side and tried to put each spadeful of soil into as neat a heap as he could. Carey sat under the tree and watched him, drinking the last of his tea. Presently Armstrong called him over. 'How deep is this thing supposed to be?'

'About two feet.'

'I'm down two and a half and there's still nothing.'

'Carry on,' said Carey. 'Meyrick could have been in error.'

Armstrong carried on. After a while he said, 'I'm down another foot and still nothing.'

'Let's see what the gadget says.' Carey put on the earphones and lowered the detector into the hole. He switched on and hastily adjusted the gain. 'It's there,' he said. 'Must be a matter of inches. I've just had my ears pierced.'

'I'll go down a bit more,' said Armstrong. 'But it'll be difficult without enlarging the hole.' Again he drove the spade into the earth and hit something solid with a clunk. 'Got it!' He cleared as much as he could with the spade and then began to scrabble with his hands. After five minutes he looked up at Carey.

'You know what we've found?'

'What?'

Armstrong began to laugh. 'A water pipe.'

'Oh, for God's sake!' said Carey. 'Come out of that hole and let me see.' He replaced Armstrong in the hole and felt the rounded shape of the metal and the flange. He dug away more earth and exposed more metal, then he got out of the hole.

Armstrong was still chuckling, and Carey said, 'Fill in that hole and go gently. It's an unexploded bomb.'

Armstrong's laughter died away thinly.

'250 kilograms, I'd say,' said Carey. 'The equivalent of our wartime 500-pounder.'

29

They were grouped around Denison who lay prone on the ground. 'Don't move him,' warned Harding. 'I don't know what he'll have apart from concussion.' Very carefully he explored Denison's skull. 'He's certainly been hit hard.'

Diana looked at McCready. 'Who by?' McCready merely shrugged.

Harding's long fingers were going over Denison's torso. 'Let's turn him over – very gently.' They turned Denison over on to his back and Harding lifted one eyelid. The eye was rolled right back in the head, and Lyn gave an involuntary cry.

'Excuse me, Doctor,' said Diana, and her hand went to Denison's shirt pocket. She got up off her knees and jerked her head at McCready. They walked back to the middle of the camp. 'The plan and the notebook are gone,' she said. 'He carried them in the button-down pocket of his shirt. The button has been torn off and the pocket ripped. The question is by whom?'

'It wasn't the Yanks,' said McCready. 'I saw them well off down-river. And it wasn't the other mob, either; I'll stake everything on that.'

'Then who?'

McCready shook his head irritably. 'By God!' he said. 'There's someone around here cleverer than I am.'

'I'd better not comment on that,' said Diana tartly. 'You might get annoyed.'

'It doesn't really matter, of course,' said McCready. 'We were expecting it, anyway.'

'But we were expecting to use it to find out who the opposition is.' She tapped him on the chest. 'You know what this means. There are three separate groups after us.' She ticked them off on her fingers. 'The

Americans; another crowd who is vaguely Slav – Russians, Poles, Bulgarians, Yugoslavs, take your pick – and now someone mysterious whom we haven't even seen.'

'It's what Carey was expecting, isn't it?'

'Yes, but it's worrying all the same. Let's see how Denison is.'

They went back to the rock where Lyn was saying worriedly, 'It's just concussion, isn't it?'

'I'm not too sure,' said Harding. 'Lyn, you'll find a black box in my pack about half-way down. Bring it, will you?'

Lyn ran off and McCready went down on his knees by Denison. 'What's wrong with him apart from a crack on the head?'

'His pulse is way down, and I'd like to take his blood pressure,' said Harding. 'But there's something else. Look at this.' He took Denison's arm by the wrist and lifted it up. When he let go the arm stayed there. He took the arm and bent it at the elbow, and again it stayed in the position into which he had put it.

McCready drew in his breath sharply. 'You can mould the man like modelling clay,' he said in wonder. 'What is it?'

'A form of catalepsy,' said Harding.

That did not mean much to McCready. 'Does it usually accompany concussion?'

'Not at all. It's the first time I've seen it induced by a knock on the head. This is most unusual.'

Lyn came back and held out the box to Harding. 'Is this what you wanted?'

He nodded briefly, took out an elastic bandage of a sphygmometer and bound it around Denison's arm. He pumped the rubber bulb, and said, 'His blood pressure is down, too.' He unwrapped the bandage. 'We'll carry him back and put him into a sleeping bag to keep him warm.'

'That means we don't move from here,' said McCready.

'We can't move him,' said Harding. 'Not until I can find out what's wrong with him, and that, I'm afraid, is mixed up with what's been done to him.'

A bleak expression came over McCready's face. If they stayed at the camp they'd be sitting ducks for the next crowd of international yobbos.

Lyn said, 'Is he conscious or unconscious, Doctor?'

'Oh, he's unconscious,' said Harding. 'Blanked out completely.'

Harding was wrong.

Denison could hear every word but could not do a thing about it. When he tried to move he found that nothing happened, that he could not move a muscle. It was as though something had chopped all control from the brain. He had felt Harding moving his limbs and had tried to do something about it but he had no control whatever.

What he did have was a splitting headache.

He felt himself being lifted and carried and then put into a sleeping bag. After a few minutes he was lapped around in warmth. Someone had tucked the hood of the bag around his head so that sounds were muffled and he could not hear what was said very clearly. He wished they had not done that. He tried to speak, willing his tongue to move, but it lay flaccid in his mouth. He could not even move his vocal cords to make the slightest sound.

He heard a smatter of conversation. '. . . still breathing . . . autonomic functions unimpaired . . . side . . . tongue out . . . choking . . . ' That would be Harding.

Someone rolled him on to his side and he felt fingers inserted into his mouth and his tongue pulled forward.

After a little while he slept.

And dreamed.

In his dream he was standing on a hillside peering through the eyepiece of a theodolite. Gradually he became aware that the instrument was not a theodolite at all – it was a cine camera. He even knew the name of it – it was an Arriflex. And the small speck of blue lake in the distance became one of the blue eyes of a pretty girl.

He pulled back from the view finder of the camera and turned to Joe Staunton, the cameraman. 'Nice composition,' he said. 'We can shoot on that one.'

Great slabs of memory came slamming back into place with the clangour of iron doors.

'It's no good, Giles,' said Fortescue. 'It's becoming just that bit too much. You're costing us too much money. How the hell can you keep control when you're pissed half the time?' His contempt came over like a physical blow 'Even when you're not drunk you're hung over.' Fortescue's voice boomed hollowly as though he was speaking in a cavern. 'You can't rely on the Old Pals Act any more. This is the end. You're out.

Even in his dream Denison was aware of the wetness of tears on his cheeks.

He was driving a car, the familiar, long-since-smashed Lotus. Beth was beside him, her hair streaming in the wind. 'Faster!' she said. 'Faster!' His hand fell on the gear lever and he changed down to overtake a lorry, his foot going down on the accelerator.

The scooter shot, insect-like, from the side road right across his path. He swerved, and so did the lorry he was overtaking. Beth screamed and there was a rending, jangle of tearing metal and breaking glass and then nothing.

'Sorry about that,' said Staunton. 'This would have been a good one, but Fortescue won't have it. What will you do now?'

'Go home to Hampstead and get drunk,' said Denison.

Hampstead! An empty flat with no personality. Bare walls with little furniture and many empty whisky bottles.

And then . . .!

In his dream Denison screamed.

He stirred when he woke up and opened his eyes to find Lyn looking at him. He moistened his lips, and said 'Beth?'

Her eyes widened and she turned her head. 'Dr. Harding! Dr. Harding – he's awake.' There was a break in her voice. When she turned back to him he was trying to get up. 'No,' she said. 'Lie quietly.' She pushed him back.

'I'm all right,' he said weakly.

Harding appeared. 'All right, Lyn; let me see him.' He bent over Denison. 'How are you feeling?'

'Not too bad,' said Denison. 'Hell of a headache, though.' He put up his hand and tenderly felt the back of his head. 'What happened?'

'Somebody hit you.'

Denison fumbled with his other hand inside the sleeping bag, groping for his shirt pocket. 'They got the plan.'

'It doesn't matter,' said Lyn. 'Giles, it doesn't matter.'

'I know.' He levered himself up on one elbow and accepted the pills Harding gave him and washed them down with water. 'I think I gave you a shock, Doctor.'

'You were aware?' asked Harding in surprise.

'Yes. Another thing – I've got my memory back.'

'All of it?'

Denison frowned. 'How would I know? I'm not sure.'

'We won't go into that now,' said Harding quickly. 'How do you feel physically?'

'If you let me stand up I'll tell you.' He got out of the sleeping bag and stood up, supported on Harding's arm. He swayed for a moment and then shook himself free and took three steps. 'I seem all right,' he said. 'Except for the headache.'

'The pills ought to clear that up,' said Harding. 'But if I were you I wouldn't be too energetic.'

'You're not me,' said Denison flatly. 'What time is it? And where are the others?'

'It's just after midday,' said Lyn. 'And they're scouting to see if anyone else is around. I think the doctor is right; you ought to take it easy.'

Denison walked to the edge of the bluff, thinking of the perturbation in McCready's voice when he discovered that, because of the attack on himself, the party was pinned down. 'I ought to be able to cross the river,' he said. 'That might be enough.'

30

Armstrong was digging another hole. He had filled in the first one and left Carey to replace the turf. Carey did his best but still the lawn in that place was bumpy and uneven and, in the circumstances, he did not feel like stamping it down too hard. He looked towards Armstrong who appeared to be systematically wrecking a flower bed. 'Found anything?'

'Not yet.' Armstrong pushed again with the spade, and then stooped quickly. 'Wait! I think there's some –' before he finished the sentence Carey was by his side – 'thing here.'

'Let me see.' Carey put his hand down the hole and felt a flat surface. Flakes of something came away on his fingers and when he brought up his hand his fingertips were brown. 'Rust!' he said. 'This is it. Careful with that spade.'

He looked back at the house and thought it was fortunate that Mrs. K. had gone shopping and taken her son with her. A bit of good for a lot of bad. Earlier in the afternoon she had been out in the garden hanging out the weekly wash to dry, and then she had come over and chatted interminably about the iniquities of the planning authorities, the ridiculous prices in the shops and other matters dear to the housewifely heart. A lot of time had been wasted.

He said, 'If the trunk is corroded we might be able to rip open the top and take out the papers without making the hole any bigger.'

'I forgot my tin opener,' said Armstrong. 'But this might do.' He put his hand to the side of his leg and from the long pocket of the overalls designed to take a foot rule he extracted a sheathed knife. 'Bought it in

Helsinki; thought it might come in handy.'

Carey grunted as he saw the design. He took the knife from the sheath and examined the broad blade and the simple wooden handle. 'The Yanks think Jim Bowie invented these,' he said. 'Don't ever try to tackle a Finn with one; they're better at it than you. And probably the Russians, too, in these parts. It'll do quite nicely.'

He cleared earth from the top of the trunk until about a square foot of rusty metal was showing then he stabbed at it with the sharp point of the knife. The metal was rotten and the knife punched through with ridiculous ease. He enlarged the hole and bent up the metal into a tongue which he could hold in his fingers. He gripped it and pulled and there was a tearing sound.

Within five minutes he had made a hole in the trunk big enough to take his hand, and he groped inside and touched a hard square edge. His fingers curled around what felt like a book but when he tried to pull it out he found he was in the position of the monkey gripping the nut inside the bottle. The book was too big to come through the hole so he dropped it and concentrated on making the hole bigger.

At last he was able to get the book out. It was a school exercise book with hard covers and, when he flicked the pages, he saw mathematical symbols and lengthy equations in profusion. 'Jackpot!' he said exultantly.

The next thing out of the lucky dip was a roll of papers held by a rubber band. The rubber snapped at a touch but the papers, long rolled, held their curvature and he unrolled them with difficulty. The first pages were written in Finnish in a tight handwriting and the first mathematical equation came on the fourth page. From then on they were more frequent until the final pages were solid mathematics.

'How do we know what we're looking for?' asked Armstrong.

'We don't – we take the lot.' Carey dived into the hole again and groped about. Within ten minutes he had cleared the box which proved to be only half full but, even so, the books and papers made a big stack.

Carey took some folded paper bags from his pocket. 'Fill that hole; I'll take care of the loot.' He looked at his watch with worried eyes. 'We haven't much time.'

He filled three stout kraft-paper bags with documents and sealed them with sticky tape. Armstrong said, 'There's not enough earth to go back. It's filling the trunk.'

'I'll see to that,' said Carey. 'You nip along and fetch that wheelbarrow. You know where it's planted.'

'The empty house at the end of the street. I hope young Virtanen parked it in the right place.'

'You'll soon find out. Get going.' Carey began to fill in the hole and, as

Armstrong had said, there was not enough earth, so he took more from other parts of the flower bed and took care not to pack it too tightly. It took him quite a while but when he had finished Armstrong had not yet returned.

He took the brown paper bags from where they had been lying among the long-stemmed flowers and hid them more securely in some shrubbery. His watch told him that time was running out; they had to get back to the paper mill and smuggle the papers aboard the bus. That had been arranged for but it would take time and there was little of that left.

Impatiently he went to the front gate and was relieved to see Armstrong trudging back with the wheelbarrow. 'What kept you?'

'The damn fool *hid* it,' said Armstrong savagely. 'What did you tell him to do?'

'To put it just inside the wall and out of sight.'

'He put the bloody thing in the cellar,' said Armstrong. 'I had to search the house to find it.'

'A misunderstanding – but we've got it. Come on.'

They put the documents into the wheelbarrow and covered the bags with dirty sacking. Armstrong put the spade and the detector on top and picked up the handles of the wheelbarrow. He was about to push off when he stopped. 'Someone's coming.'

Carey turned. A man was coming up the garden from the side of the house. His whole attitude was one of suspicion. 'What are you doing in my garden?'

Carey stepped forward. 'Grazhdaninu Kunayev?'

'Yes.'

Carey reeled out his story, then said, 'Your wife knows about it, of course. We've made very little disturbance.'

'You've been digging holes? Where?'

Carey pointed. 'There – on the lawn.' He refrained from drawing attention to the flower bed.

Kunayev walked over and prodded at the turf with his toe. 'You've been neat, I will say that.' He stamped hard with his foot, and Armstrong winced, thinking of the bomb below. 'Does this mean you'll be coming in earlier?'

Carey frowned. 'How do you mean?'

'With the bulldozers.'

'Not that I know of, comrade. That's not my department. I'm concerned only with water pipes.'

Kunayev looked at the house. 'I've liked living here; it's a good place. Now they want to pull it down and put up another damn factory. I ask you; is that right, comrade? Do you think it's right?'

Carey shrugged. 'Progress sometimes means sacrifice.'

'And I'm doing the sacrificing.' Kunayev snorted. 'I'm being transferred to the new housing development on the other side of town. A cheap, rotten, new house. Not like this house, comrade; those Finns knew how to build houses.'

'Meaning that Soviet workers don't?' asked Carey suavely.

'I didn't say that,' said Kunayev. He walked towards the wheelbarrow and picked up the detector. 'Is this your water diviner?'

Carey tightened his lips. 'Yes.'

'Like the mine detector I used during the war. I was at Stalingrad, comrade. Fourteen years old I was then.' He strolled towards the fence separating his garden from the one next door, still holding the detector. 'Boris Ivanevitch, are you there?'

'For Christ's sake!' whispered Armstrong. 'What do we do now?'

A woman called back. 'He's just going on duty.'

'Good afternoon, Irina Alexandrovna; ask him to come round here. I have something to show him.'

'Let's just leave,' urged Armstrong.

'We can't leave without that detector,' said Carey through his teeth. 'It would look too suspicious.'

Kunayev came back from the fence. He had put on the earphones. 'Seems to work just like a mine detector, too. Not as big and heavy, of course; but they're clever with their electronics these days.'

'It works on a different principle,' said Carey. 'But we've finished here, Grazhdaninu Kunayev; we must go about our work.'

'No great hurry, comrade,' said Kunayev carelessly. He walked over to the patch of relaid turf. 'You say you found your water pipe here?'

'A pipe junction,' said Carey, gritting his teeth.

Kunayev flicked a switch and walked back and forth several times. 'It works,' he said. 'I could find that junction blind-fold – see if I can't.' He closed his eyes and walked back and forward again. 'Am I there?'

'Right on the spot,' said Armstrong.

Kunayev opened his eyes and looked past them. 'Ah, Boris Ivanevitch,' he said. 'You'll be interested in this.'

Carey turned around and felt a sinking feeling in his stomach. Boris Ivanevitch was a policeman.

31

'The chief study here at Sompio is the ecology of wetlands,' said Dr. Matti Mannermaa. 'In northern Finland we have many marshes caused by the slow drying out of the shallow lakes. Sompio was chosen as a nature preserve because it not only has such a marsh but also has high ground of an altitude of over five hundred metres and a small part of Lake Loka. Thus we have a varied habitat for many creatures, especially birds.'

'Very interesting,' said McCready, hoping the interest showed in his face. He was bored to death.

'I am an ornithologist, of course,' said Dr. Mannermaa. 'My work here is similar to that done at your English research station at Slimbridge.'

'I've been there,' said Harding with enthusiasm.

'So have I,' said Dr. Mannermaa. 'I spent many months there investigating British methods. We have adopted the rocket-driven net for use here. We ring a lot of birds for the study of migratory patterns.'

McCready indicated the rack of shotguns on the wall of Mannermaa's office. 'I see you shoot them, too.'

'We must,' said Mannermaa. 'We have a continuing study in pesticide residues in body fat. We break a lot of eggs, too, Mr. McCready – to study the thickness of the shells. Decreasing shell thickness is mainly a problem with the raptors, of course.' He laughed. 'I am not a sentimentalist about birds; I like roast duck just as much as anyone else.'

'I'm a wildfowler,' said Harding. 'We get good shooting in Norfolk.'

'I hope you don't take a shotgun into Sompio,' said Mannermaa. There was a twinkle in his eye which belied the gravity of his voice. 'Well, now; let us look at the map and decide what is best for you to do.'

He stood up and went to a wall map. For a few minutes they discussed routes and possibilities. 'Here there is a hut,' said Mannermaa. 'On the edge of the marsh just below Nattaset – that's the mountain here. It's equipped with bunks and cooking facilities – rough living but better than tenting.'

'Most kind of you,' said McCready. 'Thank you very much.'

'A lot of our technical equipment is stored there. Please try not to disturb it.'

'We won't touch anything,' promised McCready. 'Thank you for everything, Dr. Mannermaa.'

As they shook hands Mannermaa said, 'I hope your companions are successful in their shopping here. Vuotso is a small place and the range of choice may be restricted.'

'All we need are basic rations.'

'If you run out you'll find some tinned food in the hut,' said Mannermaa. 'You can pay for it when you get back.'

McCready and Harding left the office and emerged on to the main street of Vuotso. Harding said, 'Co-operative chap, isn't he? Those credentials Carey supplied must be really high-powered.'

'But we mustn't take a shotgun into Sompio,' said McCready. 'I wish we could take a machine-gun.'

'Do you think we'll be followed here?'

'It's a certainty – we left a trail like a bloody paper chase. Carey's plan is working and that's just fine for Carey, but I have a feeling that we're left holding the sticky end.' McCready sounded angry. 'It's all very well for him to set us up as targets but who likes being shot at? His plan that I should be an outside guard has already broken down. I have to sleep some time. It's too big a job for one man.'

'You'll be with us this time, then?'

McCready nodded. His brow was furrowed as he tried to cover all the angles. 'Another thing – how will Denison hold out?'

'He's got remarkable resilience,' said Harding. 'That crack on the head stirred things up and a lot of the blocks on his memory have been shaken loose. He's remembering more and more as time goes on, but he seems to have the ability to handle it.'

'What happens when he gets it all back? Does he crack up and go back on the bottle?' asked McCready sourly.

'I don't know. I tried him on whisky last night. He seems to have a positive aversion to it.'

McCready grunted. 'I hope he stays that way.'

In fact, Denison felt remarkably well. As they went on foot into the Sompio nature preserve he tried to analyse the reasons for his feeling of well-being and came to the conclusion that it was because of the absence of panic when he probed into his past. And then, of course, there was the immediate environment. He stopped and took a deep breath of the cool clean air and looked about him.

They were skirting the mountain called Nattaset and keeping to the high ground. Below there was a vista of the northern wilderness breathtaking in its beauty. Where there was firm ground the ever-present birches grew, but in between a multitude of islets there was a lacework intricacy of watercourses reflecting the blue of the sky, and in the distance an island-dotted lake shone like silver. Closer at hand white wreaths of last winter's snow lay all about.

Denison turned and saw McCready trailing about half a mile behind.

He, too, appeared to have stopped and Denison thought he was doing a search with field glasses – and not just to look at the view. If beauty is in the eye of the beholder then, as far as McCready was concerned, this view would be bleak indeed. There were far too many places for a man – or even a regiment – to hide.

Denison hitched his pack to a more comfortable position and set off again, keeping up a fast pace so as to catch up with the others. He drew abreast of Lyn, and said, 'It's lucky no one took a crack at us when we were leaving Kevo. I was so woozy I wouldn't have been much help.'

Lyn looked at him worriedly. 'How are you feeling now?'

'Fine,' he said lightly. 'I feel a lot better now I can remember things. This morning I remembered the name of the man in the flat above mine; Paterson – a nice chap.'

'And you remember being a film director?'

'Yes.' He laughed. 'Don't run away with the idea that I was one of your big-time movie moguls – my stuff wasn't shown in the West End. I make educational films mostly.' He frowned. 'Or, at least, I did. I was fired from my job.'

'Don't worry about that, Giles,' she said quietly.

'I'm not worrying; I have more important things on my mind at the moment. All the same,' he said, looking into his past. 'I don't seem to have been a nice character.'

There was violence in her voice. 'Forget it!' she said crossly.

He glanced at her face in profile. 'You worry about me, don't you?' There was a tinge of wonder in his voice; it had been a long time since anyone had worried about what happened to him. All Fortescue had worried about was whether the job would get done – he hadn't given a damn about Denison himself.

'What do you expect me to do? Cheer when you get slugged on the head?' She walked on a few more paces. 'You should never have agreed to this mad scheme.'

'Carey talked me into it – he's a very persuasive man. But you talked yourself into it. Nobody asked you to come. Now why did you do that?'

She offered him a wan smile. 'You know, you're rather like Hamlet; you let yourself be pushed around.'

He grinned. 'Ah, the fair Ophelia.'

'Don't class me with that damned ninny,' she snapped. 'I'm not going to go mad in white satin. But I still think that if Hamlet had had someone to give him advice, to put some backbone into him, things would have turned out differently. As it was, all he had was that wet, Horatio.'

He felt suddenly depressed. 'Are you offering to supply backbone?'

'All I'm saying is that you mustn't depend on this gang of Whitehall thugs. Don't believe everything Carey tells you. He's in business for himself, not you.' She seemed angry.

He was silent for a while. 'You could be right,' he said at last. 'I have no illusions about this job. I know I was thrown into it involuntarily but I carried on of my own will and with my eyes open. I know I'm being used and I don't particularly like it. At the same time when Carey put the proposition I was mixed up, to say the least, and I dare say Carey took advantage. I don't blame him for it – I was all he had.'

'But you're becoming better,' said Lyn. 'You'll be getting ready to make your own decisions.'

'We'll see,' said Denison thoughtfully. 'We'll see.' He hitched the pack on his back. 'When do we get to this hut?'

They pressed on late that night because Diana wanted to reach the hut. 'No point in staying in the open when we can have a roof over our heads,' she said. Travelling late was no problem; the light never left the sky and they were able to move as fast at midnight as at midday and they saw the hut at two in the morning.

It was built of birch logs and was bigger than they had expected. It was in the form of a letter 'H', wings having been added as was necessary. The living quarters were in the cross-bar of the 'H' and they were glad to divest themselves of the heavy packs. The two women began to prepare a meal and sent the men to get water.

Harding and Denison took buckets and went outside, and Harding stopped just outside the hut and looked across the marsh which seemed to consist of reeds and water for as far as the eye could see. 'Good wildfowling country,' he said appreciatively.

Denison slapped at his neck. 'Good mosquito country,' he grumbled.

'Don't worry; they're not malarial.'

'You mean I'm merely being eaten alive?' Denison slapped at himself again. 'Let's get the water.'

They went down to the water's edge and Harding inspected it critically. 'It looks all right; but we'd better boil it to make sure.' They filled the buckets and then Harding straightened. 'I wonder what that is.'

Denison followed the direction of his gaze and saw a low wooden hut on the water's edge about a hundred yards away. 'A sauna probably. The Finns like to have them on the edge of the water so they can jump right in. You won't catch me in there.'

'It doesn't look tall enough to be a sauna,' said Harding. 'The roof's too low. I think I'll take a look.'

'The girls will be screaming for water.'

'I won't be a minute.' Harding walked away following the shore line, and Denison shrugged. He picked up a full bucket and took it up to the main hut. Upon being told there was an insufficiency of water he went back for the other bucket. Harding called, 'Denison; look what I've found.'

Denison walked towards the little hut and thought Harding was probably right – the roof was so low that there would be barely sitting room in the hut, let alone standing room. He walked around it and found Harding squatting on his heels.

'What is it?'

'It's a gun punt,' said Harding. 'Haven't seen one for years.'

From this side Denison could see that the hut consisted of roof only and was merely a shelter over a flat boat which looked like an enlarged Eskimo kayak. 'So?'

Harding shook with laughter. 'Mannermaa told us not to bring a shotgun, and all the time he had this here. The old devil!'

Denison bent down beside Harding. 'I don't see what's funny.'

'You wouldn't. I bet the gun is up at the hut. I'll have to see if I can find it.' Harding pointed to the foredeck of the punt. 'Look there; that's where the breech ropes go.'

Denison looked at the two eyebolts – they told him nothing. 'You're not being very comprehensible.'

'I don't suppose I am. These things have gone out of fashion. There are a couple still in use on the east coast back at home, but I didn't expect to see one in Finland. You'll understand better when you see the gun, if I can find it.' Harding stood up. 'Let's go back.'

They went back to the hut, taking the second bucket of water. On the way they encountered McCready who was just coming in. He seemed tired and depressed. 'Not a sign of anyone,' he said. 'But that's not surprising.' He waved a hand at the marsh. 'How deep would you say that water is?'

'Not very deep,' said Harding. 'Not at the edges, anyway. Two or three feet, perhaps.'

McCready nodded. 'You could hide a bloody army in those reeds,' he said glumly. 'What's for supper?'

Denison smiled slightly. 'I'll lay you ten to one it's bully beef stew.'

'That's not very funny,' said McCready as he went into the hut.

After he had eaten McCready felt better. It had not been bully beef for once and, with his belly full, he felt sleepy. He glanced at the bunks in the corner of the room where Diana and Lyn were already asleep, huddled in their sleeping bags. 'Well, here we are – right in the middle of the bullseye,' he said. 'I suppose someone should keep watch.'

'You get some sleep,' said Denison. 'I'll toss with Harding as to who takes first watch.'

'Where is he?'

'Looking around for some kind of gun.'

McCready came alert. 'A gun?'

'Something to do with a boat he found. He's a wildfowler, you know. He didn't make much sense.'

'Oh, a sporting gun.' McCready lost interest. He stretched for the coffee pot, refilled his cup and then produced a flask. He laced the coffee with whisky and offered the flask to Denison. 'Want some?'

'No, thanks.'

'Lost the taste for it?'

'Seems so.'

McCready put away the flask and sipped his coffee. 'You can keep watch from the hut,' he said. 'Take a turn outside once every half-hour and keep an eye on the hillside. Not that it matters but it would be nice to have warning of anyone coming.'

'They'll come?'

'If not today then tomorrow. We give them what they want and maybe they'll go away. Maybe.' He shrugged. 'I'm not getting killed for the sake of a scrap of paper that doesn't mean a damned thing. Anyway, we've got her to think about.' He nodded towards the bunk where Lyn lay asleep.

'Nice of you to be so considerate,' said Denison.

'Don't be so bloody snippy,' said McCready without rancour. 'We didn't ask her to come – she forced it.' He stretched. 'I'm going to bed.'

Denison picked up the binoculars. 'I'll do a check outside.'

He went out of the hut and looked around, studying the hillside through the glasses, especially in the direction from which they had come. There was nothing to be seen. Next he turned his attention to the marsh. A long way out there were dots on an open stretch of water which, through the glasses, proved to be birds. They were unmoving and apparently asleep. Too big to be ducks they were, perhaps, geese. Harding might know. Not that it made any difference.

After a while he went back into the hut, moving quietly so as not to wake anybody. Harding had just come back; he beckoned to Denison and said in a low voice, 'I've found it – and look!' He opened the palm of his hand and revealed a dozen small copper cylinders rather like .22 cartridge cases without the bullets.

'What are they?'

'Detonators,' said Harding. 'I can't find any powder, though. Come and have a look at the gun.'

'All right,' said Denison. It was something to do until he had to go outside again.

He went with Harding into a room at the side of the hut which was used as a store. Rolled up netting hung neatly on pegs on the wall, and there were a lot of boxes which had been pulled away from the wall, presumably by Harding.

'I found it behind there,' said Harding. 'Not so much hidden as concealed from casual eyes. I knew it must be somewhere around because of the punt.'

Denison had not the faintest idea of what Harding was talking about but he obligingly stepped forward and looked behind the boxes. At first he did not realise what he was looking at; Harding had said something about a gun for a punt and that was what he expected to find – a shotgun to kill ducks. What he saw was something unexpected. True, it *was* a shotgun, as he realised as soon as his mind had shifted gear, but it was a shotgun of Brobdingnagian proportions.

'What the devil . . . ?'

Harding chuckled. 'I thought you'd be surprised.'

'Surprised isn't the word,' said Denison. 'Confounded is more like it. How long is this thing?'

'A bit over nine feet, taking in the stock. The barrel is about seven feet.'

Denison looked down at the monstrous object and bent to peer at the bore. He measured it with his thumb and found it to be over an inch and a half. He put his hand under the muzzle and lifted. 'It's damned heavy. How the hell can you shoot a thing like this? You couldn't get it to your shoulder.'

'You certainly couldn't,' agreed Harding. 'I estimate the weight as something over a hundred and twenty pounds. It'll fire about a pound and a half of shot.'

'Well, how *do* you shoot it?'

'It's a punt gun,' said Harding. 'It lies on the foredeck of that punt. You can see that the breech ropes are attached – they run through the ring bolts on the punt and take up the recoil. The stock is merely for aiming it; if you put your shoulder to it when firing you'd end up with a broken shoulder.'

Denison scratched his jaw. 'An impressive piece of artillery. I've never heard of anything like this.'

'It was developed early in the nineteenth century,' said Harding. 'The idea is that you lie flat in the punt and propel yourself with paddles rather like ping-pong bats. It's quite easy because once all the weight is in the punt it has a free-board of only about four inches. You stalk the birds on the water – going among the reeds – and you aim by pointing the whole punt. When you're in range you fire and, God willing, you get yourself a dozen birds.'

'Not very sporting,' commented Denison.

'Oh, it isn't as easy as you'd think. Birds aren't as easy to stalk as all that; they have more chance of escaping than you have of killing them.'

'What kind of cartridge does it use?'

'It doesn't.' Harding grinned. 'Try going to a gunsmith some time and asking for quarter-bore cartridges – he'd think you'd gone mad. If you want cartridges you make up your own. You use ordinary black powder well rammed and with your shot on top with some wadding; you put a detonator on this nipple – I won't now because it makes quite a noise even without a charge in the barrel – and you pull the trigger. Down goes the hammer on the nipple, the detonator explodes, flame shoots down the hole in the centre of the nipple and ignites the main charge. Bang!'

'And the whole punt recoils a few feet.'

'You've got the idea,' said Harding. 'The detonator is a modern touch. The originals used flint and steel – very unreliable – but with detonators you shouldn't have one misfire in a hundred.'

'Interesting,' said Denison.

'But no use without powder.' Harding patted the heavy barrel. 'I'd have liked to try it out. Like Mannermaa, I'm not averse to roast duck.'

'Are you averse to sleep?' Denison checked his watch. 'I'm going to wake you in two hours for the second guard duty. You'd better get your head down.'

32

Denison woke up because someone was shaking him. He moaned in protest and opened his eyes to see Diana bending over him. 'Wake up – we've got a visitor.'

He sat up and rubbed his eyes. 'Who?'

'Come and see.'

McCready was at the window, binoculars to his eyes. As Denison joined him he said, 'It's one of the characters from Kevo – not the Yanks, the other crowd.'

Denison saw the man walking along the edge of the marsh towards the hut. He was about four hundred yards away. 'Alone?'

'I haven't seen anyone else,' said McCready. 'This boy has his nerve, I must say.'

'Perhaps he doesn't know we're here.'

'Then he's a damned fool,' said McCready. 'And they don't send fools on jobs like this. Diana, stand behind the door with your gun.'

The man tramped stolidly towards the hut. If it were not for his pack he would have looked like any holidaymaker on any beach. Within ten minutes he was within hailing distance and he put up his hands showing empty palms. Holding them up he came to a stop ten yards from the door and waited.

'He knows we're here,' said McCready. He took a pistol from his pack and worked the action to put a round into the breech. He went to the door and held the pistol behind his back. 'If he comes in you'll be behind him,' he said to Diana, and opened the door.

The man still had his hands raised as McCready said, 'What do you want?'

'I want to talk to Dr. Harold Meyrick.' The man's English was good but heavily accented. Denison tried to identify the accent but made nothing of it.

'What if Dr. Meyrick doesn't want to talk to you?'

'Why not let him make up his own mind?' asked the man.

'Whom shall I announce?' asked McCready suavely.

'Shall we say . . . Herr Schmidt?'

McCready had no trouble with the accent. 'I'd prefer Pan Schmidt – and even then I don't like it. Schmidt isn't a Czech name.'

The man shrugged. 'Many people in Czechoslovakia have German names.' When McCready did not respond he said, 'My arms are getting tired.'

'You put them up, you pull them down – but not just yet.' McCready made up his mind. 'All right, Mr. Smith; step into my parlour.' He opened the door wide and stepped back. The man smiled as he came forward, his hands still high.

He walked into the hut and came to a dead stop four feet inside as McCready brought up the hand holding a gun. Diana closed the door behind him. 'Search him,' said McCready.

Schmidt half-turned and smiled as he saw the pistol in Diana's hand. 'So many guns,' he said. 'I am unarmed, of course.'

'There's no of course about it,' said McCready as Diana checked. When she had finished and found nothing McCready wagged the gun. 'Now take off your pack – slowly.'

Schmidt eased the pack from his shoulders and lowered it to the floor. 'That's better,' he said, flexing his arms. 'You people use guns too easily.

That's why I came with my hands up – I didn't want to be shot by accident. Why did you shoot at me at Kevo?'

'We didn't,' said McCready. 'You ran into another crowd.'

'You expect me to believe that?'

'I don't give a damn if you believe it or not – but you started a war with the United States. I was watching it – three of you against four Yanks. One of your chaps had a broken arm and an American had a bullet in his leg. I had a ringside seat on the other side of the river.'

'So?' said Schmidt. 'The Americans also.' He smiled pleasantly at Denison and then turned back to McCready. 'What Dr. Meyrick carries must be very important.'

'And what is it to you?'

'I've come to get it,' said Schmidt composedly.

'Just like that?'

'Just like that, Mr. McCready.' He grinned. 'You see that I know your name. In fact, I know the names of everyone here. Mrs. Hansen, Dr. Harding, Dr. Meyrick and, of course, Miss Meyrick. It wasn't hard.'

'No doubt it wasn't,' said McCready. 'But what makes you think that Dr. Meyrick will give you anything?'

Schmidt looked Denison in the eye. 'I should think he values the safety of his daughter. It is unwise to go treasure hunting while in possession of a greater treasure, Dr. Meyrick.'

Denison glanced at Lyn, then cleared his throat. 'But we have you, Mr. Schmidt – if that's your name.'

Schmidt smiled and shook his head. 'I can see you're no tactician, Doctor. You see, I am no treasure. I am sure Mr. McCready is ahead of you in his thinking.'

'You've got the place surrounded, then?' said McCready.

'Of course. There are more than three of us this time.' Schmidt looked at his watch. 'The time is up in twenty-five – no, twenty-four – minutes.'

From the window Harding said, 'He could be pulling a bluff. I've seen no one.'

'The answer to that is easy,' said Schmidt. 'Call my bluff. I'm prepared to wait – if I can sit down.' He took a very slow step sideways and hooked a chair forward with his foot, never taking his eyes off McCready's pistol.

McCready leaned against the table. 'All right,' he said. 'Tell me what Meyrick has that interests you Czechs so much.'

A pained look appeared on Schmidt's face. 'Don't be stupid, McCready.' He jerked his thumb at Denison. 'He babbled about it in Stockholm. He discovered what was in his father's papers and where they were, and he talked about it to some Swedish friends. You ought to know scientists can't keep secrets. But then he realised exactly what he was talking about so he shut up and went back to England.'

He stopped. McCready's face was blank. 'Go on.'

'Why?' asked Schmidt. 'You know the answers. By then it was too late; the secret was out. Nothing travels faster than the news of a scientific breakthrough. Scientists like to believe in what they call the community of ideas, so the news got around Sweden, to Germany and to Czechoslovakia.'

'And to the United States,' commented McCready.

Schmidt hunched his shoulders. 'Everyone know the reputation of old Merikken and everyone knows his history. The guess is that he puts his papers somewhere for safe keeping. The way you're behaving leads us to think he buried them – or had them buried – somewhere in northern Finland. So it's a treasure hunt, as I said, and you've got a map with a cross on it. That or the equivalent.' He straightened. 'I want it.'

McCready slanted his eyes towards Denison. 'You see what comes of talking too much.' They were going to give in – that was the plan – but they must not collapse too easily because that would lead to suspicion. 'Let's be democratic, he said. 'We'll vote on it. Harding?'

'I think he's bluffing,' said Harding flatly. 'I don't think there is anyone out there. Tell him to go to hell.'

Schmidt smiled but said nothing. McCready looked at Denison. 'What about you, Meyrick? You know the importance of this more than anyone.'

'I'm not the only one to be considered,' said Denison. 'Let him have what he wants.'

'Very wise,' said Schmidt.

'Shut up,' said McCready unemotionally. 'Diana?'

'I'm against.'

McCready turned his head. His face was away from Schmidt and he winked at Lyn. 'What do you say?'

'I vote with my father.'

McCready turned back to Schmidt. 'It seems I have the casting vote – yours doesn't count.'

'It will.' Schmidt nodded towards the window. 'My votes are out there.'

'I think you're going to have to prove that,' said McCready. 'You might be bluffing and you might not, but I'm going to call you regardless.'

'This is more dangerous than a game of poker.'

McCready smiled. 'When you came in here you said you didn't want to be shot by accident, so my guess is that if you do have a loaded vote outside you won't use it forcibly against this hut. You see, you're inside it, too.'

'It's your guess,' said Schmidt.

'And it's your life.' McCready raised his pistol. 'If one bullet comes into this hut you're dead. If I don't kill you Diana will. And there's always Harding in reserve.'

Schmidt looked around at Diana who had a gun trained on him. He glanced at Harding who had also produced a pistol. His hand went to the pocket of his anorak. 'Do you mind if I smoke?'

McCready said nothing. Schmidt shrugged and lit a cigarette. He blew a perfect smoke ring. There was a crackling silence in the hut that went on and on.

33

Armstrong's hands sweated as he gripped the handles of the wheelbarrow and trundled it along the pavement at a speed that was positively dangerous to the pedestrian population of Enso. Beside him Carey walked quickly to keep pace, every now and then breaking into a little trot. Armstrong came to a halt at a street corner, stopped by the traffic flow.

'Damn Boris Ivanevitch!' said Carey. 'God save us all from talkative coppers. I hope he gets hell for being late on duty.'

'Not far now,' said Armstrong. 'Only another block. You can see the paper mill from here.'

Carey craned his neck and suddenly groaned. 'And I can see that bloody bus – it's just leaving.'

'Is it coming this way? Perhaps we can flag it down.'

'No, damn it! It's going away from us.' Carey checked his watch. 'Dead on time. Huovinen is chicken-livered; he could have delayed it somehow.'

There came a gap in the traffic and Armstrong jolted the barrow over the kerb. 'What now?' he asked as they crossed the street.'

'I don't know,' said Carey heavily. 'Let's find a place where we're not too conspicuous.'

'The mill is as good a place as any.'

'No; there'll be a watchman. Go around the next corner and we'll see what we can find.'

They were lucky. A trench was being dug along one side of the street. Carey said, 'Just the thing; we'll stop here.'

Armstrong stopped and lowered the barrow. 'Why here?'

Carey sighed and plucked at his jacket. 'Don't be dim. This uniform and those exposed pipes go together. We look natural.'

Armstrong glanced around. 'A good thing the gang's knocked off work for the day.'

'Yes,' said Carey. 'Jump in the hole and you'll look natural.' Armstrong dropped into the trench and Carey squatted on his heels. 'Got any bright ideas?'

'There's the empty house where I found the barrow. We could lie low in the cellar.'

'Until tomorrow?' Carey pondered and shook his head. 'The problem is the head count at the frontier post. They'll be two short and that might make it a bit unhealthy around here before long.'

Armstrong snapped his fingers. 'There's a railway goes from here to Imatra. Maybe we could get a ride.'

'Nothing doing. Railway police are notoriously efficient – especially at frontiers. All it needs is a telephone call from that frontier post to say there are two Finns missing and they'll be doubly efficient.'

'There's a copper coming up just behind you,' said Armstrong.

Carey did not turn. 'Not Boris Ivanevitch, I hope.'

'No.'

'Then have a look at that pipe and tell me what you see.'

Armstrong ducked down into the trench. His voice floated up. 'It's not cracked.'

'It must be cracked somewhere,' said Carey loudly. He heard the crunch of boots on road gravel behind him. 'We'll have to do a smoke test.' He looked up and saw the policeman. 'Good evening, comrade.'

The policeman's face was expressionless. 'Working late?'

'I always have to work late when something goes wrong,' said Carey in a grumbling voice. 'If it isn't one thing it's another, and they always pick on me. Now it's a pipe that's sprung a leak which no one can find.'

The policeman looked into the trench. 'What's this for?'

'Drainage for the new paper mill over there.'

The policeman looked at Carey. His eyes were like stones. 'You won't drain a paper mill through a pipe that size.'

'Not the main drainage for the mill,' said Carey. 'This is what you might call the domestic drainage for the lavatories and the canteen and so on.' An idea suddenly came into his mind, the brilliance of which astounded him. 'Perhaps the leak is in the mill. I might have to go in and see if I can find it there.' He stood up. 'You never can tell what a bad leak will do underground – undermine walls, anything.' He frowned. 'There's some heavy machinery in there.'

'So they tell me,' said the policeman. 'Imported from Finland.'

'I don't know why we can't use our own Russian stuff,' said Carey disgustedly. 'But Russian or Finnish, it will collapse if the foundations are washed from under it. I'd better go and have a look.'

'You're keen on your job,' said the policeman.

'That's how I got to where I am,' said Carey. He jerked his thumb at Armstrong. 'Now, take that young chap; he'll never rise to be an inspector if he lives a hundred years. He never raises a finger unless someone tells him to.' He turned to the trench. 'Come on, useless; we're going into the mill. Bring your barrow with your spade – we might need them.'

He walked away as Armstrong climbed out of the trench and the policeman fell into step beside him. 'You're right,' said the policeman. 'Some of these young chaps *are* useless.'

'Do you have many like that in your lot?' asked Carey.

The policeman laughed. 'They wouldn't last long with us. No, it's the layabouts I come across in the course of duty who grate on my nerves. Youngsters of fifteen and sixteen with hair half-way down their backs and swilling vodka until they're rotten drunk. I don't know how they can afford it. I can't – not on my pay.'

Carey nodded. 'I'm having something of the same trouble with my own son. This generation is as soft as putty, but what can you do, comrade? What can you do?'

'Well, I'll tell you,' said the policeman. 'Just tell that son of yours to keep out of my way. I'm getting a bit heavy-handed these days.'

They stopped at the mill entrance. 'Perhaps you're right,' said Carey. 'Maybe that's what's needed.'

'It is,' said the policeman. He flicked a hand in farewell. 'I hope you find your leak, comrade.'

'Just a minute,' said Carey. 'I've just thought of something. The watchman might not let us in.'

The policeman grinned. 'I'll have a word with him; it'll be all right.'

He walked into the mill and Carey winked at Armstrong. 'Not bad chaps, these Russian coppers, when you get to know them – in spite of Boris Ivanevitch. Come on.'

'Thanks for the testimonial,' said Armstrong. 'It's just the thing I need to get a job around here. Why are we going in?'

'You park the barrow near that temporary office in the corner. Then you go away and keep the watchman busy while I do a spot of burglary.'

'You can't burgle in front of a copper.'

'He won't stay around,' said Carey. 'He has his beat to cover.'

'All right; you do your burglary – then what?'

Carey grinned. 'Then we get ourselves booted out of Russia.'

Half an hour later, when they were walking up to the frontier post, Carey said, 'It was the papers that bothered me. Leaving Russia is easy, but not with Merikken's papers. Then I started talking to the copper about the mill and it gave me the idea. I'd seen those blueprints in that office this morning.'

Armstrong trundled the wheelbarrow. 'I hope it works. There's the frontier post.'

'Remember you don't know any Russian,' said Carey. 'It would be uncharacteristic in a Finn of your class.'

'I don't know any Finnish either,' said Armstrong. 'And that's bloody uncharacteristic.'

'Then keep your mouth shut,' said Carey. 'If you have to talk at all use Swedish; but don't talk if you can help it. Leave the talking to me. And hope that none of these guards are studying engineering or mathematics.'

They bore down on the frontier post at a steady three miles an hour. Armstrong was still wearing working overalls but Carey had covered his uniform. He had stopped being a Russian and was now a Finn. The guard regarded them with mild surprise as they approached. 'This is as far as you go,' he said in Russian, and accompanied the statement with a smile.

Carey answered in fast Finnish. 'Did the bus driver tell you we were coming? The fool left us behind. We've had to walk from the paper mill.'

The smile left the guard's face as he heard the Finnish. 'Where the devil have you come from?' he asked in Russian.

'I don't speak Russian,' said Carey. 'Don't you know Finnish?'

'Sergeant!' yelled the guard, passing the buck.

A sergeant came out of the guard house, leisurely fastening his belt. 'What's the matter?'

'These two Finns popped up. They came from back there.'

'Oh, they did, did they?' The sergeant stepped over and inspected them critically, his eyes dwelling for a time on the barrow. In exceedingly bad Finnish he asked, 'Where did you come from?'

'The paper mill,' said Carey, speaking slowly. 'The bus driver left us behind.' He indicated the barrow. 'We had to collect these papers to take to the boss in Imatra. It took us a while to find them and when we came out the bus had gone.'

'What are the papers?'

'Machine drawings and calculations. See for yourself.' Carey threw aside the sacking on top of the barrow and picked up the top document. He unfolded it to reveal a blueprint which he gave to the sergeant. 'That's one of the drawings.'

The sergeant studied the complexity of lines with uncomprehending eyes. 'Why take them back to Imatra?'

'For revision,' said Carey. 'It happens all the time. When you build a complicated machine it doesn't always fit together right, usually because some fool of a draughtsman has made a mistake. So the drawings have to be amended.'

The sergeant raised his head and eyed Carey and then looked at the blueprint again. 'How do I know this is what you say it is? I know nothing about paper machinery.'

'In the bottom righthand corner there's the name of our company and a description of the drawing. Can you read that much Finnish?'

The sergeant did not reply. He handed the blueprint back to Carey. 'Are they all like this?'

'Help yourself,' said Carey generously.

The sergeant bent and rooted about in the wheelbarrow. When he straightened he was holding a hardboard exercise book. He opened it and glanced at a solid block of mathematical equations. 'And this?'

'I wouldn't know until I saw it,' said Carey. 'It could be about the chemistry or it could be mechanical. Let me see.' He leaned over to look at the page the sergeant was examining. 'Ah, yes; those are the calculations for the roller speeds. This machine is very advanced – very technical. Do you know that the paper goes through at seventy kilometres an hour? You have to be very exact when you're working at those speeds.'

The sergeant flicked through the pages and then dropped the book into the barrow. 'What do you mean – chemical?'

Carey was enthusiastic. 'Papermaking is as much a chemical process as mechanical. There's the sulphite and the sulphate and the clay – all have to be worked out in exact formulae for the making of different kinds of paper. I'll show you what I mean.' He dug into the wheelbarrow and brought up a roll of papers. 'These are the calculations for that kind of thing. Look; these are the equations for making tissue paper of cosmetic quality – and here – the calculations for ordinary newsprint.'

The sergeant waved away the papers from under his nose. 'I'm sorry,' he said. 'I have no authority to let you pass. I will have to consult my captain.' He turned to go back into the guard house.

'*Perrrkele!*' swore Carey, giving the 'r' its full Finnish value. 'You know damned well by the head count that thirty-six came in and only thirty-four went out.'

The sergeant halted in mid-stride. Slowly he turned and looked at the guard who shrugged helplessly. 'Well?' he asked acidly.

The guard was out of luck. 'I haven't put it in the book yet.'

'How many went out tonight?'

'Thirty-four, plus the driver.'

'How many came in this morning?'

'I don't know. I wasn't on duty this morning.'

'*You don't know!*' The sergeant was apoplectic. 'Then what's the use of doing a head count?' He took a deep breath. 'Bring me the book,' he said arctically.

The guard bobbed his head and went into the guard house at the double. He emerged in less than fifteen seconds and handed the sergeant a small record book. The sergeant turned the pages and then gave the guard a look that ought to have frozen the blood in his veins. 'Thirty-six came in,' he said softly. 'And you didn't know.'

The luckless guard had the sense to keep his mouth shut. The sergeant checked his watch. 'When did the bus go through?'

'About three-quarters of an hour ago.'

'*About!*' the sergeant screamed. 'You're supposed to know to the second.' He slapped the page. 'You're supposed to record it in here.' He snapped his mouth shut into a straight line and the temperature fell. 'For *about* three-quarters of an hour two foreign nationals have been wandering on the wrong side of the frontier without anyone knowing about it. Am I supposed to tell that to the captain?' His voice was low.

The guard was silent. 'Well, speak up!' the sergeant yelled.

'I . . . I don't know,' said the guard miserably.

'You don't know,' repeated the sergeant in freezing tones. 'Well, do you know this? Do you know what would happen to me?' – he slapped himself on the chest – 'to me if I told him that? Within a week I'd be serving on the Chinese frontier – and so would you, you little turd, but that wouldn't make me any happier.'

Carey tried to look unconcerned; he was not supposed to know Russian. He saw the beginnings of a grin appear on Armstrong's face and kicked him on the ankle.

'Stand to attention!' roared the sergeant, and the guard snapped straight, his back like a ramrod. The sergeant went very close to him and peered at him from a range of six inches. 'I have no intention of serving on the Chinese frontier,' he said. 'But I will guarantee one thing. Within a week you'll be wishing you were on the Chinese frontier – and on the Chinese side of it.'

He withdrew. 'You'll stay there until I tell you to move,' he said quietly, and came over to Carey. 'What's your name?' he asked in Finnish.

'Mäenpää,' said Carey. 'Rauno Mäenpää. He's Simo Velling.'

'Your passes?'

Carey and Armstrong produced their passes and the sergeant

scrutinised them. He handed them back. 'Report here when you come in tomorrow. Report to me and no one else.'

Carey nodded. 'We can go?'

'You can go,' said the sergeant tiredly. He swung around and yelled at the unfortunate guard, 'Well, what are you waiting for? The grass to grow between your toes? Raise that barrier.'

The guard was electrified into sudden action. He raised the barrier and Armstrong pushed the wheelbarrow to the other side. Carey was about to follow when he paused. He turned to the sergeant and said, 'Papermaking is very interesting, you know. When the factory is working you ought to go and see it. Very spectacular.'

'I might do that,' said the sergeant.

Carey nodded pleasantly and followed Armstrong. He took a deep breath as though it was a different kind of air.

34

Schmidt consulted his watch. 'One minute.' He dropped a cigarette stub on the floor and put his foot on it.

'We'll wait,' said McCready. He nodded to Denison. 'Check the windows – see if there's anyone out there. You too, Harding.'

Denison went to the window. All was quiet and nothing moved except water ripples in the distance and the reeds which swayed stiffly in the light breeze. 'All quiet.'

'Here, too,' said Harding, who was at the back window. 'Not a thing stirring on the mountain.'

'I think you're trying to pull a fast one,' said McCready. 'It would be a hell of a joke if there was just one man out there.'

Schmidt shrugged. 'Wait for it.'

Denison saw a movement in the reed bed at the edge of the marsh. 'There's something – or someone out there. It's a man. He's . . .'

His words were cut off by staccato explosions. In front of the hut the ground danced and soil fountained under the impact of bullets. An upthrown stone hit the pane of glass in front of Denison and the glass fractured and starred. He ducked hastily.

The noise stopped, chopping off into a dead silence.

McCready let out his breath. 'Automatic weapons. At least three.'

'Five,' said Schmidt. 'Seven men – eight including me.' His hand dipped into his pocket and came out with the packet of cigarettes. 'I've just cast my vote.'

McCready casually laid down his pistol on the table. 'Power grows out of the barrel of a gun. Your guns are bigger.'

'I thought you'd see sense,' said Schmidt approvingly. 'Where's the map, or whatever it is?'

'Give it to him,' said McCready.

Denison took a folded sheet of paper from his pocket and held it out to Schmidt who examined it with interest. His interest turned to bafflement. 'Is this all?'

'That's all,' said Denison.

'This word – ' Schmidt stumblingly pronounced it – '*Iuonnonpuisto*. What does it mean?'

'A literal translation would be "nature park",' said McCready. 'The other three words mean lake, hill and gap. The numbers are co-ordinates in degrees of a circle. If you can find a lake, a hill and a gap in that exact relationship, all in a nature park, then you've solved the problem.' He smiled at Schmidt. 'I can't say I wish you better luck than we've had.'

'Not much to go on,' said Schmidt. 'And this is a photocopy.'

'Someone snatched the original at Kevo. Our friend there got a bump on the head. So it wasn't you, then?'

'Obviously it wasn't,' said Schmidt. 'The Americans?'

'I don't think so.'

'I do think so,' stated Schmidt. 'Because they aren't here. Perhaps they're back at Kevo measuring angles with a theodolite like he was doing.' He pointed at Denison.

'Maybe,' said McCready non-committally.

Schmidt stared at the paper. 'This is foolishness. Why didn't he give the name of the nature park?'

'Why should he?' asked McCready. 'He knew it. That is just an *aide-mémoire* – just for the figures. You see, Merikken *knew* where the papers were and expected to dig them up himself – he didn't expect to be killed in an air raid. But since one bit of rough country looked very much like another he took the precaution of measuring those angles.' He offered Schmidt a derisory smile. 'Those papers will be a hell of a job to find – especially with interference.'

Schmidt had a sour expression on his face as he folded the paper and put it into his pocket. 'Where's your theodolite?'

'Over there in the corner.'

'You don't mind if I borrow it?' His voice was heavily ironic.

'Go ahead; we can get another.'

Schmidt stood up, went to the door and opened it. He shouted something in Czech and came back into the room. 'Put your guns on the table.'

McCready hesitated, then said, 'All right, everybody; put your guns with mine.'

'You're showing sense,' said Schmidt. 'Neither of us can afford a shooting incident – especially if people are killed.' He laughed. 'If only I have the guns we'll both be safe.'

Diana reluctantly laid down her gun and Harding followed suit. When the door opened to admit another man there were five pistols laid out. The man was carrying an automatic rifle and when Schmidt saw that McCready was looking at it with wary interest he laughed, and said, 'We borrowed some of your N.A.T.O. weapons. They're not bad.' He spoke to the man and pointed at the back packs, then he picked up the pistols, put three of them into his pockets and held the other two in his hands.

'You spoke of interference,' he said to McCready. 'You will not interfere. You are out of the game.'

The other man was dumping the contents of the packs on to the floor. He gave a startled exclamation as he came upon McCready's collapsible rifle. Schmidt smiled, and said, 'Always trying, Mr. McCready – but that I expect. You will stay in this hut. If you attempt to leave it there is a grave danger of being shot dead.'

'How long for?'

Schmidt shrugged. 'For as long as I consider necessary.'

Diana spoke up. 'We'll need water.'

Schmidt regarded her speculatively, then nodded abruptly. 'I am not an inhumane man.' He pointed to Harding and Denison. 'You and you will bring water now. The rest will stay here.'

Denison picked up the two empty buckets, and Harding said, 'We'll need as much as possible. I'll take the bowls.'

The man with the automatic rifle slung it over his shoulder together with McCready's rifle. He picked up the theodolite and its tripod and left the hut followed by Denison and Harding, and Schmidt brought up the rear, a gun in each hand.

McCready watched them go down to the edge of the marsh, and cocked an eye at Diana. 'They seem to have bought it,' he said softly. 'For the next few weeks all the nature parks in Finland will be crawling with Czechs wielding theodolites. That ought to make the Finns properly suspicious.'

Denison walked down to the marsh acutely aware that the man behind him was holding a pair of pistols. He bent down and began to fill the buckets. Schmidt lobbed the pistols one at a time into the marsh, using an overarm throw like a cricketer. He spaced them well out and Denison knew they would be irrecoverable. He straightened his back and said, 'How will we know when it's safe to come out of the hut?'

There was a grim smile on Schmidt's face. 'You won't,' he said uncompromisingly. 'You'll have to take your chances.'

Denison stared at him and then looked down at Harding who shrugged helplessly. 'Let's go back to the hut,' he said.

Schmidt stood with his hands on his hips and kept his eyes on them all the way to the hut. The door closed behind them and he hitched his pack into a more comfortable position, spoke briefly to his companion, and set off along the edge of the marsh in the same direction from which he had come, keeping up the same stolid pace as when he had arrived.

35

It seemed to Denison that of all the episodes he had gone through since being flung into this hodge-podge of adventures the time he spent in the hut at Sompio was characterised by a single quality – the quality of pure irritation. The five of them were pent up – 'cribbed, cabined and confined', as Harding ironically quoted – and there was nothing that any of them could do about it, especially after McCready tested the temperature of the water.

After two hours had gone by he said, 'I think we ought to do something about this. I'll just stick my toe in and see what it's like.'

'Be careful,' said Harding. 'I was wrong about Schmidt – he doesn't bluff.'

'He can't leave his men around here for ever,' said McCready. 'And we'd look damned foolish if there's no one out there.'

He opened the door and stepped outside and took one pace before a rifle cracked and a bullet knocked splinters from a log by the side of his head so that white wood showed. He came in very fast and slammed the door. 'It's a bit warm outside,' he said.

'How many do you think there are?' asked Harding.

'How the hell would I know?' demanded McCready irritably. He put his hand to his cheek and pulled out a wood splinter, then looked at the blood on his fingertips.

'I saw the man who fired,' said Denison from the window. 'He was just down there in the reeds.' He turned to McCready. 'I don't think he meant to kill. It was just a warning shot.'

'How do you make that out?' McCready displayed the blood on his hand. 'It was close.'

'He has an automatic rifle.' said Denison. 'If he wanted to kill you he'd have cut you down with a burst.'

McCready was on the receiving end for the first time of the hard competency which Carey had found so baffling in Denison. He nodded reluctantly. 'I suppose you're right.'

'As for how many there are, that's not easy to say,' said Denison. 'All it needs is one at the front and one at the back, but it depends on how long Schmidt wants to keep us here. If it's longer than twenty-four hours there'll be more than two because they'll have to sleep.'

'And we can't get away under cover of darkness because there isn't any,' said Harding.

'So we might as well relax,' said Denison with finality. He left the window and sat at the table.

'Well, I'm damned!' said McCready. 'You've got it all worked out, haven't you?'

Denison looked at him with a half-smile. 'Have you anything to add?'

'No,' said McCready disgustedly. He went over to Diana and talked to her in a low voice.

Harding joined Denison at the table. 'So we're stuck here.'

'But quite safe,' said Denison mildly. 'As long as we don't do anything bloody foolish, such as walking through that door.' He unfolded a map of the Sompio Nature Park and began to study it.

'How are you feeling?' asked Harding.

'Fine.' Denison looked up. 'Why?'

'As your personal head-shrinker I don't think you'll be needing me much longer. How's the memory?'

'It's coming back in bits and pieces. Sometimes I feel I'm putting together a jigsaw puzzle.'

'It's not that I want to probe into a delicate area,' said Harding. 'But do you remember your wife?'

'Beth?' Denison nodded. 'Yes, I remember her.'

'She's dead, you know,' said Harding in an even uninflected voice. 'Do you remember much about that?'

Denison pushed away the map and sighed. 'That bloody car crash – I remember it.'

'And how do you feel about it?'

'How the hell would you expect me to feel about it?' said Denison with suppressed violence. 'Sorrow, anger – but it was over three years ago and you can't feel angry for ever. I'll always miss Beth; she was a fine woman.'

'Sorrow and anger,' repeated Harding. 'Nothing wrong with that.

Quite normal.' He marvelled again at the mysteries of the human mind. Denison had apparently rejected his previous feelings of guilt; the irrational component of his life had vanished. Harding wondered what would happen if he wrote up Denison's experiences and presented them in a paper for the journals – 'The Role of Multiple Psychic Trauma in the Suppression of Irrational Guilt'. He doubted if it would be accepted as a serious course of treatment.

Denison said, 'Don't resign yet, Doctor; I'd still like to retain your services.'

'Something else wrong?'

'Not with me. I'm worried about Lyn. Look at her.' He nodded towards Lyn who was lying on her back on a bunk, her hands clasped behind her head and staring at the ceiling. 'I've hardly been able to get a word out of her. She's avoiding me – wherever I am, she's not. It's becoming conspicuous.'

Harding took out a packet of cigarettes and examined the contents. 'I might have to ration these,' he said glumly. 'I've also been wondering about Lyn. She is a bit withdrawn – not surprisingly, of course, because she has a problem to solve.'

'Oh? What's her problem? Apart from the problems we all have here?'

Harding lit a cigarette. 'It's personal. She talked to me about it – hypothetically and in veiled terms. She'll get over it one way or another.' He drummed his fingers on the table. 'What do you think of her?'

'She's a fine person. A bit mixed up, but that's due to her upbringing. I suppose the problem has to do with her father.'

'In a manner of speaking,' said Harding. 'Tell me; what was the difference in age between your wife and yourself?'

'Ten years,' said Denison. He frowned. 'Why?'

'Nothing,' said Harding lightly. 'It's just that it could make things a lot easier – your having had a wife so much younger than yourself, I mean. You used to wear a beard, didn't you?'

'Yes,' said Denison. 'What the hell are you getting at?'

'I'd grow it again if I were you,' advised Harding. 'The face you're wearing tends to confuse her. It might be better to hide it behind a bush.'

Denison's jaw dropped. 'You mean . . . Diana said something . . . she can't . . . it's imposs . . .'

'You damned fool!' said Harding in a low voice. 'She's fallen for Denison but the face she sees is Meyrick's – her father's face. It's enough to tear any girl in half, so do something about it.' He stood up. 'Talk to her, but go easy.' He went to the other end of the room and joined McCready and Diana, leaving Denison staring at Lyn.

McCready organised watches. 'Not'that anything is likely to happen,' he said. 'But I'd like advance notice if it does. Those not on watch can do what they like. My advice is sleep.' He lay on a bunk and followed his own advice.

Harding wandered off into the storerooms and Denison resumed his study of the map of Sompio. From time to time he heard scrapings and bangings as Harding moved boxes about. Diana was on watch at a window and she and Lyn conversed in low tones.

After a couple of hours Harding came back looking rumpled and dishevelled. In his hand he carried what Denison took to be a gallon paint can. 'I've found it.'

'Found what?'

Harding put the can on the table. 'The powder.' He prised the lid off the can. 'Look.'

Denison inspected the grainy black powder. 'So what?'

'So we can shoot the punt gun. I've found some shot, too.'

McCready's eyes flickered open and he sat up. 'What gun?'

'The punt gun I was telling you about. You didn't seem interested in it at the time.'

'That was when we had guns of our own,' said McCready. 'What is it? A shotgun?'

'You could call it that,' said Harding, and Denison smiled.

'I think I'd better look at it,' said McCready, and swung his legs over the side of the bunk. 'Where is it?'

'I'll show you.' Harding and McCready went out, and Denison folded the map and went to the window. He looked out at the unchanging scene and sighed.

'What's the matter?' asked Diana. 'Bored?'

'I was wondering if our friends are still around.'

'The only way to find out is to stick your head outside.'

'I know,' said Denison. 'One of us will have to do it sooner or later. I think I'll have a crack at it. It's three hours since McCready tried.'

'No,' said Lyn. The word seemed to be torn out of her involuntarily. 'No,' she said again. 'Leave that to the . . . the professionals.'

Diana smiled. 'Meaning me? I'm willing.'

'Let's not argue about it,' said Denison peaceably. 'We're all in this together. Anyway, it's a sure cure for boredom. Keep your eye on those reeds, Diana.'

'All right,' she said as he walked to the door. Lyn looked at him dumbly.

He swung open the door slowly and waited a full minute before going outside, and when he did so his hands were above his head. He waited, immobile, for another minute and, when nothing happened, he took another step forward. Diana shouted and simultaneously he saw a movement in the reeds on the edge of the marsh. The flat report of the rifle shot coincided with a clatter of stones six feet in front of him and there was a shrill *spaaang* as the bullet ricocheted over his head.

He waved both his hands, keeping them over his head, and cautiously backed into the hut. He was closing the door when McCready came back at a dead run. 'What happened?'

'I was just testing the temperature,' said Denison. 'Somebody has to do it.'

'Don't do it when I'm not here.' McCready went to the window. 'So they're still there.'

Denison smiled at Lyn. 'Nothing to worry about,' he assured her. 'They're just keeping us in a pen.' She turned away and said nothing. Denison looked at McCready. 'Well, what do you think of Harding's gun?'

'He doesn't think much of it,' said Harding.

'For God's sake!' said McCready. 'It's not a shotgun – it's a light artillery piece. Even if you could lift it – which you can't – you couldn't shoot it. The recoil would break your shoulder. It's bloody useless.'

'It's not meant for waving about,' said Harding. 'It's designed for use on the punt, like a 16-inch gun on a battleship. You don't find many of those on land because of the difficulty of absorbing the recoil – but you can put half a dozen on a ship because the recoil is absorbed by the water.'

'Just my point,' said McCready. 'It's as useless as a 16-inch gun would be if we had one. The powder is something else; maybe we can do something with that.'

'Like making hand grenades?' queried Denison sardonically. 'What do you want to do? Start a war?'

'We have to find a way of leaving here.'

'We'll leave when the Czechs let us,' said Denison. 'And nobody will get hurt. They've fallen for your fake treasure map, so what's the hurry now?' There was a cutting edge to his voice. 'Any fighting you do now will be for fighting's sake, and that's just plain stupid.'

'You're right, of course,' said McCready, but there was an undercurrent of exasperation in his voice. 'Your watch, Harding; then Denison and then me.'

'You don't mind if I mess about with the gun while I keep watch?' asked Harding. 'It's of personal interest,' he added apologetically. 'I *am* a wildfowler.'

'Just don't cause any sudden bangs,' said McCready. 'I don't think my heart could stand it. And no one goes outside that door except on my say-so.'

Denison stretched his arms. 'I think I'll try to sleep for a while. Wake me when it's my watch.' He lay on his side on the bunk and for a while regarded Harding who had struggled in with the punt gun. He had some paper and appeared to be making small paper bags.

Denison's eyelids drooped and presently he slept.

He was awakened by Harding shaking his shoulder. 'Wake up, Giles; your watch.'

Denison yawned. 'Anything happening?'

'Not a thing to be seen.'

Denison got up and went to the window. Harding said, 'I think I've figured out the gun. I've even made up some cartridges. I wish I could try it.' There was a wistful note in his voice.

Denison looked about the room. The others were asleep which was not surprising because it was midnight. 'You'd better rest. When we move we'll probably move quickly.'

Harding lay on his bunk and Denison inspected the view from the window. The sun shone in his eyes, just dipping over the horizon far over the marsh; that was the lowest it would set and from then on it would be rising. He shaded his eyes. The sun seemed to be slightly veiled as though there was a thickening in the air over the marsh, the slightest of hazes. Probably a forest fire somewhere, he thought, and turned to the table to find the results of Harding's handiwork.

Harding had made up six cartridges, crude cylindrical paper bags tied at the top with cotton thread. Denison picked one up and could feel the small shot through the paper. The cartridges were very heavy; he bounced one in his hand and thought its weight was not far short of two pounds. A pity Harding could not get his wish but, as McCready had pointed out, firing the gun was impossible.

He bent down and picked up the punt gun, straining his back and staggering under the weight. He cradled it in his arms and attempted to bring the butt to his shoulder. The muzzle swung erratically in a wild arc. It was impossible to aim and the recoil as two pounds of shot left the barrel would flatten the man who fired it. He shook his head and laid it down.

An hour later the view from the window was quite different. The sunshine had gone to be replaced by a diffuse light and the haze over the marsh had thickened into a light mist. He could still see the boathouse where the punt lay, and the reeds at the marsh edge, but farther out the light was gone from the water and beyond that was a pearly greyness.

He woke McCready. 'Come and look at this.' McCready looked at the mist thoughtfully, and Denison said, 'It's been thickening steadily. If it keeps to the same schedule visibility will be down to ten yards in another hour.'

'You think we ought to make a break?'

'I think we ought to get ready,' said Denison carefully. 'And I think we ought to find out if our friends are still there before the mist gets any thicker.'

'We meaning me,' said McCready sourly.

Denison grinned. 'It's your turn – unless you think Harding ought to have a go. Or Diana.'

'I suppose I volunteer – but let's wake up the others first.'

Ten minutes later it was established beyond doubt that the besiegers were still there. McCready slammed the door. 'That bastard doesn't like me; I felt the wind of that one.'

'I saw him,' said Denison. 'The range is a hundred yards – not more. He could have killed you, but he didn't.'

'The mist has thickened,' said Diana. 'Even in the last ten minutes.'

'Let's get everything packed,' said McCready.

They started to repack their gear, all except Denison who went to the window to stare out over the marsh. Fifteen minutes later McCready joined him. 'Aren't you coming?'

'Visibility down to fifty yards,' said Denison. 'I wonder what would happen if someone went outside now.'

'If Johnny is still in those reeds he wouldn't see.'

'What makes you think he's still in the reeds? If he has any sense he'll have closed in. So will the others.'

'Others?'

'Logic says there are at least four – two to watch back and front, and two to sleep.'

'I'm not so sure of that,' said McCready. 'It's only theory.'

'Try climbing out of the back window,' said Denison drily. He rubbed his jaw. 'But you're right in a way; it doesn't make sense, does it? Not when Schmidt could have put two men right here in the hut with us. He'd have saved two men.'

McCready shook his head. 'He's too wise a bird to fall for that. When you have a rifle that'll kill at a quarter mile you don't guard at a range of three yards. Guards that close can be talked to and conned into making a false move. We can't talk to these jokers outside and they talk to us with bullets.'

He tapped on the glass. 'But Schmidt didn't reckon on this mist. It's thickening rapidly and when the visibility gets down to ten yards I think we'll take a chance.'

'Then you take it on your own,' said Denison flatly. 'If you think I'm going to go stumbling around out there when there are four men armed with automatic rifles you're crazy. They might not want to kill us by design but they could sure as hell kill us by accident. I don't go – nor does Lyn. Nor does Harding, if I have any say.'

'A chance like this and you won't take it,' said McCready disgustedly.

'I'm not in the chance-taking business, and in this case it doesn't make sense. Tell me; suppose you leave this hut – what would you do?'

'Head back to Vuotso,' said McCready. 'We couldn't miss it if we skirted the edge of the marsh.'

'No, you couldn't,' agreed Denison. 'And neither could the Czechs miss you. You'd be doing the obvious. Come over here.' He walked over to the table and spread out the map, using Harding's cartridges to hold down the corners. 'I'm not recommending leaving the hut at all – not the way things are now – but if it's necessary that's the way to go.'

McCready looked at the way Denison's finger pointed. 'Over the marsh! You're crazy.'

'What's so crazy about it? It's the unexpected direction. They wouldn't think of following us across there.'

'You're still out of your mind,' said McCready. 'I had a good look at that marsh from up on the mountain. You can't tell where the land begins and the water ends, and where there's water you don't know how deep it is. You'd stand a damned good chance of drowning, especially if you couldn't see ten yards ahead.'

'Not if you took the punt,' said Denison. 'The two girls and one man in the punt – two men alongside pushing. Where the water becomes deep they hang on and are towed while the people in the punt paddle.' He tapped the map. 'The marsh is two miles across; even in pitch darkness you could get through in under four hours. Once you're across you head west and you can't help but hit the main road north from Rovaniemi.' He bent over the map. 'You'd strike it somewhere between Vuotso and Tankapirtti, and the whole journey wouldn't take you more than seven or eight hours.'

'Well, I'll be damned!' said McCready. 'You've really been working all this out, haven't you?'

'Just in case of emergency,' said Denison. He straightened. 'The emergency hasn't happened yet. We're a bloody sight safer here than we would be out there. If there was a life and death reason for getting out of here I'd be in favour of it, but right now I don't see it.'

'You're a really cool logical bastard,' said McCready. 'I wonder what it takes to make you angry. Don't you feel even annoyed that we're being

made fools of by those Czechs out there?'

'Not so annoyed as to relish stopping a bullet,' said Denison with a grin. 'Tell you what – you were so keen on the democratic process when you were stringing Schmidt along, so I'll settle for a vote.'

'Balls!' said McCready. 'It's either the right thing to do or it isn't. You don't make it right just by voting. I think you're right but I don't . . .'

He was interrupted by a single shot from outside the hut and then there was a sustained rapid chatter of automatic fire. It stopped, and McCready and Denison stared at each other wordlessly. There was another report, a lighter sound than the rifle, and a window of the hut smashed in.

'Down!' yelled McCready, and flung himself flat. He lay on the floor of the hut and then twisted around until he could see Denison. 'I think your emergency has arrived.'

36

All was silent.

Denison lay on the floor and looked at McCready who said, 'I think that was a pistol shot, it sounded different. I hope it was.'

'For God's sake, why?'

McCready was grim. 'Just pray they don't start shooting at this hut with those bloody rifles. They're N.A.T.O. issue and they pack a hell of a wallop. In Northern Ireland the army found they were shooting through houses – through one wall and out the other.'

Denison turned his head. 'Are you all right, Lyn?'

She was flat on the floor by her bunk. 'I . . . I think so.' Her voice was tremulous.

'I'm not,' said Harding. 'I think I was hit. My arm is numb.'

Diana crossed the hut at a low run and flopped down beside Harding. 'Your face is bleeding.'

'I think that was the flying glass,' he said. 'It's my arm that's worrying me. Can you have a look at it?'

'Christ!' said McCready savagely. 'One lousy bullet and he has to get in the way. What do you think now, Denison? Still think it's not time to leave?'

'I haven't heard anything more.' Denison crawled over to the window and cautiously raised himself. 'The mist is much thicker. Can't see a damned thing.'

'Get down from there,' snapped McCready. Denison pulled down his head but stayed in a crouch below the window. 'How's Harding?'

Harding answered. 'The bone is broken,' he said. 'Can someone get my black box? It's in my pack.'

'I'll get it,' said Lyn.

McCready crawled over to Harding and inspected his arm. Diana had torn away the shirt sleeve to get at the wound, a small puncture. Harding's arm was a curious shape; it seemed to have developed an extra joint. 'It was a pistol shot,' said McCready. 'If you'd have been hit by one of those rifle bullets at that range you'd have no arm left.'

Again came the sound of automatic fire but from a greater distance. It sounded like a noisy sewing machine and was interspersed with other single shots. It stopped as quickly as it had begun.

'Sounds like a battle,' said McCready. 'What do you think, Denison?'

'I think it's time to leave,' said Denison. 'We've had one bullet in here – we might get more. You and I will go down to the punt; Diana and Lyn can help Harding along as soon as we've made sure it's safe. We leave the packs and travel light. Bring a compass, if you have one.'

'I've got one in my pocket.' McCready looked down at Harding and saw he had filled a syringe and was injecting himself in the arm. 'How are you, Doctor?'

'That will keep it quiet,' said Harding, taking out the needle. 'If someone can slap a bandage around it.'

'I can do better than that,' said Diana. 'I can make splints.'

'Good,' said Harding. 'I have a broken arm – not a broken leg. I can walk and I'll be ready to move in five minutes. Did you say something about going by punt?'

'Denison's idea.'

'Then why don't we take the gun?'

'Haul that bloody great ... !' McCready stopped and glanced at Denison. 'What about it?'

Denison thought of two pounds of birdshot. 'Might give someone a fright.'

'Tie that tighter,' said Harding to Lyn. 'Then bring me those cartridges from the table.' He raised his head. 'If you are going scouting we'll have the gun loaded when you get back.'

'All right,' said McCready. 'Let's go.' All the frustration had dropped from him now that he had something to do. 'When we go out of the door we go flat on our bellies.'

He opened the door and wreaths of mist drifted into the hut. When he put his head around the corner of the door at floor level he found the visibility to be ten to fifteen yards, shifting in density as the mist drifted in from the marsh. He wriggled out and waited until Denison joined him, then put his mouth to Denison's ear and whispered, 'We separate but keep in sight of each other – ten yards should do it. We go one at a time in ten-yard runs.'

At Denison's nod he went forward, then dropped to the ground ten yards ahead and, after a moment, waved Denison on. Denison angled away until he was parallel with McCready; he lay and stared into the mist but could see nothing. McCready went ahead again and dropped and then Denison followed, and so on until Denison put his hand wrist-deep in cold water. They were at the edge of the marsh.

He lay there, turning his head from side to side, trying to penetrate the pearly mist, his ears strained for the slightest sound. When he looked up he could see the tops of the stiff reeds, and all he could hear was a rustling as the lightest of airs brushed through them. From the marsh came the occasional call of a bird.

McCready edged up next to him. 'Where's the punt?'

'To the left – a hundred yards.'

They went slowly and separately, McCready leading because of his experience. At last he stopped and when Denison drew up with him he saw the loom of the boathouse through the mist. McCready put his lips next to Denison's ear. 'There could be someone in there. I'll take it from the other side. Give me exactly four minutes then close in from this side.'

He wriggled away and was lost to sight.

Denison lay there watching the sweep second hand on his watch. Four minutes seemed a hell of a long time. At exactly two minutes there was a renewed burst of firing which made him start; it seemed to come from the direction of the hut but he could not be sure. He found he was sweating despite the cool clamminess of the mist.

At four minutes he went forward carefully and looked into the dimness under the roof of the boathouse. He saw no one until a movement on the other side made his stomach roll over until he realised it was McCready. 'All safe,' said McCready.

'We'd better take the punt out and run it up on to the beach,' said Denison in a low voice. He waded into the water, trying not to splash, and floated out the punt. Between them they ran it up on to the shingle which crunched loudly. 'For Christ's sake, be quiet!' whispered McCready. 'Did you hear that last lot of shooting?'

'I thought it came from behind me.'

'I thought it came from the marsh,' said McCready. 'You can't tell with mist, though. It distorts sounds. Let's go back and get the others.'

They made it back to the hut uneventfully. McCready closed the door and said, 'There doesn't seem to be anyone out there – not towards the marsh, anyway. That idea of yours might be a good one.'

'I wouldn't go in any other direction,' said Denison briefly. 'Ready to move, Lyn?'

Her face was pale but her chin came up in the resolute gesture he had come to know. 'I'm ready.'

'McCready and I will go first. You follow and help Harding if he needs it. We won't be going too fast if we're carrying the gun.'

'It's loaded – but quite safe,' said Harding. His face was drawn. 'It can't be fired until it's cocked and a detonator cap put on the nipple.'

'We'd better know what we're going to do,' said McCready. 'Are you sure this gun will shoot, Doctor? I don't want us to be lumbered with a load of old iron.'

'It'll shoot,' said Harding. 'I tested the powder and it burns well; and I tested a detonator while they were shooting out there.'

Denison did not know what sound a detonator would make but that might account for his impression that a shot had come from the direction of the hut. He said, 'I think we ought to play safe until we get well into the marsh. Harding ought to go in the punt from the beginning because of his wound – and you, too, George, in case there's shooting. The girls and I will tag on behind.'

McCready nodded, but Harding said, 'I want Denison in the punt with me.'

McCready stared at him. 'Why?'

'Put it down to crankiness or, maybe, loss of blood,' said Harding. 'But that's the way I want it. Believe me, I know what I'm doing.'

McCready looked blankly at Denison. 'What do you say?'

'All right with me. If that's what he wants, that's what he gets.'

'Good,' said Harding. 'Come over here.' He took Denison to where the gun lay. 'It's all ready for going on the punt. There'll be no difficulty in fixing it – it just drops into place and I have the breech ropes all ready to reeve through the eye-bolts.' He paused. 'There are two important items to remember when you shoot one of these things.'

'Go on.'

'First; keep your head well back when you pull the trigger. There'll be a blowback from the touch-hole which could make a nasty burn on your face. Secondly; you'll be lying flat on your belly when you shoot, and you've got a limited amount of lateral aim by shifting the butt – there's enough play in the breech ropes to allow for that. But just before you pull the trigger raise your knees from the bottom of the punt. That's important.'

'Why?'

Harding shook his head. 'I don't think you realise yet what sort of gun this is. If your knees are in contact with the punt when the recoil comes you're likely to have a couple of shattered kneecaps. Watch it.'

'God Almighty!' said Denison. He looked at Harding curiously. 'Why did you pick me instead of McCready?'

'McCready knows too much about guns,' said Harding. 'He might fall into the error that he knows about this one. I want somebody who'll do exactly as I say without contaminating it with what he thinks.' He smiled wryly. 'I don't know whether we're going to fire this gun – under the circumstances I hope not – but, believe me – when you pull that trigger you'll probably be just as surprised as the man you're shooting at.'

'Let's hope it never happens,' said Denison. 'How's your arm?'

Harding looked down at the improvised sling. 'It'll be fine as long as the drug holds out. I'm leaving my kit but I have a syringe loaded with pain-killer in my pocket. Just one more thing. If we shoot in the marsh it's going to be difficult to reload the gun. It will have to be done in shallow water with McCready at the front of the punt with a ramrod. I'll have a word with him about that.'

He went to McCready and Denison bent to examine the gun. It was suddenly much more real, no longer looking like an old piece of iron piping but a weapon deadly of purpose. He straightened to find Lyn at his side. 'An extra sweater,' she said, holding it out. 'It's always cold on the water.'

'Thanks,' he said, and took it from her. 'It'll be even colder in it. You shouldn't have come, Lyn; this is no place for you. Will you promise me something?'

'That depends.'

'If we get into trouble out there – shooting, perhaps – promise to duck out of it. Get down among the reeds and out of sight. Don't take any chances you don't have to.'

She nodded towards Harding. 'And what about him?'

'Leave him to the professionals. They'll look after him.'

'If it weren't for me he wouldn't be here,' she said sombrely. 'And you're a fine one to talk about not taking chances.'

He shrugged. 'All right – but there is something you can do for me. Find a ball of string. Harding might know where there is some.'

McCready came over. 'We're ready to move. Help me with the gun.' As they lifted it they heard several shots. 'What the hell's going on out there?' said McCready. 'We're not being shot at – so who is?'

Denison took the strain at the butt end of the gun. 'Who cares? Let's take advantage.'

It was better this second time despite the hampering weight of the gun; they had a better sense of direction and knew where to go. Within five minutes they were lowering the gun on to the foredeck of the punt; it slotted neatly into place and Harding, hovering over it, wordlessly indicated how to fit the breech ropes.

Denison uncoiled the thirty-foot length of string that Lyn had found. He gave one end to McCready. 'Keep at the end of that,' he whispered. 'If you get into trouble tug and I'll stop. Two tugs and I'll back water.'

'Bloody good idea.'

Denison tapped Harding on the shoulder. 'Get in before we launch her.' Harding obeyed and Denison and McCready pushed the punt forward until it floated. Again there was the crunch of shingle and they waited with held breath to see if they had attracted attention. Denison climbed aboard over the stern and settled behind the gun. He gave the other end of the string to Harding. 'If you feel a tug let me know. Where are the paddles?'

'On the bottom boards next to the gun butt.'

He scrabbled and found them, short-handled and broadbladed. Before he put them into the water he stared ahead. He was lying prone with his eyes not more than a foot above the level of the water. Ahead of him, on the foredeck, stretched nine feet of gun. It looked less clumsy on the punt, more as if it belonged. The weapons system was complete.

'Wait!' whispered Harding. 'Take this needle and push it down the touch-hole.'

Denison stretched out his hand and drew back the hammer. It clicked into place at full cock and he jabbed the needle into the hole in the nipple and felt it pierce the paper cartridge. He waggled it about to enlarge the hole which would allow the flame to reach the powder, and then passed it back to Harding who gave him a detonator cap. Harding whispered, 'I'd keep that in your hand until you're ready to shoot. It's safer.'

He nodded and picked up the paddles and took a short, easy stroke as quietly as he could. The punt moved forward, more quickly than he had expected. Ripples ran backwards vee-shaped from the bow as the punt glided into the mist.

Denison had already determined to stay close to the banks of reeds. From the point of view of paddling the punt he would have been better in mid-channel but there he would be more exposed. Besides, he had the others to think of; they were wading and the water was more likely to be shallow by the reeds.

Harding whispered, 'McCready gave me his compass. What's the course?'

'North-west,' said Denison. 'If we have to make any course changes try to make them north rather than west.'

'Then steady as you go.'

It was an awkward position in which to paddle and he quickly developed aches, particularly at the back of his shoulders. And his breastbone ground against the bottom boards until he thought he was rubbing the skin off his chest. Whoever used the punt must have had a cushion there.

When he estimated they had travelled about two hundred yards he stopped and rested. From behind he could hear faint splashes and, when he looked back, he saw the faint figures of the other three. Beyond there was nothing but greyness. McCready came alongside, water up to his waist. 'What have you stopped for?'

'It's bloody hard work. Unnatural position. I'll be all right.'

From the land came a series of rapid shots, the stammer of an automatic rifle. McCready breathed, 'They're still at it. I'd like to know what . . .'

There was another shot, so shockingly close that McCready instinctively ducked and Denison flattened himself even closer to the bottom of the punt. There was a splashing noise to the left as though someone was running in shallow water; the sound receded and everything was quiet again.

McCready eased himself up. 'That was right here in the marsh. Let's move.'

Denison pushed off again quietly and the punt ghosted into the mist. He was aware that Harding had not said anything, so he turned his head. 'Are you okay?'

'Carry on,' said Harding. 'A bit more to the left.'

As they penetrated the marsh there were flaws in the mist – sudden thinnings and thickenings of the vapour apparently caused by a light air which stroked Denison's cheek with a delicate touch. Visibility would be no more than five yards and then, ten seconds later, the mist would swirl aside so that he could see, perhaps, forty yards. He did not like it; it was unpredictable and could not be relied on.

Behind, McCready plodded thigh-deep in the water. The footing was treacherous – mostly rotting vegetation but with the occasional ankle-twisting stone or, sometimes, an unexpected hole. He cast a glance over his shoulder and saw that Lyn, much shorter than he, had the water to her waist. He grinned at her and she smiled back at him weakly. Diana brought up the rear, turning her head constantly to look back.

They went on for fifteen minutes and then there was a choked cry from behind McCready. He looked back and saw that Lyn was neck-deep and already beginning to swim. Since he himself was in the water to his armpits this was not surprising so he gave two sharp tugs on the string. The punt ahead drifted back silently as Denison back-paddled gently, and came to a halt alongside McCready.

'You'll have to change course. We're getting out of our depth.'

Denison nodded and silently pointed the way he intended to go, keeping close to the reeds and heading towards what seemed to be a promontory about fifty yards away. As the mist closed in again to blot it out he commenced paddling again.

Once more the gentle, vagrant wind parted the mist and Denison, peering forward along the barrel of the gun, saw a movement and dug both paddles into the water as quietly as he could. The punt slowed to a halt. Again the mist closed in but he waited, hoping that McCready would have the sense not to come forward again to find out what was wrong.

When he felt the slight air pressure on his cheek increase he was ready for the diminution of the mist and the suddenly increased visibility. There was a man standing on the promontory which was just a shingle bank out-thrust into the channel. Another man was walking towards him, splashing through water, and they waved to each other.

Denison put forth his hand and slipped the detonator cap on the nipple below the hammer, and with his other hand wielded a paddle gently. The punt came around slowly and with it the gun barrel. As the primitive foresight drifted across the target he back-paddled one stroke to arrest the movement.

His finger was on the trigger but he was hesitant about firing. For all he knew these men were innocent Finns caught up in a fortuitous battle with those gun-happy, crazy Czechs. One of the men turned and there was a sharp cry and Denison knew the punt had been seen. The other man brought up his arm stiffly and he saw two brief flashes just as the mist began to close in again.

That did it – no innocent Finn would shoot on sight. He squeezed the trigger, only remembering at the last moment to pull back his head and jerk up his knees from the bottom boards.

There was a pause of a single heart beat and then the gun went off. Flame flared from the touch-hole under the hammer and dazzled him but not so much that he could not see the monstrous flame that bloomed from the muzzle of the gun. Orange and yellow with white at its heart, it shot out twelve feet ahead of the punt, blinding him, and was accompanied by a deep-throated *booom*. The punt shivered and jerked back violently in the water and the bottom boards leaped convulsively under him. Then it was gone and a cloud of black smoke lazily ascended and there was the acrid stink of burnt powder in the air.

Although deafened by the concussion he thought he heard a shriek from ahead. Retinal images danced before his eyes as he tried to penetrate the suddenly dense mist and he could see nothing. An automatic rifle hammered from behind and suddenly the water ahead fountained in spurts right across the channel as someone traversed in a blind burst. There was a whipping sound overhead and bits of reed dropped on to his face as he looked up

The rifle fire stopped.

After a moment Harding said weakly, 'What about reloading?'

'How long?'

'Five minutes.'

'Christ, no!' Denison burst into activity. 'We've got to move and bloody fast.' He brought up his legs and sat on his haunches so as to give the paddles a better grip in the water. This was no time to hang around and dead silence was not as important as getting clear. He jabbed the paddles into the water and made the punt move. As he skirted the promontory he kept a careful watch, not wanting to run aground, and still less wanting to meet whoever had been there.

The violence of that single shot was seared into him. What, in God's name, could it have been like at the receiving end? He looked sideways but there was only the drifting mist, and all he could hear was the quickened splashing of the others as they increased their pace to his speed.

He paddled until he was thoroughly weary, occasionally changing course as the channel wound among marshy islands or as Harding dictated from the compass. After half an hour at top speed he was exhausted and stopped with his shoulders bowed and paddles trailing in the water. His breath rasped in his throat and his chest felt sore.

Harding touched him on the shoulder. 'Rest,' he said. 'You've done enough.'

McCready came up, half wading and half swimming. 'Jesus!' he said. 'You set a pace.'

Denison grinned weakly. 'It was that last rifle burst. A bit too much for me. All I wanted to do was to get away.'

McCready held on to the side of the punt and surveyed the gun. 'When this thing went off I was sure the barrel had burst. 'I've never seen anything like it.'

'How far have we come?' asked Denison.

Harding used his good hand to fish in the bottom of the punt. He came up with the map, soggy and running with water, and gave it to Denison who unfolded it. He pointed over Denison's shoulder. 'I think we've just crossed that wide bit of water.'

'It was deep as well as wide,' said McCready. 'We had to swim.'

'That's much more than half-way,' said Denison. 'Dry land not far ahead.'

Diana and Lyn splashed up along the reeds in the shallower water. They were soaked and bedraggled. Denison pushed with a paddle and eased the punt towards them. 'You all right?' he asked quietly.

Diana nodded wearily and Lyn said, 'How much more of this?'

'Not far,' said Denison. 'You can travel the rest of the way in the punt.'

McCready nodded. 'I think we've got clear. I haven't heard any shooting for quite a while.'

Harding was still doing something at the bottom of the punt. 'I'm afraid we're in trouble,' he said. I thought this water was the accumulated drips from the paddles, but I think we have a leak. The punt is sinking.'

'Oh, hell!' said McCready.

'My fault,' said Harding unhappily. 'I think I overloaded the gun. The strain on the punt was too much.'

Denison blew out his breath. McCready could have been right; the barrel *could* have burst. He said, 'It seems you'll have to walk the rest of the way, Doctor. Do you think you can make it?'

'I'll be all right when I've given myself another injection.'

'We'll jam the boat into the reeds,' said McCready. 'And then get going. I think the mist is lifting and I want to be out of this swamp by then.'

37

Carey strolled through a stand of tall timber and looked towards the house. It was not the sort of house you'd expect to see in Britain because the architecture was all wrong, mainly in matters of detail, but he supposed that if it had been in England it would have been called a manor house – one of the lesser stately homes.

He stopped and lit his pipe, ruminating on history. In the days when Finland was a Grand Duchy and part of Imperial Russia the house would have been the residence of one of the minor nobility or, possibly, a bourgeois Swedish Finn of the merchant class. More recently it had belonged to a company in Helsinki who used it as a holiday home for top staff and as a venue for executive conferences. Now it was rented by British Intelligence for their own undisclosed purposes.

Certainly Carey, as he strolled in the grounds clad in Harris tweed and puffing contemplatively on his pipe, looked every inch – or centimetre – the squire or whatever was the Finnish equivalent. He struck another match and, shielding it with his hand, applied it to his recalcitrant pipe. If he was worried it did not show in his manner. With the back of his mind he worried about McCready and his party who had not yet shown up, but with the forefront he worried about what was happening back in London. Apparently his boss, Sir William Lyng, had been unable to do much about Thornton and the in-fighting in Whitehall was becoming severe.

He achieved satisfaction with the drawing of his pipe and glanced towards the house again to see Armstrong approaching. He waited until he was within easy conversational reach, then said, 'Is that boffin still fiddling with those equations?'

'He's finished.'

'About time. Has he found it?'

'No one tells me anything,' said Armstrong. 'But he wants to see you. Another thing – George McCready phoned in. He couldn't say much on the phone but I gather he has a tale to tell. He wants medical supplies for a bullet in the arm.'

'Who?'

'Dr. Harding.'

Carey grunted. 'Any other casualties?'

'None that George mentioned.'

'Good! Let's go to see the boffin.'

Armstrong fell in step with him. 'And there's a man to see you – a chap called Thornton.'

Carey's pace faltered. 'He's here now?'

'I put him in the library.'

'Has he seen the boffin?'

'I don't think so.'

'He mustn't.' Carey looked sideways at Armstrong. 'Do you know anything about Thornton?'

'I've seen him around,' said Armstrong. 'But not to speak to. He's a bit above my level on the totem pole.'

'Yes,' said Carey. 'One of the Whitehall manipulators and as tricky as they come. These are my specific instructions regarding Thornton. You're to go back to the library and offer him tea – he'll like that. You're to keep him busy until I see him. I don't want him prowling around; he makes me nervous. Got that?'

'Yes,' said Armstrong. 'What's the trouble?'

'There's a bit of an argument about policy going on back home and Thornton is pushing a bit too hard. It's nothing that should concern you as long as you obey orders – my orders. If Thornton tries to order you around refer him to me.'

'All right,' said Armstrong.

'I'll tell you something about Thornton,' said Carey candidly. 'He's a bastrich – that's a word worthy of Lewis Carroll. It means a combination of a bastard and a son of a bitch. So you don't say a word about this operation in Thornton's presence. That's another order from me.'

'Not even if he asks me directly?'

'Refer him to me,' said Carey. 'And you won't get into trouble. I know he's high-powered and you are but an underling, but you are in a different department. If he tries anything on just tell him to go to hell in a polite way, and I'll back you up.' He smiled. 'And Lyng will back me so you have support all the way to the top.'

Armstrong looked relieved. 'That's clear enough.'

Carey nodded shortly. 'Good. You attend to Thornton. I'll see the boffin.'

The man whom Carey called the boffin was Sir Charles Hastings, F.R.S., a physicist not without eminence. Carey, whose opinion of scientists was low, treated him robustly and with a lack of deference which Sir Charles, who had a sense of humour, found refreshing. Carey now, on entering the room, said, 'What's the score?'

Sir Charles picked up a set of papers. 'The answer is unequivocal. This is the crucial document. In it Dr. Merikken outlines the germ of an idea, and develops it in a most interesting way. As you may know, the concept of the grazing angle has been utilised in the X-ray telescopes we now use, but Merikken took the idea much farther – which is strange considering he worked so many years ago.'

Sir Charles paused, contemplating a vision of genius. 'Merikken not only worked out the theory but subjected it to tests in the laboratory – the only way, of course. Here is a list of his tests, the results of which are frankly astounding. In his first test he was able to obtain an X-ray reflectance of nearly 25 per cent of the incident illumination.'

'Hold on a minute,' said Carey. 'How does that compare with what we've been able to do up to now?'

Sir Charles laughed shortly. 'There's absolutely no comparison. Apart from anything else, this is going to revolutionise X-ray astronomy; it makes possible an X-ray lens of considerable resolution. But that was just the first of Merikken's tests; in his final test before he ended the series he'd done considerably better than that – and his apparatus was not up to modern standards.'

Carey felt his hands empty and took out his pipe. 'So if we put a team on to this, give it a hell of a lot of money and a a reasonable amount of time, we could improve on what Merikken did. Would you agree with that, Sir Charles?'

'Indeed I would. There's nothing in here that offends any of the laws of physics. It reduces itself to a matter of engineering – advanced engineering, mark you, but nothing more than that.' He spread his hands. 'The X-ray laser has now moved from the barely possible to the probable.'

Carey gestured with his pipe. 'Anything else of value in those papers?'

Sir Charles shook his head. 'Nothing at all. This, for instance – ' he picked up the hardbound exercise book – '. . . this is a series of calculations of nuclear cross-sections. Quite primitive and totally useless.' His voice was a trifle disparaging. 'All the rest is the same.'

'Thank you, Sir Charles.' Carey hesitated. 'I'd be obliged if you would stay in this room until I return. I don't think I'll be more than a few minutes.' He ignored Sir Charles's expression of polite surprise and left the room.

Outside the library he paused and squared his shoulders before opening the door. Thornton was lounging in a leather chair and Armstrong stood at the window. Armstrong looked harassed and was visibly relieved when he saw Carey. 'Good morning.' said Thornton. His voice was cheerful. 'I must say you have your staff well trained, Carey. Mr. Armstrong is a positive oyster.'

'Morning,' said Carey curtly.

'I just popped in to find out how Sir Charles Hastings is doing. You must know we're all very keen to see the results of your labours.'

Carey sat down, wondering how Thornton knew about Sir Charles. More and more he was certain there was a leak in Lyng's office. He said blandly, 'You'll have to get that from Sir William Lyng.'

Thornton's cheerfulness diminished a shade. 'Well, I'm sure we can excuse Mr. Armstrong while we have a discussion on that matter.' He turned to Armstrong. 'If you don't mind.'

Armstrong made as though to move to the door but stopped as Carey snapped, 'Stay where you are, Ian.'

Thornton frowned. 'As you know, there are certain . . . er . . . details which Mr. Armstrong is not entitled to know.'

'He stays,' said Carey flatly. 'I want a witness.'

'A witness!' Thornton's eyebrows rose.

'Come off it,' said Carey. 'When this operation is finished I make out a final report – including what I hear in this room. So does Armstrong – independently. Got the picture?'

'I can't agree to that,' said Thornton stiffly.

'Then you don't have to talk. What you don't say Armstrong can't hear.' Carey smiled pleasantly. 'What time is your plane back to

London?'

'I must say you're not making things easy,' said Thornton querulously.

Carey was blunt. 'It's not my intention to make things easy. You've been getting underfoot all through this operation. I haven't liked that and neither has Lyng.'

All cheerfulness had deserted Thornton. 'I think you misunderstand your position, Carey,' he said. 'You're not yet so big that you can't be knocked over. When the Minister reads my report I think you'll be in for a shock.'

Carey shrugged. 'You make your report and I'll make mine. As for the Minister I wouldn't know. I don't rub shoulders with the Cabinet – I leave that to Lyng.'

Thornton stood up. 'After this is over Lyng may not be around. I wouldn't rely on him to protect you.'

'Lyng can fight his own battles,' said Carey. 'He's been very good at it so far. Ian, will you escort Mr. Thornton to his car. I don't think he has anything more to say.'

'Just one small item,' said Thornton. 'There are, of course, people other than those in your department who have been involved. You had better made sure that Denison and the Meyrick girl are silenced. That's all I have to say.'

He stalked out, followed by Armstrong. Carey sighed and took out his matches to light his pipe but stared at it in disgust and put it down unlit. Presently he heard a car door slam and the sound of tyres on gravel. When Armstrong came back he said, 'He's gone?'

'Yes.'

'Then give me a cigarette, for God's sake!'

Armstrong looked surprised but produced a packet of cigarettes. As he held a match for Carey, he said, 'You were a bit rough on Thornton, weren't you?'

Carey puffed inexpertly, and coughed. 'It's the only way to handle a bastard like that. He's the biggest con man in Whitehall, but if you hit him over the head hard enough he gets the message.'

'I'm surprised he took it from you. Aren't you afraid he'll jerk the rug from under you? I thought he was a big boy in the corridors of power.'

'Corridors of power!' Carey looked as though he was about to spit. 'I wonder if C. P. Snow knew he was coining *the* cliché of the twentieth century. I'm not afraid of Thornton; he can't get at me directly. Anyway, I'm coming up to retirement and I'll spit in his eye any time I feel like it.'

He drew on the cigarette and expelled smoke without inhaling. 'It's nothing to do with you, Ian. You just soldier on and don't worry your head about policy.'

'I don't even know what it's all about,' said Armstrong with a smile.

'You're better off that way.' Carey stood up and stared out of the window. 'Did you notice anything odd about that conversation?'

Armstrong thought back. 'I can't say that I did.'

'I did. Thornton got so mad at me that he slipped.' Carey drew on the cigarette and blew a plume of smoke. 'How did he know about Denison? You tell me that, my son, and you'll win a big cigar.' He held out the cigarette and looked at it distastefully, then stubbed it out in an ashtray with unnecessary violence. He said curtly, 'Let me know when Denison and McCready arrive.'

38

Denison lay in the old-fashioned bath with steaming water up to his ears. He lay passively letting the hot water untie all the knots. His shoulders still ached abominably because of the paddling in the marsh of Sompio. He opened his eyes and stared at the elaborately moulded ceiling and then looked at the ceramic stove in the corner, a massive contraption big enough to heat a ballroom let alone a bathroom. He deduced from that that winters in Finland could be chilly.

When the water turned tepid he got out of the bath, dried himself and put on his – or Meyrick's – bath robe. He looked down at it and fingered the fabric. From what Carey had said in the few brief remarks he had offered his days of high living were over. That suited Denison. In the past few days there had been less chance of high living than of low dying.

He left the bathroom and walked along the panelled corridor towards the bedroom he had been given. It seemed that British Intelligence was not averse to a spot of high life; this country house reminded him of those old-fashioned detective plays in which the earl was found dead in the study and, in the last act, it was the butler what done it. Playwrights in those days seemed to think that everybody but butlers had butlers.

He was about to go into his room when the door opposite opened and he saw Lyn. 'Giles, do you have a moment?'

'Of course.' She held the door open in invitation and he went into her bedroom. 'How is Harding?'

'He's quite a man,' she said. 'He took out the bullet and set the arm himself. He said it wasn't as bad as taking out his own appendix, as some doctors have had to do. Diana and I helped to bandage him.'

'I don't think he'll encounter any more bullets,' said Denison. 'From what I gathered from Carey this job is just about over. He said something about us flying back to England tomorrow.'

'So it was successful – he got what he wanted?'

'Apparently so. There was a scientist here who checked the stuff. Diana and Ian Armstrong went back with him to England.'

She sat on the bed. 'So it's all over. What will you do now?'

'Go back into films, I suppose.' He rubbed his jaw and felt the unshaven stubble. 'Carey said he wanted to talk to me about that because it might not be too easy, not with someone else's face. He waved his arm largely. 'All this Scandinavian stuff is supposed to be kept secret, so I can't very well go back to Fortescue as I am. He'd ask too many questions which I can't answer. The trouble is that the film world is small and if it isn't Fortescue asking awkward questions it will be someone else.'

'So what's the answer?'

'A man called Iredale, I suppose,' he said morosely. 'He's a plastic surgeon. I can't say I fancy the idea; I've always had a horror of hospitals.'

'Do it, Giles,' she said. 'Please do it. I can't . . .'

He waited for her to go on but she was silent, her head averted. He sat next to her and took her hand. 'I'm sorry, Lyn. I'd have given anything for this not to have happened. I didn't like the deception I played on you, and I told Carey so. I was about to insist that it be put to an end when you . . . you found out. I wish to hell we could have met under different circumstances.'

She still said nothing and he bit his lip. 'What will you do?'

'You know what I'll do. I've got a not very good degree so I'll teach – as I told my father.' Her voice was bitter.

'When will you start?'

'I don't know. There's a lot to be straightened out about Daddy's death, Carey said he'll pull strings and make it easy from the legal angle, but there'll still be a lot to do – his will and things like that. There's a lot of money involved – shares in his companies – and there's his house. He once told me that the house would be mine if he died. That was just like him, you know – he said "if" instead of "when".'

Arrogant bastard, thought Denison. He said, 'So you won't start teaching for a long time.'

'Those different circumstances,' said Lyn. 'Perhaps they could be arranged.'

'Would you like that?'

'Oh, yes; to start again.'

'To start again,' mused Denison. 'I suppose it's a wish we all have from time to time. Usually it's impossible.'

'Not for us,' she said. 'After you've had the operation you'll be convalescent for a while. Come to the house and stay with me for that time.' Her hand tightened on his. 'If I could see Giles Denison's face in my father's house perhaps we could start again.'

'A sort of exorcism. It might work.'

'We can try.' She brought her hand up to his face and touched the scar on his cheek. 'Who did this to you, Giles? And who kidnapped my father to let him drown in the sea?'

'I don't know,' said Denison. 'And I don't think Carey knows, either.'

In the room directly below McCready was giving his report to Carey. He had nearly finished. 'It was a right shambles,' he said. 'The Czechs were shooting up everything in sight.' He stopped and considered. 'Except us.'

'Who were the opposition?'

'I don't know. They were armed with pistols, nothing bigger. We only saw them once in the marsh when Denison tickled them up with that overgrown shotgun. Remarkable man, Denison.'

'I agree,' said Carey.

'He keeps his cool in an emergency and he's a good tactician. It was his idea that we cross the marsh. It was a good idea because we didn't run into the Czechs at all. When the punt sank he led us out.' McCready grinned. 'He had us all lined up on a thirty-foot length of string. And his estimation of speed was accurate; we hit the main road just seven hours after leaving the hut.'

'Did you have any trouble in Vuotso?'

McCready shook his head. 'We nipped in quietly, got into the cars, and drove out. Not far from Rovaniemi we changed into decent clothing to make ourselves presentable for the flight south.' He grimaced. 'There's a Dr. Mannermaa in Vuotso – a bird watcher. He's going to be a bit. peeved about losing his punt and gun.'

'I'll straighten that out,' said Carey. 'You said the Czechs were also at Kevo.'

'Czechs, Americans – and a crowd of Germans hovering on the outskirts. I didn't tell the others about them because they never really came into the game.'

'East Germans or West Germans?' asked Carey sharply.

'I don't know,' said McCready. 'They all speak the same lingo.'

'And then there was the chap who knocked Denison on the head and took the original map.'

'I never spotted him from start to finish,' said McCready. 'I think he was a singleton – working on his own.'

'Four groups,' said Carey thoughtfully. 'And we can't identify any

Russians for certain.'

'Five,' said McCready. 'There's the gang that substituted Denison for Meyrick. They wouldn't have come chasing after us to Kevo and Sompio. They knew better.'

Carey grunted. 'I have my own ideas about who did the dirty on Denison and Meyrick – and I don't think the Russians came into it.'

'You said Thornton was here. What did he want?'

'I didn't find out,' said Carey. 'I wouldn't let him speak to me except in front of a witness and he turned chicken. He's too fly to be caught that way. But he knew about Sir Charles Hastings, and he knew about Denison.'

'Did he, by God? We'll have to seal that leak when we get back to London. What did Hastings say?'

'Oh, we've got the goods all right. He's taken photocopies back to London. Now we can prepare for the next stage of the operation. I hope nothing happens tonight because I'd like to get Denison and the girl out of it. They're leaving tomorrow on the ten o'clock flight from Helsinki.'

'Where are the original papers now?'

'In the safe in the library.'

'In that antique? I could open it with my grandmother's hat-pin.'

Carey smiled blandly. 'Does it matter – under the circumstances?'

'No, I don't suppose it does,' said McCready.

39

Denison went to bed early that night because he had a lot of sleep to catch up on and because he had to get up fairly early to catch the flight to London. He said good night to Lyn and then went into his bedroom where he undressed slowly. Before getting into bed he drew the curtains to darken the room. Even though he was now below the Arctic Circle there was still enough light in the sky to make falling asleep annoyingly difficult. It would get darker towards midnight but never more than a deep twilight.

He woke up because someone was prodding him, and came swimming up to the surface out of a deep sleep. 'Giles; wake up!'

'Mmmm. Who's that?'

The room was in darkness but someone looked over him. 'Lyn,' she whispered.

He elbowed himself up. 'What's the matter? Turn on the light.'

'No!' she said. 'There's something funny going on.'

Denison sat up and rubbed his eyes. 'What sort of funny?'

'I don't really know. There are some people in the house – down in the library. Americans. You know the man you introduced me to – the man you said was a bore.'

'Kidder?'

'Yes. I think he's down there. I heard his voice.'

Kidder! The man who had interrogated him in the hotel in Helsinki after he had been kidnapped from the sauna. The man who had led the American party at Kevo. The overjovial and deadly boring Jack Kidder.

'Christ!' said Denison. 'Hand me my trousers – they're on a chair somewhere.' He heard a noise in the darkness and the trousers were thrust into his groping hand. 'What were you doing prowling in the middle of the night?'

'I couldn't sleep,' said Lyn. 'I was standing at my bedroom window when I saw these men in the grounds – there's still just enough light to see. They didn't seem to be up to any good – they were dodging about a bit. Then they all disappeared and I wondered what to do. I wanted to find Carey or McCready but I don't know where their rooms are. Anyway, I looked down the stairs and there was a light in the library, and when I got to the door I heard Kidder's voice.'

'What was he saying?'

'I don't know. It was just a rumble – but I recognised the voice. I didn't know what to do so I came and woke you.'

Denison thrust his bare feet into shoes. 'There's a sweater on the back of the chair.' Lyn found it and he put it on. 'I don't know where Carey's room is, either. I think I'll just nip downstairs.'

'Be careful,' said Lyn. 'I've heard enough shooting already.'

'I'll just listen,' he said. 'But you be ready to scream the place down.'

He opened the bedroom door gently and went into the dimness of the corridor. He trod carefully on his way to the stairs to avoid creaking boards, and tiptoed down, his hand running along the balustrade. The door to the library was closed but illumination leaked out from under the door. He paused by the door and listened and heard the deep sound of male voices.

He could make nothing of it until he bent and put his ear to the keyhole and then he immediately recognised the gravelly voice of Kidder. He could not distinguish the words but he recognised the voice. Another man spoke in lighter tones and Denison knew it was Carey.

He straightened up and wondered what to do. Lyn had spoken of men in the plural which would mean there were others about besides Kidder. He could cause a disturbance and arouse the house but if Kidder was holding up Carey at gunpoint that might not be good for Carey. He thought he had better find out what was really going on before doing anything drastic. He turned and saw Lyn standing by the staircase and he put his finger to his lips. Then he took hold of the door knob and eased it around very gently.

The door opened a crack and the voices immediately became clearer. Carey was speaking. '. . . and you ran into trouble again at Sompio?'

'Jesus!' said Kidder. 'I thought we'd run into the Finnish Army but it turned out they were goddamn Czechs – we wounded one and he was cussing fit to bust. Who the hell would expect to find Czechs in the middle of Finland? Especially carrying automatic rifles and some sort of crazy flame-thrower. That's why I'm bandaged up like this.'

Carey laughed. 'That was our crowd.'

Denison swung the door open half an inch and put his eye to the crack. He saw Carey standing by the safe in the corner but Kidder was not in sight. Carey said, 'It wasn't a flame-thrower – it was a bloody big shotgun operated by no less than the eminent Dr. Meyrick.'

'Now, there's a slippery guy,' said Kidder.

'You shouldn't have snatched him from the hotel in Helsinki,' said Carey. 'I thought you trusted me.'

'I trust nobody,' said Kidder. 'I still wasn't sure you weren't going to cross me up. You were playing your cards close to your chest – I still didn't know where the papers were. Anyway, I got nothing out of Meyrick; he gave me a lot of bull which I nearly fell for, then he nearly busted my larynx. You breed athletic physicists in Britain, Carey.'

'He's a remarkable man,' Carey agreed.

Kidder's voice changed and took on a more incisive quality. 'I reckon that's enough of the light conversation. Where are Merikken's papers?'

'In the safe.' Carey's voice sharpened. 'And I wish you'd put that gun away.'

'It's just window dressing in case anyone snoops in,' said Kidder. 'It's for your protection. You wouldn't want it getting around that you're . . . shall we say . . . co-operating with us, would you? What's with you, Carey? When the word came that you were willing to do a deal no one would believe it. Not such an upright guy like the respected Mr. Carey.'

Carey shrugged. 'I'm coming up to retirement and what have I got? All my life I've lived on a thin edge and my nerves are so tight I've got a flaming big ulcer. I've shot men and I've been shot at; during the war the Gestapo did things to me I don't care to remember. And all for what? When I retire I get a pension that'll do little more than keep me in tobacco and whisky.'

'Cast away like an old glove,' said Kidder mockingly.

'You can laugh,' said Carey with asperity. 'But wait until you're my age.'

'Okay, okay!' said Kidder soothingly. 'I believe you. You're an old guy and you deserve a break. I know your British Treasury is penny-pinching. You should have worked our side of the fence – do you know what the C.I.A. appropriation is?'

'Now who is making light conversation?' said Carey acidly. 'But now that we're talking of money you'd better make sure that the sum agreed goes into that Swiss bank account.'

'You know us,' said Kidder. 'You know we'll play fair – if you do. Now how about opening that safe?'

Denison could not believe what he was hearing. All the mental and physical anguish he had suffered was going for nothing because Carey – Carey, of all people – was selling out. It would have been unbelievable had he not heard it from Carey's own lips. Selling out to the bloody Americans.

He considered the situation. From what he had heard there were only the two of them in the library. Carey was where he could be seen, over by the safe. Kidder faced him and had his back to the door – presumably. It was a good presumption because nobody conducts a lengthy conversation with his back to the person he is talking to. But Kidder had a gun and, window dressing or not, it could still shoot.

Denison looked around. Lyn was still standing in the same position but he could not ask for her help. He saw a large vase on the hall table, took one step, and scooped it up. When he got back to the door he saw that Carey had opened the safe and was taking out the papers and stacking them on top.

Kidder was saying, '. . . I know we agreed to chase Meyrick and McCready just to make it look good but I didn't expect all those goddamn fireworks. Hell, I might have been killed.' He sounded aggrieved.

Carey stooped to pull out more papers. 'But you weren't.'

Denison eased open the door. Kidder was standing with his back to him, a pistol held negligently by his side, and Carey had his head half-way inside the safe. Denison took one quick pace and brought down the vase hard on Kidder's head. It smashed into fragments and Kidder, buckling at the knees, collapsed to the floor.

Carey was taken by surprise. He jerked his head and cracked it on top of the safe. That gave Denison time to pick up the pistol which had dropped from Kidder's hand. When Carey had recovered he found Denison pointing it at him.

Denison was breathing heavily. 'You lousy bastard! I didn't go through that little bit of hell just for you to make a monkey of me.'

Before Carey could say anything McCready skidded into the room at top speed. He saw the gun in Denison's hand and where it was pointing, and came to a sudden halt. 'Have you gone m . . .'

'Shut up!' said Denison savagely. 'I suppose you're in it, too. I thought it strange that Carey should have got rid of Diana and Armstrong so fast. Just what's so bloody important in London that Diana should have been put on a plane without even time to change her clothes, Carey?'

Carey took a step forward. 'Give me that gun,' he said authoritatively.

'Stay where you are.'

From the doorway Lyn said, 'Giles, what is all this?'

'These bloody patriots are selling out,' said Denison. 'Just for money in a Swiss bank account.' He jerked the gun at Carey who had taken another pace. 'I told you to stay still.'

Carey ignored him. 'You young idiot!' he said. 'Give me that gun and we'll talk about it more calmly.' He went nearer to Denison.

Denison involuntarily took a step backwards. 'Carey, I'm warning you.' He held out the gun at arm's length. 'Come any closer and I'll shoot.'

'No, you won't,' said Carey with certainty, and took another step.

Denison's finger tightened on the trigger and Carey's arm shot out, the hand held palm outwards like a policeman giving a stop sign. He pressed his hand on the muzzle of the pistol as Denison squeezed the trigger.

There was no shot.

Denison found his arm being forced back under the steady pressure of Carey's hand against the muzzle of the gun. He pulled the trigger again and again but nothing happened. And then it was too late because Carey's other hand came around edge on and chopped savagely at his neck. His vision blurred and, at the last, he was aware of but two things; one was Carey's fist growing larger as it approached, and the other was Lyn's scream.

McCready's face was pale as he looked at the sprawled figure of Denison. He let out his breath in a long whistle. 'You're lucky he had the safety catch on.'

Carey picked up the pistol. 'He didn't,' he said shortly.

Lyn ran over to where Denison lay and bent over his face. She turned her head. 'You've hurt him, damn you!'

Carey's voice was mild. 'He tried to kill me.'

McCready said, 'You mean the safety catch *wasn't* on. Then how . . .'

Carey bounced the pistol in his hand. 'Kidder went shopping for this locally,' he said. 'On the principle of "patronise your local gunsmith", I suppose. It's a Husqvarna, Model 40 – Swedish army issue. A nice gun with but one fault – there's about a sixteenth of an inch play in the barrel. If the barrel is forced back, the trigger won't pull.' He pressed the muzzle with palm of his left hand and pulled the trigger. Nothing happened. 'See!'

'I wouldn't want to stake my life on it,' said McCready fervently. 'Apart from that will it shoot normally?'

Carey cocked an eye at him. 'I suppose Kidder has friends outside. Let's invite them in.' He looked about. 'I never did like that style of vase, anyway.' He raised the gun and aimed it at a vase at the other end of the room, a companion to the one Denison had broken over Kidder's head. He fired and the vase exploded into pieces.

Carey held the gun by his side. 'That ought to bring them.'

They waited quietly in an odd tableau. Lyn was too busy trying to revive Denison to pay much attention to what was happening. She had started at the shot and then resolutely ignored Carey. Kidder lay unconscious. The bandages around his lower jaw had come adrift revealing what seemed to be bloody pockmarks from the birdshot he had received in the marsh of Sompio. Carey and McCready stood in the middle of the room, silent and attentive.

The drawn curtain in front of the french window billowed as though blown by a sudden breeze. A woman's voice said, 'Drop the gun, Mr. Carey.'

Carey laid down the pistol on the table and stepped aside from it. The curtains parted and Mrs. Kidder stepped into the room. She was still the same mousy, insignificant little woman but what was shockingly incongruous was the pistol she held in her hand. There were two large men behing her.

'What happened?' Her voice was different; it was uncharacteristically incisive.

Carey gestured towards Denison. 'Our friend butted in unexpectedly. He crowned your husband – if that's what he is.'

Mrs. Kidder lowered the gun and muttered over her shoulder. One of the men crossed the room and bent over Kidder. 'And the papers?' she asked.

'On top of the safe,' said Carey. 'No problems.'

'No?' she asked. 'What about the girl?' The gun came up and pointed at Lyn's back.

'I said it and I meant it,' said Carey in a hard voice. 'No problems.'

She shrugged. 'You're carrying the can.'

The other man crossed to the safe and began shovelling papers into a canvas bag. Carey glanced at McCready and then his eyes slid away to Kidder who was just coming round. He muttered something, not loudly but loud enough for Carey to hear.

He was speaking in Russian.

The mumbling stopped suddenly as the man who was bending over Kidder picked him up. He carried him to the french window and, although Carey could not see properly, he had the strong impression that a big hand was clamped over Kidder's mouth.

The man at the safe finished filling the bag and went back to the window. Mrs. Kidder said, 'If this is what we want you'll get your money as arranged.'

'Don't make any mistake about that,' said Carey. 'I'm saving up for my old age.'

She looked at him contemptuously and stepped back through the window without answering, and the man with the canvas bag followed her. Carey waited in silence for a moment and then walked over and closed the window and shot the bolts. He came back into the middle of the room and began to fill his pipe.

'You know that Kidder tried to con me into believing he was with the C.I.A. I always thought that American accent of his was too good to be true. It was idiomatic, all right, but he used too much idiom – no American speaks with a constant stream of American clichés.' He struck a match. 'It seems the Russians were with us, after all.'

'Sometimes you get a bit too sneaky for me,' said McCready.

'And me,' said Lyn. 'Giles was right – you're a thoroughgoing bastard.'

Carey puffed his pipe into life. 'George: our friend, Giles, has had a rough day. Let's put him to bed.'

40

Denison walked across St James's Park enjoying the bland, late October sunshine. He crossed the road at the Guards Memorial and strolled across Horse Guards Parade and through the Palace arch into Whitehall itself, neatly avoiding a guardsman who clinked a sabre at him. At this time of the year the tourists were thin on the ground and there was not much of a crowd.

He crossed Whitehall and went into the big stone building opposite, wondering for the thousandth time who it was wanted to see him. It could only have to do with what had happened in Scandinavia. He gave his name to the porter and stroked his beard while the porter consulted the appointment book. Not a bad growth in the time, he thought somewhat vaingloriously.

The porter looked up. 'Yes, Mr. Denison; Room 541. I'll get someone to take you up. Just sign this form, if you please, sir.'

Denison scribbled his signature and followed an acned youth along dusty corridors, into an ancient lift, and along more corridors. 'This is it,' said the youth, and opened a door. 'Mr. Denison.'

Denison walked in and the door closed behind him. He looked at the desk but there was no one behind it and then he turned as he saw a movement by the window. 'I saw you crossing Whitehall,' said Carey. 'I only recognised you by your movements. God, how you've changed.'

Denison stood immobile. 'Is it you I've come to see?'

'No,' said Carey. 'I'm just here to do the preparatory bit. Don't just stand there. Come in and sit down. That's a comfortable chair.'

Denison walked forward and sat in the leather club chair. Carey leaned against the desk. 'I hope your stay in hospital wasn't too uncomfortable.'

'No,' said Denison shortly. It had been damned uncomfortable but he was not going to give Carey even that much.

'I know,' said Carey. 'You were annoyed and worried. Even more worried than annoyed. You're worried because I'm still with my department; you would like to lay a complaint, but you don't know who to complain to. You are frightened that the Official Secrets Act might get in the way and that you'll find yourself in trouble. At the same time you don't want me to get away with it – whatever it is you think I'm getting away with.' He took out his pipe. 'My guess is that you and Lyn Meyrick have been doing a lot of serious talking during the last fortnight. Am I correct?'

Carey could be a frightening man. It was as though he had been reading Denison's mind. 'We have been thinking something like that,' he said unwillingly.

'Quite understandable. Our problem is to stop you talking. Of course, if you talk we could crucify you, but by then it would be too late. In some other countries it would be simple – we'd make sure that you never talked again, to anyone, at any time, about anything – but we don't do things that way here.' He frowned. 'At least, not if I can help it. So we have to convince you that talking would be *wrong*. That's why Sir William Lyng is coming here to convince you of that.'

Even Denison had heard of Lyng; he was somebody in the Department of Defence. 'He'll have his work cut out.'

Carey grinned and glanced at his watch. 'He's a bit late so you'd better read this. It's secret, but not all that much. It represents a line of thought that's in the air these days.' He took a folder from the desk and tossed it into Denison's lap. 'I'll be back in a few minutes.'

He left the office and Denison opened the folder. As he read a baffled look came over his face, and the more he read the more bewildered he became. He came to the end of the few pages in the folder and then started to read from the beginning again. It had begun to make a weird kind of sense.

Carey came back half an hour later; with him was a short, dapper man, almost birdlike in the quickness and precision of his movements. 'Giles Denison – Sir William Lyng.'

Denison got up as Lyng advanced. They shook hands and Lyng said chirpily, 'So you're Denison. We have a lot to thank you for, Mr. Denison. Please sit down.' He went behind the desk and cocked his head at Carey. 'Has he . . . ?'

'Yes, he's read his homework,' said Carey.

Lyng sat down. 'Well, what do you think of what you've just read?'

'I don't really know,' said Denison, shaking his head.

Lyng looked at the ceiling. 'Well, what would you call it?'

'An essay on naval strategy, I suppose.'

Lyng smiled. 'Not an essay. It's an appreciation of naval strategy from quite a high level in the Department of Defence. It deals with naval policy should the Warsaw Pact and N.A.T.O. come into conflict in a *conventional* war. What struck you about it? What was the main problem outlined?'

'How to tell the difference between one kind of submarine and another. How to differentiate between them so that you can sink one and not the other. The subs you'd want to sink would be those that attack shipping and other submarines.'

Lyng's voice was sharp. 'Assuming this country is at war with Russia, what conceivable reason can there be for *not* wanting to sink certain of their submarines?'

Denison lifted the folder. 'According to this we wouldn't want to sink their missile-carrying submarines – the Russian equivalent of the Polaris.'

'Why not?' snapped Lyng.

'Because if we sank too many of them while fighting a conventional war the Russians might find themselves losing their atomic edge. If that happened they might feel tempted to escalate into atomic warfare before they lost it all.'

Lyng looked pleased and glanced at Carey. 'He's learned the lesson well.'

'I told you he's a bright boy,' said Carey.

Denison stirred in the chair. He did not like being discussed as though he were absent.

Lyng said, 'A pretty problem, isn't it? If we don't sink their conventional submarines we stand a chance of losing the conventional war. If we sink too many of their missile-carriers the war might escalate to atomic catastrophe. How do you distinguish one submarine from another in the middle of a battle?' He snapped his fingers. 'Not our problem – that's for the scientists and the technologists – but do you accept the validity of the argument?'

'Well, yes,' said Denison. 'I see the point, but I don't see what it's got to do with what happened in Finland. I suppose that's why I'm here.'

'Yes, that's why you're here,' said Lyng. He pointed to the folder in Denison's hand. 'That is just an example of a type of thought. Do you have anything to say, Carey?'

Carey leaned forward. 'Ever since the atomic bomb was invented the human race has been walking a tightrope. Bertrand Russell once said, "You may reasonably expect a man to walk a tightrope safely for ten minutes; it would be unreasonable to do so without accident for two hundred years."' He hunched his shoulders. 'Well, we've walked that tightrope for thirty years. Now, I want you to imagine that tightrope walker; he carries a long balancing pole. What would happen if you suddenly dropped a heavy weight so that it hung on one end of the pole?'

'He'd probably fall off,' said Denison. He began to get a glimmer of what these two were getting at.

Lyng leaned his elbows on the desk. 'A man called Merikken invented something which had no application when he invented it. Now it turns out to be something capable of carving up missiles in mid-flight. Mr. Denison, supposing Russia developed this weapon – and no one else. What do you think might happen?'

'That depends on the ratio of hawks to doves in the Russian government, but if they were sure they could stop an American strike they might just chance their arm at an atomic war.'

'Meyrick blabbed in Stockholm before he came to us,' said Carey. 'And the news got around fast. Our problem was that the papers were in Russia, and if the Russians got to them first they'd hold on tight. Well, the Russians *have* got the papers – but so have we, in photocopy.'

Denison was suspicious. 'But you sold them to the Americans.'

'Kidder was a Russian,' said Carey. 'I let it be known that I was willing to be bought, but the Russians knew I'd never sell myself to them. After all, I do have certain standards,' he said modestly. 'So they tried to pull a fast one. I didn't mind.'

'I don't quite understand,' said Denison.

'All right,' said Carey. 'The Russians have the secret and they'll know, when we tell them, that we have it, too, and that we'll pass it on to the Yanks. And we'll let the Yanks know the Russians have it. We drop the heavy weight on *both* ends of the balancing pole.'

Lyng spread his hands. 'Result – stalemate. The man remains balanced on the tightrope.'

'There were a lot of others involved but they were small fry,' said Carey. 'The Czechs and the West Germans.' He smiled. 'I have reason to believe that the man who bopped you on the head at Kevo was an Israeli. The Israelis would dearly like to have a defence against the SAM III missiles that the Syrians are playing around with. But, really, only America and Russia matter. And maybe China.' He glanced at Lyng.

'Later, perhaps.' Lyng stared at Denison. 'This country has just lost an Empire but many of its inhabitants, especially the older ones, still retain the old Imperial habits of thought. These modes of thought are not compatible with the atomic era but, unfortunately, they are still with us. If it became public knowledge that we have handed over to the Russians what the newspapers would undoubtedly describe as a super-weapon then I think that one of the minor consequences would be the fall of the government.'

Denison raised his eyebrows. 'Minor!'

Lyng smiled wintrily. 'The political complexion of the government of the day is of little interest. You must differentiate between the government and the state; governments may come and go but the state remains, and the real power is to be found in the apparatus of state, in the offices of Whitehall, in what Lord Snow has so aptly described as the corridors of power.'

Carey snorted. 'Any day I'm expecting a journalist to write that the winds of change are blowing through the corridors of power.'

'That could very well happen,' said Lyng. 'The control of power in the state is not monolithic; there are checks and balances, tensions and resistances. Many of the people I work with still hold on to the old ideas, especially in the War Office.' He looked sour for a moment. 'Some of the senior officers in the Navy, for instance, were destroyer commanders during World War II.'

His hand shot forward, his finger pointing to the folder in Denison's lap. 'Can you imagine the attitude of such men, steeped in the old ideas, when they are expected to issue orders to young officers to sink one type of enemy submarine and not another?' He shook his head. 'Old habits die hard. They're more likely to say, in the old tradition, "Full speed ahead, and damn the torpedoes." They fight to win, forgetting that no one will win a nuclear war. They forget balance, and balance is all, Mr. Denison. They forget the man on the tightrope.'

He sighed. 'If the news of what has been done in Finland were to be disclosed not only would the present government fall, a minor matter, but there would be a drastic shift of power in the state. We, who strive to hold the balance, would lose to those who hold a narrower view of what is good for this country and, believe me, the country and the world would not be the safer for it. Do you understand what I am saying, Mr. Denison?'

'Yes,' said Denison. He found that his voice was hoarse, and he coughed to clear it. He had not expected to be involved in matters of high policy.

Abruptly the tone of Lyng's voice changed from that of a judge reviewing a case to something more matter-of-fact. 'Miss Meyrick made a specific threat. She derided the efficacy of "D" notices and said that the students of twenty universities would not be bound by them. I regret to say that this is probably quite true. As you know, our student population – or some sections of it – is not noted for its coolheadedness. Any move towards implementing her threat would be potentially disastrous.'

'Why don't you talk to her about it?' said Denison.

'We will – but we believe you have some influence with her. It would be a pity if Miss Meyrick's anger and compassion were to cause the disruption I have described.'

Denison was silent for a long time then he sighed, and said, 'I see your point. I'll talk to her.'

'When will you see her?' asked Carey.

'I'm meeting her at the Horse Guards at twelve o'clock.'

'That's in ten minutes. You talk to her, and I'll have a word with her later.' Carey stood up and held out his hand. 'Am I forgiven?'

'I wanted to kill you,' said Denison. 'I very nearly did.'

'No hard feelings,' said Carey. 'I seem to remember hitting *you* pretty hard.'

Denison got up and shook Carey's hand. 'No hard feelings.'

Lyng smiled and busied himself with the contents of a slim briefcase, trying to efface himself. Carey stood back and looked at Denison critically. 'I wouldn't have believed it – the change in you, I mean.'

Denison put his hand to his face. 'Iredale unstuck the eyelid – that was easy – and took away the scar. He had a go at the nose and that's still a bit tender. We decided to leave the rest – getting the silicone polymer out would amount to a flaying operation so we gave it a miss. But the beard covers up a lot.' He paused. 'Who did it, Carey?'

'I don't know,' said Carey. 'We never did find out.' He looked at Denison quizzically. 'Has Iredale's handiwork made much difference with Lyn?'

'Er . . . why, yes . . . I think . . .' Denison was unaccountably shy.

Carey smiled and took out a notebook. 'I'll need your address.' He looked up. 'At the moment it's Lippscott House, near Brackley,

Buckinghamshire. Can I take it that will be your address until further notice?'

'Until further notice,' said Denison. 'Yes.'

'Invite me to the wedding,' said Carey. He put away his notebook and glanced through the window down into Whitehall. 'There's Lyn,' he said. 'Admiring the horses. I don't think there's any more, Giles. I'll keep in touch. If you ever need a job, come and see me. I mean it.'

'Never again,' said Denison. 'I've had enough.'

Lyng came forward. 'We all do what we think is best.' They shook hands. 'I'm glad to have met you, Mr. Denison.'

When he had gone Lyng put his papers back into his briefcase and Carey stood at the window and lit his pipe. It took him some time to get it going to his satisfaction. Lyng waited patiently, and then said, 'Well?'

Carey looked down into Whitehall and saw Denison crossing the street. Lyn ran towards him and they kissed, then linked arms and walked past the mounted guards and under the arch. 'They're sensible people; there'll be no trouble.'

'Good!' said Lyng, and picked up the folder from where Denison had left it.

Carey swung around. 'But Thornton is a different matter.'

'I agree,' said Lyng. 'He's got the Minister's ear. We're going to have a rough ride with this one regardless of whether Denison keeps silent.'

Carey's voice was acid. 'I don't mind if Thornton plays the Whitehall warrior as long as the only weapon he shoots is a memorandum. But when it comes to a deliberate interference in operations then we draw a line.'

'Only a suspicion – no proof.'

'Meyrick's death was bad enough – although it was accidental. But what he did to Denison was abominable and unforgivable. And if he'd got hold of Merikken's papers his bloody secret laboratories would be working overtime.'

'Forget it,' said Lyng. 'No proof.'

Carey grinned. 'I told a lie just now – the only lie I've told to Denison since I've known him. I've got the proof, all right. I've got a direct link between Thornton and his crooked plastic surgeon – Iredale was able to put me on to that one – and it won't be long before I find the sewer of a psychologist who diddled around with Denison's mind. I'm going to take great pleasure in peeling the skin off Thornton in strips.'

Lyng was alert. 'This is certain? Real proof?'

'Cast iron.'

'Then you won't touch Thornton,' said Lyng sharply. 'Let me have your proof and I'll deal with him. Don't you see what this means? We can neutralise Thornton – he's out of the game. If I can hold that over him I can keep him in line for ever.'

'But . . .' Carey held himself in. 'And where does justice come in?' he asked heavily.

'Oh, justice,' said Lyng indifferently. 'That's something else again. No man can expect justice in this world; if he does then he's a fool.' He took Carey by the elbow and said gently, 'Come; let us enjoy the sunshine while we may.'